Krishna Deities and Their Miracles

How the Images of Lord Krishna Interact with Their Devotees

Krishna Deities and Their Miracles

How the Images of Lord Krishna Interact with Their Devotees

Stephen Knapp

Ocean Books Pvt. Ltd.
ISO 9001:2015 Publishers

Published by
Ocean Books (P) Ltd.
4/19 Asaf Ali Road,
New Delhi-110 002 (INDIA)
e-mail: info@oceanbooks.in

ISBN 978-81-8430-505-0
KRISHNA DEITIES AND THEIR MIRACLES
by Stephen Knapp

Edition
2025

Price
₹ 500.00 (Rupees Five Hundred only)

Printed at
Print Media, New Delhi

Dedicated to all those who are trying to attain higher levels of spiritual experience. This is to show that raising our love of God brings God closer to us, and He can reveal Himself to whoever He wants in whatever way He wants.

Introduction

The reason why we are using the word "miracles" in the title is because many people are familiar with this word and its connotation to that which is out of the ordinary or of a special nature in the area of spiritual or religious topics. And many of the pastimes that we relate in this book can be considered in that way. Herein we will read some of the pastimes about how the temple Deities act in personal ways in the lives of Their devotees, both in waking life as well as in dreams that affect the existence of such devotees. This is with one's personal Deities as well. But for the Indian Vedic community, especially those who follow the deeper aspects of Santana-dharma, many of these descriptions are not so much miracles, but are considered common events that many people experience as part of their devotion to the Deities in the temple.

It is understood in the Vedic tradition that a person who raises his or her consciousness through spiritual practice can attain the perception of various levels of the spiritual realm, as well as perceive the higher dimensions of existence. But this depends on how sincere and steady they are in their spiritual practice. However, for one who has not endeavored in this way, all of this may seem like a mirage, a misconception, or simple buffoonery. They may be convinced that such things cannot happen, or that the Deity is not real, only a statue. But such people only reveal themselves to be both without knowledge of God or a perception of the higher dimension, and certainly without any spiritual experience. Thus, if people like this advocate a view that such things are not possible while being without knowledge or perception, or remain closed to the potential that such things can happen, then they remain but fools, closed to the evidence, the scriptural instructions, and the stories of personal experiences from those who have had them.

However, even those who blindly accept that God can interact with us without having perceived it, must also go deeper than that. They must also participate in the genuine spiritual path that uplifts or spiritualizes their consciousness so they can also begin to perceive that which is spiritual. That is what makes the difference and opens them up to the possibilities and probabilities of them having their own spiritual experiences in any number of ways, including the likes of those described herein.

These descriptions of miracles, or the interactions between the Deities of Krishna and the devotees, will cover a wide range of occurrences. Some of these miracles may be considered minor or more ordinary, while others may be a special spiritual phenomena that shows the definite interplay of the Supreme Being with His devotees and the spiritual dimension overlapping into the material realm.

These descriptions of Krishna Deities and His various forms and other Divinities include traditional pastimes that have been recorded from years ago, as well as those that are more recent. It shows how great or even minor devotees can have experiences with Krishna as long as they have two qualities, which is great faith and love. A variety of situations are provided in these descriptions, which shows the many ways that the Lord can reveal Himself, and the favor that is shown by Him to those who worship Him.

Why should some of these descriptions of the activities of these Deities be considered special, which involve what are often viewed as mere images in the temples? Because it shows how the Supreme Being and His expansions can reveal Him or Herself in many ways to the amusement and to the awe of the devotees, based on the devotees' love and devotion. Some of these revelations are like the play or pastimes of the Supreme Lord, while others are for heightening the realizations or guidance of the devotees, and those who hear about such pastimes. It is to our benefit to consider the information that is provided, and to listen or read these stories to get a better understanding of the potential relations that take place between the Supreme and His devotees. It also gives an indication of the possibility of what can happen to any of us. You will notice that the basis of all these experiences that are related in the stories that follow is but one thing, and that is love. The more there is love for the Lord by the devotee, the more compelled the Lord is to reveal Himself or interact in the lives of those devotees. Why? This will be explained later in the book.

Contents

1
The Antiquity of Deity Worship in The Vedic Tradition

There have been some people who have declared that the worship of Deities or images or the *murti* in the temples is but a recent invention of Vedic culture. However, that is not an accurate point. It is true that according to the different *yugas* or ages (such as Satya-yuga, Treta-yuga, Dvapara-yuga, and Kali-yuga) there are different processes for spiritual development that have been more recommended than others. For example, meditation was the recommended process for Satya-yuga, when people lived much longer and could sit in concentration or in *samadhi* for long periods of time. Then in Treta-yuga it was best to engage in various and extravagant rituals, *havans*, *yajnas*, or fire ceremonies. Then in Dvapara-yuga it was best to engage in elaborate worship, with opulent offerings to the Deities and prayers and mantras sung to the Deities. So, all of these processes have continued down through the ages to some degree or another. However, in Kali-yuga, though we still see all of these processes used, it is now the chanting of mantras, especially the Hare Krishna mantra, that is the most highly efficient and recommended process of spiritual growth in this age.

So, Deity worship as seen in the temples has been around for thousands of years. And as evidence of that, we can find references in the Vedic texts, as well as in the historical holy sites around India.

HISTORICAL SITES OF ANCIENT DEITY WORSHIP

For example, seven kilometers south of Gokula, not far from Mathura, is the Dauji temple. Dauji is the Deity of Lord Balarama that was originally installed 5,000 years ago by King Vajranabha, Krishna's great-grandson. From Lord Krishna and His queen Rukmini was born the great warrior Pradyumna, one of His prominent sons, who married the daughter of Rukmi, Rukmavati. They gave birth to Anirudha. Anirudha married Rukmi's son's daughter, Rachana, and from her was born Vajra, who would remain among the few survivors of the Yadus' battle. (*Bhagavatam* 10.90.35-37)

In fact, King Vajra established a number of Krishna Deities in the area. The present Dauji temple that we see today was built 200 years ago by Shyama Das of Delhi. Many people also attend this temple to get *darshan* of the single Deity of the 6 feet tall Lord Balarama. From the other side of the temple you can see the Deity of Revati, Lord Balarama's wife. Nearby is the Balabhadra Kund or Kshira (milk) Sagara (sea) where the Deity of Lord Balarama had been hidden during the Moghul invasion. Near this kund is a temple to Harideva, and in the bazaar is another temple to Krishna as Banke Bihari.

There is also much history on the site of Krishna's birth, the Krishna Janmasthana in Mathura. Historical records indicate that the first temple here was also built by King Vajranabha. This temple lasted for many years. The next temple was supposedly built by King Vikramaditya in 400 BCE. That was destroyed by the infamous Mahmud Ghazni in 1017-18. Ancient descriptions relate that such a magnificent building would have taken 200 years of great toil by the world's greatest craftsmen. Thereafter, a third temple was built by a citizen named Jajja during the time of King Vijayapalavadeva, ruler of Mathura, according to an inscription on a stone slab discovered in the area. Sri Chaitanya visited this temple during His visit in 1515. Unfortunately, that was destroyed by the Muslim Sikander Lodi shortly thereafter. The next temple was built by Raja Virsinghadeva Bundela during the reign of Jehangir (around 1650). It is said that this temple stood 250 feet tall and was a stately structure made of intricately carved red sandstone, costing some 33 lakhs of rupees. But again it was destroyed by the fanatic Muslim Aurangzeb in 1669-70. Then it its place a mosque was built, which still stands today. The next temple over the place of Krishna's birth appeared later in the mid-20th century.

Also in Mathura, not far from the Dwarkadish Mandira, there is the temple of white Sweta-Varaha, and another of Adi-Varaha. According to local history as explained by local pandits, back in Satya-yuga this Deity had been given to Lord Indra who worshiped Him in Swarga, his heavenly abode. The Deity was later taken by Ravana when he defeated Indra who took Him to Sri Lanka. Then, after Ravana was defeated by Lord Ramachandra, the Deity was taken to Ayodhya by Lord Ramachandra. Lord Ramachandra gave it to His brother Satrughna who brought it to Mathura when he was dispatched to conquer Madhu Daitya and Lavanasura. After defeating the demonic father and son, Madhu and Lavanasura, he installed the Deity of Adi-Varaha here. This story is more fully explained in Chapter 163 of the *Varaha Purana*.

East of Mathura is Vrindavana, and in Vrindavan is the Radha-Govindaji temple that is another of the seven major temples of Vrindavan. It is across the road and a little farther down the street from the Rangaji temple. It was established by Rupa Gosvami where he discovered the Gopala Deity. The beautiful temple is made out of red sandstone and was completed in 1590. The temple is now only two storeys tall but once reached up to seven storeys. The Muslim fanatic Aurangzeb, doing his dirty work, dismantled the upper five storeys of the temple due to his envy. While his men were destroying the temple, there was a loud thunderous noise that shook the ground. This put fear into the hearts of the men and they immediately stopped and ran away. Due to fear of the Moghuls, before they arrived the devotees moved the original Deities to Jaipur where today many pilgrims go to see them. So the temple now has *pratibhuh* Deities, or representative expansions, of the original Radha-Govindaji that are worshiped. The original Govindaji Deity is said to have been installed in Vrindavan thousands of years ago by Vajranabha.

Also, in Vrindavan, farther into the eastern part of town, are many other temples, including the large and ornate Lala Babu Mandir with Deities of Radha, Krishna, and Lalita. Then at the corner where we turn off from Loi Bazaar to go toward the Banke Bihari Mandir, we find the Gopishwara Mahadeva Shiva temple with a Shiva *linga*, said to have been originally installed by Krishna's great-grandson, Vajranabha, and is the place where Lord Shiva did austerities in hopes of entering the *rasa-lila* dance as a *gopi* (cow-herd girl). In the morning devotees wash the *linga* with milk and other items, and then later the *pujaris* dress the *linga* in bright colored clothes.

A few miles from Barsana is Nandagram, another place where Krishna performed many childhood pastimes described in the *Bhagavatam*. On top of the hill is the main temple that has Deities of Krishna, Balarama, Nanda Maharaja (Krishna's father), Mother Yashoda, Srimati Radharani, and two of Krishna's friends. There is also a Shiva *lingam* in a small shrine across from the temple called Nandisvara, which again is said to have been installed by Vajranabha many hundreds of years ago. It is considered that this hill is an incarnation of Lord Shiva. From the top of the walls that surround the temple we can get good views of the area, and someone who is familiar with it can point out other nearby places connected with Krishna's pastimes that we may want to visit.

Now, let us go into the foothills of the large Girnar Hill in Gujarat where we find the Radha-Damodara temple with beautiful Deities of Krishna's four-armed form. As Lakshmi-Narayana, the Deities are formed of the typical black and brown stone, and are described in the *Skanda Purana* as being self-manifested over 12,000 years ago. Next to the main temple is another for Lord Balarama and Revati, His consort. The original temple at this site is said to have been built 4500 years ago by Vajranath, Lord Krishna's grandson. Not far away is a place where lived Vallabha, the 16th century Vaishnava *acharya*.

Another interesting story is in regard to Guruvayoor in Kerala, South India, which has the Deity of a four-armed standing Vishnu with a *chakra* in the right hand, conchshell in the left, and mace and lotus flower in the other two. Sri Krishna showed this form of His only twice during His appearance on earth: once to Arjuna just before the battle of Kurukshetra while speaking the *Bhagavad-gita*, and once to His parents, Vasudeva and Devaki, at the time of His birth. This Deity is said to have been worshiped by Lord Krishna Himself at Dwaraka thousands of years ago. The legend is that when Krishna left this world, He gave the Deity to His devotee Uddhava to look after it. He then ordered Brihaspati, the guru or spiritual teacher of the demigods, and Vayu, demigod of the wind, to take care of this Vishnu Deity and to install it somewhere for the benefit of humanity. When they arrived at Dwaraka to get the Deity, the city of Dwaraka had already sunk into the sea. After searching in the water, they found the Deity and went south. Not knowing where to go, they sat down by the side of a lake and began to meditate. Soon, Shiva appeared and after some discussion they decided to start a new temple for the Deity of Vishnu near the Rudratirtha Lake. Since that time 5,000 years ago, the place has been known as Guruvayoor (guru for Brihaspati and vayoor for Vayu). Hundreds of devotees visit the temple everyday for seeing the Deity. Western devotees, however, are not allowed in without a letter of permission from the Arya Samaj.

Going eastward we go to Simhachalam. There we find the Jiyada Narasimha temple. It is here where Lord Narasimha's devotee Prahlada is said to have built the original shrine when he was saved from his father Hiranyakashipu. The story is that the hill at Simhachalam is the one from which the demon Hiranyakashipu had his devotee son thrown from it in an attempt to kill him. The mountain was also placed over Prahlada, but the Lord saved him by jumping over the hill and lifting Prahlada from the sea. The hill may seem somewhat lopsided since it is also accepted that the Lord had lifted the hill enough for Prahlada to escape from underneath it. Thereafter, Prahlada asked the Lord to assume a Deity form as both Lord Narasimha (the lion form) who would soon kill Hiranyakashipu, and Lord Varaha (the boar *avatara*) who had already killed Hiranyakshya, the brother of Hiranyakashipu. Thus, the Deity is of Varaha Narasimha.

When Hiranyakashipu was later killed by Lord Narasimha, Prahlada built a temple around the Deity where worship was conducted. In time, however, the temple was neglected and earth covered the Deity. Much later, the king of the lunar dynasty, Pururava, was drawn to Simhachalam and rediscovered the Deity under the earth. Hearing a voice, it instructed him to cover the Deity with sandalwood paste and worship Him, and only uncover Him once a year. This practice has continued and they have an annual festival when everyone can see the Deity without it being covered in sandalwood. Pururava also rebuilt the temple and established the worship of the Deity again, which has continued to this day.

Also, we can take note of the famous Kanaka Durga temple on the hilltop that overlooks the town of Vijayawada. This Deity is considered to be self-manifested. It is said that Adi Shankara had worshiped the goddess here, as well as Agastya Muni, Markandeya, and even the Pandavas, all of which suggests how old this Deity is. Legend relates that she killed the powerful demon Durgama in this area, and is presently accepted as the protector of the city. This is an interesting temple and many people come to see it. You can see families arrive to see the Deities and to perform their *puja* together.

At the nearby Mangalagiri hills, the Pana-Narasimha temple is at the top of a flight of 600 steps on the hillside. The Deity called Pana Narasimha is worshiped only with offerings of water mixed with jaggery, which is a mixture of raw cane sugar, camphor, cardamom, and black pepper. He drinks only half of the offerings while the other half goes for the devotees. It is said that in times long ago other ingredients used to be offered. This is explained in a story. The sage Kashyapa Prajapati had one son, Namuchi, who was a cruel demon. To acquire powers, Namuchi underwent severe austerities which produced intense flames from his body. The fire became so powerful that it began to flow through the universe. The demigods could not withstand the heat that was spreading, so they went to Brahma about this matter. Brahma went to Namuchi to appease him by granting him a boon. Namuchi asked to never be killed by anything either wet or dry, which Brahma granted. After that he was overconfident and began harassing the demigods, who then had to go to Lord Vishnu. He assured them that Namuchi's end would come at the right time.

Later, during a battle which involved Indra killing the armies of Namuchi, Lord Vishnu in His form as Lord

Narasimha took His disk and dipped it into some foam, which was neither wet nor dry, and then gave it to Indra who threw it at Namuchi. Namuchi fled and even went into a cave at Mangalagiri, hiding by giving up his physical form. But the disk followed and killed him there. The blood that began to flow turned into a stream called Raktakalya that spread into the area. Red soil surrounds the temple to this day. The Devas were fearful of the Lord as Narasimha, so they offered Him divine nectar to drink. He drank only half of it and said that in Satya-yuga he would drink only half of the nectar offered to Him. In Treta-yuga He would drink ghee. In Dvapara-yuga He would drink milk from a Kamadhenu cow, and in Kali-yuga He would drink half of the sweet jaggery water that was offered to Him. This is why He only accepts half of the offering, leaving the rest as *prasada* to be accepted by the devotees.

The next place we can go is 200 kilometers south from Hyderbad to Srisailam. This town is next to the Krishna River. It is found on Rishabhagiri Hill. It is mentioned in the *Mahabharata* and the *Puranas*, which indicates its antiquity. It has the Mallikarjuna (Shiva) temple, known as one of the 12 *jyotirlinga* (self-manifesting *linga*) temples in India. It is a large temple, built in 1404-5 by King Harihara Raya. There is a hall of finely carved stone work, beautiful silver doors, and a huge Nandi. The original Shiva *linga* is to the right of the main temple. This temple was visited by Adi Shankara and later by Lord Chaitanya, as well as by Lord Narasimha's devotee Prahlada and Lord Rama, who is said to have installed the Sahasra *linga*, noticeable by the three-headed Naga which surrounds it. Therefore, it is an extremely ancient site. There are also the Panchapandavas, the five *lingas* installed by the five Pandava brothers found in the courtyard. The Parvati (Bhramarambika) temple, one of the 54 *Shakti-peeths*, is up a flight of stairs behind the Shiva temple. Parvati took the form of a bee to kill the Mahisasura demon, the buzzing of which you can still hear by putting your ear to a small hole in the back wall of the sanctum. Other shrines around the temple are for Chandramamba, Rajarajeshwari, Virabhadra, and Annapoorni.

Tirupati, in the Tirumalla Hills, has one of the most famous of the ancient temples. The legend behind the temple to the Deity of Lord Balaji is summarized as follows: Once Bhrigu insulted Mahavishnu, which annoyed Goddess Lakshmi. She then went to earth and did penance in Kolhapur, a location of another famous temple for Lakshmi. The Lord then came in search for the Goddess and arrived at these hills and stayed as Srinivasa. Here He met Padmavathi, an incarnation of Bhudevi and a princess of Narayanapuram, whom He had promised to marry when He appeared as Lord Rama. When He married Her, it was a huge wedding, and the pastime was that He needed extra funds. He borrowed it from Kubera, the treasurer of the demigods. Kubera insisted on repayment with interest. Hence, the devotees in Andhra Pradesh call the Deity Vaddi Kasulaswamy (the Lord of interest), repaying Kubera's interest which never ends. The demigod Kubera is enshrined in the Govindaraja Swamy temple, believed to be there collecting the interest with a brass measure. Thus, somehow, many funds are always coming into the temple. In this way, this temple at Tirupati represents a tradition that goes back many, many hundreds of years.

Thirukkovilur is our next stop of temples with Deities that go back many years. It is located about 35 kilometers south of Tiruvannamali and 40 km west of Villupuram. Its history makes it occupy a distinct place in Vaishnava history. It is one of the 108 Divya Desams of Lord Vishnu. The Kshetra Khanda section in the *Padma Purana* discusses some of the glories of this holy place. It is associated with the Trivikrama *avatara* of Lord Vishnu. After Trivikrama or Lord Vamana had taken the whole universe with three steps from Bali Maharaja, ablution to Trivikrama's feet was performed by Brahma with the sacred waters of the Ganges. That water trickled off His feet and took the form of the sacred tank called the Chakra Tirtha. Indra is said to have had a dip in that water tank, and regained his lost possessions that had been taken by Bali.

Vaithisvarankoil is a small village about 25 to 30 miles south from Chidambaram, and just south of Sirkazhi. The stone temple has long halls with numerous columns. At the sanctum, I easily entered and the guard there was kind enough to show me around and explain a few things. I was able to get *darshan* of the main temple sanctum of Sri Vaidyanathaswamy, as well as the other smaller shrines for the other divinities. The shrine for Murugan is said to be where he received his trident. And the Jatayu Kundam or pond found off the southern hallway is where Jatayu, the great devotee bird of Lord Rama, had his last rites performed by Lord Rama.

Tirucherai is a small village located 15 kilometers southeast from Kumbakonam on the main road to Tiruvarur. Tirucherai, which like many villages may not be on the map, is one of the 108 Divya Desams of Lord Vishnu. It is here at the Saranatha Perumal temple where the Deity of MahaVishnu resides.

The temple compound occupies 1½ acres of land (116 meters in length, 72 meters wide). In front of the temple is the large Sara Pushkarini water tank, which also occupies the same dimensions. The front gate of the temple complex has a fine looking nine-tiered *gopuram* that rises 120 feet tall. Inside the front gate is an additional but smaller *gopuram* of two tiers that leads into the temple. The sanctum is guarded by two sculpted *dwarapalas* or guards. Inside the sanctum, Saranatha Perumal, the presiding MahaVishnu Deity appears in a standing pose that is twelve feet tall while facing east. He is carved from black stone but is adorned with silver hands and chest plate. It is very auspicious to have *darshan* of this Deity. On the left side is the personification of the Cauvery River, and on the right is the sage Markandeya. In front is the smaller *utsavar* festival Deity of Saranatha, accompanied by Bhudevi, Sridevi, and Neeladevi. Actually, the presence of all five consorts of Vishnu, namely Sridevi, Neeladevi, Bhudevi, Saranayaki Amman, and Mahalakshmi within the same temple is a unique feature that is not found in other Vaishnava temples.

Many other shrines also exist within the temple, so there are numerous blessings we can receive by visiting each of them. First, another Deity of Vishnu as Sri Rajagopalaswamy occupies a separate shrine, and is accompanied by His consorts Rukmini and Satyabhama. Another shrine has Lord Venkatesha as Thiruvenkatamudayan. The metal Deities of Sri Rama, Sita, and Lakshmana are in another shrine, as well as Lakshmi-Narasimha. Other shrines are for Kaliyamardhana, Balasaranatha, Senai Mudaliar, Manavala Munigal, Ramanuja, and the twelve Alwars. At the southwestern corner of the Sara Pushkarini lake is a separate shrine for Cauvery who is seen embracing the child form of Vishnu. Images of Brahma and MahaVishnu are also there. This represents the austerity Cauvery Devi performed in order to gain the favor of the Lord.

Texts such as the *Brahmanda Purana*, the *Bhavishya Purana* (Chapters 68-72), and the *Maheswara Narada Samvardha* offer descriptions of the importance of this *tirtha* and pastimes related to it. One of the pastimes is described how Lord Shiva explained the significance of Tirucherai to the sage Narada Muni. The story is that on the eve of the universal deluge MahaVishnu ordered Brahma to safely keep the sacred Vedic texts, like the *Vedas, Agamas, Sashtras,* and *Puranas* in an enormous earthen pot. But with every attempt the pot would brake. He felt discouraged and prayed to MahaVishnu about this. Vishnu then told him that there are twelve Vaishnava holy places that are the most sacred. These included Sri Rangam, Tirupati, Kanchipuram, Tirunarayanapuram, Sri Mushnam, Naimisaranya, Kumbakonam, Vrishabathri, Ayodhya, Badarikashrama, and Sara Kshetram (Tirucherai). Out of all of these, He regarded Sara Kshetra as the most sacred. The hallowed center is graced with nine sacred *tirthas* of which the Sara Pushkarini Lake is the highest. So he instructed Brahma to journey to this place and take a dip in the Sara Pushkarini Lake and form a pot from the clay found in the lake. This would be successful. This is the lake located across the street in front of the temple.

So Brahma went there and he felt greatly satisfied. He then had a dip into the sacred lake and formed a pot from its clay. The earthen pot stood firm, much to his surprise. Brahma then stored all the major Vedic texts within it and kept them safe. Thus, his mission was complete. It is also believed that the seven great *rishis*, namely Bhrigu, Sowraga, Vyasa, Markandeya, Parasara, Vamadeva, and Baninthrathiya, continue to perform penances here to preserve the holy sanctity of the place. Thus, the antiquity of this temple and its holy shrines go back many hundreds of years.

The Senneriappa Iswara temple, a noted Shiva temple, can also be found in this town along the southern bank of the Cauvery River. This is not far from the Vishnu temple described above. It is smaller but no less sacred, and the priests are glad to see visitors. In front of the temple is a lake that is said to have been formed by a drop of ambrosia. It is called Jnanavavi or Bindhusuda. It has a small three-tiered *gopuram* over the second entrance into the temple. Passing through a few hallways one can reach the place of the presiding Deity. This is the Shiva *linga* known as Senneriappar or Sara Parameswara. It was the sage Markandeya who, so many years ago, installed a *linga* in this temple, which is now in the inner sanctum. The sage worshipped it everyday. Surya the Sun-god also is said to have atoned for his participation in Daksha's ritual here. Every year the rays of the sun grace the presiding *linga* for three days in the month of Masi (Feb-Mar). In the inner hallway are other shrines for various Shaivite saints. There are also three images of Durga and two of Chandeswara that are also in this temple. The outer walls of the main shrine have lovely sculptures that depict the pastimes of this place.

If you have stayed at Thiruvarur, then it is easy to take a morning bus for a short day trip east to Nagappattinam. It is on the seashore 24 km east of Thiruvarur, or 70 km east of Tanjore. This town has a Vishnu temple with three full sized Vishnu Deities that are standing, sitting, and lying on Ananta Sesha. It is a Divya Desam, one of the 108 most important Vishnu temples in India. You go in the front entrance, down a hallway and into the main temple hall and then into the sanctum. This is surrounded by a courtyard wherein we find a few other shrines, such as to Lakshmi. Once inside the sanctum you can see the smaller brass standing Vishnu Deity with Sridevi and Bhudevi at His sides. Behind Them is the main Deity, Sundaryarajan, who stands over 15 feet tall. He is spectacular, made of shiny black stone, but He and His ornaments and weapons are covered with solid silver, with a gold Lakshmi on His chest. He is really something to see and I was in awe gazing at Him. This was the whole reason for coming here, and I was glad to do so. After the crowd moved on, I was able to get a close up view. Afterwards I was able to circumambulate the temple and view the other shrines.

The *Brahmananda Purana* explains that this temple, called the Soundarvaraja Perumal temple, has existed in all four *yugas*, beginning with Satya-yuga. The legend is that Nagapattinam was originally called Soundaranyam. The name Nagapattinam, which means City of the Serpent, is derived from the fact that Adisesha, in Satya-yuga, performed austerities here to get the blessing to be able to stay forever in the presence of his Lord, Vishnu. The *Purana* also relates how Dhruva also performed austerities in this place. Dhruva's intention was to get the Lord to appear before him and then ask for the blessing of becoming ruler of the entire world. However, when Dhruva saw Lord Vishnu, he was so overwhelmed by the Lord's beauty that he was entirely content and forgot his materialistic wish. He then simply requested the Lord to remain in Nagapattinam as Soundarya Rajan, "The King of Beauty," and bless the devotees. This is how the temple was manifested.

Another important and ancient temple is in Tiruchirappali, otherwise called Trichy or Sri Rangam. It is said the town was originally known as Tirusirappally, named after the three-headed *asura* Tirusiras who got a blessing from Lord Shiva after worshiping him here. Trichy has three major attractions. One is the Rock Fort temple in the heart of the old city. To get there we board the bus near our hotel and ride to a place several blocks away from the hilltop temple. We walk past the Teppakulam water tank and find the entrance to the Rock Fort temple in the Chinna Bazaar. We leave our shoes at the shoe minder's stall and proceed up more than 400 steps that are cut through the rock of the hill. It is a steep and laborious climb to the summit 273 feet up where the views are great. If it is not too hazy, you can see the Sri Rangam temple to the north. Westerners are, unfortunately, not allowed inside the hilltop temple to see the image of Vinayaka, known here as Uchi Pillayar.

Nonetheless, the Puranic legend of this Deity, as explained in the *Sri Ranga Mahatmya*, is that after Lord Brahma had done penance to help in the creation of the universe, when Brahma was in a state of deep meditation, Lord Vishnu was pleased with him. So Lord Vishnu manifested Himself as the Deity of Lord Ranganatha, known as Ranga Vimana, a form of Vishnu reclining on Seshanaga, the Lord's great serpent servant. Brahma worshiped Lord Ranganatha for many years and later gave the Deity to Vivasvan, the sun-god, who later handed the Deity over to Svayambhuva Manu. Manu passed on the Deity to King Ikshvaku, the great leader of the solar dynasty in which Lord Krishna would later appear as Lord Ramachandra.

Lord Ramachandra gave the Deity to Vibhishana, who was a great devotee and brother of the demon Ravana of the *Ramayana* epic. Vibhishan was returning to Sri Lanka from Ayodhya with the Vishnu Deity that had been presented to him by Lord Rama. However, he had been told that if he should set the Deity down on the ground, he would not be able to move it again. However, the gods were not pleased that the Deity would be taken away from the area of India and devised a plan to keep the deity in Bharat. Thus, when Vibhashan stopped at Sri Rangam to take bath and perform his worship on the banks of the Kaveri River at a holy place called Chandra Pushkarini, he gave the Deity to a brahmana boy with instructions not to place it on the ground. But the boy, who was Lord Ganesh in disguise, placed it on the earth anyway. Then the Deity became firmly fixed to the ground and could not be moved from the spot where it remains to this day. Vibhishan became angry and chased the boy who ran to the summit of the hill that is the Rock Fort today. There Vibhishan caught and struck the boy, who then revealed his real form and stood transformed as Vinayaka. Even though Vibhishan begged to apologize before going on to Sri Lanka, the image of Vinayaka still has a depression on his face where he had been struck.

Another part of the tradition is that a king, Dharma Varma, had seen Lord Ranganatha in Ayodhya, Lord Ramachandra's capital, and prayed to worship Him. So the Lord blessed the king to stay at Sri Rangam. Nonetheless, the Deity also blessed Vibhishana by promising to always look toward his kingdom. This is why the Deity reclines with His head to the west, looking toward the south in the direction of Sri Lanka, Vibhishana's kingdom.

King Dharma Varma and his dynasty of the Chola kings built a large temple around Lord Ranganatha. The worship was quite opulent. But, unfortunately, things declined and gradually the temple was forgotten and covered over by a thick forest. The Deity was only discovered thousands of years later by a Chola king who accidently found it while chasing a parrot. The parrot explained that Lord Ranganatha was buried in the sand. So the king excavated the temple and restored it. It was the king who again established the Sri Rangam temple. Over time, many other Chola kings again expanded the temple, which is presently one of the largest temples in India.

However, the 14th century saw the invading Moghuls plunder most of the Lord's treasures from this temple. The Vijayanagar and Nayak rulers again revived it in the 15th and 16th centuries. Then in the 17th and 18th centuries, the Muslims, French, and then the British used the fortress in furthering their domination over the area. Only after India gained independence in 1947 did the Indian government and the Ramanujas or Sri Vaishnavas finally gain control to oversee the temple properly.

Another ancient temple is found at Tiruthangal (Tiruttangal), a town located two kilometers north of Sivakasi, which is about 18 km east from Srivilliputtur. It is reached by bus from places like Madurai, Srivilliputhur, Sankarankoil, and Virudhunagar. It has the Ninra Narayana Perumal temple.

The temple faces south on a small 100-foot tall hill in the northern part of town. Climbing the stairs, one reaches the spacious entranceway. A sculpture of Narayana Ramanuja, who was the person who spent much of his money to build this hallway, adorns one of the pillars. In the back and to the west is the cave temple wherein we find the Deity of Pallikonda Perumal, Lord Vishnu in His reclining pose. Sridevi and Bhudevi are at His feet while sages like Markandeya and Bhrigu are on either side. The history of this place is that once Lord Ranganatha journeyed to Srivilliputhur to seek Sri Andal for marriage and spent the night here.

The history of this place goes back to a time when the three main Devis, namely Sridevi, Bhudevi, and Neeladevi, wondered who was most favored by Lord Vishnu. Sridevi (Lakshmi) wanted to prove her supremacy and retreated to a secluded spot in order to engage in deep meditation. Many devotees and sages came to that spot to have *darshan* of this Goddess of wealth. In response to their devotional requests, she agreed to reside there eternally as Arunakamalamahadevi. Realizing that living there in isolation would be improper, she prayed for the appearance of Lord Vishnu. The Lord was pleased and agreed to also reside there. Bhudevi and Neeladevi followed in His footsteps and reconciled with Sridevi. It was actually the desire of Lord Vishnu to bless His devotees at this spot, along with His Devis. Thus, this drama was enacted only to accomplish His desire.

Another piece of history of this place deals with Banasura. Many years ago he was the ruler of Mahishmathi and a zealous devotee of Lord Shiva. He had the strength of 1000 arms that adorned his shoulders. His daughter Usha was a devotee of Parvati, who prayed to the goddess for a suitable husband. That night after praying, she dreamed she met a prince of unparalleled charm, but after awaking, she did not know who he was. Her good friend Chitralekha knew the art of painting the images of all the eligible princes. When Usha saw the portrait of Aniruddha, the grandson of Lord Krishna, she greatly blushed. Chitralekha then used her skills of conjuration to transport Aniruddha to the palace of Usha. There they merrily spent a few days together.

Banasura soon detected something was amiss and was infuriated to learn what was going on. Banasura took his army to find and crush Aniruddha, but Lord Krishna also brought His army to find His grandson. Then, due to the entreaties of Banasura, even Lord Shiva appeared to offer assistance. It looked as if Shiva and Krishna would engage in battle. But by Lord Krishna's power, Banasura lost his 1000 arms and was left with only two. After realizing his mistake in the matter, the marriage of Usha and Aniruddha was allowed to take place in grand style. The *Sthala* (or local) *Purana* relates that it was here at Tiruthangal where the extraordinary wedding took place. Thus, the images of Usha and Aniruddha are also found in the main shrine.

Ramesvaram is easy to reach after seeing Madurai and the surrounding area, where we can catch the early morning train for Ramesvaram. It is a relaxing ride (about six hours) as we head toward the coast. Ramesvaram is a tropical island surrounded by coral reefs and sandy beaches with coconut palms and tamarind trees. It is a major center of pilgrimage for both Vaishnavas and Shaivites. The Sri Ramanathaswamy temple is one of the most important in India. It is a massive complex with a number of shrines, holy wells, *gopurams*, and several long hallways, one reaching 4000 feet in length, the longest in the country. The halls are adorned with many large pillars, some of which are covered with scroll work, lotus designs, animals, and other figures, and colorfully painted medallions are on the ceilings.

According to legends, this temple was originally started by Lord Ramachandra. Lord Rama had gone to Sri Lanka to rescue His wife, Sita, and engaged in a great battle during which He killed the demon Ravana. Afterward, He wanted to absolve Himself of the sin by installing a *lingam* at Ramesvaram. He sent His most trustworthy servant

Hanuman to get a Shiva *lingam* from Mount Kailash, but Hanuman was delayed in his return. Since Shiva had to be worshiped by a certain time, Sita made a Shiva *lingam* (known as Sri Ramanatha) out of sand. When Hanuman returned with a *linga,* he was disappointed and angry to find another *linga* already installed. To pacify Hanuman, Rama had the Hanumath *lingam* (known as Visvalingam) installed next to the Ramanatha *lingam.* Then He ordered that all worship should first go to the Visvalingam. So, in this complex the main shrines are for Visvalingam and the Sri Ramanatha *lingam.* It is now the seat of one of the 12 *jyotirlingas.* Thus, the worship here goes back many thousands of years.

The Ramesvaram temple is also where Sri Chaitanya Mahaprabhu found the *Kurma Purana.* Within it He found a verse stating that Ravana kidnapped an illusory Sita, and the real Sita was safely hidden by Agni. This information has greatly relieved many devotees of Sri Sri Sita-Rama.

The Channekeshvara temple at Belur (155 km from Mysore) is the only one of the remaining Hoysala temples that is still a functioning temple. This temple is over 800 years old, started in 1117, and was built entirely of green chlorite by Vishnuvardhana after his victory over the Chola armies. It is said to have taken nearly 103 years to complete it. The temple enshrines the beautiful, four-armed deity of Keshava, which is said to have been worshiped by Lord Brahma at his abode of Satyaloka. Later, King Indradyumna is said to have brought the Deity here and worshipped Him until he left this world, after which the Devas continued the worship until King Vishnuvardhana began the worship. The king discovered the Deity when he was traveling through the area and one of his servants took a bath and was cured of leprosy while bathing in the lake known as Vishnu Samudra, which is situated on the outskirts of town. Legend says that the lake appeared from a drop of nectar that fell from Garuda's pot. The king understood that this was a special place, which was confirmed when the Deity of Keshava appeared in the dreams of both King Vishnuvardhana and Ramanujacharya, telling them to build a temple for Him. Thereafter, as instructed, the king discovered the Deity at Chandra Drona Hill, from where he took the Deity to Sri Narayanapura and then on to Velapura, now known as Belur. The Deity of Chenna Keshava is four-armed, holding the disc and conch shell in the upper hands, and lotus and club in the lower. One interesting thing is that there is a large pair of chappals in a glass case in the front *mandapam* hall. The local cobblers believe the Lord walks to Bababudangiri hill daily to visit Lakshmi who resides there. It is said that the Lord appears in the dreams of the cobblers when the chappals need replacing. They spread red kumkum on the ground so that His footprints appear when He walks through it. Then they prepare new chappals according to the size. This is all quite miraculous for most people, but is common in the pastimes of Sri Krishna.

At another place known as Kankroli, 18 kilometers north of Nathdwara, there is the temple of Lord Dwarkadisha, managed by the Vallabhacarya *sampradaya*. The legend is that the Deity came from Mathura where He was worshiped many thousands of years ago by the great devotee King Amburisha. The temple is located on the banks of the man-made lake of Raja Samand.

Many other examples could be given of the stories and legends of Deities that are found in various temples throughout India, or holy places where temples have been established thousands of years ago, that show how long ago the process of Deity worship has been going on. There are also many additional references in the Vedic texts themselves which show the importance of Deity worship from many thousands of years ago, some of which we will review next.

SCRIPTURAL REFERENCES TO DEITY WORSHIP

Even in the *Puranas*, for example, there are stories that include and relate the importance of worshiping Deities. For starters, in the *Bhagavata Purana* (4th Canto, 8th Chapter) there is the popular story of the great sage Narada Muni teaching Dhruva Maharaja the best way to become spiritually realized. Therein he explains the form of the Lord upon which to meditate and how to worship the Deity or Sri Murti of the Lord. The interesting thing here is that the *Bhagavata Purana* was composed by Srila Vyasadeva about 5,000 years ago, and the incident of Dhruva Maharaja is known to have taken place thousands of years before that. So, this gives some indication of how long Deity worship has been going on.

Narada Muni describes, "The Lord's form is always youthful. Every limb and every part of His body is properly formed, free from defect. His eyes and lips are pinkish like the rising sun. He is always prepared to give shelter to the surrendered souls, and anyone so fortunate as to look upon Him feels satisfaction. The Lord is always worthy to be the master of the surrendered soul, for He is the ocean of mercy. The Lord is further described as having the mark of Shrivatsa, or the sitting place of the goddess of fortune, and His bodily hue is deep bluish. The Lord is a person, He wears a garland of flowers, and He is eternally manifest with four hands, which hold [beginning from the lower left hand] a conchshell, disc, club, and lotus flower. The entire body of the Supreme Personality of Godhead, Vasudeva, is decorated. He wears a valuable jeweled helmet, necklaces and bracelets. His neck is adorned with the Kaustubha jewel, and He is dressed in yellow silk garments." (*Bhag*. 4.8.46-48)

This gives a little idea of the descriptions from Narada Muni to Dhruva Maharaja. Yet, he goes on to explain that yogis who meditate on this form very soon are freed from material contamination. The mantra *Om namo bhagavate vasudevaya* is also worthy of chanting in one's meditation. But the physical form [Deity] of the Lord should also be installed. Then Narada describes how the Deity should be worshiped and with what procedures and paraphernalia. He also says, "It is possible to worship a form of the Lord made of physical elements such as earth, water, pulp, wood, and metal. In the forest one can make a form with no more than earth and water and worship Him according to the previous instructions." (*Bhag*. 4.8.56) This shows some of the elements of which a Deity can be made. But a devotee who seriously engages in this process becomes blessed by the Lord according to whatever is his desire.

Furthermore, in the 11th Canto, Chapter 27 of the *Bhagavata Purana*, Lord Krishna explains to Uddhava the details of Deity worship, how it is important, the benefits of someone installing a Deity in the temple, maintaining it, or the harm that comes to one for dishonoring the Deity or the temples.

Therein, Uddhava relates that all the great sages, including Narada Muni, Srila Vyasadeva, and Brihaspati, have declared that such worship brings the greatest benefit possible in human life. The instructions for this process first emanated from the Lord Himself, and were thereafter also spoken by Lord Brahma to his sons, headed by Bhrigu, and by Lord Shiva to his wife, Parvati. Thus, according to the conclusion he was presenting, this method of worship is appropriate for all orders of society.

Then Lord Krishna begins to explain some of the important points of Deity worship to Uddhava. Some of what He relates are that a person should worship only after cleaning the body with water and the use of mantras. One may worship the Deity form, or a form on the ground, in fire, in the sun, in water, or within the worshiper's own heart, and offer the appropriate paraphernalia in loving devotion. The Deity form appears in eight varieties, such as in stone, wood, metal, earth, paint, sand, with jewels, or in the mind wherein the offerings are provided mentally. A Deity may be temporary or permanent, the latter of which, once installed, should never be sent away. The Deity may be cleaned or bathed, and, thereafter, once the devotee has purified himself and the items, offered the appropriate things according to the type of Deity it is.

"Even very opulent presentations do not satisfy Me if they are offered by non-devotees. But I am pleased by any insignificant offering made by My loving devotees, and I am certainly most pleased when nice presentations of fragrant oil, incense, flowers, and palatable foods are offered with love." (*Bhag*.11.27.18)

In this way, the instructions of Lord Krishna continue in how to care for the Deity and what is to be offered, by which a person can receive both material enjoyment and liberation. Afterwards, "Singing along with others, chanting loudly and dancing, acting out My transcendental pastimes, and hearing and telling stories about Me, the devotee should for some time absorb himself in such festivity.

"The devotee should offer homage to the Lord with all kinds of hymns and prayers, both from the *Puranas* and from other ancient scriptures, and also from ordinary traditions. Praying, 'O Lord, please be merciful to me!' he should fall down flat like a rod to offer his obeisances.

Placing his head at the feet of the Deity, he should then stand with folded hands before the Lord and pray, "O my Lord, please protect me, who am surrendered to You. I am most fearful of this ocean of material existence, standing as I am in the mouth of death." (*Bhag*.11.27.44-46)

In this way, Lord Krishna concludes: "By worshiping Me through the various methods prescribed in the *Vedas* and *tantras*, one will gain from Me his desired perfection in both this life and the next. The devotee should more fully establish My Deity by solidly constructing a temple, along with beautiful gardens. These gardens should be set aside to provide flowers for the regular daily worship, special Deity processions and holiday observances.

"One who offers the Deity gifts of land, markets, cities and villages so that the regular daily worship and special festivals of the Deity may go on continually will achieve opulence equal to My own. By installing the Deity of the Lord, one becomes king of the entire earth, by building a temple for the Lord one becomes ruler of the three worlds, by worshiping and serving the Deity one goes to the planet of Lord Brahma, and by performing all three of these activities, one achieves a transcendental form like My own. But one who simply engages in devotional service with no consideration of fruitive results attains Me. Thus, whoever worships Me according to the process I have described will ultimately attain pure devotional service unto Me." (*Bhag*.11.27.49-53)

The process of Deity worship is so important and special to the Lord, that He also gives a warning to anyone who may try to impede in this process: "Anyone who steals the property of the demigods or the brahmanas [priests], whether originally given to them by himself or someone else, must live as a worm in stool for one hundred million years. Not only the performer of the theft, but also anyone who assists him, instigates the crime, or simply approves of it must also share the reaction in the next life. According to their degree of participation, they each must suffer a proportionate consequence." (*Bhag*.11.27.54-55)

Also, Sukadeva Goswami, over 5,000 years ago, explained in the *Srimad-Bhagavatam* the means for worshiping the physical Deity of the Lord, starting with this prayer: "'My Lord Vishnu, full of six opulences, You are the best of all enjoyers and the most powerful. O husband of mother Lakshmi, I offer my respectful obeisances unto You, who are accompanied by many associates, such as Vishvaksena.

I offer all the paraphernalia for worshiping You.' One should chant this mantra every day with great attention while worshiping Lord Vishnu with all paraphernalia, such as water for washing His feet, hands and mouth, and water for His bath. One must offer Him various presentations for His worship, such as garments, a sacred thread, ornaments, scents, flowers, incense, and lamps." (*Bhag*.6.19.7.)

He also emphasized the importance of worshiping the Deity of Lakshmi-Narayana, where he explains: "If one desires all opulences, his duty is to daily worship Lord Vishnu with His wife, Lakshmi. With great devotion one should worship Him according to the above-mentioned process. Lord Vishnu and the goddess of fortune are an immensely powerful combination. They are the bestowers of all benedictions and the sources of all good fortune. Therefore, the duty of everyone is to worship Lakshmi-Narayana." (*Bhag*.6.19.9)

One other example is in the popular story of Prahlada Maharaja and the Lord's half-lion avatar of Lord Narasimhadeva. Therein, Prahlada explains the nine processes of bhakti-yoga, devotional service, to the Lord. The verse is:

sri-prahrada uvacha
shravanam kirtanam vishnoh
smaranam pada-sevanam
archanam vandanam dasyam
sakhyam atma-nivedanam

"Prahlada Maharaja said: Hearing and chanting about the transcendental holy name, form, qualities, paraphernalia, and pastimes of Lord Vishnu, remembering them, serving the lotus feet of the Lord, offering the Lord respectful worship with sixteen types of paraphernalia, offering prayers to the Lord, becoming His servant, considering the Lord one's best friend, and surrendering everything unto

Him–these nine processes are accepted as pure devotional service." (*Bhag*.7.5.23) In this verse, the word *archanam* means "offering the Lord respectful worship" in the form of the Deity, the *archa-vigraha*.

A further recommendation for engaging in Deity worship is found in the *Bhagavata Purana* on the occasion of the solar eclipse at Kurukshetra, when many sages gathered to participate during the time of Lord Krishna. Upon being questioned about the best way to become free from the karmic bondage to fruitive and sensual activities, they replied: "It has been definitely concluded that work is counteracted by engaging in Vedic sacrifices [rituals] as a means of worshiping Vishnu, the Lord of all sacrifices, with sincere faith. Learned authorities who see through the eye of scripture have demonstrated that this is the easiest method of subduing the agitated mind and attaining liberation, and that it is a sacred duty which brings joy to the heart. This is the most auspicious path for a religious householder of the twice-born [brahminical] orders–to selflessly worship the Personality of Godhead with wealth honestly obtained." (*Bhag*.10.84.35-37)

Many of these stories that we are relating herein are also repeated in other texts, such as the *Vishnu Purana*, *Padma Purana*, *Varaha* and *Brahma Puranas*, and others. So, they are not exclusive to the *Bhagavata Purana*, which shows how important they are.

The following verse also begins to show the process that is involved in worshiping the *archa-vigraha*, or the Deity form of the Lord: "One should worship the Deity along with each of the limbs of His transcendental body, His weapons such as the Sudarshan Chakra, His other bodily features and His personal associates. One should worship each of these transcendental aspects of the Lord by its own mantra and with offerings of water to wash the feet, scented water, water to wash the mouth, water for bathing, fine clothing and ornaments, fragrant oils, valuable necklaces, unbroken barleycorns, flower garlands, incense and lamps. Having thus completed the worship in all its aspects in accordance with the prescribed regulations, one should then honor the Deity of Lord Hari with prayers and offer obeisances to Him by bowing down." (*Bhag*. 11.3.52-53)

All in all, this shows that Deity worship has been a serious aspect of the Vedic process for spiritual development for many thousands of years. Thus, as it is further said, anyone who engages in the worship of the Deity in the temple is said to have reached the truth of studying all of the *Vedas*.

DIFFERENCE BETWEEN IDOL AND DEITY WORSHIP

What we have been describing is called, in certain cultures, such as the Abrahamic religions (Judaism, Christianity and Islam) idol worship, which immediately has the connotation of something bad, false, evil, wicked, and certainly misdirected, as if it will take one to hell. It can conjure in the mind something to do with pagan worship of the devil, or other aberrations as something being a false god. It is, however, most peculiar that none of these religions have, nor do they offer, a clear concept of what is God or what He looks like. But they seem to offer a clear conception of the imaginary idea of what is the devil or Satan. They cry against the process of Deity worship, when that has been outlined most precisely in the Vedic texts, but they cannot give a substantial description of God or the various ways in which He can be worshiped. Christianity is responsible for this more than any other sect.

There is certainly a difference between idol worship and worship of the Deity in the temple. So, let us briefly clarify this point. In this age of Kali-yuga, the worship of and desire for the almighty dollar is certainly a popular but easily recognized form of idol worship in this age. The idol that is worshiped and striven for is the dollar itself. And this extends itself in many ways and forms. Worship of a product of our imagination is also a form of idol worship, which should be avoided. We cannot make up just any form and expect suitable results from worshiping it. But we must understand that the authorized Deity is not someone's imagination, but is formed according to the precise descriptions in the Vedic texts, and is installed according to the exact processes as outlined therein as well. That is what makes the difference. It is similar to the authorized mailboxes set up by the government. If you put your mail in one of them, it will be picked up to be delivered to the address that is on your envelope. However, if you make up your own mailbox and put it on a street corner somewhere, the letter placed therein will go nowhere. Similarly, a pure devotee or *acharya* who is qualified to communicate with God is also qualified to install Him in the Deity form. This is also done through the prescribed Vedic rituals, such as the *prana prathistha* or installation ceremony. Then Krishna accepts that form as His expansion to receive service, prayers, obeisances, and worship from His devotees through this authorized means.

The thing to understand is that once the Deity in the temple has been established through the sacred rituals that call the Divinity to occupy the Deity, the Deity then becomes an expanded form of the Lord. Thus, by worshiping the *archa-vigraha* or Deity form of the Lord, one can approach the Lord who then accepts the service of a devotee by His omnipotent energy. The *archa-vigraha* of the Lord descends upon the request of the *acharyas*, the spiritual masters, and works as an expansion of the Lord in allowing us to view the spiritual form of God with material eyes, and in accepting the service of the devotees. Otherwise, for most people, it is very difficult to see that which is spiritual with material senses, at least until we are qualified with a spiritual consciousness. Thus, the Deity is also the Lord's causeless mercy on us.

Foolish people who have no spiritual perception, or no knowledge of spiritual scripture, consider that the Deity is merely made of material elements, and is, thus, something material, not spiritual. But they do not know or realize that the Lord, being the controller of both material and spiritual energies, can turn what is material into something spiritual, and what is spiritual into something material again. Thus, He can appear as both spiritual or material, but His spiritual nature is never compromised in any way. That is the difference, and that is what must be perceived. When a person begins to realize that, then the act of *darshan*, or seeing the Deity is not a mere exercise in respect and veneration, but it opens the relations between the devotee and God so that it becomes seeing the Deity and being seen by the Deity. There is a special reciprocation between the devotee and Divine which opens to a new level of experience, and new level of a loving devotional relationship. That is when the Deity is no longer mere stone, paint, or wood, jewels, etc. It is the Divine, vibrant with life that is revealed by the Infinite Supreme to the infinitesimal living being.

In many places, as we have seen in the previous section and will further uncover in later chapters, there are stories connected with particular Deities and various temples across India and beyond of how the Deity acted in various ways in reciprocation to the love of the devotee, or in other ways to show the supreme spiritual nature of the Lord in His Deity form. The Lord Jagannatha Deities in Jagannatha Puri, for example, is one such place with myriad pastimes that have taken place between Them and the devotees. Many of these are recorded and can be read and enjoyed, which show that such pastimes with the Deity, of which some people would call miracles, have continued from ancient times down to the present day.

In the Vedic tradition, there have been numerous spiritual authorities and *acharyas* who have attained high levels of realization, love of God, and relations with the Lord through the Deity. These include Ramanujacharya, Madhvacharya, Vallabhacharya, Sri Chaitanya, along with Saint Jnanadeva, Namadeva, Tulasidas, Meera Bai, Ekanatha, Tukaram, Ramadas, and many others who have pastimes with the Deity that have been recorded. Reading the biographies of such advanced devotees can be especially inspiring.

Even Sri Adi Shankaracharya had specific relations with the Deity in the temple. Some people may question how this could be since Shankaracharya was an impersonalist, one who accepts that God has no ultimate form but remains impersonal as in the Brahman effulgence. However, if we study a little of his history, we will see that he not only had special communications with the Deity of the Lord, but he also established Deities in various temples.

He was known for having installed a Shiva *linga* at his matha at Gokarna, worshiped the Deity at Ramesvaram, constructed the Kamakshiamam temple and installed the image of Devi therein at Kanchipuram, visited Tirupathi and recited *slokas* or verses that glorified the form of the Lord, Bhagavan Venkateshwara, from foot to head. He built the Sringeri Matha after having constructed a Sri Chakra on a rock and worshiped the image of Sarada Devi. He had also established a temple of Lord Krishna, his family Deity, at his birthplace of Kaladi for his mother, which you can still see today. He had also visited the Guruvayur temple many times. Near the end of his travels, Sri Shankara went to Badrinath where Lord Vishnu appeared to him and explained that His Murti or Deity form was in the Alakananda River, which should be taken out and established in a temple that Shankara was to build. Thereafter, Shankara had the Deity of Lord Vishnu, Badrinarayana, taken from the river and then constructed and consecrated a temple and installed the Narayana Deity therein. The *pujas* or worship ceremonies were established and Shankara brought suitable Brahmana priests from Kerala and appointed them the traditional temple priests after giving them proper training.

In this way, it is clear that Sri Shankara recommended and established Deity worship in various parts of India for the practice and preservation of Sanatana-dharma, and for the personal spiritual development of the people.

In conclusion, with the kind of evidence as provided above, the importance and the antiquity of temple Deity worship in the Vedic tradition cannot be denied.

□

2
Darshan and the Significance of Deity Worship

Deities, called *murtis* in Sanskrit, are an important part of Vedic temples and the Vedic tradition, but what is the significance of Deities and Deity worship? One thing to understand is that all the images of the Deities in the Vedic pantheon, as found in the temples, are made according to explicit details and instructions found in the Vedic texts called *Shilpa Shastras*. From these instructions we find the means to portray the proper stance, hand gestures, and other factors in the image of the Deity. In this way, Deities are not formed according to whim but in compliance to the scriptural regulations. Then they are installed in the temple in an elaborate ceremony known as *prana pratishta*, wherein the divine personalities are called to appear in the form of the Deity. Some of the Deities are demigods, while others, such as Krishna, Vishnu, Ramachandra, are of the Supreme Being.

Some people, however, do not believe that God has a form. But many verses in the *Puranas* and, particularly, the *Brahma-samhita* establish that the Supreme Being does have a specific form. These texts also describe His variegated features, which include His spiritual shape, characteristics, beauty, strength, intelligence, activities, etc. Therefore, it is considered that the authorized Deities of the Supreme that are shaped according to these descriptions provide a view of the personal form of God.

Those who have no knowledge of God or His form will certainly consider the temple Deities as idols. But this is the effect of their foolishness. They think that the Deities are simply the products of someone's imagination, or merely made of material elements. Of course, there are those who say that God has no form, spiritual or material, or that there is no Supreme Being. Others think that since God must be formless, they can imagine or worship any material form as God, or they regard any image as merely an external manifestation of the Supreme. But images of the demigods are not additional forms or representations of an impersonal God, nor are they equal to God. All such people who think in the above mentioned ways have resorted to their own imagination to reach such conclusions and are, therefore, idolaters. The imaginary images and opinions of God that are formed by those who have not properly learned about, seen, or realized God are indeed idols, and those who accept such images or opinions are certainly idolaters. This is because these images or opinions are based on ignorance and are not a likeness of His real form.

Nonetheless, God is described in the Vedic literature, which explains that God is *sat-chit-ananda vigraha*, meaning the form of complete spiritual essence, full of eternity, knowledge, and bliss, and is not material in any way. His body, soul, form, qualities, names, pastimes, etc., are all nondifferent and are of the same spiritual quality or energy. This form of God is not an idol designed from someone's imagination, but is the true form, even if He should descend into this material creation. And since the spiritual nature of God is absolute, He is nondifferent from His name or any other aspect of Himself. Thus, the name Krishna is an *avatara* or incarnation of Krishna in the form of sound. Similarly, His form in the temple is not merely a representation, but is also qualitatively the same as Krishna as the *archa-vigraha*, or the worshipable Deity form.

Some people may question that if the Deity is made from material elements, such as stone, marble, metal, wood, or paint, how can it be the spiritual form of God? The answer is given that since God is the source of all material and spiritual energies, material elements are also a form of God. Therefore, God can manifest as the Deity in the temple, though made of stone or other elements, since He can transform what is spiritual into material energy, and material energy back into spiritual energy. Thus, the Deity can easily be accepted as the Supreme since He can appear in any element as He chooses, whether it be stone, marble, wood, gold, silver, or paint on canvas. In this way, even though we may be unqualified to see God, who is beyond the perceptibility of our material senses, the living beings in this material creation are allowed to see and approach the Supreme through His *archa-vigraha* form as the worshipable Deity in the temple. This is considered His causeless mercy on the materially conditioned living beings that He would allow Himself to appear to humanity as a Deity to accept our worship and service.

In this manner, the Supreme Being gives Himself to His devotees so they can become absorbed in serving, remembering and meditating on Him. Thus, the Supreme comes to dwell in the temple to accept our worship and attract the eyes to concentrate and meditate on the Deity, and the temple becomes the spiritual abode on earth. In time, the body, mind and senses of the devotee become spiritualized by serving the Deity, and the Supreme becomes fully manifest to him or her. Worshiping the Deity of the Supreme and using one's senses in the process of bhakti-yoga, devotional service to the Supreme, provides a means for one's true essential spiritual nature to unfold. The devotee becomes spiritually realized and the Deity reveals His spiritual nature to the sincere souls according to their evolutionary spiritual development. This can continue to the level in which the Supreme Being in the form of the Deity engages in a personal relationship and performs reciprocal, loving pastimes with the devotee, as has previously taken place with other advanced individuals.

At this stage, *darshan* is not simply a matter of viewing the Deity in the temple, but to one who is spiritually realized it is a matter of experiencing the Deity and entering into a personal, reciprocal exchange with the Supreme Personality in the form of the Deity. At that stage, you may view the Deity, but the Deity also gazes at you, and then there is a spiritual exchange wherein the Deity begins to reveal His or Her personality to you. This is what separates those who are experienced from those who are not, or those who can delve into this spiritual exchange and those who may still be trying to figure it out. For those who have experienced such an exchange with the Supreme or His Deity, at this stage the worship of the Supreme Being in the Deity moves up to a whole different level, with no limits as to the spiritual love that can be shared between the devotee and the Deity.

□

3
Why God Reveals Himself to His Devotees

When it comes to the *jiva* or individual soul attracting the attention of the Supreme Being who is *atmarama* or completely self-satisfied, how is it possible? What would the infinitesimal soul have that the Supreme Being would want? Why would the Lord, the Absolute Truth, be attracted to anyone, even if they are advanced in doing austerities, yoga, *pranayama* or breath control, Vedic and spiritual studies, going on long and difficult pilgrimages, or anything else? How would that gain the attention from the Supreme Being?

The fact is that in so many places in the Vedic scriptures, Lord Krishna explains specifically that the only way to attain Him is through love and devotion, *bhakti*. That is the process of bhakti-yoga.

Lord Krishna explains, "It is not possible to attain Me through *jnana* (knowledge, contemplation, or mental speculation), yoga, renunciation, penance, study of scriptures, or the performance of duty in the same way in which it is possible to attain Me through *bhakti*." (*Bhagavata Purana* 11.4.21)

"The devotees are My heart and I am the heart of My devotees. They know nothing except Me. I also do not know anything except them." (*Bhagavata Purana* 9.4.68)

"Like one who has no freedom at all, I am completely under the subjection of My devotees, as if they always hold Me in their fist." (*Bhagavata Purana* 9.4.63)

In the *Bhagavad-gita,* one of the most important of all spiritual texts of India, Sri Krishna explains so many times that it is through *bhakti* that one can reach the ultimate perfection and know Krishna in full, such as in 18.55. On the other hand, the path to understand and reach the formless aspect of God, which is highly acclaimed by many, is still missing the means of attracting the Supreme Being to us. The thing to realize is that such systems as jnana-yoga, which consists of the attainment of spiritual knowledge and discrimination between the material and spiritual, can lead to the Brahman, or the formless and attributeless aspect of God. Karma yoga or adopting all our actions into pious purposes, leads us to heaven, as long as the good karma we have acquired does not run out. Yoga and the system of *yamas* and *niyamas,* meaning the rules and regulations of conduct and preparation for higher perception, or *pranayama* and breath control, leads to the realizations of the Paramatma or Supersoul within us all. But none of these by themselves leads us to Bhagavan, the Supreme Person.

It is *bhakti* which purifies and spiritualizes both the mind and senses and the intellect so that they can perceive the higher dimensions in which the Absolute Truth exists. Sri Krishna says in the *Srimad-Bhagavatam,* "Just as by the continuous application of the eye-ointment the eyes become clean and can see clearly those things that may be difficult to see, the constant reading of the sacred texts that relate My pastimes, or listening to them, purify the heart and the devotee is able to see Me, who is otherwise too subtle to be seen with ordinary senses." (*Bhagavata Purana* 11.10.26)

In this way, it is the *bhakti* or love and devotional service, or actions that are absorbed and performed in loving thoughts of Lord Krishna, that creates the force of attraction of Lord Krishna towards His devotee. Krishna is charmed by this loving devotion when it resides in His devotee and gains more pleasure from it than from His own natural blissful potency. As soon as the desire to serve Krishna arises in the heart of the devotee, it generates a corresponding desire in Him to relish that service. The more pure love is aroused in the devotee for serving Krishna, the more Krishna wants to go there and experience that loving attitude and engage in reciprocating with that devotee. The intensity with which Krishna is drawn to that devotee is reciprocal to the intensity of the devotee's *bhakti* or eagerness to serve Krishna.

How can Krishna accept the devotee's service if He remains on the transcendental plane and the devotee on the phenomenal if he has no need for such service and feels neither thirst, hunger, heat or cold? The attraction of the devotee's loving service makes Him come down to the devotee's level in the form of Sri Vigraha, or the Deity form in the temple, and accept all its limitations in order to receive the offerings of food, drink, *arati* rituals, or clothes that are lovingly offered to Him by the devotees. In this way, the Deity actually begins to feel the hunger or thirst, or the need for the service offered by the devotees. Then the Lord in the Deity form relishes the love and service that is offered. This is also the grace of God for the devotee, which paves the way for the devotee to move forward in his or her spiritual progress to attain the spiritual realm of God.

This grace or mercy of God is first developed by *sadhana* or spiritual practice according to the principles of that practice for the devotee's purification, but such grace of God is over and beyond *sadhana* alone, but is dependent more on the love that is developed and offered to the Supreme. It is the warmth of that love from the devotee that causes the heart of Bhagavan to melt and flow toward the devotee in the form of grace.

This is why the Supreme Being will take up residence in the form of the Deity, and in this way turns what appears to be a material form into something that is spiritual and reciprocal to those who are devoted in a loving way that attracts the Lord to them. Then the Lord may reveal Himself by so many ways to show the devotee that He is accepting their service, or even in need of their service, or in dreams to help guide them in their service, and so many other ways. Through this means the Lord kindles and urges the love the devotees have for Him to even higher levels of expression, up to and including not being able to exist without engaging in their offerings of devotional service to the Supreme. When this happens, the devotees feel their life is empty without being able to continue their offerings to the Lord in the Deity form. This is only some of the ways the Lord actually inspires deeper levels of love within the devotee, which attracts Him all the more, from which the devotee also continues to become increasingly attracted to the Supreme.

Therefore, the exchange between the Lord in the form of the temple Deity and the service offered by the devotees invokes the same spiritual atmosphere as found in Lord Krishna's own supreme transcendental abode of Goloka Vrindavana. The Lord accepts the service of the devotee through His Deity form and inspires the devotees to service in deeper levels of love, which enlivens the Lord, which thus enlivens the devotees, like a spiritual competition of greater and greater levels of loving ecstasy for everyone. This is the epitome of loving relations for which the soul is always seeking. This is also why the Lord begins to reveal Himself to be the divine personality within the Deity, showing not only that the Deity is more than mere stone or material elements, but actually reciprocates with the devotee as the Supreme Person. No other process can draw or attract the Supreme Lord as this loving devotional service. There are many examples that have happened, and many that continue to happen throughout the world in the way and for the reasons we have described. What follows are just some of them. Many more examples could be included because they happen in many ways, but I hope this will be enough to convey the variety of such interactions between the Deities and their devotees.

□

4

Stories of Deities and Their Reciprocation

Deities can be considered as another channel or portal through which the higher dimension or the Supreme Being directly reveals Himself to those in the material realm. Without understanding this, or without becoming qualified to perceive it, no one will actually realize the deeper character or nature that can be within the Deities, and the reciprocation with Them that can be attained. However, we know that there will be many who are simply too dull-headed to be able to comprehend this. In spite of all the explanations and information that is supplied, they will remain full of doubt and scepticism, believing or perceiving nothing but what can be viewed with their faulty material senses. Thus, the finer aspects of the spiritual realm will remain aloof from such people, and they will never fathom how the Deity of the Lord can show Himself or interact with those of us who are still residing in the material world but are on the spiritual path. So what follows are various examples of how the Deities have revealed Themselves to Their devotees in various ways.

Historically, there are numerous temples throughout India that are important, or that have significance in the way they were established and what parts were played in their development, or are related to events from ages ago that took place at the present location. And as we travel the length and breadth of India we can take note of the various temples wherein the Deities have exhibited activities with their devotees in various ways. These show that the Deity is not ordinary or mere stone or marble or wood, but is imbibed with personality of the Divine Being and can make what is material into that which is spiritual, and, thus, do whatever the Deity wants to do to reveal Himself or Herself to the devotees.

Furthermore, it has been my own experience that as you travel through India visiting these temples, there are still so many spiritual experiences that you can have if you are spiritually qualified and open to them. By that I mean if you are practicing a spiritual path as in a regular *sadhana*, and have developed some appreciation for what lies in the spiritual dimension and beyond mere sense perception, then you also become eligible to have reciprocation in many ways with the Deities of these temples, if the Deity so desires. There is nothing but whatever blockages we have in our own mind that excludes us from such experiences.

THE TEMPLES OF VRINDAVANA

Let us first start with the temples in Vrindavana, the land of Lord Krishna. To recognize the spiritual significance of the holy *dhams*, or places of spiritual energy, may not be so easy for neophytes. As I said earlier, in order to perceive the spiritual atmosphere in places like Vrindavan you have to receive the blessings of the resident devotees and become qualified so that Vrindavan reveals itself to you. An example of this was related to me by a friend. When he visited the holy place of Radha Kund which is near Vrindavana, he met an old *sadhu*, a saintly man who had retired from material life and was now living at Radha Kund. My friend asked the *sadhu* some questions and at first the man hesitantly explained that he did not work or attempt to maintain himself. He simply depended on Krishna and chanted the Lord's holy names at Radha Kund. How he got his food was that a small boy would come by and give him some food every day. The man explained that as a person becomes more and more spiritual, he will recognize the eternal atmosphere that pervades Vraja, especially at Radha Kund, and he will not feel the need to take so much care of the body. My friend then asked him if he could actually see the spiritual world or if he had ever seen Krishna at this holy place. The old man said he had not seen Krishna, but sometimes he could here the *gopis* talking with Krishna or discussing amongst themselves how Krishna looked and what He was doing.

My friend then asked the old *sadhu* how it was possible for him to perceive such things? The man then began talking quite readily and convincingly told my friend that Radha Kund was indeed the spiritual world; you simply had to remove your materialistic vision. Then the old man took my friend's hand and pushed it flat to the ground on the banks of the Radha Kund and said, "Just touch this land and you can feel the spiritual nature of it." My friend told me that at that moment a charge went up his arm from the ground and he could actually feel the difference, that this was indeed a spiritual place. But before my friend got the blessings of this sage, he could not really feel the difference. And that is what is necessary. Until you can actually perceive it, all you can do is to try to understand with your mind and imagine how Krishna performed so many pastimes here, and how this place is spiritual. But the actual realization of such things goes much further and much deeper than that. It is a matter of re-establishing your spiritual identity and connection with the spiritual realm. It is the reawakening of your spiritual consciousness and actually perceiving the subtle nature of spiritual reality. That is our real nature, our real home. It should not be so difficult to re-establish our connection with it. It is only a matter of freeing ourselves of lifetimes of material conditioning. And that is, essentially, what the spiritual path is all about. When you begin to rise above this material influence, the habitual thoughts patterns that have become so hard to resist, and you begin to see what you really are as a spiritual entity, then you can also begin to enter into the perception of spiritual reality

The Deities of Sri Sri Radha-Damodara that used to be in Vrindavana, but are now in Jaipur.

and see that, actually, it is all around us. It is everywhere. It is what we are, and the Supreme Reality is only waiting for us to rise to that level of understanding and witnessing this spiritual truth. Even a glimpse of this reality will change our lives, and that is when we can become open to receiving the reciprocation with this Supreme Reality, some of which we will discuss now.

RADHA DAMODAR

There are many, many temples that have significant histories and pastimes related to them in the area of Mathura/Vrinavana, or what is called Vrajamandala. For example, in Vrindvana, there is the Radha-Damodar Mandir. The original Deities of Radha-Damodar were installed by Rupa Gosvami in 1542, but were later taken to Jaipur where they are now worshiped. The present Deities are considered equal to the original. There is also a stone or *shila* from Govardhana Hill in the temple that has an actual footprint of Krishna on it. Krishna personally appeared to Sanatana Gosvami to give him the *shila*. He told Sanatana that because he was having difficulty from old age he should stop his daily circumambulation of Govardhana Hill and simply circumambulate the *shila*. The footprint became part of the stone when Krishna stood on it and caused the stone to melt from the sweet sound of His flute playing. Now pilgrims circumambulate the temple four times, which is equal to walking once around the 15 mile path of Govardhana Hill. You can ask the *pujari* (priest) at the temple for Giriraja *darshan* and for a few rupees he will bring this Govardhana *shila* for you to see.

RADHA SYAMASUNDARA

Not far away is the Radha-Shyamasundara temple, which is one of the seven main temples of Vrindavan and has some very beautiful Deities. It was established by Shyamananda PrabhuShyamananda Prabhu who was a a very elevated *bhakta* and disciple of Sri Chaitanya Mahaprabhu. In fact, one time he saw Srimati Radharani, Lord Krishna's closest devotee. Shyamananda Prabhu would regularly clean the little forest area of Nidhibana and once happened to find an ankle bell. He thought it must be Radharani's since he knew Krishna and Radha often spent Their evenings there. This is because Their pastimes continue to go on there in the spiritual dimension, even thousands of years after They were known to have lived here.

When Radharani discovered one of Her ankle bells was missing, she sent Lalita to find it. At Nidhibana, Lalita saw Shyamananda Prabhu and asked him if he had found an ankle bell. He said he had and asked if it was hers. Lalita said it belonged to her sister and asked to have it. Shyamananda said he would not give it to her but only to her sister. Lalita insisted that he give it to her, and Shyamananda continued to refuse. So Lalita returned to Radharani and Radha decided to personally go for the ankle bell Herself. Approaching Shyamananda, Radha asked for the ankle bell and he was happy to give it to Her. Radha, being pleased with his service, revealed Her identity to him and by impressing Her ankle bell into his forehead with Her hand personally gave him a *tiloka* mark. Later, the other devotees and *bhaktas* criticized him for wearing a new style of *tiloka*. But that night Srimati Radharani appeared to Jiva Gosvami in a dream and told him that She was the one who gave Shyamananda the *tiloka* mark. Then all the devotees went to Shyamananda to ask for forgiveness and accepted that he actually saw Srimati Radharani. This is another story signifying that the eternal pastimes of the spiritual realm are continually taking place in Vrindavan.

PISI MA AND HER DEITIES OF LORD CHAITANYA AND LORD NITYANANDA

Down a few doors from the temple of Bana-Khandi

Mahadeva near Loi Bazaar in Vrindavana, around a few corners from the Radha Syamasundara Temple, is the little temple of Gaura-Nitai (Lord Caitanya and Lord Nityananda) of Pisi Ma Gosvamini. She belonged to the famous Mukhopadhyaya family, the landlords of Delagrama in the district of Nadiya in Bengal. Before Pisi Ma became a devotee of Gaura Nitai, she was known as Chandrashashi. Once she happened to go to Siuri and stay in a house near a temple in which the Gaura-Nitai Deities of Murari Gupta, an associate of Sri Chaitanya Mahaprabhu, were served by Balarama dasa Babaji, a *siddha* or perfected saint. She saw the beautiful images of Gaura-Nitai and developed motherly affection for Them. She also started offering Them khira, a sweet made from 40 kgs, of milk every day.

Once the Deities said to her in a dream, "Ma! We are hungry. We want to eat *khira* prepared by you." When she told Balarama dasa Babaji about this he said, "The scriptures forbid the cooking of food for the Deities by a person not duly initiated." Therefore, she got herself initiated by Balarama dasa Babaji and started offering *khira* prepared by herself to Gaura-Nitai. Gaura-Nitai were now very happy to have a mother who loved Them so much. But Chandrashashi was not to stay in Siuri for long. Gaura-Nitai knew this. They trembled at the very thought of her going away. One night she saw in a dream that both Gaura and Nitai were holding the loose end of her sari and saying "Ma! You do not go away from here. If you go, who will give us *khira* everyday? You are Our mother and We are your children. How can children live without the mother?"

Chandrashashi, like a good but helpless mother, caressed Them lovingly but pleaded her inability to stay on in Siuri indefinitely and asked Them to leave her sari. But They would not leave. In a tug of war that ensued, a piece of her sari was torn off and remained in the hand of Gauranga. When Chandrashashi woke up, she saw that a piece of her sari was actually torn off. Immediately she went to Balarama dasa Babaji and told him about it.

The day had just dawned and the door of the temple was closed. Balarama dasa Baba opened the door. Both he and Chandrashashi were surprised to see the torn off piece of the sari in the hand of Gauranga.

Chandrashashi was overwhelmed with a strong current of ecstatic love that in a moment swept away her attachment to home and all its glory and splendor. With determination never to go back she began to live in the temple and serve Gaura-Nitai with motherly affection. How could she do otherwise after finding children like Gaura-Nitai?

Chandrashashi was only twenty years old at this time. Her staying alone in the temple with Babaji aroused suspicion in the minds of people who began to talk slanderously about her and Babaji. This pained her very much. One night before going to sleep she wept before Gaura and Nitai and complained to Them of her plight.

That same night, Gaura-Nitai appeared to her in a dream and said, lovingly throwing their arms around her neck, "Ma! Let us go to Vrindavana."

So Chandrashashi and Balarama dasa Babaji took Them to Vrindavana, where they are now worshipped in a temple in Vanakhandi. Once in Vrindavana, the people began to call Chandrashashi Pisi Ma, meaning father's sister. (From *Experiences in Bhakti*, p. 70)

In this way, she renounced her family and all her wealth at the age of twenty and came to live in Vrindavana with Them. Pisi Ma served Gaura-Nitai as if They were her own children. However, when she became a hundred years old, it was no longer possible for her to continue her service to Them. So she deputed Sripada Gopeshvara Gosvami, a descendent of Lord Nityananda for the service. He was very dedicated and he served in the mood of a friend to the Deities. But Gaura Nitai were accustomed to the motherly affection of Pisi Ma and did not immediately adjust Themselves to the friendly attitude of Gopeshvara Gosvami. Pisi Ma would bathe Them in warm water, while Gopeshvara used cold water. So the Deities caught a cold.

Pisi Ma, who lived in a room upstairs, could tell something was wrong and learned about the cold the Deities were suffering from. So she came down to see Them and saw Their red eyes and phlegm flowing from Their noses. She wiped the phlegm with a corner of her sari and touched Their bodies, feeling that They had a fever. She called Gopeshvara Gosvami and told him, "What have you done? You have bathed Them in cold water and made Them ill. See what severe cold They have caught and how Their nose is running?"

As she said this, she showed Gopeshvara the corner of her sari stained with Gaura-Nitai's phlegm. But Gopeshvara did not believe this. So Pisi Ma in anger held the other corner of her sari near the nose of Gauranga and said, "Baba, sneeze a bit." Gaura sneezed and again phlegm came out of his nose, and the temple was filled with its supernatural aroma. Gopeshvara Gosvami, realizing the real position of Pisi Ma, fell down at her feet in penitence. (From *Experiences in Bhakti*, p. 32)

I will describe one final miracle with Pisi Ma and her Gaura-Nitai Deities that I know. When Pisi Ma gave her Gaura-Nitai Deities to Gopeshvara Gosvami he wanted to serve Them in the mood of a friend, called *sakhya-rasa,* but he said They were too small and looked more like little children, which was not appropriate for his mood. He told Pisi Ma that the small size of the Deities failed to arouse his friendly sentiment, thus he could not serve Them to his full satisfaction. Then, to solve this difficulty, Pisi Ma entered the temple, held the chins of Gaura-Nita with her hands and pulled Them upwards. The Deities allowed Themselves to be pulled and assumed Their present form, which is taller, as they are seen to this day in Their temple in Vrindavana.

RADHARAMANA

Another important temple nearby is the Radharamana Mandir, founded by Gopala Bhatta Gosvami. Gopala Bhatta had been worshiping a *shalagrama-shila,* which is Krishna or Vishnu in the form of a stone he had gotten while on pilgrimage in Nepal. These special *shalagrama-shila*s are found in the Gandaki River there. However, Gopala Bhatta longed to have a Deity of Krishna to worship and dress. Then one day in 1542 the Deity of Radharamana spontaneously manifested from the *shalagrama-shila,* thus fulfilling Gopala Bhatta Gosvami's desire. You can still see the stone or *shila* on the back of the Deity, from which He manifested Himself. This is one of those miracles of *bhakti.*

LOKANATHA GOSWAMI AND THE DEITY OF RADHAVINODA THAKURA

Lokanatha Gosvami was one of the closest associates of Sri Chaitanya Mahaprabhu, and was commissioned by Him to go to the area of Vrindavana to rediscover the holy places connected with the pastimes of Lord Krishna. Vraja-Vrindavana was at that time covered with forests. So he went from forest to forest looking for the necessary evidence. While he was engaged like this, his mind was set on Krishna and His pastimes, and he always shed tears in such remembrance.

Once when he was staying under a Tamala tree near Kishori Kund, a pond in the forest of Chatravana, a thought came to his mind. He thought if he had with him Sri Krishna Himself in the form of His *vigraha* or Deity form, he could serve and please Him so that He might also help him in his explorations. The moment he thought in this way, Krishna felt attracted towards him and became restless to receive his service. He thought of a clever way to reach him immediately in the form of the Deity. He went to Lokanatha Swami in the guise of a tribesman with his own image and said, "Maharaja, this is my Thakura (Deity) Radhavinoda.

The little Deity of Radharamana of Vrindavana that manifested from a shalagram-shila stone by the fervent prayers of Gopal Bhatta Goswami.

I have been serving Him since a long time ago. Now I have become old and cannot serve anymore. I am leaving Him with you. I shall be happy if you kindly serve Him."

This was like a bolt from the blue for Lokanatha. The benign Lord had responded to his desire and come to him of his own. Tears of love and gratitude streamed out of his eyes. He took the image, clung it close to his heart and was for some time lost within himself. On regaining outer consciousness, he looked all round for the man who had brought the Deity, but he was nowhere to be seen. Who was he and where had he gone after doing him that great favor? The thought was plaguing his mind when the Deity of Radhavinoda smiled and said, "Who could bring Me? I have brought Myself. I was lying in Kishori Kund nearby. Since you desired eagerly to serve Me, I have come. I have been forcibly drawn by your love. I could not resist the temptation of enjoying your loving service. I am very hungry. Give Me something to eat."

Radhavinoda remained with Lokanatha till the end. Lokanatha made a bag from the fibre of some plant, in which he carried Him wherever he went. Radhavinoda felt happier in it than even in His celestial abode in Vaikuntha or Goloka. It is said that He was of great assistance to Lokanatha in discovering His own pastime places, *lila-sthalis*. Narayana Bhatta Gosvami writes in his *Vraja-bhakti-vilasa* that Lokanatha Goswami discovered as many as 333 forests and places connected with the *lila* of Sri Krishna. (From *Experiences in Bhakti*, p. 54)

LALA BABU AND THE KRISHNA CHANDRAMA DEITY

Lala Babu was born in 1775 in great wealth. His grandfather Ganga Govinda Sinha was owner of a large state and the Governor of Bihar. He inherited the property of his grandfather, thus becoming the richest and most respected man in Eastern India of his time. But the spirit of *bhakti* always dwelt in his mind. Therefore, one day he renounced everything and moved to Vrindavana. That is when he built the beautiful Lala Babu temple in Vrindavana, which you can still see there. He installed beautiful Deities of Radha and Krishna. The name of the Krishna Deity was Sri Krishna Chandrama.

After the installation of the Deities a strange thought came to him and he asked the *pujari* priest to keep a small lump of butter on the head of Sri Krishna Chandrama. His idea was that if the butter actually melted, it would indicate if the Deity was really alive. If the Deity was alive, then the heat of the Deity would melt the butter.

The *pujari* did as asked, and after a little while the butter actually melted and flowed down the Deity's cheeks. The *pujari* and the other devotees in the temple began to cry aloud with tears of joy. Lala Babu also become so overwhelmed with *bhava,* ecstatic love for Krishna, that he fell on the ground unconscious. (From *Experiences in Bhakti*, p. 31)

BANKI BEHARI

The Banki Behari Mandir is one of the most popular temples of Vrindavan. Haridas Gosvami found the Deity of Banki Behari at the bottom of Visakha Kunda in Nidhiban after Haridas had a dream in which the Deity appeared to him and told him where to look. When you visit the temple of Banki Behari you will see that the curtain in front of the Deity is closed for a few seconds every minute. This is because the Deity once walked off the altar and out of the temple to follow a great devotee who had come for *darshan*. Apparently the devotee and Deity gazed at each other too long and the Deity became fond of the devotee and later walked off the altar to find him. When the temple priests found the Deity of Banki Behari missing from the altar, they went out looking for Him. After finding Him in the forest of Vrindavana, they placed Him on the altar again but began closing the curtain at short intervals to keep the Deity from getting too attached to any of the visiting devotees. This tradition has continued ever since then.

The beautiful Deity of Sri Syamasundara, made from black marble, at the Krishna Balarama Mandir in Vrindavana.

The beautiful Deity of Srimati Radharani who accompanies Sri Syamasundara at the Krishna Balarama Mandir in Vrindavana.

MADANA GOPALA AND SANATANA GOSWAMI

The Madana Mohana temple, located on a hill near the old river bed of the Yamuna, was established by Sanatana Gosvami. This was one of the first temples erected after Sri Chaitanya's visit to Vrindavan. According to records, it was originally Sri Adwaitacharya who had discovered the Deity of Madana-Mohana in the hill, called Dwadashaditya. It is also said that the original Deity was fashioned by the architect of the demigods Vishwakarma, under the direction of King Pariksit's mother, Uttara, many years ago. The Deity was called Madana Gopala when He was under the care of Sri Adwaita. It was Sri Adwaita who later gave the Deity to a priest in Mathura named Purushottama Chaube.

Sanatana Gosvami was entrusted by Sri Chaitanya Mahaprabhu with the task of rediscovering the holy places in Vrindavana. He lived there on Aditya-tila on the bank of the Yamuna River. But he would go to Mathura for *madhukari*, begging from door to door for something to eat because there were few people in Vrindavana at that time. Once he happened to go to the house of Damodara Chaube. There he saw the beautiful image of the Deity of Madana Gopala. The priest had treated the Deity like one of his children and when Sanatana Gosvami saw this he criticized the priest for not following the many rules and regulations for Deity worship. Then in a dream Madana Mohan told Sanatana that He had been happy with the priest's spontaneous love, but now He was no longer happy with all these rules that were supposed to be followed.

Nonetheless, the Deity stole the heart of Sanatana and he was lost in *bhava-samadhi*, totally absorbed in ecstatic love thinking of the Deity. He wanted to offer his loving service to this Deity of Madana Gopala, but he tried to suppress his desire. Certainly, the Chaube family would not give away their Deity to him. But even if they did, how would he get the means to serve Him as well as the Chaube family?

However, it was not possible for him to suppress this desire. It grew stronger all the time, and the Deity was in his mind always. He would go to the Chaube's house on the excuse of *madhukari* to get the *darshan* of Madana Gopala. Madana Gopala could not remain unaffected by the seed of *bhava* and *bhakti* that had sprouted in the heart of Sanatana, for it evoked a similar desire in the mind of Madana Gopala.

There was no end to Sanatana's happiness and astonishment when one day Chaube's wife, who had motherly affection for Madana Gopala and served Him lovingly, said to him in a sorrowful mood and with tears coursing down from her eyes, "Baba! From today you have to accept the responsibility of the service of Madana Gopala. Gopala has grown up and become restive and unmanageable. He does not want to remain under the protection of His mother. He asked me in a dream yesterday night to give Him to you. I have also become old and imbecile and cannot serve Him well. It is in His interest that I entrust Him to someone, who can serve Him well and with affection." Fortune smiled on Sanatana. He returned to his *kutir* (cottage) with the treasure of his heart.

At first Sanatana used to keep Madana Mohan in a tree because he had no where else to keep Him. Later, Sanatana built another hut of straw near his own as his temple in which he installed Madana Gopala. For offerings to His Deity, Sanatana still had to depend on doing *madhukari,* and from whatever flour he got he prepared *bati.* This was prepared by kneading flour, rolling it into balls and baking them on fire. He would then offer them to Madana Gopala with saltless and spiceless vegetable, prepared from leaves he collected in the forest. Madana Gopala somehow kept accepting and swallowing this fare for a few days, hesitating to complain about it. But one day he said to Sanatana in a dream, "Sanatana, I find it difficult to swallow this *bati* of flour and leaves boiled without salt. I have to push them down My throat forcibly. Why not give me some salt along with these?"

Tears trickled down from the eyes of Sanatana. In utter helplessness he said in all humility with folded hands,

"Prabhu! You know that Your humble servant is a recluse, without any wherewithal for your service. You ask for salt today. Tomorrow You may ask for molasses and then for *raj-bhoga* (a large royal offering of food). How shall I manage? I have been enjoined by Chaitanya Mahaprabhu to follow the ideal of a Vaishnava Vairagi (a Krishna devotee renunciant), who is supposed to not ask for anything from anyone and remain content with whatever he gets from *madhukari*. You know that in *madhukari* people give flour, but no salt."

Did Madana Gopala feel humiliated? Did He think of going back to the house of Damodara Chaube where He got better things to eat? No. Greedy persons do not mind humiliation. His greed was for the loving service of Sanatana was so great that He preferred to suffer humiliation and eat the poor and saltless food he gave rather than leave him. For Him the love behind the food he offered was more precious than the food itself. (Based on *Experiences in Bhakti*, p.56)

To continue the story, just then a rich merchant was taking a boat loaded with salt down the Yamuna River. By Krishna's will the boat became stuck in the shallow river. Madana Mohan then changed into a cowherd boy who led the merchant to Sanatana. Sanatana could do nothing to help the merchant, so the merchant prayed to Madana Mohan that if his boat became free he would sell his salt and return to use the money to build a nice temple for Sri Madana Mohan. After praying, the merchant returned to his boat and found that it was no longer stuck. When the merchant sold the salt, he returned to build the temple. So this is how the temple was erected. Later, this was the Deity from which Krishnadas Kaviraja got the inspiration to write the *Caitanya-caritamrta*.

Unfortunately, in 1670, due to the threat of fanatic Muslims, the original Radha-Madana Mohan Deities were moved to Jaipur, and then again moved to Karauli where a nice temple was built for them. *Pratibhuh* or replacement

Deities were later installed in the Vrindavana temple. You can still see the *bhajan kutir,* or place of worship, of Sanatana Gosvami, along with a well said to have been dug by Krishna Himself for Sanatana's water. This shows the exquisite relations that the Deities of Krishna can display with His devotees.

The Deity of Madana Mohana as He now appears in Karauli.

MADANA MOHANA IN KARAULI

After Sanatana Gosvami's Deity of Madana Gopala became Madana Mohana and was later moved from Vrindavana to Jaipur and then to Karauli to be protected from the Muslim invaders in 1730, the activities of the Deity continued.

Taja Khan, a person in the court of Karauli, was a devout Muslim. He lived in piety and went to the mosque every day to say his prayers. He spent most of his time in reading the Koran and meditating on God. The Muslims revered him as a true Muslim, and the Hindus as a pious man.

One day he was sent by the court to the temple of Madana Mohana to deliver a message to the Gosvami in the temple. Then he happened to see the Deity through a window in the temple. He was so struck by its beauty that he kept on looking at it for sometime. After he had delivered the message through the gatekeeper, he returned. But as he returned, he could not help but look again and again at Madana Mohana, and Madana Mohana looked back at him. He went back to the court and then went home and to the mosque. Wherever he went he found the image of Madana Mohana pursuing him in his mind until it was securely seated in the temple of his heart. He even forgot his prayers, Kalama and Koran. He only thought of Madana Mohana and kept his mind's eye always fixed on Him.

Taja Khan was born a Muslim and brought up in a culture which is averse to the Deity worship of the Hindus. How is it that the image of Madana Mohana captured his heart the moment he saw Him? It may be because of the pious *samskaras* or impressions from his past life which were revived the moment he saw Madana Mohana; or it may be that Madana Mohana Himself took to a liking for Taja Khan.

Taja Khan's heart, which was now full of love for Madana Mohana often spilt over in the forms of poems. He once sang in Urdu:

Oh! How my heart yearns for Thee
Unthwarted by hunger, thirst or sleep,
O Madana Mohana! Give *darshan* to me.
Each moment without Thy *darshan*
Appears like a *yuga* to me.
The sidelong glances thrill my heart.
Cast Thy glance but once at me.
Listen, O son of Nanda with moonlike face,
Taja Thy servant stands begging at Thy gate
for Thy *darshan* and Thy grace.

Taja Khan could not now remain long without looking at Madana Mohana. He tried to go and see Him every time the temple opened. He kept standing at the gate and looking at Him through the window. When the temple was closed, he peeped into the temple of his heart, of which the gates always remained open, and saw Madana Mohana sitting there, always looking and smiling at him.

The way of *bhakti* is sweet, yet at times beset with difficulties, trials and tribulations. Taja Khan also had to face them. His Muslim brethren came to know of his *bhakti* towards Madana Mohana. They declared him a Kafir (infidel) and excommunicated him. The Gosvami of the temple barred him from going to the temple and seeing Madana Mohana even from outside because he was a Muslim. One day he was going up the stairs of the temple when the gatekeeper pushed him down. He felt so much aggrieved that for three days he did not eat anything. He did not go to the court and remained lying at home, all the time weeping and sobbing in remembrance of Madana Mohana.

For three days Madana Mohana also remained cheerless without seeing him. One can imagine how deeply He felt his absence from what He did on the third day. Every night, according to the tradition in the temple, the *pujari* kept a silver *thala* or plate full of eatables near the bed of Madana Mohana when He went to sleep. That way the Deity may eat if He felt hungry. However, that day at midnight when everyone was asleep, Madana Mohana got up from the bed, took the plate of food, and in the guise of the attendant of the temple started towards the house of Taja Khan. On reaching the house, He knocked at the door. When Taja Khan opened the door, He extended the plate towards Taja Khan and said, "Gosvami has sent this sacred food (*prasada*) and said that you must come for *darshan* at the time of *shringar arati* tomorrow. No one will object to your coming. He has also said that when you go you should carry this plate with you."

Taja Khan was taken aback by this. He kept gazing at the young attendant who seemed to have a divine luster on his face. He took the plate from His hands and said, "Has Gosvami sent this? Has he really called me for the *darshan* of Madana Mohana?"

"Yes, yes, it is he who has sent it and he who has called you for *darshan*. Do come," said the attendant, who then went away.

All this was a mystery to Taja Khan. He was not sure to believe all this or not. But he was hungry and ate the food and then cleaned the plate. In the meantime, Madana Mohana said to Gosvamiji in a dream, "Taja Khan has not eaten since you pushed him away from the temple. I have given him the plate full of eatables that the *pujari* had kept for me, so that he may have something to eat. He will come for My *darshan* tomorrow. Do not prevent him."

In the morning when the pujari priest went to open the altar room, he was surprised to seer the silver plate missing. Trembling with fear he went to the Gosvamiji and said, "Maharaja! Thakura's (the Deity's) silver plate has been stolen. Believe me, I kept it with the eatables for Him near Thakura's bed at night and locked the door of the altar room from outside. Please do not suspect me."

"Do not worry," said the Gosvamiji. "The thief has confessed the theft. The plate will come."

Gosvamiji went to Maharaja Gopala Singhaji, who was the ruler of Karauli at the time, and reported everything to him. Maharaja was overwhelmed with *bhava* (ecstatic love) to hear about Madana Mohana's concern for His devotee and the trouble He took for his sake. He was also filled with love and veneration for Taja Khan, whose *bhakti* had subjugated Madana Mohana to that extent.

Taja Khan started for the temple with the plate in hand before the time of the *shringara arati*. But he was staggering on account of fear because he was still not sure that he was called by Gosvamiji. He apprehended that the young man who gave him the plate might have stolen it and given it to him for fear of being caught. He might even be one of the gang of his Muslim adversaries who might have hatched a plot against him so that he might be accused of the theft of the plate. As he reached the temple, he saw the Maharaja and Gosvamiji standing at the gate. He was all the more struck with fear. How could he think that they were standing there to honor and not to punish him? As he bent low to salute the Maharaja, the Maharaja came forward and embraced him. He said with tears in his eyes, "Taja Khan! You are blest. Madana Mohana has been so kind to you." Gosvamiji also embraced him and said, "Taja Khan! Forgive me for barring you from the *darshan* of Madana Mohana. I thought you did not deserve His *darshan* because you were a Muslim. Now I know that if there is anyone in Karauli who really deserves His *darshan*, that is you."

As the large number of people who had gathered on the scene saw the Maharaja and Gosvamiji embracing with love the poor person of the court of Karauli, they shouted with joy, "Taja Khan ki jaya!" Taja Khan stood bewildered. The whole thing was still a mystery to him. "Why this sudden outburst of affection for me?" he thought. "How am I blest? How has Madana Mohana been kind to me?" Suddenly a wave crossed his mind. With a start he asked Gosvamiji,

"Gosvamiji! Where is that servant whom you sent with the plate?"

Gosvamiji said, pointing towards Madana Mohana, "He sits there on the altar. But is He now the servant? He is the master of all, the creator and controller of the universe. Blessed are you because your love made Him the servant of the servant of His servant."

As Taja Khan heard this, his body trembled like a tree struck by storm. Tears streamed down from his eyes. His heart pained and he looked pityingly at Madana Mohana at the thought of the trouble He had taken for him.

After this, Taja Khan became so famous that it became difficult for him to live peacefully in seclusion. He left Karauli and no one knows where he went. But the people of Karauli still sing a song describing Madana Mohana as the servant who stole the *thala* (plate) for Taja. (Based on *Experiences in Bhakti* p. 137)

RADHA-GOVINDAJI

The Radha-Govindaji temple of Vrindavana is another of the seven major temples of Vrindavan. It was established by Rupa Gosvami where he discovered the Deity. The original Deity of Sri Govinda was installed in Vrindavana nearly 5000 years ago by the great grandson of Lord Krishna, King Vajranabha. The Deity had somehow become lost for many years but revealed where He was buried to Rupa Gosvami in a dream. Rupa Gosvami, using the directions he received from Govindaji in his dream, found the Deity and installed Him on the hill where he had found Govindaji in what became the Radha-Govindaji temple in Vrindavana 450 years ago in 1590.

The beautiful temple is made out of red sandstone. The temple is now only two storeys tall but once reached up to seven storeys, tall enough that it is said to have been visible all the way from Agra on a clear day. The Muslim fanatic Aurangzeb, doing his dirty work once again, dismantled

The Deities of Sri Sri Radha-Govinda, now in Jaipur.

the upper five storeys of the temple due to his envy. While his men were destroying the temple, there was a loud thunderous noise that shook the ground. This put fear into the hearts of the men and they immediately stopped and ran away. However, the Deities had already been moved. Due to fear of the Moghuls, before they arrived the devotees moved the original deities to Jaipur where today many pilgrims go to see them. So the temple now has *pratibhuh* deities, or representative expansions, of the original Radha-Govindaji that are worshiped.

When the Radha-Govindaji Deities were moved to Jaipur by Jai Singh, to protect Them from the Muslims, Sewai Jai Singh II first was residing in the building that later became the temple. It is explained that in a dream the king was kicked out of bed and was instructed that the building he was in was meant to be the residence of the Deities. When the king woke up on the floor next to his bed, he arranged to install the Deities in the present building and that his own palace would be across the park from the temple. This way he could watch the daily *aratis* to the Deities. In fact, Maharaja Jai Singh accepted spiritual initiation from Vrajananand Swami of the Ramanuja *sampradaya*.

Presently, this temple of Sri Sri Radha-Govindaji, located on the north side of the City Palace, is one of the most important of all temples in Jaipur. It is very opulent and the Deities are very beautiful. There is also a small Krishna Deity, Gaura-Govinda, that was worshiped by Kasiswara Pandit. This temple is extremely popular and is visited both morning and evening by hundreds of devotees. People will crowd around the altar to see the Deities, and after the *arati* the priests will hand out *maha-prasada* to the guests who try to scramble to get some. Devotees can also purchase offered food, *prasadam*, from the nearby stalls after the noon *arati*. In the early morning or evening there may be a lecture given by one of the local holy men, and afterward there will be the final *arati* for the day. Several other Deities from Vrindavana are also now situated in Jaipur, so that Jaipur is now considered part of Greater Vrajamandala.

GOVINDA DEVA AND THE GARDENER'S POMEGRANATE

As can be seen from the above description, the Deities of these Radha Govinda Deities have quite a lively history. To illustrate further, here is another story about Them.

After Maharaja Jai Singh built a new temple for Govinda Deva, he appointed Sri Govinda Charana Gosvami as the *pujari* priest in charge of the Deity's service. One morning when Gosvamiji opened the door of the altar-room for the early morning service of *mangala-arati*, he was surprised to see that the dress of Govinda was torn. It was not torn when the Deity was dressed the night before. The cut was long and straight, so it was not the work of a mouse. It actually looked like Govindaji had gone out somewhere in the night and torn His dress because it got entangled in something. Could Govindaji do that, even when the door was closed and locked from outside? No one else could have done that.

Gosvamiji did not take long to solve the mystery because he was not an ordinary priest, but a *siddha* saint. While in his *samadhi* meditation, Radharani appeared to him and said, "Last night both of Us went to a garden to pluck pomegranates. Lalaji (Krishna) had plucked only one when the gardener came to know. He ran after Us with his staff and We fled away. The pomegranate was green, but still Lalaji ate it all." Gosvamiji then looked around the altar of the Deity and was surprised to see the rind of the pomegranate and its seeds scattered all over.

Immediately Gosvamiji called the gardener. He asked him, "Did anyone go to your garden to pluck pomegranates last night?"

"Yes, Maharaja! A boy and a girl, both had gone. When I ran towards them with my staff, they fled."

"Oh, how fortunate you are, gardener, yet how unfortunate! Thakura (Krishna) and Thakurani (Radharani) Themselves went to your garden and you ran after them with your staff! Come and see what is lying here on the altar–the seeds of the unripe pomegranate They brought and ate."

The gardener was a great devotee of Govindaji. He went to the temple for the *darshan* of Govindaji at the time of every *arati*, unmindful of the sun, rain or storm. He had planted for the Govinda Deity several pomegranate trees in his garden. He would anxiously wait for the day when the trees would grow and bear the fruits so he could offer them to the Deities. The gardener would closely watch the trees, and his heart sprang with joy upon the sight of the flowers on the trees, which gradually turned into fruits. The fruits would take time to ripen, but Govinda did not have the patience to wait till then, He went to the garden anyway, plucked a green pomegranate and ate.

When Gosvamiji told the gardener about this pastime of Govinda and the gardener saw the seeds of the unripe pomegranate lying near the altar of Govinda, he was overwhelmed with emotion. Tears began to stream down from his eyes. Hairs stood on end. He kept looking at the Deity of Govinda. He could not say anything but "Govinda! Govinda!" and fell unconscious. On regaining consciousness he said, "Thakura! You came, but I could not recognize You, but I ran after You with my staff. I thought You were the children of some maid-servant of the palace and began to shower abuses on You. The trees and the pomegranates are Yours. They were planted for You. But You came like a thief, perhaps because You did not want that I should recognize You. What did You gain by concealing yourself from me, and from hearing all my abuses?"

The gardener did not know that Govinda enjoyed the abuses of a devotee even more than his praises. He did not know that He enjoyed to steal what belonged to a devotee more than to beg for it. When did He beg for the butter of the *gopis* (milk maids) of Vraja? He always stole it. He was, therefore, called the butter-thief (*Makhana-chora*). A thief feels offended if you call him a thief, but this thief is different from others. He feels happy when you call Him a thief. That is the nature of Krishna's mischievous side when it is exhibited toward His devotees. That is His loving pastimes, to forget that He is the Supreme and to act like an ordinary little child.

When Maharaja Jai Singha came to know about the theft, he gave the gardener a piece of land in reward because he had grown trees of which the fruits Govinda could not help but steal. His descendants enjoy the yield of the land to this day. (Based partly on *Experiences in Bhakti* p. 80 and other sources)

UDUPI KRISHNA

The famous temple of Krishna in Udipi, established by Madhvacharya, is known for being an important religious center for teaching the Dvaita or Tatvavada philosophy, especially as presented by Madhvacharya. It is also known for that activities of the Deity here. One famous story is that of Kanakadasa, a staunch devotee of Lord Krishna. It was in the 16th century when Kanakadasa came to the temple to worship the Deity of Lord Krishna. However, he was not allowed to enter the temple because he was of a low caste, and at that time only the higher castes could go in the temple to offer worship. It did not upset him when he was not allowed inside, but he went to the side of the temple and prayed with intense devotion. The Deity of Lord Krishna was so pleased that He turned Himself in the direction of Kanakadasa and also made the wall to crack, forming a few holes in the wall so Kanakadasa could still see the Deity. In this way, the Deity reciprocated with His devotee and allowed Kanakadasa to see Him. Even today, it is the tradition that when pilgrims first come to the temple, they go to the side of the temple and view the Deity through the same hole in the wall, now known as Kanakakhind, before going inside the temple for a closer *darshan*. Nowadays, this Kanakakhind is decorated with colorful carvings depicting the ten main *avatars* of Vishnu.

□

5
Deities in Other Areas of India

There are many other temples in the area of India that also have noteworthy stories to tell about the Deities that reside in them. For example, another place we want to see to the north of Kathmandu by 11 kilometers is Budhanilkantha at the foot of Shivapuri hill. Here we find the large Deity of sleeping Vishnu that was carved out of solid rock in the 11th century. One legend relates that the Deity was found when a farmer was tilling his field and saw blood oozing up from the ground after his plough struck something. The people dug into the ground and found the Deity. So there is no telling how old this Deity is. Many pilgrims now come here. We reach it by getting a bus near the National Theatre, a pleasant ride, but the bus stops often to pick up passengers. When the bus makes its final stop, the Deity is only a few minutes away. Anyone is allowed in the courtyard and can see the Deity, but the central pool, where the Deity is reclining on Seshanaga, is for Hindus only, which means those who are born Hindu. At the feet of Lord Vishnu, the devout chant their prayers and make offerings of rice, where the pigeons wait to eat it up. It is considered that the Deity sleeps continuously for four months in the rainy season, and in November there is a festival when thousands of devotees come to participate when the Deity wakes up.

JAGANNATHA MANDIR IN MAYAPUR

In Mayapur, about a four hour ride north of Kolkata, and a short ride away from the Chand Kazi *samadhi* by cycle ricksha, we turn down a dirt road. After a ten minute ride we arrive at the Mayapur Jagannatha Mandir in the village of Rajapur. The Deities here are very special and have revealed Themselves to the surrounding devotees in many ways.

A summary of the story about Them must be told. At the time of Lord Chaitanya, 500 years ago, there lived in Navadvipa a great Vaishnava named Jagadisha Ganguli. He would walk 600 miles to Puri each year to participate in the Ratha Yatra festival. But he was an old man and was affected with a disease that left him blind. Thereafter, his friends advised him not to attempt the long trip to Puri since it would be too dangerous.

Feeling despondent he thought of committing suicide. But Lord Jagannatha appeared to him in a dream and spoke to him one night and told him that while bathing in the Ganges the next day a log floating down the river would bump his head at which time his sight would be restored. Then he should take the log to a particular devotee carpenter and ask him to carve the Deity of Lord Jagannatha. When all this had happened, he took the log to the person to carve the Deities, but the carver was very hesitant to take up the task since he was a leper. Not only did he feel unqualified to do it, but it would also be extremely painful since his hands were diseased. Jagadisha insisted, however, explaining that Lord Jagannatha Himself had ordered this. So the carver began the work. To his surprise, as he worked he became cured of his leprosy.

Jagadisha brought the Jagannatha Deities to where They are now located and established Their worship. But after the disappearance of Jagadisha, the worship of the Deities decreased until They were forgotten. Over the years They became completely covered over by a termite mound.

Centuries later the local villagers noticed a beautiful flower growing on the mound. When they went near it they could hear a voice saying, "Please bring me water, I'm thirsty."

Thus, some years ago, the villagers cleared away the dirt and found the Deities unharmed, even though They had been neglected for many years. In spite of the fact that the Deities were carved from wood and covered by a termite mound, They were still intact. The villagers then established a simple temple for Lord Jagannatha, Lord Balarama, and Lady Subhadra to resume worshiping Them.

The Deities of (left to right) Lord Balarama, Lady Subhadra, and Lord Jagannatha, in Mayapur.

Since that time the Deities had been worshiped by Phatik Chaterjee. But in 1979 the aging priest realized he would soon die. After much consideration he decided to make sure the Deities would continue being properly worshipped by giving Them to the care of the devotees of Iskcon. Phatik died shortly thereafter. Now the Deities have a nice, new temple and are visited by many pilgrims from around the world. Many come here to try the *maha-prasada* (food preparations offered to the Deities) and relish its spiritual taste. The scriptures state that Sri Ksetra, or Jagannatha Puri, is eternally manifest in this area of Mayapur. Thus, one gets the same benefits of visiting Jagannatha Puri by visiting this Jagannatha Mandir in Mayapur. And here you get the special blessings of being allowed into the temple to see the Deities, whereas in Puri itself, not everyone is allowed entrance into the temple.

When we visit this Jagannatha temple we can see the Deities in their nice new temple, which has an open *kirtana* hall in front of Them. In front of the *kirtana* hall is a series of diorama displays which relate the story of these Deities and how They were established here. Behind the new temple is the old one where the Deities used to stay. This is still used when the Deities play the part of getting colds and fever after Their bathing ceremony during Their annual Ratha Yatra celebration. Next to the road which is separated by a wall and in front of the old temple is the old *kalpavriksha* tree. It is said that Shiva and Parvati came here to perform austerities and still come here. Under this tree you will also see a Shiva *lingam* known as Kshetrapala. This *lingam* has revealed itself as Lord Shiva to the devotees here in a number of ways. So devotees come here to pray to Shiva and Parvati for *krishna-prema*, ecstatic love for Radha and Krishna.

Ever since the Jagannatha Deities were recovered, many people have continued to experience rare pastimes with Them. Many examples could be cited, but here are a few.

One devotee by the name of Jaimini Ghosh would serve the Deities regularly. But once he fell asleep outside the temple, and when he woke up, he found that he had somehow been transported to Jagannatha Puri during the time of the Rathayatra festival. So he enjoyed the festival there for several days. Then he remembered his parents and how they must be worried since they did not know where he was. However, he did not have the money for the fare back to his home in Rajapur. When he explained his situation to some local pandits, they said that if Lord Jagannatha brought him here, then go to the Deities and ask that He take you back. After going before Lord Jagannatha in Puri, he fell asleep at night and awoke to find himself back in Rajapur.

Another time there was an epidemic in the area and many were dying from it. Then one night Lord Jagannatha appeared in a dream to the *pujari* and explained how to make the proper medicine that would cure the people. Then the *pujari* told everyone so they could gather the ingredients, but one ingredient could not be found. Later in the day, one small boy who had never been seen before came to the *pujari's* wife and gave her a special branch from an herb. When the *pujari* saw it he was very happy because that was the last ingredient that they had been looking for. Then they made the medicine and everyone overcame the epidemic. From that day even the non-Hindus held great respect for Lord Jagannatha.

Another story that I had heard while visiting the Rajapur temple of Lord Jagannatha was when a ricksha driver came to the temple and ate some *maha-prasada* and took some with him for his friend, who was a Muslim. But when the driver offered his friend the *prasada,* the Muslim threw it on the ground saying that he does not eat food offered to idols. That night in a dream the Muslim saw Lord Balarama sitting on him and strangling him. As He was beating the man, Balarama asked, "Don't you know that My brother is worshiped by honoring *maha-prasadam,* and you threw it on the ground? I will kill you!" Subhadra was also in the dream saying "Kill him! Kill him!" But Lord Jagannatha merely laughed and said "No, no, no, don't kill him."

The next day the Muslim came to the temple and very humbly went before the Deities and offered respect to Lord Jagannatha and then asked for some *maha-prasada* while relating the story, but no *prasada* was available. "There must be something," the man pleaded. So the *pujari* found some scraps in a pot, and the Muslim gladly accepted it.

Once one of the Iskcon *pujaris* forgot to bring tulasi leaves for the offering to the Deities. Such leaves are important to include in each offering. He did not know what to do and did not want to leave the plate of food in case some children or an animal might come and spoil it. So he offered the food anyway while praying that the Lord would accept it without tulasi leaves. When he came back in time to do the *arati*, he saw there was a ten inch branch of tulasi leaves sticking up from the mound of rice.

Another time there was a Muslim girl who had very poor eyesight. In fact, it gradually got worse and the doctors said it was incurable. The family, having heard about the power of Lord Jagannatha, brought the girl before the Deities and she prayed to the Deities for help. Then after drinking the *caranamrita* or water that had been used to bathe the Deities for seven days her vision was miraculously cured. Even into her old age her eyesight was clear.

Another time a devotee, Sadhana Siddhi Prabhu and his family moved to the temple. One day his son Dalim came running to his mother crying hysterically. After she calmed the boy down he explained that he saw a beautiful broach on Lady Subhadra and wanted to take it for himself. But when he reached over to grab it, Lord Balarama swung His arm and slapped the boy across the face sending him tumbling out of the room.

There are many other pastimes that are told about these Deities, others you can read about in the book "The Pastimes and History of Lord Jagannatha in Rajapur" by Pankajanghri Dasa, published by Gouranga Releases, in Scotland.

SRILA BHAKTISIDDHANTA SARASVATI THAKUR IN MAYAPUR

There were many experiences that were had by Srila

Bhaktisiddhanta Sarasvati Thakur, the spiritual master of His Divine Grace Srila A.C. Bhaktivedanta Swami Prabhupada, in the holy dham of Mayapur. As explained in the *Sri Bhaktisiddhanta Vaibava* (Volume 1, pages 61-2) by Bhakti Vikas Swami, in November of 1915, Srila Bhaktisiddhanta Sarasvati Thakur, had experienced the loss of his spiritual master, Srila Gaura Kishora dasa Babaji. This, along with other dilemmas he was facing in the Vaishnava devotee community after the disappearance of his father, Srila Bhaktivinoda Thakur, sixteen months earlier, made him feel disappointed and hopeless. He decided to keep to himself. With little food or sleep, he remained engaged in intense *bhajana* while wrestling with the problems.

Srila Bhaktisiddhanta's heart reverberated with Srila Bhaktivinoda's order that he continue with his service to Sri Chaitanya Mahaprabhu. And seeing the mass of people spoiling their valuable human lives, simply taking birth and then dying without information of or interest in the incomparable spiritual boons offered by Chaitanya Mahaprabhu, Sri Bhaktisiddhanta Sarasvati was unceasingly contemplating the need to preach. Yet, having experienced the kind of malicious opposition he would have to face for speaking the truth, he was reluctant to return to public life.

Then one day a gust of wind blew before him an extract from the *Sri Caitanya-caritamrita* which described how Lord Chaitanya instructed Sanatana Gosvami to compose transcendental literature, renovate the forgotten holy places, institute service to Lord Krishna, and propagate *bhakti-rasa*, the knowledge of the yoga of devotion. Taking this as a divine instruction, but feeling depressed and incapable, Sri Siddhanata Sarasvati pondered, "I have no public support, nor wealth, learning, or the intelligence required to awaken interest in the populace. How can I convey to the inhospitable world the pure teachings of Sri Chaitanya and establish the spiritual teachings as yearned by my gurus?"

Shortly afterward, one night at the Yogapitha, the place of Sri Chaitanya's birth, in a dreamlike revelation he saw approaching him from the east the Pancha-Tattva, consisting of the divine personalities of Sri Chaitanya, Sri Nityananda, Sri Advaitacharya, Sri Gadadhara, Srivasa, along with the six Gosvamis of Vrindavana, as well as Srila Jagannathaa dasa Babaji, Srila Bhaktivinoda Thakur, Srila Gaura Kishora dasa Babaji, and numerous other great devotees who had already left their physical forms. They told him:

"Sarasvati! Why are you worrying? Begin the task of establishing *shuddha-bhakti,* pure devotional service. Distribute the teachings of Lord Chaitanya universally. Expand the service to the transcendental name, holy place, and teachings of Lord Sri Chaitanya. With unbreached enthusiasm broadcast the perfection of *bhakti,* devotional yoga. We are eternally with you, ready to help. The support of unlimited people, immeasurable opulence, and boundless scholarship awaits the blessing to serve your mission. All will manifest when required. Come forward with full strength to distribute the message of Sri Chaitanya Mahaprabhu's *prema-dharma* throughout the globe. No worldly hindrance or menace will be able to obstruct this undertaking of yours. We are forever with you."

It was the next morning when the few young disciples he had gathered saw for the first time in many days his face refulgent in happiness. He related to them the vision he had seen. After that his determination to preach was fully rekindled and unretractable.

At another time, as told in *Sri Bhaktisiddhanta Vaibava* (Volume 1, page 388), while staying at the Yogapitha, Srila Bhaktisiddhanta came out of the Bhakti Vidya Bhavan at nearly two in the morning and called out, "Everyone, look! See over there! Gauranga (Sri Chaitanya) and Nitai (Lord Nityananda) are going on *sankirtana* (congregational singing of the Lord's holy names)! Follow Them! Follow Them! Come and see!" All of the devotees rushed out, but no one else could see Them. This is but an example of how he could perceive the spiritual dimension that appears in such holy *dhamas* and the spiritual activities that go on there.

Another time in the middle of the night, Srimat Tirtha Maharaja roused the devotees: "Get up! Look at what is going on!" Srila Bhaktisiddhanta Sarasvati also awoke and said, "Just see! The Pancha-Tattva are going by, chanting and performing *sankirtana*! Come, let us follow Them!" The devotees accompanied their guru out into the darkness, but only Srila Bhaktisiddhanta Sarasvati and Srimat Tirtha Maharaja could see Them. Such incidents were not uncommon in the pastimes of Srila Bhaktisiddhanta Sarasvati, especially in the holy place of Navadvipa *dhama* in Mayapur.

EKACHAKRA

The Birchandrapur side of Ekachakra, the birthplace of Sri Nityananda, can be reached from the central arch in the village. From there we go to the left and then make a quick right, and straight down the street through the houses we shortly arrive at the Bankim Raya temple. This temple was established by Nityananda's son, Virabhadra Gosai, to house Bankim Raya, the Deity that Sri Nityananda had found when He returned to Ekachakra after being absent for 30 years. When you get up to the altar you will see the small Krishna Deity in the center with Srimati Radharani on His left and Jahnava Devi on His right. It is said that Lord Nityananda left this world by entering into this Krishna Deity. There is also a Deity of Yogamaya on a separate throne to the right. The Radharani Deity was also found in Bhaddhapur about ½ mile to the west in the region of Birchandrapur. After that She was installed with Bankim Raya and called Bhaddhapurera, the mistress of Bhaddhapura.

SAKSI-GOPALA

About six miles from Puri is the Saksi-gopala temple,

located between the Jagannatha Puri and Khurda Road Junction railway stations. A new station called Saksi-gopala is there where people get off to visit the temple. The Saksi-gopala Deity is the Gopala Deity who walked from Vrindavana to Vidyanagara, a town located 20 to 25 miles from Rajahmundry on the banks of the Godavari River. How this happened was that two brahmanas were traveling and visiting the holy places. One was poor and young and was serving the older and richer brahmana. The older one was so satisfied with the charitable service of the younger brahmana that he vowed in front of the Gopala Deity that he would give his daughter to the younger brahmana to be his wife. The younger brahmana protested, but the older one insisted. Later, when they returned home, the older brahmana hesitated to fulfill his promise due to pressure from his family who disagreed with the idea. The older brahmana then began to say he could not remember any such promise, while his son called the younger brahmana a liar and thief. There was some controversy about this between the two brahmanas and the younger one was concerned to uphold the dignity of the elder. In a meeting with the townspeople it was agreed that if the Deity Gopala came to testify as a witness, the older brahmana would give his daughter as promised.

The younger brahmana went all the way back to Vrindavana and related the situation to the Gopala Deity who at first said "I have never heard of a Deity walking from one place to another." The younger brahmana said, "That is true, but how is it that You are a Deity and talking to me now, although you are a Deity? Actually, you are Lord Krishna, the son of Maharaja Nanda. You are not a statue. For the sake of the old brahmana You can do something You have never done before." So, finally the Deity agreed to walk. He told the brahmana that He would follow him and that the sound of His ankle bells would indicate He was there, but if the brahmana turned around to look, He would walk no farther. So for 100 days they walked toward Vidyanagara, then the sound of the Deity's ankle bells ceased to be heard. The brahmana became worried and looked back, and the Deity was standing there smiling. The brahmana went to gather the people of the town who were amazed to see the Deity. Then the older brahmana agreed to give his daughter in marriage as promised and a temple was built for the Deity. After the marriage ceremony the Deity of the Lord informed both brahmanas "You two have been My eternal servants birth after birth." That is how the Deity of the Lord became famous as Sakshi Gopala, the Deity who acted as a witness.

Later, the King of Orissa, Purusottama, was insulted by the King of Kataka (Cuttack). So Purusottama fought and defeated the King of Kataka and took charge of the city. He then brought the Gopalaji Deity from Vidyanagara to Kataka and built a temple there. The Deity also stayed in the Jagannatha temple for some time, but then was moved to a village about six miles from Puri, called Satyavadi. Some time after that a new temple was constructed where we find the Saksi-gopala Deity today. Though the temple does not allow foreigners inside, many people visit this temple with the understanding that whether the Supreme is in the spiritual strata or expands Himself in the material realm in the form of a stone Deity, He can change what is spiritual into material and vice versa whenever He wants. That is why a stone Deity can do what is considered miraculous things, like walk, talk, etc. Thus, it is accepted that the bona fide Deity of the Supreme is non-different from the Supreme Himself.

REMUNA

Remuna is a short distance from Balasore, south of Kolkata. Some pilgrims will want to stop at Balasore in order to take an hour long bus or auto-ricksha ride to Remuna. In Remuna is the temple of Ksira-cora-gopinatha, which is an important place of pilgrimage. This is the Deity who hid a pot of sweet rice (*ksira*) for His devotee Madhavendra Puri. The story is that once Madhavendra Puri, while visiting Vrindavana, was told in a dream by Krishna that a Deity of Gopala had been placed in a thick bush by a temple priest to keep Him hidden from the Muslim invaders. Gopala wanted Madhavendra Puri to find Him and establish a temple.

So Madhavendra Puri gathered the local residents and was able to find the Deity in the woods and built a temple. Later, in another dream the Deity told Madhavendra that He was still very hot from so many years of living outside and needed some sandalwood paste to help cool Him. So Madhavendra Puri traveled all the way to Jagannatha Puri to get some nice sandalwood to bring back to Vrindavana.

On his way, he stopped at the Remuna Gopinatha temple, which is known for a special kind of sweet rice, called *amrita-keli* that they offer to the Deity. He was attracted to the idea of learning how to make it the way the cooks prepare it there so he could make similar sweet rice for his own Gopala Deity. But thinking that he was offensive for wanting to taste the preparation that was to be offered to the Deity, he decided not to taste any at all. However, that night the Deity Gopinatha told the temple priest in a dream to wake up and find a pot of sweet rice that the Deity had hidden behind His dress and to give it to Madhavendra Puri. When the priest awoke and looked behind the Deity's dress, there was the pot of sweet rice. Then the priest went out and after calling the name of Madhavendra Puri found him and gave him the sweet rice. From that time the Gopinatha Deity at Remuna has been known as Ksira-cora-gopinatha, the Deity who stole the pot of condensed milk for His devotee.

Furthermore, after Madhavendra Puri had secured a large amount of sandalwood and was on his way back to Vrindavana, he again stopped at Remuna. Then the Gopala Deity in Vrindavana spoke to Madhavendra Puri in a dream telling him that he should simply turn the sandalwood into paste and offer it to the Gopinatha Deity at Remuna. Since Krishna as Gopinatha in Remuna or as Gopala in Vrindavana or wherever He might be are equally the same, offering the paste to Gopinatha would also cool Gopala in Vrindavana. Thus, Gopala relieved His devotee Madhavendra Puri from the task of bringing the heavy load such a great distance back to Vrindavana. So Madhavendra offered sandalwood paste every day to the Deity until all the sandalwood and camphor were gone. A few months later Madhavendra Puri left this world and his *samadhi* tomb is located in Remuna a few minutes away from the Ksira-cora-Gopinatha temple.

All pilgrims traveling through Orissa should stop to see the temple of Ksira-cora-gopinatha at Remuna, who stands with Deities of Govinda on His right and Lord Madana-Mohana on His left. Also, the *samadhi* tomb of Madhavendra Puri is a short distance from the temple.

In this way, we can see that the Krishna Deities of this region, such as Jagannatha, Saksi-gopala, and Ksira-cora-gopinatha, are very active Deities and display Their supernatural qualities in a way that attracts many pilgrims to the temples of this area.

Also within the compound of the Ksira-cora-gopinatha temple is the *samadhi* tomb of the great Vaishnava devotee Rasikananda. Rasikananda was an important disciple of Syamananda. He had also helped bring numerous writings of the Vrindavana Goswamis to Bengal. Actually, it was Rasikananda who had found the Gopinatha Deity in the nearby pond after Gopinatha had been placed there to keep Him hidden from the Muslim king. After that, Rasikananda renovated the temple after the previous one had been destroyed by Muslim invaders, which had been built by King Gajapati Maharaja Langula Deva.

All this is elaborated by Sri Kaisoranandadeva Goswami, a disciple of Rasikananda. He explains that it all started in Treta-yuga while Lord Ramachandra and Sita were living at Chitrakoot. They had taken shelter of the ashrama of some sages during a rain storm. There were many cows in the ashrama. This reminded Lord Rama of His pastimes as Lord Krishna, for which He carved some figures of those pastimes on a black rock. Sita wanted to see these figures. So upon Her request, He showed them to Her along with the Deity of Gopal that He had made to exhibit His form when He would again appear on earth. He showed this along with figures of Krishna's eight main *gopis* and four other maid-servants. Other scenes included Lord Balarama wrestling Mustika, Lord Krishna wrestling Chanura, along with twelve cows and a few other scenes. Pleased by this, Sita began to worship the Deity.

When Rama and Sita left Chitrakoot, Lord Brahma took up the worship of this Deity, all the way through to the age of Kali-yuga. Lord Ramachandra and Sita had previously visited Remuna when They were returning from Lanka after Lord Rama had killed the demon Ravana. They liked this place and Sita wanted to bathe in the Ganga. So Lord Rama shot seven arrows into the ground to bring up the Ganga River. That is now called Saptashara (seven arrows) in Remuna. That is where the *murti* of Shiva as Gadegadeshwara was installed. The image of Durga Devi is in the nearby temple of Ramacandi. Because Lord Rama felt pleasure (*ramana*) here, it became known as Remuna.

It was in the thirteenth century when King Langula Narasimhadeva from Orissa stopped at Chitrakoot during his travels and happened to see this Gopala Deity. He was amazed that no one seemed to be worshiping the lovely Deity, not knowing that Lord Brahma was still arriving everyday to do the *puja*. But that night the king had a dream in which the Deity of Gopala requested to be taken to a more inhabited place. So the king decided to take Him to Jagannatha Puri. However, while passing through Remuna, the Deity again appeared to the king in a dream and asked to be installed there. So the king arranged it. The queen noticed the eight principal *gopis* on the stone of the Deity, so she called Him Gopal.

Shortly after the time of Sri Chaitanya Mahaprabhu, there was a Muslim king who would go and smash the Deities in temples. People of Remuna heard he was coming there, so they took the Gopala Deity and hid Him in a pond three miles away. Being upset that he could not find the Gopala Deity, the Muslim king assaulted and partially broke the Ramacandi Durga Deity.

Later, the great devotee Rasikananda had a dream in which he was ordered to excavate the pond to recover the Deity of Gopinatha. After doing so, he built a temple for the Deity and established the worship. Later, when Rasikananda had made up his mind that it was time for him to leave this world, he entered the temple of Gopinatha and disappeared. Seven of his associates who had been performing *sankirtana* with Rasikananda also gave up their bodies to follow him into the spiritual realm when they became so spiritually distressed after hearing that Rasikananda had gone. Their *samadhi* tombs are also next to Rasikananda's in the temple courtyard.

ALALARNATHA

About 14 miles from Jagannatha Puri is the Alalarnatha temple at Brahmagiri. Lord Alalarnatha is a four-handed form of Lord Vishnu. Whenever the Jagannatha Deities in Puri would be removed from the altar before the Ratha-Yatra festival for two weeks, Sri Chaitanya would stay here. This is a temple where, at the end of the *kirtana* hall in front of a Deity of Sadbhuja (a form of the combination of Lord Krishna, Lord Rama, and Sri Chaitanya Mahapurabhu), there is a large stone slab with the imprint of Sri Chaitanya's body. Once when He fell onto the stone in an ecstatic trance, the stone melted leaving the imprint of Sri Chaitanya's body as we find it today.

Across from the Alalarnatha temple is another Gaudiya-Math temple that was established by Srila Bhaktisiddhanta. It is also here where we find a much smaller Alalarnatha Deity that was uncovered during excavations around the main Alalarnatha temple. How this Deity was found is that once when Srila Bhaktisiddhanta was staying at his temple, the priest at the Alalarnatha shrine had a dream in which the Lord came to him and said that He wanted to accept the worship of Srila Bhaktisiddhanta. Then the priest brought the small Alalarnatha Deity to Srila Bhaktisiddhanta who worshiped Him, and where the little Deity has remained since then.

YADAGIRI-GUTTA

Yadagiri-gutta is 60 kilometers northeast of Hyderabad, reached by bus (2 hours). Upon arrival at Yadagiri-gutta, you either walk a half-hour, or get an auto-rickshaw, or take another very crowded bus to the top of the hill.

Yadagiri was named after a sage named Yadava who performed heavy austerities to see Lord Vishnu as Narasimha. Being pleased with him, the Lord self-manifested and appeared in order to give him *darshan* in three forms: Jwala Narasimha, Gandabheranda Narasimha, and Yogananda Narasimha. Yadava begged for the Lord to remain on the hill in these forms. Thus, you have the Lakshmi-Narasimhadeva temple on the hilltop with Deities of the Lord in all three forms embedded in stone in the main cave. Actually, it is a cave about 12 feet high by 30 feet long, located in back of the temple hall, by the rear pillar. You take a stairway down into the chamber and then toward the back. Jwala Narasimha is in the shape of a serpent, while Yogananda Narasimha appears sitting in meditation in a yoga pose. You will also see silver Deities of Lakshmi-Narasimha, which are quite striking in appearance and lends presence to the experience of seeing Them. To the right of the temple's main door is a Hanuman temple. You will see a long horizontal gap in the rock just below Hanuman. This is said to be where Gandabheranda Narasimha manifested. This is a very popular temple. It is said that any wish of the sincere devotee visiting this temple will be fulfilled. On weekends the lines to see the Deity can be very long. So it is best to go during the week. Plus, places to stay are few, therefore, consider taking a day trip from Hyderabad.

KANCHIPURAM

This is an important place with many temples to see, one of which is the large Vishnu temple for Varadaraja. It is one of the 108 Divya Desams, or holiest sites for Lord Vishnu. The Varadaraja temple is said to be on the site where Lord Brahma performed a fire (*yajna*) ritual to invoke Lord Vishnu. The central enclosure of the temple is supposed to conform to the raised altar that Brahma had used for the ritual. This shows how ancient this tradition is at this location. The temple is built on a small hill and has two high *gopurams* on the east and west sides of the temple compound that lead into the first enclosure, and a smaller gate leads into the inner enclosures. As you enter through the main gate, you will first see a separate *mandapa* hall which houses 96 elaborately carved columns that show many figures, such as dancers, animal riders, and scenes of the Vaishnava iconography. Some of them also produce musical tones when struck. There is some excellent sculptor work here. In the back of the hall is a *kund* or pond, called Ananta Thirtam. This is because Lord Ananta is said to have created it so He could recline in it and observe the pastimes of Lord Varadaraja. There is also a story that once during the summer's intense heat, the original Deity of Lord Varadaraja felt overly hot and appeared to a priest in a dream requesting to be put into the water. So they keep the Deity in a silver chest in a shrine inside this pond. Every forty years the Deity is taken out and worshiped in a grand way for forty-eight days. Around the pond are several shrines, among which include a temple in which the main Deity is Lord Narasimha on one side, and a Deity of the Sudarshan chakra on the back. A shrine to Ramanujacharya is also nearby.

THIRUATTUR (OR THIRUVATTUR OR THIRUVATTAR)

Thiruattur, about 50 kilometers south of Trivandrum, has the Adi Keshava temple located near the banks of the Payasvini River. Thiruattur is a small town, but many pilgrims stop in to see the temple. The easiest way to visit Thiruattur and Suchindram is to take a taxi from Kanyakumari. It is 46 kilometers from Kanyakumari, or a 1 ½ hour taxi ride. You can also reach it by getting a bus from Trivandrum going to Nagarcoil or Kanyakumari, and stopping at Marthandum, and then get another bus to Thiruattur. Thiruattur is on the Thoduvetti Kulasekharam Road. The temple is only about ten minutes from the bus stop in a calm and isolated area.

The Adi Keshava temple has beautiful architecture but is not as large as the one in Trivandrum, though the style is similar. The architecture here, as with several other temples in Kanyakumari district, resembles that of the temples of Kerala, using a combination of wood and stone. This temple has been glorified by a decad of 11 verses composed by Nammalwar in the first millennium CE. It is an important center of worship and is also referred to as Adi Anantam and Dakshina Vaikuntham.

The legend behind this temple involves Lord Brahma. It is described that once when Brahma wanted to have *darshan* of MahaVishnu, he performed a penance, but he failed to perform it properly in regard to the rules in the Agamas. Thus, from the sacrificial fire came a demon named Kesha, along with his sister, Keshi. They immediately had one thing in mind, and that was to mitigate their enormous appetites. Brahma granted them the blessing of long life and that they could go anywhere in the universe in search of prey. Then the demons went everywhere, subjecting even the virtuous and pious to fear and suffering. The great sages could no longer cope with the atrocities that were being committed and prayed to MahaVishnu to save the world from this terror. Upon hearing the prayers of the devout sages, MahaVishnu and Adisesha both descended to the Earth planet. A battle ensued and the demon was soon forced to give up his pride and surrender to the Lord. MahaVishnu ordered Adisesha to coil himself over the body of the Kesha demon. Then MahaVishnu reclined on Adisesha and, in this way, keeps the demon bound up, otherwise his influence would escape and again wreak havoc over the planet.

However, the demon's sister, Keshi, vowed vengeance for her brother. She is said to have taken the form of the Tamraparni River, and then made the Tamraparni River flood the land. MahaVishnu, however, directed Bhudevi, the Deity of the Earth planet, to raise the level of the land, thus ending the attempts of the river to immerse the area. Humbled by this course of events, the Tamraparni offered obeisances to the Lord and went around His abode, like a garland that wrapped the temple with water. The place where the river divided itself to form a circle is called "Moonattu Mugam" and "Kothai Pirali." And the place where the river circles around it is called Thiruattur.

Shiva is believed to have taken on 12 forms to witness the battle that went on between Vishnu and Kesi, and to worship Vishnu. A pilgrimage to all of the 12 main Shiva temples here is considered complete only after visiting this temple at Thiruattur.

The temple at Thiruattur is situated on a platform in a compound of 1½ acres. It is surrounded by a massive 30-foot tall wall. Nearby on three sides is the Tamraparni River and its tributaries. On the western side is the *ghat* where a dip is considered to relieve one of numerous sinful reactions.

The temple still maintains the old traditions and male members must wear a *dhoti*. Entrance with pants or trousers is not allowed. You enter the temple through the eastern doorway after climbing about 25 steps. The gate is a lovely structure of tiles and wood, typical of the Kerala style of architecture, but similar to the South Indian temple *gopurams*. From the entrance, one goes south to the shrine of Sri Butanatha. Next is a room in the southwest corner where we find Deities of Adikeshava, Devi, and Venkatachalapathi. Walking along the outer hallway, we reach the place of the copper flagstaff, the *dwajasthamba*. This was installed by Maharaja Mulam Tirunal of Travancore in 1895. Next we come to the Nalambalam, the circumambulatory passage around the sanctum (Sri Balippuram), which is a hall with 224 ornately carved granite pillars. These have lovely images of Deepalakshmis, which are the Lakshmis (the goddess of fortune) that carry the lamps. No two images are the same, each one differing in hairstyles or in positions.

In front of the sanctum is the Mukhamantap hall, which is shaped out of a single piece of black granite. This is three feet thick and 17½ by 15 feet long. It certainly shows the skill of which the stone carvers had during the day when this temple was built. The pillars nearby in the Balipeeta Mantap have life-size images that include Vishnu, Lakshmana, Indrajit, Venugopal, Nataraja, and Parvati, and even Brahma playing the veena, as well as others. There is also a shrine to Tiruvambadi Krishna. Additional shrines to Adi Kesava, Venkatachalapati, and Taayaar are also found. And the flag staff of copper was built by the Travancore royal family.

The sanctum faces west, although the main temple entrance is to the east. In this inner sanctum is the Deity of MahaVishnu who is 18 feet long and lies on Seshanaga. The Deity faces west as It is said that He is looking toward the Sri Padmanabhaswamy temple in Trivandrum. For a full *darshan*, the Deity must be viewed through three doors. The sanctum has been designed so that the rays of the setting sun illuminate the face of the Deity. MahaVishnu lets His left hand hang down. The hoods of Adisesha rising over the head of MahaVishnu can also be seen. The Deity is beautifully made out of a combination of ingredients that is known as Katusarkara yogam. This requires that the Deity is not washed with water, but the smaller or festival Deity is regularly worshiped, anointed, and dressed in ornaments and flowers. One man there told me the Deity was made of 16,108 *shalagram shilas*. This Deity is also accompanied by Lakshmi and Bhudevi on either side. A separate shrine is found in which the Deity of Alambadi Krishna is located.

The *Padma Purana* describes the original temple at this location as having been built in Treta-yuga many thousands of years ago, originating before the Sri Padmanabhaswamy temple in Trivandrum. This temple is also one of the 108 Divya Desams (most holy places of Lord Vishnu) of the Vaishnavas. This is also the Krishna temple which Sri Chaitanya Mahaprabhu visited on His tour of South India and found a copy of the ancient *Brahma-samhita*. This has become an important text for all Vaishnavas.

According to the descriptions in "15 Vaishnava Temples of Tamil Nadu" by M. Rajagopalam, this temple is noted for particular miracles that have taken place here. One example is that in 1674, the Muslim vandals chose Thiruattur as one of their targets of attack. Queen Rani Umai Ammai Nachair, the ruler of this area, found herself unequal to the task of thwarting the attack. She went to the warrior-king Kerala Varma of Kottayam for support, but he was not hopeful for his chances at victory. He went to the Adikeshava temple and chanted fourteen verses to invoke the Lord to grant success for his endeavor. These verses are known as the *Bhakta Sangeerthanam* and are recited even today by the devotees. After chanting them, the ruler felt that a soldier clad in green armor had left the sanctum of the Lord. As the Muslim army approached, they were attacked by hoards of wasps. Their commander was stung to death. Thereafter, the demoralized forces ran for their lives and the attack was thwarted.

Another example is that in 1741 Marthanda Varma, the king of Travancore, was engaged in a bitter struggle with the Dutch at Colachel. Before embarking on the venture, he placed his sword at the feet of Adikeshava and sought His blessings. He emerged triumphant in the battle. Dilanoi, the Generalissimo of the Dutch forces, became his captive. Later, Dilanoi became an admirer of Marthanda Varma and was appointed the commander of the Travancore army.

In the eighteenth century the temple was again the target of the Muslim invaders. The army of the Nawab of Arcot desecrated the temple and defaced it of its ornaments. The smaller Utsava Deity was also captured and stored in a lumber room along with other articles. The Deity, however, would appear on top of the pile everyday, pushing aside all the weights that were put on it. The perplexed Nawab had it chained down, boring two holes in the pedestal. At that time the Begum of the Nawab was afflicted with a disease. She was unable to withstand the excruciating pain. The physicians could do nothing about it. Then the Deity appeared to the Azhathi or guard of the temple, and told him to recover the small festival or *utsava* Deity. Explaining the greatness of the Lord, the Azhathi convinced the Nawab that the disease would be cured once the Deity was restored to its original place in the temple. The Nawab complied and was surprised that the disease in his Begum had disappeared. The Nawab repented for his blasphemous deeds and as a token of gratitude, he offered a pillow, crown, and a plate of gold. A special *puja* or worship was performed wherein a cap that is used to crown the Deity is fashioned like the Muslim head-dress. This was instituted by the Nawab and is still performed during the two annual Utsavams.

During the original *puja*, the Azhathi carrying the Deity placed it alongside the Shiva temple at a place called Thali and had a bath. On return he was dismayed to find the Deity could not be moved. The Maharaja came to know of this strange phenomenon and decided to take the Deity of Adikeshava to Thali every year for performing an *arati* worship. Only after this decision was made could the Deity be moved. This incident is commemorated every year during the Aippasi festival performed at Thali.

TRIVANDRUM (TIRUVANANDAPURAM)

Here we find the Sri Padmanabhaswamy temple, a large ornate structure built about 400 years ago. It is popular and busy. It is dedicated to Sri Vishnu as He reclines on His servant, Ananta or Adisesha. In fact, the name Trivandrum is short for Tiruvanandapuram, which means the abode of the serpent Anantha (Sesha). The temple is a Divya Desam, or one of the 108 most important temples to Lord Vishnu. The Deity of reclining Vishnu in the sanctum is flanked on all sides by Sri Devi, Bhudevi, Niladevi, and different sages. From His navel sprouts a lotus on which is Lord Brahma. The Deity, made from 12,000 *shalagramas*, always had a

A print of the large Deity of Sri Padmanabhaswamy, a Vishnu Deity reclining on Seshanaga, who can be seen through three doors.

black complexion, but He displays gold feet, hands, and crown. This place is mentioned in five of the *Puranas*, namely the *Padma*, *Skanda*, *Vayu*, *Varaha*, and *Brahmanda Puranas*.

The Deity is 20 feet long and lies in a compartment that has three doors in the front: one for His upper body, one showing His midsection, and another for His legs and feet. To get a full view, one has to do obeisances at all three doors. There are other shrines throughout the temple for Krishna, Narasimha, Subramanya, Ganesh, etc. It is open only to Hindus who must wear or rent a *dhoti* to go in. Men must remove their shirts as well. However, Westerners or white-skinned Hindus are forbidden to enter. Nonetheless, they can go in if they follow the procedure to get and sign a form stating their respect for Hinduism. But the procedure seems to change every few years.

Once in the temple, the halls are cavernous and there are beautifully carved columns and stone and woodwork. The hall that leads to the sanctum has 324 carved pillars. The Kulashekara Mandapam hall has 24 columns of excellent quality, four of which give musical sounds when tapped. It would be a photographer's delight if only you could take photos. But no cameras are allowed inside.

The origin of this temple is prehistoric. There is no clear evidence of when this temple was established or who had installed the Deity. However, according to the late Dr. L.A. Ravi Varma, a great historian, the original temple was built on the first day of Kali-yuga and is at least 5000 years old. From records such as *Grandahavali* and the *Ananthasayana Mahatmya*, it appears that the temple was constructed on the 950th day of Kali-yuga by the saint Divakar Muni from Tuludesh (Mangalore). The story in brief is that the sage was doing penance offering prayers to his favorite Deity. Suddenly, Lord MahaVishnu appeared before him as a little child. The saint became so fascinated and affectionate to the child that he could hardly think of anything else. He pleaded to the child not to leave him and it was agreed that the child would stay under certain conditions that there could be no misconduct by the sage. But one time the child began to chew on the sage's *shalagrama shilas* and acted in a most mischievous manner, and the sage got angry. Then the child said "If you want to see me, you must go to Ananthankadu," and immediately disappeared. Then the sage understood who the child was. The sage became so remorseful and began searching for the child. Finally, he saw the child disappear into the hollow of a big Alappa tree near the sea coast. The tree fell to the ground and assumed the shape of a huge reclining Vishnu, extending as much as 13 kilometers. His head was at the town of Tiruvallam (about 5 km from the present temple) and His feet at Trippapur (8 km in the opposite direction). Elated with joy, the sage prayed to the Lord to shorten His huge form so that it could be seen within the view of one's eyes. So the Lord shortened His form to equal three times the length of the sage's staff or dunda. The sage then began to happily worship this wooden form of the Lord.

Much later, after 1731 during some of the renovation of the temple, the Deity was replaced with a bed of 12,000 *shalagrama shilas* molded into the shape of the Deity with the help of kadukusarkara, which is a kind of mortar. This is the Deity that is worshiped to this day.

Thiruvananthapuram is mentioned in the *Bhagavata Purana* as Syanandoorapuram in descriptions of the pilgrimage of Lord Balarama. The temple has undergone various stages of renovation and reconstruction over the years, but is a sign of the great antiquity of Deity worship and the miracles that can be manifest through the Deities.

KARAMADAI

Karamadai is a significant Ranganatha temple. Karamadai is on the Coimbatore Mettupalayam highway about 23 kilometers from Coimbatore and just south of

Mettupalayam, a good stop on our way to Mysore or Bangalore. The temple itself is not far from the bus station.

The temple is not the largest but occupies about one acre of land. The main eastern entrance has no tower, but the 40-feet tall *gopuram* rises over the northern entrance. However, they were building a new *gopuram* for the east entrance, which is probably finished now. This temple is rather modern, being constructed by Mr. Thiruvenkatavan Chettiar of Udagamandalam in 1944. Usually Vishnu is shown in detail only in standing, sitting, or reclining poses. However, the unique point about this temple is that the main Deity of Vishnu here shows Himself as a *linga* but wears the Vaishnava *tilak*. This is seen nowhere else. It is said that thousands of years ago Bhrihaspati performed an arduous penance and gained the favor of the Lord, who appeared in this way according to the sage's wishes. In other parts of the temple, there is the Deity of a two-armed form of Vishnu, Ranganayaki Thayar, whose charms attract numerous devotees. Also, the smaller *utsavar* or festival Deity shows Himself in a sitting posture. Other shrines are found in the temple and the outer walls of the sanctum have three niches with lovely images. Sculptures of the Dasavatars of Vishnu also adorn the pillars of the main hallway, all of which reveal extraordinary craftsmanship.

In historic times, the area used to be dense forest that was filled with Karai trees. So the region was called Karaivana. Settlements of the Thottiar tribe were here, and their livelihood was raising cattle. One of them owned a cow that hardly gave any milk. So after watching it for a time, they found that it emptied its utter on a particular anthill. Thus, with utensils the tribesman tried to dig up the anthill but found that blood gushed forward. The main instigator of the dig also lost his eyesight and collapsed to the ground. His kinsmen sought advice from the spiritual preceptor, Vedavyasabhattar. Under his instruction, they built a temple to accommodate the Deity of the Lord that they found who appeared at this place of his own accord.

However, they could not understand who exactly this Svayambhumurti (self-manifesting Deity) was. Some felt that He was Lord Shiva, while others felt He was MahaVishnu. Then MahaVishnu appeared in the dream of a devotee named Pitchu Mandradiar and requested him to cover the Deity with sandal paste before dawn. While the sandal paste was being applied, Lord Vishnu gave *darshan* with the conch and disc in His hands, showing that He was certainly Vishnu.

Another interesting story is that during the time of the British rule, there was one man who was in charge of mapping the route for the railroad tracks. He prepared the tracks in such a way that it would be damaging for the temple and the water tank. Then in a dream, Lord Vishnu, mounted on a horse, appeared to him and hit him with a cane. The man then lost his eyesight. He repented for his irreverence to the Lord's temple and rearranged the route of the train tracks. Thereafter he regained his eyesight. As a token of gratitude, he gifted the temple with a horse *vahana* and arranged to re-lay the floor of the main shrines.

MELKOTE (OR MALAKOTE OR MAILKOTE)

Melkote is a small town 48 km north of Mysore. It has little in the way of accommodation, so it is best to be visited as a day trip from Mysore or Srirangapatnam. It is a sacred hill shrine with a temple of Madhvacharya, which has a Deity of Vishnu made of pure gold, standing 1 foot tall. Tiru Narayana is the name of the main temple. The Puranic names for Melkote are Vedadri (which means Veda Hill from which the *avatara* Dattatreya instructed his disciples), Narayanadri (the hill of Narayana), Yadavagiri (Yadu Hill where Krishna and Balarama of the Yadu dynasty worshiped the Lord in Dvapara-yuga), Tirunarayanapura (abode of Lord Vishnu), Bhulokavaikuntha (the realm of Vaikuntha on earth), Doddagarudanahalli (place of elite warriors), Doddagurugalahalli (place of great teachers, Ramanuja), Jnanamantapa (house of knowledge), Vaikunthavardhana Kshetra (the place which increases the population of Lord Vishnu's abode), Dakshina Badrikachalam (the southern Badrinatha), and Yathisailam.

The main Deities are said to have been given to Brahma by Lord Vishnu Himself. Tradition, as the *Naradiya Purana* explains, is that Lord Brahma once performed penance here, and Lord Narayana responded by coming to Melkote and assumed the form of a divine temple. Also, many thousands of years ago, Brahma gave one Deity to Sanatkumara. Lord Vishnu ordered Seshanaga to take the form of a hill at Melkote and wait for His arrival. Sanatkumara then installed the Deity and the temple complex in Bhuloka, planet Earth, at Melkote for the benefit of mankind. He later gave the Deity to Lord Rama, and Rama worshiped this Deity and later gave it to His son Kusha. Kusha also gave the Deity as his daughter's dowry when she married a prince of the Yadu dynasty.

When Lord Krishna appeared in the Yadu dynasty, He also worshiped this Deity. It was during this time that, while residing in the milk ocean, Lord Vishnu's diamond crown was stolen by Virocana, the son of Prahlada. Garuda killed Virocana and recovered the crown. However, while returning he saw Lord Krishna playing in Vrindavana with His friends. Garuda gave Lord Krishna the crown, known as Vajramukti. Krishna then gave the crown to the Deity Ramapriya.

When Lord Balarama, Krishna's brother, returned to Dwarka from one of His pilgrimages, he related to Lord Krishna that the Deity in Melkote was the same as their own family Deity. So they took the Deity to Melkote and found no difference between the two Deities. So Krishna installed the Deity of Ramapriya in Melkote and the Yadu family regularly came there to worship that Deity.

The lovely and large Deity of Lord Vishnu, made of black stone but covered with jewels and golden hands, with rich paraphernalia, as found in the temple in Melkote, in South India.

Later, the story goes that in the 11th century, the Jain King Bittideva embraced Vaishnavism with the training and influence of Sri Ramanuja, and changed his name to Vishnuvardhana. However, at that time, because of the Muslim invaders, Narayanapuram was in ruins. Both the main Deity of Narayana and the smaller Deity of Ramapriya were lost. But Ramanuja had a vision in which Lord Vishnu showed him where the Deity could be found. Thus, he located the larger Deity among some Tulasi trees in an ant-hill in Yadavagiri, and then installed the Deity in the temple. As a service to his guru, Vishnuvardhana renovated the Tiru Narayana temple and built five shrines to Lord Vishnu known as the PanchaNarayana temples.

The smaller Vishnu Deity or Ramapriya had been given to a king who gave it to his daughter who became very attached to it as one of her dolls. Then later, when the sages wanted to install it in the temple, Ramanuja came to ask for it back. The king laughed and said, "I have so many dolls. You call it and if it comes, then you can have it." So he called it by name and the Deity practically flew into his arms. So then he took the Deity and it was also installed in the temple. The king's daughter, however, was so attached to it, but she was a Muslim and could not be allowed into the temple. Nonetheless, she also came to Melkote and there attained *mukti*, liberation. She is known as Beebu Nachiyar and is one of the saints of the temple. Her image is shown near the Deity.

Now when you go to this temple you can see that the main Deity of Lord Vishnu is black stone and shows Him holding a shanku (conch), chakra, and gadha (club). These are all covered in gold as are the Deity's hands, feet, chest, and crown. He also wears a colorful outfit, gold bead necklaces, bright garlands, and a large string of *shalagrama shilas* hang to His feet. So He is quite lovely to see. He is directly in front of you as you enter the temple and stands nearly five feet tall. The Deity of Ramapriya is in the Ranga Mandapam hall in front of the sanctum, on the right side of the entrance. This Deity was worshiped with great love by Lord Ramachandra. Shrines for the Deities of Vaikunthanatha, Chakrathu Alwar, and Anjaneya are on the *parakramas*, or walkways of the temple. And the Goddess Yadugiri Nachiyar (Lakshmi) and Kalyani Nachiyar have separate shrines in a *mandapam* hall of beautifully carved stone pillars in the back right corner of the complex.

On the hilltop at the other end of town, many steps up, is a temple to Lord Narasimha sitting in the Yoga position, so He is called Yoga Narasimha. He is nearly three feet tall and beautifully dressed and adorned in gold, with gold hands, feet, and crown with large flower garlands covering His chest. This Deity, according to the *Naradiya Purana*, is said to have been installed here thousands of years ago by Prahlada Maharaja, Narasimha's devotee and son of Hiranyakashipu. Beneath the temple is a small cave, just under the Deity, where Prahlada is said to have meditated. From this temple you can get a great view over Melkote. The town also has the Academy of Sanskrit Research, which has a large library of old Sanskrit manuscripts and palm leaves.

NATHDWARA

By taking short excursions away from Udaipur we can reach several other places we want to visit, such as Nathdwara, which is a very holy town. You can easily reach it by bus 48 kilometers northeast of Udaipur. It is the home of the famous Deity, Sri Nathji. Sri Nathji is Lord Krishna as He is depicted at the age of seven while He was in the act of lifting Govardhan Hill. Actually, Sri Nathji used to be called Gopalaji and had been worshiped near Vrindavana before being moved to Nathdwara. The story of how Gopalaji was discovered is described in the *Caitanya-caritamrita*. It was Srila Madhavendra Puri who came to Govardhan Hill and, after he went around the hill and began preparing for evening rest near Govinda Kund, a local cowherd boy visited him with a pot of milk. The beautiful boy made Srila Madhavendra Puri forget his hunger and thirst. Madhavendra asked the boy how he knew he was fasting, and the boy replied that he resided in this village and in his village no one fasts.

That night in a dream, the same boy came to Madhavendra and lead him to a bush and explained that he was in the bush and suffered from severe cold, heat, rain, and wind. So Madhavendra was thus instructed by that boy to find the Deity with the help of the local villagers, who Madhavendra realized was Lord Krishna Himself. The Deity of Sri Gopalaji had been hidden in the bushes for some years and was discovered by Madhavendra. Then in a grand festival, the Deity was installed, using the water from Govinda Kund for the bathing ceremony. The Deity of Gopalaji stands with His left arm raised in the air in the pose Krishna took in the famous pastime of when He lifted Govardhan Hill as an umbrella to protect the local residents from the fierce rains sent by the demigod Indra.

Many people came to the place, named Jatipura (meaning "the home of the saint" in reference to Madhavendra Puri), to see and worship Gopalaji. A huge festival was started wherein the local residents brought offerings in large quantities of vegetables, fruits, grains, and many other preparations. This festival has continued in Jatipura to this day. Then a member of the royal family constructed a temple for the Deity on top of the hill.

After a few years, the Deity appeared in a dream and ordered Madhavendra to go to Jagannatha Puri to get sandalwood, which could be used to cool the Deity who was still feeling feverish from being in the ground for so many years. So Madhavendra left Jatipura to perform this service. When he arrived in Shantipur, near Mayapur, Sri Advaitacharya, an associate of Sri Chaitanya, asked him for initiation.

When Madhavendra arrived north of Jagannatha Puri, he stopped at the temple of Gopinatha in Remuna. The story of what happened there can be found in the descriptions of Remuna and the Kshira-cora-gopinatha Deity.

After Madhavendra Puri left this world, the worship of Lord Gopalaji at Jatipura was taken over by Srila

Vallabhacarya, who had been initiated in the disciplic succession coming from Sri Vishnuswami, and taught the ideals of *pushti-marg*, or the worship of Lord Krishna in His childhood form. It was during this time that the Deity of Gopalaji started being called Sri Nathji by the devotees.

As with other Deities who were moved from Vrindavana to escape the fanatic Muslim Aurangzeb's destruction of Hindu temples, Lord Sri Nathji was moved from His hilltop temple, which can still be seen on top of Govardhan Hill, to the land of Mewar from Jatipura. The Deity was first moved to Agra where the devotees kept Him in secret for six months, and then moved Him farther west. As the Deity was being moved, He reached a place where He could be moved no farther. The Maharana Sri Raj Singh accepted it as a sign from the Deity Himself, so he made arrangements to build a temple there. This is the place that later developed into the village of Nathdwara, which means the doorway to the Supreme Lord. This city has become one of the important pilgrimage places for the worshipers of Lord Krishna, especially for the followers of Vallabhacarya.

PANDHARPUR

Pandharpur is famous for its temple where the Deity of the Supreme Being is worshiped in His form named Vithobha, Panduranga, or Sri Vitthala. This place is called Bhu-Vaikuntha, the manifestation of the spiritual world on earth. The town is located along the Bhima River, which is considered as sacred as the Ganges and locally known as the Chandrabhaga. There is a short road with many shops on it that connects the temple of Sri Vitthala to the river. There are 14 bathing *ghats* along the river, but the main one is Maha Dvara Ghata.

How Lord Krishna came to Pandharpur many years ago is an example of how much affection the Lord can have on His devotees, as explained in the *Skanda* and *Padma Puranas*. It was while He was living in Dwaraka when Srimati

Radharani, His consort from the village of Vrindavana, came to visit Him. But when Krishna's queen, Rukmini, saw how Krishna was dealing more intimately with Radharani

Lord Vitthala, standing on the brick set there by His devotee Pundarika, as found in Pandharpur.

than He had with her, Rukmini left Dwaraka and went to Dindirvana, a forest near Pandharpur. So Krishna went to find her, but His apology had no effect. So Krishna went to see one of His devotees at Pandharpur.

This most fortunate devotee was Pundarika, or Pundalika as He is known in Maharashtra. When Krishna saw him, he was engaged in taking care of his elderly parents. Pundarika, being a simple devotee, gave Krishna a brick to sit on and asked that He wait until he was finished serving his parents. So Krishna stood there waiting. In the mean time, Rukmini also joined Krishna and They both decided to stay in Pandharpur and accepted the forms of Deities. Now devotees from all over can come to Pandharpur and see Krishna as He stands on the same brick that was given to Him by Pundarika.

The present Vitthala temple complex faces east toward the river in the center of town. When you approach it from the west, you have to go around it to reach the entrance. There you find many flower vendors and little shops selling the usual assortment of holy paraphernalia, such as photos of the Deities, incense, beads, etc. In the very front of the temple on the steps is a brass bust of Namdev, the 13th century poet. People do not place their feet on the step on which the bust is located. It is stated that Namdev wanted to be on these steps in order to receive the dust of the feet of Vitthala's devotees. Out of respect, people come and worship the bust of Namdev, and you can watch as they offer incense, coconut, flowers, or place their heads on the base of the shrine.

Namdeva was a famous saint and devotee poet of Lord Vitthala. The most famous story about Namdeva is when he was a child and was instructed to care for the family Deity at home while his father was away. When it came time to offer a plate of food to the Lord on the altar, he expected the Deity literally to eat the whole offering, leaving nothing as *prasada,* or sacred food remnants. Namdeva waited to see if the Deity would eat, but after a while when the Deity still had not eaten, Namdeva went into the Deity room and insisted that if the Lord did not eat, he would smash his own head against the wall. Then the Deity ate the food, using His own hands to feed Himself. Of course, when his family returned, they expected to see the remnants from the Lord's offerings, so they did not believe Namdev when he told them that the Deity ate the offering. Only after they witnessed the Deity directly eating the offering were they convinced.

To enter the temple you must go through a gate on the left side to reach the doorway. Inside, you pass by a shrine to Lord Ganesh where you stop and pray that he removes any obstacles in your devotional service. The temple's courtyard is surrounded by a colonnade and in the middle are several altars and a pavilion for Garuda. Crossing the courtyard you will see the aisles where the queue of people line up to enter the temple's main hall. In the morning and on festival days the line of pilgrims can be very long. But in the evening of this ordinary day I was able to go right in with no waiting.

You enter the temple's sanctuary through two columned hallways. Embossed silver plates cover many of the 16 columns and doorways. Although most of the temple dates from the 17th century, parts of it date back to the 12th and 13th century. On either side of the door to the sanctuary are huge images of Jaya and Vijaya who guard the entrance to Vaikuntha, the spiritual world. I had prearranged to get some Deity *prasada,* so the temple assistants gave me some Deity flower garlands, *tulasi* leaves, a coconut and sugar sweets, which they instructed me to take home and distribute to my whole family. Then I went inside the sanctum to see the Deity of Lord Vitthala.

The Deity of Sri Vitthala is said to be 5,000 years old and self-manifested, without being carved or installed, as previously related. In the sanctuary you can see Lord Vitthala as He stands on a brick, slightly smiling, and dressed in fine, colorful garments, and wearing a *vaijayanti* garland. His hands are on His hips, His right holding a lotus flower and His left clutching a conchshell. He is a Deity of black stone, about three feet tall, and always attended by two or three priests. When you see Him, you grasp His ankles and place your head right on His feet. This is very special because in most temples you can only see the Deity from a distance, never being allowed on the altar or touching the Deity. However, in the morning hundreds and even thousands of pilgrims want to see Lord Vitthala, so you have to get there early, move fast, and put up with the crowd.

As everyone exits the hall, the devotees pray to the Lord to forgive any offenses they may have committed. They may also embrace the Garuda Stambha pillar and pray that Garuda will carry them back to the spiritual world at the end of their life. Also in the hall are additional shrines to Rama and Lakshmana, Kashi Viswanatha, and Kal Bhairava. Hanging from the ceiling near the hall's exit is the *Pandurangastakam*, the eight prayers composed by Shankaracarya that he wrote that glorify the qualities and devotees of the Lord when he visited Pandharpur. After we've seen Lord Vitthala, we circle around the main temple to the shrine of Srimati Rukmini, wife of Lord Vitthala, to offer our respects to her. As you wind your way through the halls and carved stone pillars of the temple, you see a few other shrines, such as one to Mahalakshmi, one to Vishnu or Balaji, another for Radha and Satyabhama, and so forth. Then you go out the back door facing town, which means you have to go around the temple and back to the entrance to get your shoes.

DWARAKA

Along with Badrinatha, Jagannatha Puri, and Ramesvaram, Dwaraka is one of India's four main holy places where, it is said, the spiritual realm overlaps into this material world. It is also said to be one of the Saptapuris, or seven holy places, which also includes Ayodhya, Mathura, Haridwara, Kashi (Varanasi), Ujjain, and Kanchipuram. Shankaracharya established one of his four *mutts* or centers here, and even Ramanujacharya and Madhavacharya came here on pilgrimage. Dwaraka is the remains of Krishna's capital city, which He established around 3000 BCE. It was one of the most developed and advanced cities anywhere. Descriptions of it are found in many Vedic texts, including the *Mahabharata, Bhagavata Purana, Vishnu Purana, Vayu Purana, Harivamsha,* and in 44 chapters of the *Skanda Purana.* It is described as having been full of flower gardens and fruit trees, along with beautiful singing birds and peacocks. The lakes were full of swans and lilies and lotus flowers. The buildings were also beautiful and bedecked with jewels. There were temples, assembly halls, residential homes, and as many as 900,000 palaces. While Lord Krishna lived here, the people of the town would often see Him. By local tradition, the present people of Dwaraka are considered to be family descendants of Lord Krishna, or members of the Yadu dynasty.

Dwaraka existed for nearly 100 years while Krishna lived here. This is where He appeared with 16,108 palaces for 16,108 queens. Although the city came under attack from local warlords, they could never conquer Dwaraka. When Lord Krishna was making final arrangements to depart from this world, when He left His capital the island fortress was covered by the sea, as Krishna said it would be. Presently, major excavations and archeological digs have uncovered varieties of artifacts that give evidence for the location and advanced nature of the city. On shore digs, conducted by the Deccan College of Pune, they found evidence of a settlement dating back to the first century. Further findings brought forth evidence that a city certainly could have been existing there from as long ago as 5000 years.

Offshore excavations, started in 1981 by the National Institute of Oceanography, brought forth evidence of a number of things. The sea level at Dwaraka was 60 yards lower 5000 years ago. A large fortification was found under the water. Other findings include pottery, bronze statues, terra cotta beads, and so on. The dates of some of the finds go back to the Harrapan Age.

The Times of India News Service also released an article on April 7, 1997, called *Krishna's Dwarka May Not be a Myth*. In the article, Mr. S. R. Rao, who heads the Dwaraka underwater excavation project and is a consultant to the Marine Archaeology Centre of the National Institute of Oceanography in Goa, remarked on some of the findings. The remains of three temples and a township on the seashore near today's Dwaraka compare well with descriptions of Dwaraka found in the *Mahabharata* and the *Harivamsha*. Another major township was also found nearly 30 kilometers away at a depth of 30 feet, spread over a four-kilometer area near the island of Beyt Dwaraka during underwater excavation. Mr. Rao identified Beyt Dwaraka as Kusasthali where the first town of Dwaraka was built under the direction of Lord Krishna as described in the *Mahabharata*. Excavations on the island reveal that civilization was active here as far back as the Harappan culture in the 2nd millennium B.C.E.

The findings they have made concerning ancient Dwaraka make it clear that the stories in the ancient Vedic texts, such as the *Mahabharata* and the *Puranas*, are not mere myths or fables. Dwaraka was a highly sophisticated and well organized city. Remnants of the wealth of the old town still affects life in Dwaraka today since gold fragments wash up on shore. More excavations were scheduled to begin at the end of 1997.

The main temple here for Lord Dwarakadisha is the center of attention in Dwaraka and many people have had various spiritual experiences here in relation to the Deity, including myself.

When we find the temple, we will make our way through a high archway and into the temple courtyard. The main temple is said to be 5,000 years old and built in one day by Visvakarma, architect of the demigods. However, most of the present day temple is said to have been built in the 16th century, but there are parts of the sanctuary walls that date from the 12th century, and the temple sanctum is said to date back at least 2500 years. It is supported by 72 pillars and reaches up to 235 feet tall. The temple is covered by ornate stone carvings, columns, and ornamentation. Like many temples in India, no photography is allowed inside. But once seeing it, the beauty of the place will stay with you for a long time. It is certainly a temple you will remember.

The temple is visited by many hundreds of pilgrims, local as well as from all over India. As you enter it, you first notice the smell of incense and the hum of the pilgrims chanting *mantras* and prayers. As you look around, the ceilings have many beautiful paintings of the pastimes of the Lord based on the descriptions in the *Puranas*. The floor is made of pink and black marble that is set in lovely patterns. The Deity of Dwarakadish is in the central shrine and has four hands. He represents the four-armed form of Vishnu called Trivikrama. This Deity is very old and is mentioned in the *Varaha Purana*, and He is worshiped with much opulence and reverence.

To see Lord Dwarakadish, you can stand in the central viewing area with the growing crowd of devotees. One side is for men, the other side for women, and the back is for everyone. When the curtain opens behind a silver doorway, the Lord is revealed in His beautiful four-armed form and the *arati* begins. Lord Dwarakadish stands five feet tall and is dressed in colorful clothes and beautiful gold, silver, and jewels. Around the Deity arc priests who sing Sanskrit verses that relate the glories, characteristics, and pastimes of the Supreme Being. Above the altar are two-winged angels or Gandharvas who help protect the Deity. The priest then begins to offer such articles as ghee lamps, incense, and chamara fan. Everyone gazes at the Deity with the utmost respect. Some chant prayers and sing while others are very quiet in spiritual contemplation.

As you go around the complex, you will see other shrines, all of which contain a myriad of deities of demigods and goddesses, and various forms of Lord Vishnu and Krishna and Their consorts. All of Them are said to be very old. To the right of the main Deity is a small temple of Lord Balarama, Krishna's elder brother. To the left of the main temple is a smaller temple with a large deity of Pradyumna and a small deity of Anirudha, Krishna's son and grandson. Across from this is another temple of Purushottama (Vishnu). Another temple dedicated to Shiva as Kuseswara Mahadeva is next to this. Directly across from the main temple is a small temple for Devaki, Krishna's mother. And next to that is another for Veni-madhava (Vishnu). Once you visit these temples you can go behind the main temple to a rectangular building that has several altars around the sides with the Deities of Radhika, Jambavati, Satyabhama, Lakshmi, Sarasvati, and Lakshmi-Narayana. Seeing the temple at night is also very beautiful because it is lit up very brightly with many spotlights. Many people visit at this time as an uplifting way to end the day.

There are also other significant temples here, a few of which we will note. One is the Nageshwar Mahadev temple, which contains one of the 12 Shiva *jyotirlingas* (self-manifesting *lingas*) in an underground chamber. It is on the route from Dwarka to the Beyt Dwarka island. The *Shiva Purana* explains that the Nageshwar temple is in a place called Darukavan.

One legend connected with this temple is that a devotee named Supriya was attacked by the demon Daruka who imprisoned him and several others at his capital Darukavan, where he resided with his wife, Daruki. But Lord Shiva appeared as the *jyotirlingam* and destroyed the demon with the weapon known as the Pasupatastram.

Another legend is that Shiva, being sad over the death of his wife Sati, lived at Darukavan for some time in the guise of a sage. Darukavan was a land of snakes, and they cursed him to become a *linga* when their wives were enchanted by him. They were not aware of who he was. From the curse of the nagas, the *linga* was cast into the *kund* (water pool) and came to be known as the Nageshwara *jyotirlinga*. This *linga* was installed here in Dvapara-yuga when the Pandavas found this unique form of Shiva. Lord Krishna told them it was Bholenath's (Shiva's) *jyotirlinga*, and that its worship will benefit the world. To diminish the brilliance that emanated from the *linga*, Lord Krishna instructed the Pandavas to bring sand from Ramesvaram to cover it. They removed the *linga* from the *kund* and installed it as Nageshwara *jyotirlinga*.

In this *linga* dwells both Vishnu and Shiva, so it is also called Hari/Hareshwar. This temple's main door is to the west, unlike other temples. This is because the devotee Namdev was in the eastern doorway and the priest asked him to move. So he went to the back of the temple on the west side and worshiped there. Then Hari/Hareshwar turned and faced west to accept his devotee's worship.

BADRINATH

Regarding the holy place of Badrinath in the Himalayas, it is said that Narada Muni and the demigods come to the Badrinatha temple here during the winter months to continue the worship of Badrinath, the Deity of BadriNarayana when the other priests leave for the winter and go to Joshimath. In the middle of November the priests perform one last *puja,* leave the ghee lamps lit, and close the temple. Badrinath stays closed 6 months a year from Deepavali all the way until the full moon day in the month of Chittirai (late spring in the Himalayas). Then in May they return, open the temple, and the ghee lamps are still burning, thanks to the demigods.

The tradition of this temple is explained as follows: Since the history of this temple is so old, the only way we can understand how it came to be is by the explanations in the *Puranas.* In Satya-yuga, the Lord lived at Badarikashrama (Badrinatha) in a visible form. In Treta-yuga, the sages saw the Lord through the practice of yoga. Then during the age of Dvapara-yuga, it became difficult even for the sages to see the Lord. So then the sages and even the demigods prayed to the Lord, "You are our only supporter, please do not leave this place and ourselves."

Being pleased by their devotion, the Supreme said, "My dear ones and saints! After some time Kali-yuga will start. People in that age will be full of sins, wickedness, pride, and without any pious action. So I cannot stay in a visible form before them. But here under Narada Shila in the Alakananda [River], there is a divine image of mine, which you may take and establish. If one sees that image, he will get the same reward of seeing me in visible form."

After that, Brahma and the other gods took that image out of the Narada Kund in the river and asked Visvakarma, the architect of the gods, to build a temple, after which they established the Deity there. Narada Muni was made their official priest, and a rule was made that the Deity would be worshiped for six months by human beings, and the other six months by the gods. And this rule is still followed to this day.

In the *Skanda Purana* another story is told relating how the Deity of Badrivishal was established. Therein it is explained that Lord Shankar (Shiva) told his son Skanda that in Kali-yuga, in his incarnation as a saint (Shankaracharya), he would take the Deity from Narada Kund and install it. Thus, by seeing that Deity, all the sins of a person will be removed in a moment, just as the heard of elephants run away by seeing a lion. So after some time, Lord Shankara took birth as Shankaracharya and established the Deity of Sri Badrinathji for the general good of all people.

How this happened is further related. At the tender age of twelve, Shankaracharya went to Badarikashrama after a hard three months of travel up into the mountains with his pupils. He took bath in the hot springs of Taptakund and went into the temple, but the four-armed form of Narayana that had been established by the rishis in Satya-yuga was not there. In its place was a *shalagram-shila* stone, which is considered the same as the Lord. But Shankaracharya went outside the temple with a heavy heart, followed by the temple priests. He asked them, "Why is the temple without Narayana's form? I have heard that the Lord resides here in this pious place for the last four *yugas*."

The priests replied, "Because of the tyranny of Chinese robbers, our ancestors hid that form of the Lord in the nearby *kund*. But after that it was difficult to find. So from that time on we have allowed the *shalagram-shila* to reside on the altar." So Shankaracharya asked them if the form of the Lord could be found, would they install and worship it in the temple. The priests all agreed.

Then Shankaracharya went to the *kund* and meditated, and then went into the water. The priests asked him not to go since there was a current below in which many people had lost their lives. But Shankaracharya did not listen. He went deep into the *kund* and pulled out a Deity of Lord Narayana to everyone's astonishment. But the fingers on the right hand of the Deity were broken, so he went back in and pulled out another Deity, but the same fingers were broken. Then he did that a third time and became perplexed until a voice told him, "Shankara, you need not be confused. In this Kali-yuga, only this broken form will be worshiped." So in this way, Shankaracharya came out of the water with the lost Deity and installed it in the temple in a solemn manner. He established one of his disciples, Nambudri Brahmana, for doing the worship. In this way, the Deity and the temple were again established by Sri Shankaracharya. Today, people of all races, creeds, religions, and communities go there with respect to see the Deity of Lord Narayana, Badrivishal.

This story shows the antiquity of the temple and of Deity worship itself, and how Shankaracharaya, in his most inner sentiments, did not follow his teachings of impersonalism but was instead a great devotee of Lord Vishnu or Krishna and also advised the process of Deity worship for the benefit of everyone.

TIRUPATI

There are many, many stories about the Deity of Lord Vishnu at the hilltop temple at Tirupati, and how people offer this Deity their prayers or donations for their wishes to come true, whatever they may be. Unfortunately, many such prayers are for varieties of material facility, but He listens to them all. I knew one friend who climbed the hills and was determined not to ask the Deity for anything, only pure devotional service. But as he was climbing the stairs, he had a severe tooth ache. He could not help but keep thinking about the pain and wishing it would go away. Then when he reached the top and went to see the Deity, he noticed that his toothache had completely gone. No pain at all. He felt that though he did not ask for it intentionally, the Deity still heard his thoughts and removed his pain.

The powerful and very opulent Deity of Lord Vishnu at Tirupati, also known as Sri Venkateshvara or more simply as Sri Balaji.

6

Stories of Lord Jagannatha in Puri

The temple of Lord Jagannatha in Jagannatha Puri is a most important place for the devotees of Lord Krishna and pilgrims who long to visit this place. It is known that Lord Jagannatha is a most lively Deity, showing Himself to many devotees in many ways. So we give a special chapter to relate a few stories just on Lord Jagannatha.

The significance of Jagannatha Puri and the story of how the Deities first appeared goes back many hundreds of years to the time of King Indradyumna, who was a great devotee of Lord Vishnu. One time in his court the King heard from another devotee about an incarnation of Lord Vishnu, named Nila-madhava. (Nila-madhava is the Deity form of Lord Vishnu.) The King very much wanted to see this form of the Supreme and sent many brahmanas to search for Nila-madhava. All came back unsuccessful except for Vidyapati, who did not come back at all. He had wandered to a distant town which was populated by a tribe of people known as Shabaras of non-Aryan heritage. He had stayed in the house of Visvasu, and later, at Visvasu's request, married his daughter, Lalita.

After some time Vidyapati noticed that Visvasu would leave the house every night and return at noon the next day. Vidyapati asked his wife about this. Though her father had ordered her not to tell anyone, she told Vidyapati that Visvasu would go in secret to worship Nila-madhava. After repeated requests, Vidyapati finally got permission to go see Nila-madhava, only if he went blindfolded. But Vidyapati's wife had bound some mustard seeds in his cloth so that a trail could be left to follow later. When they reached the shrine, Vidyapati saw the Deity Nila-madhava after the Shabara took off the blindfold, and he felt great ecstasy.

The story continues to relate that while Visvasu was out collecting items for worship, Vidyapati saw a bird fall into the nearby lake and drown. The soul of the bird suddenly took a spiritual form and ascended back to the spiritual world. Vidyapati wanted to do the same and climbed the tree to jump in the lake. Then a voice from the sky declared that before he jumped he should tell Indradyumna that he had found Nila-madhava.

When Visvasu returned to worship the Deity, Nila-madhava spoke and said that He had accepted the simple worship from him for so many days, but now He wanted to accept the opulent worship that would be offered by King Indradyumna. When Vidyapati went back to tell the King, Indradyumna immediately went to find Nila-madhava but could not locate Him. So the King arrested Visvasu, but a voice told him to release the Shabara and that he should build a temple on top of Nila Hill where the King would see the Lord as Daru-brahman, the wooden manifestation of the Absolute.

After great endeavor, King Indradyumna built the temple at Sri Kshetra, now known as Jagannatha Puri, and later prayed to Lord Brahma to consecrate it. However, Lord Brahma said that it was not within his power to consecrate the temple since Sri Kshetra is manifested by the Supreme's own internal potency and is where the Lord manifests Himself. So Brahma simply put a flag on top of the temple and blessed it, saying that anyone who from a distance saw the flag and offered obeisances would easily be liberated from the material world. So now, anyone who merely sees the flag on top of the present temple and in the mood of devotion offers obeisances to it can be freed from material existence. Nonetheless, after much waiting the King had become anxious since Nila-madhava had not manifested Himself. Thinking his life was useless, the King decided he should end his life by fasting. But in a dream the Lord said that He would appear floating in from the sea in His form as Daru-brahman.

The King went to the shore and found a huge piece of wood that had the markings of a conch, disc, club, and lotus. This was Daru-brahman. But try as they might, the men could not budge the wood. In a dream the Lord spoke to the King and instructed him to get Visvasu and put a golden chariot in front of Daru-brahman. After doing this and forming a *kirtana* party to chant the holy names, and praying for Daru-brahman to mount the chariot, Daru-brahman was easily moved. Lord Brahma then performed a sacrifice where the present temple now stands and installed a Deity of Lord Narasimhadeva, the half-man and half-lion Deity that is now on the western side of the temple.

From the wooden Daru-brahman, the King requested many expert carvers to carve the form of the Deity, but none could do so for their chisels immediately broke when they touched the wood. Finally, the architect of the demigods, Visvakarma, (some say the Lord Himself) arrived as an old artist, Ananta Maharana, and promised that he would carve the Deity form of the Lord inside the temple in three weeks if the King would allow him to work behind closed doors. But after 14 days the King became very anxious because he could no longer hear the sounds of the carving. Finally, he could stand it no more. On the advice of the queen, he personally opened the doors of the temple to see what was happening. Then he saw the forms of Lord Jagannatha, Lord Balarama, and Lady Subhadra. But because the King had opened the doors sooner than he was supposed to, the Deities were not completed: Their feet and hands had not yet been carved. Thus, the Supreme manifested Himself in this form.

Lord Jagannath as He is seen on the last night of the great Ratha festival as He stands on the Ratha Yatra cart wearing His Suna Vesha outfit and with golden ornaments and hands that hold His golden chakra and conch shell.

The King felt he had committed a great offense for having opened the doors before the allotted three weeks had passed, so he decided to end his life. But in a dream Lord Jagannatha told the King that though he had broken his promise, this was just a part of the Supreme's pastimes to display this particular form. Occasionally, the King could decorate the Deity with golden hands and feet. Yet, those devotees who were filled with love would always see the form of Lord Jagannatha as the threefold bending form of Syamasundara, Krishna, holding a flute. Thus, the Supreme appeared in this form so that people could approach and see Him, especially as He rides on the huge carts during the Ratha-Yatra festival.

This next story and the following two are from "The Lilas of Lord Jagannatha" by Mr. Somanath Khuntia, a writer and priest who serves in the temple. His book contains many stories of actual miracles that have happened in the temple, or to devotees connected with Lord Jagannatha. These are but a few.

LORD JAGANNATHA AND DASIA BOURI

It is useless to ask whether Dasia Bouri was of sound mind to offer a coconut to the Deity of the Lord, and then ask, "Please return it to me if the Lord does not accept it happily." This was certainly strange. Is there such a God who can take offerings in His own hands from devotees?

Anyone who goes to the temple offers such things as coconuts, mangos, bananas, and other items, but it is accepted that they are sanctified through many rituals before the offering is made, which makes them eligible for being accepted by the Deity. So how is it that a coconut was offered to the Lord Himself as if He were in dire need of it? So Dasia Bouri instructed the priest, "Let it be offered as it is. Otherwise, it is to be returned."

The chief priest of Dasia Bouri's village entered the temple a second time with the coconut in his hand. Already he had *darshan* of the Lord, and all the *bhoga* or unoffered food had been offered to the Deity. However, the priest had forgotten the coconut. Just for the sake of formality, he was going to show the coconut before the Deity of the Lord to fulfill Dasia Bouri's request and then return it to him.

Inside the inner sanctum of the temple, there was a big rush. Near the Garuda-stambha was a little free space. So the priest moved there to have a clear view. He prayed, "Oh Lord, accept this offering from Dasia Bouri from the nearby village of Baligram. He is of a caste that is excluded from the temple. But he has requested that if You don't accept it in Your own hands, then it must be returned unoffered."

While people were crowding around the priest, he held up the coconut before Lord Jagannatha. He felt as if his hands were frozen around it. Suddenly, the coconut began slipping out of his grasp! Then it disappeared miraculously! The priest and everyone else were awestruck by this miracle.

The priest wondered, "Dasia Bouri is a devotee of colored caste, an untouchable. How was it possible in this age of Kali-yuga for the Lord to take such a man's offering in His own hands?"

Suddenly, another priest near Lord Jagannatha's altar shouted, "Oh, what a catastrophe! Pieces of coconut shell are falling all around here!"

The details of this incident quickly became known by all. Everyone wondered about it, and thought it was a trick. But this mattered little to the Lord and His devotee. "You cannot realize God except through faith," Dasia Bouri's father had told him.

Dasia belonged to the nearby village of Baligram, which exists even today some 30 miles from Puri. Life in the village goes on much as it did then in the 1790s. Dasia had a wife but no children. He was a weaver by occupation.

Usually, he sang hymns to the Lord in the evening in his simple hut. Singing was spontaneous to him and new songs to Jagannatha were always pouring from his lips, even though he could not read or write. He felt the reverberations from these songs throughout his body. He often felt as if he were being embraced by God and once heard the utterance, "I have created everybody. All are My sons and daughters. There is no untouchability and no separation between Me and anyone."

The time of the Rathayatra or Chariot Festival was nearing. Jagannatha would come outside so that people of all castes and religions could see Him. Eagerly that morning Dasia Bouri also set out on foot for Puri, 30 miles away. He sang sweetly all the way, charming his fellow pilgrims with his devotional songs. When the group arrived, it was already time for the pulling of the chariots to begin. So he waited near Balagandi Street, halfway down the Grand Road of Puri, instead of going nearer to the temple. It is the fervent belief of devotees that one can be purged of all sins at the slightest touch of the ropes used in pulling the chariots. Dasia Bouri felt as if he were being pulled toward the chariot of Lord Balabhadra, instead of himself pulling it. Then as if in a vision, he saw Subhadra's chariot approaching. To his God-intoxicated mind, Subhadra's chariot appeared to be running ahead.

Decorated in gorgeous colors, the chariot of Lord Jagannatha followed last, to the resounding thunder of clanging cymbals and blowing conch shells. The chariot was headed by four white wooden stallions and was being pulled vigorously by tens of thousands of devotees.

"What a gracious countenance! What large, loving eyes! Oh, such a face! It is like the dark sky itself! How inviting His smile, reaching out His big arms to embrace us all!" Dasia Bouri thought to himself. He wished to go up to the chariot, but his wish could never be fulfilled, for he was an untouchable. "Is it an offense to touch Jagannatha, who is Lord of the entire cosmos?" Dasia's only consolation was that he was seeing Jagannatha before him on the best of days and in the Lord's best mood. To be near His divine presence was all Dasia could think of.

The Lord's image fully held Dasia Bouri's attention. He was overwhelmed with feelings of intense love and devotion. In such a state, Dasia Bouri walked back to his village, with the Lord's songs on his lips and the Lord's image imprinted on his heart.

His wife was waiting for him. She had prepared simple rice water for his meal. In the middle of the bowl of white rice, one dark leaf of spinach was floating. In his highly elated state, Dasia saw it as one of the big round eyes of Jagannatha.

The entire atmosphere of the home was saturated with the Lord's divine presence. Seeing her husband dancing, the wife thought he must have become possessed by some ghost.

"The food resembles my Lord! How can I eat it?" was all Dasia could reply.

Then Lord Jagannatha appeared to Dasia Bouri and spoke, "Oh, Dasia! I am always with you. I have no need for a diamond pedestal. Ask whatever you like. I am prepared to bless you!"

At bedtime, Dasia Bouri whispered to Lord Jagannatha, "Oh, Lord. I only ask this. Please accept my offerings of Your own accord, whenever I offer You anything." The Lord gave a nod of agreement and disappeared.

The next morning Dasia Bouri procured a coconut from his landlord, bartering a piece of cloth for it. The coconut must be offered to the Lord, only then could his dream be verified. But how could the coconut be sent to Jagannatha? By the Lord's arrangement, the head priest of his village happened to be going that very day to Puri with a group of devotees bearing many offerings. Dasia humbly approached the brahmana priest, asking, "O friend, please take this to Lord Jagannatha on my behalf, as I am unable to go inside the temple. If He does not take it, please return it to me when you come back."

After the illuminating incident in the temple, all realized, including the village priest himself, that the Lord and His devotee are inseparable. "Where there is a pure devotee, I Myself am present."

Once Dasia Bouri went to Puri on his own with a basket of mangos for the Lord. On arriving in Puri, he envisioned the image of Jagannatha sitting inside the blue wheel on top of the temple, called Nila-chakra. Jagannatha accepted the fruit of his own accord, and the basket was immediately emptied. A group of temple priests saw this miraculous disappearance of the mangos and rushed to Jagannatha to ascertain the genuineness of the incident. To their utter amazement, they found mango skins and pits lying on the altar, and drops of mango juice running down the face of Jagannatha!

Who will label such a devotee as "low" or "untouchable." There was such complete union between this devotee and Lord Jagannatha, like a lover and his beloved! Is not such a person blessed?!

After the death of Dasia Bouri, the King of Puri granted his descendants a role in the annual Chariot Festival. They alone would be allowed to carry the wooden horses and the three charioteers to the chariots. This service is performed to this day only by members of his family.

LORD JAGANNATHA AND BANDHU MOHANTI

Bandhu Mohanti was a non-brahmana, but he was a great devotee of Lord Jagannatha. As poor as he was, he believed that Lord Jagannatha was his true friend and would come to help him in his hour of need.

Bandhu Mohanti used to spend most of the day only reading about Lord Jagannatha, forgetting his wife and children. His wife did not even know that her husband was a devotee of Lord Jagannatha. She only thought that he has some local friend known by the name of Jagannatha. She was much annoyed when Bandhu Mohanti wanted to spend more time with his friend than with her. One day the wife asked, "Who is that friend?"

Bandhu Mohanti replied, "You do not know and you cannot know. He is very rich, having a great building. He is a king and His dress, His behavior, His life style, everything about Him is royal. He is also very kind."

"Let us go see him some time!" the wife requested.

"How can you go in such a poor dress?" the husband answered. "If we want to go, we must take with us some gifts, and our children must wear good clothes. You must wear a gold necklace and bangles, otherwise the gatekeeper of my friend's house may not allow us to enter. Since I have no money to buy such things, I am not going to meet Him," he added. Bandhu Mohanti's wife replied, "If your friend is true and faithful, he will respect you and accept you in whatever dress you wear. Since you are so poverty stricken, why don't you approach him for help?"

Bandhu Mohanti paid no attention to what his wife said, and so his wife became very angry again. Even more difficult times were coming. The whole village was suffering from a bad harvest, as no rain had come, many might die of starvation. It was the year 1392, and like Bandhu Mohanti, most of the villagers were farmers. All were greatly worried. Bandhu Mohanti was often telling them, "My friend is rich. If He wishes, we can be saved." So his wife forcibly made Bandhu Mohanti go and meet this great friend.

It was after dark when Bandhu Mohanti, accompanied by his wife and three children, started out for Puri to meet Lord Jagannatha. The wife was thinking, "If we come to any town, at least someone will give the children some food." So they came walking from the village Shatapada to Puri, nearly 30 miles away. Only a few grains of rice were shared with them by the pilgrims who passed them on the road that night.

After three days, they finally reached Puri. Bandhu Mohanti took them straight to the temple of Lord Jagannatha, but as it was the middle of the night, the doors were closed. So they rested at Pejanala on the southern side of the temple. This is the outside watering trough where cows come to drink the rice water drained from the temple kitchen.

"Where is he, your rich friend here at Puri? Where is his house? When are we going there?" asked his wife anxiously.

"He is very nearby now," Bandhu Mohanti replied. He did not wish to tell her that he meant Lord Jagannatha was his friend. The children were hungry and crying. So the wife gave them rice water to drink from Pejanala, where the cows come to drink. Afterwards they went to sleep. Bandhu Mohanti also slept. But as his wife was feeling so worried for the children, she woke up. Suddenly she saw a young dark brahmana carrying many different types of food over his head on a golden tray. He came near, shouting, "Where is Bandhu Mohanti? Where is Bandhu Mohanti?" The wife heard this, as he was shouting in a loud voice. "Yes, we are here. What is the matter?" she asked.

The young brahmana smiled mysteriously and said, "The friend of Bandhu Mohanti has sent him this food. Please take it as I have a lot of other work to do." The wife was not in position to know what to do. Bandhu Mohanti was fast asleep. She did not think it proper to disturb his sleep after such a long journey. The young brahmana was about to leave, so she had no time to ask anything. She accepted all the food on the golden plate and woke her children. They all ate this huge feast, then fell asleep again, their stomach fully satisfied.

When Bandhu Mohanti awoke, he was told everything. He began to cry profusely, "Why didn't you wake me up? You are blessed to see Him. I am unfit to ever meet Him!" His mind was reeling from the magnitude of what had just happened to them. The wife did not understand what the matter was. As she was more worldly-minded, she could not grasp the deep meaning of the incident.

Bandhu Mohanti, in great ecstasy, ate from the golden tray all that was left by the children. "But what should I do with the gold plate?" he asked himself. He cleaned it and with deep devotion he placed it under his pillow that night, lest it be stolen.

In the morning, there was much commotion inside the temple. The costly golden tray used by Lord Jagannatha was missing. The matter was immediately reported to Virakishora, the King of Puri, who is considered to be the "moving Jagannatha" and sole authority on matters of the Jagannatha Temple.

The police caught Bandhu Mohanti as he slept that morning outside the temple walls. The golden tray was returned to the temple, and the King was about to deliver harsh punishment. Bandhu Mohanti's wife and children cried and pleaded. "It was all the doing of Bandhu Mohanti's rich friend!" the wife said, trying to defend her husband. Bandhu Mohanti could not help but cry also. Never did he expect that such a calamity would happen to them. The King announced that he would give the sentence the next day.

That night the King of Puri had a miraculous dream. Lord Jagannatha Himself appeared in the dream, saying, "Oh, King, if a friend come to your house, is it not right that you greet him with a fine meal? Bandhu Mohanti is My friend, so what fault have I done to give him food on My golden tray? Will you sentence Me also? Please, release him at once."

The King was astonished to see Lord Jagannatha come in his dream and tell him all this. He released Bandhu Mohanti forthwith. He also ordered that Bhandhu Mohanti and also his descendants be allowed to serve in the temple itself.

Even now in the temple, descendants of Bandhu Mohanti cook the first meal of the day for Lord Jagannatha. It is a preparation of sweet rice and ghee, known as khecheda. After cooking this *prasada,* Bandhu Mohanti himself was given the privilege of carrying this offering on that very golden tray to the Deities. After the food was offered, he would lead the procession of *maha-prasada* being taken to the devotees, carrying the golden try over his head. Even today there are cooks in the temple with the surname of Mohanti who are direct descendants of Bandhu Mohanti, still carrying out this service.

What is surprising is that Bandhu Mohanti was a non-brahmana and never held any hereditary service in the temple before. Of the more than 15,000 worshipers of the Jagannatha temple today, this can only be said of him. He had simply considered Lord Jagannatha to be his friend.

A WISH FULFILLED

On the first day of a young man's service in the temple of Lord Jagannatha, another miraculous *lila* or pastime occurred. When he was standing before the Deities in the evening, a newly married couple who cam from the state of Bengal met him. The man's name was Deepen Ghosh and the wife's name was Shubhashree.

The husband asked the priest who later retold this event, "Is the one with the black face Jagannatha? Can He really hear prayers and answer them? Perhaps not, because He is made of wood and has no ears to hear with. You, being the priests of Jagannatha, only cheat the innocent pilgrims who come from distant places. You are only interested in taking money from them in His name. But He never answers any of our prayers."

As this was only his first day in the temple, the young *khuntia* or servant could not understand what Mr.

Ghosh meant. He simply replied with much feeling, "Yes, Jagannatha does hear, if your prayer is sincere."

Deepen Ghosh was a wealthy businessman and he was very skeptical of these ancient traditions. So he sarcastically rebuffed the young man, "I am sincere, but you are not. What is the use of doing *puja* and prayer to that log of wood? The father has told the son to do this, and the son has told his son. Like that, it goes on and on. The one whom you call Jagannatha can never hear you."

When the man became more adamant to challenge Jagannatha, the young priest consulted with the head priest, who was decorating Lord Jagannatha with flower garlands at that time. The head priest advised, "Tell him to come again for the Chandana Lagi ceremony of Jagannatha after midnight. At that time, Jagannatha's forehead is smeared with sweet-smelling sandal before He retires to bed. If any person prays to Him at this particular hour, He grants the prayer."

When Mr. Ghosh again began to abuse Lord Jagannatha with sarcastic remarks and loud laughter, his young wife bowed her head in prayer. When he left the temple, she silently followed. To the amazement of all, this same Mr. Ghosh and his wife turned up for the Chandana Lagi ceremony that very night. He met the young priest there and put the same question again, "So, is this a good time for Jagannatha to listen? If so, I have something to ask Him."

The young priest inquired as to what he wanted. Mr Ghosh retorted, "Can He give it to me? You ask Him first!" The priest, being disgusted with this difficult man, told him, "Yes, He will grant it to you, just tell Him what you want."

Mr. Ghosh looked a moment at his beautiful young wife. Her skin was light and her face shone like that of a goddess. She was wearing a rich Benares silk saree and her face was half-covered with its cloth. Then, half in joke and half in deep sincerity, he turned to Lord Jagannatha and asked, "Tell Him to give me salvation. Tell Him I am asking for His *moksha*."

The young *khuntia* went to the head priest, who was putting sandalwood paste on Lord Jagannatha's forehead at that moment. It is but natural that at such an enjoyable moment Lord Jagannatha would be in a good mood and happy to grant anything asked for. The *khuntia* communicated all the details about the man to the head priest. His name, his native place, his wife's name, and the prayer itself.

Then in a big voice so that the man himself could hear, the priest asked Lord Jagannatha, "Oh, Jagannatha, this man Deepen Ghosh from Bengal asks that You grant him liberation. Please grant this."

The young priests returned and told the man that his prayer would be granted.

Mr. Ghosh replied, "Hah! This wooden Deity! It granted my prayer! Wonderful! Don't cheat me, please. Don't cheat me. Don't think I am so stupid, I can't be fooled so easily."

Months passed. This incident slipped from the young priest's mind. Some six months later, he was returning home from his work at school. As he passed by the main East Gate of the temple, he heard his name announced over the temple loudspeakers. "Sri Somanatha Khuntia, please come to the information counter because a lady from Bengal has come to meet you."

The *khuntia* was very surprised. "What lady wants to meet me?" He went quickly to the information counter. On seeing the lady, he could not recollect ever meeting her before. She was wearing a plain white sari, without any makeup or gold ornament. She was a widow in mourning. More than this, he could not gather.

Seeing the young priest coming, the lady rushed to him and fell at his feet out of respect for a priest of the temple. She also put 101 rupees at his feet. In tears, she said, "Actually, your Jagannatha is very great. He hears just like a man, and now I am a widow, as my young husband, Deepen Ghosh, died suddenly only last month." The young priest then remembered everything and stood speechless. This is the miraculous power and personality of the Deity who is indeed able to see and hear everything, and do anything when He wants.

□

7

More Recent Personal Experiences

This chapter contains a few of the more recent and personal stories that I have heard from people who have had their own experiences with Deities of the Supreme, or His various incarnations and forms.

Sometimes devotees are humble and are hesitant to share what are intimate experiences with the Deities due to fear of them being misunderstood. And some will share but will prefer that they remain anonymous out of either humility, or that others will view them as being unqualified for such events in their lives. But the interactions with Deities happen to many people on a regular basis, for many reasons. Sometimes their health is in grave or serious condition, which is then alleviated after doing serious prayers to the Deities. Or sometimes couples who have not been able to have children pray sincerely to the Deities and later find that they are expecting a child.

Even with the Deities at the nearby Krishna temple here in Detroit, called Devasadan Mandir, I have seen where people have had difficulties with their immigration status and have but a week or two before they must leave America. Then I have instructed them to drop their ego and open their hearts and go in front of the Deities that we have here of Sri Sri Radha-Kunjabihari and express their fear and concerns, and ask for help. Another week or so later they came back to let me know that their immigration

The lovely and most merciful Deities of Sri Sri Radha-Kunjabihari at the Krishna temple in Detroit, Michigan.

status had been resolved. Or in another case, a couple was trying to have children, but nothing had yet developed. Later, after praying to the Deities, they had a healthy baby. I have also seen where practically impossible projects had been proposed to the Deities, such as making a new hall, or different developments around the building, and so on, and when the devotees wished and prayed devotedly enough, difficult things came together very quickly by the blessings of the Deities.

These kinds of things have happened all over the world, but I have seen this happen several times here in Detroit in relation to our Sri Sri Radha-Krishna Deities, or with our Deities of Lord Jagannatha, Balarama and Subhadra. These Deities have done miracles for Their devotees in the past and continue to do so. All it takes is to go before the Deities and open up to the blessings They can provide. But first you must humble yourself and then reveal your hearts with faith, and then with trust be open for whatever may happen, and miracles can and have taken place. This is especially beneficial and shows that the Deities are real. This also increases the faith and devotion of the persons who experience or witness this. But extra merit is earned when a person simply prays for continued devotional service to the Deity and deeper levels of love for God.

LADDU GOPAL AT SRI KHANDA

This is from a lecture by H.H. Jayapataka Swami, a story that has been told many times.

There is a Deity of Gopal Krishna, a small Gopal, "laddu Gopal" we call Him. This is in Sri Khanda. There lives Mukundananda and his wife, and their son was Raghunanda. The father had to go and see some disciple who was on his death bed. So he quickly gave the initiation to his son with the *ugranaya*, first mantra of the Gayatri mantra, and instructed, "You can worship the Deity. Your mother will tell you what to do. I have to go to see my disciple, to help him remember Krishna at the time of death." The he went off.

The mother said, "You just go in, you ask the Deity to accept the laddus, then you come back with the plate."

So he went to the Deities, put the laddus there, and asked the Deity to accept: "Please accept these laddus." But it seemed that the Deity wasn't accepting them. He didn't see, so he cried, "hhuhh huhhh."

The Deity asked, "Why are you crying?"

"You are not taking the laddus."

"You want me to eat?"

"Oh, yes. My mother said you would eat."

Then the Deity became a little boy and started eating the laddus. The boy came back with an empty plate to his mother.

The mother looked at the empty plate. "Where are the laddus?"

"Oh, the Deity ate them," said the boy. She was wondering what's happening? This was going on every day, and the Deity was taking every day.

When Mukundananda came back, the mother told him this is happening. He said, "I'll hide in the temple and watch what is happening." Then he came behind the Deity, and was listening. He heard the boy say, "Please accept these laddus. Eat them." Then he didn't hear anything. He looked up, and he saw the Deity eating the laddus. The Deity had become like a little boy and was eating the laddus.

"Huh!" he gasped. After all, in most cases you don't expect to see the Deity eating laddus like that. He was shocked. When He heard the gasp, the Deity became stone again. But in his hand He had a half-eaten laddu.

Since then they offer the Deity half a laddu.

So the boy became very famous. The Deity was eating from his hand.

When Raghunanda grew up, he established the Lord Chaitanya dancing Deity in Khatwa, at the place where Lord Chaitanya took sannyasa.

GOPAL GIRI

Gadai Giri had only one son, who was named Gopal Giri. Gopal Giri was influenced by the devotional qualities of his father and was very devoted to Lord Jagannath. Every year he would go to Puri to see the Ratha-Yatra festival. He was also very attached to performing *sankirtan,* and was expert in many different styles of *kirtan.*

Gopal Giri had a desire to worship a Deity of Gopal. Unable to find such a Deity, he decided to go to Puri, thinking that if he would render service to Lord Jagannath there, then somehow Gopal would come to him. Arriving in Puri, he stayed in the area known as Kundei Benta Sahi, near Grand Road. As he was very scholarly, he easily obtained service in the office of the king, where he became the poddar, or cashier, for the Temple of Lord Jagannath.

Gopal Giri led a very regulated life. While staying in Puri he would daily go to see Lord Jagannath, and at the temple he would sit on the *bais pahaca*, the twenty-two steps inside the compound leading up to the main *darshan* area, and there he would read *Srimad-Bhagavatam*. In the evening he would take *prasad* and go home. Every Sunday he would go to the Satalahari Math, a temple near the ocean, where he would sit and read *Srimad-Bhagavatam* and chant *harinam*, the Lord's holy names. He was very attached to *Srimad-Bhagavatam*.

During the Ratha-Yatra festivals in Puri, he would approach devotees and *sadhus* coming from Vrindavana and ask them to bring him back a Deity of Gopal. They would readily agree. "Yes, yes," they would say. "Next time I will bring a Gopal Deity for you." But no one ever brought a Deity. At this same time, in Vrindavana there was one renounced devotee who was worshiping a Deity of Gopal. One night this Gopal Deity appeared in the sannyasi's dream and spoke to him.

In this regard, Sri Srimad Gour Govinda Swami tells this story:

"Gopal Giri was serving in Puri as a government cashier. He was always thinking in his mind, 'If I can get a Gopal Deity, I'll offer worship to Him.' But he thought, 'How can I go to Vrindavan?' He had a strong desire to get a Deity.

"At that time this Deity of Gopal was in Vrindavan with a sannyasi Vaishnava, a renunciant. He was doing *madhukari*, begging, and he was keeping that Deity in his *jhola* (a cloth tied as a bag). During the day, he would go out and do *madhukari*, then in the evening he would cook whatever he had begged and offer it to Gopal. In this way, he was leading his life.

"One night this Gopal Deity told the Vaisnava, 'You take me to Gopal Giri, the son of Gadai Giri. He wants to offer Me worship. I want to go there. Take me there.'

"But the Vaishnava sannyasi thought that it was only a dream. He did not take it seriously. After a few days Gopal came again in a dream and beat him with a cane on his legs. It was such a severe beating that his legs were bleeding. The sannyasi Vaishnava woke up and begged, apologizing, 'Please forgive me for my offense. I did not take Your order seriously. But You have beaten me so severely, how can I go there with such wounds on my legs?'

"Gopal said, 'When Gopal Giri touches you, it will be healed, otherwise you cannot be cured. You go there at once. Don't make any delay.'

"So he started walking. At that time there was no communication system, no train or bus. The only way was by walking. It took him two and a half months to reach Puri. At this time Gopal Giri was staying in a rented house at Kundhei Benta Sahi in Puri. The Vaishnava reached Puri in the evening and stayed near the Jagannath temple. Early the next morning he inquired, 'Who is Gopal Giri? I want to meet him.'

"Many people knew Gopal Giri. He was famous as the cashier of the Jagannath temple. So he quickly found Gopal Giri at his rented house.

"Gopal Giri had just finished his bath and was putting on *tilak*. The Vaisnava arrived and offered his obeisances to Gopal Giri. He then took the Deity from his bag and presented Him to Gopal Giri. Gopal Giri was amazed. 'What is this? Who are you, and where has this Deity come from?'

"The Vaisnava replied, 'You wanted Gopal to worship, so Gopal has come from Vrindavana. I was in Vrindavana carrying this Gopal. He told me to hand Him over to you, and He beat me when I did not listen.' He showed Gopal Giri his legs and said, 'If you touch it, it will be cured; otherwise it will not be cured.' So Gopal Giri immediately touched him and the injury was gone.

"Gopal Giri was very happy that Gopal had fulfilled his desire. He couldn't go to Vrindavana, but Gopal had come to him. Gopal Giri went to the market and purchased rice, dal, and vegetables. He prepared *prasad* and gave some to the Vaishnava. Then he went to the king and offered his resignation, saying, 'I don't want to serve any more.'

"When he returned to his room he opened his bag and told that Vaishnava, 'You can take as much money as you want.' The Vaishnava said, 'No, I don't want any money. I only want to do service for Gopal. Wherever Gopal goes, I will go. I want to go and serve Him. I am not one to sell Gopal. I am a servant. I won't take any money.'

"Later on, Gopal Giri again went to see the king. The king asked him, 'Why did you resign?' 'I have a Temple in my village and I had a desire to get a Deity of Gopal to worship.' The king was very pleased and said, 'All right, your desire is very noble. I have no objection. But sometimes you must come to Puri with your *kirtan* party and chant in Jagannath's temple.'

The king gave Gopal Giri some extra months of salary and allowed him to go. Gopal Giri then sent a message to Gadeigiri for a *kirtan* group to come to Puri to accompany Gopal to His new home. When the Gajapati king heard the *kirtan* of the Gadeigiri villagers he became very pleased. It is written in the *Mada La-panji*, the history book of the Temple of Lord Jagannath, that whenever the *kirtan* party from Gadeigiri comes they should be allowed to perform *kirtan* in the temple.

Gopal Giri installed the Gopal Deity in Gadeigiri and requested the renunciant from Vrindavana to perform Gopal's daily worship. After serving Gopal for twenty years, the renunciant departed this world and was given *samadhi*, ritual burial, near Gopal's temple. After this, Gopal Giri engaged other renounced Vaishnavas in the daily worship of Gopal.

HOW GOPAL CAME TO ISKCON

The following story is about how Gopal came to Iskcon,

adopted from the book *Gopal Jiu-The Beloved Deity of Srila Gour Govinda Swami* (by Gopal Jiu publications, pages 55-61).

Ghanashyam Giri's father, Gopinath Giri, departed this world in 1964. From 1964 until 1992 Ghanashyam Giri was entrusted with serving Gopal. He worked very hard to make Gopal happy, but after some time he found that there was very little help. Concerned about how Gopal's service could be maintained, he remembered his cousin-brother Braja-bandhu Manik who had become a *sannyasi-guru* in Iskcon and was now known as Gour Govinda Swami Maharaja. Ghanashyam Giri thought that since Gour Govinda Swami had so much devotion for Gopal, he would be the appropriate person to whom to pass on the service of Gopal.

In the meantime, Gour Govinda Swami was regularly coming to Gadeigiri for *darshan*. Before and after traveling abroad for his preaching tours he would always seek the blessings of Gopal. In 1989 Gour Govinda Swami began bringing devotees from the large Iskcon Temple in Bhubaneswar to Gadeigiri to celebrate Radhastami, the appearance festival of Srimati Radharani. This developed into a grand festival of *kirtana,* lectures and *prasad* distribution, and many of the local villagers would enthusiastically participate. Again, Ghanashyam Giri decided to give Gopal to Gour Govinda Swami. They discussed the matter and Gour Govinda Swami happily agreed to accept the responsibility. But shortly thereafter Ghanashyam Giri began again to have second thoughts. If he gave Gopal to the guru of so many Westerners, would Gopal then belong to the Western corner? One year went by, and seeing his reluctance Gour Govinda Swami became disappointed.

Ghanashyam Giri describes the incident that changed his mind: About 2:30 one morning I had a dream. Gopal came and was standing near my head. He said, "Why are you sleeping? Wake up! So many troubles have come to you, but have you felt any difficulty? No, because I am always behind you. Now you are alone. How can you arrange all types of festivals for Me? I am always very interested to hear *nama-sankirtana*. Gour Govinda Swami is your own relative. Why don't you give Me to him? So, now tell Me, will you give Me or not?"

In the dream I said, "Yes. Yes. I will give. I will give." Suddenly my wife woke me up and said, "What are you saying? What will you give? To whom will you give? You are speaking like a madman. What happened?" I told her that Gopal had just come and asked me if I was going to give Him to Gour Govinda Swami or not and I said, "Yes. Yes. I will give. I will give." I told her, "Gopal was standing near that window. He just left."

My wife said gently, "Go and donate Gopal to Srila Gurudeva. Whatever property you have you should also give to him. If he takes Gopal, then Gopal will be happy and He will be taken care of nicely. You will be able to see Gopal here every day. Why are you hesitating?" In this way, my doubt was cleared.

The next day I was preparing to go to Bhubaneswar to see Gour Govinda Swami, but I heard that Gurudeva was coming to Gadeigiri. So I stayed and waited for his arrival. He came a few days later and I met with him. He asked me, "How are you? What about Gopal?" I said, "I have been waiting for you to come, to give Gopal to you."

Gurudeva looked at me for a moment and laughed. He said, "What has happened to you? What has brought about this change?" He said, "Has Gopal spoken to you?" I said, "Yes, Gurudeva, Gopal spoke to me." Then Gurudeva asked me, "What day was it that He spoke to you, and what time?" I told him, "Twelve days before, at 2:30 in the morning." Gurudeva nodded his head up and down. "Gopal came and spoke with me on the same morning at 2:00 am, then at 2:30 He came to you. That morning I was translating the *Bhagavatam* into Oriya. I dozed off for a few moments.

"Gopal came to me and said, 'You installed Radha-Gopinath here. Has Gopinath replaced Me in your life?'" (Srila Gour Govinda Swami had commissioned a sculptor to make Deities of Radha and Krishna to be exactly the same height, width, standing position, etc., as Radha Gopal in Gadeigiri, and installed them on the Iskcon property at Bhubaneswar, naming them Radha-Gopinath).

Gopal again asked Srila Gurudeva, "Is Gopinath the same for you as me?" With folded hands Gurudeva replied, "No." Then Gopal said, "You are worshipping here, but I can't come here. Gadeigiri is the house of My devotees. They have no wealth, but there mind is always on Me. Even if they only offer Me a tulasi leaf and a little water I am happy there. They are always saying, 'Gopal! Gopal!' I cannot leave them and come here. You are not doing any service for Me because Ghanashyam has not given Me to you. He promised, 'Unless Gopal tells me to give Him.'"

Gopal then said, "I will speak to Ghanashyam. First I have met with you and now I am going to Ghanashyam."

While Gurudeva and I were speaking, one of my family members was there. They said, "You are always talking about donating Gopal, but your are only speaking and not giving." I said, "No, today I must donate Gopal to Gurudeva. Bring tulasi and water and chant mantra." Gurudeva asked, "How will you donate to me?" I said, "As *Srimad-Bhagavatam* describes that Bali Maharaja donated to Lord Vamanadev, like that I will donate Gopal to you. You place your hand under mine and I will donate three times with water and tulasi leaf." I called for a brahmana who put tulasi and water in my hand. I said, "First I donate to you Radha Gopal Jiu. Secondly I give you all of Gopal's paraphernalia. Thirdly I donate the property to you. From tomorrow you will take charge."

Gour Govinda Swami immediately accepted Gopal and the property, and on the 15 of November, 1993 he recorded everything in the name of Iskcon, the institution of his spiritual master.

Gour Govinda Swami then sent two of his disciples to Gadeigiri. They arranged to fix the broken temple building and make nice arrangements for Gopal's worship. The existing temple for Gopal was very small and simple. Now that Gopal was under his care, Gour Govinda Maharaja wanted to build something nice for Gopal. He was very eager to see the work begin. On November 23, Fakir Charan went to see Gour Govinda Swami in Bhubaneswar.

Fakir Charan remembers: When he saw us he started scolding us. He said, "The registration was finished eight days ago, where have you been? My dear Gopal's work is not going on correctly. Gopal is beating me." He then showed us his back, which bore fresh marks from a beating. I was shocked. We both begged forgiveness for the delay. He then replied, "The devotee of Krishna never fears anyone. This is service for Krishna, so where is the fear?"

On January 17, 1994 Gour Govinda Swami laid the foundation stone for Gopal's new Temple and he installed a Deity of Anantasesh. On that day, in his lecture he spoke to all of the devotees as well as to the laborers and construction workers who were there to begin work on the new structure that became the new temple for the Deity of Gopal.

THE APPEARANCE OF LORD NARASIMHA IN MAYAPUR

Here is the story on how the famous Deity of Lord Narasimha manifested at Iskcon Mayapur. This story of how Lord Narasimhadeva came to Sri Mayapur Chandrodaya Mandir is adopted from the Mayapur Journal, based on a discussion with HG Atma Tattva Prabhu.

It all started when on the 24th of March, 1984, at 12.20 a.m., thirty-five dacoits armed with weapons and bombs attacked Sri Mayapur Chandrodaya Mandir. This was an event that many devotees heard about all over the world.

They harassed the devotees and treated them with derision. But the greatest shock came when the dacoits decided to steal the Deities of Srila Prabhupada and Srimati Radharani. Fearlessly the devotees challenged the attackers. How could they see Srila Prabhupada and Srimati Radharani carried away? Shots were fired, a few dacoits fell, and their plans foiled. The Deity of Srila Prabhupada was rescued, but the beautiful form of Srimati Radharani would no longer grace the main altar.

This incident really disturbed the minds of the devotees. Those involved in management were especially concerned to make some permanent solution. This was not the first time the devotees had faced violence and harassment in Mayapur. The co-director of Mayapur suggested that Lord Narasimhadeva be installed. When the dacoits had threatened devotees at the Yoga-pitha, Lord Chaitanya's birthplace just down the road, Srila Bhaktivinoda Thakura and his son, Srila Bhaktisiddhanta Sarasvati Thakura, had promptly installed Sri Sri Lakshmi-Narasimhadeva. There had been no further disturbances.

Other devotees in Mayapur were not so keen to follow so closely in these footsteps. The *pujari* of the Deity had to be a *naisthika-brahmachari* (celibate from birth), and the worship of Lord Narasimhadeva must be very strict and regulated. Who would be prepared to worship Him?

Despite such hesitancy, the co-director was enthusiastic to bring Lord Narasimhadeva to Mayapur. He asked Bhaktisiddhanta Dasa and Atma Tattva Prabhu to draw some sketches. One day quite spontaneously he said that the Deity's legs should be bent, ready to jump, he should be looking around ferociously, his fingers should be curled, and flames should be coming from his head. So Atma Tattva Prabhu sketched a Deity in this mood. The devotees liked it, and Pankajanghri Dasa agreed to be the *pujari* and do the worship.

Radhapada Dasa, a wealthy devotee from Calcutta offered to sponsor the sculpting and installation of the Deity. It seemed Lord Narasimhadeva's appearance in Iskcon Mayapur would be a simple, straight-forward affair. Radhapada Dasa promptly gave Rs.1, 30,000 and it was accepted that the Deity would be ready for installation in three months. Atma Tattva Prabhu left for south India to get things organized. By Krishna's grace Atma Tattva soon found a very famous sthapati sculptor. A sthapati not only sculpts Deities, he is also expert in temple architecture and engineering. The man was very obliging until it was mentioned that the Deity to be carved was Ugra-Narasimha, or the form of angry Narasimha. He emphatically refused to make such a Deity. Many Deity sculptors were then approached, but the answer was always the same: No. Atma Tattva Prabhu had made a number of trips between Mayapur and south India, six months had passed, but Lord Narasimhadeva had not yet manifested in His Deity form.

Radhapada Dasa was very anxious to see Lord Narasimhadeva installed in Mayapur. He asked Atma Tattva to visit the original sthapati and once again plead the case. This time the sculptor was a little more congenial and offered to read me a chapter from the *Silpashastra* (a Vedic scripture on sculpture and temple architecture) that deals with the different forms of Deities. He read aloud some verses describing Lord Narasimhadeva. A series of verses described His flame-like mane, his searching glance, and his knees bent with one foot forward ready to jump from the pillar. When he read this, it was exactly the form that was desired.

Atma Tattva Prabhu showed him the sketch he had done. The sculptor was impressed and offered to draw an outline based on the scriptural description which could be used as a guide for sculpting the Deity. He reminded Atma Tattva, though, that he would not carve the form himself.

It took him a week to complete the sketch, and it was very impressive. Atma Tattva Prabhu returned to Mayapur and showed the sketch to the temple authorities. Everyone wanted this same sthapati to carve the Deity. Once again Atma Tattva was sent back to south India to try to convince him. All that could be done was to pray to Lord Narasimhadeva to be merciful and agree to manifest Himself in the temple in Sri Mayapur Dhama.

Atma Tattva had hardly said two sentences when the man very matter-of-factly said he would carve the Deity. The story of how he came to this decision is interesting. The sthapati had approached his guru, the Shankaracharya of Kanchipuram, about the request. His guru's immediate reply was, "Don't do it. Your family will be destroyed." But then, after a moment's reflection, he asked, "Who has asked you to carve this Deity?" When he heard that it was the Hare Krishna people from Navadvipa, he became very concerned. "They want Ugra-Narasimha? Are they aware of the implications of sculpting and installing Ugra-Narasimha? Such Deities were carved over 3,000 years ago by very elevated sthapatis. There is a place on the way to Mysore where a very ferocious Ugra-Narasimha is installed. The demon Hiranyakashipu is torn open on His lap and his intestines are spilling out all over the altar. Once, the standard of worship there was very high. There was an elephant procession and festival everyday. But gradually the worship declined. Today that place is like a ghost town. The whole village is deserted. No one can live there peacefully. Is that what they want for their project?"

The sthapati replied, "They are insistent. They are constantly coming to talk to me about the Deity. Apparently they have some problem with the dacoits."

Handing his guru a sketch of the Deity, he said, "This is the Deity they want." His guru took the sketch and looked at it knowingly. "Ah, this is an Ugra category," he said, "but a Deity in this particular mood is called Sthanu-Narasimha.

He doesn't exist on this planet. Even the demigods in the heavenly planets don't worship a form like this. Yes, this Deity belongs to the Ugra category. Ugra means ferocious, very angry. There are nine forms within this category. They are all very fierce. The one they want is Sthanu-Narasimha: stepping out of the pillar. No. Don't carve this Deity. It will not be auspicious for you. I will talk with you about this later."

A few nights later the sthapati had a dream. In the dream his guru came to him and said, "For them you can carve Sthanu-Narasimha." The next morning he received a hand-delivered letter from Kanchipuram. The letter was from the Shankaracharya and gave some instructions regarding temple renovations. There was a footnote at the bottom. It read, "For Iskcon, you can carve Sthanu-Narasimha." The sthapati showed the letter and said, "I have my guru's blessings. I will carve the Deity."

Atma Tattva Prabhu was overwhelmed with joy, and gave him an advance payment and asked him how much time it would take to carve the Deity. He said the Deity would be ready for installation within six months.

Atma Tattva returned to Mayapur. After four peaceful months in the holy *dhama*, it was decided to go to South India and purchase the heavy brass paraphernalia required for the worship of Narasimhadeva and then collect the Deity. The trip was well organized and trouble-free until Atma Tattva visited the sthapati. He explained to the sthapati that all the paraphernalia required for the worship had been purchased and that he had come to collect the Deity. He looked at Atma Tattva as if he'd lost his sense and exclaimed, "What Deity? I have not even found the suitable stone!"

Atma Tattva Prabhu couldn't believe his ears. "But you told me he would be ready in six months," he exclaimed.

"I will keep my promise," the sthapati said. "Six months after I find the stone, the Deity will be ready for installation."

His reply was emphatic, but Atma Tattva just couldn't understand or accept the delay. In frustration he challenged him, "There are big slabs of stone all over South India. What's the problem?"

He looked at Atma Tattva the way a teacher would view a slow student and said very deliberately, "I am not making a grinding mortar, I am making a Deity. The scriptures tell us that only a stone that has life can be used to make a Vishnu Deity. When you hit seven points of the stone slab and they make the sound mentioned in the scriptures, then that stone may be suitable. But there is a second test to indicate whether the stone is a living stone. There is a bug that eats granite. If it eats from one side of the stone to the other and leaves a complete trail visible behind it, then the second test of living stone has been passed. That stone is a living stone, and expression can manifest from it. Only from such a slab can I carve your Narasimhadeva. Such stone speaks poetry. All features of the Deity sculpted from such stone will be fully expressive and beautiful. Please be patient. I've been searching sincerely for your six foot slab."

Atma Tattva Prabhu was amazed and a little anxious. The devotees in Mayapur were expecting the arrival of the Deity soon. How was he going to explain the "living stone" search to them? Maybe they would decide to make Narasimhadeva from marble. Atma Tattva decided to try to lighten the subject by discussing the Prahlada Maharaja *murti* with the sthapati.

"Please forgive me, but I forgot to tell you last time I came that we want a Prahlada *murti*. We want to worship Prahlada-Narasimhadeva. What do you think?"

"I don't think that will be possible," the sthapati replied matter-of-factly. Atma Tattva looked at him incredulously, not sure what to say. He smiled and continued, "You want everything done exactly according to scriptures. Your Narasimhadeva will be four feet high. Comparatively speaking, that will make Prahlada Maharaja the size of an amoeba."

"But we want Prahlada Maharaja one foot high."

"Fine," the sthapati replied, "but that means your Narasimhadeva will have to be about 120 feet high."

We began to argue back and forth about Prahlada Maharaja's form. Finally, the *sthapati* sighed in resignation and agreed to make Prahlada Maharaja one foot tall. At least now there was something positive to report when Atma Tattva returned to Mayapur.

After two months he again returned to South India. There had been no developments. Atma Tattva Prabhu shuttled back and forth from Mayapur to South India every thirty or forty days. Finally, the stone was found and the sthapati became a transformed man. For over a week he hardly spent any time at home. Hour after hour, day after day, he just sat staring at the slab. He had a chalk in hand but did not draw anything. He refused to allow his laborers to do anything except remove the excess stone to make the slab rectangular. The next time he was visited, he had made a sketch on the stone. That was all.

The Mayapur managers were becoming impatient. "Are you sure this Deity will be finished in six months?" Atma Tattva asked the sthapati in desperation. "Don't worry. The work will be done," he replied.

After returning to Mayapur, Atma Tattva Prabhu was soon back in South India to check on some details of the Deity. He found the sthapati carving the form himself with intense care and dedication. At that stage the stone had gone and the shape had come. The sthapati had just started on the armlets. He took two weeks to carve them. All the features were so refined and delicate. Atma Tattva was impressed and very happy.

In all, it took the sthapati a little over twelve months to finish the Deity. When he completed the work he didn't immediately inform anyone but decided to visit some friends for a few days. It was the monsoon season, there were few visitors, and he felt it safe to lock up Lord Narasimhadeva securely in his thatched shed. Two days later his neighbors ran to inform him that the thatched shed was on fire. There was heavy rain and everything was wet, but the coconut-tree roof had caught fire. He ran to the scene to find Narasimhadeva untouched but the shed burned to ashes.

Immediately he phoned Atma Tattva Prabhu, "Please come and take your Deity. He's burning everything. He's made it clear He wants to go NOW!"

Enthusiastically, Atma Tattva traveled to south India, hired a truck, and half-filled it with sand. He arrived at the sthapati's studio thinking this final stage would be relatively simple. However, he had foolishly forgotten that Lord Narasimhadeva is a very heavy personality: he weighed one ton! After two or three hours they managed to lift the Deity safely from the shed onto the truck. To travel across the border safely, they also needed police permission, along with signed papers from the Central Sales Tax Department, the Archeological Director, and the Art Emporium Department in Tamil Nadu. All the officers demanded to see the Deity before signing the necessary papers. Once they took *darshan* of Lord Narasimhadeva, they all became very obliging and efficient. They had all the necessary papers in hand within twenty-four hours – a miracle given the usual quagmire of bureaucracy found in government offices in India.

The trip back to Mayapur was also amazingly trouble-free and peaceful. Their protector was certainly with them. Usually the sthapati comes on the day of the installation ceremony, goes into the Deity room and carves the eyes of the Deity. This is called *netranimilanam* (opening the eyes). It was an exceptional case that Narasimhadeva's *sthapati* had already carved the eyes. He had not only carved the eyes; he had also done the *prana-pratistha* (installing the life force), a little *puja* and an *arati*. This may have been why all the papers were prepared so obligingly, and transporting the Supreme Lord was so easy. He was already present. And who could dare to say no to Lord Narasimhadeva?

The installation of Lord Narasimhadeva was very simple and lasted three days; from the 28th to the 30th of July, 1986. Atma Tattva Prabhu remembers feeling apprehensive that perhaps the installation was too simple. The grave warnings of the Shankaracharya of Kanchipuram had left deep impressions. But soon it was apparent that everything was fine by the loud, dynamic *kirtana, sankirtana-yajna,* the only true opulence of Kali-yuga, that was dominating the scene. Everyone felt enlivened and satisfied. Lord Narasimhadeva, the protector of the *sankirtana* mission, had finally decided to manifest at Sri Mayapur Chandrodaya Mandir.

LORD NARASIMHADEVA RECIPROCATES INSTANTLY

Installing this Deity of Lord Narasimha in the temple was only the first step. What happens after the Deity is installed continues to show the presence of the personality of Lord Narasimha on a regular basis. So, here are a few stories as related by Pankajanghri das of Mayapur, the *pujari* or priest who takes care of the Deity, that shows how this Deity reveals Himself to His devotees.

As Pankajanghri das describes, I have been asked to recount some stories in connection with Him, the Deity of Lord Narasimhadeva, but unlike the *sastras* (scriptures), these "lilas" (pastimes) have no authority except for the testimony of the devotees who told them. In most cases there were no other witnesses. Although I am generally quite skeptical when it comes to accepting other people's mystical experiences as truth, just too many things started happening recently, not to sit up and take notice.

For instance, during one Gaura Purnima festival, I called over a devotee in the crowd and asked her to distribute the

The fierce but merciful Deity of Lord Narasimhadeva in Mayapur.

Lord's *charanamrita* [bathing water] to the ladies, which she did. Later, when she brought the *charanamrita* pot back, she remarked that Lord Narasimhadeva was very merciful to reciprocate so quickly.

"I was praying this morning that I might be able to offer some direct service to Him, and now you have given me this service."

"Yes," I said, "desires are quickly fulfilled in the holy *dham*. Just see, the same day you desire, it happened."

"No, not the same day—the same moment," she replied. "The very instant I expressed that desire to serve Him, you called me over." "Wow! That is amazing," I acknowledged. "Did you hear about how one devotee's eye problem was cured at the same time that Lord Narasimhadeva's original eyes were placed back, after one donor had bought Him new eyes?"

"Oh, yes," she told me. "As a matter of fact, I was staying in the same building when Lord Narasimhadeva spoke to her." She added, "You know, there was so much energy around that night that nobody could get any sleep."

Just a few days later, another devotee revealed how Lord Narasimhadeva helped him. "I was suffering intensely. I could not even stand without supporting myself on the column in front of Lord Narasimhadeva's altar. I prayed, 'Please help me. Take away this suffering condition so that I may serve You fully.' I then felt all my pain moving up and flowing out of my body. It just left."

While I was hearing this, I noticed another devotee who had come for the *darshan* of the Lord. Earlier in the morning this devotee had asked my advice what to do, for she had been afflicted for about two weeks with a severe problem that contaminated her body that wouldn't allow her to paint some Deities in Assam, although she had already been commissioned to do it and had an air ticket to go.

"Mataji," I exclaimed while walking over to her, "Lord Nrsimhadeva is giving instant benedictions. Why don't you ask Him to remove your problem?"

The very next morning, when she saw me, she said, "Thank you so much for the advice! You know, when I arrived home from the temple yesterday, my problem had completely disappeared."

Some days later another devotee came to the *pujari* room and told us about a dream, wherein Lord Narasimhadeva walked and talked with her just like a father. When she asked how she could serve Him, He told her to offer Him some mangoes. It wasn't the mango season, but she managed to get some, and we offered them for her. This was the year that His Holiness Gour Govinda Swami left his body in Mayapur.

A few days after this tragedy she came again and said, "Actually, I only told you half of the dream. Lord Narasimhadeva also said to me, "My *pujari* is very dear to Me, and I am going to take him back with Me."

"Oh, don't do that, please," she fearfully exclaimed to the Lord. "We want him to stay here."

"No, I think I will take him back," He said.

"So after my pleading with Him for a long time, the Lord firmly announced. 'All right, then, I will take one of the gurus instead.'"

She concluded by saying, "I told my spiritual master about this dream, and he advised me not to tell anyone. But now, because it has come true, I think I can tell you."

When I repeated this story to my friend, Visvambhar from Carolina, he said, "This is amazing! My wife also dreamed about Lord Narasimhadeva and mangoes. You see, yesterday, while she was walking outside the Mayapur campus, she saw a jar of mango pickles in a shop and desired to buy them for Lord Narasimhadeva. But doubting the purity of the contents, she refrained. However, last night, Lord Narasimhadeva appeared in her dream and asked, "Where are My mango pickles?"

When Lord Narasimhadeva first came to Mayapur, all the *pujaris* were reluctant to worship His awesome form.

Bhava Siddhi das was particularly frightened and always very nervous worshiping Him. One night, after putting the Lord to rest, he was leaving the altar when he heard such a tremendous sound that it made his hairs stand on end. Looking back fearfully, he saw that everything was in place. So he quickly left, locked the door and paid his obeisances, praying for forgiveness for any offense he might inadvertently have committed. At the end of that night he was awakened by the shaking of his bed. Bhava Siddhi was sleeping on the top of a bunk bed. So he thought it must be the *pujari* below him getting up for *mangala-arati* (morning worship).

However, when he opened his eyes, he saw Lord Narasimhadeva sitting on his bed. That fortunate *pujari* became very fearful, practically to the point of panic. As he tried to get up, Lord Narasimhadeva placed His two hands, which felt like the weight of the universe, on his shoulders. "Be peaceful, be calm," the Lord consoled him. "I have just come to tell you that when you worship Me in the temple, there is no need to fear Me. Please, give up this fear."

The Lord then disappeared, but Bhava Siddhi began to run up and down the veranda of the Long Building, where he slept.

"What happened?" asked some concerned devotees. But they received only incoherent replies. They started to think maybe he had gone mad or become haunted by a ghost. Finally, Bhava Siddhi ran over to the temple and prostrated himself before the door where Lord Nrsimhadeva is worshiped and offered heartfelt prayers. After some time he became a little pacified, and began walking back to his room. "I wonder why everyone is staring at me," he thought. When he looked down, the answer was obvious: He had gone to the temple in his night dress.

I saw Bhava Siddhi at the Gaura Purnima festival—he was living in America—and asked him about that incident. "Yes," he said. "I still have those two marks from Lord

Nrsimhadeva on my shoulders. They are almost gone now, but they are still visible."

He wasn't the only one to claim to have seen Lord Narasimhadeva. Once, a devotee from a nearby Gaudiya Math temple came to offer worship to Lord Narasimhadeva and told our head *pujari*, Jananivas, that on Narasimha Caturdasi (the Appearance Day of Narasimhadeva), he had been staying up all night chanting. Then, at the end of the night, Lord Narasimhadeva manifested Himself in his room. It was the form of Narasimhadeva from the Iskcon temple, and He appeared to be smiling very sweetly at me. My Guru Maharaj said I was very fortunate and should come here and worship Lord Narasimhadeva.

Another time the frantic parents of a runaway boy, after searching all over the country, finally heard that their son was at our Mayapur center. They immediately came and spent the whole day looking for him, inquiring at the reception desk and from individual devotees, but they were not at all lucky in tracing him.

At the end of the day, during the *sandhya arati* (evening worship) of Lord Narasimhadeva, his mother was praying with folded hands, "My dear Lord, the last time I came here, I happily participated in the chanting and dancing, but now my heart is broken because of my lost son, and I find no pleasure in life anymore. My Lord, if only my son could be returned to me, then I would also raise my hands and chant 'Haribol, Hare Krishna.'"

As these words left her mouth, a figure passed and stepped before her and Lord Narasimhadeva: it was her lost son. Both parents have now accepted Vaishnava initiation, started a *nama hatta* preaching center, and are enthusiastically preaching the Lord's glories.

There are other stories—some I would be hesitant to repeat, and others that I can't, having been told them in confidence. The devotees who told these stories have had their faith and conviction strengthened, and certainly mine was, too, by hearing them. So, if others derive the same benefit from reading them—even though they are not *sastra* (scripture)—it will be most beneficial. They help us advance in Krishna consciousness.

(These stories are just a few selections from http://narasimhalila.com/home.html, where you can find many more pastime descriptions)

Once, Lord Narasimhadev's worship in Mayapur was going on as usual when the *pujari* noticed that one flower fell from Narasimhadev's garland. The *pujari* asked the visitors if anyone was offering any special prayers to Lord Narasimhadev. The visitors in front did not say anything, but from the back one lady came forward with tears in her eyes. She said, "My daughter got married about four or five years ago and she has no issue. The people in my son-in-law's house consider it inauspicious. So I was praying to Narasimhadev that He might help her in her desperate situation." Then the *pujari* said, "Your prayer is granted, the symptom is that this flower fell from Narasimhadev's garland. Please take this and keep it nicely. You can wash this flower and give the water to your daughter to drink." Then the lady left, and later the *pujari* forgot the incident.

After one year, the same devotee, along with her daughter, son-in-law and a newborn baby came smiling to Narasimhadev. She reminded the *pujari* about the prayer she made one year back, as a result of which her daughter gave birth to a very nice baby boy, whom they named Prahlad. And once again they offered a very nice *puja* (offering) to Lord Narasimhadev.

(From http://narasimhalila.com/pastimes1.html)

MIRACLES IN MAYAPUR

To show further examples about the miracles that can take place with Krishna Deities, here are two little stories that relate how Deities can intercede and change the health and recovery of those who have been injured. This is again in regard to Lord Krishna's form as Lord Narasimhadeva, but it also exemplifies the sincerity of the people involved and the power of the faithful *pujaris*, such as Jananivas das and Pankajanghri das who have become famous simply for their devotion and dedication to the Deities in Mayapur. And I take great pleasure in helping spread examples that show the potency, glories and mercy of the Deities in this way. The following story is told with gratitude and love by Racitambara dasi.

On April 22, 2005, Revati Sundari devi dasi, age 8, was climbing on the roof of the bamboo playhouse in the Grihastha park in Sri Mayapur *dham*. To her great surprise she fell through the roof, landing on her head, and the roof caved in on top of her. She was in shock for an hour, shaking and crying and incoherent. She also had concussion. Gaura Baba, our wonderful homeopathic Vaishnava doctor, treated her for concussion and shock and suggested a scan.

After three days, Revati woke up in the night vomiting black blood. We rushed her off to Kolkata. On the way, clear fluid was leaking from her nose, then violent nosebleeds started.

We took her straight to a good pediatrician, who immediately called in the top neurologist in the city. He ordered a CT scan and then, seeing the results, he sent us to a very good neurosurgeon, who has his own private hospital. Revati was admitted straight away.

The symptoms continued through the night, and we found out that the clear fluid from her nose was the brain fluid (CFS) leaking out. The scan clearly showed a fracture in the floor of her brain, from which the brain fluid was escaping. Also her brain was swollen and blood was pooling there, causing pressure. She had extreme pain in her head which was unabated since the accident. The doctors worked on her for a couple of days, giving her medicine intravenously. The whites of her eyes became totally red. She was like a limp rag with little interest in anything.

Finally the doctors said that the next morning, early, they would do a special scan showing all the sections of her brain to determine the exact extent of the injuries and then would probably decide to operate to repair the damage. They would tell us their decision by 9 am.

I phoned Pankajanghri Prabhu, explaining the situation and asking him to please pray to Lord Nrsimhadev. He immediately said he would do a full *puja* (offering) between 5 and 7 am, complete with *abhisekha* (bathing ceremony) and everything else. This was the time of the special scan.

The next morning when I met the doctors, they were looking amazed and said that the new scan showed that the injuries were miraculously almost healed. All the symptoms such as pain, violent nosebleeds, brain fluid leakage, vomiting, etc., had abruptly stopped.

When I went in to see Revati, she was sitting up in bed looking bright-eyed and fresh, and her eyes were fully white again. Thank you, Lord Nrsimhadev!

Another example is that on October 28th, 2006, Chakravarty Raj, the 14 year old son of Radha Kanta Gopal das and Padma Radhika devi dasi was injured when a fire cracker burst in his face. He was immediately rushed to hospital. The doctors said that he suffered from 2nd degree burn injuries on his face and suggested (1) facial dressing immediately, (2) chemical crafting after a fortnight and then (3) plastic surgery after 6 months or 1 year.

Next morning, the parents requested Pankajanghri Prabhu to offer special offerings to Lord Narasimhadev for the speedy recovery of Chakravarty Raj, which were duly performed.

For the next 2 days, he was just lying in bed without much movement. He could not even open his eyelids. He was then taken to Disha eye hospital at Barackpur, where they found that the carina (the white portions of the eyes) took the burn injury and the pupils were unharmed. Hence, there would be no problem with his sight and a treatment of 15 days would cure the carina.

On 2nd November morning, Padma Radhika devi dasi approached her Guru Mahraja, His Holiness Jayapataka Swami, and told him of what had happened. He gestured that he will pray for him and applied Narasimha oil on her forehead. The same morning, Chakra was taken to Kolkata for treatment of his facial injuries.

After getting an opinion at the Apollo Hospital in the morning, Chakravarty was taken to the Railway Hospital at Howrah. One of the senior Doctors tested him and confirmed that it was a second degree burn and sent him to the dressing room for initial facial dressing. But within 3 minutes one of the staff from the dressing room rushed out yelling and took the parents inside. Upon seeing Chakravarty the parents stood there motionless, struck with wonder and amazement. There was Chakra, standing and smiling, with no trace of any injury or mark on his face!! Narasimhadev ki jai!!

When asked for clarification, the doctor and others present in that place could not give any valid reason. One of them said, "You can go back in your temple and ask you Lord about it. *Yeh tho apke Bhagavan ka chamarkar hai.* This is your Lord's miracle."

LORD NARASIMHA IN SOUTH AFRICA

Here is a true story that happened in 1998 in South-Africa. The father and the daughter who experienced this event told this story to a friend, a sannyasi and devotee of Lord Narasimhadev. This story was also found in the newspapers, and several witnesses of this truck-accident after this incident became devotees of Lord Narasimhadev.

This happened to a simple Vaishnava family that lives there. They had a 5-year old daughter. This girl was a great "fan" of Lord Narasimhadeva, she found Him simply funny, as he looked half-lion and half-man and felt very attracted to Him. She often told her playmates about her favorite God, a lion, and the kids always wondered about what kind of God this could be.

What can a five year old girl know about God? She wasn't initiated, not even her parents Although the father of the family followed a guru and was close to a small Hindu-community.

What happened was that one day the girl was playing outside with her ball along with some other kids near the street. The ball, however, landed in the street, and the girl ran after her precious ball. There was hardly any traffic on this rarely used country road. But this time a very fast truck came running down the way. The girl in her play didn't see the truck coming.

The father was in the first floor of the house and saw his baby girl running on the street, but he also saw the huge truck coming, closing in on his daughter with great speed. The father yelled at her, but she didn't hear him. So he jumped out of the window to save his daughter and broke both his legs, laying on the ground in pain.

Then, helpless, he had to watch how his little girl was hit by the truck and thrown through the air, landing some 20 meters away. All of the children and neighbors around who observed this froze with shock. The father later said that when he saw this his only desire was to die.

From the other direction came a police car that also witnessed the accident. The truck went on and the policeman drove his car across the street to stop him. The truck-driver was barely able to stop his truck and seemed to be very drunk. The policeman immediately called the ambulance and ran over to the motionless girl laying in the grass. The closest hospital was a small private clinic. The ambulance came, but refused to take the girl, being afraid they wouldn't have the necessary machines to help the injuries the girl must have. They advised the policeman to call the main hospital, as only they could efficiently help her, as they suspected that her spine must be broken, etc. The policeman was in despair, not even knowing where the father of the girl was. Actually, he didn't even know if the girl was still alive, and he didn't dare to touch her, not knowing how injured she was. However, in the end she was brought to a good hospital, and the policeman accompanied the girl, along with her father who also arrived there.

The chief-doctor heard what had happened to the girl, and they immediately X-rayed her to see the results. The policeman wanted to be assured of how the girl was doing, and waited to see the results. Everybody was shocked to hear of what a terrific accident that had happened to the girl.

However, when the nurse brought the X-ray pictures to the doctor, he became very upset and started yelling at the nurse that she should, for-God's sake, at least bring the right pictures. After all, this was about life or death. He even threatened to fire her, as it was unacceptable to make such mistakes. The nurse was scared and didn't understand what was happening. Yet, those were the correct pictures of the five year old girl who had been hit by the truck. The nurse wasn't aware yet of what had happened to the girl. When the doctor viewed the X-rays, he said that they could not be the right pictures because they showed that there was not a single broken bone. The doctor kept saying all the time, again and again, that it was impossible, it can't be.

Then suddenly the girl awoke from her faint and, in full awareness, told a story which made its tour through the media.

She explained that in the moment she picked up the ball from the street, she saw the truck coming up to her. And the only thing she could do was to yell out for help. She didn't call for mommy or daddy, but for her Narasimhadev. In that moment, when the truck hit her, she suddenly saw how Narasimhadev picked her up from the ground, smiled at her, and said, "Don't be afraid, nothing will happen to you." The girl continued her story that the Lord had put her on the other side of the street into the grass. But when putting her down, He accidentally scratched her waist, which still hurt her a bit.

She spoke about how beautiful Narasimhadev was, His hair, His eyes, etc., but his claws were very sharp and He should cut them. She also spoke about how He wore a golden dhoti, etc. The doctor didn't understand anything and told the policeman she still was in shock and hallucinated, which is normal.

So, the girl was profoundly checked for any injuries, but the only injury they found on her body were those scratches. The doctor said this must be from a wild animal like a lion, as he had cases like this before. So, he was disturbed and asked if they had been the ones who brought the girl to hospital since she was injured by a wild animal, not a truck. Nobody was clear on how to explain it. However, later the same doctor and nurse who took care of her became devotees after they learned from the parents who "that lion" was.

So, as we can see, miracles still happen today. These are not mere stories from the *Mahabharata, Puranas* or *shastras* that are thousands of years old. This was simply because the little girl was very attracted to this form of God, and in her despair she called Him for help. Lord Narasimhadev did not consider if she was initiated or had the right to call His name. He protects His devotees that sincerely worship Him in their hearts.

The little girl was obviously no common soul, and who can say what she did in her previous life to have such an experience.

SRI SRI RADHA GANDHARVIKA GIRIDHARI IN MAYAPUR

At the Sri Caitanya Math, on Bhaktisiddhanta Road a few kilometres North of Iskcon Mayapur, the Deities here were personally installed and worshiped by Srila Bhaktisiddhanta Saraswati Thakur.

As it was told by Vrajanath Prabhu, from the Sevak office in Iskcon Mayapur, there was one maker of Deities in Jaipur who had a dream. He had many finished Deities, but one particular Deity appeared to him in the dream and said, "Tomorrow my very great devotee will come to take me away."

The next day, Srila Bhaktisiddhanta Saraswati visited the Deity maker looking for Deities. The man immediately took Srila Bhaktisiddhanta to the Deities and said, "Here are your Deities."

When Srila Bhaktisiddhanta Saraswati asked why he had said these were his Deities, the Deity maker told him about the dream. Srila Bhaktisiddhanta joyfully accepted the Deities and worshiped them for the rest of his life. This happened in 1922.

He named them Sri Sri Gandharvika Giridhari. The name *Gandharvika* means, "She who sings like a Gandharva" meaning Her voice is so sweet, like a Gandharva, which indicates Srimati Radharani. And *Giridhari,* as you know, is the one who lifted Govardhan Hill.

THE BALA GOPALA DEITY AND KRISHNA PREMA DAS

Krishna Prema (Ronald Noxon) served for a time as a priest or *pujari* in the temple of Bala Gopala, the Deity of his guru, Yashoda Ma in Mirtola, a village in the Himalayas. One night while asleep, Krishna Prema heard someone calling "Dada, Dada." He suddenly got up and looked around but saw no one. Thinking that it was nothing, he again closed his eyes and laid down. But again he heard the sweet call "Dada," meaning elder brother. This time he could understand that it came from inside the temple. But no one was inside. So how could this be? Yes, as he went near the temple he heard, "Dada, I am feeling cold. The window is open."

Then Krishna Prema went into the temple and found that the window was indeed open. So he closed the window and carefully covered the body of Bala Gopala with a quilt. When he said, "Thakura, You feel so cold," a stream of tears flowed from the eyes of the Deity, making Krishna Prema feel petrified. But here was the Supreme Lord accepting the position of the child Deity who was completely dependent on the loving care of his "Dada," wanting to be loved and enjoy this sweet, intimate relationship between them.

KICKED BY THE KARTAMASHA DEITY

As told by Pusta Krishna Prabhu: When I first came to Krishna consciousness movement in Gainesville, Florida in 1970, I had never seen an ISKCON temple. I took one Hinduism course which showed a movie about Deity worship of Sri Sri Radha Krishna in India. I remember going back to speak with Gargamuni Swami and I asked him if he did that also. He said "Yes". Coming from the Jewish tradition where idolatry was frowned upon, I was uneasy. So, in February 1971, we started our hitch-hiking trip up to New York, on the way to East Pakistan on Srila Prabhupada's orders. When I first arrived in the Brooklyn temple, it was night-time. The following morning, I went to my first *mangala-aratik*. I was really shaken seeing the odd forms of the Jagannath Deities. I had literally joined the movement under a tree in the Plaza of the Americas in Gainesville.

Anyway, the years passed, I took sanyasa in 1972 at age 22. Some months later, I was at the Los Angeles Temple. The current temple room was then the old church with pews. At the front of the room was the single Deity of Kartamasha, Krishna as an elephant herds boy. While I was taking rest one afternoon, that Kartamasha Deity appeared in my dream. I looked down at His lotus feet and noticed He was making circles with His big toe. I thought to myself, "the Deity can't move His toe!" I bent down in my dream to take a closer look, and He kicked me in the head with His foot!!! I was immediately transported to the Brahman plane, very laughingly liberating knowing that my Lord had such a wonderful and charming sense of humor. Needless to say, I never looked upon another Deity the same way again. Although They may stand still on the altar…I know They do so at Their own sweet will, being capable of wonderful activities if They so choose.

SAVED BY GAURA NITAI

This story is from Malati devi dasi, a disciple of Srila A.C. Bhaktivedanta Prabhupada who had helped start the Hare Krishna Movement in Europe. She relates, as recorded in class at Detroit in April, 2011: At one point I was in charge of a group of ladies traveling and doing book distribution in Belgium and Holland. We had a wonderful set-up inside a Mercedes van with installed Deities of Sri Sri Gaura Nitai (Lord Chaitanya and Nityananda). So we would have a regular morning program for Them in the van and then the whole day we were out distributing books. Then we would come back in the evening and see the Deities again and then go to sleep. A simple life, and very blissful.

However, it was one winter in Holland in which they said it was the coldest winter in 53 years. So we would sleep in our sleeping bags and coats and we were still cold in that van. So we went to a camping store and purchased a heater, and we were really excited that we were finally going to be warm. So we looked around and I found a place under some trees to park the van for the night where there were no houses around. Then, in anticipation, that evening we closed the windows to make sure they were really tightly closed so we would not lose one bit of heat. And we happily went to sleep that night.

Later, after I had been asleep for a while, I saw myself in a dream lying on a road. And I saw Sri Sri Gaura Nitai coming down the road, but when They came to me They started kicking me in the side. And They were saying, "Get up! Get up! It's time for *mangala arati*, get up!" And I was feeling Them kicking me in my side, and so I tried to wake up, but I couldn't wake up, and I realized something was wrong. Now it was no longer a dream, I was trying to get up but I couldn't get up. I was sleeping by the door and I managed to get the door opened and I rolled out onto the ground.

That night it had snowed so I fell into the snow and as my head started to clear, I started pulling the other women out of the van yelling, "Get out! Get out of the van!" One of the women were saying, "Leave me alone, I don't want to get up now." And I responded by saying, "Get out! You have to get out now, something is wrong!" And we all had these horrible, horrible headaches.

So, to make a long story short, by closing the windows there was no oxygen, and the heater had burned up all the oxygen. So, if Gaura Nitai had not come and woke me up, we would have all died. It was the Deities who saved us.

Then, a funny part of the story, the police came and surrounded us with dogs. The police were all speaking in Dutch and none of us spoke Dutch, except for Hello, and Good Day, just enough to get by. It turned out the place where I parked was a place where they trained the dogs, the K-9 forces. So they saw us there wondering what is going on. When they realized what had happened, they took us right away to a hospital to be checked out. We got better, but it was Gaura Nitai who saved our lives that day. But as I look back on it, it was so amazing and so wonderful to be kicked in the side by the lotus feet of Sri Sri Gaura Nitai.

The Little Lord Jagannatha Deities (Lord Balarama, Lady Subhadra and Lord Jagannatha) of Chintamani devi dasi.

LORD BALARAMA SHOWS HIS PRESENCE

This is told by Chintamani devi dasi, who helped open the first Hare Krishna temple in Japan. As she explains:

Little Lord Jagannatha, Little Lord Balarama and Lady Subhadra, as They are lovingly called (all about 10 inches tall), arrived at the Japan temple in 1970. I don't know where They came from, probably from somewhere in India. I just remember that we opened a box we got in the mail and there He was, with Little Lord Balarama and Lady Subhadra. We made an altar for Them and started doing *aratis* and offering food, although we did not have any clothes for Them.

I'll describe one special incident that involves Little Lord Jagannatha. In Japan, we had Lord Jagannatha on a little altar and there was no one else in the house we used as a temple. One day I was cooking the offering, and the offerings in Japan were pretty much on time, but they weren't exact. On this occasion I was cooking and I was thinking, "Is Lord Jagannatha really eating this food? How do I know He is really eating this food?"

I happened to be late for the offering and I heard a noise come from another part of the house, like a thud. Although I knew there was no one else in the house, I stopped for a minute. But then I kept cooking and about a minute later I heard the same noise again. Then I was scared and wondered what it was, and whether somebody else was in the house that I didn't know about. So I looked in the front room and the back room of this tiny Japanese house, and then I looked in the temple room and saw Lord Balarama standing on the bottom shelf of the altar, which was three shelves high. I wondered how He had gotten there. It was as if He took two steps down. Then the only thought that was in my mind was that maybe He was hungry because I was late for the offering and maybe He was trying to show me He was eating it.

So I put Lord Balarama back up on the altar and went back to the kitchen and finished the offering really fast to keep the Deities from waiting. When the brahmacharis came back from *sankirtana*, I told them what happened but they just looked at each other like, "Yeah, sure." But that's what appeared to happen.

This is just one of many other incidents that have happened with these particular Deities that she will be glad to tell you if you see her. Due to the mercy of Srila Prabhupada, these Deities became Chintamani's personal Deities in 1972 when he ordered her to take Them wherever she went.

LORD JAGANNATHA IN LONDON SOHO

One time the *pujaris* were preparing to offer a flower set to Sri Sri Radha London-Isvara (Radha & Krishna). This means that the whole outfit of the Deities are made of flowers. A donor had offered the funds required.

Then that night while one of the *pujaris* was sleeping, Lord Jagannath appeared to her in a dream. He said, "I am God just as much as He is! I want a flower set also."

"But Lord Jagannath," she pleaded nervously, "Someone donated the money for the flower set. We don't have the money to buy a flower set for You."

"Don't worry," Lord Jagannath said. "Radharani will arrange everything."

Then the next day someone came to the temple and donated the money needed to buy Lord Jagannath's flowers, and the devotees enthusiastically prepared a flower set for Lord Jagannath as well.

A FEW STORIES BY ANJU KEJRIWAL

Anju is from Bombay and was raised in a spiritual family, so she always had Balgopal (the Deity of child Krishna) in the house and they would serve Him. She explains:

I have got a small Balgopal at home and one time a friend got some laddu sweets, and she started opening them. But I said "No, no. Let me do an offering of them to my Balgopal, and then we can all take." And then she said "You and your Krishna," like she was laughing at me.

Then she came into my temple room and she asked "Does Krishna really eat?"

I replied, "Of course He eats. How can you say He does not eat?" Even from my childhood we always accepted that Krishna eats through His Deity. But my friend thought I was crazy, but I said nonetheless, let me do the offering.

She had come to stay with us, and the next day she was sleeping where my Deity room was and she got up in the morning and she was praying there a little bit, and then she herself saw two laddu crumbs on the clothes of my Balgopal Krishna Deity. And then she called me to come and see. She said, I don't believe your Krishna eats. But the evidence was there, so she saw this herself and became convinced. And then she looked at the laddus herself that were left in the bowl and she could see like two little teeth had pricked the laddus where Krishna would have taken a few bites out of them, before the crumbs were on His clothes. So then her faith started to build up, and she decided that I was not totally mad.

Another time I went out of town. I give my Deity of Balgopal hot milk every night. My maids were in the house and they were alone, but they knew the routine to give the Deity offerings. If I'm not there, then my daughter would do it, or even the maids would do it.

So when I got back from out of town my maid told me, "Your Krishna is real." So I asked what happened. She said that she forgot to give Them milk in the night. She explained, "At 2 A.M. in the night He was kicking me and telling me to 'Give Me milk.'" The maids were busy watching TV because no one else was there. So they did not give the Deities milk but He woke her up and told her to "Give Me milk." Then she got up and give Him some hot milk.

So when I got back she was so scared and said that your Krishna is real. I said "See, He is not just stone. So whatever we eat, we first feed Him."

RADHA-KRISHNA IN MY DREAMS

This is told by Madhava Lata devi dasi from Italy. She explains:

I saw myself in a huge temple room, and there were many, many devotees. Some were chanting, others were talking, walking, admiring the Deities. The Deities were on this big altar but not very much raised from the floor level, just one step, and without any sort of boundaries. They were completely dressed and bedecked in white and also made of white marble, but they were actually moving. Krishna was bent as usual in His *tribanga* (three curved bending) form, but instead of holding the flute He had in one hand (His right) a long little box, and in the other hand a thin brush. He was putting on kajjhal, and with a sidelong glance He was looking into the little mirror that Radharani was holding for Him. Also, Radharani was holding a mirror in her right hand, and looking into it with the side of her eye and shyly giggling. So while Krishna was putting on the kajjhal, They were playfully looking into each others eyes in the little hand-mirror.

Many devotees were uttering exclamations of delight and joy at this pastime of the Divine Couple. I was also watching but I was taken by so much emotion that tears were coming down from my eyes, so I started to walk towards the side door because I did not want the devotees to see my emotions. But there were so many of them that I had difficulties in making my way through the crowd, so much so that I fell down long on the floor. Then I started to crawl towards the door with difficulty since I was blinded by my tears and, when I made it, on the doorway stood the same Radha-Krishna in the same white dress, but there They were entwined in a dance. At that point I just put my head on their Lotus Feet.

I always think and meditate on this form of the Lord, even though I never read of this pastime, at least in my limited knowledge. I have also found a name to remember this pastime as Sri Sri Radha Kajjhal Kanu. I don't even know if this is correct in Sanskrit, but it reminds me of the mood of the Lord in this pastime. Now it is two years that I am thinking of having a painting made depicting this vision.

SAVED FROM NIGHTMARES BY BALARAMA

I used to have nightmares in black and white, all of my life (til teen-age) about being chased, living in a war zone, etc. Then after reading the "Krishna" book regularly every night before bedtime for several days (70s trilogy), one night I had a dream in which Balarama slammed his mace and then suddenly ever after that I would dream in color and never had those hellish type of dreams again. (From a person who preferred to be anonymous)

BALARAMA WINKS

I had been chanting *japa* meditation for maybe one-and-a-half to two years while I was a *brahmacharini* in the temple and had recently come to the San Francisco temple in 1971. We were reading from the *Nectar of Devotion* in the morning, and we read the story of Lord Balarama drinking His *varuni* honey beverage and becoming intoxicated. When I read this, I was so amazed, and I asked in my heart to Lord Balarama on the altar there, "Is our Lord Balarama really here?"

Then He winked one of His huge lotus eyes to let me know it was indeed Him. It was a huge, huge wink. Jaya Jaya Lord Balarama!

Many years later - more than 20 years ago, I had lent my small Jagannath Deities (about 8 inches tall) to someone but had done so with the caveat that I might ask for Them back sometime when I was able to care for Them. Finally, my life had settled, and I asked for the Deities back (how They arrived to me in the first place is another story). The person didn't remember that I had only "loaned" Jagannath, Balarama and Subhadra to them. I begged and pleaded to no avail. Several years went by. I could not forget my Deities. So finally, one day my husband and I got in our car and drove the 400 miles to where the Deities were – on a shelf as decorations, not on an altar - and "stole" Them, replacing Them with other new and similar Deities. We were so scared someone would catch us, but the adults of the house were not in the room.

We quickly drove off feeling like the worst sinners and criminals but I was forced from inside to do this. On our way up the mountains, the full moon started to rise behind the clouds and naturally I was praying to Krishna for protection and forgiveness if I had done wrong. Then the clouds opened up some holes - the exact replica of Lord Jagannath's beautiful face appeared in the clouds – two large round eyes and one perfect big smile underneath; except one of the large eyes was half closed in a wink. This lasted just for a minute or two. Amazing, but absolutely true. (From Anonymous)

THE HUNTER'S BLESSING

This recipient of Krishna's mercy was a hunter residing in Nigeria, Africa and this is a recent incident. One morning the hunter drew an arrow in his bow to shoot a bird. Just as he did this, he actually heard a clear, loud voice say: "Don't do that."

He complied with the voice and ceased to shoot. Then later that night, he had a dream where he was directed by a man to visit a temple in another African city, maybe South Africa. He again obliged the direction and went to visit that temple. As soon as he arrived, he was astonished to recognize the man from his dream, Srila Prabhupada, sitting high as a *murti*, or image. In fact, as soon as he entered the temple, he was stunned and immediately shouted out his discovery: "That's the man from my dream." With such a startling introduction to Krishna and the mercy of the pure devotee, he stopped his hunting and is now becoming a devotee. (This story was described by His Holiness Bhakti Vasudeva Swami.)

SRI GOVINDAJI RECIPROCATES

One of my miracles with Krishna occurred very early in my devotee career. Though I lived outside the temple at the time, as well as most times in my devotional life, I'd quickly acquired the habit of attending the *mangala arati* and found the whole atmosphere of the (early morning) *brahma muhurta* period simply enchanting. This was taking place in the Brooklyn, New York temple, and because the *kirtans* there were so exquisite and energetic, my ecstasy was almost uncontainable. Because of this, I soon began skipping across the whole width of the temple, maybe 20 or 25 feet, and I'd usually do this at top speed. Having been an athlete most of my life, this was done pretty fast. I was in such ecstasy in fact that I'd just go back and forth, skipping rapidly across the floor to release my reverie and hopefully, if I could, please the Lord.

I can't say exactly how or when, but pretty soon after I started doing this, I noticed that one of the Deities on the altar was skipping along with me. I could actually see this with my peripheral vision, and I was totally flabbergasted seeing this, but also very thrilled and so enlivened. Doubters will of course doubt this testimony, but I could care less. I don't doubt it because I saw with my own eyes the shadow of a large Deity moving across the floor with me at about the same speed. I was very far away from the altar, because I always did this in the very rear of the temple where I hoped no one would see me, but there's no doubt in my mind that the shadow and figure I saw moving across the altar with me was none other than the Deity of Sri Govindaji, who reciprocated my excitement. (By Raga Devi Dasi)

TRANSPORTED TO GOLOKA VRINDAVANA

I recall one night I was immediately "implanted" in Goloka Vrndavana. All I could experience was unlimited pure living entities chanting or actually vibrating the holy name with their entire beings. I was surrounded by them, like being in an ocean and I was one particle, also chanting with all my being. I recall that everyone was very, very excited as "Krsna and Balarama are coming!" There was a mood of ever-increasing happiness – that the transcendental brothers were coming. There was an intensity and heightened expectation that increased again and again and again. The intensity continued to rise and so did the happiness. That was a simultaneous understanding, along with the complete "immersion" of all entities in vibrating the holy name. There was ever-increasing bliss with no cessation, simply increasing, increasing, increasing. I did not get to wait until They came, as the experience also ended abruptly.

Again, I did not "see" anything, but understood I was "experiencing" transcendental activity amongst the pure souls in the spiritual world.

Conclusion: I have absolutely no qualification for any of these experiences, and it has been over 10 years since these events occurred. However, I have been fortunate enough to have been given a glimpse of reality and that keeps me going in my darkest hours. I have not made these experiences widely known, due to them being easily misunderstood. However, I hope that some people may gain strength from what I experienced. My final conclusion of the entirety of these events is that Krishna Consciousness is for each of us, not just for the pure souls in the Vedic literature. Krishna has come, Lord Chaitanya has come, Srila Prabhupada has come for each and every one of us to go back home. What we read about can be experienced by us, by the grace of the devotees of the Lord, guru and Krishna. This philosophy is not merely theoretical, neither is it exaggeration. If it happened to me, let me assure, it can happen to anyone as I am no one special. I am not saying this out of humility, it is just a simple fact. Please take heart that you can also be transferred to the spiritual world, in this very life, and that the spiritual world is very real, and that Srila Prabhupada is unlimitedly merciful. (Preferred anonymous)

STORIES OF A FAMILY'S SPIRITUAL BLESSINGS

Here is a story from a family in Metro Detroit in which they explain the series of events that propelled them along in their spiritual development. They now conclude that these events are the direct blessings of the Deities. The wife first tells her part:

Some years ago, before we became involved in Krishna consciousness or bhakti-yoga, we had been married for about 8 to 9 years. So I was finishing my fellowship and my husband had just finished and was working really hard, doing as many cases as possible, even if someone called him at two in the morning. Someone told him that you have to make yourself very approachable and available to make a surgeon's practice flourish. So he was starting completely new. So it was a very hectic and stressful lifestyle for both of us. So under that stress we started arguing more and reached a stage where we were not very happy with each other. So things started going bad until things could take a turn for the worse.

So on January 1, 2007 we went to a New Year's Party. I was wearing an overcoat and just before leaving, I took out a picture of Radha-Kunjabihari from my pocket. My in-laws would go to the temple once in a while and gave the picture to me, and I had that. So when the people started wishing everyone else a happy new year, I took out the picture and prayed and asked for a good year. But starting from that day, things just got worse between us. So it reached a point where the marriage had to improve or it just wasn't going to last.

Six months later I got a job at the hospital and was doing research for a month. So I was able to leave early and do other things. So on the way back home I would stop by the temple, not because I was so attracted to it, or knew that this is where I would be later in life, but just because it was convenient. I could not settle myself anywhere else, so I would stop there at the temple. Usually the *darshan* of the main Deities would be closed at the time I would often arrive, so I would sit in front of Sri Nathji and the Lakshmi-

Narayana Deities and cry to Them, or lament in my heart that things are not going right and that something has to happen for things to get better, or ask "Why are you doing this to me?" So that went on for a few months when I would just stop in and see the Deities, or sit in the main hall in front of Radha-Kunjabihari even if the curtains were closed. So it wasn't like love for Krishna, but I was asking Them to do something.

Then I met the wife of one of the devotees who was working in the same office as I was. I never knew she was into Krishna Consciousness, and we would only talk business. Then one day she asked me if I wanted to go to a program at someone's home. And I really did not think I would want to go to someone's home on a weekend just because of one invitation. Later, on the day of the event, she called me to see if I was interested, so I asked my husband and he said sure. I was pretty convinced that he wouldn't go, and I don't know what made him say yes. So we went, and when we got there, one devotee was giving a talk on "Who am I." And it was very nice, and we became very interested in the whole philosophy.

Then, while talking to my friend at work, she asked if I want to come for Krishna Janmastami (the festival of Krishna's appearance). They were going to New Vrindavana in West Virginia, and would we like to go. But I was thinking no, I don't think we would go to a temple for a weekend vacation, and driving so far and all of that. So I said that I would ask my husband, and again he said sure. Maybe it would be good to get out of the house for a bit. So we went, and that's when things really began to happen in our spiritual development.

Now when I look back, I realize that when I was at the temple in front of the Deities, asking the Deities why are You doing this to me, and asking Them to change things and make things better, that is when the transition started and progressed to the point where I'm now at the temple every weekend doing service to the Deities, and I'm attached to the temple, and things are so much nicer and good now. So I think it is the Deities' direct mercy that we are now in this process of spiritual development. And people think that things with us in our marriage are perfect, and now they are perfect. I just cannot imagine how things could be so bad and now things are so good, and things could change so much.

Now when I see others struggling with things like that, I can completely understand and I try to help if I can. I think others go through the same thing. But we were very blessed to get this kind of spiritual association.

Now the husband explains how things continued:

My first Deity pastime begins in the year 2007. This was during the Janmastami celebration when we first got involved in Krishna Consciousness. That is when we made our first visit to the New Vrindavan temple. When we went to view the Narasimha Deity, I was amazed at the Deity, how big He was, but there was a large crowd in front of the Deity and I could not get close enough to get a good view. So I was wishing for a better view of the Deity. Then suddenly the flames of the *arati* lamp fell in front of the crowd, and everybody just scattered and moved out of the way. That allowed me the room to just move up in front of the Deity and get a good, clear *darshan*. So Lord Narasimha created a situation and granted my wish to see Him.

The very next day they had a *japa* session to teach people how to chant the Hare Krishna mantra after *mangala arati*. So as everybody was leaving the temple room in a line, there was one devotee who was handing out beads to chant on, if anyone was interested. That was before I had started chanting. So I was thinking, "Oh, chanting. We don't need this chanting." So I was thinking I will not take the beads. So he was asking everyone if they wanted beads. But when

I got up to him, he didn't even ask me, he just handed them to me. So I said, "How come you are asking everyone but you are not asking me?"

So I stood there looking at him and he looked at me. So he asked, "You want beads?" and I answered "OK."

Then he said, "Sixteen rounds." So that's when I started chanting 16 rounds daily, that same day.

The next pastime was during Krishna Janmastami in 2008 here in Detroit at the Hare Krishna temple. So by now I was really into it. It was a weekday for the festival, which went on until after 12:30 at night. But the next day I knew I had a very busy schedule with a major 6 to 8 hour surgery to perform, and I had to be in the hospital by 7:30 AM. So I needed to be fresh and clear-headed. I had been in the temple until 10 PM that night, and I just felt really bad leaving, but it was a major operation that I was expected to do and I didn't want to be drowsy. So I had this tussle in my mind, do I operate or do I stay at the festival until one or two AM and just take a chance that I will be all right. I thought Krishna would be happy if I just went home early and did my karma, or what I was duty-bound to do.

So just as I walked into the house there was a voicemail from my assistant saying that he could not be there for me tomorrow. So that was easy, because if he could not be there, I cannot do the operation. Then I called my patient and told him that I am without my assistant and you don't want me to do the operation without my assistant, so we have to reschedule. So I went right back to the temple just in time for the Janmastami celebration. In this way, Sri Sri Radha-Kunjabihari granted my wish.

Their son tells this pastime of how their own Deities of Gaura-Nitai came to their house.

It was a few weeks before we were going to Mayapur and it had been a year-and-a-half since we had taken up bhakti-yoga, Krishna consciousness, and many of our friends already had Deities in their homes. So I was asking my parents why don't we have Deities, and they said we'll get Them when the time comes, when Krishna thinks we are ready. So I said "OK."

When we reached Mayapur, it was during Radhanatha Swami's *yatra*. So I was asking if this wasn't the perfect place and situation to get Deities?

Then the day before we left India, we were coming back home from the *yatra*, all the devotees from Michigan were scheduled to meet with Radhanatha Swami. There were also ten to fifteen sets of Deities lined up on a bench outside the ashrama where Swamiji was staying so he could come out, meet the devotees, and then give names to all these sets of Gaura-Nitai Deities that the devotees would take back with them.

Then one devotee, Yugal Kishore, told everyone to hold their Deities when Swamiji would give names for Them, and we held one set of Deities as well, even though we had not purchased any set for ourselves, and the ones we were holding were actually meant for Yugal Kishore's mother. Then when Radhanatha Swami was coming down the line, giving each set of Deities Their name, he came to us and asked my father, "Is this set of Deities for you?"

He said , "Yes." He couldn't say no.

He said, "OK, these Deities are for you, and they are Sri Sri Nitai-Mayapur Bihari."

So, after all the Deities got names, we had to tell Yugal Kishore that these are our Deities now, because Swamiji confirmed it. So my desire to have Deities was fulfilled.

After that, we took the Deities into the main temple room to show Them to the main Deities of Pancha-Tattva and to Srila Prabhupada, since it was also the observance of Srila Prabhupada's disappearance day. And then so many of the local devotees just thronged us, lined up to see our new Deities saying how beautiful They were.

Then in the evening we went to Srila Prabhupada's *samadhi* for kirtan, but it was so packed with people that we decided to better use our time to get some Deity outfits before we leave Mayapur. While we were shopping, Radhanatha Swami had come out of the *samadhi* and saw us, stopped, said some kind words, and then gave us the garland he was wearing, which had come from the Deity of Srila Prabhupada in the *samadhi*. So that was very special, and we still have that garland to this day.

The husband now continues to relate some of the additional pastimes that have happened. These are just a few.

Many pastimes have happened since we have acquired our Deities. I was chanting my rounds in front of my Deities one morning, and I had to be at the hospital fairly early. So I knew I would not be able to finish my rounds of *japa* meditation before I had to leave, and the day was so busy that I knew I would not be able to get back to it until 10 PM at night in order to finish. So I was asking the Deities if there was something They could do so I could simply finish my rounds of *japa*, chanting the Hare Krishna mantra. I had to be at the hospital by 9 AM, but I called the operating room at 7:45 AM to see what the status of my case was, and the person says, "Your case got canceled, did you know?"

I said, "Really? I never canceled it."

So I called the patient and asked if he canceled, but he said, "No. Your office called to cancel it."

I replied, "My office does not open until 8:30, and I never told my office to cancel it." And there is only one other lady besides me in my office, and she won't do anything like that without confirmation from me. So how did that happen? My Deities answered my prayers again. So I was able to go and finish my rounds of *japa* meditation very nicely.

This next pastime was in regard to the nice programs we just had with Radhanatha Swami while he was here in Detroit, 2011. I always spend some time with my own Gaura Nitai Deities before I go to bed. I had really wanted the program to be at the Grosse Pointe War Memorial because the venue is good, location is nice, and I thought everyone would like it. So I went there to ask how to book the facilities, but the lady there said, "First of all, we have only one date open, and that is June 28."

I said, "Really. That's the only day I want." Because normally they are booked one to two years in advance. But they have a very strict rule that no outside food or drinks are permitted, you have to get it there from their own chef. That's the way they make their money. So that was a bit of a dilemma. But we started brainstorming to see what kind of vegetarian food we could get from them that would meet our standards. Then we gave them a big list of the restrictions and standards we wanted, and the lady said she would give it to their chef. After two weeks we still did not hear from them, so we called and she said, "You know what? This is a very complicated affair. Why don't you do whatever you want. Because we cannot accommodate your request, we allow you to do what you need to do."

I said, "That's what we have been asking."

The next fear was how many people would come to the presentation. We wanted to have a decent turnout for the event, and that is what I was deliberating over when I was in front of my Deities. So I also have a photo of Srila Prabhupada in my temple room, and while I was discussing this with my Gaura Nitai Deities, the garland from Srila Prabhupada's photo fell from it, which it had never done before. So I took that as a sign of blessings and that now we did not have anything to worry about. In the end, everything came together very nicely, from having the date we wanted, being able to bring our own food, which they never allow, and then having a good turnout for the attendance of the event, including the mayor of the town. It was very successful. The Deities fulfilled all our requests.

LORD JAGANNATHA WANTS WATERMELON

As told by Inna. It was a really hot day, July 19, 2011. I was going home from work, and on the way home I stopped to buy groceries for my Lord Jagannatha Deity. For some reason, I kept thinking that Lord Jagannatha wanted a watermelon in this hot temperature. So I picked a big one for Him. When I got home, I felt too tired from work and from being outside, so I put the groceries in the refrigerator and put the watermelon on the kitchen counter. Right after that I entered Lord Jagannatha's room, paid obeisances and said: "Dear Lord Jagannath, if You could please forgive me, I feel so exhausted and need some rest. Let me please have some rest and then I will go to the kitchen and make my offerings to You."

After saying these words, I went to my office, set at my home computer and began going through my unread emails and watching some news. I do this when I feel tired and can't concentrate on anything else. However, as I sat there, I kept feeling guilty that Jagannatha was waiting for me, like He wanted the watermelon. About a half-an-hour later I heard this sudden noise as if something was hit. The sound came from the kitchen. So I rushed to the door to find nobody and nothing there. I began looking around until my glance fell on the watermelon on the counter. The watermelon was cracked in half, and produced a great scent of a red-ripe watermelon! Immediately, I realized what happened and said, "Oh, My Lord Jagannatha, please forgive me, I will bring it to You right away!" I rushed to the back yard, picked two tulasi leaves, detached the two halves of the watermelon, and put one Tulasi leaf on each half. While doing all this I kept talking to my Jagannatha and laughing at the entire situation. Carrying half of the watermelon in each hand, I entered the altar room to put this on the offering table. Much to my delight and amazement, when I looked at the Deities, all Three of Them were laughing! It was so obvious! And, as I was pronouncing the mantras to offer the watermelon to Them, I kept laughing. I even thought that my Deities of Krishna and Narasimhadeva also laughed.

□

Conclusion

So herein I have provided the relevant explanations on the authority and antiquity and importance of Deity worship in the Vedic tradition, and for a person's spiritual development and for attaining a stronger connection with the Divine. I have also presented various stories of people's experiences, both old and recent, which show the unique and multiple ways Krishna will reveal Himself through the Deity forms. There are many more stories that could be used, and new experiences between the Deity and His devotees are happening all the time. But, as previously explained, this shows how Krishna reciprocates or engages in pastimes with people in many ways and at all times, and is not merely a stone image, but acts as He likes and when He likes in personal ways.

The Deity is also a manifestation of the Lord's causeless mercy on all the conditioned souls, or even those devotees who are trying to develop deeper levels of appreciation, love and devotion for the Lord. Thus, the Deity can also give evidence of the reality of the Supreme's existence in the spiritual dimension, the same dimension to which we all naturally belong.

Of course, it takes a certain level of spirituality, in most cases, to perceive this, without which our consciousness is far away from the spiritual plane of existence. What I mean by that is explained in the following verse from the *Padma Purana*:

arcye vishnua shila-dhir gurushu nara-matir vaishnave jati-buddhir vishnor va vaishnavanam kali-mala-mathane pada-tirthe 'mbu-buddhihi

shri-vishnor namni mantre sakala-kalushahe shabda-samanya-buddhir vishnau sarveshvareshe tad itara-samadhir yasya va naraki shah

This verse essentially means that "Persons who consider the Deity of the Supreme Lord to be dead matter, made out of wood, stone or metal, or the spiritual master, who is an eternal associate of the Supreme Lord, to be an ordinary man who is prone to die, or the Vaishnava to be coming from some caste, or the water that washes the feet of the pure devotee or the Supreme Lord [or His Deity] to be ordinary water, although such water has the potency to destroy all the evils of the age of Kali, or considers the holy name of the Supreme Lord or mantras dedicated to Him, which are able to destroy all sins, to be ordinary sounds, or thinks the Supreme Lord of all, Lord Vishnu, to be on the same level as the demigods, is considered to possess a hellish mentality. A person who thinks in this way is certainly a resident of hell."

This means that a person who lacks the proper understanding about the spiritual nature of the Deity simply lives in an ephemeral world full of temporary forms and elusive ideas that occupy his mind with no ultimate conclusion or solution. But by understanding the spiritual characteristics of the Deity and those who are connected with the Divine in this way, ultimately reach the goal of life.

On a personal level, I have also had numerous experiences with the Deities. I have been a *pujari* (priest) and in close contact with Deities and caring or worshiping Them for many years. I often consult with the Deities for answers to questions or guidance in various situations or projects, or simply for blessings. And many times I have received answers I needed, sometimes immediately and directly as telepathic messages, and other times later in other ways.

For example, once I was in Vrindavana at the Krishna-Balarama Mandir during the evening *arați* and standing in the back of the crowd, just chanting *japa* and looking at the Deities as I often do while there. I was feeling that I should give up on a certain project I had been thinking about, which would take a long time to develop and much thought and energy. It would just be easier not to start it. Then, suddenly, I got a telepathic message that went something like, "How dare you think of quitting! How do you think anything will change if you quit?"

This was a message that came directly from the Deity of Lord Krishna. I was shocked at the directness of it. But it was all I needed to hear to understand that obviously Lord Krishna has a plan and that I was a part of it, and though I'm still not sure exactly how it will manifest, I should continue to work on it and help be the catalyst for it. Once I heard that message, I did not need any further instruction to know what Krishna expected of me and what I was supposed to do. Everything instantly became very clear. This was just one of many such circumstances that has happened to me.

Another time was during my stay in Chicago back in 1978. I had gotten married to Chintamani devi dasi and was greatly attracted to her little Jagannatha Deities. I had great fun in purchasing items for increasing the opulences of Little Lord Jagannatha. Chintamani and I took pleasure in taking turns dressing the Deities, after she had trained me how to do it. And I liked buying beads and crystals to make more necklaces and belts for Their Lordships. I really was focused on keeping everything neat and organized. One time I went on a marathon for six weeks of making all kinds of beaded belts and necklaces for the Deities. I was in a world of my own, and greatly ecstatic. With all that happened in Chicago, the Deities' paraphernalia, which had been rather minimal up to then, easily doubled or tripled during that time.

Various spiritual pastimes continued to happen with Little Lord Jagannatha. One time I was doing the evening *arati* at the Krishna temple where I was serving and Chintamani came down from the upstairs women's *ashrama* to see her Little Lord Jagannatha Deities before going to cook the milksweets. Her Jagannatha Deities were on the main alter in the temple room at the time. I happened to learn that someone else was already cooking the milksweets that evening when I had gone to get the offering from the kitchen to offer to the Deities before doing the *arati*. I thought that if she found someone else cooking them she might get upset. So when I was offering the *arati* in front of Little Lord Jagannatha, I felt I really wanted to tell her about it but couldn't because I couldn't stop the *arati*. Later she told me that when she was standing there, she had received a telepathic message from Little Lord Jagannatha that she wouldn't have to cook the milksweets, and then when she went up to the kitchen she indeed saw that someone else was already doing them. So somehow Little Lord Jagannatha had fulfilled my desire to convey to her the message. These kinds of incidents were always happening from time to time with these Little Lord Jagannatha Deities.

Another time that was quite noteworthy for me was when I was in Dwaraka. I had gone there on one of my typical photographic pilgrimages, and wanted to spend several days there. I had gone to the temple for *darshan* early one day, but it had been quite crowded, so I did what I could at the time to see as much as possible, but I could not get very close for a good view. Then one evening *arati* that I attended was not so crowded and I was able to get to the very front to watch the ceremony. The temple assistant saw me and gave me lots of offered sugar sweets and *tulasi* leaves. I was very surprised at this and felt that this was special mercy from the Lord. As I stood there and watched,

I became very ecstatic. Soon it was as if I was seeing nothing else but the Deity. My whole consciousness was focused strictly on the Deity of Lord Dwarakadish. In fact, I could not take my eyes off Him. It became a very powerful *darshan* and meditation in which I felt I was not only looking at Lord Dwarakadish, but He was also looking at and seeing me. I had not experienced such an exchange in a long time. It was very moving and the feeling and energy I got from it made me feel like I was literally floating for days. I was in a different consciousness that made me feel I was no longer merely wandering on this planet earth, but I would walk around town and see other temples while feeling I was in the spiritual realm. That is a taste and experience that you do not forget.

When I started thinking about writing this book I thought I would not include any of my own experiences, but simply focus on what I have heard and learned from others. But now I have broken that idea and have also included a few of my own stories and experiences. But this is possible for anyone. It is all up to Lord Krishna and the other Divinities as to who They offer their blessings. You simply have to be open to it, especially with love. There is another world out there, all around us. And this is one of the ways in which that spiritual dimension can open up for us. I take great pleasure in explaining and relating these stories that show the glories, potency and causeless mercy of the Lord in this way.

□

Glossary

Acarya—the spiritual master who sets the proper standard by his own example.

Advaita—nondual, meaning that the Absolute Truth is one, and that there is no individuality between the Supreme Being and the individual souls which merge into oneness, the Brahman, when released from material existence. The philosophy taught by Sankaracharya.

Agni—fire, or Agni the demigod of fire.

Agnihotra—the Vedic sacrifice in which offerings were made to the fire, such as ghee, milk, sesame seeds, grains, etc. The demigod Agni would deliver the offerings to the demigods that are referred to in the ritual.

Ahimsa—nonviolence.

Akarma—actions which cause no *karmic* reactions.

Ananda—spiritual bliss.

Ananta—unlimited.

Arati—the ceremony of worship when incense and ghee lamps are offered to the Deities.

Arca-vigraha—the worshipable Deity form of the Lord made of stone, wood, etc.

Asana—postures for meditation, or exercises for developing the body into a fit instrument for spiritual advancement.

Asat—that which is temporary.

Ashrama—one of the four orders of spiritual life, such as *brahmacari* (celibate student), *grihastha* (married householder), *vanaprastha* (retired stage), and *sannyasa* (renunciate); or the abode of a spiritual teacher or *sadhu*.

Ashvamedha—a Vedic ritual involving offerings to God made by brahmana priests.

Atma—the self or soul. Sometimes means the body, mind, and senses.

Atman—usually referred to as the Supreme Self.

Avatara—an incarnation of the Lord who descends from the spiritual world.

Aum—*om* or *pranava*

Ayurveda—the original wholistic form of medicine as described in the Vedic literature.

Badrinatha—one of the holy places of pilgrimage in the Himalayas, and home of the Deity Sri Badrinatha along with many sages and hermits.

Bhagavan—one who possesses all opulences, God.

Bhajan—song of worship.

Bhajan kutir—a small dwelling used for one's worship and meditation.

Bhakta—a devotee of the Lord who is engaged in *bhakti-yoga*.

Bhakti—love and devotion for God.

Bhakti-yoga—the path of offering pure devotional service to the Supreme.

Bhava—preliminary stage of love of God.

Brahmacari—a celebate student, usually five to twenty-five years of age, who is trained by the spiritual master. One of the four divisions or *ashramas* of spiritual life.

Brahmajyoti—the great white light or effulgence which emanates from the body of the Lord.

Brahmaloka—the highest planet or plane of existence in the universe; the planet where Lord Brahma lives.

Brahman—the spiritual energy; the all-pervading impersonal aspect of the Lord; or the Supreme Lord Himself.

Brahmana or brahmin—one of the four orders of society; the intellectual class of men who have been trained in the knowledge of the *Vedas* and initiated by a spiritual master.

Brahminical—to be clean and upstanding, both outwardly and inwardly, like a *brahmana* should be.

Caitanya-caritamrta—the scripture by Krishnadasa Kaviraja which explains the teachings and pastimes of Lord Chaitanya Mahaprabhu.

Caranamrita—the water that has been used to bathe the Deity and is offered in small spoonfuls to visitors in the temple.

Chaitanya Mahaprabhu—the most recent incarnation of the Lord who appeared in the 15th century in Bengal and who originally started the *sankirtana* movement, based on congregational chanting of the holy names.

Chakra—a wheel, disk, or psychic energy center situated along the spinal column in the subtle body of the physical shell.

Cit or *chit*—eternal knowledge.

Darshan—the devotional act of seeing and being seen by the Deity in the temple.

Dashavatara—the ten incarnations of Lord Vishnu: Matsya, Kurma, Varaha, Narasimha, Vamana, Parashurama, Rama, Krishna, Buddha, and Kalki.

Deity—the *arca-vigraha*, or worshipful form of the Divinity in the temple.

Deva–a demigod, or higher being.

Devaloka—the higher planets or planes of existence of the devas.

Devas—demigods or heavenly beings from higher levels of material existence, or a godly person.

Dham—a holy place.

Dharma—the essential nature or duty of the living being.

Dharmachakra—Buddhist wheel of law, the first sermon given by Buddha at Sarnath.

Diksha—spiritual initiation.

Divya Desam–One of the 108 most important Vishnu temples in India.

Diwali—festival of lights, marks the end of the rainy season. Dualism—as related in this book, it refers to the Supreme as both an impersonal force (Brahman) as well as the Supreme Person.

Dwaita—dualism, the principle that the Absolute Truth consists of the infinite Supreme Being along with the infinitesimal, individual souls.

Ganesh—a son of Shiva, said to destroy obstacles (as Vinayaka) and offer good luck to those who petition him. It is generally accepted that the way Ganesh got the head of an elephant is that one time Parvati asked him to guard her residence. When Shiva wanted to enter, Ganesh stopped him, which made Shiva very angry. Not recognizing Ganesh, Shiva chopped off his head, which was then destroyed by one of Shiva's goblin associates. Parvati was so upset when she learned what had happened, Shiva, not being able to find Ganesh's original head, took the head of the first creature he saw, which was an elephant, and put it on the body of Ganesh and brought him back to life. The large mouse carrier of Ganesh symbolizes Ganesh's ability to destroy all obstacles, as rodents can gradually gnaw their way through most anything.

Gangapuja—the *arati* ceremony for worshiping the Ganges.

Ganges—the sacred and spiritual river which, according to the *Vedas*, runs throughout the universe, a portion of which is seen in India. The reason the river is considered holy is that it is said to be a drop of the Karana Ocean outside of the universe that leaked in when Lord Vishnu, in His incarnation as Gaudiya—a part of India sometimes called Aryavarta or land of the Aryans, located south of the Himalayas and north of the Vindhya Hills.

Gaudiya *sampradaya*—the school of Vaishnavism founded by Sri Caitanya.

Gayatri—the spiritual vibration or *mantra* from which the other *Vedas* were expanded and which is chanted by those who are initiated as *brahmanas* and given the spiritual understanding of Vedic philosophy.

Goloka Vrindavana—the name of Lord Krishna's spiritual planet.

Gompa—Buddhist monastery.

Gopuram—the tall ornate towers that mark the gates to the temples, often found in south India.

Gosvami—one who is master of the senses.

Govardhana-shila—a sacred stone from Govardhana Hill, considered as a direct form or expansion of Lord Krishna.

Govinda—a name of Krishna which means one who gives pleasure to the cows and senses.

Govindaraja—Krishna as Lord of the Cowherds.

Grihastha—the householder order of life. One of the four *ashramas* in spiritual life.

Guru—a spiritual master.

Hanuman—the popular monkey servant of Lord Rama.

Hare—the Lord's pleasure potency, Radharani, who is approached for accessibility to the Lord.

Hari—a name of Krishna as the one who takes away one's obstacles on the spiritual path.

Haribol—a word that means to chant the name of the Lord, Hari.

Harinam—refers to the name of the Lord, Hari.

Impersonalism—the view that God has no personality or form, but is only an impersonal force (Brahman) which the individual souls merge back into when released from material existence.

Impersonalist—those who believe God has no personality or form.

Incarnation—the taking on of a body or form.

Jagannatha—Krishna as Lord of the Universe, especially as worshipped in Jagannatha Puri.

Jai or *Jaya*—a term meaning victory, all glories.

Japa—the chanting one performs, usually softly, for one's own meditation.

Jyotirlinga—the luminous energy of Shiva manifested as a self-manifested *lingam* at one of 12 places, such as Kedarnatha, Patan, Ujjain, and Varanasi.

Kali-yuga—the fourth and present age, the age of quarrel and confusion, which lasts 432,000 years and began 5,000 years ago.

Kalki—future incarnation of Lord Vishnu who appears at the end of Kali-yuga.

Karma—material actions performed in regard to developing one's position or for future results which produce *karmic* reactions. It is also the reactions one endures from such fruitive activities.

Karma-kanda—the portion of the *Vedas* which primarily deals with recommended fruitive activities for various results.

Karma-yoga—system of yoga for using one's activities for spiritual advancement.

Karmi—the fruitive worker, one who accumulates more *karma*.

Keshava—Krishna with long hair.

Kirtana—chanting or singing the glories of the Lord.

Krishna—the name of the original Supreme Personality of Godhead which means the most attractive and greatest pleasure. He is the source of all other incarnations, such as Vishnu, Rama, Narasimha, Narayana, Buddha, Parashurama, Vamanadeva, Kalki at the end of Kali-yuga, etc.

Krishnaloka—the spiritual planet where Lord Krishna resides. *Kshatriya*—the second class of *varna* of society, or occupation of administrative or protective service, such as warrior or military personel.

Ksirodakasayi Vishnu—the Supersoul expansion of the Lord who enters into each atom and the heart of each individual.

Kumbha Mela—the holy festival in which millions of pilgrims and sages gather to bathe in the holy and purifying rivers for liberation at particular auspicious times that are calculated astrologically. The Kumbha Mela festivals take place every three years alternating between Allahabad, Nasik, Ujjain, and Hardwar.

Kuruksetra—the place of battle 5,000 years ago between the Pandavas and the Lakshmi—the goddess of fortune and wife of Lord Vishnu.

Lila—pastimes.

Lilavataras—the many incarnations of God who appear to display various spiritual pastimes to attract the conditioned souls in the material world.

Madana-mohana—name of Krishna as one who fills the mind with love.

Mahabharata—the great epic of the Pandavas, which includes the *Bhagavad-gita*, by Vyasadeva.

Maha-mantra—the best *mantra* for self-realization in this age, called the Hare Krishna *mantra*.

Maha-Vishnu or Karanodakasayi Vishnu—the Vishnu expansion of Lord Krishna from whom all the material universes emanate.

Mandir—a temple.

Mantra—a sound vibration which prepares the mind for spiritual realization and delivers the mind from material inclinations. In some cases a *mantra* is chanted for specific material benefits.

Maya—illusion, or anything that appears to not be connected with the eternal Absolute Truth.

Moksha—liberation from material existence.

Murti—a Deity of the Lord or an image of a demigod or spiritual master that is worshiped.

Narasimha—Lord Vishnu's incarnation as the half-man half-lion who killed the demon Hiranyakashipu.

Narayana—the four-handed form of the Supreme Lord. Nityananda–the brother of Sri Chaitanya, and *avatara* of Lord Balarama.

Om or *Omkara—pranava,* the transcendental *om mantra,* generally referring to the attributeless or impersonal aspects of the Absolute.

Paramatma—the Supersoul, or localized expansion of the Lord.

Parampara—the system of disciplic succession through which transcendental knowledge descends.

Parthasarathi—Krishna as Arjuna's chariot driver.

Prana—the life air or cosmic energy.

Pranayama—control of the breathing process as in *astanga* or *raja-yoga.*

Pranava—same as *omkara.*

Prasada—food or other articles that have been offered to the Deity in the temple and then distributed amongst people as the blessings or mercy of the Deity.

Prema—matured love for Krishna.

Puja—the worship offered to the Deity.

Pujari—the priest who performs worship, *puja,* to the Deity. Radha—Krishna's favorite devotee and the personification of His bliss potency.

Ramachandra—an incarnation of Krishna as He appeared as the greatest of kings.

Ramanuja—Vaishnava philosopher.

Ramayana—the great epic of the incarnation of Lord Ramachandra.

Rasa—an enjoyable taste or feeling, a relationship with God.

Ravana—demon king of the *Ramayana.*

Rishi—saintly person who knows the Vedic knowledge.

Sac-cid-ananda-vigraha—the transcendental form of the Lord or of the living entity which is eternal, full of knowledge and bliss.

Sadhana—a specific practice or discipline for attaining God realization.

Sadhu—Indian holy man or devotee.

Samadhi—trance, the perfection of being absorbed in the Absolute.

Samsara—rounds of life; cycles of birth and death; reincarnation.

Sanatana-dharma—the eternal nature of the living being, to love and render service to the supreme lovable object, the Lord.

Sankirtana-yajna–the prescribed sacrifice for this age: congregational chanting of the holy names of God.

Sannyasa—the renounced order of life, the highest of the four *ashramas* on the spiritual path.

Satya-yuga—the first of the four ages which lasts 1,728,000 years. *Shabda-brahma*—the original spiritual vibration or energy of which the *Vedas* are composed.

Shalagrama-shila–the sacred stone that is accepted as a direct form of Lord Vishnu.

Shastra—the authentic revealed Vedic scripture.

Shiva—the benevolent one, the demigod who is in charge of the material mode of ignorance and the destruction of the universe. Part of the triad of Brahma, Vishnu, and Shiva who continually create, maintain, and destroy the universe. He is known as Rudra when displaying his destructive aspect.

Sikha—a tuft of hair on the back of the head signifying that one is a Vaishnava.

Sravanam—hearing about the Lord.

Srimad-Bhagavatam—the most ripened fruit of the tree of Vedic knowledge compiled by Vyasadeva.

Sruti—scriptures that were received directly from God and transmitted orally by *brahmanas* or *rishis* down through succeeding generations. Traditionally, it is considered the four primary *Vedas*.

Sudra—the working class of society, the fourth of the *varnas*.

Surya—Sun or solar deity.

Svami—one who can control his mind and senses.

Tilok—the clay markings that signify a person's body as a temple, and the sect or school of thought of the person.

Tirtha—a holy place of pilgrimage.

Treta-yuga—the second of the four ages which lasts 1,296,000 years.

Trivikrama—Lord Vishnu as Vamadeva, the *brahmana* dwarf who covered the entire universe in three steps.

Tulasi—the small tree that grows where worship to Krishna is found. It is called the embodiment of devotion, and the incarnation of Vrinda-devi.

Upanishads—the portions of the *Vedas* which primarily explain philosophically the Absolute Truth. It is knowledge of Brahman which releases one from the world and allows one to attain self-realization when received from a qualified teacher. Except for the *Isa Upanishad,* which is the 40th chapter of the *Vaikunthas*—the planets located in the spiritual sky.

Vaishnava—a worshiper of the Supreme Lord Vishnu or Krishna and His expansions or incarnations.

Vaishnava-*aparadha*—an offense against a Vaisnava or devotee, which can negate all of one's spiritual progress.

Vaisya—the third class of society engaged in business or farming.

Varaha—Lord Vishnu's boar incarnation.

Varna—sometimes referred to as caste, a division of society, such as *brahmana* (a priestly intellectual), a *kshatriya* (ruler or manager), *vaisya* (a merchant, banker, or farmer), and *sudra* (common laborer).

Varnashrama—the system of four divisions of society and four orders of spiritual life.

Vasudeva—Krishna.

Vedanta-sutras—the philosophical conclusion of the four *Vedas.*

Vedas—generally means the four primary *samhitas; Rig, Yajur, Sama, Atharva.*

Venktateshvara—Vishnu as Lord of the Venkata Hills, worshiped in Tirumala.

Vishnu—the expansion of Lord Krishna who enters into the material energy to create and maintain the cosmic world.

Vishvakarma—demigod architect of the heavens.

Vrindavana—the place where Lord Krishna displayed His village pastimes 5,000 years ago, and is considered to bc part of the spiritual abode.

Yamuna—goddess personification of the Yamuna River.

Yashoda—foster mother of Krishna.

Yatra—a pilgrimage to the holy places.

Yuga-avataras—the incarnations of God who appear in each of the four *yugas* to explain the authorized system of self-realization in that age.

□

References

Art of Sadhana: A Guide to Daily Devotion, by Swami B.P. Puri Maharaja, Mandala Publishing Group, San Francisco, CA.

Bhagavad-gita As It Is, translated by A.C. Bhaktivedanta Swami, Bhaktivedanta Book Trust, New York/Los Angeles, 1972

Bhakti-rasamrita-sindhu, (Nectar of Devotion), translated by A.C. Bhaktivedanta Swami, Bhaktivedanta Book Trust, New York/Los Angeles, 1970

Bhakti Rasamarita Sindhu, by Srila Rupa Gosvami, trans. By Bhanu Swami, Sri Vaikuntha Enterprises, Chennai, 2003

Caitanya-caritamrta, translated by A.C. Bhaktivedanta Swami, Bhaktivedanta Book Trust, Los Angeles, 1974

Darshan, Seeing the Divine Image in India, Diana Eck, Anima Books, Chambersberg, PA, 1985

Experience in Bhakti: The Science Celestial, by Dr. O.B.L. Kapoor, Published by Sri Badrinarayana Bhagavata Bhushana Prabhu, 1994.

Gopal-tapani Upanishad, by Krsna Dvaipayana Vedavyasa, commentary by Visvanatha Cakravarti Thakura, translated by Bhumipati dasa, Ras Bihari Lal & Sons, Loi Bazaar, Vrindaban, UP, 281121, India, 2004

The Gosvamis of Vrindavana, O.B.L. Kapoor, Sarasvati Jayasri Classics, Delhi, 1994

The Hidden Treasure of the Holy Dham Nabadvipa, Srila Bhaktivinoda Thakura, Ananta Printing and Publishing and Mandala Media Group, Soquel, CA, 1993

The Lilas of Lord Jagannatha, by Somanath Khuntia, Vedic Cultural Association, 1990

Pastimes and History of Lord Jagannatha in Rajapur, by Pankajanghri Dasa, Gauranga Releases, Scotland, 2007

Seeing Spiritual India, by Stephen Knapp

Sri Jagannatha: The Pastimes of the Lord of the Universe, by Bhakti Purusottama Swami, Bhaktivedanta Book Trust, Sri Mayapur Dham, India, 2006

Srimad-Bhagavatam, translated by A. C. Bhaktivedanta Swami, Bhaktivedanta Book trust, New York/Los Angeles, 1972

Story of Rasikananda, Gopijanavallabha dasa, edited by Bhakti Vikas Swami, Mumbai, 1997

□□□

INDIAN RELIGIONS SERIES: 6

FAITH & PHILOSOPHY OF JAINISM

Arun Kumar Jain

KALPAZ

Faith & Philosophy of Jainism

ISBN: 978-81-7835-856-7

Published in 2010 in India by
Kalpaz Publications
C-30, Satyawati Nagar,
Delhi-110052
E-mail: kalpaz@hotmail.com
Phone: 9212729499

Printed at : Salasar Imaging System, Delhi

Contents

Preface

This book is an exposition on Jainism from its origin to modern times. It is a conscientious piece of work exploring different aspects of Jainism in the light of modern viewpoint. It emphasizes on the historical developments of Jainism from its earliest time to its latest version outlining several factors, which led to such a growth. As one of the world's major religions, founded on the spiritual principles of non-violence (ahimsa), truth, and righteous conduct, Jainism has today a very long history of a splendid living tradition, with a well-defined world view, philosophy, and code of ethics. This volume covers its beginnings, antiquity, doctrines, Tirthankaras, spread and among other aspects, its contribution to world's culture and art heritage.

Jainism stands for brotherhood and unity between all beings without distinction of colour and creed and the most characteristic feature is a gracious and winning tolerance which is common in all forms of Jainism. Jainism is not only deeply philosophical, but also possesses a system of evolution. This book is therefore offered as a modest contribution to a cause which every true lover of humanity must have at heart.

This book covers all important standards of Jainism such as; basic teachings, life of all Tirthankaras, The main sects and lay practices, Important Jain scriptures, Influential Jain scholars, Sacred Jain sites, Jain prayers and pilgrimages, beliefs, rituals and ceremonies. A detailed introduction provides a holistic overview of Jainism. An extensive bibliography and references at the end of each chapter guides interested readers to in-depth resources on various topics. This volume is most interactive and highly educative and we hope that it will be very useful and popular among scholars, students and readers who are interested in Jainism.

1

Jainism: An Introduction

Jainism is one of the oldest living religions of India. It predates chronicles as per recordings in the Hindu Holy Scriptures. It is a distinctive system, quite different and independent from other systems of Indian philosophy. Jainism is a religious faith of strictly human origin and is preached and practiced by one who has achieved ideal knowledge, nirvana and self-control by his own individual efforts and has been released from the shakels of corporeal existence, the cycle of births and deaths. Such human beings are regarded as Gods of Jainism. The idea of God as a creator, protector, and destroyer of the world doesn't exist in Jainism. The concept of God's rebirth as a human being to demolish the devils is not accepted in Jainism. In short Jainism doesn't believe in creator God, but it is not an atheistic religion because it believes in many Gods who are self realized persons and who have achieved nirvana. In older times it was known by many names such as Saman tradition, or the religion of Nirganth or Jin.

Jin means a vanquisher, i.e, one who has vanquished the corporeal passions like craving, hate, anger, greediness, and arrogance by one's own individual efforts. Jin is a human being and not a supernatural being or an avatar of a powerful God. Some of the Jins founded religious order, they are known as Tirthankar and there exist the divine lineage of the twenty-four Tirthankars of whom the ascetic sage Bhagwan Mahavir was the last. All human beings have the capability to become Jin.

Ancientness of Jainism

History of Jainism starts with Bhagwan Rishabh Dev or Adinath. He was the first of the twenty-four Tirthankar. As per Jain philosophy, Bhagwan Rishabh Dev was the first Tirthankar of the current age (Avasarpini). Because of this, he had the name of Adinath - the first Bhagwan. He became a Siddh, an enlightened soul which has demolished all of its karma.

Bhagwan Rishabh Dev has been cited in the Hindu text of the Bhagavath-Puran as an incarnation of Vishnu. He is cited in all the Vishnu/Shiv Purans, and also in some other texts. As per Bhagavata, he was born to show the individuals of this world the way of redemption. It was he who advised the individuals to follow the path of undying happiness, instead of indulging in a life of corporeal delights and enjoyment. He is the founding father and promoter of Sramanic culture. In the depth study of the vedas and Purans, which contain many references to Bhagwan Rishabh Dev.

Contemporary scholars share the view that Bhagwan Rishabh Dev was a historical person established on many archeological and literary proof. In his Indus Valley Civilization and Hindu Culture, the reputed scholars says that the first Jain Tirthankar belonged to Indus Valley Civilization. For a long time Bhagwan Rishabh Dev proceeded to spread his religious faith having the five great vows as its fundamental theme. When he saw that all his remaining Karmas are nearing their end he proceeded to the Ashtapad mountain. On the thirteenth day of the dark half of the month of Magh, a little before noon time, Bhagwan Rishabh Dev, along with ten thousand other monks, was maintaining a six day fasting without water. He was sitting in the meditation in the Paryanka pose. When the moon entered the Abhijit lunar sign he got enlightenment and got released from all griefs. The lord of Gods, Saudharmendra, Emperor Bharat, many Gods and men assembled and celebrated the propitious event of Bhagwan Rishabh Dev's Nirvana.

About 2600 years ago Bhagwan Mahavir or Vardhaman (599 to 527 BC.), the twenty fourth and the last Tirthankar of this age rejuvenated the Jain faith preached by his predecessor Bhagwan Parshva (950 to 850 BC.) in India. He elaborated the guidelines and implemented daily rituals for his devotees relevant to his time. The current Jain Holy Scriptures reflect only his teachings.

Bhagwan Mahavir was a prince and his childhood name was Vardhaman. Being son of an Emperor, he had many corporeal delights, amenities, and services at his command. But at the age of thirty, he left his household and royal family, gave up his corporeal belongings, and become an ascetic in search of an answer to purge pain, grief, and sufferings from life.

Bhagwan Mahavir spent the next twelve and half years in profound silence and meditation to overcome his cravings, feelings, and attachments. He carefully avoided injuring or bothering other life forms including animals, birds, insects and plants. He also did not eat food for long periods of time. He was tranquil and serene against all agonizing rigorousnesses. During this period of time, his divine powers fully developed and at the end he realized ideal perception, ideal knowledge, ideal power, and total happiness. This realization is known as Kewal-Gyan or the ideal nirvana.

Bhagwan Mahavir spent the next thirty years travelling on bare foot around India preaching to the masses the undying truth he realized. The ultimate aim of his teaching is how one can achieve total liberty from the cycle of birth, life, pain, despair, and death, and attain the permanent blissful state of one's self. This is also known as deliverance, enlightenment, absolute liberty, or Moksh.

At the age of 72, Bhagwan Mahavir achieved enlightenment and his purified soul left his body and attained complete nirvana. He became a Siddha, a pure consciousness, an enlightened soul, living eternally in a state of complete happiness. On the night of his enlightenment, people celebrated the Festival of Lights (Dipawali) in his honour. This is the last day of Hindu and Jain calendar year known as Dipawali Day.

In short Jainism existed before Bhagwan Mahavir, and his teachings were established on those of his predecessors. Therefore, unlike Bhagwan Buddha, Bhagwan Mahavir was more of a reformer and propagator of an existing religious order than the founding father of a new religion. He pursued the well-established doctrine of his predecessor Tirthankar Parshvanath. Nevertheless, he did reorganize the philosophical principles to correspond to his times.

Tirthankars

In Jainism, a Tirthankar or Jin is a human being who attains nirvana through austerity and who then becomes a role-model teacher for those seeking divine guidance. A Tirthankar is an arhat someone who has totally vanquished anger, arrogance, deceit, craving, etc. A Tirthankar is so called because they are the founding father of a Tirth ford, a Jain community which acts as a bridge across the river of human despair.

After attaining nirvana, a Tirthankar shows others the way to nirvana. The Tirthankar's spiritual teachings form the Jain canons. The inner knowledge of all Tirthankars is ideal and same in every sense, for the teachings of one Tirthankar don't oppose those of another. Nevertheless, the degree of elaboration varies as per divine advancement and purity of humans during that period. The higher the divine advancement and purity of mind, the lower the elaboration required.

At the end of his human life-span, a Tirthankar attains nirvana (moksh), ending the cycle of endless births and deaths. Jainism states time has no beginning or end. It goes like the wheel of a cart. There have been an endless number of time cycles before our current age and there will be an infinite number of time cycles after this age. At the commencing of the twenty first century, we are about 2,530 years into the fifth era of the current half cycle.

Twenty four Tirthankars are born in each half cycle of time (i.e. forty eight in each full cycle), in this part of the world. In our present descending half cycle of time, the first Tirthankar Rishabh Dev, lived billions of years ago and achieved deliverance (moksh or nirvan) towards the end of the third era.

The next Tirthankar in our part of the world will be born at the beginning of the third era of the next ascending half cycle of time, in about 81,500 years. As Tirthankars direct us to nirvana, their statues are worshipped in Jain temples by Jains aiming to attain nirvana. Tirthankars are not God or Gods. Jainism doesn't believe in the existence of God in the sense of a creator, and Gods are beings superior to humans but, however, not fully enlightened.

Depictions in different forms, including images, statues, etc., of the Tirthankars are always presented as seated with their legs crossed in front, the toes of one foot resting close upon the knee of the other, and the right hand lying over the left in the lap. Only two are presented otherwise one that of Parsvanatha, the twenty-third, who has snake-hoods over him, and Suparsva, the seventh, who the Digambars portray with a smaller group of snake-hoods.

Digambar representations are quite nude, while those of the Shvetambar's are clothed and adorned with crowns and ornaments. They are further differentiated from one another in representations by their helper Yakshas and Yakshinis, and also by their related chihnas (symbols) carved on the cushions of their thrones.

All but two of the Jains are attributed to the Ikshvaku family or Kula or Kul which in Sanskrit means heart community or intentional or chosen community or household. Munisuvrata, the twentieth, and Neminatha, the twenty-second, were of the Harivamsa race.

All (except Bhagwan Rishabh Dev) received diksha (consecration) and Gyan (nirvana) at their native places. Bhagwan Rishabh Dev became a Kewalin at Purimatala, Nemi at Girnar, and Bhagwan Mahavir at the

Rijupaluka River. Twenty Tirthankars died or obtained Moksh (deliverance) on Sameta Sikhara. Nevertheless Bhagwan Rishabh Dev,the first, attained enlightenment on the Kailash Mountain of the Himalayas; Vasupujya died at Champapuri in north Bengal; Neminatha on Mount Girnar; and Bhagwan Mahavir, the last, at Pavapur.

Twenty-one of the Tirthankars are said to have achieved Moksh in the Kayotsarga posture; Rishabh,Nemi; and Bhagwan Mahavir on the padmasana (lotus throne).

The twenty-four Tirthankars are:

1. Bhagwan Rishabh Dev (Adinath)
2. Shri Ajitnath
3. Shri Sambhavanath
4. Shri Abhinandannath
5. Shri Sumatinath
6. Shri Padmaprabha
7. Shri Suparshvanath
8. Shri Chandraprabha
9. Shri Pushpadanta
10. Shri Sheetalnath
11. Shri Shreyansanath
12. Shri Vasupujya
13. Shri Vimalnath
14. Shri Anantnath
15. Shri Dharmanath
16. Shri Shantinath
17. Shri Kunthunath
18. Shri Aranath
19. Shri Mallinath
20. Shri Munisuvrata
21. Shri Nami Natha
22. Shri Neminatha
23. Shri Parshva
24. Bhagwan Mahavir

Beliefs

As per Jainism the fate of every being is a result of its actions. Souls are unborn and uncreated. They are also undying and equal. They exist in both animate and inanimate objects of existence. They all are capable of become free or achieving Moksh, through their individual efforts. The deliverance of each soul depends upon its own karma and purity of effort. There is no such thing as divine intervention or grace of a guru. Jains venerate Tirthankars as a mark of gratitude for the teachings left by them. they are are pure beings, who manifest upon earth from time to time as per an established pattern to teach masses the philosophy of nirvana and show them the way through their own example.

Jainism considers the whole existence as sacred, since it is infused with countless souls, some bound and some released. We should thus, think and act responsibly towards all existence. The pure soul of each life form is looked upon as Endless Knowledge, Perception, Consciousness, and Bliss (Ananta Gyan, Ananta Darshana, Ananta Caritra, and Ananta Sukha). In Jainism there is no place for an all-powerful Supreme Being, Creator or Doer, but rather in a undying world governed by natural laws and inhabited by countless souls in varying degrees of bondage and nirvana.

Compassion to all fellow life forms (along with humans) is fundamental to Jain belief. Jainism is the only religious faith wherein all devotees, both monks and practicing lay persons of all denominations and traditions, are required to be vegetarian. In areas of India with strong Jain influence, often the bulk of the population is vegetarian. In many towns, the Jains run animal shelters. In Delhi, there is a bird hospital run by a Jain temple. Many historians believe that different sects of Hinduism adopted vegetarianism due to the strong influence of Jainism and Buddhism.

Jains cover their mouths to check the possibility of inhaling insects and small organisms, a practice linked with their belief in ahimsa and the possibility of unintentional bad karma. As a part of its stance on ahimsa, Jainism goes even step beyond vegetarianism, in that the Jain diet also excludes most root vegetables, as Jains consider such vegetables have an endless number of personal souls, invisible to the naked eye. Jains also don't eat certain other foods believed to be unnecessarily injurious. Many Jains are also vegan, due to the cruelty, and violence inherent in modern dairy farms. Observant Jains don't eat, drink, or travel after sunset, and always rise before sunrise.

History suggests that different sects of Hinduism became vegetarian due to strong Jain influences. Jains run animal shelters all over India. For instance, Delhi has a bird hospital run by Jains. Every city and town in Bundelkhand has animal shelters run by Jains where all manner of animals are sheltered, although the shelter is usually known as a Gaushala.

Jains hold that this temporal world is full of sorrow and grief and hence in order to achieve lasting happiness one must transcend the cycle of transmigration. Otherwise, one will remain forever caught up in the ceaseless cycle of transmigration. The only way to break out of this cycle is to practice detachment through judicious perception, judicious knowledge, and judicious behaviour.

The Jain religious faith places great importance on Karma. Basically, it means that all jivas reap what they sow. A happy or miserable existence is determined by actions in former births. These results may not occur in the same life, and what we sow is not limited to physical actions. Physical, verbal, and mental activities affect future situations. Karma has long been a necessary part of Jainism, and other Indian religions such as Buddhism, Hinduism and Sikhism. It is believed usually that an all-knowing Tirthankar can foretell all things, long before science.

Tattvas

The backbone of the Jain beliefs are seven central ideas (Tattvas). Please note that some Jain commentators include two more additional concepts to the following seven namely merit (punya) and demerit (papa) karmas. Without knowing these seven fundamental concepts, one can't progress towards nirvana. They are:

Jiva: Souls and living beings

Ajiva: Non-living things

Asrava: Influx of karma

Bandha: The bondage of karma

Samvara: The stoppage of influx of karma

Nirjara: Shedding of karma

Moksh: Nirvana or Redemption

Fasting

Fasting is common amongst Jains and a part of Jain festivals. Most Jains fast at special times, during festivals, and on holy days. Pajushan is the most important festival, lasting eight days in Shvetambar Jain custom and ten days in Digambar Jain custom during the monsoon. The monsoon is a time of fasting. Nevertheless, a Jain may fast at any time, especially if he or she feels some mistake has been committed. Variations in fastings encourage Jains to do whatever they can to maintain self-discipline.

Some Jains revere a special practice, where an individual who is aware that he or she may expire soon, and feels he has completed all his duties, ceases to eat or drink until death. This form of dying is called santhara or sallekhana. It is regarded as to be extremely divine and creditable. This has recently led to a controversy in India, where in Rajasthan, a lawyer petitioned the High Court of Rajasthan to declare sallekhana illegal. Jains see sallekhana as divine detachment. It is a declaration that an individual has finished with living in this world and now chooses to leave.

Rituals

Every day most Jains bow and say their universal prayer, the Namokara Mantra, aka the Navkar Mantra. Jains have built temples, or Basadi or Derasar, where images of Tirthankars are worshiped. Jain rites may be elaborate because symbolic objects are offered and Tirthankars praised in song. But some Jain denominations refuse to enter temples or worship images. All Jains accept that images of Tirthankars are merely symbolic reminders of the path that they have to take, in order to achieve Moksh. Jains are clear that the Jins live in Moksh and are completely detached from the world. Jain rites include: Pancakalyanaka Pratishtha, Pratikramana, Samayika, Guru-Vandana, Chaitya Vandana, and other sutras to honour monks.

Cosmology

As per Jain philosophy, the world was never created, nor will it ever cease to exist. Thus, it is shaswat (infinite). It has no start or end, but time is cyclical with progressive and regressive spirituality phases.

Jains divide time into Utsarpinis (Progressive Time Cycle) and Avsarpinis (Regressive Time Cycle). An Utsarpini and an Avsarpini constitute one Time Cycle (Kalchakra). Every Utsarpini and Avsarpini is divided into six unequal periods of time known as Aras. During the Utsarpini half cycle, humanity develops from its worst to its best: morals, progress, bliss, strength, health, and religion each begin the cycle at their worst, before finally completing the cycle at their best and starting the process again. During the Avsarpini half-cycle, these ideas deteriorate from the best to the worst. Jains believe we are currently in the fifth Ara of the Avsarpini phase, with about 19,000 years until the next Era. After this Avsarpini phase, the Utsarpini phase will start, continuing the endless repetition of the Kalchakra.

Jains believe that at the upswing of each time cycle, masses will lose religious faith again. All wishes will be granted by wish-granting trees (Kalpavrksa), and individuals will be born in sets of twins (Yugalika) with one boy and one girl who stay together all their lives: a symbol of an integrated human with male and female features balanced.

Jain doctrine is established upon undying, universal truths. During the first and last two Aras, these truths lapse amongst humanity and then reappear through the teachings of enlightened humans, those who have reached Moksh or total knowledge (Kewal-Gyan), during the third and fourth Aras. By tradition, in our world and in our time, Bhagwan Rishabh Dev is regarded as the first to realize the truth. Bhagwan Vardhamana (Bhagwan Mahavir) was the last Tirthankar to achieve nirvana. He was preceded by twenty-three others, making a total of twenty-four Tirthankars.

It is important to note that the above description stands true "in our world and in our time" for Jains believe there have been endless sets of 24 Tirthankars, one for each half of the time cycle, and this will continue in the future. Hence, Jainism doesn't trace its origins to Bhagwan Rishabh Dev , the first, or finish with Bhagwan Mahavir, the twenty-fourth, Tirthankar.

As per Jainism, the World consists of endless amount of Jiva (life force or souls), and the design resembles a man standing with his arms bent while resting his hands on his waist. The narrow waist part comprises different Kshetras, for vicharan (roaming) for humans, animals and plants. Currently we are in the Bharat Kshetra of Jambu Dweep (dweep means island).

The Dev Lok (Heavens) are at the symbolic 'chest' of Creation, where all Devas (demi Gods) live. Similarly below the 'waist' are the Narka (Hell). There are seven Narka Lokas, each for a variable degree suffering a jiva has to go through to face the aftermaths of its paap karma (sins). From the first to the seventh Narka, the degree of suffering increases and light reaching it decreases (with no light in the seventh Narka).

The sidhha kshetra or Moksh is situated at the symbolic forehead of the creation, where all the jivas having achieved enlightenment live in a state of total peace and undying bliss. Outside the symbolic figure of this creation nothing but aloka or akaasha (sky) exists.

Spread

Scholars agree in general that by the close of fourth century BC., the Mauryan Emperor Chandragupta and a band of Jain monks led by Sruthakewalin Bhadrabahu, expecting a severe famine in their country, migrated to Sravanabelagola where from they started spreading the gospels of the Tirthankars. Later on, after the demise of Chandragupta and Bhadrabahu, their followers under the leadership of Visakhacharya moved to the Chola and Pandya countries in order to spread Jainism, and most probably, this southward movement could have taken place in the beginning of the third century BC. Contemporary epigraphic evidence in Karnataka testifying such a southward migration of the Jain mendicants, although absent, the early brahmi inscriptions found in Madurai, Tirunelveli and Pasumpon districts would prove beyong doubt the antiquity of Jainism in Tamil Nadu much earlier than the second century BC.

Some are of the opinion that there was a large number of sravaks (Jain householders) in the south to support the emigrant monks, as it was a custom of the monks not to accept food from individuals other than the Jain folk.

Jainism crossed India from South India at about eighth century BC, if not earlier, and become one of the most prominent religions of Ceylon, which was known in those days by the name of Lanka, Ratnadvipa or Simhala. The Mahavamsa refers to the existence of Jainism in Ceylon even before the arrival of Buddhism. As per it, Pandukabhaya built a house at Anuradhapur for the Nigantha Jotiya and Giri and some more Niganthas, Jain custom takes the history of Jainism in Ceylon even prior to its Aryanization, or the Arrival of the Aryans. Ravana, an Emperor of Lanka long ago is said to have erected a Jain temple there at Trikutagiri. Another statue of Parsvanatha, the twenty-third Jin found in the caves of Terapur is also said to be from Sri Lanka. Jainism was a living religious faith of Sri Lanka up to the tenth AD.

Kalakacharya, another Jain monk, is said to have visited Burma or Svarnabhumi. Rishabh Dev is said to have travelled to Bali (Bacteria), Greece, Svarnabhumi, Panhave (Iran), eto. Tirthankar Parsvnatha also went to Nepal. The existence of Jainism can also be proved in Afghanistan. Tirthankar images in the Kayotsarga, or meditating pose have been found in Vahakaraj Emir (Afghanistan). Digambar Jain monks have been in Iran, Siam, and Philistia. Greek writers also mention their existence in

Egypt, Abyssinia and Ethyopia. It had also spread in Kabul, Campa, Bulgaria and some other foreign countries.

Sects

It is usually believed that the Jain sangha divided into two major denominations, Digambar and Shvetambar, about two hundred years after Mahavir's enlightenment. Some historians believe there was no clear division until the fifth century. The best available information indicates that the chief Jain monk, Acharya Bhadrabahu, foresaw famine and led about 12,000 Digambar devotees to southern India. Twelve years later they returned to find the Shvetambar denomination, and in 453 the Valabhi council edited and compiled the traditional Shvetambar Holy Scriptures.

The differences between the two denominations are minor and relatively obscure. Digambar Jain monks don't wear clothes because they believe clothes, like other belongings, increase dependency and craving for material things, and craving for anything ultimately leads to grief. Shvetambar Jain monks, contrarily, wear white, seamless clothes for sensible reasons, and believe there is nothing in Jain scripture that condemns wearing clothes. Sadhvis (nuns) of both denominations wear white. In Sanskrit, ambar refers to a covering usually, or a garment in particular. Dig, an older form of disha, refers to the cardinal directions. Digambar thus means "covered by the four directions, or sky-clad. Svet means white and Shvetambars wear white garments.

Digambars believe that women can't achieve Moksh in the same birth, while Shvetambars believe that women may achieve nirvana and that Mallinath, a Tirthankar, was a woman. The difference is because Digambar asceticism requires nudity. The earliest record of this belief is contained in the Prakrit Suttapahuda of the Digambar mendicant Kundakunda.

Digambars believe that Bhagwan Mahavir was not married, whereas Shvetambars believe Bhagwan Mahavir was married and had a daughter. The two denominations also differ on the origin of Mata Trishala, Bhagwan Mahavir's mother.

Sthanakavasis and Digambars believe that only the first five lines are formally part of the Namokara Mantra (the main Jain prayer), whereas Shvetambars believe all nine form the mantra. Other differences are minor and not established on major points of philosophy.

Excavations at Mathura revealed many Jain statues from the Kushana period. Tirthankars, presented without clothes, and monks with cloth wrapped around the left arm are identified as Ardhaphalaka and cited in some texts. The Yapaniya denomination, believed to have started from the Ardhaphalaka, follows Digambar nudity, along with several Shvetambar philosophy.

Shvetambars are further divided into sub-sects, such as Sthanakavasi, Terapanthi and Deravasi. Some are murtipujak (revering statues) while non-Murtipujak Jains refuse statues or images. Shvetambar follow the 12 agam literature (voice of all-knowing).

Most simply call themselves Jains and follow general traditions rather than specific sectarian practices. In 1974 a committee with representatives from every denomination compiled a new text called the Samana Suttam.

While Jains represent less than 1% of the Indian population, their contributions to culture and society in India are considerable. Jainism had a major influence in growing a system of beliefs and morals that had a major impact on all aspects of Indian culture in all ages; from Upanishads to Mahatma Gandhi. Scholarly research and proof have shown that philosophical ideas regarded as typically Indian – Karma, Non violence, Moksh, Rebirth and like - either originate in the sramana school of thought or were spread and developed by Jain teachers. These ideas were later assimilated in Hinduism and other religions, often in a different form and with different meanings.

Jains have also wielded great influence on the culture and language of Karnatak, Southern India and Gujarat most significantly. The earliest known Gujarati text, Bharat-Bahubali Ras, was written by a Jain monk. Some prominent individuals in Gujarat's Jain history were Acharya Hemacandra Suri and his pupil, the Chalukya ruler Kumarapala.

Jains are amongst the wealthiest Indians. They run many schools, colleges and hospitals and are prominent patrons of the Somapuras, the traditional temple architects in Gujarat. Jains have greatly influenced Gujarati cuisine. Gujarat is mainly vegetarian, and its food is mild as onions and garlic are omitted.

Jains encourage their monks to do research and obtain higher education. Jain monks and nuns, especially in Rajasthan, have published many research monographs. This is distinctive amongst Indian religious groups and parallels Christian clergy. The 2001 census states that Jains are India's most literate community and that India's oldest libraries at Patan and Jaisalmer are preserved by Jain institutions.

REFERENCES

Acaranga-sutra, Anga-sutrani I: Vacana Pramukha, Acarya Tulasi, Editor Yuvacarya Mahaprajna, Jaina Vishvabharati, Ladnun, First Edition, 1974.

Amar, Muni: *Jainatva ki Jhanki, Sanmati Grantharatnamala No. 12*, Sanmati Gyanpeeth, Seventh Edition, Agra, 1987.

Basham, A.L.: *A Cultural History of India,* Clarendon Press, Oxford.

Caillat, C.: *Jainism,* Macmillan Company of Upadhye, A.N., andIndia, Delhi, 1974.

Chakravarti, A.: *Samayasara of Sri Kundakunda*, Translation with Introduction. Bharatiya Gyanpeeth, Delhi, 1971.

Diwakar, R.R.: *Bihar Through Ages,* Calcutta, 1959.

Dwivedi, R.C.: *Contribution of Jainism to Indian Culture,* Motilal Banarsidass, Varanasi, 1975.

Jacobi, H.: *Introduction to Kalpa-sutra.*

Jacobi, H.: *Jaina Sutras, Part 1, The Akaranga Sutra, The Kalpa Sutra, Part2, The Uttaradhyana Sutra,The Sutrakritanga Sutra. 2 vols,* Dover Publications, New York, 1968.

Jain, Champat Rai: *Householder's Dharma,* Bijnore, 1931.

Jain, H., and Upadhye, A.N.: *Mahavira, his Times and his Philosophy of Life,* Bharatiya Gyanpeeth, New Delhi, 1975.

Jaini, Jugmandar Lal: *Outlines of Jainism,* Cambridge, 1916.

Jaini, P.S.: *The Jaina Path of Purification,* Berkeley: University of California Press, 1979.

Jaini, Padmanabh, S.: *The Jaina Path of Purigication,* California, 1979.

Lalwani. K.C.: *Kalpa Sutra of Badrabahu Svami,* Motilal Banarsidass. Delhi, 1979.

Latthe, A.B: *An Introduction to Jainism,* Bombay, 1905.

Law, B.C: *Mahavira: His Life and Teachings,* London, 1937.

Padmarajiah, Y.J.: *Jain Theories of Reality and Knowledge,* Bombay, 1963.

Pancastikaya-sara: Kunda-kunda, Edited by A.Chakravarti (Sacred Books of the Jainas, No. 3), Central Jaina Publishing House, Arrah, First Edition, 1920.

Pandey, V.: ed. *The World of Jainism*, pub. by the Author, Bombay, 1976.

Stevenson. S.: *The Heart of Jainism*, Munshiram Manoharlal, New Delhi, 1970.

Tahtinen, U.: *Ahimsa, Non-violence in Indian Society*, Rider, London, 1976.

Talib, G.S.: ed. *Jainism*, Punjabi University, Patiala, 1975.

2

History

Jainism arose in seventh century BC Eastern India. It was a time and place of religious regeneration, in which several groups reacted against the formalized rites and hierarchical organization of traditional Hinduism. It was in this fertile phase that Buddhism developed as well. Jains believe that twenty-four historical figures have lived and taught Jain truths in this age.

The twenty-third Tirthankar, Parshvanath, is thought to have lived in the seventh century and founded a Jain community established on renunciation of the world. Bhagwan Mahavir, the twenty-fourth and last Tirthankar to appear in this age, is usually regarded as the founding father of Jainism. He is by tradition thought to have lived from 599 to 527 BC., but some scholars believe he was a contemporary of the Buddha in the early fifth century BC.

Like the Buddha, Bhagwan Mahavir was born into the warrior class. At the age of thirty, he renounced the world to seek divine truth in ascetic solitude. He found nirvana after thirteen years of renunciation, and soon made eleven converts. All were former Brahmans and became followers of Bhagwan Mahavir. Bhagwan Mahavir is said to have fasted to death.

THE ANCIENTNESS OF JAINISM

The kayotsarga stance of Yogisvara Rishabh Dev found in the ruins of Mahenjo-daro has compelled the historians to think as far back as the first Tirthankar Rishabh Dev. In the excavations at Mahenjo-daro, there is ample evidence about the existence of yoga and the tradition of yoga and vairagya (detachment) is asmuch linked with the name of Rishabh Dev of the Jain pathas Shakti is with Shiva in the Hindu tradition. For this reason, it is not unreasonable for some Jain scholars to suggest that even though Rishabh Dev has been noticed in the Vedas, he is pre-Veda. The antiquity of the Jain religious tradition and the Tirthankars has been clearly noticed at several places in the earliest works of the Vedic tradition, the Vedas and the Puranas. There is evidence to show that so far back as the first Century BC. There were people who were worshipping Rishabh Dev, the first Tirthankar. There is no doubt that Jainism prevailed even before Vardhaman or Parsvanath. The Yajurveda mentions the names of three Tirthankars-Rishabh Dev, Ajitanath and Aristanemmi. The Bhagavat Purana endorses the view that Rishabh Dev was the founder of Jainism.

Prof. Virupaksa Wadiyar, writes:

"The naturalist Marichi was a close relation of Rishabh Dev. The hymns written by him are to be found in the Vedas, the Puranas and other texts, and at places therein, he has mentioned the Tirthankars. There is no reason then not to admit the existence of Jainism during the Vedic period.

The Bhagavat Purana has noticed Rishabh Dev with great respect. To quote:

"For running the administration of the world, Rishabh Dev placed his son Bharat on the throne, and himself became completely detached to propagate bhakti (devotion), gyan (knowledge) and vairagya (detachment), the religion of the great Seers (Paramahansas) who themselves had attained the height of non-involvement and detachment."

Dr. Budhprakash writes in his book "Indian Religion and Culture":

"In the list of a thousand names of Vishnu contained in the Mahabharata are included Sreyans, Anant, Dharma, Shanti and Sambhav, and in that of Shiva are included Rishabh, Ajit, Anant and Dharm. Both Vishnu and Shiva have been given a name as Subrata. All these are the names of the Tirthankars. It seems that in the atmosphere of synthesis of the Mahabharata, effort was made to present the Tirthankars as Vishnu and Shiva and thus establish the religious unity in the country. This shows that the tradition of the Tirthankars is very old."

Major-General L C. R. Furlong writes in his book "The Short Study, in Science of Comparative Religion":

"Innumerable number of years prior to Jesus Christ, Jainism was widely spread in India. When the Aryans had reached Central India, they found that the Jains were already there."

P. C. Roy Choudhury writes in his book "Jainism in Bihar":

"Some modern writers have indulged in a common-place error by writing that Jainism was born out of the widespread discontent against the Brahmanical religion. This wrong notion originated another which was that Vardhaman Mahavir was the founder of Jainism. This is factually wrong. Jainismhad originated earlier and was fairly widespread, and Mahavir helped it to spread further, and this is the reason why such a wrong notion was entertained by some reputed scholars.

Not only Mahavir, not even the first Tirthankar, Rishabh Dev, was the founder of Jainism. It is not the function of a Bhagwan to propound a religion; rather, sheltered in religion, the Soul is elevated to the status of Paramatman (Bhagwan). According to the Jain belief, Bhagwans may be infinite in number, but in a single age, in the land of Bharata, the number of Tirthankars is 24 only. Every Tirthankaris of necessity a Bhagwan, but not vice versa. One may become a Bhagwan without becoming a Tirthankar.

According to Dr. H. Jacobi, "The interest of Jainism to the students of religion consists in the fact that it goes back to a very early period and to Primitive currents of religious and metaphysical speculations, which gave rise also to the oldest philosophies Sankhya, Yoga and to Buddhism."

Jainism was in existence long before Mahabharata, Ramayana and even Vedic period. Rigveda, Atherva Veda, Yajur Veda, Sarna Veda, Bhagwat Purana, Ramayana, Mahabharata, Manusmarati, Shiv Purana, Vishnu Purana, Markanda Purana, Agni Purana, Vayu Purana, Garuda Purana, Narad Purana and Sikandha Purana etc. almost all the sacred books of Hindus, Brahmins and Buddhists frequently mention the names of Jinendras, Arhantas and Jain Tirthankars with great honour and respect. Modern researches have proved beyond doubt that the religion of Oravidas was Jain.

Prof. A. Chakravarti, also informs, "First Tirthankar Bhagwan Rishabh's religion evidently was prevalent in whole India before the Aryan's invasion as is evidenced by various references found in Rigveda."

Eminent historians like Vincent Smith, R. C. Majumdar and R. K. Mookarji regard Parshva Natha as a historical personage and a great preacher of Jaina religion. The predecessor of ParshvaNatha was Nemi Natha or Arishtanemi, the 22nd Tirthankar and the historicity of Nemi Natha like that of Parshvanatha, could be easily established. Nemi Natha was the real cousin of the famous Lord Krishana of Mahabharata.

ORIGIN

Like Buddhism, Jainism also started at a time when the Later Vedic period (1000 BC-600 BC) had come to an end and there was a rise of empires and small kingdoms. The rise of the first kingdoms was marked by the surfacing of the ruling class in each kingdom, which belonged to the Kshatriya or the warrior caste. While the Kshatriyas ruled these kingdoms and protected the rest of the masses, the Brahmin or the priestly caste provided the religious and educational needs of the masses, and also sanctified the rule of the Kshatriyas.

The Kshatriyas and Brahmins in tandem maintained their power over the masses in general and the masses belonging to the lower caste in particular. The lowermost strata of the society could not question the power of the Brahmins and the Kshatriyas. Except for the struggle with the masses belonging to the lower caste, there was a rift between the Brahmins and the Kshatriyas to take control of the reigns of the society. The Kshatriyas were alarmed by the rising power of the priests, who in turn wanted to usurp the power of the Kshatriyas. The rise of Buddhism and Jainism during this period was a natural outcome to the counter the threat of the Brahmanical Hindu order, as the founders of these religions were themselves Kshatriyas or warriors.

Jainism is not an offshoot of Vedic Brahminism. It belonged to the masses who were basically agriculturist and valued bulls and cows. They thus had simple living and could practice non violence and austerities. In contrast, the Vedic Aryans were basically pastoral people and they were used to animal-sacrifice.

Naturally the Aryan and non-Aryan people of India were always in conflict, and, so in their religious philosophy too they held opposite opinions. In the long nil, the Vedic Aryans accepted all that was of importance in Jainism and Buddhism. The current Hinduism is a commingled stream of Aryan and non-Aryan cults.

Jainism is basically a religious faith of Tirthankars. Jainism has come from the word 'Jin' which means one who has vanquished his passion. It basically means the conquest of one's own self in bondage. Again, a Tirthankar is one who has built a ford which takes one across the ocean of bondage and suffering. A Tirthankar has not only vanquished himself, but has taught masses, the way out of this ocean of suffering. These twenty four Tirthan-karas have been cited, namely:

Name	Place of Birth	Place of Nirvana	Emblem
1) Rishabh Dev	Ayodhya	Mount Kailash	Bull
2) Ajitnath	Ayodhya	Sammed Sikhar	Elephant
3) Sambhav Nath	Sravasti	Sammed Sikhar	Horse
4) Abhinandan-Nath	Ayodhya	Sammed Sikhar	Monkey
5) Sumatinath	Ayodhya	Sammed Sikhar	Curlew
6) Padmaprabha	Kaushambi	Sammed Sikhar	Red Lotus
7) Suparshvanath	Kasi (Banaras)	Sammed Sikhar	Svastika
8) Chandra-Prabha	Chandrapuri	Sammed Sikhar	Crescent
9) Pushpadanta	Kakandi	Sammed Sikhar	Dolphin
10) Shitalnath	Bhadrikapuri	Sammed Sikhar	Wishing Tree
11) Shreyamsanath	Simhapuri	Sammed Sikhar	Garuda
12) Vasupujya	Champapuri	Champapuri	Buffalo
13) Vimalnath	Kampilya	Sammed Sikhar	Boar
14) Anantanath	Ayodhya	Sammed Sikhar	Bear
15) Dharmanath	Ratnapuri	Sammed Sikhar	Vajardanda
16) Shantinath	Hastinapura	Sammed Sikhar	Deer
17) Kunthunath	Hastinapura	Sammed Sikhar	He Goat
18) Aranath	Hastinapura	Sammed Sikhar	Fish
19) Malinath	Mithilapuri	Sammed Sikhar	Waterpot
20) Munisuvrata	Kusagranagara	Sammed Sikhar	Tortoise
21) Naminath	Mithilapuri	Sammed Sikhar	Blue Lotus
22) Neminath	Sauripura	Mount Girinar	Conch
23) Parshvanath	Kasi (Banaras)	Sammed Sikhar	Serpent
24) Mahavira	Kundalpura	Pava Puri	Lion

Bhagwan Rishabh Dev has been identified with the image of an ascetic God on a seal amulet of Indus Valley Civilization. Nevertheless, this can't be Bhagwan Rishabh Dev as this God is linked with linga-worship. Excepting Parshanath and Bhagwan Mahavir, other Tirthankars are more legendary figures than historical persons.

EARLY HISTORY

History of Jainism starts with Bhagwan Rishabh Dev or Adinath. He was the first of the 24 Tirthankar. He belonged to the House of Ikshwaku, which was also known as the "House of the Sun". As per Jain philosophy, Bhagwan Rishabh Dev was the first Tirthankar of the current age (Avasarpini). Because of this, he had the name of Adinath - the first Bhagwan. He became a Siddha, an enlightened soul which has demolished all of its karma.

Bhagwan Rishabh Dev was born to Emperor Nabhi Raja and Queen Marudevi at Ayodhya in the Ikshvaku clan. As per Jain philosophy,

Bhagwan Rishabh Dev existed before civilization developed. He taught masses agriculture, tending of animals, cooking, and more. He had one hundred and one sons.

His eldest son Bharat was a chakravarti Emperor - the vanquisher of the known world. In the later part of his life he retired to become an ascetic and achieved Moksh. Since he became a siddha, he is occasionally worshipped. As per Jain philosophy, India was named Bharata-varsha or Bharata after him. This has been mentioned in various Vedic Puranas such as Agni Purana, Vishnu Purana, Markandeya Purana, Brahmanda Purana, Matsya Purana, Kurma Purana, Shiva Purana and Skanda Purana.

His second son was Bahubali, whose statue stands at Shravanabelagola, Karnataka and also at Karkala. Marudevi mother of Adinath was the first person to attain Moksh - even before Bhagwan Rishabh Dev himself. Bhagwan Rishabh Dev's grandson Marichi's soul later became Mahavir. He achieved 'kevalgnan' or endless knowledge at Palitana and achieved nirvana (Moksh) at Ashtapad mountain in Himalayas.

Bhagwan Rishabh Dev has been cited in the Hindu text of the Bhagavatha-Puran as an incarnation of Vishnu. He is cited in all the Vishnu/ Shiv Purans, and also in some other texts. As per Bhagavata, he was born to show the masses of this world the path of redemption. It was he who advised the masses to follow the path of undying happiness, instead of indulging in a life of corporeal delights and enjoyment. He is the founding father and promoter of Sramanic culture. In the depth study of the vedas and Purans, which contain many references to Bhagwan Rishabh Dev .

Modern scholars are of opinion that Rishabh was a historical person established on many archeological and literary proof. They puts the date of Rishabh Dev at the end of Stone Age and beginning of Agriculture age. The modern historians are of opinion that there exists some link between Bhagwan Rishabh Dev and Indus valley civilization. Terracotta seals and other evidences unearthed at the ancient cities of Harrapa and Mohenjo Daro provide a link between Rishabh and Indus Valley Civilization.

In his Indus Valley Civilization and Hindu Culture, the reputed scholars says that the first Jain Tirthankar belonged to Indus Valley Civilization. Prof. Ram Prasad Chanda, who supervised Indus Valley Civilization excavations, states in his article Mohen-jo-Daro: Sindh 5000 Years Ago in Modern Review (August, 1932) that, "Not only the seated deities on some of the Indus seals are in Yoga posture and bear witness to the prevalence of Yoga in the Indus Valley Civilization in that remote age, the standing deities on the seals also show Kayotsarga (a standing or sitting posture of meditation) position. The Kayotsarga posture is peculiarly Jain. It is a posture not of sitting but of standing. In the Adi Puran Book,the Kayotsarga posture is described in connection with the penance of Rishabh, also known as Vrishabh."

For a long time Bhagwan Rishabh Dev proceeded to spread his religious faith having the five great vows as its fundamental theme. When he realized that all his remaining Karmas are nearing their end he proceeded to the Ashtapad mountain. On the thirteenth day of the dark half of the month of Magh, a little before noon time, Bhagwan Rishabh Dev, along with ten thousand other monks, was maintaining a six day fasting without water. He was sitting in the meditation in the Paryanka pose. When the moon entered the Abhijit lunar mansion he got enlightenment and got released from all griefs. The lord of Gods, Saudharmendra, Emperor Bharat, many Gods and men assembled and celebrated the propitious event of Bhagwan Rishabh Dev's Nirvana.

MEDIEVAL HISTORY

Bhagwan Mahavir is the twenty-fourth Tirthankar. He was born in 599 BC. at Kshatriyakund which was a part of the well known Vaish republic. His father's name was Emperor Siddhha and his mother's name was Queen Trishal. They were very religious people and were devotees of Bhagwan Phvan. Queen Trishal had fourteen dreams when she conceived Bhagwan Mahavir. While she was pregnant, the prosperity of Emperor Siddhha grew. The parents attributed their success to the baby. So when the baby was born, he was named Vardhaman, which means continuously increasing.

He was very brave and while playing he once saved his friends from a snake. Another time, a heavenly angel joined them in the cover of a young boy. As per rules of the game, Vardhaman had a chance to ride on the boys back. While he was riding, the boy turned into a monster in order to scare him. Vardhaman nevertheless overcame the monster. The heavenly angel then appeared in his true form. He praised Vardhaman for his boldness and called him "Bhagwan Mahavir" meaning very brave.

Although Bhagwan Mahavir was born with corporeal comforts and luxuries, they never attracted him. He lived a simple life. So when his parents died, he decided to be an ascetic. He asked for permission from his brother. His brother was still mourning the loss of their parents. He thus requested Bhagwan Mahavir to wait for a couple of years before leaving. Bhagwan Mahavir waited for two years, during which he led a totally detached life.

After realizing this, his brother gave him permission to become an ascetic. Bhagwan Mahavir was thirty years old when he gave up his corporeal life and all corporeal activities. He spent most of his time in austerity and in meditation. He suffered a great deal of physical pain and torture from different sources. Amongst them, the most severe was the biting by the highly poisonous snake Chandakaushik. Bhagwan Mahavir remained tranquil and serene in the midst of all these torturous events. He never lost his serenity and never developed hate for anyone. He magnanimously forgave all of them. He led such a highly austere life for twelve and a half years. At the age of forty-two he achieved nirvana, Kewal-Gyan. He became Jin, the twenty-forth Tirthankar of the current age. As all-knowing he knew everything of the past present and future.

As the last Tirthankar, he rejuvenated the religious order (Tirth) consisting of monks, nuns, Shravaks and Shravikas. This order is known as the Jain Sangh. His first follower, called Ganadhar, was Gautamswami. He was a well known Brahmin scholar of the time. Bhagwan Mahavir had eleven Ganadhars. Those Ganadhars compiled twelve Holy Scriptures established on what Bhagwan Mahavir taught.

As per Jainism, ontologically there are two kinds of substances, namely, Jiva and Ajiva. A jiva is either nitya-Siddha, siddha or Baddha. A jiva in his pure nature has endless Gyan (knowledge), ananta darshana (endless perception), ananta charitra (pure conduct) and ananta virya (endless power): Through karmas of beginning-less rebirths, the soul it soiled, for these karmas stick to the soul, make its vision and action limited, obscured and obstructed in every way. Naturally, the original soul in its pure nature is pure spirit and karmas are like material particles. Usually no material particles can stick to the pure spirit. Along with this materialized view of the spirit in its embodied body remains either small or big. For instance, in an ant, the jiva is small in size, but in an elephant it is big in size. Hence, a jiva has also special features.

Again, the karmic matter may hinder the perception of a jiva by restricting its sense-organs. As per development of baddha jivas there is an ascending order of one-sensed, two-sensed, three sensed, four sensed and five sensed jivas. One sensed jiva remains immobile like plants and man is said to be five sensed jiva because he has the traditionally five sense-organs of eye, nose, ear, tongue and skin. But a jiva might win his own redemption by shedding off all the karmic matter. He becomes a siddha (perfect). And a perfected siddha who has laid down scriptural teaching and preaching is called a Tirthankar, and, they are 24 in number, and Bhagwan Mahavir is the last and most illustrious of all of them. But a nitya-siddha is one who is forever free and has not been a baddha at all.

For a century or so after the passing away of Bhagwan Mahavir, Jainism remained an insignificant denomination with no great following worth speaking. With Buddhism on the ascendance and its increasing popularity amongst the lay folk, with many other rival denominations such as the Ajivakas, the Lokayatas, the Samkhya Vadins competing vigorously and trying to outdo each other, Jainism remained in the back ground, with a small but highly committed following of its own.

As a religious faith it appealed to few and offered but little comfort to those who wanted to continue their old materialistic ways but at the same time dabble a little bit in religious faith so as to whet their divine appetite or allay their fears of retribution or falling into hells.

With its heavy importance on the cultivation of highest virtues, offering no compromises on the question of austerities and ascetic discipline, Jainism could not make much head way especially in times when the middle path of the Buddha was becoming increasingly popular, offering the much needed divine comfort to the materialistically inclined and socially and financially well placed trading and ruling classes.

During this period, the denomination survived because of the dedicated work of many spiritual leaders referred in the Jain texts as Gandharas. Because of their sustained efforts the denomination seemed to have gained some recognition by the time the Mauryas came to power in the fourth century BC. Tradition states that their first Emperor, the celebrated and legendary Chandragupta Maurya, became a Jain in the later part of his reign and died as a Jain monk. Bhadrabahu, a Jain monk of highest virtue, was instrumental in this conversion.

Foreseeing an impending famine of serious dimensions in northern India, Bhadrabahu seemed to have persuaded Chandragupta Maurya to accompany him to the south, where the monks could pursue their activities and also spread Jainism in the south. The Emperor consented and they all travelled to a place now called Sravanabelagola in the south. Chandragupta Maurya ended his life there, in the true Jain custom, fasting himself to death.

At the same time, when Bhadrabahu was in the south with his devotees, a group of monks remained in the north, facing the famine, under the leadership of Sthulabhadra. He said to have diluted some of the teachings of Bhagwan Mahavir as compromise, in view of the suffering and bewilderment caused by the severity of the famine.

When the group headed by Bhadrabahu eventually returned to the north they were disillusioned at the changes that took place in the Order. A confrence was convened at Pataliputra to sort out the differences and preserve the teachings of Bhagwan Mahavir. But Bhadrabahu did not attend the confrence. He proceeded to Nepal, where he died in the true Jain custom, fasting himself to death.

Jainism spread to south India during the post Mauryan period, chiefly because of the dedicated work of the Jain monks who migrated to the south. Many south Indian kings became converted to Jainism and patronized the religion.

It also spread to the eastern coastal belt of India now constituting, parts of Andhrapradesh and Orissa. About 450 BC., an assembly was organized at Vallabhi under the leadership of Devarddhi, which recognized eighty-four works as the main canonical literature.

In the west, in Gujarat, Jainism became well-liked mainly during the medieval period when Kumarapala ascended the throne and ruled from Gujarat. The invasion of the Muslims from outside did affect Jainism also, especially in Gujarat and Rajasthan, but it survived because of the high degree of ascetic control and the dedication of its monks to the life they had chosen.

MODERN HISTORY

Jainism is the religion followed by the Jains, so called since they follow the path practiced and taught by the Jins. The term is an English image of the original Jain-dharma or Jin dharma. German Jainologists, like, Leumann, Winternitz and Schubring, prefer the Jinism, which they consider to be the etymologically right rendering. Both the forms are, nevertheless, correct, Jainism meaning the religion of the Jains and Jinism that of the Jin, though the former is more popular and in present use both in literature and common parlance.

Jainism is a prominent, fully developed and well-recognized religious and cultural system, strictly native to India. It is the oldest living representative of that antique Sramana current of Indian culture, which was, in its origin, non-vedic and probably non-Aryan and even pre-Aryan.

Scholars of Eastern religions are also of the view that Jainism was related to the ancient philosophy of India, because of certain of its metaphysical conceptions, animistic belief, hero-worship in the form of worship as deities of perfected mortals, and of its being a very undemanding religion, be it in worship, rites or morals. It has also been described as a very original independent and systematic philosophy, of which the realistic and rationalistic tone doesn't fail to attract notice of even a casual observer. Moreover, unlike many other indigenous religious denominations, Jainism has succeeded in preserving down to the current time its integrity as a separate world religious faith in the midst of preponderant Hinduism. The Jains have extended their activities beyond the sphere of their religious literature to a far greater extent than the Buddhists have done, and they have memorable accomplishments in the secular science to their credit, in doctrine, grammar, lexicography, poetics, mathematics, astronomy and astrology, and even in the science of politics. In one way or other there is always some connection even of these 'profane' works with religious faith.

In Southern India, the Jains have also given services in developing the Dravidian languages, Tamil and Telugu and particularly the Kanarese literary language. They have, besides, written considerable amount in Gujarati, Hindi, and Marwari. Therefore we see that they occupy no mean position in the history of Indian literature and Indian thoughts. It is a total system with all the necessary branches, such as dogma or ontology, metaphysics, philosophy, epistemology, mythology, morals, rite, and the rest, and is divided into several denominations and sub-sects indicative of a long process of development. It has its own deities, gurus and Holy Scriptures, its own temples, places of worship and pilgrimage, and its own festivals and fairs. Besides devotees, it possesses well-organized ascetic orders, comprising both male and female monks.

The Jain community, with its distinctive cultural heritage, has formed from the days of yore a prominent section of the Indian masses and has been drawing adherents from almost all the different races, castes and classes inhabiting the different parts of this ancient country. In theory, Jainism admits of no caste distinctions, but owing to the growing influence of orthodox Hinduism in medieval times, its caste system came to be more or less adopted by the Jains as well, although still not so rigidly. At present, the bulk of the community is confined to more than two dozen subdivisions of the Vaishya caste, although stray members of the Brahmana, Kshatriya and Sudra castes and of several unidentified caste-groups are also here and there seen professing Jainism. The Jains have for long abstained from active proselytization and there is no regular Jain mission working in this direction, yet several Hindus, Muslims and

Christians are known to have converted to Jainism in the past hundred years or so.

Since the days of Bhagwan Mahavir and the Buddh (sixth century BC.) till the advent of Islam in India, the doctrine of the Nirgranthas, Jins or Tirthankars, i.e. Jainism, maintained its position as one of the three major religious faith of the country, the other two being Brahmanism (Hinduism) and Buddhism. Even during this period it lost members and many a time royal patronage and popular support, due to the greater proselytizing of the Buddhist and of the Shiv and Vaishnava denominations of Brahmanism, which sometimes look the form of violent religious persecutions. Thus, it went through a process of decay. A variety of internal and external factors made the community suffer both in influence and numbers, till at the current time it can count a bare eight to ten million souls as its members.

Without doubt, they form part of an elite and thriving section of the Indian middle classes, and are engaged in business, industry, banking, trade and commerce, the different learned professions, services and politics, and are present all over the World, living mainly in all the big towns, capital cities and trade centres.

The percentage of literacy and education is relatively very high and that of crime very low. They are well known for their philanthropy, charitable institutions and works of public welfare. In the food habit, the Jains are prefect vegetarians, rather lacto-vegetarians, don't eat meat, fish or egg, nor drink spirituous liquors.

Jains follow in general such trade and vocations as don't involve injury to life, upholding the philosophy of non-violence as best as they can, and avoid hurting or killing any life form.

The members of the ascetic order, both male and female, are on the whole, saintly, puritanical, altruistic, possessionless, and austere in the observance of their vows and the rules of their order. The custom for the monk is very rigorous, and a speedier release is thus possible. During the rainy season he seeks shelter in a monastery of the order, for then life is more abundant and movement pregnant with danger to it. For the remaining eight months he takes the road and wanders barefoot and bareheaded; he may not sleep in a bed nor take any conveyance, and may have as his only belongings his cloth, bowl, broom, and sacred books-indeed, these are not reckoned his own. He may not touch money; he must drink no wine, light no fire, and take no bath except in pure water. He may not disturb the insects or vermin that neither torment his flesh, nor do anything that may harm even potential life. Therefore, Jain monks are expected to walk gently, so as not to crush the living atoms.

The two principal denominations are the Digambar (sky-clad) and the Shvetambar (white-clad), so-called because the male monks of the former in the highest stage go about naked and those of the latter wear scanty, unsewn white cloths. Each of the major denominations is further divided into at least three different subsects, the Digambar into Terahapantha of Suddhamnaya, the Bisapantha, and the Taranapanth or Samaiya, and the Shvetambar into the Samvegi or temple-worshipper, the Sthanakavasi or Sadhumargi and the Teranpanth. The Digambar Terahapantha is so-called because it enjoins strict devotion to the thirteen (teraha) rules of ascetic behaviour, and is more puritanical and austere, even in the temple worship. The Bisapantha, then again, is much more elaborate and lax in worship and not so strict even in ascetic discipline.

The Samaiya or Taranapantha is a medieval product, doesn't insist on temple or image worship, and possesses practically no ascetic order. The Samvegis amongst the Shvetambars are temple worshipers and constitute the bulk. The Sthanakavasis, who came into being about the same time as the Digmbara Taranapanthis, in the 15th century AD., are like them opposed to image and temple worship and instead emphasize the adoration of ascetic gurus. Buildings reserved for the latter's exclusive stay are called Sthanakas. A later derivation from the Sthanakvasi denomination is the Svethambara Terapantha, which differs from the parent doctrine only in certain ascetic practices and usages. The organization of the order in this subsect is more rigid and unitary, being subject to the dictates of only one man, the Acharya or chief pontiff.

Certain misconceptions about the character, position, genesis, and history of Jainism may be noticed prevailing amongst even some of those who are supposed to be educated and well informed. There are individuals who have failed to comprehend the Jain doctrine of Anekanta, its Syadvadic mode of predication, the Jain metaphysics, and the theory of karma, or to appreciate the scope and significance of the Jain philosophy of non-violence. The cultural contributions of Jainism have not been duly evaluated, nor has the role of Jainism in the context of current day world problems been properly assessed.

Certain seals as old as perhaps five to eight thousand years, belonging to the pre-historic Indus valley civilization and bearing the figures of a nude yogin in the typically Jain kayotsarga posture along with the bull emblem, as also the nude male Harappan torso, seem to point to the prevalence of the worship of Rishabh or Adinath (the First Bhagwan) of Jain custom in that remote age. The growth of Vedicism, when the early Vedic hymns collected in the Rigveda were composed belongs to a later period. In a number of hymns of the Rigveda, which is supposed to be the earliest known or available book in the world's library, Rishabh is alluded to directly and indirectly, as is also the case with the other Vedas. Beside him, several other Tirthankars, who succeeded him, find mention in the Vedic literature, and the Brahamanical Purans have treated Rishabh as an early avatar of the God Vishnu. In the philosophical literature of ancient India, Jainism finds place as a prominent non-Brahmanical system. The Buddhist literary custom is no less explicit in indicating the prevalence of Jainism in the time prior to the growth of Buddhism (sixth century BC.) in fact, the last Tirthankar, Bhagwan Mahavirs, was a senior contemporary of Buddha. Many records, literary references, monuments and antiquities belonging to subsequent centuries speak eloquently of the prominent and major role Jainism has played during the last two thousand and five hundred years in the life and culture of the Indian subcontinent.

Alexander the Great is himself said to have come in contact with certain nude Jain monks. Terms like gymnosoph, gymnetai and gennoi used by the Greek writers, beginning with Megasthenes have usually been taken to have referred to the naked Jain saints of ancient India. The Chinese pilgrims of the fourth to seventh centuries AD. and the Arab merchants and traders of the seventh to fourteenth centuries were well acquainted with the Jain and distinguished them from the devotees of Brahmanism and even Buddhism. The European adventurers and travellers of the fifteenth to eighteenth centuries don't appear to have noticed the distinction between the two communities, the Hindu and the Jain, because, looking superficially, there was none. The Muslim chroniclers of medieval times also usually suffer from the same lapse, but not all of them. Abul Fazal Allami's account of Jainism is his Ain-I-Akbari is tolerably full and elaborate for such a work.

Coming to comparatively modern times, Oriental or Indological studies by Western scholars commenced about the beginning of the last quarter of the eighteenth century. The first regular notice of the Jain appears to be one published by Lt. Wilfred in the Asiatic Researches in 1799 and the contemporary existence of monuments, literature, and adherents of Jainism was first brought to light by Col. Colin Mackenzie and Dr. F. Buchanan Hamilton in 1807, followed by H.T. Colaebrooke's "Observation on the Jain." This the most reputed Sanskritist of his times, whose individual collections of Sanskrit manuscripts included a fair number of Jain texts, gave a more or less accurate account of this religious faith together with a hint that it must be older than Buddhism.

As time went, the Jain system of religious faith and culture came to be studied more and more intensively and also extensively, and its literature, art and architecture, archaeological remains, principles, practices, history and traditions became subjects of specialized studies. A host of learned person worked in the field, most notable amongst them being Albrecht Weber, Leumann, Fleet, Guerinot, Wilson, Jacobi, Buhler, Hoernle, Hertel, Burgess, Jarl Charpentier, Vincent Smith, Schugring and Zimmer. It is due to the sincere efforts put in by these orientalists and many others who drew inspiration from them or pursued in their footsteps that now Jainology has come to be a prominent branch of Indology and Oriental studies, and a bibliography on any branch of Indology can hardly do without a reference to Jain works on the subject, and no account of prominent religions of the world, or a comparative study of religions, is complete without Jainism included in it. Its independent existence, greater antiquity in relation to not only Buddhism but even Brahmanism, and the wholesome, abiding values inherent in its doctrine, principles and way of life, with a universal appeal and message of peace and goodwill for all and every one, have become admitted facts.

REFERENCES

Amar, Muni: *Jainatva ki Jhanki, Sanmati Grantharatnamala No. 12*, Sanmati Gyanpeeth, Seventh Edition, Agra, 1987.

Avasyaka-sutra: Editor Madhukar Muni, Jinagama Granthamala, No.24 Agama Prakashan Samiti, Byavar, First Edition, 1985.

Bhargava, D.: *Jain Ethics,* Motilal Banarsidass, Delhi, 1968.

Bhattacharya, B.C.: *Jaina Iconography,* 2nd ed, Motilal Banarsidass, Delhi, 1974.

Chatterjee, A.K.: *Comprehensive History of Jainism (up to 1000 A.D.),* Firma KLM, Calcutta, 1978.

Dasavaikalika-sutra: Editor Madhukar Muni, Jinagama Granthamala, No. 23, Agama Prakashan Samiti, Byavara, First Edition, 1985.

Gopal, S.: *Outlines of Jainism,* New Delhi, 1973

Gopalan, A.S.: *Outlines of Jainism,* Willey Eastern (P) Limited, New Delhi. First Edition. 1973.

Guseva, N.R: *Jainism*, Bombay, 1971.

Jain, Jyoti Prasad: *Jainism: The Oldest Living Religion*, Banaras, 1951.

Jain, Jyoti Prasad: *Religion and Culture of the Jains*, New Delhi, 1977.

Jain, K.C.: *Lord Mahavira and his Times*, Motilal Banarsidass, Delhi, 1974.

Malavania, Pt. Dalasukhabhai: *Jainism (Some essays)*, Translated by Dr. A.S.Gopani, Prakrita Bharati Academy, Jaipur, First Edition, 1986.

Mehata, M.L.: *Jaina Culture*, Varanasi, 1969.

Ramchandran, T.N.: *Jain Monuments of India*, Calcutta, 1944.

Rampuria, S.C.: *The Cult of Ahimsa*, Calcutta, 1947.

Sangave, Vilas A.: *The Sacred Shravan-belagola: A Socio-Religious Study*, New Delhi, 1981.

Sarvartha-siddhi: Pujapada Devanandi, Edited by Pt. Phoolachandra Siddhantashastri, Bharatiya Gyanpeeth, Durgakund Road, Varanasi, 1955.

Warren, H.: *Jainism in Western Garb, as a Solution to Life's Great Problems*, Edited, with notes, by N.J. Shah. 2nd. ed. Shree Vallabhsuri Smarak Nidhi, Bombay, 1983.

Warren, Herbert: *Jainism*, Arrah, 1916.

Williams, R.: *Jaina Yoga: A survey of Medieval Sharavakachara*, London, 1963.

3

Philosophy

Mainly Jainism assumes that the world, with all its components, is without a beginning or an end, being everlasting and undying. The wheel of time incessantly revolves like a pendulum. In the first half circle from the descending to the ascending stage where human prosperity, bliss, and life span increases and in the second half circle from the ascending stage to the descending stage where prosperity, bliss, and life span decreases.

Bhagwan Mahavir explained that from eternity, every human (soul) due to its ignorance is in bondage of karmic atoms known as karma. These karma are continuously accumulated by our actions of body, mind and speech. Under the influence of karma, the soul is habituated to seek delights in materialistic possessions and belongings. This is the deep-rooted cause of self-centered violent thoughts, deeds, anger, hate, greediness, and such other vices. Which results in further accumulation of karma.

The philosophy of karma occupies a significant position in the Jain doctrine. It provides a judicious and satisfying explanation to the obviously inexplicable phenomena of birth and death, bliss and despair, inequalities in mental and physical attainments, and of the existence of different species of life forms. It explains that the principle governing the successions of life is karma. Our actions of body, mind, and speech bind us.

One can get rid of karma and achieve nirvana by simultaneously following the path of right faith (samyak-darshana), right knowledge (samyak-Gyan), and right behaviour (samyak-charitra). The proper knowledge of the six universal substances (six Dravya) and the nine basic truths (nine Tattva) is called right knowledge and true faith in that knowledge is called right faith. The right behaviour includes ahimsa, self-purification, compassion, penance, austerity, and meditation.

BASIC PHILOSOPHY

The Jain philosophy bases its philosophy on the absolute need of conquering the lower nature for the realisation of Truth. The Jains don't accept the power of the Vedas. Jainism divides the whole world into two main divisions viz., sentient beings (Chetana, also called Jiva or Soul) and non-sentient things (Jada, also called Ajiva or non-soul).

Soul is that element which thinks, knows and feels. It is the divine element in the life form. The true nature of the soul is right knowledge, right faith and right behaviour. The soul is undergoing evolution and involution, so long as it is subject to transmigration. Whatever is not soul is non-soul (Ajiva).

The combination of the Jiva and the Ajiva causes all diversities in this world. Their interaction or interplay is the cause of the world-process or evolution. When the soul is stripped of all its Ajiva bondage, it becomes pure and achieves its ultimate Mukti.

Jainism divides the whole world into two main divisions viz., sentient beings (Chetana, also called Jiva or Soul) and non-sentient things (Jada, also called Ajiva or non-soul). Soul is that element which thinks, knows and feels. It is the divine element in the life form. The true nature of the soul is right knowledge, right faith and right behaviour. The soul is undergoing evolution and involution, so long as it is subject to transmigration. Whatever is not soul is non-soul (Ajiva).

As per Jain thought, the fundamental constituents of reality are souls (jiva), matter (pudgala), motion (dharma), rest (adharma), space (akasa), and time (kala). Jainism doesn't regard God as a Creator. Why did God create this world or this cosmos? Only he can be called God who is all-knowing, all-powerful, and who is devoid of cravings, and passions. If God has created such a world impelled by his craving or curiosity, then the question arises whether he can be called God at all if he is a thrall to passions and cravings. How can we say that God is "Karunanidhi"(treasure of benevolence) if he causes grief to others for his pleasure? The Jain concept of Godhood is the perfected Soul (Siddha), the enlightened soul (Mukta). The Jains worship these enlightened souls (Tirthankars) who have demolished all Karmas and achieved redemption, as their God. The Gods and other superhuman beings are all just as subject to karma and rebirth as human beings are. By their actions, souls accumulate karma, which is understood to be a kind of matter, and that accumulation draws them back into a body after death. Hence, all souls have undergone an infinite number of former lives, and-with the exception of those who win release from the bondage of karma-will continue to reincarnate, each new life determined by the kind and amount of karma accumulated. Finally it unfolds its absolute purity by breaking the shakels of Karma and achieves perfection, Nirvana or Mukti. The Jains regard the Jain Tirthankar to be free from faults. He is true God. He is the knower of all things and the revealer of Dharma. He is free from the 18 kinds of blemishes viz., hunger, thirst, senility, disease, birth, death, fear, arrogance, attachment, aversion, infatuation, worry, conceit, hate, uneasiness, sweat, sleep and surprise.

Every living being has a soul, so every living being can be harmed or helped. For purposes of assessing the worth of actions, living beings are classified in a hierarchy as per kinds of senses they have; the more senses a being has, the more ways it can be harmed or helped. Plants, different one-celled animals, and 'elemental' beings (beings made of one of the four elements-earth, air, fire, or water) have only one sense, the sense of touch. Worms and many insects have the senses of touch and taste. Other insects, like ants and lice, have those two senses plus the sense of smell. Flies and bees, along with other higher insects, also have sight. Human beings, along with birds, fish, and most terrestrial animals, have all five senses. This total set of senses makes all kinds of knowledge available to human beings, including knowledge of the human condition and the need for deliverance from rebirth.

There are six real substances, which make the world. These six are space, time, matter, souls, Dharmastikaya (fulcrum of motion) and Adharmastikaya (fulcrum of stability, or rest). Space serves as a receptacle for the other substances. It is infinite. Time is real. It is beginningless and endless. Material objects consist of atoms.

The proper goal for a Jain is release from death and rebirth, and rebirth is caused by the accumulation of karma, all Jain morals aims at purging karma that has been accumulated, and ceasing to accumulate new karma. Like Buddhists and Hindus, Jains believe that good karma leads to better conditions in the next life, and bad karma to worse. Nevertheless, since they conceive karma to be a material substance that draws the soul back into the body, all karma, both good and bad, leads to rebirth in the body. No karma can help an individual attain deliverance from rebirth. Karma comes in different kinds, as per kind of actions and intentions that attract it. In particular, it comes from four fundamental sources:

- Attachment to corporeal things.
- The passions, such as anger, greediness, fear, arrogance, etc.

- Sensual enjoyment.
- Ignorance, or false belief.

The philosophy of Karma occupies a very important place in the Jain doctrine. Punya is the effect of virtuous deeds (Subha Karma). Papa is the effect of evil deeds (Asubha Karma). If a man has abundance of good actions, his bliss increases; if he has abundance of evil deeds, his sorrows and pain increase. When both the good and evil deeds are purged, he achieves emancipation or Moksh.

The Jains believe in rebirth, the companion of the philosophy of Karma. The philosophy of rebirth alone can explain the inequality seen in the world. Why is one man born rich and the other poor? Why is one man healthy and strong, and another man weak and unhealthy? Why one man lives for 30 years, and another for 85 years? Why one man is an Emperor and another a labourer in the field? What is the cause of this obvious injustice? Karma. Good Karmas give good birth. Evil Karmas give rise to low births.

Moksh is the total elimination of Karma from the Jiva. The Jiva gets freedom as soon as it achieves this stage. The enlightened state is known as Mukti. The Jiva achieves ideal, unlimited, undying bliss, untouched by cares and worries. Moksh implies liberty from matter. The enlightened soul goes to the abode Siddhakshetra, which is at the top of this world.

The three pronouncements: Right faith, right knowledge and right behaviour constitute the path to Nirvana. Wrong beliefs, wrong knowledge and wrong behaviour prolong the bondage of the souls. Right knowledge reveals the nature of things as it is and with certainty. That noble soul who has right knowledge on account of right faith starts to practise the rules of right behaviour, to achieve the state of desirelessness by eradicating likes and dislikes, which demolish the five kinds of sin viz. Himsa (injury), falsehood, theft, unchastity and attachment to ordinary objects.

Universal Tenets of Jainism: Non-violence (non-injury), Satyam (truthfulness), Asteya (non-stealing), Brahmacharya (celibacy) and Aparigraha (non-covetousness). The wheel on the palm, symbolizing the Jain Vow of Non-violence, represents ahimsa or ahimsa. Right in the centre of the palm is written "Ahimsa". The wheel represents the dharmacakra, to halt the cycle of rebirth through relentless pursuit of truth. Jain monks walk barefoot and sweep the ground in front of them to avoid killing any insect. While performing holy deeds, Shvetambar Jains wear cloths (Muhapatti) over their mouths and noses to avoid saliva falling on texts or revered images. As per earliest Jain documents, plants both are and contain life forms, though one-sensed beings, so even a vegetarian life does harm. This is why the ideal way to end one`s life, for a Jain, is to sit motionless and starve to death. Bhagwan Mahavir himself, and other great Jain saints, are said to have died this way. That is the only way to be sure you are doing no harm to any life form.

DIVINE LAWS

In Jainism blissfulness consists not in dependence but in independence; the dependence is in the life of the world and if that life of the world is a part of religious faith then we may express the concept by the English word, but the life which is the highest life, is that in which we are individually independent, so far as binding or disturbing influences are concerned. In the Highest State the soul, which is the highest being, is independent.

The first prominent concept connected with it is the concept of world. Is it everlasting or non-everlasting? Is it permanent or transitory? We say that we can't study any concept unless we look upon it from all standpoints. We may express this concept by symbols or forms; we have expressed it by the story of the elephant and the seven blind men who wanted to know what kind of animal the elephant was, and each, touching a different part of the animal, understood its form in so many different ways and thereupon became dogmatic. If you wish to understand what kind of animal an elephant is, you must look upon it from all sides, and so it is with truth. Thus we say that the cosmos from one standpoint is undying and from another one-everlasting.

The totality of the cosmos taken as whole is undying. It is a collection of many things. That collection contains the same particles every moment, thus as collection it is undying; but there are so many parts of that collection and so many entities in it, all of which have their different states which occur at different times and each part doesn't retain the same state at all times. There is change, there is destruction of any particular form, and a new form comes into existence; and thus if we look upon the cosmos from this standpoint it is non-everlasting. With this doctrine there is no concept, and no place for the concept, of creation out of nothing. That concept, really speaking, is not entertained by any right-thinking individuals. Even those who believe in creation believe from a different standpoint than this.

It can't come into being out of nothing, but is an emanation coming out of something. The state only is shaped. This text in a sense is created because all its particles are put together, having been in a different state. The form of the text is created. There was a beginning of this text and there will be an end. In the same manner, with any form of matter, whether this form lasts for moments or for centuries, if there was beginning of this text and there will be an end. In the same manner, with any form of matter, whether this form lasts for moments or for centuries, if there was a beginning there must be an end.

We say there are both preservation and destruction in the many forces working around us all these forces are working ever moment in the midst of us and around us, and the collection of these entities is called by the Jains God.

If the law are fixed why do individuals bow down to these energies? Why do they consider the collective energy as a God or as God? There is always an concept of the power to do evil in the beginning of this concept. When railroads were first introduced into India ignorant individuals who did not know what they were, who had never seen in their lives that a car or carriage could be moved without the horse or the ox, thought that there was some divinity in the engine, some God or Goddess. and some of them even bow down before the car; and even to this day you will find in some parts of India, amongst the pariahs or low class, that there are individuals who entertain this concept. So to these energies in our primitive state we are liable to attribute individuality; and after a long course of growth we symbolize our thought in the form of pictures and explain them in that way to make them more intelligible to others.

In the ancient times there was not rain but a rainer, not thunder but a thunderer, and in that way, individuality is attributed, or living consciousness and character, to those forces. There may be conscious entities in these forces, as there may be living entities on the planets, but these forces themselves are not living entities. This, nevertheless, expresses the concept in the beginning; these energies were classed as creative, preservative and destructive, and these three entities were regarded as to be component parts of one being called Brahma by the Hindus. Really, creation in this is in the sense of emanation, preservation is used in the sense of preserving the form, and destruction in the sense of demolishing the form.

The concept of matter is something that can be handled or perceived by the senses and the energies must be material energies, as cohesion, magnetism, electricity, but to consider these God would be the most materialistic concept, and thus the Jains discard this concept so far as the Godhead or Godlike character is concerned. They naturally admit the existence of these energies, that they are indeed to be found everywhere, but they are subject to fixed laws which can't be interfered with by any person, not that these energies consciously influence our destinies with regard to good and evil. To say that they do so influence us is only to show our ignorance with regard to their laws. These energies collectively we call substantiality.

There are countless qualities and attributes in matter itself, and they manifest themselves at different times and ways. We are not able selves at different times and ways. We are not able without further growth to know what energies are inherent in matter, and when any new thing comes to view we are surprised, and whatever is surprising is regarded as to be something coming from divinity; but where we understand scientific percepts the surprise is removed and it is all as simple as the daily rising and setting of the sun. Thousands of years ago the different phenomena of nature were regarded as in different parts of the world to be the working of different Gods and Goddesses, but when we understand science these phenomena become simple and the concept of theses beings as characters of the highest divine power goes away.

We know that there is something besides matter; we know that the body exhibits many qualities and powers not to be found in common material substances, and that the some thing which causes this, departs from the body at death. We don't know where it goes; we know that when it lives in the body the powers of the body are different from what they are when it is not there. The powers of nature can be assimilated to the body at death. We don't know where it goes; we know that when it lives in the body the powers of the body are different from what they are when it is not there. The powers of nature can be assimilated to the body when that some thing is there. That being is viewed by us the highest and it is the same inherently in all life forms. This principle common to us all is called divinity. It is not fully developed in any of us, as it was in the saviours of the world, and thus we can them divine beings.

So the collective concept derived from observations of the divine character inherent in all beings is by us called God. While there are so many energies in the material world and in the divine and putting those two energies together we give them the name of nature we separate the material energies and put them together; but the divine energies we put together and call them collectively God. So where the form of the Jain prayer is given the object is not a receive anything from that being or from that divine nature, but to become like that power." So where the form of the Jain prayer is given the object is not to receive any thing from that being or from that divine nature, but to become one like that; not that divine being will make us, by a magic power, become like itself, but by following out the ideal which is before our eyes, we shall be able to change our own individuality; it will be regretted, as it were, and will be changed into a being which will have the same characters the divinity which is our concept of God. So we worship God, not as being who is going to give up something, not because it is going to do something or please us, not because it is lucrative in way; there is not any concept of selfishness; it is like practicing virtue for the sake of virtue and without any other motive.

The common concept of soul substance is that in order for thing to exist it must have formed, it must be perceived by the senses. This is our common experience. Really speaking it is the experience only of the aesthetic part of the being, the lowest part of the human being, and from and experience we derive conclusions and think that these conclusions apply to all substance. There are substances, which can't be perceived by the senses; there are subtler substances and entities and these can be known only by the consciousness, by the soul. Such a substance which can't be seen, heard, tasted, smelt or touched, is a substance which need not occupy space and need not have any tangibility, but, it may exist though it may not have nay form.

Sight is an effect made on the nerves of the eye by vibrations sent forth form the object perceived and this impression which we call sight, if there are no vibrations coming out of the object, is naturally not produced; but if this substance influences us in certain ways the implication is that there is something moving or producing vibrations, and these can't exist unless there is some materialistic substance which is vibrating. The very fact that something is moving in some way and influences us in some peculiar way implies that there is something materialistic about this. If there are no vibrations the substance is not materialistic. It need not exist in a form, which will give us the impression of any colour, smell, etc. There is nothing, which can partake both the attributes of soul and of matter; the attributes of matter are directly contrary to those of the soul. While one has its life in the other, it doesn't become the other.

How can that soul reside in matter when its attributes are of a different nature? By our own experience we know that, we are obliged to reside in surrounding which are not congenial to us, Which are not of our own nature. People feel that they are not related to their surroundings, there must be some reason for their being obliged to reside in those surroundings, but there must be a reason in the intelligence itself; it can't be in the materialistic substance. We know that this is fact, because intelligence can't proceed from any thing, which is strictly materialistic. No materialistic substance has given any evidence of having possessed intelligence; it might have done so when there was life in it, but without this it has no intelligence.

PRIMARY BELIEFS

Jainism maintains that every soul is capable of achieving perfection if it wilfully exerts in that direction. But the real situation is that from time undying the soul is bound with matter and it is the objective of every person to get the soul rid of matter so that soul can assume its true state. This divine emancipation requires the knowledge of the beatific condition and of the causes which stand in the way of its attainment. To find out these causes it is necessary to understand what are the existing elements or substances of nature and mode of their interaction. Jainism believes that the whole world can be divided into two categories, viz., Jiva, i.e., soul and Ajiva, i. e. non-soul. These two - Jiva and Ajiva - exhaust between them all that exists in the world and Jain doctrine is established on the nature and interaction of these two elements. It can be said in short that the living and the non-living, by coming into contact with each other, forge certain energies which bring about birth, death and different experiences of life; this process could be stopped, and the energies already forged demolished, by a course of discipline leading to redemption. There are seven propositions called the seven tattvas (realities) in Jainism. These seven tattvas are as follows:

1. Jiva (Living substance).
2. Ajiva (matter or non-living substance).
3. Asrava (the influx of Karmic matter in the soul)
4. Bandha (bondage of soul by Karmic matter).
5. Samvara (stopping of Asrava).
6. Nirjara (gradual removal of Karmic matter).
7. Moksh (attainment of ideal liberty or redemption).

Much importance has been given to these seven tattvas as every would be aspirant for Moksh has to understand the nature of these tattvas. Again, out of these seven tattvas the substances are really two viz., soul and non-soul, and amongst these two, the non-soul is all that is not soul, i. e., devoid of sentiency. Thus, amongst these two substances, the really sentient object is the Jiva, i.e., the soul. Naturally, the living substance, viz. Jiva, assumes highest importance in the context of Non-violence.

Jiva

As regards the features of Jiva, i.e., the soul, it is stated that there is an infinite number of souls; in fact, the whole world is literally filled with them. The souls are substances and as such they are timeless. Again, their characteristic mark is intelligence, which can never be demolished. Further, the soul is ever all ideal, all powerful; but by ignorance it identifies itself with the matter and hence its degradation and troubles begin. Souls are of two kinds; Samsari (ordinary souls) and Siddha or Mukta (enlightened souls).

Out of these, the samsari jivas, i. e. the ordinary souls, are the embodied souls of life forms in the world and are still subject to the cycle of Births and Deaths and the Siddha or Mukta Jivas are the enlightened souls.

Also, from the Metaphysical point of view the difference between the Samsari-Jiva, i.e., the ordinary soul, and the Mukta Jiva i.e. the enlightened soul, consists in the fact that the former is permeated with subtle matter known as Karma, while the latter is absolutely pure and free from any material alloy.

The ordinary souls are also divided into two groups from another point of view, viz. 'Sthavara Jivas' are the immobile or one-sensed souls, that is, having only one sense, i.e. the sense of touch; and 'Trasa Jivas' are the mobiles, many- sensed souls, that is, having a body with more than one sense. Again, the mobile souls are those which being in fear have the capacity of moving away from the object of fear, and immobile souls don't have this ability.

Ajiva

Jain doctrine starts with a perfect division of the world into living and non-living substances, Jiva and Ajiva. These living and non-living substances are called Dravyas in Jain Doctrine.

A Dravya has got three features. First, Dravya has the quality of existence. Secondly, it has the quality of permanence through origination and demolition. Thirdly, it is the substratum of attributes and modes. The Dravya is therefore un-created and indestructible, its necessary qualities remain the same and it is only its Paryaya or mode or condition, that can and does change.

Asrava

The third principle Asrava signifies the influx of Karmic matter into the constitution of the soul. Combination of Karmic matter with Jiva is due to Yoga. Yoga is the activity of mind, speech and body. Therefore Yoga is the channel of Asrava. The physical matter which is actually drawn to the soul can't be perceived by the senses as it is very fine.

Bandha

When the Karmic matter enters the soul, both get imperceptibly mixed with each other. Bandha or bondage is the assimilation of matter which is fit to form Karmas by the soul as it is linked with passions. The merger of spirit and matter doesn't imply a total annihilation of their natural properties, but only a suspension of their function, in varying degree, as per quality and quantity of the material absorbed.

Therefore, the effect of the fusion of the spirit and matter is manifested in the form of a compound individuality which partakes of the nature of both, without actually demolishing either.

Samvara

Effective states of craving and aversion, and activity of thought, speech or body are the conditions that attract Karmas, good and bad, towards the soul. When those conditions are removed, there will be no Karmas nearing the Jiva, that is total Samvara - a sort of protective wall shutting out all the Karmas is founded round the self. Therefore Samvara is the stoppage of inflow of Karmic matter into the soul. There are several ways through which the stoppage could be effected.

Nirjara

Nirjara means the falling away of Karmic matter from the soul. The soul will be rendered free by the automatic falling out of the Karmas when they become ripe. But this is a lengthy process. The falling away may be intentionally brought through the practice of austerities.

Therefore, Nirjara is of two kinds. The natural maturing of a Karma and its separation from the soul is called Savipaka Nirjara and inducing a Karma to leave the soul, before it gets ripened by means of ascetic practices is called Avipaka Nirjara.

Moksh

Moksh or nirvana is the liberty from all Karmic matter, owing to the non-existence of the cause of bondage and the shedding of all the Karmas. Therefore total liberty of the soul from Karmic matter is called Moksh.

Moksh is achieved when the soul and matter are separated from each other. The separation is effected when all the Karmas have left the soul, and no more Karmic matter can be attracted towards it.

From the fundamental tenets of Jainism it is evident that the inherent powers of the soul are crippled by its association with Karmic matter and that is why we find every person in an imperfect state. The real and everlasting bliss will be obtained by an individual only when the Karmas are completely removed from the soul and Jainism firmly believes that although man is imperfect at present, it is quite possible for him to rid himself of the Karmas by his own personal efforts without any help from an outside agency. The highest bliss is to escape from the Cycle of Births and Deaths and be an enlightened soul, that is, to obtain Moksh. This world is full of sorrow and trouble and it is quite necessary to achieve the aim of transcendental happiness by a sure method.

When the goal has been fixed the next question arises regarding the way how to achieve that objective. To this question Jainism has a definite answer. It emphatically states that Samyag-darsana, i.e., right belief, Samyag-jnana, i.e., right knowledge, and Samyak-charitra, i.e., right behaviour together constitute the path to salvation. Right belief, right knowledge and right behaviour are called Ratnatraya or the three jewels in Jaina works.

According to Jainism these three things must be present together to constitute the path to salvation. Since all the three are stressed equally and since the Mokshamarga is impossible without the comprehension of all the three, it is apparent that Jainism is not prepared to admit anyone of these three in isolation as means of salvation. This position in Jainism is quite distinct from many religious faiths in India. For instance, there are religious schools in Hinduism which lay all the importance on Bhakti, i.e., devotion, or on jnana, i.e., knowledge, or on Karma, i.e., ethical behaviour. The denomination of Bhagavatas mainly emphasizes the Bhakti aspect, the denomination of Advita Vedantins the Jnana aspect and the denomination of Purva Mimamasaksa the Karma aspect. But according to Jainism no such one-sided importance can be accepted as the correct path.

In this respect Jainism has clearly laid down that with a view to attaining deliverance all the three must be simultaneously pursued. It is strongly contended that to effect a cure of a malady, faith in the efficacy of a medicine, knowledge of its use, and actual taking of it; these three together are necessary, so also to get emancipation, faith in the efficacy of Jainism, its knowledge and actual practicing of it: these three are quite indispensable. This Jaina path to deliverance is compared to a ladder with its two side poles and the central rungs forming the steps. The side poles are right belief and right knowledge and the rungs or steps are the gradual stages of right behaviour. It is possible to ascend the ladder only when all the three are sound. The absence of one makes the ascent impossible.

Therefore, a simultaneous pursuit of correct belief, right knowledge and right behaviour is emphatically enjoined by Jainism upon the people. Apparently on this path, Jainism has based its distinctive ethical code for its followers - both householders and monks.

ETHICS

The Jain code of ethics is a natural result of a judicious approach established upon the central principles of Jainism. It is not a 'system of laws' or commandments handed down by a higher power. Jains are expected to study the Holy Scriptures and grasp the ideas of judicious perception, judicious knowledge and judicious behaviour. Then they should consider their own experiences and realize that passions such as anger, arrogance, deception and greediness make a major impact on their lives. It is observed that if a person accepts success and failure, pain and pleasure, sickness and health, union and separation, victory and defeat as part of the corporeal existence, he/she has mild passions. This leads to contentment and peace of mind.

In this manner, a person can transform unpleasant-feeling-producing karma into pleasant-feeling-producing karma. Then again, one who is upset, discontent, angry, egotistic, selfish, conniving, greedy or vindictive has no peace of mind. Such a person might transform pleasant-feeling-producing karma into unpleasant-feeling-producing karma. Fear of the legal system or some higher power or karma involves passion - the cause of painful karmic bondage. Even philanthropy tarnished with ego, intrigue, exploitation and greediness for tax relief leads to the influx of undesirable karma.

All persons aspire to genuine bliss and peace of mind. All realize from their experiences that bliss arises from contentment and equanimity. Anger, revenge and violence only fuel the cycle of violence. Jainism believes that no overall good of persons or society can arise from violence. Jainism promotes a culture of ahimsa in which a person's thoughts and actions originate from a judicious mind and pure heart, without any ego, arrogance, fear, intrigue or greediness. A culture of ahimsa is the process of improving and refining our lives through our practice of ahimsa.

Violence is of two kinds: physical violence and mental violence. Physical violence is killing or causing bodily injury to a life form. It is gross violence. Mental violence is the violence of thoughts, feelings and emotions. It is subtle, abstract, and intangible. It consists of causing anxiety, suspicion, fear, etc. Therefore anger, arrogance, intrigue and greediness constitute abstract violence. Fear, suspicion, hate, lies, thievery, cheating, possessiveness and taking more than one's fair share lead to violence of thoughts, feelings and emotions; of self and of other persons. It should be pointed out that violence aimed at others is invariably accompanied by mental violence of self. Further, Jainism teaches that untruth, stealing, unchastity and possessiveness are also aspects of violence. Therefore the foundation of the culture of ahimsa is laid on the following five vows:

- Ahimsa (Non-violence) which consists of not obstructing the life processes of self or of any other life form. This embodies the principle of freedom and equality of all life forms.
- Truth (Satya) which means always speaking the truth and supporting what is true as per one's own perception and experience.
- Non-stealing (Achaurya) which entails not taking anything which doesn't belong to us, accepting only one's fair share, and, being honest in business dealings.
- Purity of body and mind (Brahmacharya), which entails total celibacy for monks and nuns, and, partial celibacy - no premarital or extramarital sexual activity, for laypersons.
- Non-possessiveness (Aparigrah) which entails limiting our materialistic belongings and cravings.

These vows help us minimize all violence, physical and mental, direct and indirect, intentional and unintentional, which we are apt to commit through the activities of body, speech and mind. We also create an atmosphere of trust and goodwill in society by practicing these virtues.

Jains believe that vegetarianism is the first necessary feature of the culture of ahimsa. Vegetarianism not only helps purge intentional and avoidable physical violence of animals but also the violence of self. Poor health and illness lead to mental violence. It has been established by many researchers that a non-vegetarian diet is not good for health. One can maintain a well-balanced, protein-rich, low-fat, low-cholesterol vegetarian diet, which is good for health. Therefore vegetarianism is necessary for minimizing physical and also mental violence. Everybody knows that alcohol, tobacco and drugs are the roots of significant violence, physical and also mental. Alcohol and drugs impair the ability to think and discriminate between undesirable and desirable actions. This is violence of the subtle life processes which may lead to violence of others as well. Alcohol and drugs are not 'clean fun' by any standards. Hence one must stay away from them at all costs. Jainism teaches to avoid all situations and actions which may lead to violence.

The Jain texts present a number of vows that basically promote the practice of ahimsa. For instance, a householder is expected to follow the augmenting vow (Gunavrat) of limiting needless activities (Anarthadand Vrat), which basically promotes conservation of natural resources and environmental protection.

METAPHYSICS

Jain metaphysics asserts the existence of principle of sentient or consciousness, called as Jiva or soul, characterised by knowledge and perception. There are infinite, independent souls categorised into: enlightened and non-enlightened. Infinite knowledge, perception and happiness are the inherent qualities of a soul. These qualities are completely enjoyed uninterrupted by enlightened souls, but clouded by karmas in the case of non-enlightened souls, resulting in karmic bondage. This bondage further results in a continuous co-habitation of the soul with the body. Therefore, an embodied non-enlightened soul is found in four territories of existence - heavens, hells, humans and animal world - in an un-ending cycle of births and deaths, also known as samsara. The soul is in bondage since time immemorial; nevertheless, it is possible to achieve nirvana through judicious perception, judicious knowledge and judicious behaviour.

As per Jain metaphysics, the soul is the master of its own fate. One of the qualities of the soul is total lordship of its own fate. The soul alone selects its actions and soul alone reaps its consequences. No God, prophet or angel can intervene in the actions or the fate of the soul. Moreover, it is the soul alone who makes the required efforts to achieve nirvana without any Godly grace. Amongst the twelve contemplations of Jains, one of them is the loneliness of one's soul and nature of the World and rebirth. Therefore, only by purifying one's soul by one's own actions can one help oneself.

Jain metaphysics is also established on seven (sometimes nine, with sub-categories) truths or key tenets, also known as tattva, which are an effort to explain the nature and solution of human plight. The first two are the two ontological categories of the soul and the non-soul, namely the axiom that they exist. The third truth is that through interaction, called yoga, between the two substances, soul and non-soul, karmic matter flows into the soul, adheres to it, becomes converted into karma and the fourth truth acts as a factor of bondage bandha, restraining the manifestation of the consciousness inherent to it. The fifth truth states that an arrest (samvara) of new karma is possible through austerity, through practice of right behaviour, faith and knowledge. An intensification of austerity burns up the existing karma - this sixth truth is conveyed by the word nirjar. The final truth is that, when the soul is released from the influence of karma, it reaches the goal of Jain teaching, which is nirvana or Moksh. Some authors add two additional categories: the meritorious and demeritorious acts, related to karma (punya and paapa). These nine categories of primal truth, called navatattva, form the basis of entire Jain metaphysics.

Everything can be looked upon from two standpoints, the substance and the manifestation. If the state of the soul itself is to be taken into consideration that state has its beginning and its end. The state of the soul as living in the human body had a starting at birth and will have an end at death, but it is a beginning and an end of the state, not of the thing itself. The soul taken as a substance is timeless; taken as a state every state has its beginning and end. So this beginning of a state implies that before this beginning there was another state of the soul. Nothing can exist unless it exists in some state.

The state may not be permanent, but the thing must have a state at all times. if thus the current state of the soul had beginning, it had another state before the beginning of this state, and after the end of this state it will have another state. So the future state is something that comes out of or is the consequence of the current state. As the future is to the present, so the present is to the past. The present is only the future of the past. What is true with regard to the future state is true with regard to the past and current state. The acts of the past have determined our current state, and if this is true the acts of the current state must determine the future state.

Incarnation, which means literally becoming flesh; and, really that which is spirit is always spirit or soul. The spirit doesn't become flesh. If rebirth means to become flesh there can be no rebirth, but if it means simply the life in flesh for a short time, then there is rebirth. Rebirth means also to be born in some state again and again. Metempsychosis means in Greek only change; that the animal itself, body and soul, everything together, is changed into some other thing and so on. That is the concept of metempsychosis.

Transmigration of souls is, especially in the concept of the Christians, the concept of the human soul going into the animal body, as if this were a need. But that is not the real concept; the real concept is simply going from one place to another or from one body to another, but not necessarily going from the human body to the animal body, but simply travelling. It implies the concept of form. Nothing can travel unless it has form and occupies space and is materialistic; so in our doctrine we reject all these terms if that is the concept connected with these terms, and use the concept of rebirth; that is, the soul is born in some other body, and the birth doesn't imply the same conditions [as those] applying to the human birth

There are certain circumstances in which human beings are born; the seed itself takes several months to ripen and then there is the birth. This may be due to certain acts or forces, which are generated by human beings? These are in a condition to be observed by beings whose forces will take them to some other planet, and we say that there is another condition of birth there.

There is no need for gestation and fecundation. The karmic body has in itself many powers and has a force to take to itself another body, which is in the case of the human beings a gross body, but in the case of other beings a subtle body is generated and this body is changeable so far as its form and dimensions are concerned. Thus, if the forces generated, while we live any kind of life are of different kinds then in the case of some being it may be necessary that he should be born in the human condition and pass through the actual circumstances which must be obeyed if the human being is to be born, while if the forces generated are different in their character he may be born on some other planet, where birth is manifested in different way, without any need of the combination of the male and the female principle.

There are so many different planes of life that the mere study of the human life ought not to be made to apply to all the affairs of life. We have studied only a few forms of the life of animals, human beings, etc., but that is only the part which under the current growth of our science of our eyesight even, we are able to study. We are not able to study other forms of life, countless in the world, and thus we ought not to apply the laws therefore discovered to all forms of life.

Our study is introspective because our concept is that soul is able to know everything under the right circumstances. The knowledge acquired under these circumstances is of the sounder nature and a more correct kind because the obstacles, which come in the way science, are not there. Science has to commit errors and think that they don't; still knowledge is derived from inferences which we draw from certain premises which may not be right or if the premises are right the inference may be wrong. We don't mean to say that there are always errors in the knowledge, which is acquired through sensation or through matter, but sometimes it is possible, and while it may be correct knowledge in many cases we can't rely on that.

The highest knowledge is immediate knowledge, derived by the soul without the assistance of any external thing, and the knowledge of enlightened souls, as well as the knowledge of human beings who are just on the point of being enlightened, or have passed through the course of discipline, mental, ethical and spiritual, and have nearly exhausted past forces, at the same time generating divine forces, and on account of control and sees everything when this state is arrived at; it knows means that it is something, some reality, and there can be no reality unless it can differentiate itself from other realities.

Only the one universal thing could not know itself, because knowledge implies comparing one with another, and if that itself, because cognition implies comparing one with another, and if that is not done there is no individuality. We say thus that the soul in its highest existence knows, that it is perfectly separate form other things, so far as experience and knowledge are concerned, but in so far as its nature is concerned, so long as there is a sense of separateness, there is no occasion or chance for the soul to rise higher because when the soul thinks that it is living a different existence for its own sake it is considering its own self to be dissimilar from another person and thinks that this is its own and a part of its nature, its own being, and thus anything done in regard to these surroundings will benefit or injure its own.

It even thinks that its very life consists in doing goods and in loving other souls and taking active measures for carrying into effect the very plan of the sole. Then it comes higher, and ultimately reaches the highest condition. The condition of the soul, as I have said, is the highest in which there is ideal consciousness, there is infinite knowledge and infinite happiness; we express these three ideas in Sanskrit as existence infinite, happiness infinite and knowledge infinite. That condition of the soul can't be described by us because description is something which proceeds from a finite mind and when the soul becomes infinite no finite mind and when the soul becomes infinite no finite mind can fully express the conditions of that infinite state. The attributes we give thus to that condition of the soul are always full of comprehension. We shall always leave out many things; we have not the power to express all our thoughts. How can we express, then, this state of a soul, which so far as its power and knowledge are concerned is infinite?

The Jains have studied the nature of the soul and the world from these standpoints and have derived a beautiful principle, and so far as this is concerned there is this difference between this country and other countries and other religions, they can understand all these from these standpoints. The Bible says, 'Thou shalt not kill', and Jains practice universal love so that this also means that we should not kill any beings. If we say that the Bible doesn't mean that we take away a part of the bible. Why should we interpret the laws of any religious faith from the narrowest standpoint? We should take into consideration the nature, attributes and working of all things. We can't derive laws, which are to be applied to the whole world simply by our observation of a part of the conscious nature of the world. If you wish to state correctly the nature of the world you will study the nature of all the different parts of the world and then the laws will be relevant to all parts of it.

We think that we are superior to other things because our tenants who reside on the ground floor are inferior to us, but we have no right thus to crush those tenants, who later on will acquire the right to inhabit the second and third floors and eventually the highest floor. One living on the highest plane has no right to crush those who reside on the lowest plane. If one thinks that he has a right to do this, which he has, not sufficient strength to reside without demolishing life, our doctrine says that it is still sin to destruct life, and it remains only to choose the lowest form, the less evil, We will in business take such a kind of business as will yield the most profit and will cause us to lose the least, in which we have the less liabilities; and the highest condition will be that in which we have no liabilities and no creditors, the state in which we may reside without any creditors or in a perfectly free condition. That is the enlightened condition.

The concept of Karma is very complicated. The one chief point is that that theory is not the theory of fatalism, not a theory in which the human being is tied down to some, one, bound down by the force of something outside itself. In one sense only will there be fatalism; if we are free to do many things we are also not free to do other things, and we can't be freed from and results of our acts. Some results may be manifested in great strength, others very weakly; some may take a very long time and others a very short time; some are of such a nature that they take a long time to work out, while the influence of others may be removed by simply washing with water and that will be the case in the matter of acts done incidentally without any settled purpose or any fixed craving.

In such a case with reference to many acts we may counteract their effects by willing to do so. So the theory of karma is not in any sense a theory of fatalism, but we say that all of us are not going to one goal without any craving on our part, not that we are to reach that state without any effort on our part, but that our current condition is the effect of our acts, thoughts and words in the past state.

To say that all will reach the ideal state merely because some one has died that they might be saved, merely from a belief in this person, would be a theory of fatalism, because those who have lived a pure and virtuous state and have not accepted a certain theory will not reach the perfected state simply for that reason and no other the faith in saviors is simply this, that by following out the divine principle which is in our selves when this is fully developed we also shall become Christ's, by the crucifixion of the lower nature on the altar of the higher.

We also use the cross as a symbol. All life forms have to pass through or evolve from the lowest, the monadic, condition to the highest state of existence and can't reach this unless they obtain possession of the three things necessary; right belief, right knowledge and right behaviour. The right, belief, really speaking, is not that there is no passing through forms after death, but the soul keeps progressing always in its own nature without any backward direction at all.

We have expressed this in clear language without any parables or metaphors, but when we preach these truths to the ignorant masses some story or picture might be necessary for them and after that the explanation of the real meaning; as well have all allegory in the Pilgrim's Progress. It is just like reaching the Celestial City in that text, but we must all understand that these things are parables. Others may need music to assist their religious faith, but when we understand the esoteric meaning which underlies all religion there will be no quarrelling and no need of names or of forms; and this is really the object of all religions.

Jainism: A Scientific Religion

Jainism is the only religious system that recognizes clearly the truth that religion is a science. It is the only man made religion, the only one that reduces every thing to the iron laws of Nature and with modern science.

The pursuit of science by looking at facts alone and ignoring the ultimate purpose of life has resulted in a lop sided growth. Science has made the world a wonderland, built up a glittering human civilization, opened up innumerable avenues for the growth of mental and physical powers, added to the power of man to such an extent that man has become almost a supreme power to triumph over and shape his physical environment- a geological force changing the face of the planet earth chemically, physically and in many other ways. However, under all this pomp and show, some vital element is found missing. Science has failed to impart man knowledge of ultimate purpose and even an understanding of any immediate purpose in life.

It is wrong to suppose, as science does that the world is a mere mechanical movement and man a purposeless force. Life is not the product of mechanical laws. The current of life drives man onward and upward on the path of evolution and the driving power lies not outside him but within him. But the scientist does not comprehend the real nature of this driving power. His electrons and protons do not resolve the mystery of soul. Besides, God and soul cannot be treated as mathematical equations. Our deepest convictions, for which we are sometimes ready to die, are not the results of cold rational calculations. What makes man a man is not his physical and material richness but his sense of eternal, immortal voice within him for the sake of which even kings and multimillionaires have abandoned their empires, renounced the world and become wandering mendicants. Science deals with the domain of positive knowledge but the temper, which it should produce, goes beyond that domain. The ultimate purpose of man may be said to be to gain knowledge, to realize truth, to appreciate goodness and beauty. But the scientists proclaims the world of truth, beauty and Goodness to be no more than a product of accidental combination of atoms destined to end as it began in a cloud of hydrogen gas. For him life is not the designed plan of a divine artist, but an outcome of the peculiar combinatin and collusion of whirling atoms. Infect, men of science believe in nothing but what the can prove by scientific methods. But science alone cannot explan the mysteries of life and existence. It is with the temper and approch of science allied to philosophy and with reverence for all that lies beyon that we must try to understand all life and universe.

Hence, a co-ordination between science and religion both is essential for smooth sailing of life in the universe. Indeed, nature preaches the lesson of mutual co-existence in every sphere. It has to be admitted beyond doubt that science can give us comforts and articles of luxury but it cannot give happiness. Our material achievements, our control of physical forces have not added to the peace of mind or brought laughter back to life, or answered any question about here and hereafter. Religion comes to our rescue to provide us real peace and happiness, and guide us on the path of salvation-the ultimate goal of life.

Jainism ordains its followers to drink water after proper distillation, because besides making water more compatible for consumption, it avoids the killing of germs of water. Scientists have found through microscopes that it contains innumerous tiny germs invisible to the naked eye moving to and fro in water. It is why the modern scientists and medical experts advise the use of filtered water. How strange it is that that the great Jain Acharyas knew about this fact through their absolute knowledge and perception without the aid of any implement.

Difference between Jainism and Vedic Hindu Religion

If we compare Jainism and Hinduism, we find that the differences between them are great and that their agreement is in respect of a few particulars only concerning the ordinary mode of living. Even the ceremonies which appear to be similar are in reality different in respect of their purport if carefully studied. Hence the significant differences between Jainism and Hinduism can be briefly noted as follows:

The sacred books of the Hindus like *Vedas, Smrtis, Puranas* etc. are not accepted by the Jainas and the Hindus also do not recognize even a single scripture of the Jainas.

While the Jainas regard the world as eternal, the Hindus hold it to have been made by a creator.

In Jainism, worship is not offered to an eternal and eternally pure God, but to those great ones who have realized their high ideal and attained Godhood for themselves; in Hinduism worship is performed of many forms of one God who is the creator and the ruler of the world.

The significance of worship in Hinduism is also not the same as that in Jainism. In Jainism, there is no offering of food and the like, nor is a prayer made to the deity for boons. On the other hand, in Hinduism the attainment of the desired object is by the will of certain divine beings who are to be propitiated.

As Hinduism is a sacrificial religion, the performance of several sacrifices for a variety of reasons and for different duration has got an important place in it. This is not the case with Jainism and especially the animal sacrifices practiced by the Hindus have absolutely no place in Jainism.

While the Hindus believe that Gods alone can attain salvation, the Jainas consider that it is, the right of human beings only.

The path of salvation prescribed by Jainism is only one and it is known as *Ratnatraya-marga,* i.e., the threefold path of Right Belief, Right Knowledge and Right Conduct, which is to be simultaneously pursued by all persons. But in Hinduism, there is no prescription of one single, definite and clear path of salvation. Instead, in Hinduism different ways have been laid down for the attainment of salvation by various religious preachers in different periods of time.

The Hindus regard *Karma* as an invisible power but the Jainas think it as a form of matter which can stick to the soul.

In Jainism there are various concepts like *dharma, adharma, lesya, gunasthana* etc., which are not found in Hindu spiritual ideology.

The peculiar Hindu practices like *niyoga,* i.e., levirate and *sati,* i.e., ascending the funeral pyre of the husband, are not approved by the Jainas. Further, a large number of Hindu religious practices. which are repugnant to Jainism, have been termed as *mudhatas* or stupid customs and beliefs and the true Jainas are required to be absolutely free from them. They are sun-worship, bath during eclipses, giving away money at the end of eclipses, fire-worship, the worship of edifices, ceremonial bathing in rivers and the ocean, adoration of trees, sacred offerings of boiled rice, religious suicide by falling from a precipice, bowing at the tail of a cow and taking cow's urine, etc.

REFERENCES

Avasyaka-sutra: Editor Madhukar Muni, Jinagama Granthamala, No.24 Agama Prakashan Samiti, Byavar, First Edition, 1985.

Bool Chand: *Lord Mahavira,* Banaras, 1948.

Bothra, P.: *Jain Theory of Perception,* Motilal Banarsidass, Delhi, 1976.

Brown, Percy: *Indian Architecture,* Bombay, 2nd Edn.

Jacobi, H.: *Studies in Jainism,* Ahmedabad, 1946.

Jain, C. R.: *Fundamentals of Jainism,* Veer Nirvan Bharti, Meerut, 1974.

Jain, Champat Rai: *Fundamentals of Jainism*, Meerut, 1974.

Jain, J. P.: *Religion and Culture of the Jains*, Bharatiya Gyanpeeth, New Delhi, 1975.

Madhav Rao, N.: *Jainism A New Look.*

Mehta, M. L.: *Outlines of Jaina Philosophy*, Jaina Mission Society, G. 146, Chickpet, Bangalore - 2, October, 1954.

Mookerjee, S.: *The Jain Philosophy of Non-absolutism, a Critical Study of Anekantavada. 2nd. Ed*, Motilal Banarsidass, Delhi, 1978.

Nahar and Ghosh: *An Epitome of Jainism*, Calcutta 1917.

Saletore, B.A: *Medieval Jainism*, Bombay, 1938.

Samaya-sara: Kunda-kunda, Bharatiya Gyanpeeth, Durgakund Road, Varanasi, First Edition, 1950.

Sangave, V.S.: *Jaina Community, a Social Survey. 2nd. ed.* Popular Prakashan, Bombay, 1980.

Sangave, Vilas A.: *Life and Legacy of Mahavira:* A Social Study, Meerut, 1974.

Tattvartha-sutra: Umasvati, P.V. Research Institute, Varanasi, Reprint Second Edition.

Thomas, F.W.: *Sri Mallisenasuri, Syad-Vada-Manjari*, Motilal Banarsidass Delhi, 1968.

Trsastisalakapurusacaritrani: Canto 10, Hemacandra, Jaina Dharma Prasaraka Sabha, Bhavanagar, First Edition, 1908.

4

Concept of God

Mainly Jainism assumes that the world, with all its components, is without a beginning or an end, being everlasting and timeless. The wheel of time incessantly revolves like a pendulum. In the first half circle from the descending to the ascending stage where human prosperity, bliss, and life span increases and in the second half circle from the ascending stage to the descending stage where prosperity, bliss, and life span decreases.

Bhagwan Mahavir explained that from eternity, every life form (soul) due to its ignorance is in bondage of karmic atoms known as karma. These karma are continuously accumulated by our actions of body, mind and speech. Under the influence of karma, the soul is habituated to seek delights in materialistic possessions and belongings. This is the deep-rooted cause of self-centered violent thoughts, deeds, anger, hate, greediness, and such other vices. Which results in further accumulation of karma.

The philosophy of karma occupies a significant position in the Jain philosophy. It provides a judicious and satisfying explanation to the obviously inexplicable phenomena of birth and death, bliss and despair, inequalities in mental and physical attainments, and of the existence of different species of life forms. It explains that the principle governing the successions of life is karma. Our actions of body, mind, and speech bind us.

One can get rid of karma and achieve nirvana by simultaneously following the path of right faith; samyak-darshana, right knowledge; samyak-Gyan, and right behaviour; samyak-charitra. The proper knowledge of the six universal substances six Dravya and the nine basic truths; nine Tattva is called right knowledge and true faith in that knowledge is called right faith. The right behaviour includes ahimsa, self-purification, compassion, penance, austerity, and meditation.

DEFINING GOD

Jainism believes that world and all its substances or entities are timeless. It has no beginning or end with respect to time. World runs own its own accord by its own cosmic laws. All the substances change or modify their forms continuously. Nothing can be destructed or created in the world. There is no need of some one to create or manage the affairs of the world. Hence Jainism doesn't believe in God as a creator, survivor, and destroyer of the world.

Nevertheless Jainism does believe in God, not as a creator, but as an ideal being. When an individual destructs all his karmas, he becomes an enlightened soul. He lives in an ideal blissful state in Moksh eternally. The enlightened soul possesses infinite knowledge, infinite vision, infinite power, and infinite happiness. This life form is a God of Jain religious faith.

Every life form has a potential to become God. Hence Jains don't have one God, but Jain Gods are countless and their number is continuously increasing as more life forms achieve nirvana.

Jains believe that since the beginning of the time every life form (soul) is attached with karma and also it is in delusion (ignorant) state of its true nature. The main objective of the religious faith is to remove this delusion through self-knowledge and self-effort. This knowledge will remove karma which are linked with it from the beginning of time. When all karma get removed, the soul becomes enlightened soul.

There are many types of karma. Nevertheless they are broadly classified into the following eight categories:

Mohniya karma: It generates delusion in the soul in regard to its own true nature, and makes it identify itself with other external substances.

Gyan varaniya karma: It covers the soul's power of ideal knowledge.

Darasna varaniya karma: It covers the soul's power of ideal visions.

Antaraya karma: It obstructs the natural quality or energy of the soul such as charity and will power. This prevents the soul from achieving nirvana. It also prevents a life form from doing something good and enjoyable.

Vedniya karma: It obscures the blissful nature of the soul, and thereby produces pain and pleasure.

Nama karma: It obscures the non corporeal existence of the soul, and produces the body with its limitations, qualities, faculties, etc.

Gotra karma: It obscures the soul's features of equanimity, and determines the household, social standing, and individuality.

Ayu karma: It determines the span of life in one birth, therefore obscuring soul's nature of timeless existence.

While travelling on the path of divine progress, an individual destructs all eight types of his karmas in the following sequence:

First Mohaniya (delusion), then Gyan varaniya (knowledge), Darasna varaniya (vision), and Antaraya (natural qualities) all three together. At this time, he achieves Kewal-Gyan and he is known as Arihant, which is also known as Tirthankar, Jin, Arhat, Kewali, or Nirgantha.

Lastly the remaining four karmas namely Vedniya (pain and pleasure of the body), Nama (body), Gotra (social standing), and Ayu (life span) are destructed. At this time, he achieves total nirvana and he is known as Siddha.

The first four karmas are called Ghati karmas because they obscure the natural qualities of the soul. The last four karmas are known as Aghati karmas because they don't affect the qualities of the soul, but they are associated to the physical body of the soul. Once an individual destructs all his Ghati karmas, he will definitely destruct all of his Aghati karmas before his death. No fall back can occur after the destruction of Ghati karmas.

Arihant

When an individual destructs his four Ghati karmas, he achieves Kewal-Gyan. He has regained the original attributes of his soul, which are ideal knowledge, vision, power, and happiness. He is all-knowing of the past, present and future forms of all entities (living and nonliving beings) of the world. He is still a human being. He remains in the state of blissful condition for the rest of his life. Arihants are classified into two categories:

- Tirthankar
- Kewali

Tirthankar: Immediately after achieving Kewal-Gyan, if an individual establishes the four fold religious order of monks, nuns, sravaks (male householder), and sravikas (female householder) is known as Tirthankar. He preaches the Jain doctrine, religion, morals, conducts to his devotees.

Jainism believe that Twenty four Tirthankars are born during each descending and ascending part of the time cycle in this region

Bharat Kshetra) of the world. No two Tirthankars exist at the same time. Usually a Tirthankar is born when the religion is at its depression state. The new Tirthankar revives the same Jain doctrine. He gives a different form to the religion practice, which depends upon the time, place, and the social behaviour of the human society of that time.

Simple kewali: The only difference between Tirthankar and simple kewali is that the latter doesn't establish the religious order. He remains in the state of ideal blissful condition for the rest of his life after achieving Kewal-Gyan.

In the religious scriptures, the name Arihantas and Tirthankars are interchangeably used because simple kewalis don't play any active roles in the religious order. Tirthankar is also known as Jin, Arihant, Arhat, Arhant, or Nirgrantha.

Tirthankar: Founding father of four-fold order of monks, nuns, laymen, and laywomen.

Jin: One who has vanquished his, inner passions such as craving and hate.

Arihant: One who has destructed his inner enemies such as greediness, anger, craving, and hate.

Arhat: One to whom nothing can be secret.

Arhant: A divine acquirement leading a man to the state of an Arihant.

Nirgrantha: A religious faith of One who has gotten rid of all knots or attachments.

Both Tirthankars and Simple kewalis (all Arihants) become Siddha after nirvan (death). All Siddhas are equal in qualities.

Siddha

Both the Tirthankars and simple kewalis (all Arihants) destruct the remaining four Aghati karmas at the end of their current life. After their nirvan (death) all of them are known as Siddhas. They are totally free and enlightened. They are free from the birth and death cycle. They don't possess body. They don't feel pain and pleasure, or joy and grief. They live as a pure soul in an ever-lasting blissful condition at the top of the world (Lokakas) known as Moksh. The quality and attributes of all Siddhas are same. Nevertheless, they still maintain their distinctive identity and form.

Both Arihants and Siddhas are regarded as Gods of Jain religious faith. Arihats are ideal human beings and preach the Jain religious faith to the individuals after achieving Kewal-Gyan. After death they become Siddhas. All Siddhas are perfected souls, living eternally in a blissful state in Moksh.

In the Namok ar Mantra we pray to the Arihants (Tirthankar) first and the Siddhas second. Although the Siddhas are perfected souls, have destructed all (both Ghati and Aghati) Karmas, and are at the highest divine stage. While the Arihantas have destructed only four Ghati Karmas and are at a lower (thirteen gunasthan) divine stage.

Arihants (Tirthnkaras) after achieving Kewal-Gyan (after destructing four ghati karmas), establish the four fold order of Jain religious faith. They preach the Jain doctrine, ethics and behaviour. They explain the path of nirvana and the qualities of the perfected soul or Siddhas. Without the teachings of Arihantas we would not have known Siddhas or nirvana. For this reason we pray Arihantas first and Siddhas second.

DIMENSIONS OF GOD

Jainism believes that cosmos and all its substances are everlasting. All substances continually undergo changes. Former forms give way to new ones without loosing their own inherent qualities. Jains believe that the cosmos is without beginning or end. The cosmos did not start at any time and it will not end at any time. There is no need of some almighty to create or manage the affairs of the cosmos. The cosmos runs on its own accord by its own cosmic laws.

Jains believe that God did not create the cosmos. If God has created the cosmos, he has to have a craving to create. The craving makes God imperfect and he can't be imperfect. From another angle, if God carries out the task of creation and destruction without any objective then it becomes a game. If he carries out this work as a game, he has to be deemed a child. Thus, he could not have created the world. If he carries out all this work on account of his supreme grace he would have made all Jivas (souls) happy and he would have created things that would have given bliss to all. But we have 87% of the people of earth living in poverty and despair and only 13% people are well off. Thus, God must not be managing the cosmos. Since God is all-knowing, all-powerful, and devoid of cravings, and passions, He could not be interested in the matters of cosmos. Some claim that all creatures are God's images and we are all parts of Him?" If so, we should all have unlimited happiness, ideal perception, ideal knowledge and ideal behaviour. But it isn't so. Thus, we can't be a part of the God or his images. If We accept that God created the earth, he manages the earth and he decides who gets what, then countless questions are raised and we don't have judicious answers to these questions. Thus, it appeals to our common sense that God did not create the cosmos.

As per Jain belief, God has absolute knowledge. Thus, he reveals the necessary and real form of the cosmos. He revealed that the world is without a beginning or end. The cosmos does undergo continuous change. Production and disposal are always going on. Behind this timeless process there doesn't exist any plan or organization. The whole cosmos is self-regulated. For life forms Karmas play prominent role. Karma is the finest matter that our soul attracts established on our thought, speech and/or action. Bad Karma pollutes the inherent qualities of the soul. The bondage and deliverance of each person depends upon himself or herself. Every person experiences bliss or unhappiness according to his past Karma, his current destiny has been decided, and his future will be decided established on his current or past Karma.

Jains believe in different type of God. The God is Jin. The word Jin literally means "the Victor" or "the Liberator". One who has freed himself from the bondage of Karma by conquering raaga (attachment, deceit and greediness) & dvesha (aversion – anger and ego) is Jin. Bhagwan Mahavir was the last reformer of Jainism.

He should not be mistaken as the founding father of Jainism. We had first Tirthankar, Rushabha in the third era of this Avasarpini (regressive) half cycle (millions and millions years ago). Each time cycle has two half cycles, Utsarpini (progressive) and Avasarpini (regressive). There have been infinite time cycles before (time without beginning) and there will be infinite time cycles (without any end) in future. The word Tirthankar means one who lays down the divine order to cross over the corporeal sea of suffering. The remaining twenty three Tirthankars lived during the fourth era of the present Avasarpini. At present, we are in the fifth era. The basic truths of Jainism were therefore laid down long back.

DEITIES

Jains worship idols of Jins, Tirthankars, who are reverend as supreme beings but as the time passed by Jains also started worshipping many other deities, Yaksas and Yaksinis, in Jain temples.

They are not same as Jin, Arihant, or Tirthankars who have vanquished the inner passions while these deities (Yaksas and Yaksinis) are full of passions and are wandering through the cycles of births and death just like us. They are also called shashandevtas, gaurdian deities. They are heavenly beings of Vyantar group who have supernatural powers including changing capabilities of their form and size.

Jains believe that these Yaksas and Yaksinis were appointed by Indra to look after the well beings of Tirthankars. Thus, they were always found around Jins and that has reflected their presence in Jain temples also around the idols of Jins. They are found in pair of a male (yaksha) and a female (yakshini). Yaksa usually found on the right side of the Jin idol while yaksini on left side. In the earlier period they were regarded chiefly as devotees of Jin but as the time passed by, individuals started to worship them too.

Not all Yaksa are benevolent, because some can be malevolent. Just as some Yaksa paid homage to Bhagwan Mahavir and protectd him from some sufferings, Yaksa Sulpani troubled Bhagwan Mahavir in his mediation and inflicted much suffering and similar stories are available where yaksa troubled others too. The residential place (bhavana) of Yaksa is also known as chaitya or ayatana. It could be anywhere, outside the city, on the hill or a mountain, on the tree, by the water reservoir, at the gate of a city, or within a city in a house or a palace. The celebrated Yaksa Angulimala was living on the tree in the forest and when reformed for a better he had a place at the city gate.

The humans are opportunistic and since Jins would not reward no matter how sincerely one may worshiop them, Jains looked at yaksas and yaksanis for the immediate returns, and to self serve Jains gave them the places in their temples. Some Yaksa were and are known for lending fertility and wealth upon their devotes. Thus, they had become very popular and their idols had been placed in Jain temples and Jains worship them. Jains offer them different things in favour of boons for children, wealth or liberty from fear, illness or disease.

The earlier Holy Scriptures like the Sthanagansutra, Utradhyayansutra, Bhagwatisutra, Tattvarthsutra, Antagadasasaosutra, and Paumacariya have frequent references to the Yaksa. Their reference as Shasandevatas in the Harivamsapuran (783 AD.) made the beginning of this idea. Amongst all the yakshas, Manibhadra and Purnabadra yakshas and Bahuputrika yakshini have been the most favoured one. Manibhadra and Purnabadra yakshas are cited a chief of demigods, Manibhadra of

Northern horde and Purnabadra of Southern horde. Bahuputrika (having many sons) is named as one of the queen of Manibhadra. Harivamsapuran also explains the capability of yakshas and yakshnins to mollify the injurious power of rogas, grahas, raksasas, bhutas and pisachas.

The individuals also believed that they bestow favours to those who worship them and because of that became more popular then Jins for some. Thus, the individuals started worshipping them for materialstic cravings which could not be fulfilled by the worship of Vitaraga Jin. Due to this, between tenth and thirteenth centuries AD. yaksha Saarvanubhuti, or Sarvahna and yakshini Cakreshvari, Ambika, Padmavati, and Jvalamalini became so popular that independent cults developed around them. Different temples were erected just to worship them and you can see that even now.

The Jain works from sixth to the tenth century A. D. mention only some of the iconographic features of Yaksharaja (Sarvahna or Sarvanubhuti) and Dharanendra Yaksha and Cakreshvari, Ambika, Padmavati, Yakshi.

The list of twenty-four Yaksa-Yaksi pairs was finalized in about eight-ninth century AD. as found in Kahavali, Tiloyapannatti, and Pravacanasaroddhara while their independent iconographic forms were standarized in eleventh - twelfth century AD. as cited in the Nirvankalika, the Trisastisalakapurusacaritra, the Pratisthasara-samgraha, Pratisthasaroddhara, the Pratisthatilaka and acaradinakara and a number of other texts. Nevertheless, we find much difference between Shvetambar and Digambar traditions as to the names and iconographic features of Yaksas and Yaksis. The names and the iconographic features of the bulk of the Yaksas and Yaksis bear the influence of the Brahminical and Buddhist Gods and Goddesses. The Jains seem to have adopted either the names or the distinct iconographic features, sometimes both, in such cases two.

The original Agamas don't mention about the Jin idol and idol worship, even then for last 2500 years Jains have constructed thousands of excellent temples at tremendous cost and have installed idols to respect the Tithankars. Thus the concept of idol and idol worship, even that of the Jins, was anathema to the very spirit and words of the Jins. But now by erecting and worshipping Yaksas and Yaksinis, and asking for materialistic gains from them, Jains are distracted from divine path and digging their own graveyard to false belief (Mithyatva). Jainism objective is to be free from materialistic attachment.

For a moment even if we look at the materialistic gain by their worship then everybody who worships should get it but that doesn't happen. Thus, one lives in mithyatva. One should not forget that if at all materialistic gain is achieved then that is from maturation of one is own shubh (good karmas). Somadeva might have felt that these sasana-devatas may replace ratherr than being complementary to the Jins as the object of worship cautioned; anyone who worship them equal to Jin is heading downwards. Asadhara declares that an individual with true insight would never worship Yaksas even when beset with great calamities. Because Jains believe that our calamities are our own doing and we should bare down such calamities with calmness to stop the whirlpool of reaction which would do nothing but will bring more calamities. In conclusion in Jainism, the guidlines are set which tell us what is right and wrong, but it is upto every person to decide which idles to worship to and which ones we should just admire.

Yakshas and Yakshanis

Chakreshware Devi: She is the dedicated attendant deity of Bhagwan Adinath (Bhagwan Rishabh Dev). She is also called by another name i.e. Apratichakra. The colour of this Goddess is golden. Her Vehicle is the eagle. She has eight arms. In her four right hands she holds the blessing mudra, arrow, rope and wheel. In her four left hands she holds the rein, the bow, the protective weapon of Indra and the wheel.

Ambika Devi: She is the dedicated deity of Bhagwan Neminath the 22nd Tirthankar. She is also called Ambai Amba and Amra Kushmandini. Her colour is golden and the lion is her vehicle. She has four arms. In her two right hands she carries a mango and in the other a branch of a mango tree. In her one left hand she carries a rein and in the other she hasher two sons.

Padmavati Devi: She is the dedicated deity of Bhagwan Parshvanath, the 23rd Tirthankar. Her colour is golden and her vehicle is the snake with a cock's head. She has four arms and her two right hands hold a lotus and a rosary. The two left hands hold a fruit and a rein.

Saraswati Devi: Saraswati, the Goddess of knowledge, is regarded to be the source of all learning. This divine energy is the source of divine light, remover of all ignorance and promoter of all knowledge. She is respected and adored by all faiths, worldly persons and saints. She has four arms, one holding a text, the other a rosary and two hands holding a musical instrument Veena. Her seat is a lotus and the peacock is her vehicle representing equanimity in prosperity. In some places it is cited that the swan is her vehicle.

Lakshmi Devi: Goddess Lakshmi represents wealth. People worship her as the Goddess of wealth, power, money etc. In the upper two hands, she is holding a lotus with an elephant, in the lower right hand a rosary and in the lower left hand a pot.

Manibhadra Dev: Shri Manibhadra is originally a yaksha, worshipped by Indian masses from very old times and his introduction in Jainworship is only a later adaptation. It is an image of six armed yaksha with an elephant as his vehicle.

Ghantakarna Veer: This deity is worshipped for protection and for driving away the evil influence created by lower types of negative energy. His arrow indicates penetration of evil forces. The bow gives forceful momentum to the arrow. His symbol is the bell that resounds to create propitious sounds in the atmosphere. Sometimes individuals who are not aware of the facts call him by error Ghantakarna Bhagwan Mahavir that creates confusion between Bhagwan Mahavir and Ghantakarna Veer. He is not connected to Bhagwan Mahavir in any way.

Nakoda Bhairava: This is the tutelary deity of Bhairava. This deity is usually found near the entrance of the temple. Individuals from far and near, visit the shrine and make offerings to the deity on fulfilment of their materialistic cravings. It is the positive force around the temple.

Bhomiyaji: This deity is in the shape of a mountain. It is the natural positive energy of the mountain Sametshikharji. This energy inspires and guides the believer and the traveller.

PHILOSOPHY OF GOD

The Jain morality and ethics are embedded in its metaphysics and its usefulness towards the soteriological aim of nirvana. Jain ethics germinated out of the rules for the monks which are capsuled in the mahavratas or the five great vows which we have discussed above.

The ethics are administered not only through the instrumentality of physical actions, but also through oral action and thoughts. Hence, non-violence has to be observed through mind, speech and body. The other rules of the monks and laity are deduced from these five key vows. Jainism doesn't call forth the fear of God as an explanation for ethical behaviour. Observance of the ethical code is not necessary merely because it is a commandment of a God or any other Supreme Being. Neither, is its observance necessary just because it is conducive to general welfare of the state or the community. While it is true that in Jainism ethical and religious injunctions were founded as law by Arhats, who have attained perfection through their supreme ethical efforts, their obedience is just not to please a God. It is because the life of the Arhats has presented that such commandments were conducive to Arhat's own welfare, helping him to achieve divine victory. Just as Arhats attained Moksh or nirvana by observing the ethical code, so can anyone, who abides by this path.

MESSENGERS OF GOD

The idea of God is distinctive in Jains. This distinctive idea also has an impact on the meaning of prayer, bhakti and worship which attach to pure soul and obscure its natural qualities. Pure soul's natural qualities include nirvana and happiness. Based on the type and amount of karma, a soul takes a body form and has four minor categories of karma with it which define the body, life span, social standing, pain and pleasure. The cycle of birth/death continues until the removal of all Ghati Karma. The path of removal of karma is the Jain path of purification or divine progress which ultimately leads to perfection or Godhood.

Jains don't believe in God taking part in creation, destruction, or maintenance of the cosmos. Also, it doesn't believe in avatar of God. Jainism is not Atheism or "Nastika-Darshan" as it is sometimes labelled. Jains believe in God - as the Supreme State of Beings. If western semitic sense of "Theism" is taken, requiring creation theory, then Jains may be considered an atheism but further explanation must be provided. It follows that Jains don't believe in prophets as Creator God's messengers. God is not involved in providing materialistic things to the asking devotee. Therefore, the God in Jains may be loosely equated to the Christian or Hindu God (not demigods) minus creation.

Jains emphasizes potency of karma as the fundamental principle of Samsara (relative world) resembling Purva Mimamsa. It also emphasizes that each personal soul is a potential Parmatman (all-knowing ultimate state) resembling Uttar Mimamsa, i.e. Vedanta.

Godhood is the perfected state of soul and supreme manifestation of human excellence. Godhood is latent in common persons (souls) who become God upon removal of karma by their own effort. Upon total removal of all four categories of Ghati Karma, the perfected human being becomes Arihanta God. At this state, the God remains human and has ideal knowledge (without bounds of time and space). When the life span of this last body form is completed, soul is said to reach Nirvana or Moksh and is referred to as Siddha God. This state of soul is the ultimate and linked with it are ideal power and happiness.

Tirthankar

Arihant God is also called Jin, the word from which the word "Jain" has been derived. The words Arihanta and Jin mean the victor of soul's inner enemies of attachment and aversion. Becoming Arihanta, Jin or Kewali, removing of four Ghati Karma, and achieving Kewal-Gyan (Nirvana) are all equivalent. A lot of souls have become Arihanta. A limited number of Arihanta Gods become Tirthankars, who reestablish religious order (consisting of male and female monks and lay devotees) and become well known. Most recent Tirthankar Bhagwan was Bhagwan Mahavir (not born as a God or an avatar of God, not a founding father of Jainism). Like other Arihanta Gods, Tirthankar Gods reach Siddhahood upon completion of life-span as a human. All Arihanta souls are equal in the qualities of soul. To be an all known (knowledgable) human, one must make divine progress to remove all Ghati Karma and become Arihanta. Only through Arihanta can the truth be revealed about issues unknown to humans.

For instance, Bhagwan Mahavir, after becoming a Tirthankar, could tell about prior Tirthankars and future Tirthankars. Other souls became Arihanta and Siddha Gods, while Bhagwan Mahavir was Tirthankar himself. Bhagwan Bahubali, whose tall monolith statue is quite celebrated, was an Arihanta and the son of Tirthankar Rishabnath-Adinath.

Prior to Bhagwan Mahavir, (twenty-fourth of recent era), Parshvanath (twenty-third Tirthankar), Arishta Neminath (twenty-second Tirthankar, are said to be cousins and contemporary of Shri Krishna), Naminath (said to be a contemporary of Shri Rama) and other Tirthankars have been known. First Tirthankar of recent era. Rshbhnath is cited in the early vedas. The lives and teachings of Bhagwan Parshvanath (about 850 BC.) and Bhagwan Bhagwan Mahavir are historical facts and prior Tirthankars are known through literary accounts. All Tirthankars teach the same tenets of Jain Dharma through ahimsa, at different times and circumstances. At the current time, there are no Tirthankars or common Arihanta in our region (Bharat-Kshetra) of the cosmos. Nevertheless, in another region (Mahavideh Kshetra) there are twenty Tirthankars. The first present Tirthankar's name is Shri Simandhar Swami.

God has no cravings or attachments and loves all souls equally. Therefore, a Tirthankar is unaffected by the kind or mean actions to him/her by surrounding beings. God doesn't participate in performing miracles for the devotee to fulfil materialistic cravings. Worship, prayer, and rites are for the devotee's self-purification and divine aspirations. The praise of God's qualities and remembering of Tirthankar's life are for inspiration. God's idol is always in the meditation posture and without garments, ornaments or weapons. Therefore, the idol represents purity and Godhood.

NIRVANA

Nirvana in Jainism means final release from the karmic bondage. When an enlightened human, such as, an Arhat or a Tirthankar extinguishes his remaining aghatiya karmas and therefore ends his corporeal existence, it is called enlightenment. Technically, the death of an Arhat is called enlightenment of Arhat, as he has ended his wordly existence and achieved nirvana. Moksh, that is to say, deliverance follows enlightenment. An Arhat becomes a siddha, the enlightened one, after achieving enlightenment. Nevertheless, the word nirvana is often used to mean Moksh, as well. Hence nirvana means; Death of an Arhat, who becomes enlightened thereafter, and Moksh.

REFERENCES

Amar, Muni: *Jainatva ki Jhanki, Sanmati Grantharatnamala No. 12*, Sanmati Gyanpeeth, Seventh Edition, Agra, 1987.

Avasyaka-sutra: Editor Madhukar Muni, Jinagama Granthamala, No.24 Agama Prakashan Samiti, Byavar, First Edition, 1985.

Basham, A.L.: *Post-script, attached to the article on Hinduism in Cultural History of India*, Oxford University Press.

Bhagavati (Vyakhyaprajnapti) in Anga-sutrani II: Editor Yuvacarya Mahaprajna, Jaina Vishvabharati, Ladnum, First Edition, 1974.

Bhattacharya, N.N.: *Jain Philosophy, Historical Outline.* Munshiram Manoharlal, New Delhi, 1976.

Einstein Albert: *Ideas and Opinions*, Bonanza Books, No.9.

Ferfusson, J.: *History of Indian and Eastern Architecture*, London.

Fischer, E., & Jain, J.: *Art and Rituals, 2500 Years of Jainism in India*, Sterling Publishers, New Delhi, 1977.

Garbe, R.: *Encyclopaedia of Religion and Ethics*, T. & T. Clark, 38 George Street, New York, 1920.

Ghosh, A.: *Jaina Arts and Architecture*, New Delhi, 1974.

Glassenapp, H.V: *Doctrine of Karman in Jaina Philosophy*, Bombay, 1942.

Jain, Muni Uttam Kamal: *Jain Sects and Sub-sects*, New Delhi, 1975.

James, William: *Principles of Psychology, Vol. I*, Macmillan & Co., London, 1918.

Jindal, K.B: *The prefaces*, Calcutta, 1958.

Kalghatagi, T.G.: *Jaina View of Life*, Sholapur, 1969.

Kapadia, H.R.: *Jaina Religion and Literature*, Lahore, 1944.

Kapashi, V.J.: *In Search of the Ultimate*, V.K. Publications, Harrow, 1984.

Radhakrishnan. S.: *Indian Philosophy. 2nd.ed, 2 vols*, Allen and Unwin, London, 1929,1931.

Rosenfield, C.: *Gurudev Shree Chitrabhanu, a Man with a Vision*, New Jain Meditation Intemational Center, York, 1981.

Roy Chowdhari, P.C.: *Jainism in Bihar*, Patna, 1956.

Roy, A.K.: *History of the Jains*, Gitanjali Publishing House, New Delhi, 1984.

Schubring, W.: *The Doctrine of the Jains*, Motilal Banarsidass, Delhi, 1962.

Upadhye, A.N.: *Lord Mahavira and his Teachings. 2nd. Ed*, Shree Vallabhsuri Smarak Nidhi, Bombay,1983.

Uttaradhyayana-sutra: Editor Madhukara Muni, Jinagama Granthamala No. 19, Agama Prakashan Samiti, Byavara, First Edition, 1984.

Williams. R.: *Jaina Yoga*, Motilal Banarsidass, Delhi, 1983.

Winternitz, M.: *The Jainas in the History of Indian Literature*, Ahmedabad, 1946.

5

Main Figures

The Jains formulated their own history, the Deeds of the 63 Illustrious Men (the Universal History). The most prominent figures in this history are the 24 Tirthankars, perfected human beings who appear from time to time to preach and embody the faith. Other prominent figures in the history are from the Hindu custom, most notably Krishna—regarded by the Jains as a cousin of the 22nd Tirthankar, Arishtanemi—and the hero Rama, who is treated as a pious, nonviolent Jain. By incorporating yet redefining such prominent Hindu figures, the Jains were able to both remain part of and separate from the surrounding Hindu world.

MAIN FIGURES IN EARLY PERIOD

Bhagwan Rishabh Dev In Jainism, Bhagwan Rishabh Dev or Adinath (other names used: Richabh, Richabhanath, Rushabh, Rushabhdev, Adinath or Adishwar; Sanskrit [cabha meaning best, most excellent) was the first of the 24 Tirthankar.

As per Jain philosophy, Bhagwan Rishabh Dev was the first Tirthankar of the current age Avasarpini. Because of this, he had the name of Adinath - the first lord. He became a Siddha, an enlightened soul which has destructed all of its karma.

Bhagwan Rishabh Dev was born to Emperor Nabhi Raja and Queen Marudevi at Ayodhya in the Ikshvaku clan. As per Jain philosophy, Rishabh existed before civilization developed. He taught people agriculture, tending of animals, cooking, and more. He had one hundred and one sons.

His eldest son - Bharat - was a chakravarti Emperor - the vanquisher of the known world. In the later part of his life he retired to become an ascetic and achieved Moksh. Since he became a siddha, he is occasionally worshipped. As per Jain philosophy, India was named Bharata-varsha or Bharata after him.

His second son was Bahubali, whose statue stands at Shravanabelagola, Karnataka and also at Karkala. Marudevi mother of adinath was the first person to attain Moksh - even before Rishabh himself. Rishabh's grandson Marichi's soul later became Bhagwan Mahavir. He achieved Kewal-Gyan or infinite knowledge at Palitana and achieved nirvana or Moksh at Ashtapad Mountain in Himalayas.

Bhagwan Rishabh Dev has been cited in the Hindu text of the Bhagavatha-Puran as an incarnation of Vishnu. He is cited in all the Vishnu/ Shiv Purans, and also in some other texts.

As per Bhagavata, he was born to show the individuals of this world the path of redemption. It was he who advised the individuals to follow the path of timeless happiness, instead of indulging in a life of corporeal delights and enjoyment. He is the founding father and promoter of Sramanic culture. The vedas and Purans, contain many references to Bhagwan Rishabh Dev.

As per Bhagvata Puran: In the womb of Merudevi, wife of Nabhi, Rishaba had his eighth incarnation. He showed himself in a form that is to be worshipped by all Shramanas.Bhagavata mentions body his only belonging, wearing the sky, wearing the wind.

Ajitnath

Ajitnatha was the second Jain Tirthankar of the current age - Avasarpini. As per Jain philosophy, he became a siddha, an enlightened soul which has destructed all of its karma.The soul that became Bhagwan Ajitnath, in its earlier avatar, was the great Emperor Vimalvahan of Susima city in Mahavideh area. He led a pious life in spite of the available princely grandeur. At an appropriate time, he became an ascetic under Arindam Suri.

Ajitnatha was born to Emperor Jitashatru Raja and Queen Vijaya at Ayodhya in the Ikshvaku clan.Queen Vijaya Devi saw fourteen propitious dreams. Vaijayanti, the wife of Emperor Jitshatru's younger brother, Sumitra, also saw the same fourteen dreams. This was a queer coincidence. When the augers were consulted they informed that Vijaya Devi will give birth to a Tirthankar and Vaijayanti to a Chakravarti -Emperor.

During the period of the queen's pregnancy, the influence of Emperor Jitshatru enhanced to an extent that even the enemy kingdoms sought and negotiated friendly treaties with him. It became a common practice to say Emperor Jitshatru is invincible, Ajit.

The queen gave birth to a son on the eighth day of the bright half of the month of Magh. Inspired by the popular lore, the Emperor named the new born as the Ajit. The same night vaijayanti also gave birth to a son who was named Sagar. Then both the princes came of age they were married. Time passed with the fusion of bliss.

When Emperor Jitshatru became old and wanted to devote the last part his life to divine pursuit, he called his younger brother and asked him to take over the throne. Sumitra had no craving for the kingdom, he too wanted to become an ascetic. Both the princes were called and offered the kingdom. Ajit Kumar was a naturally detached person since childhood, and so he too declined. At last prince Sagar ascended the throne.

Ajit Kumar became an ascetic in his youth and went into remote and dense forests for his meditation and penance. His individuality and the intensity of his lofty practices cast a pacifying influence all around. Natural enemies in the animal kingdom, like lion and cow, wolf and deer, snake and mongoose used to come and sit around him serenely.

After a twelve year period of profound meditation and other divine practices achieved nirvana on the eleventh day of the bright half of the month of Paush. The Gods created the divine pavilion and Bhagawan Ajitnath gave his eloquent and magnetic discourses. Thousands of individuals accepted the path of renunciation.

Emperor Sagar, during this period, vanquished the six continents and became Chakravarti. Emperor Meghvahan and Vidyadhar Bhim, the ruler of the island of Rakshasas, demons, were the illustrious contemporaries of Emperor Sagar. Once they went to a discourse of Bhagwan Ajitnath. There, Vidyadhar Bhim was drawn towards divine life. He became so detached that he gave his kingdom including the celebrated cities of Lanka and Patal Lanka to Emperor Meghvahan. He also gave all his knowledge and miraculous powers to Meghvahan. Besides this he gave a divine necklace of nine large and shining beads. Meghvahan was the first Emperor of the Rakshas clan in which the famous Emperor Ravana was born.

Emperor Sagar had thousands of queens and sixty thousand sons. Eldest amongst them was Janhu Kumar. Once all the princes went for an outing. When they arrived at the base of Astapad hills, they dug up large ditches and canals. In their youthful abandon they flooded these canals with the water of river Ganges. This flash flood inundated the houses and villages of the lower Gods known as Nag Kumars. The Emperor of these Gods, Jwalanprabh came and tried to stop them in vain. The unruly princes were intoxicated with the regal power. At last Jwalanprabh lost his temper and turned all the sixty thousand princes to ashes.

This sudden death of all his sons was a traumatic experience for Emperor Sagar. He handed over the empire to his eldest grandson, Bhagirath, and took Diksha from Bhagwan Ajitnath.

When his last moments were nearing, Bhagwan Ajitnath went Sammetshikhar. With one thousand other monks, he commenced his final meditation. He achieved Nirvana on the fifth day of the bright half of the month of Chaitra.

The 2nd Jain Tirthankar Ajitanatha,was born in Ayodhya. The Yajurveda mentions the name of Ajitanatha, but the meaning is not clear. His younger brother as per Jain traditions was Sagara who became the second Chakravarti. He is known from the traditions of both Hinduism and Jainism as found in their respective Hindu Holy Scriptures Purans.

Sambhavnath

Sambhavanath was the third Jain Tirthankar of the current age - Avasarpini. As per Jain philosophy, he became a siddha, an enlightened soul which has destructed all of its karma. Sambhavnath was born to Emperor Jitari Raja and Queen Saina Rani at Sravasthi in the Ikshvaku clan. His birth date was the fourteenth day of the Margshrsha shukla month of the Hindu calendar. A long time after the Nirvana of Bhagwan Ajitnath, the city of Kshempuri in the Airavat area of Mahavideh was ruled by Emperor Vipulvahan. He was a soft hearted and compassionate ruler who loved and cared for his subjects.

Once when there was a devastating draught and the population was deprived even of a few drops of water, the Emperor opened his grain yards for the public, his kitchen for the monks and ascetics and his treasury for the import of food grains. He instructed the caretaker of his individual kitchen that the doors of his kitchen should be open to all and sundry. All guests should be given priority over himself. Whatever little is left should be served to him. If nothing is left he would be contented with the pleasure of serving his guests. During the drought there were many occasions when the Emperor remained unfed and thirsty.

As a consequence of this sublime feeling of compassion, Vipulvahan acquired distinctive purity of soul and earned the Trithankr-nam-and-gotra-karma. Though, after the drought normalcy returned, the torture of the living world by the nature left a mark on Vipulvahan's psyche. One day while he was standing on the roof top he witnessed dense rain clouds being scattered by wind. A feeling of intense detachment grew in him. He handed over his kingdom to his son and took Diksha from Svayamprabh Suri. After completing his age he reincarnated in the Anat dimension of Gods.

From the Anat dimension, the being that was Vipulvahan descended into the womb of Queen Sena Devi, wife of Emperor Jitari of Shravasti. While this being was still in the mother's womb there were sufficient rains and abundant crop. One day when the Emperor and queen were happily watching the lush green vegetation all around, from their roof top, the Emperor said, This time even the waste-land is filled with grain crop. It seems that all this that is impossible, has been made possible, Sambhav due to the propitious influence of the pious soul you carry in your womb. We shall call our son- Sambhav.

On the fourteenth day of the bright half of the month of Margshrish, the queen gave birth to a healthy son and he was ceremoniously named Sambhav Kumar. The little prince grew up in royal comfort but he hardly ever took more than cursory interest in the luxurious life style. At the appropriate age Sambhav Kumar was married and coronated. After a long and quit reign he became an ascetic on the fifteenth day of the bright half of the month of Margshrish. After a fourteen year period of divine practices, he achieved nirvana. Arhat Sambhavnath gave his first discourse on the ephemeral nature of the ordinary existence. For a long period he worked for the spread of religion. He got Nirvana on the fifth day of the bright half of the month of Chaitra.

Abhinandannatha

Abhinandannatha or Abhinandan Swami was the fourth Tirthankar of the current age -Avasarpini. As per Jain philosophy, he became a siddha, an enlightened soul which has destructed all of its karma.

Abhinandannath was born to Emperor Sanvara Raja and Queen Sidharta Rani at Ayodhya in the Ikshvaku clan. His birth date was the second day of the Magh shukla month of the Hindu calendar. Mahabal was the Emperor of Ratnasanchay or Mangalavati town in Purvavideh. Though an Emperor, he was a simple and humble person. When someone criticized him he would humbly said you are my true well-wisher and a friend who helps my progress by pointing out my faults. When a feeling of detachment grew in him, he found an opportunate moment and took Diksha from Vimal Suri. Due to his simplicity and humility he became a very popular and ideal Sharman in his group. It is said that as a consequence of this rare disposition and profound mediational practices he purified his soul to an extent that he acquired the Tirthankar-nam-and-gotra-karma. Completing his age, he reincarnated as a God in the Vijay dimension.

When the being that was Mahaval left the Vijay dimension, he descended into the womb of queen Siddharth, wife of Emperor Samvar of Ayodhya. As a consequence of the simplicity of attitude inherited from the earlier birth, the soul in the womb of the queen had a soothing and pacifying influence on the outer world. The people of the kingdom were suddenly filled with the feelings of humility and fraternity. Irrespective of age, caste, creed and status every one started greeting and honouring others. Politeness and polished manners became the thing in vogue. The augurs and other scholars confirmed that as the aura of a pious soul influences all the individuals around, the effusion of politeness was caused by the soul in the womb.

The queen gave birth to the future Tirthankar on the second day of the bright half of the month of Magh. As the influence of this soul was evident in the overt mutual greetings, the Emperor named his son as Abhinandan, greeting.

As time passed Abhinandan lead normal ordinary life with least indulgence. He ascended the throne when his father became an ascetic. After a long and quit reign, he became an ascetic and indulged in rigorous penance and lofty divine practices. He achieved nirvana on the fourteenth day of the dark half of the month of Paush. For a long period Bhagwan Abhinandan moved around to show the right path to millions of beings. On the eighth day of the bright half of the month of Vaishakah he achieved Nirvana at Sammetshikhar.

Sumatinatha

Sumatinatha was the fifth Jain Tirthankar of the current age, Avasarpini. As per Jain philosophy, he became a siddha, an enlightened soul which has destructed all of its karma.

Sumatinath was born to Emperor Megh Raja and Queen Mangala Rani at Ayodhya in the Ikshvaku clan. His birth date was the eighth day of the Vaishakh shukla month of the Hindu calendar Vijayasen was the Emperor of Shankhpur town in the Purva Mahavideh area. He had a son named Purushasimha. While he had gone for a walk in the garden one day, the prince listened to the discourse of Acharya Vinayanandan Dev. He became detached and a turned ascetic. Due to vigorous penance and higher divine practices, he earned the Tirthankar-nam-and-gotra-karma. Completing his age, he reincarnated as a God in the Vijayant dimension.

From Vijayant dimension, the soul that was Purushasimha descended into the womb of queen Mangalavati/Sumangala, wife of Emperor Megh of Ayodhya. The news of the queen being pregnant made the atmosphere of Ayodyha live with bliss and joy.

One day two women and a little boy came to the Emperor's court to seek justice. One of the women put forth her case before the Emperor; we both are wives of a rich seafaring merchant. Our husband has left for his heavenly abode leaving behind us two, a son, and heaps of wealth. The child truly belongs to me but this second wife of the merchant claims to be her. This is nothing but a conspiracy to grab the wealth that would be inherited by the child. Save me, I seek my son and justice from you.

The story narrated by the other woman was also the same. Shouting charges and counter charges at each other, both the women claimed the possession of the child. The child could not indicate his true mother as he had got equal affection from both. As the boy was born in some remote place, there was no eye witness available.

The Emperor was in a quandary. Even after a lot of probing and weighing the evidence he could not solve the problem. Any ill conceived solution could end up in doing injustice to the innocent. The Emperor and his ministers all could end up in doing injustice to the innocent. The Emperor and his ministers all were in a fix. The night was nearing and the Emperor was getting late for his dinner. He adjourned the case and went into the palace for dinner.

The queen asked him why he was late for dinner that day. The Emperor narrated the case of the two women and their child and told that no one is able to say firmly, which one of the women is the real mother of the child and which one is the pretender.

The queen told that let a woman solve the problems of women. Send the case to me and allow me to resolve the issue. Next morning the queen herself came to the Emperor's court. Both the women and their son were produced before the queen. There was no obvious indication in the behaviour and disposition of the two women that could give any sign of the genuineness of one. All of a sudden, the queen got an insight and she said, this enigma has no simple solution. There is one object and two claimants. The object, being an individual, can't be split into two. Under the circumstances the only solution I can think of is to keep the matter pending. I carry a pious soul in my womb. Let us wait till it is born and is ready to resolve this issue. During the period of waiting, let the son and the property of the deceased be taken into the custody of the state. Till then the claimants may wait.

Hearing this, one of the claimants readily accepted the arrangement but the other started weeping. In a choked voice she cried, Please do not separate me from my son. I will not be able to survive without my son for such a long period, I withdraw my claim. Let the other woman take the child and also all the possessions of my husband. My only submission is that I may be allowed to at least meet the child. I will be contented with that only.

The queen recognized the pain and concern of a mother's heart. She gave her judgment; the woman who immediately agreed to my proposal is the impostor. Her attachment is not to the child but to the wealth. She may be imprisoned. The one who wants to surrender her claim is the real mother. The child and the wealth may be given to her with all honours.

Everyone present in the assembly was dumbstruck by this witty method of judgment. The impostor pleaded guilty and submitted to be pardoned. On the eighth day of the bright half of the month of Vaishakh, the queen gave birth to a son. A wave of peace and goodwill swept the whole world. Appreciating the fact that the marked improvement in wisdom and sense of judgment during the pregnancy was the influence of the presence of the illustrious and pious soul, Emperor Megh named the new born as-Sumati wisdom or right thinking.

When he became a young man, Sumati Kumar was married, and in due course inherited the kingdom. Emperor Megh became an ascetic. After a long and quit reign Sumatinath, too, became an ascetic. He achieved nirvana under a Priyangu tree on the eleventh day of the bright half of the month of Chaitra. He founded the four pronged religious ford and became a Tirthankar. On the ninth day of the bright half of the month of Chaitra he got Nirvana at Sammetshikhar.

Padmaprabha

Padmaprabha was the sixth Jain Tirthankar of the current age, Avsarpini. As per Jain philosophy, he became a siddha - an enlightened soul which has destructed all of its karma.

Padmaprabha, also known as Padhmaprabhu swami was born to Emperor Shridhar Raja and Queen Susimadevi at Koushambi in the Ikshvaku clan. His birth date was the twelfth day of the Kartik Krishna month of the Hindu calendar. Maharaj Aparajit ruled over Susima town in the Purvavideh area. He was a simple and religious person. He got detached after listening to the discourse of an Arhat and took Diksha from Acharya Pihitashrava. Due to long divine practices he earned Tirthankar-nam-and-gotra-karma. Completing his age, he reincarnated as a God in the Graiveyak dimension.

From the dimension of Gods, the being that was Aparajit descended into the womb of queen Susima, wife of the Emperor Kaushambi. One day queen Susima had a craving to sleep on a bed made up of lotus flowers. As this was a craving of a pregnant mother, the Gods made arrangements for its fulfillment. On the twelfth day of the dark half of the month of Kartik the queen gave birth to a son. The new born had a soft pink glow like lotus flowers. The Emperor named him as Padmaprabh.

In due course the prince became young and was married. When his father left for divine practices, Padmaprabh ascended the throne. After a long and successful reign, when through his three fold knowledge he knew that the right moment has come, he became an ascetic. After six months of divine practices, on the full moon day of the month of Chaitra he achieved nirvana under a banyan tree. Propagating right religious faith for a long time, Bhagwan Padmaprabh wandered around and at last arrived at Sammetshikhar. He got Nirvana on the eleventh day of the dark half of the month of Margshirsh.

Suparshavnatha

Suparshvanath was the seventh Jain Tirthankar of the current age, Avasarpini. As per Jain philosophy, he became a siddha, an enlightened soul which has destructed all of its karma.

Suparshvnath was born to Emperor Prathisth Raja and Queen Prithvidevi at Banaras in the Ikshvaku clan. His birth date was the twelfth day of the Jayesth shukla month of the Hindu calendar.

There are some legends about the all the Jain Tirthankars which may contain some historical matter. In the Mahavagga, there is a mention of a Jain temple of Bhagwan Suparsva, the seventh Tirthankar situated at Rajagrih of Bihar state of India in the time of Bhagwan Buddha. At Mathura, there is an old stupa of the Jains with the inscription of 157 AD. This inscription records that an image of the Tirthankar Aranath was set up at the stupa built by the Gods.Therefore, in 157 AD., this stupa was so old that it was regarded as the work of the Gods. It was probably, thus, erected several centuries before the Christian era. The later authors give us some information about this stupa.

Jinprabha in the Tirtha Kalpa, a work of the 14th century established on ancient materials mentions that the stupa originally of gold was erected in honour of the 7th Jain Tirthankar Suparsvanatha by the Kubera for two Jain Saints named Acharya Dharmaruchi and Dharmaghosh. In the time of 23rd Jain Tirthankar Parsvanatha, the golden stupa was enclosed in bricks and a stone temple was built outside. Even Somadeva, the author of the Yasastilaka who is nearly four hundred years earlier than Jinaprabha refers to it as built by Gods.From this type of legendary account, it seems that there was the worship of Suparsvanatha several centuries before the Christian era.

When Suparshva became young he was married and later ascended the throne. He ably conducted the affairs of he state and looked after the well being of his individuals. One day while he was enjoying the nature sitting at the roof top, he observed the falling of leaves and wilting of flowers. Suddenly he became aware of the transient nature of life. This gave a rising to the feeling of detachment and craving for divine upliftment. He gave his kingdom to his son and became an ascetic. After nine months of disciplined practices he became knowledgable on the sixth day of the dark half of the month of Phalgun. For a long period he worked for the spread of right knowledge. He got enlightened on the seventh day of the bright half of his month of Palgun at Sammetshikhar.

Chandraprabha

Chandraprabha was the eighth Jain Tirthankar of the current age,Avasarpini. As per Jain philosophy, he became a siddha, an enlightened soul which has destructed all of its karma.

Chandraprabha (also known as Chandraprabhu Swami) was born to Emperor Mahasen Raja and Queen Lakshmana Devi at Chandrapuri in the Ikshvaku clan. His birth date was the twelfth day of the Posh Krishna month of the Hindu calendar. In his birth as Emperor Padma of Mangalavati town of Dhatkikhand, the being that was to become Bhagwan Chandraprabh earned Tirthankar-nam-and-gotra-karma. Spending a life time as a God in Anuttar Vijay dimension he descended into the womb of queen Lakshmana, wife of Emperor Mahasen of Chandranana town.

Chandraprabh was apathetic towards the ordinary delights and princely grandeur. After he ascended the throne his reign was short lived. He became an ascetic in the prime of his youth and just after three months of acute divine practices he became knowledgable. For a considerably long period he proceeded to enlighten the people and spread the true religious faith. When his end approached he went to Sammetshikhar and after a month of long fasting and meditation got enlightened.

Pushpadanta

Pushpadanta, also known as Suvidhinath, was the ninth Jain Tirthankar of the current age,Avasarpini. As per Jain philosophy, he became a siddha, an enlightened soul which has destructed all of its karma.

Pushpadanta was born to Emperor Sugreev Raja and Queen Rama Rani at Kakandi in the Ikshvaku clan. His birth date was the fifth day of the Margshrsha Krishna month of the Hindu calendar. In the tradition started by Bhagwan Rishabh Dev the ninth Tirthankar re-founded the four pronged religious ford was Bhagwan Suvidhinath During his earlier avatar as Emperor Mahapadma of Pushkalvati Vijay purified his soul to he extant of earning Tirthankar-nam-and-gotra-karma. He took birth in the Vijayant dimension of Gods and from there he descended into the womb of queen Rama Devi, wife of Emperor Sugriva of Kakandi town.

During the period of pregnancy queen Rama developed a strange capacity to develop processes for doing even the most difficult of tasks. Everyone got astonished at her skill. When the child was born the Emperor accordingly named him as Suvidhi, correct procedure. During the teething period of the child the mother got a craving for playing with flowers. As such, he was also popularly known as Pushpadant, flower-tooth.

Sheetalnath

Sheetalnath was the tenth Jain Tirthankar of the current age, Avasarpini. As per Jain philosophy, he became a siddha, an enlightened soul which has destructed all of its karma.

Sheetalnath was born to Emperor Dradhrath Raja and Queen Nanda Rani at Bhaddilpur in the Ikshvaku clan. His birth date was the twelfth day of the Magh Krishna month of the Hindu calendar. The being that was to be Bhagwan Sheetalnath, in his former but one birth was the Emperor of Susima town in the Pushkarvar Island. His name was Padmottar. When his son reached adulthood the religious Emperor gave his kingdom to the son and took Diksha from Tristadha Muni. Vigorous divine practices and worship of the pious states as cited in the Holy Scriptures resulted in his acquiring the Tirthankar-nam-and-gotra-karma. Completing his age he reincarnated as the Emperor of the Pranat dimension of Gods.

Sheetalnath was born on the twelfth day of the dark half of the month Magh. When he grew older he married at the request of his parents.

At proper time, Emperor Dridhrath coronated him and took Diksha. After a long and successful reign Sheetalnath left his home and became an ascetic. He achieved nirvana under a Peepal tree on the fourteenth day of the dark half of the month of Paush. After wandering and preaching for a long time, he came to Sammetshikhar and achieved Nirvana on the second day of the dark half of the month of Vaishakh.

Shreyansanath

Shreyansanath was the eleventh Jain Tirthankar of the current age, Avasarpini. As per Jain philosophy, he became a Siddha - an enlightened soul which has destructed all of its karma.

Shreyansanath was born to Emperor Vishnu Raja and Queen Vishnu Devi Rani at Sinhpuri in the Ikshvaku clan. His birth date was the twelfth day of the Falgun Krishna month of the Hindu calendar.

In his earlier avatar, the being that was to become Bhagwan Shreyansnath purified his soul as Emperor Nalingulm, and went to the Mahashakra dimension of Gods. From there he descended and took birth as Shreyans Kumar, the son of Emperor Vishnuraja and queen Vishnu Devi of Simhapur. Shreyans Kumar was born on the twelfth day of the dark half of the month of Bhadrapad.

He had a normal princely life and ascended the throne when Vishnuraja retired. After a long reign Shreyans Kumar became a Shraman and within a short span of two months achieved nirvana on the fifteenth day of the dark half of the month of Magh under a mango tree. He got Nirvana at Sammetshikhar on the third day of the dark half of the month of Shravan.

It was during his period that the being that was to be Bhagwan Bhagwan Mahavir reigned as the first Vasudev Triprishta. After the death of Triprishtha, his brother Baldev Achal became a follower of Dharmghosh who was a devotee of Shreyansnath. Achal got enlightened in this birth.

Vasupujya Swami

Vasupujya Swami was the twelve Jain Tirthankar of the current age, Avasarpini. As per Jain philosophy, he became a siddha, an enlightened soul which has demolished all of its karma.

Vasupujya was born to Emperor Vasupujya Raja and Queen Jaya Devi Rani at Champapuri in the Ikshvaku clan. His birth date was the fourteenth day of the Falgun Krishna month of the Hindu calendar. Emperor Padmottar ruled over Mangalavati town of Ardhapushkar island. He was an individual devoted to divine pursuits. In later part of his life he took Diksha from Acharya Vajranabh. Reducing the tarnish of Karma by penance and divine practices he earned the Tirthankar-nam-and-gotra-karma and incarnated as a God in the Pranat dimension.

Vasupujya was the Emperor of Champa town in the Bharat sub-continent. His queen was Jaya Devi. Besides being a great warrior Emperor Vasupujya was a compassionate and charitable person. The queen too was benevolent and she inspired the Emperor in his charitable activities.

The being that was Padmottar was born to Queen Jaya Devi. It is said that when the queen was pregnant, the Emperor of Gods came to convey his veneration to the future Tirthankar and his mother. As Indra is also known as Vasu, the new born was named Vasupujya venerated by Vasu.

As Vasupujya grew, so grew his inherent detachment and apathy for ordinary affairs. He had no attraction for the regal splendor and grandeur. When he became young his parents wanted him to marry but he declined. He even conveyed that he had no intention of ascending the throne. In spite of all persuasions from his household members, he renounced the corporeal life and became a Shraman on the fifteenth day of he dark half of the month of Phalgun along with six hundred other persons.

The intensity of his divine practices was so profound that he became knowledgable within one month. At that moment he was practicing under a Patal tree in a garden outside Champa town. He founded the four pronged religious ford and preached for a long period.

The second Vasudev, Dwiprishtaha, was his devotee. He and his brother Baldev Shrivijay vanquished Prativasudev Tark and brought his oppressive rule to an end. Shrivijay later joined the ascetic order of Bhagwan Vasupujya.

Bhagwan Vasupujya got Nirvana in Champa town on the fourteenth day of the bright half of the month of Ashadh.

Vimalnath

Vimalnath was the thirteenth Jain Tirthankar of the current age, Avasarpini. As per Jain philosophy, he became a Siddha, an enlightened soul which has demolished all of its karma.

Vimalnath was born to Emperor Kratvarm Raja and Queen Shyama Devi at Kampilaji in the Ikshvaku clan. His birth date was the third day of the Magh Sukla month of the Hindu calendar. Emperor Kritvarma and

Queen Shyanan Devi of Kampilpur were both spiritualists and devotees of the Jin. The queen one day saw fourteen propitious things in her dream and the augurs announced that she will give birth to a Tirthankar. It was the pious soul that in its earlier birth was Emperor Padmasen of Mahapuri town in Datakikhand and had descended into the queen's womb from the Mahardhik dimension of Gods.

During her pregnancy the queen radiated a soothing glow. Her temperature also became congenial, kind, and generous. When the child was born the whole atmosphere was also filled with a soothing glow. Inspired by this spread of purity, the Emperor named his new born son as Vimal,pure or untarnished.

In due course, prince Vimal Kumar became young, was married, and then ascended the throne. After a long and successful reign he became a Shraman along with one thousand other kings and princes on the fourth day of the bright half of the month of Magh. After two years of divine practices he achieved nirvana and founded the religious ford. Merak Prativasudev, Svayambhu Vasudev, and Bhadra Baldev were his contemporaries. Bhagwan Vimalnath got Nirvana at Sammetshikhar on the seventh day of the dark half of the month of Ashadh.

Anantnath

Anantnath was the fourteenth Jain Tirthankar of the current age, Avasarpini. As per Jain philosophy, he became a siddha, an enlightened soul which has demolished all of its karma.

Anantnath was born to Emperor Raja Sinhsen and Queen Suyasha Rani at Ayodhya in the Ikshvaku clan. His birth date was the 13th day of the Vaishakh Krishna month of the Hindu calendar. Queen Suyasha Devi, wife of Emperor Simhasen of Ayodhya, gave birth to an illustrious son on the thirteenth day of the dark half of the month of Vaishakh. During her pregnancy the queen dreamt of a very long strand of beads whose ends were not visible. The power and the glory of the Emperor also increased manifold during this period. Accordingly the new born was named Anant, endless Kumar.

After leading a normal life, first as a price and then as the Emperor he became an ascetic along with one thousand other persons. He became knowledgable on the fourteenth day of the dark half of the month of Vaishakh under an Ashok tree. In his first discourse he elaborated the subject of the fundamentals-matter and life. He had fifty chief followers including the senior most named Yash. Purushottam Vasudev and Suprabh Baldev reigned during his period of influence. Bhagwan Anantnath got

Nirvana at Sammetshikhar on the fifth day of the bright half of the month of Chaitra.

Dharmanath

Dharmanath was the fifteenth Jain Tirthankar of the current age, Avasarpini. As per Jain philosophy, he became a siddha, an enlightened soul which has demolished all of its karma.

Dharmanath was born to Emperor Bhanu Raja and Queen Suvrata Rani at Ratnapuri in the Ikshvaku clan. His birth date was the third day of the Magh Sukla month of the Hindu calendar. The being that was to become Bhagwan Dharmnath was Emperor Dridhrath of Bhaddilpur in Mahavideh area, in its earlier avatar. Though he had enormous wealth and a large kingdom, he led a detached and pious life like a lotus in a pond. Even great saints praised him as the embodiment of religious faith. During the later part of his life Emperor Dridhrath became an ascetic and due to his unblemished character and sincere divine practices he earned the Tirthankar-nam-and-gotra-karma. Completing his age he reincarnated as a God in the Vaijayant dimension.

This being then descended into the womb of queen Suvrata, wife of Emperor Bhanuraja of Ratnapur. During the pregnancy the queen devoted all her time in religious activities. Even the Emperor and all other members of the household were inclined to devote maximum time to different religious activities like charity, righteousness, penances, studies etc. On the third day of the bright half of the month of Magh a son was born to the queen. Due to the religious influence during the pregnancy period, the Emperor gave him the name Dharmnath. In due course he became young, was married and then ascended the throne. He ruled successfully for a long period.

One day he terminated all corporeal attachments and became and ascetic. After two years of divine practices he became all-knowing. His first religious discourse was attended by the fifth Vasudev Purush Simha and Sudarshan Baldev.

In his first discourse he chiefly dealt with the subject of form and ill effects of passions. A large audience was benefited by this eloquent discourse. At last he went to Sammetshikhar and got Nirvana.

Shantinath

Shantinath was the sixteenth Jain Tirthankar of the current age,Avasarpini. As per Jain philosophy, he became a siddha, an enlightened soul which has demolished all of its karma.

Shantinath was born to Emperor Viswasen Raja and Queen Achira Rani at Hastinapur in the Ikshvaku clan. His birth date is the thirteen day of the Jyest Krishna month of the Hindu calendar. The account of the earlier incarnations of Bhagwan Shantinath indicates that his being had taken the path of discipline that lead toward purity of soul many births before. Due to this uplifting during his incarnations as Shrisen and Vajrayudh it was born as Meghrath, the son of Emperor Dhanrath of Pundarikini town in Purva Mahavideh area. At the proper time, Emperor Dhanrath gave the kingdom to Meghrat and became an ascetic.

Emperor Meghrath, then, coronated his son and took Diksha from Arhat Dhanrath. Due to his increasing purity in meditation in the face of many afflictions, he earned the Tirthankar-nam-and-gotra-karma. Completing his age he reincarnated in the Sarvarthsiddha dimension of Gods.

After wandering as an ascetic for one year he returned to the same jungle and there, on the ninth day of the bright half of the month of Paush, he achieved nirvana under a Nandi tree. His first discourse was on the subject of disciplining the senses. He came to Sammetshikhar after a long period wandering and propagating true religious faith. There, along with nine hundred other monks, he observed a month long fasting that started his final meditation. On the thirteenth day of the dark half of the month of Jyeshta, Bhagwan Shantinath achieved Nirvana.

Kunthunath

Kunthunath was the seventeenth Jain Tirthankar of the current age, Avasarpini. As per Jain philosophy, he became a siddha, an enlightened soul which has demolished all of its karma.

Kunthunath was born to Emperor Shursen Raja and Queen Srirani Rani at Hastinapur in the Ikshvaku clan. His birth date was the 14th day of the Vaishakh Krishna month of the Hindu calendar. The name of the powerful and illustrious Emperor of Khadgi town in Purva Mahavideh area was Simhavaha. He was a very devoted and religious person when his son became young and capable; he handed over his kingdom to the son and took Diksha from Samvaracharya. Due to his vigorous penance and devotion for the Arhat, he earned the Tirthankar-nam-and gotra-karma. Completing his age he reincarnated in the Sarvarthsiddha dimension of Gods.

From the dimension of Gods he descended into the womb of Queen Shri Devi, wife of Emperor Shursen of Hastinapur. During her pregnancy the queen saw a heap of gemstones known as Kunthu in her dreams. This inspired the Emperor to name him Kunthu Kumar. The pious deeds of earlier birth resulted in unlimited power and grandeur for Kunthu Kumar. After Shursen became an ascetic, Kunthu Kumar ascended the throne. Soon the disc weapon appeared in his armory and he proceeded to conquer the world with his mighty army. Without any confrontation all the kings accepted his sovereignty and Kunthunath became a Chakravarti. Many mighty kings and princes used to be present in his court all the time. After a long and quit reign of twenty three thousand seven hundred and fifty years he became an ascetic along with one thousand kings immediately after Diksha he acquired Manahparyav Gyan. He spent sixteen years as a common ascetic. Indulging in penances and other divine practices, he achieved nirvana on the third day of the bright half of the month of Chaitra under a Tilak tree in Sahasramara jungle outside Hastinapur. His first discourse was on the subject of inner purity.

As knowledgable ascetic Kunthunath wandered around and preached true religious faith for a very long period. He then went to Sammetshikhar and observed a month long fasting before breathing his last. His devotees were deeply devoted to him. As such, a large crowd was present at the moment of his Nirvana and cremation ceremony. They witnessed the ceremony with heavy hearts and tear filled eyes. The mortal remains of Bhagwan Kunthunath were taken away by the Gods for worship.

Aranath

Aranath was the eighteenth Jain Tirthankar of the current age, Avasarpini. As per Jain philosophy, he became a siddha - an enlightened soul which has demolished all of its karma.

Aranath was born to Emperor Sudarshan Raja and Queen Devi Rani at Hastinapur in the Ikshvaku clan. His birth date was the 10th day of the Migsar Krishna month of the Hindu calendar. Emperor Dhanpati of Susima city in Mahavideh area took Diksha from Samvar Muni and after acquiring Tirthankar-nam-and gotra-karma he reincarnated in the Graiveyak dimension of Gods. From here he descended into the womb of Queen Maha Devi, wife of Emperor Sudarshan of Hastinapur. Besides the fourteen great dreams that precede the concept of a Tirthankar, Queen Maha Devi also saw a gem studded wheel Ara. Accordingly, after the birth the boy was named Ara Kumar.

When Ara Kumar became young he was married to many beautiful princesses. Later Emperor Sudarshan gave the kingdom to Ara Kumar and became an ascetic. For some years Arnath ruled as a regional Emperor. Gradually his power and glory increased and one day the disc weapon appeared in his armory. He vanquished the six continents and became a Chakravarti. In his attendance were thirty two thousand kings.

After a long and successful rule, one day Emperor Aranath was thinking about the ever changing seasons. This activated a chain of sublime thoughts that lead to total detachment. He renounced all the wealth, power and glory and became an ascetic. He did divine practices and wandered around. After three years he arrived in the Sahasramra jungle outside Hastinapur and stood in mediation under a mango tree. With the fire of higher meditation he burnt one after another the four vitiating Karmas including illusory, knowledge obstructing, perception obstructing, and power hindering. Consequently he achieved nirvana. His first discourse after achieving nirvana was on the subject of how to win over the enemies like attachment and aversion.

In this first religious assembly thousands of persons became monks including his 32 chief followers headed by Kumbh. Spending a long period of twenty one thousand years wandering and promoting religious faith, he eventually arrived at Sammethshikhar and achieved nirvana.

Mallinath

Mallinath was the nineteenth Jain Tirthankar of the current age, Avasarpini. As per Jain philosophy, Mallinath became a siddha - an enlightened soul which has demolished all of its karma. As per members of the Shvetambar denomination, she was female, making her the only female to become a Tirthankar during the current age. Digambars believe that Mallinath was male.

Mallinath was born to Emperor Kumbha Raja and Queen Prabhavati Rani at Mithila in the Ikshvaku clan. His birth date was the 5th day of the Shravan Sukla month of the Hindu calendar.

Malli Kumari became an ascetic along with three hundred males and equal number of females. Immediately after her Diksha, she acquired Vipulmati Manahparyav Gyan (the ultimate Pra normal capacity and started profound meditation. The same afternoon she achieved nirvana. In her first discourse she discussed on the subject of doctrine of equanimity. The six kings took Diksha during this first discourse. After enhancing the spread of religious faith for a long period she achieved Nirvana on the fourth day of the bright half of the month of Chaitra at Sammetshikhar.

MAIN FIGURES IN MEDIEVAL PERIOD

Unisuvrata

Unisuvrata Swami was the twentieth Jain Tirthankar of the current age, Avasarpini. As per Jain philosophy, he became a siddha, an enlightened soul which has demolished all of its karma.

Munisuvrata was born to Emperor Sumitra Raja and Queen Padmavati Rani at Mithila in the HariVansh clan. His birth date was the 15th day of the Shravan Sukla month of the Hindu calendar. The being that was to be Bhagwan Munisuvrat purified its soul during his birth as Surshreshta, the Emperor of Champa city in Mahavideh. He then reincarnated in the Pranat dimension of Gods.

Bhagwan Munisuvrat's period was a prominent period of Jain pre-history. His illustrious contemporaries and devotees included stalwarts like the ninth Chakravarti-Mahapadma, the eighth Prativasudev, Baldev, and Vasudev, Ravan, Rama and Lakshman respectively. The elder brother of Bahagavan Munisuvrat, ascetic Vishnu Kumar, also became famous for his pioneering effort of saving the Jain organization from the oppressions of mister Namuchi; the Raksha Bandhan festival is celebrated in the memory of that event.

Naminath

Naminatha was the twenty-first Jain Tirthankar of the present era. As per Jain philosophy, he became a siddha, an enlightened soul which has demolished all of its karma.

Naminatha was born to Emperor Vijay Raja and Queen Vipra Rani of the Ikshvaku dynasty, who were the rulers of Mithila at that time. His birth date is the 8th day of Shravan Krishna in the Hindu calendar.

As per Jain custom, the soul that would one day be the God Bhagwan Naminath purified itself during its avatar as Emperor Siddharth of the town of Kshambi in eastern Mhavideh. He reincarnated as a God in the Aparajit dimension, and later reincarnated as the child of Queen Vipra and Emperor Vijay. As the queen had seen fourteen propitious things in her dream at the moment of conception, the augurs declared that the unborn child was going to be a Chkravarti or a Tirthankar.

During Vipra's pregnancy, Mithila was attacked by a group of powerful kings. Peace-loving Emperor Vijay was at a loss to find a quit solution, until an expert augur told the Emperor that the pregnant queen should go to the roof of the palace and look at the attacking armies. The queen pursued these instructions and threw a loving glance at the large armies stationed on the fields outside the town. The aura of the pious soul in her womb was so powerful that it cast a pacifying spell on the attackers. The kings, who had been sure of winning the battle, surrendered and bowed before Emperor Vijay.

This incident inspired the Emperor to name his new-born child Naminath. Born on the eighth day of the dark half of the month of Sravan, Naminath had a happy childhood. When he matured, he was married and later was given the reign of the kingdom. After a long and quit reign, he became an ascetic on the ninth day of the dark half of the month of Ashadh. After nine months he achieved nirvana under a Bakul Tree in a garden near Mithila. His first discourse was on the subject of right perception. After a long period of religious and divine activities, he went to Sammetsikhar, where he became enlightened on the tenth day of the dark half of the month of Vaishakh.

The literary account seems to be supported by epigraphic evidence. In the Kathiawar peninsula, a copper plate has been discovered on which there is an inscription about Emperor Nebuchadnezzar (940 B C.). As per inscription, Nebuchadnezzar, who was also the Bhagwan of Reva-nagara in Kathiawar, Gujarat and who belonged to the Sumer tribe, had come to the city Dwarka of the Yaduraja. He has built a temple and paid homage and made the grant perpetual in favour of Bhagwan Neminatha, the paramount deity of Mt. Raivata.

Neminatha

Neminatha was twenty-second Jain Tirthankar of the current age, Avsarpini. As per Jain philosophy, he became a Siddha, an enlightened soul which has demolished all of its karma.He also known as Aristhnemi. He along with Rishab or Adinath is cited in the Rig Veda Samhita.

Neminatha was born to Emperor Samudravijay Raja and Queen Shivadevi Rani at Souripur in the HariVansh clan. His birth date is the 5th day of Shravan Sukla in the Hindu calendar.

There seems to be no doubt about the existence of Jainism in the 7th century BC. but the history of Jainism goes back even earlier than of Parsvanatha. The Jain record mentions the names of twenty two Tirthankars before him. Neminatha, the 22nd Tirthankar of the Jains, was the son of Samudra Vijaya and grandson of Andhakavrishni. Many Jains and some Hindus is said to be a cousin of Krishna, the Bhagwan of the Bhagavad Gita.

As per both religions, Krishna negotiated his marriage with Rajamati, the daughter of Ugrasena, but Neminath, empathizing with the animals which were to be slaughtered for the marriage feast, left the procession suddenly and renounced the world. Some writers of the Jain Holy Scriptures say that Tirthankar Neminath was the master of Krishna.

It is cited in the Chhandogya Upanishads III, that the sage Ghora Angirasa imparted certain instructions of the divine sacrifice to Krishna, the son of Devaki. The liberal payment of this sacrifice was austerity, liberality, simplicity, ahimsa and truthfulness. These teachings of Ghora Angirasa seem to be the principles of Jainism. Hence, Ghora Angirasa seems to be a Jain sadhu. The word Ghora Angirasa seems to be an epithet given to him because of the extreme austerities he undertook. It may be possible to suggest that Neminatha was his early name and when he had obtained redemption after hard austerities, he might have been given the name of Ghora Angirasa. He is said to be the contemporary of Krishna, the hero of Mahabharata.

Parshavanath

Parshvanath was the twenty-third Tirthankar in Jainism in 7th century BC. He is the earliest Jain leader usually accepted as a historical figure.

As per Jain custom he died 250 years before the death of Bhagwan Mahavir, the last Tirthankar. The chronology accepted by most Jains Shvetambars places Bhagwan Mahavir's death in 527 BC. Parshva was the son of Emperor Ashvasena and queen Vama of Varanasi. He renounced the world and became an ascetic when he was 30 years old. He attained Nirvana atop Sammet Sikhar. He was called purisadaniya beloved of men, a name which shows that he must have been a genial individuality.

Bhagwan Parshvanath is always represented with the hood of a snake shading his head. In Jain canonical literature, Parshvanatha is represented in padmasana, lotus posture – both palms and feet, with propitious lotus marks on them, placed upward. He has blue-black complexion – the colour of the cosmos. The seven-hooded serpent Shesh – umbrella-like unfurling its hoods over the deity, represented elements of the earth and the ocean and has hence a similar body colour. Parshvanatha has been represented as wearing a gem-studded crown and other ornaments. He has a golden throne as a seat and a rich canopy above.

Bhagwan Mahavir

Bhagwan Mahavir, Great Hero (599 – 527 BC.) is the name most commonly used to refer to the Indian sage Vardhamana who founded what are today regarded to be the fundamental principles of Jainism. As per Jain tradition, he was the 24th and the last Tirthankar. He is also known in texts as Vira or Viraprabhu, Sanmati, Ativira,and Gnatputra. In the Theravada Buddhist Holy Scriptures he is referred to as the Nirgrantha Nathaputta - the naked ascetic of the Jnatr clan.

In a place called Kundagram in the ancient kingdom of Vaishali modern day Bihar, India, Bhagwan Mahavir was born to Emperor Siddartha and Queen Trishala on the 13th day under the rising moon of Chaitra April 12 as per Gregorian calendar. While still in his mother's womb it is believed he brought wealth and prosperity to the entire kingdom, which is why he was also known as Vardhaman. An increase of all good things, like the abundant bloom of beautiful flowers, was noticed in the kingdom after his conception. Queen Trishala had 14 (16 in Digambar Denomination) propitious dreams before giving birth to Vardhaman, signs foretelling the advent of a great soul.

Jain tradition states that after his birth, Indra bathed him in celestial milk with rites befitting a future Tirthankar and he was returned to his mother, Trishala.

Vardhaman's birthday is celebrated as Bhagwan Mahavir Jayanti, the most prominent religious holiday of Jains around the world. Bhagwan Mahavir Jayanti is celebrated with prayers, decorations, processions and festivity.

As Emperor Siddartha's son, he lived as a prince. Nevertheless, even at that tender age he exhibited a virtuous nature. He started engaging in meditation and immersed himself in self-contemplation. He was interested in the core philosophy of Jainism and started to get further away from corporeal matters.

At the age of thirty Bhagwan Mahavir renounced his kingdom and household, gave up his corporeal belongings, and spent twelve years as an ascetic. During these twelve years he spent most of his time meditating. He gave utmost regard to other life forms, including humans, animals and plants, and avoided injuring them. He had given up all corporeal belongings including his clothes, and lived an extremely austere life. He exhibited exemplary control over his senses while enduring the penance during these years. His courage and braveness earned him the name Bhagwan Mahavir. These were the golden years of his divine journey, at the end of which he attained Kewal-Gyan. He was now an individual of infinite harmony, knowledge and self-control.

Bhagwan Mahavir devoted the rest of his life to preaching the timeless truth of divine liberty to people around India. He travelled barefoot and without clothes, in the hardest of climates, and people from all walks of life came to listen to his message. At one point he had over 400,000 devotees. Bhagwan Mahavir's preaching and efforts to spread Jain doctrine is regarded the real catalyst to the spread of this ancient religious faith throughout India and into the mainstream.

At the age of 72 years and 4.5 months, he achieved Nirvana end of life cycle, and leaving the body, achieving and living in pure soul form. This is not regarded as death, since death means having re-birth again in some physical bodily form. When Nirvana is achieved, the soul reaches to the highest point of the cosmos and stays there eternally. In Jainism, this is called as Moksh in the area known as Pawapuri on the last day of the Indian and Jain calendars, Dipavali. Jains celebrate this as the day he achieved nirvana or Moksh. Jains believe Bhagwan Mahavir lived from 599-527 BC., although some scholars prefer 549-477 BC.

Bhagwan Mahavir's doctrine has eight principal cardinals - three metaphysical and five ethical. The aim is to elevate the quality of life. These independent tenets reveal exceptional unity of objective, and aim at attaining divine excellence by ethically sound behaviour and metaphysical thought. Bhagwan Mahavir's metaphysics consist of three tenets - Anekantavada, Syadvada, and Karma; and his Panchavrats, five codes of behaviour - Non-violence, Satya, Asteya, Brahmacharya, and Aparigraha. He talks of Tri-ratnas - three gems, which are the means and the goal.

Bhagwan Mahavir preached that from eternity, every life form, soul is in bondage of karmic atoms accumulated by good or bad deeds. Under karma, the soul seeks temporary and illusory pleasure in materialistic belongings, which are the deep rooted causes of self-centered violent thoughts, deeds, anger, hate, greediness, and other vices. These result in further accumulation of karmas.

To liberate one's self, Bhagwan Mahavir taught the need of right faith, samyak-darshana, right knowledge, samyak-Gyan, and right behaviour, samyak-charitra. Bhagwan Mahavir stated men and women are spiritually equal and that both may renounce the world in search of moksh or ultimate bliss.

Bhagwan Mahavir attracted individuals from all walks of life, rich and poor, men and women, touchable and untouchable. He organized his devotees into a fourfold order; monk (Sadhu), nun (Sadhvi), layman (Shravak), and laywoman (Shravika). This order is known as Chaturvidh Jain Sangh.

Bhagwan Mahavir's sermons were orally compiled by his immediate followers in the Agam Sutras. These Agam Sutras were orally passed on to future generations. In the course of time many Agam Sutras have been lost, demolished, or modified. About one thousand years later the Agam Sutras were recorded on Tadpatris, leafy paper used in those days to preserve records for the future. Shvetambar Jains accept these sutras as authentic teachings while Digambar Jains use them as a reference.

Jainism existed before Bhagwan Mahavir, and his teachings were established on those of his predecessors. Therefore Bhagwan Mahavir was a reformer and propagator of an existing religious faith, rather than the founding father of a new faith. He pursued the well established creed of his predecessor Tirthankar Parshvanath. Nevertheless, Bhagwan Mahavir did reorganize the philosophical principles of Jainism to correspond to his times.

A few centuries after Bhagwan Mahavir's death, the Jain religious order, Sangh grew more and more complex. There were schisms on minor points, though they did not affect Bhagwan Mahavir's original philosophies. Later generations saw the introduction of rites and complexities that some criticize as placing Bhagwan Mahavir and other Tirthankars on the throne similar to those of Hindu deities.

MAIN FIGURES IN MODERN PERIOD

Kundakunda

Kundakunda was a celebrated Jain Acharya, Jain scholar monk, 2nd century AD., composer of divine classics such as: Samayasara, Niyamasara, Pancastikayasara, Pravacanasara, Atthapahuda and Barasanuvekkha. He occupies the highest place in the tradition of the Jain acharyas.

He belonged to the Mula Sangh order. His proper name was Padmanandi, he is popularly referred to as Kundakunda because he was born in a place named Kaundakunda in south India. He is closely linked with the Digambar denomination, also in recent decades, his texts have become popular amongst Shvetambars also. He was known also as:

1. Padmanandi
2. Elacharya
3. Vakragriva
4. Grddhapiccha

For Digambars, his name has propitious significance and occupies third place after Bhagwan Bhagwan Mahavir and Gautama Ganadhara in the sacred litany. Kundakunda wrote in Shauraseni Prakrit. Amongst the modern devotees of Kundakunda, two names are notable, Banarasidasa, a 16th century lay poet from Agra who began his divine quest after reading kundakunda's "Samayasara"; and Rajachandra, the Gujarati merchant who trod famously on the divine path highlighted by Acharya Kundakunda.

Acharya Hemachandra

Hemachandra Suri was an Indian Jain scholar, poet, and polymath who wrote on grammar, doctrine, prosody, and contemporary history. Noted as a prodigy by his contemporaries, he gained the title Kalikal Sarvagya, (all-knowing of the Kali age).

He was born in Dhandhuka, Gujarat about 100 km south west of Ahmadabad), to Chachadev (father) and Pahini Devi(mother). They named him Changdev. The Jain temple of Modhera Tirtha is located at his birthplace. As a young man, Chandradeva was initiated as an ascetic at a Jain temple, and he took the name Somachandra (Somachandra). He was trained in religious discourse, doctrine, logic and grammar. In 1110, at the age of 21 he was ordained as an Acharya of the Shvetambar denomination of Jainism and was given the name Acharya Somchandra and popularly as Hemachandra.

At the time, Gujarat was ruled by the Solanki dynasty. Hemachandra rose to prominence under the reign of Siddharaj Jaysinh I, and was an advisor to his successor Kumarapala (1143–1173). During Kumarapala's reign, Gujarat became a reputed centre of culture. Starting in 1121, Hemachandra was involved in the construction of the Jain temple at Taranga. His influence on Kumarapala resulted in the Jain religious faith becoming the official religion of Gujarat, and animal slaughter was banned.

Taking an approach of anekantavada, Acharya Hemachandra is said to have displayed a broad minded attitude and pleased the Kumarapala, the Emperor of Gujarat. Certain Brahmins who were jealous of Hemachandra's rising popularity with the Emperor complained that Hemachandra was a very arrogant person, that he did not respect the Hindu Gods, and that he refused to bow down to Bhagwan Shiva. When called upon to visit the temple of Shiva with the Emperor, Hemachandra readily bowed before the idol of Shiva, but said: "I am bowing down only to that God who has demolished the passions like attachment and hate which are the cause of corporeal life, whether he is Brahma, Vishu, or

Jin." He ensured that he remained true to principles of Jainism, namely, that a Jain should bow down only to a passionless and detached God such as a Jin, and at the same time managed to please the Emperor. Ultimately, the Emperor became a devoted devotee of Hemachandra and a champion of Jainism.

REFERENCES

Acaranga-sutra, Anga-sutrani I: Vacana Pramukha, Acarya Tulasi, Editor Yuvacarya Mahaprajna, Jaina Vishvabharati, Ladnun, First Edition, 1974.

Buhler, G.: *Indian Sect of the Jainas*, Edited by Burgess, Jas, Luzac & Co., 46, Great Russell Street, 1903.

Chakravarti, A: *The Religion of Ahimsa*, Bombay, 1957.

Hume, Robert Earnest: *Thirteen Principal Upanisads (Trans.)*, Oxford, 1921.

Jacobi, H.: *Mahavira and His Predecessors.*

Jain, J., and Fischer, E.: *Jaina Iconography, Part One, The Tirthankara in Jaina Scriptures, Art and Rituals, Part Two, Objects of Meditation and the Pantheon. 2 vols.* E.J.Brill, Leiden, 1978.

Jain, Kailash Chand: *Jainism in Rajasthan*, Sholapur, 1963.

Jain, Kamata Prasad: *The Religion of Tirthankaras*, Aliganj, 1964.

Kausambi, *Dharmananda: Bharatiya Sanskrti aur Ahimsa.*

Lalwani, K.C.: *Sramana Bhagavan Mahavira, Life and Doctrine.*

Lenin: *Collected Works of Lenin, Vol. 14.*

Nevaskar B.: *Capitalists without Capitalism, the Jains of India and the Quakers of the West*, Greenwood Publications, Westport, 1971.

Nyayavatara: Siddhasena, Translated by Vijayamurti Sastracarya, Paramashruta Prabhavaka Mandal, Jauhari Bazar-Bombay, First Edition, 1950.

Paul Marett: *Jainism Explained*, Liececiter 1988.

Shah, Umakant P.: *Studies in Jaina Art*, Banaras, 1955.

Sharma, S.R.: *Jainism and Karnataka Culture*, Dharwar, 1940.

Sheth, C.B.: *Jainism in Gujarat*, Bombay, 1953.

Siddhahemasabdanusasanam: Acarya Hemacandra, Bherulal Kamhaiyalal Religious Trust, Chandanbala Apartment, Ridge Road, Valakeshwara, Bombay, Second Edition, 1985.

Smith, Vincent A.: *A History of Fine Art in India and Ceylon*, Oxford, 1915.

Sogani, K.C.: *Ethical Doctrines in Jainism*, Jaina Samskriti Samrakshaka Sangha, Sholapur, 1967.

6

Scriptures

Bhagwan Mahavir's preaching were orally compiled by his immediate followers in Jain scriptures known as Jain Agam or Agam Sutras, which consist of many texts. The Agam Sutras teach great reverence for all forms of life, strict codes of vegetarianism, asceticism, ahimsa, and opposition to war. These Agam Sutras were not documented in any form but were orally passed on to the future generations.

In course of time many of the Agam Sutras have been were remembered and some were altered. About one thousand years later the memorized Agam Sutras were recorded on leafy papers (Tadpatris). Shvetambar Jains have accepted these Sutras as an authentic version of Bhagwan Mahavir's teaching while Digambar Jains did not accept them as authentic. Digambars follow two main texts (Shatkhand Agam and Kasay Pahud) and four Anuyogs (consist of about 20 texts) written by great Acharyas (scholars) during 100 to 800 AD.

Bhagwan Mahavir's preaching was orally complied by his followers into many texts. This knowledge was by word of mouth transferred from acharyas (gurus) to the followers over the course of about one thousand years. In olden times, monks rigorously pursued the five great vows of Jainism. Even religious scriptures were considered belongings and thus knowledge of the religion was never documented. Also, during the course of time many learned acharyas (elder monks) complied commentaries on the different subjects of the JainJain religious faith.

Around 500 AD., which was one thousand years after Bhagwan Mahavir's nirvana (death), Jain acharyas realized that it was extremely difficult to keep memorizing the entire Jain literature complied by the many scholars of the past and present. In fact, significant knowledge was already lost and the rest was polluted with modifications and mistakes. Hence, they decided to document the Jain literature as known to them. In this time period two major denominations, namely Digambar and Shvetambar, were already in existence. A thousand years later (1500 AD.), the Shvetambar denomination divided into three subsects known as Shvetambar Murtipujak, Sthanakvasi, and Terapanthi. Differences exist amongst these denominations in their acceptance of the validity of the documented Jain Holy Scriptures and literature.

Jain literature is classified into two major categories:

Agam Literatur: This consists of original Holy Scriptures complied by Gandharas and Srut-kewalis. They are written in the Prakrit language.

Non-Agam Literature: This consists of commentary and explanation of Agam literature and independent works, complied by elder monks, nuns, and scholars. They are written in many languages such as Prakrit, Sanskrit, Old Marathi, Gujarati, Hindi, Kannad, Tamil, German, and English.

DIVINE WORDS

Jainism denies the existence of God as the creator, sustainer, and the ethical governor of the world. As per Jain dharma, the goal of life is to achieve nirvana. The Jain scripture, Jain Agamas Siddhantas, preaches the philosophy of Non-violence or ahimsa. As per this philosophy, all objects have a soul, and should not be hurt or killed.

Main teachings involves that it was the greatest sin to cause injury to creatures, and that it was the greatest virtue to renounce corporeal belongings and practice strict asceticism. Orthodox Jains could not even take to farming, because it involved tilling which killed earthworms. His message of ahimsa (Non-violence), truth (Satya), non-stealing (Achaurya), celibacy (Brahma-charya), and non-possession (Aparigraha) is full of universal compassion.

Bhagwan Mahavir was quite successful in eradicating from human intellect the concept of God as creator, protector, and destroyer. He also denounced the worship of Gods and Goddesses as a means of redemption. He taught the concept of supremacy of human life and stressed the importance of the positive attitude of life.

Bhagwan Mahavir also preached the gospel of universal love, emphasizing that all life forms, irrespective of their size, shape, and form how spiritually developed or under-developed, are equal and we should love and respect them. The prayer of Jain Religion is as follows:

Namokar Mantra

Namokar Mantra is the central prayer in Jainism and can be recited at any time of the day. While praying by reciting this mantra, the devotee bows with respect to Arihants, Siddhas, spiritual leaders (Acharyas), teachers (Upadyayas) and all the monks. This worship the virtues of all the supreme spiritual people instead of just worshipping one particular person. It is important to note that the Navkar Mantra doesn't mention the names of even Tirthankars and Siddhas. At the time of recitation, a Jain devotee remembers their virtues and trys to emulate them. In this mantra Jains bow down to these supreme spiritual personalities, and thus, it is also called Namokar Mantra.Every day Jains bow their heads and say their universal prayer, the Namokar Mantra. All good work and events begin with this prayer of salutation and worship.

Namo Arihantanam

Namo Siddhanam

Namo Ayariyanam

Namo Uvajjhayanam

Namo Loye Savva Sahunam

Eso Panch Namoyaro

Savva Pavappanasano

Mangalanam Cha Savvesim

Padhamam Havai Mangalam

The meaning of this mantra is as follows:

"I bow in reverence to Arihants

I bow in reverence to Siddhas

I bow in reverence to Acharyas

I bow in reverence to Upadhyayas

I bow in reverence to all Sadhus

This five-fold salutation

Destroys all sins

And amongst all propitious things

Is the most auspicious one"

In the above prayer, Jains don't ask for any favours or materialistic benefits from their Gods, the Tirthankars or from monks and nuns. They don't pray to a specific Tirthankar or monk by name. By saluting them, Jains receive the insiration from the five benevolent for the right path of true bliss and total liberty from the despair of life.

RELIGIOUS SCRIPTURES

Jains have their own scriptures called Agams, also called the Jain Shrut. Jains don't have one main scripture text but they have many.

The teachings by knowledgable Bhagwan Tirthankar to his enlighten principal followers, called Ganadhars was first composed in fourteen Purvas and then in twelve Ang-Pravishtha-Agams (an 'Ang' being a 'limb') by Ganadhars themselves. All Purvas are included in one part of the twelfth Ang, called Drastivad. It is said one Jain scripture that, "Having climbed the tree of ideal knowledge, knowledgable Bhagwan Tirthankar showers flowers of knowledge to enlighten principal followers, called Ganadhars. They collected all these flowers in the cloth of the intellect, and have interwoven them into the garland of Dvadsangi" (Dvadsangi means twelve Ang-Pravishtha-Agams).

The composition of scripture has a specific objective of showing the listener the path of everlasting bliss and nirvana. The Agam Sutras teach the everlasting truth about behaviour, equanimity, universal affection and friendship, and the everlasting truths on thinking, namely, the principle of relativity, principle of non-one-sided-ness and many divine things including great reverence for all forms of life, soul, karma, cosmos, strict codes of asceticism, rules for householders, compassion, ahimsa, non-possessiveness.

In addition to the twelve Ang-pravishtha works composed by the Ganadhars, other canonical literature (Ang-bahya-Agams) which composed by Stathviras or elder monks are also included as part of the Jain Agams.

The Jain Agams consisted of (1) 14 Purvas, (2) 12 Ang-pravishtha-Agams and (3) Ang-bahya-Agams (34 for Shwetambar Murtipujak, 21 for Shwetambar Sthanakvasi and 14 for Digambar). Agam (Canonical) literature is divided into two groups:

Ang-agams or Ang-pravista-agams: These texts contain the direct preaching of Bhagwan Mahavir. They were complied by Ganadharas.

Ang-bahya-agams (outside of Ang-agams): These texts are expansions of Ang-agams. They were complied by Srut-kewalis.

Agam Literature

Bhagwan Mahavir's preaching was methodically compiled by his devotees into many texts. These texts are collectively known as Agams, the sacred texts of the JainJain religious faith. Hence, the JainJain religious faith doesn't have one sacred text like the Bible or Koran, but it has many texts complied by many devotees.

Ang-agams

Bhagwan Mahavir's immediate followers were known as Ganadharas. All Ganadharas possessed ideal knowledge (Kewal-Gyan). They orally complied the direct preaching of Bhagwan Mahavir into twelve main texts (sutras). These texts are known as Ang-agams. Hence the Ang-agams are the oldest religious scriptures and the back bone of Jain literature.

The twelfth Ang-agam is called Drastivad. The Drastivad consists of fourteen Purva texts, also known as Purvas or Purva-agams. Amongst Ang-agams, Purvas were the oldest sacred texts. All Jain denominations believe that knowledge of the Purvas (Drastivad) were gradually lost starting two hundred years after Bhagwan Mahavir's nirvan (death). Nevertheless, the subject matter of the Purvas has been referenced by other Jain Holy Scriptures and literature.

The Digambar Jain denomination also believes that the remaining eleven Ang-agams were gradually lost. All Shvetambar Jains believe that the proper meaning and the original intent of the eleven Ang-agams survived and were properly documented by elder monks one thousand years after Bhagwan Mahavir's nirvan.

Ang-bahya-agams

Monks who had knowledge of a minimum of ten Purvas were known as Srut-kevlis. The Srut-kevlis wrote many texts (sutras) expanding the subject matter defined in the Ang-agams. Collectively these texts are called Ang-bahya-agams meaning outside of Ang-agams.

The different Jain denominations accept different numbers of Ang-bahya texts. Nevertheless the Digambar denomination believes that they were also gradually lost starting about two hundred years after Bhagwan Mahavir's Nirvan.

Classification of Ang-bahya-agams

The Shvetambar denomination has divided Ang-bahya-agams into the following categories:

Upang-agams: The scriptures which provide further explanation of Ang-agams are called Upang-agams. There are 12 Upang-agams accepted by all Shvetambar denominations.

Chhed-sutras: The subject matter described in Chhed-sutras is only for monks and nuns and not for lay persons. It relates to the conduct and behaviour of monks and nuns. It also explains how they can repent for their sins and errors. The Shvetambar Murtipujak denomination accepts 6 Chhed-sutra texts but the Sthanakvasi and Terapanthi denominations accept only 4 texts.

Mool-sutras: The scriptures which are necessary for monks and nuns to study in the earlier stages of their monkhood are called Mool-sutras. The Shvetambar Murtipujak denomination accepts 4 Mool-sutras texts but the Sthanakvasi and Terapanthi denominations accept only 3 texts.

Chulika-sutras or Sutras: The scriptures which enhance or decorate the Ang-agams are known as Chulika-sutras or Sutras. There are 2 Chulika-sutras accepted by all Shvetambar denominations.

Prakirna-agams: The scriptures which describe independent or miscellaneous subjects of the JainJain religious faith are known as Prakirna-sutra. The Shvetambar Murtipujak denomination accepts 10 Prakirna-agams texts but none are accepted by the Sthanakvasi and Terapanthi denominations.

Digambar Jain Literature

The Digambar denomination believes that there were 25 Agam-sutras (11 Ang-agams and 14 Ang-bahya-agams) complied from the original preaching of Bhagwan Mahavir. Nevertheless, they were gradually lost starting about two hundred years after Bhagwan Mahavir's enlightenment. Hence the existing Agam-sutras (which are accepted by the Shvetambar denominations) are not accepted by them as authentic Holy Scriptures.

In the absence of authentic Holy Scriptures, Digambars use the following literature as the basis for their religious practice. These Holy Scriptures were written by great Acharyas (scholars) from 100 to 800 AD. and are established on the original Agam Sutras.

- Two Main Texts:
  1. Shatkhand-agam
  2. Kashay-pahud

- Four Anuyogas:
  1. Pratham-anuyoga (Dharma-kath-anuyoga) - Religious Stories
  2. Charn-anuyoga - Conduct
  3. Karan-anuyoga (Ganit-anuyoga) - Description of the Cosmos
  4. Dravy-anuyoga - Philosophy

Shatkhand-agam

This Digambar holy scripture is also known as Maha-kammapayadi-pahuda or Maha-karma-prabhrut. It was written by two Acharyas; Pushpadant and Bhutabali around 160 AD. The second Purva-agam named Agraya-niya was used as the basis for this scripture. The scripture contains six volumes. Acharya Virsen wrote two commentary texts, known as Dhaval-tika on the first five volumes and Maha-dhaval-tika on the sixth volume of this scripture, around 780 AD.

Kashay-pahud

This scripture was written by Acharya Gunadhara. The fifth Purva-agam named Gyan-pravad was used as a basis for this scripture. Acharya Virsen and his disciple, Jinsen, wrote a commentary text known as Jaya-dhaval-tika around 780 AD.

Four Anuyogas

1. Pratham-anuyoga (Dharma-kath-anuyoga) - Religious Stories. This anuyoga consists of the following texts which contain religious stories, art, literature, history, poetry, and like literature.
2. Charn-anuyoga – Conduct. This anuyoga consists of the following texts which contain tenets of observances, conduct, behaviour, and like literature.
3. Karan-anuyoga (Ganit-anuyog) - Description of the Cosmos. This anuyoga consists of the following texts which contain geography, mathematics, astronomy, astrology, and like literature.
4. Dravy-anuyog – Philosophy. This anuyoga consists of the following texts which contain philosophical doctrine, theories, Tattvagyan, and like literature.

Details

Ang-agams: Ang-agams are the oldest religious scriptures and the back bone of Jain literature.

Acharang Sutra(Aayarang): This agam explains the conduct and behaviour of ascetic life and the description of the penance of Bhagwan Mahavir. This is the oldest agam from a linguistic point of view.

Sutrakratang Sutra (Suyagdang): This agam explains ahimsa, Jain metaphysics, and the refutation of other religious theories such as Kriyavada, Akriyavada, Ajnanavada, and Vinayavada.

Sthananga Sutra (Thanang): This agam defines and catalogues the main substances of the JainJain religious faith (defines Jain metaphysics).

Samavayanga Sutra: This agam defines and catalogues the main substances of the JainJain religious faith from a different perspective than the Sthananga Sutra.

Vhakhya Prajnapti or Bhagavati Sutra (Viyah Pannati): This agam explains the subtle knowledge of soul, matter, and other related subjects. 36000 questions and answers are presented in discussion form. It is the largest of the eleven Ang-agams.

Jnata Dharma Kathanga Sutra (Nayadhammakahao): This agam explains Jain tenets through examples and stories. This text is very useful in understanding the mode of Bhagwan Mahavir's religious preaching.

Upasaka Dashanga Sutra (Uvasagdasao): This agam explains the code of behaviour of the ten lay devotees (Shravaks) of Bhagwan Mahavir. This agam is very useful for understanding the code and behaviour of common people (Shravaka Dharma) in the JainJain religious faith.

Antah Kradashanga Sutra (Anatagaddasao): This agam tells the stories of ten sacred monks achieving nirvana (Moksh) by destroying their karmas.

Anuttaroupa Patika Dashanga Sutra (Anuttarov Vaiya Dasao): This agam contains the stories of an additional ten sacred monks who achieved the top-most paradise, known as Anuttara paradise.

Prashna Vyakrana Sutra (Panha Vagarnai): This agam explains the five great vows (mahavratas) and the five worst sins defined in the JainJain religious faith.

Vipaka Sutra (Vivagsuyam): This agam explains the results of good and bad karmas through several stories.

Upang-agams: The scriptures which provides further explanation of Ang-agams are called Upang-agams.

Aupa Patika Sutra (Ovavaiya): This agam explains the splendid procession (view) of Emperor Konika when he visited Bhagwan Mahavir. It also explains how an individual can achieve paradise in the next life.

Raja Prashniya Sutra (Raya Pasen Ijja): This agam explains the story of Monk Keshi. Monk Keshi was the Ganadhara of Bhagwan Parshvanath. He removed the doubts of Emperor Pradeshi regarding the existence and attributes of the soul. Monk Keshi made the Emperor a devotee of the JainJain religious faith. After his death, the Emperor was born as a Dev in paradise. He appeared from paradise to shower Bhagwan Mahavir with unprecedented pomp and splendor. The thirty-two dramas (plays) described in this agam throw light upon the ancient dramatic art of India.

Jivabhigama Sutra: This agam explains the cosmos and the subtle description of all life forms (souls) of the cosmos. It gives very important information to the scholars of biology and botany.

Prajnapana Sutra (Pannavana): This agam explains the form and attributes of souls from a different perspective.

Surya Prajnapti Sutra (Surya Pannti): This agam explains the Sun, the planets and the associated mathematics regarding their motion.

Chandra Prajnapti Sutra: This agam explains the Moon, the planets and the associated, mathematics regarding their motion. Both of these upangas, the Chandra Prajnapti and Surya Prajnapati, sutras are very important in understanding the astrology of olden times.

Jambudveepa Prajnapti Sutra: This agam provides a description of Jambudveepa. Jambudeepa is a place explained in Jain geography. It also provides information on ancient kings.

Nirayarvali Sutra: This agam explains the story of ten princes. All ten princes fought with Emperor Chetaka of Vaishali in cooperation with Emperor Konika. Emperor Chetaka was the son of the 10 princes' step-mother. In the end all ten princes went to hell after dying in war.

Kalpa Vatansika Sutra (Kappavadamsiao): This agam explains the story of Emperor Konika's children. They did not fight with Emperor Chetaka in the war. They renounced the world and became monks. After their death, they went to paradise.

Pushpika Sutra (Puspiao): This agam explains the former lives of certain devas (angels) who worshiped Bhagwan Mahavir.

Pushpa Chulika Sutra: This agam describes stories similar to those in the Pushpika.

Vrashnidasha Sutra (Vanhidasao): This agam explains how Bhagwan Neminath convinced ten kings in the Vrashni region to follow the JainJain religious faith.

Chhed Sutra Aagams: The subject matter described in the Chhed-sutras is for monks and nuns and not for lay persons. It relates to the conduct and behaviour of monks and nuns. It also explains how they can repent for their sins and errors.

Nisheetha Sutra (Nisiha): This agam explains the procedure of repentance (Prayashchitta) in the form of punishment for the monks and nuns who have conducted themselves badly.

Vrahat Kalpa Sutra: This agam explains which of the ten kinds of repentance (Prayashchittas) is appropriate for a particular wrong-doing by monks and nuns. It also defines in clear terms what is acceptable behaviour for monks and nuns and what is not.

Vyavahara Sutra: This agam describes the system of confession for monks and nuns who fall from proper behaviour. It explains the credentials of the listening monk or nun and with what sort of feeling the confession should be made. It also explains what sort of repentance (Prayashchitta) the monk should carry out. There are several other indication of the limits of ascetic life.

Dasha Shruta Skandha Sutra (Achardasha): There are ten chapters in this Sutra. It contains the following information:

- 20 places of Asamadhi
- 21 powerful faults bringing weakness in behaviour
- 33 Ashatanas of Guru
- 8 Sampadas of Acharyas and their kinds
- 10 places of Chitta Samadhi
- 11 Pratimas of Sravaka
- Bhiksu Pratimas
- Kalpasutra - recited during the Paryushanas
- 30 places of Maha Mohaniya karma bandhana
- 9 Nida nas (Niyane)

Panch Kalpa Sutra: This sutra explains the daily rites the monks and nuns have to perform. Only scattered chapters of this agam are now available. Nevertheless, the commentaries (Bhashya and Churni) written about this agam by some elder monks are accessible.

Mahanisheetha Sutra: This agam explains the process of confession and repentance (Prayashchitta) for monks and nuns. It explains the scale of pain one has to suffer if he or she breaks the fourth vow (chastity). It also describes and explains the behaviour of good and bad monks.

Mool-sutras: The Holy Scriptures which are necessary for monks and nuns to study in the early stages of their ascetic life are called Mool-sutras.

Avashyaka Sutra: The daily rites or routines which it is necessary to perform during the day and night for the purification of spirit are called Avashyaka. A description of the six routines (Avashyakas) are explained in this agam. The six routines are; Samayika, Chaturvinshatistava, Vandanaka, Pratikramana, Kayotsarga, and Pratyakhyana.

Dasha Vaikalika Sutra: This agam briefly describes and explains the behaviour of ascetic life.

Uttaradhyayana Sutra: This agam has the same place in Jain literature as the Dhammapada in Buddhism and the Geeta in the Hindu religion. It contains preaching regarding religious tenets and practices, and many stories, dialogues, and examples established on such tenets and practices.

Ogha Niryukti or Pinda Niryukti Sutra: This agam explains certain rules and procedures for monks with respect to travelling, staying, accepting food and other necessities from lay persons.

Chulika-sutras: The Holy Scriptures which enhance or decorate the Ang-agams are known as Chulika-sutras or Sutras.

Nandi Sutra: This agam contains an elaborate description of Tirthankars, Ganadharas, and five types of Knowledge (Gyan); Mati, Shrut, Avadhi, Manaparyay, and Kewal-Gyan.

Anuyogadvara Sutra: This agam provides the description of many rights regarding the mode of preaching.

Prakirna-agams: The Holy Scriptures which describe independent or miscellaneous subjects of the Jain religion are known as Prakirna-sutra.

Chatuh Sharana: This agam contains prayers to the four benevolent beings:

- Bhagwan Arihant - God in the form of human being
- Bhagwan Siddha - God in the form of pure consciousness
- Sadhu - All monks
- Dharma - Religion

Aatur Pratyakhyana (Aayur-Pachakhana): This agam explains differences in the death of children, youths, adults, and old people. It also describes the types of vows a wise person should take during different states of illness and how he should beg the pardon of all life forms in the cosmos.

Bhakti Parijna (Bhatta-parinna): This agam explains the process of fasting and how one should strive to feel at the time of death.

Sanstaraka (Santharag): This agam explains the process of dying by one's own craving (Santhara) and its glory.

Tandulavaitalika: This agam explains the state of pregnancy and provides knowledge about the human body.

Chandra-Vedhyaka: This agam explains the method of concentrated meditation (Dhyana) that one should observe through the description of Radhavedha.

Devendra-Stava: This agam explains the names, positions, and residences of Devas (angels) who reside in paradise. It also provides a description of the moon, sun, planets, and stars.

Ganita Vidya: This agam explains palmistry and how it is used to predict the future (Nimitta).

Mahapratyakhyana: This agam explains how to completely give up the worst sins and how to repent these sins.

Veerastava: This agam is considered lost. Nevertheless, it appears from literature referencing this agam that it contained prayers of Bhagwan Mahavir.

NON-RELIGIOUS SCRIPTURES

The Jain non-religious scriptures includes general secular topics such as sciences, history, and grammar. The Jains have used several languages at different times and in different areas of India.

- Prakrit: Prakrit literature includes the Agamas, Agama-tulya texts, and Siddhanta texts. Composition in Prakrits ceased around 10th century AD.
- Sanskrit: Writing in Sanskrit became common after about 1st century AD., starting with Tatvartha Sutra of Uma Swati. Jain Sanskrit literature includes Purans, Koshas, Shravakacharas, Mathematics, and Nighantus.

- Apabhramsha: Produced from about 10th to 15th cent AD., these texts include Kahas, rasas, and grammars. Most of the known Apabhramsha texts are of Jain origin.
- Tamil: Some of the early Tamil classics such as Tirukural, Cilappatikaram and Jivakachintamani are Jain works.
- Hindi: In the past 8-9 centuries many Jain texts in Hindi have been written, which include Ardha-kathanaka, Chhah-dhala, and Mokshamarga Prakashaka.

REFERENCES

Chandogya Upanisad: Edited by Max Muller, F. (S. B. E.) Vol. 1, Motilal Banarasidas, Delhi, Reprint Edition, 1981.

Dasgupta, S.N.: *History of Indian Philosophy, Vol. I,* Cambridge University Press, London, Second Edition (Reprint), 1932.

Desai, P.B. *Jainism in South India and some Jaina Epigraphs,* Sholapur, 1957.

Devendra Muni Shastri: *Source-Book in Jaina Philosophy,* Sri Tarak Guru Jain Granthalaya, Udaipur, 1983.

Karttikeyanupreksa: Svamikumara, Editor Dr. A.N.Upadhye, Smd. Rajchandra Ashrama, Agosa via Anand (Gujarat), First Edition, 1960.

Pramana-mimamsa: Hemacandra. Edited by Pt.Sukhalal Sanghvi, Saraswati Pustak Bhandar, Ahmedabad, Reprint Second Edition, 1989.

Radhakrishnan, S.: *Indian Philosophy, Vol. I,* George Allen & Uniwin, London, First Edition (Revised), 1929.

Schubring, Walther: *The Religion of the Jainas,* New Delhi 1966.

Shah, Chimanlal J.: *Jainism in North India,* London, 1932.

Shah, U.P.: *'Jainism', New Encyclopaedia Britannica,* Chicago, 1974.

Songani, Kamal Chand: *Ethical Doctrines in Jainism,* Sholapur, 1967.

Srimadbhagavadgita Bhasya: Translated by Dr.A.G. Krishnawarrior, Shri Ramakrishna Math, Madras, First Edition, 1983.

Srimadbhagavat (Two Volumes): Gita Press, Gorakhpur, Third Edition, 1956.

Stevenson, Sinclair: *The Heart of Jainism,* Oxford, 1915.

Tatia, Nathmal: *Studies in Jain Philosophy,* Banaras, 1951.

Tukol, T.K.: *Compendium of Jainism*, Dharwad, 1980.

Zimmer, H.: *Myths and Symbols in Indian Art and Civilization,* Edited by Joseph Campbell, Harper and Brothers, New York, First Edition, 1945.

7

Teachings

Jainism is one of the world's oldest religions. This ancient religion was passed on to us through one of the greatest religious teachers of all time, Bhagwan Mahavir. Bhagwan Mahavir was not the founding father of Jainism. What he did was to bring together in a systematic form the philosophy and doctrine of his predecessors, preach them widely throughout his home country, and lay the foundations of an organized Jain 'church' with monks and nuns and lay persons following his teachings. The social order which he created has endured to the current day.

Bhagwan Mahavir taught a scientific explanation of the nature and meaning of life and a guide as to how we should behave to draw this real nature and meaning into our own life. We must begin with three things. First, we must have Right Faith, we must believe in truth. Second, we must have the Right Knowledge, we must study to understand what life is all about. Third, we must follow Right Conduct, the conduct which our faith and knowledge show us to be correct. These are the 'three jewels', ratnatraya. of Jainism.

Right Faith is perhaps the hardest of all. Nobody can tell us what we can believe, but we can look at the message of Bhagwan Mahavir and believe that he really did know what he was talking about and that his message makes sense.

Bhagwan Mahavir's message contains the basis of Right Knowledge. Life is a puzzle. Where did we come from before birth? Where do we go after death? Nobody's life is completely and totally happy, but why do some individuals have lives of great despair and others have much joy? Bhagwan Mahavir teaches us that this is not the result of the whims of some distant God. No, each one of us is what we have made ourselves by our actions in this life and in former lives. Every person (and not only humans, but animals and plants) is basically a pure spirit or soul (jiva is the Jain word for it) which is capable of total knowledge and total liberty. But by our actions and thoughts we have, as it were, covered this pure spirit with the gross materialistic of karma which obscures our knowledge and limits our liberty and ties us down to one life after another. Though we may have a lot of bliss in life we also, all of us, have a great deal of unhappiness. We want to know the way in which we can get rid of the restrictions of karma and gain the state of total knowledge and glorious liberty which is known as Moksh or enlightenment. Though this may be a very long, very slow process for most of us, over countless lives, Bhagwan Mahavir teaches us how to make a start in freeing ourselves from the restrictions and sorrows of karma.

Now we come to Right Conduct. Strength of passions is the worst thing, passions of violence and craving and belonging. The most prominent principle which runs through the whole of Bhagwan Mahavir's attitude of life is non-violence. This is usually translated as 'ahimsa', but it goes beyond that and really means the greatest possible kindness to all living beings. This is the first and central rule which we should try to follow, to get rid of violence in all our actions and even in our thoughts. Yes, in our thoughts as well, for violent thoughts can be potentially as injurious as violent deeds.

Bhagwan Mahavir's teachings, if faithfully pursued, have two results. Firstly, they produce a better society for every creature to live in, and secondly, they enable the person to improve his or her own inner feelings and character. So, following on from non-violence, we are taught to be truthful and honest, to create both persons and a society in which lies and theft, and general insecurity, are absent. Lies and theft are the consequence of our passions and possessiveness. True peace and harmony in society and in the person are possible only if we can restrain our passions and cravings. So Bhagwan Mahavir tells us to reduce our longing for the things of the world, for materialistic belongings and for sexual activities. We can never have real peace of spirit so long as we are constantly seeking more and more belongings and delights.

These then are the five rules of conduct which Bhagwan Mahavir taught, ahimsa, truthfulness, no stealing, non- acquisition and control of sexual cravings. It is a hard program and not everybody can follow it all at once. So Bhagwan Mahavir set up a society in which some individuals, monks and nuns, try to follow his program as far as is humanly possible. Others, common lay persons, men and women, don't give up their homes and jobs and families, but they try as far as possible in the circumstances of daily life to follow the five rules of conduct. While the monk or nun can take precautions to avoid harm even to the tiniest living creature, the rule of ahimsa must mean something less for common individuals caught up in the common business of our lives. A monk or nun can give up all belongings and seek no more: for most of us non-acquisition must mean trying to reduce our craving for belongings and the delights of the world. Monks and nuns can go very much further than married men and women in subduing their attachment to sex.

Bhagwan Mahavir taught his message for thirty years until his life on earth ended and he passed on to that state of complete liberty and happiness and peace which we call Moksh. For most of us Moksh is a very long way away. But he taught us how we can approach it ourselves by rules which lead to inner peace and harmony inside ourselves and outward peace and harmony in human society. He taught more than that, a democratic organization in the society which he set up, with all men and women playing their part and with no barriers of class or caste. He also taught tolerance and an appreciation that things can be seen from more points of view than one. Above all he taught that we ourselves produce our own destiny by our own actions and emotions: we should not look outside for some God to praise or blame or ask for favours. When we honour Bhagwan Mahavir we don't ask him for current help, but we meditate on his example and teachings and seek to draw the real meaning of these into our own life and spirit.

SPIRITUAL TEACHINGS

Jain religion puts a significant stress on the thought process of a human being. An individual's behaviour and his actions are the reflection of his internal thoughts, day in and day out. It is not the action but intention behind the action results in the accumulation of Karma. One should be very careful about his thoughts, how he thinks, and the subject matter of his thought.

To make room for pure thoughts, and to drive out the evil ones, Jainism recommends to meditate the following twelve thoughts or Bhavnas. The twelve Bhavnas described here are the subject matters of one's meditation, and how to occupy one's mind with useful, religious, beneficial, serene, harmless, spiritually advancing, Karma preventing thoughts. They cover a wide field of teachings of Jainism. They are designed to serve as aids to divine progress, produce detachment, and lead the aspirants from the realm of desire to the path of renunciation. They are reflections upon the key facts of life, intended to develop purity of thought and sincerity in the practice of religion. These reflections are also called Bhavnas (aspirations).

- Anitya Bhavna - Impermanence of the world
- Asarana Bhavna - No one provides protection
- Samsara Bhavna - No permanent relationship in cosmos
- Ekatva Bhavna - Solitude of the soul
- Anyatva Bhavna - Separateness
- Asuci Bhavna - Impureness of the body
- Asrava Bhavna - Influx of karma
- Samvara Bhavna - Stoppage of influx of karma
- Nirjara Bhavna - Shedding of karma
- Loka Bhavna - Transitory of cosmos
- Bodhi-durlabha - Unattainability of right faith, Bhavna knowledge, and conduct
- Dharma Bhavna - Unattainability of true preceptor, Holy Scriptures, and religion

Anitya Bhavna: This Bhavna tells us that in this world every thing such as life, youth, wealth, property, etc. are transient or subject to alteration. Nothing in the cosmos is permanent, although the whole cosmos is constant. Divine values are thus worth striving for as soul's ultimate liberty and stability. This will help to break all earthly attachments.

Asarana Bhavna: This Bhavna tells us that he is helpless against death, old age, and disease. The only way he can overcome death and disease is by destroying all his karma. The soul is his own savior, and to attain total liberty and nirvana, one takes refuge to the true path and to the five best personalities. They are Arihanta, Siddha, Acharya, Upadhyay and Sadhus. The refuge to others are due to delusion, and must be avoided.

Samsara Bhavna: This Bhavna tells us that the soul transmigrates from one life to the other in any of the four forms, human, animal, hellish, and heavenly. The continual cycle of birth, life, and death is full of pain and sorrows, and has not yet ended. There are no permanent worldly relations like father, mother, friend, foe, etc. It is we who establish these relations and live accordingly. This kind of thought will help minimize or stop any attachments to anybody, other life forms, or objects. The soul must attain ultimate liberty from it, which is nirvana or Moksh.

Ekatva Bhavna: This Bhavna tells us that the soul is solitaire, and lonely in existence. The soul assumes birth alone, and departs alone from the life form. The soul is responsible for its own actions and karmas. The soul will enjoy the fruits, and suffer bad consequences of its own action alone. Such thoughts will stimulate his efforts to get rid of karmas by his own initiative and will lead religious life.

Anyatva Bhavna: This Bhavna tells us that soul is separate from any other objects or life forms of the world. Even his body is not his. At the time of death, soul leaves the body behind. The body is matter, while the soul is all consciousness. The soul thus should not develop attachment for worldly objects, and other life forms. He should not allow himself to be controlled by cravings, greediness, and urges of the body.

Asuci Bhavna: This Bhavna tells us about the constituent element of one's body. It is made of impure things like blood, bones, flesh, etc. It also generates impure things like perspiration, urine, stool, etc. The soul, which resides within the body, is unattached to the body. It is alone and pure. The body ultimately becomes nonexistent, but the soul is timeless. Thus emotional attachments to the body is useless.

Asrava Bhavna: This Bhavna tells us about karma streaming into the soul. Every time he enjoys or suffers through the senses (touch, taste, smell, sight, and hearing) he makes his karma increase. This thought will make him more careful, and will try to stop the influx of karmas.

Samvara Bhavna: This Bhavna tells us about stopping evil thoughts, and becomes absorbed in attaining divine knowledge, meditation, etc. This prevents the influx of karma.

Nirjara Bhavna: This Bhavna tells us about the evil consequences of karma, and striving to destroy the previously acquired karma by austerity and meditation.

Loka Bhavna: This Bhavna tells us about the real nature of this cosmos. Judging from the standpoint of substance, it is timeless but from the standpoint of modification it is transitory. Therefore all objects of the world come into existence and perish. This thought makes him understand the true nature of reality, which is necessary for right knowledge.

Bodhi-durlabha Bhavna: This Bhavna tells us that it is very difficult for the transmigrating soul to acquire right faith, right knowledge, and right conduct in this world. Thus, when one's has the opportunity to be a religious person, take the advantage of it to develop right religious talent.

This thought will strengthen one's effort to achieve them, and live accordingly.

Dharma Bhavna: This Bhavna tells us that the true preceptor, Holy Scriptures, and religion are excellent shelters in this world full of agony. All other things lead to despair and suffering.

REDEMPTION

Redemption or salvation is a religious concept referring to forgiveness or absolution for past sins and protection from timeless damnation. Redemption is common in many world religions and all Abrahamic Religions.

Redemption in Jainism means nirvana, redemption or emancipation of soul. It is a blissful state of existence of a soul, completely free from the karmic bondage, free from samsara, the cycle of birth and death. An enlightened soul is said to have achieved its true and pure nature of infinite happiness, infinite knowledge and infinite perception. Such a soul is called siddha or paramatman and regarded as supreme soul or God. In Jainism, it is the highest and the noblest aim that a soul should strive to attain. It fact, it is the only aim that an individual should have; other aim s are contrary to the true nature of soul. With right faith, knowledge and efforts all souls can achieve this state.

Where there is neither Karma, nor quasi-Karma nor the worry, nor any type of thinking which is technically called Artta, Raudra, Dharma and Sukla, there is redemption.

As per Jainism, Redemption can be achieved only in the human birth. Even the demi-gods and heavenly beings have to re-incarnate as humans and practice right faith, knowledge and conduct to attain nirvana. As per Jainism, human birth is quite rare and priceless and hence a man should make his choices wisely.

DEVOTION TO GOD

Jainism was known as Nirgrantha Dharma. It was also known as Shramana Dharma and it had many branches or schools. This Shremana tradition was different from the Brahamana Tradition. Both these currents of ancient Indian thought have sufficiently interacted and have influenced each other to a great degree in the area of Theology, Doctrine, and even socio-cultural life. The insistence of Ahinsa i.e. ahimsa and compassion towards all life forms- birds, insects and even animals, is Shramana influence over Brahamana; while then again, the Holy Scriptures, ethics, prayers, rites of Jainism and Buddhism is the Brahamana influence over the Shramanas. Both these systems have quite a good number of differences, the most fundamental and the central one of the them is the "approach" towards reality.

With the Jains happiness consists not in dependence but in independence; the dependence is the life of the world; but the life which is the highest life is that in which we are individually independent so far as binding or disturbing influences are concerned. Jainism is one of the systems that doesn't accept the Vedic authorities. Disapproval of Vedic authorities by Shramanas, and particularily by Jains, is not simply on issues related to religion and rites like Yagna and sacrifices, but also on issues which are metaphysical and epistemological by nature. Jainism doesn't accept Advait or Monism but believes in the pluralism of souls, This disapproval of Vedic power leads to the disapproval of Advait-doctrine, disapproval of Monism, and disapproval of many theistic elements. As a resent Jainism was treated as Atheistic or as we say not believing in God (niriswarvadi). The second most prominent reason that led towards the misconception is Janism's strong stress on ahimsa and thus equally strong revolt against vedic riteistic sacrifices. This led Janism, if not towards pure atheism, it definitely led it towards anti-theism of Veda and other orthodox schools of Indian Philosophy.

Jainism like other systems of Indian Philosophy accepts the concept of nirvana or emancipation. But then Jainism believes in strong efforts to break the chains of Karma which is the cause of bondage. Jainism doesn't believe in a fruit-giver God, or God that will be pleased and will shower upon us all joy and power. The way to nirvana is to make efforts for three-fold combination of Right-Faith, Right Knowledge and Right Conduct.

Jainism doesn't believe in Divine Grace as Christianity and Islam and other Theistic theosophies believe. In Jainism, there is no realisation of one's unity with God, as it is in Vedanta doctrine. In Jainism, we find neither God, as an outside agency, nor God's elegance as inevitably required to achieve the redemption. And the last, but certainly not the least, in the series of the root causes is Jainism's Law of Karma. In Jainism, we find the extreme position of Law of Karma.

The term Karma in its most universal and simple sense means action. The law or philosophy of Karma means that all deeds, good or bad, physical or mental produce their proper consequences in the life of the person who acts. It is founded on the simple law of cause and effect. No effect is without a cause, and one has to bear the fruits of his deeds, sooner or later. There is no get away from this. The law of Karma occupies a distinct place both in Indian Doctrine and in Indian spirituality. It is known as Karma-Marg (path) or Karma-vada. But then it is found at its highest degree of minuteness and in its best form of preciseness in Jainism. To Jains, in fact, the science of Karma is the real science of Spirituality, in so far as it tries to unfold the real nature of spirit or self. This extreme stress on Karma, its uncompromising sincerity and steadfast faith in dealing with Karma through penance and ousterities, has no place for God's grace or God as the dispensor of fruits of deeds. Jainism maintains that every soul in its pure form is God, having all the four Infinities: Infinite Knowledge, Infinite perception, Infinite Strength and Infinite Happiness.

Therefore the stress not on God or God's grace but on spiritual growth of soul lifting it to a higher and higher level and therefore achieving Godhood has also led many to consider Jainism as Atheism.

In the ancient period different phenomena of nature were regarded to be the working of different Gods and Godesses. There may be conscious entities in these forces as there may be living entities on a planets, but these forces themselves are not living entities. The Jains discard this concept so far as the Godhead or Godlike character is concerned. In fact, with the growth of science and with the better understanding of the science these phenomena become simple and the concept of these beings as character of the highest divine power goes away. Actually, so far we have only discussed what God of the Jains is not, what is important is what is the God of the Jains. Jainism believes in soul. It believes that: the soul exists; it is timeless; it is the agent of all actions; it enjoys the fruits of actions; the embodied soul's deliverance is possible; the means of nirvana is also available.

As per Jainism the embodied soul is a soul in bondage. The bondage is due to Karma. The soul that is polluted and is having a veil of Karma on it due to subreption, passions etc. The soul in bondage is in the state of dependence - the complete dependence of the soul is its lowest stage while the complete liberty or nirvana is its highest divine stage. As the soul becomes purer and purer from the veil of impurities of Karm on it, it becomes brighter and brighter.

As per Jainism a soul, completely released from the bondage is a soul in state of siddhahood or Godhood. In this state soul is free and enjoys four infinites: Infinite Knowledge, Infinite Perception, Infinite

Power and Infinite Happiness. The released soul is a vanquisher - a Jin as is therefore a hero. A released soul possesses all the attributes of God. Now if we interpret God as the manifestation of the highest values, highest virtues and highest morals then such released souls, are Jain Gods.

Let me also show what Jain God is an what the theistic colours are in the background of Jain Doctrine, chiefly its logic, ethics and epistemology. First we talk a but Jain logic. "The Jains admit that things are one in their universal aspect and many in their particular aspect." Therefore along with the differences, the element of universal, which is in all, becomes the pure being or "Sat" from Jain's logical point of view. We may call this the Highest Universal or "Maha Samanya"; and this universal is the Absolute. It becomes Absolute. "The whole gamut of reality, nevertheless, reveals its universal umitive nature as one existence when it is envisaged from the synthetic angle of vision."

Moreover, one of the greatest contribution of the Jain Doctrine is its theory of non-absolutism. But then the non-absolutism is relativism and there can't be relative with absolute. Relative always pre-supposes the absolute, which could be clearly understood through its Maha-Samanya or Universal. So the collective concept derived from observations of the divine characters inherent in all beings is by us called God.

Jain ethics deals with certain definite codes both for the householder and also for the monks. These codes are rigorous in insisting on spiritual growth through Right Counduct. The keynote of the system is Non-violence i.e. not hurting, not killing anyone. The sanctity of life, including that of birds, beasts and insects, itself is holy and religious. The full recognisation of this sanctity, in any form turns out to be theistic. To a Jain self-perfection or self-realization is the highest goal. Total eradication of emotions and passions is indispansible for self-realization for they disturb the tranquillity of soul. The Jain-ethics stresses meditation on love for all creatures, compassion for the distressed, pleasure at the virturous and indifference to the vicious.

It talks about the Five Great Vows and regards transcendental purity of the soul as the highest good. Like the doctrine of soul, the holy-panted, the Great Vows, Jain's Law of Karma equally strengthens Jainism as religion having theistic altitudes towards higher ethical objective. One of the definitions of religion is "the belief in the conservation of values". Jainism and Jain ethics form this point of view raises to the position of religion. Moreover, we find in all traditional theism there is devotion and the expression of devotion is through prayers, rituals and rites and also faithful obedience towards the scriptural commandments. If we go into the Jain philosophies and Jain way of life we find it satisfying all these. We are, therefore, observing that the Jain-ethics, its codes, philosophy of Karma and its doctrine of soul, all this "is the judicious conviction and deep faith in the intrinsic purity and perfection of the soul, and the capacity and capability to realise, recover and retain for Godhood through philosophical enlightment and a rigorous course of ethical and spiritual discipline" is the keynote of Jain Theism.

ETHICAL ACTIONS

We know that the proper goal for a Jain is release from death and rebirth, and rebirth is caused by the accumulation of karma, all Jain ethics aims at purging karma that has been accumulated, and ceasing to accumulate new karma. Like Buddhists and Hindus, Jains believe that good karma leads to better circumstances in the next life, and bad karma to worse. Nevertheless, since they conceive karma to be a materialistic substance that draws the soul back into the body, all karma, both good and bad, leads to rebirth in the body. No karma can help an individual attain nirvana from rebirth. Karma comes in different kinds, as per kind of actions and intentions that attract it. In particular, it comes from four fundamental sources: (1) attachment to corporeal things, (2) the passions, such as anger, greediness, fear, arrogance, etc., (3) sensual enjoyment, and (4) ignorance, or false belief. Only the first three have a directly ethical or ethical upshot, since ignorance is cured by knowledge, not by ethical action.

The ethical life, then, is in part the life devoted to breaking attachments to the world, including attachments to sensual enjoyment. Hence, the ethical ideal in Jainism is an ascetic ideal. Monks (who, as in Buddhism, live by stricter rules than laymen) are constrained by five cardinal rules, the "five vows": (1) non-violence, frequently translated "ahimsa," or "non-injuring," satya, or truthfulness, asteya, not taking anything that is not given, brahmacharya, chastity, and aparigraha, detachment. This list differs from the rules binding on Buddhists only in that Buddhism requires abstention from intoxicants, and has no separate rule against attachment to the things of the world. The cardinal rule of interaction with other jivas is the rule of non-violence. This is because injuring other jivas is caused by either passions like anger, or ignorance of their nature as life forms. Consequently, Jains are required to be vegetarians. As per earliest Jain documents, plants both are and contain life forms, though one-sensed beings, so even a vegetarian life does harm. This is why the ideal way to end one's life, for a Jain, is to sit motionless and starve to death. Bhagwan Mahavir himself, and other great Jain saints, are said to have died this way. That is the only way to be sure you are doing no harm to any life form.

While it may seem that this code of behaviour is not really ethical, since it is aimed at a specific reward for the agent—and is thus entirely self-interested—it should be noted that the same can be said of any religion-based ethical code. Furthermore, like the Hindus and Buddhists, Jains believe that the only reason that individual advantage accrues to ethical behaviour is that the very structure of the cosmos, in the form of the law of karma, makes it so.

MESSAGE OF HARMONY AND LOVE

Of all religions of the world, Jainism is the only religion which has the principle of Peace as its fundamental philosophy. The other religions also speak of Peace whenever convenient but they never offer such loyalty to the principle of Peace as is found in Jainism. In the history of world religions, Jainism alone has given a distinctive position to the philosophy of Peace and has based its ethical code entirely on the total observance of the tenet of Peace in all its aspects. Jainism is the only religion in the world which has given maximum attention to the prominent practical aspects of the theory of Peace so that Peace, in it's minutest details, can be actually observed both by the lay devotees and monks in their day to day life.

At the same time Jain religion has got the distinctive distinction, amongst the religions of the world, of ably presenting in a scholastic and scientific manner the theoretical and philosophical side of the philosophy of Peace by discussing it thoroughly not only from internal and absolute points of view but also from external and real points of view. Also, the Jain religion has earned special prestige in the world by giving equal stress on the negative and positive aspects of Peace. On this basis Jainism has shown to the world in a ideal and convincing way the worth of the philosophy of Peace by stating the fundamental principle, viz., "Ahimsa Paramo Dharmah" i. e. Non-violence is the greatest religion. That is why Jain Religion is regarded as Non-violence Religion and Jain Culture as Non-violence Culture. For understanding this utmost significance attached to the principle of Peace in Jainism, it is quite necessary to see, in brief, the outstanding features of Jain religion and the important aspects of the concept of Peace as formulated in Jain religion.

The heart of Jainism is ahimsa. Positively stated, Jainism is a religion of compassion, universal love and friendliness. It aims at the welfare of all life forms, and not of man alone. It maintains that life forms are infinite, all so called empty spaces in the cosmos are filled with minute life forms. As per it, there are countless single-sense organisms that take the subtlest possible units of materialistic elements -earth, water, fire and air - as their bodies. Fresh earth is alive but when it is baked it becomes dead. Fresh water from a well, etc. is alive but when it is boiled or influenced by mixing some other substance it becomes dead. Vegetables, trees, plants, fruits, etc. do have life but when they are dried, cut or cooked they expire. To avoid injury to them as far as possible, man is counselled to use them discreetly. He should resist from polluting water, air, etc. and thereby perpetrating violence to them. Worms, insects, animals, etc. help in keeping ecological balance therefore they help man. And domestic animals have for ages been a constant and faithful aid to man in civilizing himself.

From the critical standpoint of their original pure pristine state, all life forms are uniform in their nature. Jainism teaches to look upon them as upon one's ownself. Inflicting injury to them is inflicting injury to one's ownself.

The Jain dictum parasparopagraho jivanam, that is 'life forms render service to one another' offers an endearing alternative to the modern Darwinian formula of 'survival of the fittest.' The life of a life form is a life of mutual cooperation andassistance. Industry, labour, service and sacrifice of countless life forms are there behind the sustenance and development of a person. Therefore every person is indebted to the universal society of all beings. Even virtues and meritorious qualities can never be cultivated and fostered in isolation.

This concept of Non-violence, ahimsa, has evolved from logical thinking and from experience. It has an almost empirical basis. It has emerged from the philosophy of the equality of all souls. Everyone wants to live, nobody likes to die. Violence enters first in thought, it then manifests itself in speech and then in deeds. That is why they say that war is born in the minds of men. The quest for non-violence is centred in Anekantavada, the doctrine which accomodates a multiplicity of points-of-view and of perspectives.

In Jain doctrine Non-violence is said to be the supreme religion and himsa is considered to be source of all evil and of all sorrows. Non-violence is not limited to not injuring the human beings, it extends to all life forms. This doctrine believes in the unity of life and regards all life forms as equal. He who can be cruel to animals can be cruel to human beings too. Further, cruelty is not only an aspect of external behaviour, but it is also an inner evil tendency. He who is cruel at heart will behave cruelly towards animals and also human beings. He who is compassionate at heart, will behave compassionately towards all.

Moreover, the Jain religion believes in the cycle of birth and rebirth. The soul is in one Yoni (existence) today; it may be in another Yoni tomorrow. It may be a fly today and a human tomorrow. This being so, man has no right to harm other living creations. One should behave sympathetically towards all, friends and also foes. In fact there should be no enemy. Such is the importance of Non-violence in Jain doctrine. Nothing is higher than the Meru mountain; nothing is vaster than the sky. Similarly, there is no better religion than Non-violence.

It is one of the principles of Jainism that all life forms desire life and not death. No one has the right to take away the life of any other being; to kill a life form is the greatest of sins. Life is dear to everyone, and we must have respect for life. Not only "Love and Let Live" but "Live and Help Others Live" should be our principle. Just as the head of a household looks after the welfare of the members of the household, a human being, who enjoys the highest place in the evolution of life, should look after the welfare of other lower orders of creations.

The cosmos is full of living creations, big and small, and, thus, it is impossible to exist without killing or harming some of the smallest of the life forms. Even in the process of breathing, or drinking or eating, we almost unconsciously kill many sentient beings? Thus, as per Jainism the minimum of killing should be our ideal. Moreover, it is more serious where killing is done intentionally or through indifference. Thus, great care should be taken in all our daily activities to see that the minimum of violence is committed by our deeds, speech and mind.

In the cosmos, there are different forms, different orders, of life, such as human beings, animals, insects, trees and plants, bacteria and even still smaller lives which perhaps be seen only through the most powerful of microscopes. Jainism has classified all the life forms as per their sense organs.

Jainism firmly believes that life is sacred, irrespective of caste, colour, creed or nationality and thus not only physical or mental injury to life should be avoided, but all possible kindness should be shown towards all the living beings. This should be the true spirit of Non-violence. Jainism believes that more weapons are in no way an effective answer to weapons.

REFERENCES

Avasyaka-sutra: Editor Madhukar Muni, Jinagama Granthamala, No.24 Agama Prakashan Samiti, Byavar, First Edition, 1985.

Basham, A.L.: *A Cultural History of India*, Clarendon Press, Oxford.

Basham, A.L.: *Post-script, attached to the article on Hinduism in Cultural History of India*, Oxford University Press.

Bhagavati (Vyakhyaprajnapti) in Anga-sutrani II: Editor Yuvacarya Mahaprajna, Jaina Vishvabharati, Ladnum, First Edition, 1974.

Bhargava, D.: *Jain Ethics*, Motilal Banarsidass, Delhi, 1968.

Chandogya Upanisad: Edited by Max Muller, F. (S. B. E.) Vol. 1, Motilal Banarasidas, Delhi, Reprint Edition, 1981.

Chatterjee, A.K.: *Comprehensive History of Jainism (up to 1000 A.D.)*, Firma KLM, Calcutta, 1978.

Diwakar, R.R.: *Bihar Through Ages*, Calcutta, 1959.

Dwivedi, R.C.: *Contribution of Jainism to Indian Culture*, Motilal Banarsidass, Varanasi, 1975.

Einstein Albert: *Ideas and Opinions*, Bonanza Books, No.9.

Jacobi, H.: *Mahavira and His Predecessors.*

Jacobi, H.: *Studies in Jainism*, Ahmedabad, 1946

Jain, C. R.: *Fundamentals of Jainism*, Veer Nirvan Bharti, Meerut, 1974.

Jain, Champat Rai: *Fundamentals of Jainism*, Meerut, 1974.

Jain, Champat Rai: *Householder's Dharma*, Bijnore, 1931.

Latthe, A.B: *An Introduction to Jainism*, Bombay, 1905.

Law, B.C: *Mahavira: His Life and Teachings*, London, 1937.

Lenin: *Collected Works of Lenin, Vol. 14.*

Madhav Rao, N.: *Jainism A New Look.*

Malavania, Pt. Dalasukhabhai: *Jainism (Some essays)*, Translated by Dr. A.S.Gopani, Prakrita Bharati Academy, Jaipur, First Edition, 1986.

Mehta, M. L.: *Outlines of Jaina Philosophy*, Jaina Mission Society, G. 146, Chickpet, Bangalore - 2, October, 1954.

Sheth, C.B.: *Jainism in Gujarat*, Bombay, 1953.

Siddhahemasabdanusasanam: Acarya Hemacandra, Bherulal Kamhaiyalal Religious Trust, Chandanbala Apartment, Ridge Road, Valakeshwara, Bombay, Second Edition, 1985.

Smith, Vincent A.: *A History of Fine Art in India and Ceylon*, Oxford, 1915.

Sogani, K.C.: *Ethical Doctrines in Jainism*, Jaina Samskriti Samrakshaka Sangha, Sholapur, 1967.

Songani, Kamal Chand: *Ethical Doctrines in Jainism*, Sholapur, 1967.

Srimadbhagavadgita Bhasya: Translated by Dr.A.G. Krishnawarrior, Shri Ramakrishna Math, Madras, First Edition, 1983.

Srimadbhagavat (Two Volumes): Gita Press, Gorakhpur, Third Edition, 1956.

Stevenson, Sinclair: *The Heart of Jainism*, Oxford, 1915.

Williams. R.: *Jaina Yoga*, Motilal Banarsidass, Delhi, 1983.

Winternitz, M.: *The Jainas in the History of Indian Literature*, Ahmedabad, 1946.

Zimmer, H.: *Myths and Symbols in Indian Art and Civilization*, Edited by Joseph Campbell, Harper and Brothers, New York, First Edition, 1945.

8

Moral Value System

The Jain morality and ethics are rooted in its metaphysics and its utility towards the soteriological aim of nirvana. The ethics are governed not only through the instrumentality of physical actions, but also through verbal action and thoughts. Therefore, non-violence has to be observed through mind, speech and body. The other rules of the monks and laity are derived from these five major vows. Jainism doesn't invoke the fear of God as a reason for ethical behaviour. The observance of the ethical code is not necessary simply because it is a commandment of a God or any other supreme being. Neither, is its observance necessary simply because it is conductive to general welfare of the state or the community.

While it is true that in Jainism, the ethical and religious injunctions were laid down as law by Arhats who have attained perfection through their supreme ethical efforts, their devotion is just not to please a God, but because the life of the Arhats has demonstrated that such commandments were conductive to Arhat's own welfare, helping him to reach spirtual victory. Just as Arhats attained Moksh or nirvana by observing the ethical code, so can anyone, who follows this path.

MORAL VALUES

Jain ethics is directed toward the deliverance of the person. Its orientation is thus religious. Its end is the spiritualization of all areas of life in order to fit the person for his final goal, Its primary precept relevant to kind and commoner alike is, Do your duty and do it as humanly as you can.

Jainism permits no separation between religion (Dharma) and morality because both are concerned with the well-being of the person in the world in keeping with his own nature. The word Dharma signifies the nature of things (vatthu sahavo dhammo). It is the law which "leads, binds, or takes back a being to its necessary nature; enables it to realize the divinity inherent in itself; helps it to extricate itself from the misery of ordinary existences and reach the state of supreme beatitude." All beings seek bliss and try to avoid pain and loss. The practice of Dharma enables them to attain this end. In the words of the well-known Acharya Samanta Bhadra, "Religion is something which takes the life forms out of the corporeal despair and establishes them in the highest happiness."

This interconnection between religion and morality imparts to Jainism its unique feature. H. S. Bhattacharya finds the insistence of Jainism on divine motivation "the foundation" of all true religion and ethics and thinks it may well serve as "the basis of a universal code of ethical and religious acts." The uniqueness of Jainism "Lies not only in emphasizing this all prominent condition of all religious and ethical activities but in justifying their position by looking upon morality, not as an adjunct to human nature, but as part and parcel of it."

The connection between religion and morality is often missed because Jainism delineates the pathway to divine perfection through the practice of yoga and demarcates stages of self-realization, but the roots of that perfection are in the soul of everyday life. We have first to learn to live a good life in this world and then we can go higher to divine perfection. In order to exclude none from the need for ethical discipline, Jainism has formulated two levels of religious existence: one which sets ethical standards for laymen, and one for monks.

For one who sets out on the path toward perfection, Jainism presents the practice of ten great virtues. They are: Supreme Forbearance, Humility, Straightforwardness, Ideal Truthfulness, Purity, ideal Self-restraint, Austerity, Total Renunciation, Nonattachment, and Celibacy. These virtues are to regulate thought, speech, and action. They are a necessary part of Jain ethics, and are like "ten inextinguishable lamps" which illuminate the path of the beginner.

MORALITY IN LIFE

Jain religion encompasses a threefold path of divine practice. It includes right faith, right knowledge and right conduct. The three components are interrelated and interdependent and are known as "The Three Jewels", because of their value for redemption.

Right faith is primary. It signifies belief in the nirvana of the divine teachers. It assumes a life of principled morality on the part of the householder. The Holy Scriptures describe the eight organs of right faith. Yasastilakacampu states that right faith is the "prime cause of redemption."

Right knowledge follows from faith. It is obtained by studying the teachings of the Tirthankars. Because it is the basis of right conduct, Jain doctrine explains it minutely. It ranges all the way from sense knowledge to reasoning, clairvoyance, direct awareness of the thought forms of others and infinite knowledge (Kewal-Gyan). These represent progressive stages.

Right knowledge includes the nature of things in this world. In discussing the qualities of materialistic particles, Jainism finds they are of infinite number and that some of these are obviously contradictory. Simply stated, the qualities of a thing are not exhausted by our comprehension of it, and there is more than meets the eye. Philosophically, this is known as the theory of nonabsolutism (Anekantavada) and calls for an attitude of openness. Our limitations of knowledge dictate a style of relativity. The linguistic manner of expressing different qualities of matter is called Syadvada (the philosophy of qualified assertion). The style of Syadvada allows no room for assertions. This Jain theory of knowledge, incorporating the two tenets of nonabsolutism and relativity, has made an esteemed contribution toward liberalizing the mind of man. It elevates the mystery of life and denigrates dogmatism.

The third jewel is right conduct. Jain Holy Scriptures approach this in progressive succession -conduct for householders and for monks. For the former, the goal sought is the growth of the person and society; for the latter, it is self-realization. All aspirants dedicate themselves to proper conduct through vows (Vratas) and subvows. Vows are at the heart of Jain morality and are undertaken with a full knowledge of their nature and a determination to carry them through.

Principally, Jain ethics specifies Five Minor Vows (Anuvratas), Three Social Vows (Gunavratas), and Four Spiritual Vows (Siksavratas) to be carried out by the householder. Being twelve in number, the texts speak of them as Duvalasaviha Agaradhamma.

The Minor Vows are: ahimsa, truth, nonstealing, celibacy, and nonpossession. They are called "Minor" (anuvrata) because the householder observes them in a modified way. In their full observance by monks, they are called Mahavratas.

Ahimsa is the foundation of Jain ethics. Bhagwan Mahavir called it pure, universal, everlasting. It says: 'one should not injure, subjugate, enslave, torture or kill any animal, life form, organism or sentient being. This is the essence of religion. It embraces the welfare of all animals, visible and invisible. It is the basis of all stages of knowledge and the source of all rules of conduct. The Holy Scriptures analyze the divine and practical aspects of ahimsa and discuss the subject negatively and positively.

Premeditated violence is prohibited for all. A householder is permitted to incur violence defensively and vocationally provided he maintains total detachment. Common violence is accepted for all in the business of remaining alive, but even here, one should be careful in preparing food, cleaning house, etc. This explains the Jain's practices of filtering drinking water, vegetarianism, not eating meals at night, and abstinence from alcohol.

The primacy given to Non-violence by the Indian people has nobly contributed to their character, most dramatically by Mahatma Gandhi. "In the hands of Mahatma Gandhi, Non-violence—the sword of self-suffering—became a mighty instrument" that wielded enormous social and political power with utmost significance for the future of man kind. Jain literature is a treasury of many such characters who exemplify the human potential for living nonviolently in this world.

The second of the five minor vows is Truth. It is more than abstaining from falsehood; it is seeing the world in its real form and adapting to that reality. The vow of truth puts an individual in touch with his inner strength and inner capacities. He becomes secure and fearless. There is then no need to steal—the third vow.

Celibacy is the fourth vow, relevant to monks and householders in differing degrees. Its fundamental intent is to overcome passion and to check the waste of energy. Positively stated, the vow is meant to impart the sense of serenity to the soul. The householder fulfills this vow when he is content with his own wife and is completely faithful to her.

Nonpossession is the fifth miner vow. As long as an individual doesn't know the richness of joy and peace that comes from a consciousness of the soul, he tries to fill his empty and insecure existence with the clutter of materialistic acquisitions. But, as Bhagwan Mahavir said, security born of things is a delusion and must come to nought. To remove this delusion, one takes the vow of nonpossession and realizes the perfection of the soul, Nonpossession, like ahimsa, affirms the oneness of all life and is beneficial both in the divine and social spheres.

In addition to the Five Minor Vows, the householder observes three Social Vows that govern his external conduct in the world. Then there are four Divine vows that reflect the purity of his heart. They govern his internal life and are expressed in a life that is marked by charity (dana).

The Jain householder who observes twelve vows progresses upon the divine path until he comes to the place where he must decide whether to observe the discipline of the monk's life. To enter this higher domain, he must pass through eleven successive stages called Pratimas, Where the eleventh stage is reached, he can start the conduct of a monk.

In order to preserve the integrity of the principal vows listed above, Jain thinkers have prescribed sub-vows as precautionary means. First, there is reference to the Salyas or disturbing factors such as ignorance, deceit, and self-interest, from, which an individual should free himself. The salyas represent the negative requirements for the ideal practice of the vratas. Also, there are the four Bhavanas (virtues) that represent the positive means of supporting the Vratas. These qualities, which a votary of ahimsa must possess, are maitri (love, friendship), pramoda (joy and respect), karunya (compassion), and madhyastha (tolerance toward life forms). Third, there are the twelve sub-vows known as anupreksas (reflections). Broadly stated, they are twelve topics of meditation that cover a wide field of teaching. They are designed to serve as aids to divine progress, produce detachment, and lead the devotee from the realm of desire to the path of renunciation. They are reflections upon the central facts of life, intended to develop purity of thought and sincerity in the practice of religion.

In this way Jain ethics prescribes thirty-five rules of conduct for the householder. They are meant for the good of his entire personality. By observing these rules, he comes to possess all of the twenty-one qualities that a fully developed person must manifest.

Having observed all the rules of conduct and having passed through the eleven religious stages (pratimas, the householder is now qualified to become an ascetic. The life of an ascetic is marked by the spirit of detachment. Through the practice of yoga and meditation, he eventually achieves the highest knowledge and becomes an enlightened soul. This is the ultimate end of Jain ethics.

Viewed from the level of the life of an ascetic, Jain ethics appears to be a rigorous discipline for the person, aimed at cultivating his detachment from the world. From a broader view, including the life of the householder, Jain ethics is not just person and divine, but inclusive of all forms of life for the total upliftment of existence. The person who subjects himself to this form of ethics will be serious, good tempered, merciful, straightforward, wise, and modest. He will be sociable, careful in speech, reverent to age and custom. Renouncing ego and belongings, he will endure all manner of rigorousnesses until he achieves the highest ideal of perfection.

MORAL VALUES FOR LEADER

It must not be forgotten that the leader is in reality only an outer agent and a 'substitute', as it were, of the true leader, and that he is necessary only due to the fact that the initiate has not yet reached a certain degree of growth and so is still incapable of entering directly into conscious communication with the latter.

As significant as the role of the leader may really be - and it is not we who would dream of disputing it - we are obliged to say that such an assertion is in total false for several reasons, the first of which is that there are exceptional cases of beings for whom a pure and simple initiatic transmission, without any intervention whatsoever by a spiritual master, suffices to immediately 'awaken' the divine acquisitions obtained in other states of existence; as rare as these cases may be, they prove at the very least that this is in no way a need of principle.

No doubt this has a certain drawback, in the sense that such a path is apparently less sure and more difficult to follow than that where the initiate benefits from the constant supervision of a spiritual master; but this is a different question in total, and what is important from our current point of view is that the very existence of these initiatic forms, which necessarily offer the same goal as the others, and which consequently must offer their adherents means sufficient to reach it, provided only that they are fully qualified, amply proves that the presence of a spiritual master need not be regarded as constituting an indispensable condition in all cases.

And naturally, whether or not there is a human spiritual master, the inner spiritual master is always present, since it is one with the very 'Self'; whether, in order to manifest itself to those who are not yet capable of having an immediate consciousness of it, it takes as support a human being or a 'non-incarnated' spiritual influence is, in the final analysis, only a difference of modality that changes nothing necessary.

We have just said that where it exists, the role of spiritual master is especially important at the beginning of the effective initiation, which might seem perfectly apparent since it is natural that an initiate should have more need of guidance the less he is advanced on the path; and this remark already implicitly refutes another mistake we have noticed, which consists in the claim that there is no true spiritual master but the one who has already reached the goal of spiritual realization, that is, Deliverance.

MORAL DUTIES OF SUBJECTS

Jain society is as dualistic as the Jain cosmos. On the one hand, there are the monks, who practice severe asceticism and strive to make this life their last. Contrarily, there are the lay persons, who pursue less rigorous practices, striving only to do good deeds and hoping for a better avatar in the next life. Due to the strict ethics embedded in Jainism, the laity must choose a profession and livelihood that keeps with the faith, making the safe occupation of trade the number one occupation of choice.

In their effort to achieve their highest hope, which is the permanent release of the jiva from all involvement in worldly existence, the Jains believe that no spirit or divine being can assist them in any way. Hence Jainism is a non-theistic religion. The Jains consider that Gods (i.e., devas) and spirits can influence events of this world only. They can't help the jiva to obtain release. This has to be attained by person through their own efforts. In fact, the Gods can't even gain their own release until they are reincarnated as people and undertake the difficult life of a Jain monk.

The ethical code of Jainism is taken very seriously. Summed up in the Five Vows, they are pursued by both lay persons and ascetics. For lay persons, chastity means confining sexual experience to the marriage relationship. For monks, it means total celibacy. Non-injury commonly means veganism, but some Jains have been known to starve themselves to death in order to avoid injuring any living creature. There are even those who wear masks over their mouths and noses to avoid any possibility of breathing in tiny insects.

The Jains adopted Vedic rites for marriage and other household rituals since the Jain religion itself has neither priests nor rites. They also adopted many of the Hindu deities as a means of explaining how world events may be influenced; they do not, nevertheless, regard such Gods (devas) as ultimate in any important sense of the word. Like us, the Gods are trapped in the cycle of transmigration. Jains have built temples where images of their Tirthankars are venerated in much the same way that Hindus venerate images of God. For instance, Jains venerate Rama, incarnation of Vishnu as a Tirthankar rather than as God. Jain rites are elaborate, and include offerings of flowers, fruit and other symbolic objects, with the Tirthankars being praised in chant using passages from the Jain Holy Scriptures. One Jain symbol incorporates a wheel on the palm of the hand. Another incorporates a swastika or Om on a hand.

MORAL VALUES IN SOCIETY

Pali Literature contains only scanty and scrappy bits of information on the duties of a Jain house-holder. But they are priceless as the gradual growth of the vows could be traced with the help of such information.

The Samannaphala Sutta of the Dighanikaya refers to the Catuyamasamvara as a ppart of the philosophy of Nigantha Nataputta. This is not an accurate record, for Catuyamasamvara is of Parasvanatha, and not in the philosophy of Nigantha Nataputta We shall discuss this matter later on. The four vows of Parasvanatha were revised by Nigantha Nataputta who found it necessary to specify Brahmacharya as a separate vow in view of the laxity he observed amongst the devotees of Parsvanatha. Nigantha Nataputta, therefore, founded a discipline established on five vows as opposed to that a Parsvanatha.

A reference to five vows of Jainism is found in the Anguttara Nikaya, this mentions the five ways of falling into sin as taught by Nigantha Nataputta. The five ways are:

- Destruction of life forms.
- Taking what is not given.
- Passionate enjoyment of evil.
- Speaking lies.
- Taking liquor and intoxicants.

This, again, in only partially accurate. The first four kinds of sins are referred to correctly, although not in the Jain order.

Attachment and intention are very prominent in Jainism. They are regarded as the main sources of Himsa. If one, who abides by the rules of conduct conscientiously, walks along, carefully looking ahead, end intent on avoiding injury to the crawling creatures, were to injure an insect by trampling it under foot by chance, he would not be responsible for Himsa. And if one acts carelessly or intentionally, he would be responsible for that whether a life form is killed or not. For, under the influence of passions, the person first injures the self through the self whether there is later on an injury caused to another being or not:

Both, non-abstinence from Himsa, and indulgence in Himsa, constitute Himsa; and therefore whenever there is careless activiy of mind, body or speech, there is always injury to life form. Mere possession of a sword would not make one guilty of Himsa. Even then such possession can be the cause of some injury to somebody. Thus, to check all possibility of Himsa, one should not entertain even the craving for the possession of such objects as are likely to cause injury.

Therefore all these indicate that intention is the main source of injury in Jainism and if injury is caused by body intentionally, it will be regarded more blamable. If killing of life forms is made an offence even when it is without intention, no one on earth can be an Ahimsaka, for the entire world is full of vitalities of all types which a man may kill in large number without knowing them at all.

Pratimas

The stages of ethical evolution of a Jain house-holder are called the Pratimas and are eleven in number. Ten of them (i.e. excepting Ratribhuktityaga) are referred to indirectly in the Pali Canon. The Anguttara Nikaya gives us a list of monks who were prevalent at that time, and it refers to Nigantha, Mundasavaka, Jatilaka, Paribbajaka, Magandika, Tedandika, Aruddhaka, Gotamaka, and Devadhammika. The Niganthas are undoubtedly the devotees of Nigantha Natputta who performed very severe penances. The same Nikaya enumerates six Abhijatis and in that account the Niganthas are said to have worn one yellow stained cloth (kasayavastra). This may be a reference to Elaka or Esullaka (i.e. the vow of wearing small loin, cloth with or without a cloth to cover the upper body)

Buddhaghosa in his Commentary on the Dhammapada says that more assiduous niganthas cover their water-pots so that no soul and sand should enter it. Commoner ascetic practices are also cited in the Nikayas. Out of them, Nabhihatam (refusing to accept the food especially prepared for them), is related to the eleventh stage of Jain House-holder called Uddistatyaga Pratima. From these indirect references we come to the conclusion that at that time no such name was given to the vratis. Nevertheless, it shows that there were some types of categories of vratis.

PRACTICAL ASPECTS

The Acharyas have discussed same of the social issues that confront us today such as sexual relationships, marriage and household and the role and status of women. Modern scholars also provide us with updated interpretations of ancient tenets.

On the matter of sexual relationships, Jainism sets celibacy (Bramacharya) as the norm. For the monk, the vow is defined as total abstinence, but for the layman it means inner purity. The householder must be content with his own wife and must consider all other women as his sisters, mothers and daughters. The Acharyas had a realistic understanding of the power of sex and counseled against its indulgence through suggestive literature, sexual fantasies and intimacy. Sexual deviations were to be avoided, including contact with lower animals and inanimate objects. The Holy Scriptures provide many examples of positive sexual relationships that are relevant to the current situation.

Women have been accorded equal status to men within the Jain religion. As a matter of fact, there were more women in the order of Bhagwan Mahavir than men. The Holy Scriptures record many tributes to exceptional women. The care of women, especially in critical situations, is given a higher priority than that of men. Mothers of the Tirthankars are given special honour through communal worship. Legends abound in which heroines such as Brahmi, Sundari, Mallikumari, and Rajimati have come to the aid of men. Women have also been celebrated for their learning and have been recognized for their exceptional contributions in the field of education, culture and religion. So far as their legal and social status within the community is concerned, Jain women are on a par with their Hindu sisters.

Jain egalitarianism rejects the Hindu division of society into higher and lower castes. It finds no basis for the concept that makes one caste superior to the other. On the contrary, it finds castism an evil established on hate, arrogance, and deluded vision. Bhagwan Mahavir gave no ground for the supremacy of any caste by reason of birth. This explains why many slaves, untouchables, and low-caste people entered the Jain fold, and some were able to prove their individual merit by rising to the level of saints. Bhagwan Mahavir showed his feelings for the dignity of his fellows by eliminating the convention of caste distinctions in mutual address. He says, "Worthy beings! Take it as my command that henceforth no monk address another by the latter's caste.' He was very conscious that arrogance of caste is destructive of communal solidarity.

The eighth and ninth sermons contained in the Uttaradhasana Sutra ethicize the idea of caste so that virtue, not birth, is the hallmark of an individual's standing. It is said, "One becomes a Sramana by equanimity, a Brahmana by chastity, a Muni by knowledge and a Tapasa by penance. By one's action one becomes a Brahmana or a Ksatriya or a Vaisya or a Sudra."

In a similar vein, Acharya Amitagati said that, "Good individuals should not havc arrogance in any class as it leads to degradation, but they should observe good conduct which might give them high position.'

It is clear that there is no religious support for castism in the Jain tradition. Nevertheless, in the course of history, because of certain social factors, the Jain did form a large number of castes and subcastes. Even so, the Jain community has been foremost in social services that cross all caste barriers and it has served as a cohesive force for national unity.

Social service is an important outcome of Jain ethics. It prescribes six daily duties for every householder. These duties are, adoration of deity (Jin), veneration of the Gurus, study of literature and Holy Scriptures, practice of self discipline, observance of fastings and curbing appetites, and charity. All of these daily duties are related to the performance of social service for mankind.

The duty of charity (dana) sets the mood and manner of the layman's daily life. One performs charity, not on a cloud of sentiment, but following the details of scripture so that it is all done wisely, equitably, politely, and in a spirit of gratitude and humility.

One vow of spiritual discipline (siksavrata) that the householder takes is that of hospitality to monks, (Atithi Samvibhaga Vrata). This involves the supply of food, texts, medicine, etc. Acharya Samantabhadra calls the vow of hospitality physical service (Vaiyavrtya). It makes the householder into the parent of the monk. Sick, aged, and helpless monks are therefore taken care of in their time of need. The practice of such physical service developed especially in the area of medical charities (Ausadhi-Dana). Its effect was the creation of a communal sense of fearlessness (Abhaya-Dana).

Jain ethics also makes the study of Holy Scriptures (Svadhyaya) an important service for monk and layman. This endeavor is known as Sastra-Dana. Its objective is to advance knowledge, purge mistake, and to bring many others into its orbit of nirvana, By following the duty of scriptural charity, Jain laymen have erected prestigious libraries containing many literary treasures. These Grantha-Bhandaras are not confined to Jain works but contain collections which are of value for Indian culture at large.

This brief listing of social services should make it plain that there is no conflict in Jain ethics between personal piety and social outreach. The six daily duties of the householder are individual, but not private; they extend into the community of which the person is a part.

REFERENCES

Amar, Muni: *Jainatva ki Jhanki, Sanmati Grantharatnamala No. 12*, Sanmati Gyanpeeth, Seventh Edition, Agra, 1987.

Bhattacharya, B.C.: *Jaina Iconography*, 2nd ed, Motilal Banarsidass, Delhi, 1974.

Bhattacharya, N.N.: *Jain Philosophy, Historical Outline*. Munshiram Manoharlal, New Delhi, 1976.

Bool Chand: *Lord Mahavira*, Banaras, 1948

Bothra, P.: *Jain Theory of Perception*, Motilal Banarsidass, Delhi, 1976.

Brown, Percy: *Indian Architecture*, Bombay, 2nd Edn.

Ghosh, A.): *Jaina Arts and Architecture*, New Delhi, 1974.

Glassenapp, H.V: *Doctrine of Karman in Jaina Philosophy*, Bombay, 1942.

Gopal, S.: *Outlines of Jainism*, New Delhi, 1973.

Gopalan, A.S.: *Outlines of Jainism*, Willey Eastern (P) Limited, New Delhi, First Edition, 1973.

Guseva, N.R: *Jainism*, Bombay, 1971.

Hume, Robert Earnest: *Thirteen Principal Upanisads (Trans.)*, Oxford, 1921.

Jacobi, H.: *Introduction to Kalpa-sutra.*

Jaini, P.S.: *The Jaina Path of Purification*, Berkeley: University of California Press, 1979.

Jaini, Padmanabh, S.: *The Jaina Path of Purigication*, California, 1979.

James, William: *Principles of Psychology, Vol. I*, Macmillan & Co., London, 1918.

Jindal, K.B: *The prefaces*, Calcutta, 1958

Kalghatagi, T.G.: *Jaina View of Life*, Sholapur, 1969.

Kapadia, H.R.: *Jaina Religion and Literature*, Lahore, 1944.

Mookerjee, S.: *The Jain Philosophy of Non-absolutism, a Critical Study of Anekantavada. 2nd. Ed,* Motilal Banarsidass, Delhi, 1978.

Nahar and Ghosh: *An Epitome of Jainism,* Calcutta 1917.

Nevaskar B.: *Capitalists without Capitalism. the Jains of India and the Quakers of the West,* Greenwood Publications, Westport, 1971.

Nyayavatara: Siddhasena, Translated by Vijayamurti Sastracarya, Paramashruta Prabhavaka Mandal, Jauhari Bazar-Bombay, First Edition, 1950.

Padmarajiah, Y.J.: *Jain Theories of Reality and Knowledge,* Bombay, 1963.

Saletore, B.A: *Medieval Jainism,* Bombay, 1938.

Samaya-sara: Kunda-kunda, Bharatiya Gyanpeeth, Durgakund Road, Varanasi, First Edition, 1950.

Sangave, V.S.: *Jaina Community, a Social Survey. 2nd. ed.* Popular Prakashan, Bombay, 1980.

Sangave, Vilas A.: *Life and Legacy of Mahavira:* A Social Study, Meerut, 1974.

Sangave, Vilas A.: *The Sacred Shravan-belagola: A Socio-Religious Study,* New Delhi, 1981.

Sarvartha-siddhi: Pujapada Devanandi, Edited by Pt. Phoolachandra Siddhantashastri, Bharatiya Gyanpeeth, Durgakund Road, Varanasi, 1955.

Schubring, W.: *The Doctrine of the Jains,* Motilal Banarsidass, Delhi, 1962.

Schubring, Walther: *The Religion of the Jainas,* New Delhi 1966.

Shah, Chimanlal J.: *Jainism in North India,* London, 1932.

Shah, U.P.: *'Jainism', New Encyclopaedia Britannica,* Chicago, 1974.

Shah, Umakant P.: *Studies in Jaina Art,* Banaras, 1955.

Tukol, T.K.: *Compendium of Jainism,* Dharwad, 1980.

Upadhye, A.N.: *Lord Mahavira and his Teachings. 2nd. Ed,* Shree Vallabhsuri Smarak Nidhi, Bombay,1983.

Uttaradhyayana-sutra: Editor Madhukara Muni, Jinagama Granthamala No. 19, Agama Prakashan Samiti, Byavara, First Edition, 1984.

Warren, H.: *Jainism in Western Garb, as a Solution to Life's Great Problems,* Edited, with notes, by N.J. Shah. 2nd. ed. Shree Vallabhsuri Smarak Nidhi, Bombay, 1983.

Warren, Herbert: *Jainism,* Arrah, 1916.

Williams, R.: *Jaina Yoga: A survey of Medieval Sharavakachara,* London, 1963.

9

Movements

While Jains represent less than 1% of the Indian population, their contributions to culture and society in India are considerable. Jainism had a major influence in developing a system of doctrine and ethics that had a major impact on all aspects of Indian culture in all ages : from Upanishads to Mahatma Gandhi. The scholarly research and evidences have shown that philosophical concepts considered typically Indian – Karma, Non-violence, Moksh, rebirth and like - either originate in the sramana school of thought or were spread and developed by Jain teachers.These concepts were later assimilated in Hinduism and other religions, often in a different form and with different meanings.

Jains have also wielded great influence on the culture and language of Karnatak, Southern India and Gujarat most significantly. The earliest known Gujarati text, Bharat-Bahubali Ras, was written by a Jain monk. Some prominent individuals in Gujarat's Jain history were Acharya Hemacandra Suri and his pupil, the Calukya ruler Kumarapala.

Jains are both amongst the wealthiest Indians and the most philanthropic. They run many schools, colleges and hospitals and are prominent patrons of the Somapuras, the traditional temple architects in Gujarat. Jains have greatly influenced Gujarati cuisine. Gujarat is mainly vegetarian, and its food is mild as onions and garlic are omitted.

Jains encourage their monks to do research and obtain higher education. Jain monks and nuns, especially in Rajasthan, have published many research monographs. This is distinctive amongst Indian religious groups and parallels Christian clergy. The 2001 census states that Jains are India's most literate community and that India's oldest libraries at Patan and Jaisalmer are preserved by Jain institutions.

The diversity of denominations and sub-sects in Jainism is a characteristic feature of its long history and also of its manifestations of religious reform in the contemporary period. As one distinguished western observer of Jainism, Kendall W. Folkert, pointed out that the true nature of this great religion can be understood only if we emphasise not so much the broad divisions into Digambar and Shvetambar denominations but direct our probe into the importance and rationale of small sub-divisions. There are two major factors behind the unity of Jainism despite these divisions: one, attempts by all to unravel the original philosophy and practice of the devotees of Jin, and, two, the overarching philosophical credo of 'the many— pointed nature of truth' (anekanta and syadavad) in Jainism. There is scope for a variety of interpretations to be subsumed under the umbrella of a united Jain faith. The emergence of sub-divisions is not an attempt at deviation from the earlier charters, but a constant return to the roots and an effort to build up on those foundations what is conceived as the 'original' or authentic structure by cutting away the accretions of sectarianism and false philosophy. An examination of the nature of reform movements within Jainism further elucidates as to why the faith of the Jin has coexisted in a symbiotic relationship with Hinduism and how-unlike Buddhism, for instance, it has shown notable continuity of precept and practice within the geographical confines of India with almost negligible spread beyond Indian borders (except in very recent times).

Of the different divisions, the Shvetambar and Digambar are of ancient vintage whereas the Sthanakvasi, Terapanth and Kanji Swami divisions represent movements, which began in the fifteenth, seventeenth and nineteenth centuries respectively. Again, whereas there are separate Terapanth denominations in Shvetambar (1653 AD.) and Digambar (1626 AD) branches, the Kanji Swami denomination cuts across the two major divisions (Shvetambar and Digambar) of Jainism. The ancient divisions of Jainism have been discussed in Unit 8, but in order to trace the history of other contemporary movements we shall have to go back briefly to the late mediaeval period. Here we shall first deal with the sectarian reform movements within Jainism with special reference to the religious philosophies, practices and personages of each contemporary denomination. This will be pursued by specifically social reform activities in Jainism during the nineteenth and twentieth centuries.

RELIGIOUS MOVEMENTS

A common feature of all religious reform movements in Jainism is the use of the Hindi and Gujarati term "uddhar" which is often seen as the equivalent of English 'reform' but signifies literally 'a raising up' (it can also be used to describe the restoration of a ruined temple). This term is employed by sympathetic Jain writers in the sense both of a retrieval and reactivation of a fundamental philosophy of ahimsa and renunciation taught by Bhagwan Mahavir and a concomitant rejection of what are regarded as the debased practices, which attend this particular period of the world era. Interestingly enough, given the individualistic bias of Jainism (viz., for achieving Moksh or redemption) these reform movements are usually spearheaded by known persons who may or may not begin a line of pupillary succession. Therefore the three sectarian movements that we shall discuss were led by persons : Sthanakvasi and Terapanth (anti-image or aniconic denominations amongst the Shvetambars); Sthanakvasi by Lonka or Lonka Shah and also a merchant called Lavaji, Terapanth by Acharya Bhikshu and Kanji Swami Panth (originally Shvetambar but later on Digambar) by Kanji Swami.

The Sthanakvasi

A somewhat mysterious person in Jainism, Lonka or Lonka Shah existed in Gujarat during the fifteenth century. Tradition is unanimous that an inspection of the Shvetambar Holy Scriptures led him to deny that image-worship could have any place in true Jainism. The Sthanakvasi whose remote founding father he is see him as a rich, mighty and learned layman with powerful connections amongst the Moslem authorities in Ahmedabad, whose skills in calligraphy led to an invitation to copy the Holy Scriptures. After serious study of the Holy Scriptures he became convinced that the practice of Jainism he saw around him was without any textual basis and totally corrupt. Accepting the authority of only thirty-two of the scriptural texts and rejecting a great deal of rite of all kinds, he took some sort of ascetic initiation and became a charismatic teacher who weaned away large number of Shvetambars from their image-related practices.

A balanced picture of Lonka's career is presented recently by Pandit Dalsukh Malvania, a Sthanakvasi layman and one of the most distinguished twentieth century interpreters of the Jain intellectual tradition. The aniconic ideal of Lonka's devotees did not long survive the death of its inspiration. The pupillary descent started by him (Lonka gaccha) gradually reverted to image-worship as there is inscriptional evidence to prove the consecration of temples and installation of images by acharyas of that gaccha. Nevertheless, in 1644 the Mughal Emperor issued an edict to exclude the lay members of the Lonka gaccha from communal meals with Shvetambar community in Ahmedabad, which not only seriously impeded their business activity but also suggests that they were not fully assimilated into the image-worshipping community. The Lonka gaccha today has no fully initiated monks and exists only at the fringes of Shvetambar society.

The Sthanakvasis were formed by the seventeenth century Gujarati merchant called Lavaji who along with another merchant Dharmasimha broke away from the Lonka gaccha. As with Lonka there is some doubt about whether Lavaji took formal ascetic initiation but there is no doubt that the substance of his criticism of the Lonka gaccha was directed to its general laxity and he consequently expressed a wish to revert to the model of ascetic behaviour found in the Dashavaikalika which did not, naturally, include image-worship. The three monks who came after him in pupillary succession pursued the practice envisaged in the earliest Holy Scriptures of lodging in ruined and deserted building due to which the monks of this nascent sub sect were called Dhumdhiya, 'Searchers' (for suitable lodgings).

The Sthanakvasis, as they are known today, evolved from these monks, the name meaning 'Living in Lodging Houses (Sthanaka), a reference to the fact that the monks of this denomination shunned the upashrayas lodgings which the image-worshippers erected in the vicinity of temples. Lavaji was responsible for the introduction of a practice which has proceeded to distinguish Sthanakvasi and Terapanthi monks from those of other Shvetambar denominations : the permanent wearing of a strip of cloth across the mouth, tied behind the ears, known as muhpatti, mouth-shield (square in shape for the Sthanakvasis, rather more narrow and elongated for the Terapanthis), which by minimizing the destruction of air-bodies and tiny insects through the outflow or inflow of breath is an outward sign of the ascetic's dedication to ahimsa. Shvetambar image-worshipping monks today all possess muhpattis and one of their most conventional poses in portraits and photographs is with a book in one hand and a muhpatti in the other, symbolising knowledge and compassion.

These monks tie or hold in hand the muhpatti only on special worship or rite occasions. In fact, with the image-worshipping Shvetambars even the lay persons tie up a handkerchief over their mouth and nostrils while praying close to the image. Nevertheless, what distinguishes the practice of muhpatti by aniconic Sthanakvasis and Terapanthis is that the muhpatti be worn permanently by monks. It is worth-noting that though the ostensible reason for their emergence was a process of ascetic reform initiated by Lavaji and Dharmasimha, it has been suggested with some plausibility that those who became Sthanakvasis were in fact trying to break away from high caste domination and in reality the origins of the denomination may well lie in the realm of lay business competition. As with other Jain denominations, the Sthanakvasis split at a fairly early stage into branches, in this case as many as twenty-two established on regional and perceptorial connections. The Sthanakvasis have remained a resilient part of the Jain community whose reputation for devotion to the tenets of ahimsa and compassion is high. In the past, the Sthanakvasis were located chiefly in the north and the west in towns such as Ludhiana in Punjab and Limbdi in Gujarat.

Now, however, due to increasing internal migration by the Sthanakvasi laity in India, they have become more widespread and Sthanakvasi monks can often be found passing caturmas (the four month rainy season retreat) in the south of the subcontinent. Recently, the Sthanakvasi monk, Sushil Kumar Muni (1926-1994) gained comparative fame in public life for his attempts to intervene positively in the different communal disputes, which plague contemporary Indian society. Having been denied his wish to proselytize Jainism in the West by his religious superiors, in 1974 Sushil Muni split off the aniconic Sthanakvasi Sraman Sangha together with twenty other monks and founded his own religious order, the Arhat Sangha. He then headed to New Jersey, where he founded first the International Bhagwan Mahavir Jain Mission and later, in 1983, Siddhacalam, the first asrama for Jain monks and laity in the West. Sushil Muni also organized the first World Jain Conference in New York (1981), which was succeeded by confrences in Leicester (1983) and Delhi (1985, 1987), and Asian Jain Conferences in Bangkok (1988) and Singapore (1989).

Terapanth

Acharya Bhikshu, the eighteenth century Shvetambar reformer and founding father of the Terapanth denomination, is one of the best-documented figure in the history of Jainism. Bhikshu (often known by the Rajasthani version of his name, Bhikhanji) was born in 1726 in the desert region of Marwar in Rajasthan. It is likely that the vigorous and uncompromising variety of Jainism he preached had something to do with the rugged ecology of his birth and activity. Bhikshu belonged to the fairly many Bisa Oswal caste and originally took initiation in 1751 as a Sthanakvasi monk under Acharya Raghunathji. He maintained that the Jain path could involve nothing but total dedication and his experiences as a Sthanakvasi monk revealed to him a host of imperfections in the denomination, which led to his breaking away from it in 1759.

Along with thirteen other monks who pursued him, Bhikshu formed the Terapanth ('tera' means thirteen in Rajasthani and Hindi). In keeping with its rigorous nature, the monks of Terapanth undertook elaborate and long fasting and observed the strictest ahimsa, viz. tying the muhpatti all the time. Bhikshu made a difference between laukika (worldly) and lokottara (transcendent) religious practices and stressed the latter urging even the laity to aspire to them. The full community of Terapanthis, including lay supporters, was formed in 1765.

When Bhiksu died in 1803, he had initiated fifty-six nuns and forty nine monks which, in the light of what little is known of Shvetambar ascetic demography at the time, probably represents a reasonably significant number. What was distinctly new in Terapanth was its insistence on the centrality of the acharya, the assumption by him of all ascetic offices and the subordination of all Terapanth monks to him. The ninth acharya (from 1936 to 1998), Acharya Tulsi presided over a recent notable expansion of Terapanthi activity and was responsible for the high profile of the denomination in post-independence India. He carried out the largest number of initiations of any Terapanthi acharya and planned for the first Jain University in Ladnun, his birthplace in Rajasthan. In 1949, he established the Anuvrata movement, dedicated to raising the ethical tone of Indian public and commercial life by taking Jainism beyond the Jains, which was to become the best-known Terapanthi enterprise in India and an outward expression of the denomination's identity.

The movement had some of the trappings of an internationalist western-style peace movement. To quote Acharya Tulsi, 'If an atom (anu) has in it the monstrous power to destroy the world, amply demonstrated in the unprecedented holocaust at Hiroshima and Nagasaki, I want to tell the world that we have its counterpart in anuvrata- a small or atomic vow-which alone has the power to ward off and counter the threat of an atom bomb." (cited in Dundas, 1992). A member of this movement, as conceived by Acharya Tulsi, would take both a general, and depending on his or her status and walk of life, a modified version of the anuvratas, the lay lesser vows, which through effecting a ethical reformation would "inspire people to cultivate self-restraint irrespective of their caste, colour, creed, country and language, to establish the values of friendship, unity, peace and morality, to create an unfettered society free from exploitation." (cited in Dundas).

Another Terapanthi innovation, associated with Acharya Tulsi's successor and current head, Yuvacharya Mahaprajna, is the growth of a modern form of Jain meditation known as prekshadhyana, 'insight-meditation', which is designed to "engage the mind fully in the perception of subtle, internal and innate phenomenon of consciousness" (cited in Dundas). As Dundas has pointed out, "this system, takes its inspiration from scattered scriptural statement about perceiving the self with the self, while also drawing eclectically on a wide range of sources in other traditions, provides a meditative structure...for a religion which seems to have lost contact with its original system of contemplation at least one thousand years ago." (Dundas).

Another notable feature is the Terapanthi leadership's willingness to break with Jain tradition's longstanding prohibition of monks travelling into 'non-Aryan' lands. Here, lower-order male and female ascetics called saman and samani have been trained and granted special dispensation to travel abroad. Though they take the five Great Vows, they are unlike normal monks in that to facilitate their activities outside India they are allowed to use mechanical means of transport and to accept food, which has been specially prepared for them.

The Kanji Swami Panth

The most successful twentieth century Jain movement has unquestionably been the Kanji Swami Panth. Kanji Swami was born in 1889 into a Sthanakvasi household in a small village in the Kathiawar region of Gujarat. Orphaned at an early age, he gradually became inclined towards the ascetic life and in 1913 took initiation as a Sthanakvasi monk. Though he soon became a learned and celebrated monk, carrying the title 'Kohinoor of Kathiawar', Kanji Swami was never able to engage fully with the Shvetambar Holy Scriptures, which he felt lacked a sense of soul. The event, which changed the course of Kanji Swami's life, was his discovery around 1921 of Kundakunda's 'Essence of the Philosophy'.

Soon afterwards he studied other Digambar Holy Scriptures such as the writings of Todarmal and Shrimad Rajachandra, due to which he became convinced that Digambar Jainism was the true path. Nevertheless, for some time he led a kind of double life, nominally a Sthanakvasi monk but regarded himself as a Digambar until 1934 when his divine crisis came to an end. In that year during the celebration of Bhagwan Mahavir Jayanti in the small town of Songarh he threw away his muhpatti and proclaimed himself to be a Digambar layman. Kanji Swami never became a Digambar monk, nevertheless. Initially the Shvetambar Sthanakvasi community of Gujarat was resentful of what it conceived to be an apostasy towards Digambar philosophy in Kanji Swami's teachings as also of the movement's un-Gujarati character.

Finally the local Sthanakvasis seem to have become reconciled to Kanji Swami and indeed virtually all of the three hundred or so families who today live at Songarh and belong to the Kanji Swami Panth claim to be of Sthanakvasi background. As regards the philosophies of the Panth, there is insistence on the primacy of the higher level of truth (nishcaya naya) over the lower one of common life (vyavahara naya). For Kanji Swami, the three Jewels of right faith, knowledge and practice could only function properly on the basis of a prior experience of the soul, and the different rites and merit-making practices of Jainism were regarded as subordinate and basically irrelevant through their being linked to the passions.

As per Kanji, it was only the pure soul, which could bring about spiritual deliverance. The Kanji Swami Panth has always been a lay movement and initiated monks are accorded no special status. Nonetheless, Kanji Swami was respectful of monks since he regarded them as personifying the key tenets of Jainism. Similarly, although he was critical of elaborate worship and rites, yet he accepted the worship of images in temples of Digambar Jain tradition some of which he himself consecrated. He also undertook extensive pilgrimages (by motor vehicle) to Digambar holy places throughout India. Whereas Songarh in Gujarat was the founding place of this Panth, another leading centre was founded in Jaipur and today a large number of its devotees are found amongst the born-Digambars and also the Digambar-converts all over North India.

The Kanji Swami Panth got embroiled in the politics of the Digambar Jains but its adherents proceeded to increase. Due to its insistence on simplified procedures of rite and worship, it also became increasingly popular in the diasporic Jain community. Kanji Swami died at Mumbai in 1981. We have so far seen how sects and sub-sects arose around certain key persons in the Jain tradition. Amongst Sthanakvasis and Terapanthis, these leaders gave rise to pupillary succession. Especially amongst the Shvetambar Terapanthis the office of the acharya became the pivot of centralization and unity amongst both its lay and ascetic devotees. The Kanji Swami movement, contrarily, has remained a lay movement without initiating pupillary succession. However, Kanji Swami too started a new denomination or Panth.

Shrimad Rajachandra

Like his predecessor Banarsidas, the mystic Shrimad Rajachandra (1867-1901) was a layman who attempted to point to the truth of Jainism on the basis of direct individual experience. Raichandbhai Mohte (the honourific name Shrimad Rajachandra was to be bestowed on him by his devotees) was born in the small Gujarati port of Vavania in a household which was partly Jain (on his mother's side) and partly Vaishnava Hindu and, though it is difficult to see Rajachandra as anything other than a Jain, the influence of Hinduism coloured his writings and he often talked about God in the vocabulary of Vaishnava theism. Rajachandra claimed to have achieved memory of his former births at the age of seven. He was intellectually and spiritually a precocious youth. Having extensively read Jain and other religious literature by the time he was sixteen, he produced a variety of writing before he was twenty, which show his familiarity with the technicalities of Jain doctrine.

The major influence on Rajachandra was of Digambar texts, especially Kundakunda's writings about the true nature of the soul. He criticized sectarianism and rites in the extant brand of Jainism. In a letter written in 1887, he affirmed what his position was with regard to Jainism : "to be entirely free in whatever way from attachment and hate is my religion....Do not forget that I don't belong to any gaccha but only to my soul." Nevertheless, it is noteworthy that, despite has initial dubiety, Rajachandra came to accept the validity of image-worship as an aid to divine advancement. The main body of Rajachandra's writings includes about eight hundred letters throughout his life, which chart clearly his divine growth.

At the age of twenty, he was already making claims for himself as a spiritual leader, and in 1890 he attained what he held to be a state of realization which he described in a letter of 1897: "I am distinct from everything in all respects. I am only most pure consciousness, most exalted and unthinkable and an unadulterated pure experience-self... I direct my resultant consciousness to my soul. I absorb myself deeply within it". Rajachandra summarized his interpretation of Jainism in his 'Attainment of the Soul' (Atmasiddhi), a short verse treatise written in the course of one night in 1896. The divine climax of Rajachandra's life is regarded by his devotees as having taken place on a hill outside Idar, a small town in north Gujarat. There he practiced intense austerities and preached to seven Shvetambar monks who had become his followers, one of whom had broken his ascetic vows to follow Rajachandra, expounding his mastery of his inner being.

Rajachandra died in 1901 in Rajkot, worn out, one suspects, by effects of continual fasting. Rajachandra is best known outside the Jain community for the brief relationship he formed with the young Mohandas, later Mahatma Gandhi and it is still not uncommon in Gujarat to hear

Rajachandra described as Gandhi's guru. The two young fellow-Gujaratis were introduced in Bombay in 1891, just after Gandhi returned from studying in Britain, and he recorded his impressions of Rajachandra in his autobiography, paying tribute to the role the Jain played, at least in part, in his divine growth. While working in South Africa, Gandhi became attracted to Christianity and he was to credit Rajachandra with providing him through letters with the divine counsel, which was to lead him back to Hinduism.

Gandhi's understanding of the nature of religion and stress on ahimsa was possibly influenced by his early contact with Rajachandra. Though it is difficult to gauge the number of Rajachandra's devotees today, most Jains would regard him as a great teacher and there are Shrimad Rajachandra temples throughout India and in East Africa, Britain and North America. Rajachandra's stress upon self-experience suggest that his teachings will continue to maintain their appeal.

REFORM MOVEMENTS

Though it is difficult to separate social and religious reform movements in a world-religion like Jainism, yet it may be pointed out that the above-cited religious movements have often been either accompanied by social reform or co-existed with it.

Reform Movements in the Digambar Sect

Leaders of different denominations amongst Jains launched several reform movements pertaining to issues and problems, which they regarded imminent, and pressing both from religious and social points of view. In reform movements amongst the Digambar sect, the 'Das Pujadhikara Andolana' i.e., 'the Dasas' Right to Worship Movement' occupies a important position. The 'Dasas' are persons belonging to the 'Dasa' divisions of Jain castes. The use of 'Visa' and 'Dasa' as names of divisions of castes is common amongst the Jain castes like Agarwala, Osavala, Hummada, Porvada in northern and western India. The term 'Visa' signifies 'twenty in the score' i.e. pure, and 'Dasa' signifies 'ten in the score', i.e., half-pure.

Such Visa and Dasa divisions are treated in a descending order of social respectability and are regarded as heterogamous divisions for marital purposes. As Dasa persons were assigned a lower position in the caste system, different social restrictions were enforced on their inter- dining and inter-marriage relations. Along with these social restrictions, certain religious disabilities were also forced on them. The Dasa persons were not allowed to perform puja or worship in the temples. This form of religious discrimination and social injustice was not liked by the leading intellectuals and was strongly opposed by the Dasa persons amongst the Digambar Jains.

Pandit Gopaladasaji Baraiyya of Banaras spearheaded the movement and declared in unambiguous terms that 'in accordance with the liberal tenets of Jainism the Dasas have the equal right to worship like the non-Dasa persons'. This stand taken by the pandits and the intellectuals was opposed by rich persons and after a protracted controversy, the matter was referred to a court of law where the judge gave the decision that the Dasas have no right to worship as there is no custom or practice in prevalence to that effect. The court decision gave rise to widespread disquiet between the Visa and Dasa sections for a long time and considering the stiff and adamant attitude of the Visa sections, many Dasa persons left the Digambar denomination and joined the Shvetambar denomination.

Later, the All India Digambar Jain Parishad, Delhi, the national representative organisation of the Digamabara Jains, rejuvenated the movement and, due to its strenuous efforts, circumstances changed and the Dasa persons in practice began to enjoy in full measure their right to worship in Jain temples and even built temples from their own funds for common use. The second prominent movement of a socio-religious nature with far-reaching effects was launched by the Digamabara Jains at the beginning of the twentieth century. The movement was known as 'shastra-mudrana Virodhi Andolana' i.e. the Anti-Scripture Printing Movement and it aimed at preventing the Shastras, the sacred literature preserved in manuscript form, from being printed and published in text form. Several intellectual and social leaders from north India like Babu Suraja-bhanaji, Babu Jyotiprasadaji Jain and Pandit Chandrasen Vaidya strongly pleaded for the printing and publication of ancient Holy Scriptures on all subjects in text form so that they could be easily accessible to the general public and be useful in guiding their social and religious practices.

This was opposed by the orthodox sections because they believed that printing the Holy Scriptures in text form was an anti-religious act. They considered that it was sin to touch a printed religious text and hence they not only forbid keeping the printed religious texts in temples but also enforced a social and religious boycott on the publishers of such texts. This opposition could not stand for a long time in the changed circumstances of life when leaders of all other religions had started to make use of the printing machine.

Slowly the opposition fizzled out, the printing of ritualistic literature and sacred texts was started, separate Jain scripture publishing concerns were founded and publication of many texts under the 'Jain Sacred Literature Series' was undertaken. The commencement of this publication activity on a large scale greatly helped in ushering social reform amongst Jains in different parts of India.

Reform Movements in the Shvetambar Sect

In the Shvetambar sect also, some prominent movements of a socio-religious nature took place in the early decades of the twentieth century. Amongst the Murtipujaka Shvetambar Jains, the 'Bala-diksha Pratibandha Andolana' i.e. the 'Prevention of Initiation of Children Movement' was started by important intellectuals and social workers. It was directed against the prevailing large- scale practice of initiating adolescents and young children (sometimes children of below 10 years) to the ascetic order of the sect because it was felt that small children are not at all in a position to take an independent decision regarding the adoption of the ascetic career as a goal in their life.

The movement dragged on for a long time and, due to protracted controversies, the general public opinion moved in favour of putting a virtual ban on such initiation of children and in favour of prescribing an age limit for entry into the ascetic order. In spite of forceful propaganda and general awakening, the movement could not succeed in completely stopping the practice, but the actual frequency of such initiations became much less. The youth amongst the Shvetambar Jains took a lead in this movement and founded a new organization known as Jain Yuvak Sangh for carrying out this and other social reforms amongst Jains. Due to this agitation the old princely State of Baroda passed legislation prohibiting initiation of children in the state. Amongst the Sthanakvasi Shvetambar Jains, the 'Ek Acharya Andolan', i.e. the 'One Religious Head Movement, was started by intellectuals and social workers with a view to establishing the power of one acharya (pontiff) on the entire ascetic order of the Sthanakvasi denomination.

As we have seen, the movement succeeded and the system of supremacy of one acharya was recognised and accepted by the Sthanakvasi Jains. Accordingly, monks of the Sthanakvasi section from all over India were brought under the direct control of one acharya. This resulted in bringing necessary unity amongst the laity of the Sthanakvasi section also, as the lay members were dependent on the monks for the performance of religious rituals and ceremonies on account of the total absence of idol worship. Therefore, unity amongst the monks and lay members of the Sthanakvasi denomination under the power of one acharya was forged and proceeded. This kind of unity is not found amongst the Digambar Jains and the Murtipujaka Shvetambar Jains.

REVIVALIST MOVEMENTS

In addition to movements of a socio-religious nature cited above, from the early years of the twentieth century strictly social reform movements were also launched by intellectuals and social workers amongst Jains in different parts of India. These movements were chiefly directed towards brining about necessary reforms in the fields of marriage, education, and social customs and tradition. The chief concern of the social reform movement amongst Jains was to initiate major changes in several practices connected with different aspects of marriage, like age of marriage, preliminaries to marriage, selection of marriage partners, celebration of marriage ceremony, and widow remarriage. In the field of education also, several efforts were made by Jains from the commencement of the twentieth century, so that they did not lag behind other communities in the race for advancement started under the impact of western culture.

In the early stages, a protracted controversy raged as to whether to continue the orthodox system of religious education through 'Pathsalas' (i.e. indigenous schools) or to adopt the new system of secular education transmitted through schools and colleges especially started for the purpose by the government or by the other public bodies. The leaders of the community eventually decided to popularize and spread secular learning but, at the same time, to continue to keep the base of religious education to the maximum extent possible. As a result, along with religious education, secular education was also brought within the reach of all members of the Jain community. Residential schools and colleges known as Gurukulas were started where students are prepared for different university courses but, at the same time, care is taken that they lead a rigorously religious life.

This Gurukula system of education is becoming popular because the students trained by these institutions remain religious- minded throughout their life and are also in a position to maintain themselves. The Bhagwan Mahavir Brahmacharyashrama, the Gurukula at Karanja in Maharashtra, and the Yashovijayaji Jain Gurukul at Palitana in Gujarat are notable institutions of this kind. The number of such Gurukulas is small because of the heavy expenditure required. Where Gurukulas could not be founded, boarding houses or hostels have been started at practically all big places and centres of education throughout India. Here, residential housing is given to Jain students free of rent or on nominal rates. Students occupying such hostels are free to join any institution for their education, but they are expected to take elementary religious education for which provision is made by the authorities, and to lead a religious life (that is, to visit the temple daily, to refrain from eating at night or eating prohibited things, etc.).

Poor and deserving hostel students are given financial help in one form or another. With a view to accelerating the spread of education, special funds are constituted to give scholarships or loans to deserving Jain students wherever they may be. Usually, the scholarship amount is given on the condition that the receiver has to refund it by instalments when he completes his education and is settled in life. In awarding the scholarships, preference is shown to those who wish to pursue higher studies in Jainology or craving to take specialized courses. The spread of higher education amongst Jains at present is chiefly due to the help rendered to them through different means provided by the Jain community. Adequate attention was also paid by Jains towards the spread of female education. Like boarding houses or students' hostels for boys, Shravikashrams (women's homes) were started by Jains at prominent places.

The Shravikashrams were specially designed and organized to impart religious and secular education to female students, to provide lodgings for working women, to give residential facilities to female students enrolled in other institutions, to provide shelter to orphans, widows and deserted women and, in recent times, to arrange vocational training and run small scale industries for the benefit of women. In some places special scholarship funds have been created with a view to delivering help to poor and deserving women students and to encourage talented girls to take specialized training courses required for different careers and professions. In the field of social customs and traditions, it can be stated that many undesirable and anti-social practices, which were prevalent in other societies, were not found amongst the Jains. For instance, in ancient times, in almost all patriarchal societies, the birth of a girl was not a welcome event and this gave rise to practices like female infanticide and neglect of female children.

This custom of infanticide of girls crept into some sections of Hindu society during the medieval period and was in vogue till it was prohibited by the early British rulers. Since Jain doctrine is established on the main principle of Non-violence or non-injury to life forms, female infanticide was not even thought of in the Jain community at any time. For the same reason, female children were not purposefully neglected although sometimes they might have been regarded as a burden on the household. Similarly, the practice of 'sati' (self-immolation by widows), which was common amongst the Hindus, was conspicuous by its absence amongst the Jains.

Further, the custom of tonsure was practiced by Hindu widows from about 1200 AD. and was in vogue in many quarters till recent times. But the Jain widows never pursued this custom. Amongst the Jain women only the Sadhvis (nuns) used to be shaved in accordance with the rules of asceticism prescribed for them. In respect of observance of social customs and traditions, it may be said that several Jain associations and Jain journals and newspapers started during the British period at the national, regional and social levels tried by all means of propaganda and education to eradicate bad and irreligious practices which had crept into the Jain community from medieval times due to lack of knowledge of Jain doctrine and Holy Scriptures and the impact of devotees of other religions and customs on Jains. Chiefly due to their efforts, the worship of Hindu Gods has declined, the observance of Hindu festivals like Holi and Shitala-saptami has been discontinued, the performance of Shraddha ceremony for religious reasons is declining and undesirable social practices like bride-price, child marriage, extra expenditure on ceremonies connected with pregnancy and death, beating breasts while sorrowing over the death of an individual, etc. are becoming infrequent.

Further, interest has been generated in Jain religion, history, literature, and culture. But the efforts made have not yet succeeded in bringing about a sense of oneness amongst all Jains, irrespective of differences of denomination, caste, religion, language or occupation. We have explained how in course of its growth different denominations and sub-sects started within Jainism. As it is common in other religions that over a period of time with the changes in values and new developments new groups emerged within a particular religious faith, the same also happened in Jainism.

We have seen that in Jainism the new denominations like the Sthankavasi, the Terapanth and the Kanjipanth developed because of particular way of interpreting the Jain philosophies. Differences amongst these denominations over different religious practices nevertheless in no way weakened what is regarded as the original philosophy of Jin. Another prominent point to note is that certain key religious leaders are instrumental in bringing the reformatory spirit in Jainism. Along with movements in the sphere of religion we also find in the twentieth century pure social reform movements amongst the Jain. So we can conclude by saying that in modern times Jainism witnessed different initiatives from within to strengthen the solidarity amongst the Jains.

REFERENCES

Acaranga-sutra, Anga-sutrani I: Vacana Pramukha, Acarya Tulasi, Editor Yuvacarya Mahaprajna, Jaina Vishvabharati, Ladnun, First Edition, 1974.

Buhler, G.: *Indian Sect of the Jainas,* Edited by Burgess, Jas, Luzac & Co., 46, Great Russell Street, 1903.

Caillat, C.: *Jainism,* Macmillan Company of Upadhye, A.N., andIndia, Delhi, 1974.

Chakravarti, A.: *Samayasara of Sri Kundakunda*, Translation with Introduction. Bharatiya Gyanpeeth, Delhi, 1971.

Chakravarti, A: *The Religion of Ahimsa,* Bombay, 1957.

Dasavaikalika-sutra: Editor Madhukar Muni, Jinagama Granthamala, No. 23, Agama Prakashan Samiti, Byavara, First Edition, 1985.

Dasgupta, S.N.: *History of Indian Philosophy, Vol. I,* Cambridge University Press, London, Second Edition (Reprint), 1932.

Desai, P.B. *Jainism in South India and some Jaina Epigraphs,* Sholapur, 1957.

Devendra Muni Shastri: *Source-Book in Jaina Philosophy,* Sri Tarak Guru Jain Granthalaya, Udaipur, 1983.

Ferfusson, J.: *History of Indian and Eastern Architecture,* London.

Fischer, E., & Jain, J.: *Art and Rituals, 2500 Years of Jainism in India,* Sterling Publishers, New Delhi, 1977.

Garbe, R.: *Encyclopaedia of Religion and Ethics,* T. & T. Clark, 38 George Street, New York, 1920.

Jacobi, H.: *Jaina Sutras, Part 1, The Akaranga Sutra, The Kalpa Sutra, Part2, The Uttaradhyana Sutra,The Sutrakritanga Sutra. 2 vols,* Dover Publications, New York, 1968.

Jain, H., and Upadhye, A.N.: *Mahavira, his Times and his Philosophy of Life,* Bharatiya Gyanpeeth, New Delhi, 1975.

Jain, J. P.: *Religion and Culture of the Jains*, Bharatiya Gyanpeeth, New Delhi, 1975.

Jain, J., and Fischer, E.: *Jaina Iconography, Part One, The Tirthankara in Jaina Scriptures, Art and Rituals, Part Two, Objects of Meditation and the Pantheon. 2 vols.* E.J.Brill, Leiden, 1978.

Jain, Jyoti Prasad: *Jainism: The Oldest Living Religion*, Banaras, 1951.

Jain, Jyoti Prasad: *Religion and Culture of the Jains*, New Delhi, 1977.

Jain, K.C.: *Lord Mahavira and his Times*, Motilal Banarsidass, Delhi, 1974.

Jain, Kailash Chand: *Jainism in Rajasthan*, Sholapur, 1963.

Jain, Kamata Prasad: *The Religion of Tirthankaras*, Aliganj, 1964.

Jain, Muni Uttam Kamal: *Jain Sects and Sub-sects*, New Delhi, 1975.

Jaini, Jugmandar Lal: *Outlines of Jainism*, Cambridge, 1916.

Kausambi, *Dharmananda: Bharatiya Sanskrti aur Ahimsa.*

Lalwani, K.C.: *Sramana Bhagavan Mahavira, Life and Doctrine.*

Lalwani. K.C.: *Kalpa Sutra of Badrabahu Svami*, Motilal Banarsidass. Delhi, 1979.

Pancastikaya-sara: Kunda-kunda, Edited by A.Chakravarti (Sacred Books of the Jainas, No. 3), Central Jaina Publishing House, Arrah, First Edition, 1920.

Pandey, V.: ed. *The World of Jainism*, pub. by the Author, Bombay, 1976.

Paul Marett: *Jainism Explained*, Lieciciter 1988.

Pramana-mimamsa: Hemacandra. Edited by Pt.Sukhalal Sanghvi, Saraswati Pustak Bhandar, Ahmedabad, Reprint Second Edition, 1989.

Trsastisalakapurusacaritrani: Canto 10, Hemacandra, Jaina Dharma Prasaraka Sabha, Bhavanagar, First Edition, 1908.

10

Reformers

Jains hold the Jain philosophy to be everlasting and established on universal tenets. In the present time cycle, they trace the origins of its doctrine to Rishabh, the first Tirthankar. Post Mahavir many intellectual giants amongst the Jain monks contributed and gave a concrete form to the Jain doctrine within the paramaters set by Bhagwan Mahavir.

REFORMERS IN EARLY PERIOD

Kundakunda

Kundakunda was a celebrated Jain Acharya (monk) in second century AD. He is composer of spiritual classics such as: Samayasara, Niyamasara, Pancastikayasara, Pravacanasara, Atthapahuda and Barasanuvekkha. He occupies the highest place in the tradition of the Jain acharyas.

He belonged to the Mula Sangh order. His proper name was Padmanandi, he is popularly referred to as Kundakunda because he was born in a place named Kaundakunda in south India. He is closely associated with the Digambar denomination, also in recent decades, his texts have become popular amongst Shvetambars also.

For Digambars, his name has auspicious significance and occupies third place after Bhagwan Mahavir and Gautama Ganadhara in the sacred litany. Kundakunda wrote in Shauraseni Prakrit. Amongst the modern devotees of Kundakunda, two names are notable, Banarasidasa, a 16th century lay poet from Agra who began his divine quest after reading kundakunda's "Samayasara"; and Rajachandra, the Gujarati merchant.

Acharya Bhadrabahu

Acharya Bhadrabahu (433 BC.-357 BC.) was a Jain monk. He is more famously known as a spiritual teacher of Chandragupta Maurya and author of several texts related to Jainism, including some of the most prominent works, Upsargar Stotra and Kalpasutra.

Bhadrabahu was born in Pundravardhan, (now in Bangladesh). During this time, the secondary capital of the Mauryas was Ujjain. While there Bhadrabahu was able to predict through his nimitta Gyan (subtle cognition of causes and effects) that there would be a 12-year famine across North India. He decided the famine would make it harder for monks to survive and migrated with a group of monks to South India, bringing with him Chandragupta, the founding father of the Mauryan Empire turned Jain monk.

While Bhadrabahu was away the monks staying in the North realized that the sacred scriptures were being forgotten. An ascetic named Sthulabhadra convened an assembly to recompile the Purva scriptures. Nevertheless, because Sthulabhadra's own knowledge of these texts was imperfect, he went to Bhadrabahu to study the sections missing from his memory.

Bhadrabahu taught Sthulabhadra, but forbade him to teach the Purvaa to others upon witnessing a demonstration by Sthulabhadra of certain extra corporal powers, which suggested that with time these sacred scriptures would become corrupted. Therefore, the 14 Purvas in their original form perished with these two men.

Bhadrabahu remains an exemplar of commitment to first tenets at any cost. After him, the Sangha split into two separate teacher-student lineages of monks. Digambar monks belong to the lineage of Acharya Vishakha and Shvetambar monks follow the tradition of Sthulabhadra. Bhadrabahu composed some new texts as well. In the Shvetambar tradition, Brihatkalpa, Vyavahara, and Nisitha are considered his works.

Bhadrabahu is considered to be the last expert of 14 Purvas, of 12th Anga called Dristivaad, one of the scriptures of Jainism. Of these, 10 Purvas were passed on to Sthulibhadra, his chief disciple. Bhadrabahu went to Nepal for twelve years to perform the "Mahaprana Sadhana" a tantric exercise.

As per Digambars, he died after committing Sallekhana. Acharya Bhadrabahu had a brother named Varahmihir. Both were in the same kingdom. When a son was born to the Emperor, Varahmihira declared that he would live for a hundred years but Bhadrabahu declared that he would live for only seven days, and that he would be killed by a cat. On the eighth day the prince died because of a door's anklet falling on his head which had a picture of cat drawn on it. Due to this humiliation Varahmihira left the kingdom and died after some time.

As per story Varahmihira became evil and tortured and terrorized the Jains, especially followers and devotees of Bhadrabahu. Acharya Bhadrabahu then formed a mantric prayer to 23rd Jain Tirthankar Parshvanath called the upsarghar stotra (now known as Uvassagaharam Stotra) and called upon Dharnendra, the divine devotee (a "devta") of Parshvanath. As an effect of it, Varahmihira was defeated and Jain society was relieved. That mantric prayer is still celebrated amongst the Jains and they chant it with due respect and faith. And that prayer had made Bhadrabahu's name immortal amongst Jain monks.

Tiruvalluvar

Thiruvalluvar is a celebrated Tamil poet who wrote the Thirukkural, an ethical work in Tamil literature. He is claimed by Tamils who practice Jainism as their own. However, some consider him as a Jain showing internal textual evidence from Thirukural. Thiruvalluvar's period is between the second century BC. and the eighth century AD. Both Thiruvalluvar's faith and identity are disputed. His disputed identity includes a low-caste Hindu(Paraiyar), Jain, Buddhist, high-caste Hindu, Brahmin and half-Brahmin.

There are a few legends abound about the birthplace of Thiruvalluvar. One legend associates him to Madurai, the ancient capital of the Pandya rulers who vigorously promoted Tamil literature. As per another he was born and lived in Mylapore, a part of current day Chennai city and travelled to Madurai to submit his work, the Thirukural, for approval of the Emperor (Pandian) and his college of poets.

There are, also, traditional stories mentioning the Tamil Sangam of Madurai (the assembly/conference of reputed scholars and researchers conducted on a regular basis) as the power through which Thirukkural was introduced to the world. Thiruvalluvar might have spent most part of his life in Madurai because it was under Pandia rulers that many Tamil poets flourished.

Thirukkural is one of most revered works in the Tamil. It consists of 133 athikarams or chapters. Each athikaram consists of ten kurals (rhyming Tamil couplets) therefore making 1330 kurals in total. Each couplet consists of four seers in the first line and three seers in the second. A seer is a single or a combination of more than one Tamil word. The first Kural is Ahara Muthala Ezhuthellam Aathi; Pahavan Muthatrey Ulahu.

Thirukkural is divided into three sections. Section one deals with Aram doing things, with moral sense and honour, for the good of the less fortunate, the second discusses Porul realities or facts of life, and the third dwells on Inbam the delights that a man and a woman experience in the course of their relationship. There are 38 chapters in the first section, 70 chapters in the second and 25 chapters in the third section.

Siddhasen Diwakar

Siddhasen Diwakar was a highly intelligent Jain acharya of his time. Siddhasen could study the Holy Scriptures and realize their truth in a short time. In due course he became the most well known Jain scholar of the time. He was like the illuminating lamp of the Jain order and thus came to be known as Siddhasen Diwakar. He is credited with the authorship of many texts but most of them unfortunately are not available. Sanmatitarka is his best text on logic and is widely read even at present. The well known Kalyanmandir Stotra was also composed by him.

Approximate 2000 years ago there lived a teacher named Devarshi in the court of Emperor Vikramaditya. Devarshi's son, Kumud (this was the birth name of Siddhasen Diwakar) was very good-looking, smart and highly intelligent and so Devarshi sent him to the best monastery school of the time. There Kumud quickly mastered all the arts and sciences. Devarshi was very proud of his son. It was normal in those days to hold contests to determine who was more knowledgeable. Devarshi believed that Kumud would defeat anyone in such contests and Kumud did not belie his expectations. In a short amount of time, Kumud overcome everyone in the court of Emperor Vikramaditya. From there he went to other important courts of India and was victorious every time. Nevertheless these successive triumphs generated a sense of vanity in his mind and he started believing that there was no one was more learned than himself.

He announced for an open competition with any one who claimed superior knowledge and also vowed that if any one could beat him, he would instantly become the winner's disciple. No one nonetheless came forward to accept his challenge. This made him even more egotistical. His conceit now knew no bounds. He sewed the emblems of a lamp, a net, a fork, a ladder and a spade onto his clothes and when any one inquired about the objective of such amazing emblems, he would say that they were meant for his rivals. If any of his opponents, out of fear of defeat, escaped in the dark, he would locate him with his lamp, if one escaped in water, he would trap him with the net, if one escaped in fire, he would get him out with the fork, if one escaped in the sky, he would bring him back with his ladder and if one escaped in the nether world, he would dig him out with the spade. At that time, Jain Acharya Vriddhivadi was the head of the Jain religious order. He was very learned but because he was a Jain saint he would not come out to challenge Kumud. Someone told Kumud that his universal subjugation would remain incomplete until he vanquished the Jain Acharya.

Acharya Vriddhivadi was then camping at Mandu (Madhya Pradesh,India), a little away from Ujjayini (Ujjain). Kumud rode out to meet him; nevertheless, Jain monks don't stay at any one place very long. Consequently the Acharya happened to move towards the next camp that very morning. As Kumud arrived in Mandu, he came to know that the Acharya had left. He felt that the Acharya was scared of him and had got away knowing about his arrival. He sped towards the place where the Acharya was headed and stopped him near the river Kshipra.

He informed the Acharya that he was Kumudchandra, the most knowledgeable man of India and since the latter claimed to be very learned, he had come to have a match. The Jain Acharya was rather unresponsive but Kumud insisted upon the contest. Acharya then suggested to have the contest in the nearby court but Kumud was rather eager and insisted upon the contest right there with the ranchers of the Kshipra as their judges. Acharya had heard about Kumud and was aware of his status as a well known scholar. He saw that the knowledge of Kumud was obscured by the vanity; nevertheless he also visualized the immense contribution that Kumud could make to the religious order, if he accepted the Jain faith. Acharya thereupon agreed and asked Kumud to first make his presentation. Kumud seized that opportunity and started exposing the weakness of different schools of thought including Jainism. The rancher had no idea what he was talking about. Then came the turn of the Jain Acharya. He knew the real calibre of the ranchers and asked them to form a circle and recite a song. Then with his melodious voice he started singing a song with the following lines; Ahimsa is the path of peace; That eventually leads to happiness.

The ranchers liked the song and merrily recited the same in chorus. Simultaneously they played flute in tune. At the end of the song, Acharya said that he did not want to say anything else. Kumud was sure that he had made his exposition very well and asked the ranchers about the outcome. Ranchers unanimously declared Acharya to be the winner. Kumud immediately realized his folly. His vanity disappeared and he fell at the feet of the Jain Acharya begging him to accept him as the pupil.

Acharya nevertheless did not intend to take advantage of that unfair contest. He thus declined the offer and asked Kumud to a rematch at a nearby court. Kumud replied that the "Acharya was his true preceptor because he made him realize that the real essence of knowledge lay in equanimity of mind and not in vanity with which his own knowledge had been clouded." At the insistence of the Acharya he nevertheless agreed to have one more contest in the nearby court where Acharya decisively defeated him. So Kumud became his pupil and was renamed Siddhasen that is known as Siddhasen Diwakar.

He inspired the Jain monks to study profoundly the Jain Holy Scriptures. He himself devoted to the profound study of Jain works. He was bitterly opposed to the storage of Jain works in isolated places; he eagerly desired to bring them to light for the propagation of Jainism. He himself wrote collected and edited certain prominent Jain works. He complied the celebrated Kalyanmandir Stotra. It is a monumental work in Sanskrit poetry. Sanmatitarka is his best text on logic and is widely read even at present. He wrote well known Sakal tirth stotra with the details of all Jain Tirtha of that time. This work itself places Siddhasen Diwakar on a high pedestal of Jain scholars and pioneers of religious Acharya's of the fifth century.

REFORMERS IN MEDIEVAL PERIOD

Pujyapada

Acharya Pujyapada who lived in the 5th century AD. was a renowned grammarian and saint belonging to the Digambar tradition of Jains. Before initiation as a Jain ascetic, he was known as Devanandi. Since it was believed that he was worshiped by demigods on account of his vast scholarship and profound piety, he was named Pujyapada. He was heavily influenced by the writings of his predecessors like Acharya Kundakunda and Acharya Samantabhadra. He is rated as being the greatest of the early masters of Jain literature. He was important preceptor, with impeccable pontifical pedigree and divine lineage. "He was a great yogi, sublime mystic, brilliant poet, noted scholar, reputed author and master of several branches of learning.He wrote in Sanskrit, in prose and also verse form. He was pontiff of the Nandi sangha, which was a part of the lineage of Acharya Kundakunda. He was the tenth guru of the pontifical lineage of the Nandi Sangha. He was born in a brahmin household of Karnataka. His parents were Madhava Bhatta and Shridevi.

It is likely that he was the first Jain saint to write not only on religion but also on secular subjects, such as ayurveda and Sanskrit grammar.

When one looks at the earlier writers in the Jain tradition, notably Kundakunda and Samantabhadra, one doesn't find any secular writings. They wrote beautifully on religion and the means to achieve nirvana. Whereas Acharya Pujyapada, besides being a deep scholar of the Jain religion and a mendicant walking in the footsteps of the Jins, was a grammarian, master of Sanskrit poetics and of ayurveda. Acarya Pujyapada was said to be the guru of Emperor Durvinita of the Ganga dynasty. He is reliably dated as having lived between 464 - 524 AD.

Pujyapada is emphatic and focused that nirvana is the only way to achieve everlasting happiness. Pointing to the knotty nature of materialism, existentialism and hedonism he leads the reader to the path of divine happiness through judicious knowledge, judicious perception and judicious conduct. He is a writer of brevity and doesn't believe in highly embellished poetry. He says what he needs to in simple Sanskrit verse.

Haribhadra

Haribhadra Suri was a Shvetambar mendicant Jain leader and writer. There are multiple conflicting dates assigned to his birth. Nevertheless, given his familiarity with Dharmakirti, a more likely choice would be sometime after 650 AD. In his writings, Haribhadra identifies himself as a student of Jinabhadra and Jinadatta of the Vidyadhara Kula. There are various, somewhat contradictory, accounts of his life.

The earlier of these, which dates to the twelfth century, says that Haribhadra was an educated Brahmin who made the boast that he would become a pupil of anyone who stated a sentence which he could not understand. After hearing a Jain nun named Yakini Mahattara narrated a verse that he could not understand, he was sent to her teacher Jinabhata, who promised Haribhadra that he would instruct him if Haribhadra accepted initiation into Jainism. Haribhadra agreed, and took the name Yakiniputra, or "Spiritual Son of Yakini".

The second account, which bears similarities to the story of Akalanka Digambar, also shows the state of relations between Buddhist and Jain mendicants at the time. In this story, Haribhadra was teaching two of his nephews. These nephews went to secretly study logic at a Buddhist temple, and fled after being discovered there. One of them was killed by the Buddhists, and the other died of sorrow later. Haribhadra engaged the monks of this monastery in a philosophical debate, and emerged victorious. He then ordered the losing monks to jump into a vat of hot oil. When Haribhadra's own teacher heard of this, he ordered Haribhadra to undertake severe penances for his unseemly display of anger and attachment.

Haribhadra did so, and took the title "Virahanka", which means "having separation (or viraha, from his nephews) as a distinguishing characteristic".

Tradition ascribes some 1400 different works to him. A more creditable number is in the vicinity of one hundred, some of which are amongst the most highly regarded works in Jainism. Some have even suggested that, established on the language and subject material of the texts ascribed to Haribhadra, there were two Haribhadras, the first of which, Haribhadra Virahanka, may have lived around the sixth century, and the second, Haribhadra Yakiniputra, was an ascetic who lived in a temple around the eighth century. Scholars of the Shvetambar community itself tend to hold with the belief that there was only one Haribhadra. Amongst his prominent teachings were tolerance for other traditions, and that ultimate reality can be grasped from multiple different perspectives.

With his writings, he established that Sanskrit, rather than Prakrit, would be the language of Jain study. He used his only familiarity with the techniques of brahminical study and wrote in the same style. He is also noted for the great respect he displays toward other religious traditions. He even did what few other Jain scholars have done, and wrote a commentary on the Nyayapraveua, a text on Indian logic by the Buddhist scholar Dignaga. He does nevertheless eventually support Jain thought, arguing that the other beliefs tend to display only a one-sided view of the greater reality.

Acharya Hemachandra

Hemachandra Suri (1089–1172) was an Indian Jain scholar, poet, and polymath who wrote on grammar, philosophy, prosody, and contemporary history. Noted as a prodigy by his contemporaries, he gained the title Kalikal Sarvagya, (all-knowing of the Kali age).

He was born in Dhandhuka, Gujarat about 100 km south west of Ahmadabad), to Chachadev (father) and Pahini Devi(mother). They named him Changdev. The Jain temple of Modhera Tirtha is located at his birthplace. As a young man, Chandradeva was initiated as an ascetic at a Jain temple, and he took the name Somachandra (Somachandra). He was trained in religious discourse, philosophy, logic and grammar. In 1110, at the age of 21 he was ordained as an Acharya of the Shvetambar denomination of Jainism and was given the name Acharya Somchandra and popularly as Hemachandra.

At the time, Gujarat was ruled by the Solanki dynasty. Hemachandra rose to prominence under the reign of Siddharaj Jaysinh I, and was an advisor to his successor Kumarapala (1143–1173). During Kumarapala's reign, Gujarat became a reputed centre of culture. Starting in 1121, Hemachandra was involved in the construction of the Jain temple at Taranga. His influence on Kumarapala resulted in the Jain religion becoming the official religion of Gujarat, and animal slaughter was banned.

A prodigious writer, Hemchandra wrote grammars of Sanskrit and Prakrit, texts on science and logic and practically all branches of Indian philosophy. His best known work, the epic poem Tri-shashthi-shalaka-purusha-charitra (Lives of Sixty-Three Great Men), is a hagiographical treatment of the sequence of teachers and their pupils who were instrumental in defining the Jain philosophical position, their ascetisicism and eventual nirvana from the cycle of death and rebirth, and also the legendary spread of the Jain influence. It still serves as the standard synthesis of source material for the early history of Jainism.

Hemachandra, following the earlier Gopala, presented what is now called the Fibonacci sequence around 1150, about fifty years before Fibonacci (1202). He was considering the number of cadences of length n, and showed that these could be formed by adding a short syllable to a cadence of length (n–1), or a long syllable to one of (n–2). This recursion relation $F(n) = F(n-1) + F(n-2)$ is what defines the Fibonacci sequence.

REFORMERS IN MODERN PERIOD

Acharya Bhikshu

Acharya Bhikshu was one of the great revolutionary saints of Jainisim. He was the founding father and first spiritual head of Jain Shvetambar Terapanth denomination. He was a staunch disciple of Bhagwan Mahavir and completely immersed his life onto the path given by Bhagwan Mahavir. In the initial phase of his divine revolution, he moved out from the group of Sthankvasi Acharya Raghunath ji. That time he had thirteen saints, thirteen devotees and thirteen fundamental rules. This coincidence results in the name of "Terapanth"

The different beliefs and teachings of the religious orders of those times greatly influenced his thinking and he choose to follow the way of the search for truth and to understand it. He studied and analyzed the different disciplines of the Jain religion thoroughly and on this basis he compiled his own ideologies and tenets of the Jain way of life. Based on the philosophies propagated, Acharya Bhikshu rigorously pursued the tenets and therefore set an example for all to follow. He showed the importance of discipline, purity and self-control. It was this way of life that was demonstrated by Acharya Bhikshu which became the foundation principle of Terapanth. The Letter of Conduct was written by him is still pursued in the same manner with due respect with slight changes as per the time & situation. The original copy of letter written in rajasthani language is still available. His devotees piously referred this great visionary monk as 'Swamiji'.

The life of Acharya Bhikshu was a prodigy of ups and downs that tested and molded him to become a supreme person. While in the first half of the life, he faced ordeals and difficulties, the second half reveals (unfolds) the success and accomplishments.

Acharya Bhikshu had a very broad vision who was far ahead of his times. He rose above the current circumstances of the society and strived to present an example to the people of all times of a life of discipline and truth. In pursuit of this aim , he sacrificed materialistic goals, honour and luxuries.He revolutionized the different tenets which had become meaningless with the passing of time and gave conception and birth to these tenements.

He visualized a systematic, well established and orderly religious denomination and saw it taking shape through Terapanth. To organize and stabilize this religious order he propagated the ideology of one guru and brought to an end the concept of self discipleship. In this way his ideology of one Acharya, one principle, one thought and similar thinking became the ideal for other religious denominations. Acharya Bhikshu showed the way from desire to desirelessness. He said the common man should understand and practice true religion which would take him to the path of redemption.

In the middle of the 18th Century, Acharya Bhikshu led a reformist movement in a society griped in fundamentalist religious philosophy and blind faith. A philosopher, writer, poet and social reformer, the Jain leader wrote 38,000 shlokas (hymns), now compiled in two volumes as Bhikshu Granth Ratnakar. His Nav Padarth Sadbhav, which advocated a society free from exploitation, is regarded as a significant philosophical composition that deals exhaustively with the nine gems of Jain doctrine.

Acharya Rajendrasuri

Acharya Rajendrasuri (1827-1906) was the major reformer of 18th and 19th century in Shvetambar denomination of Jainism. Acharya Rajendrasuri was born on 3 December 1827 at Bharatpur in Rajasthan. In 1880 AD., as the leader of the Tapa Gachchha, he lead a movement to restore orders of wandering monks, leading to near extinction of the Jain Yati institutions. Afterwords he restore shraman sanstha by reopening of Agam gachchha or Samakit gachchha, which is now known as "Tristutik" gachchha. He opposed worship of other Gods and Goddesses in spite of Jain Tirthankars. He wrote many texts on Jainism, the most celebrated being "Aabhidhan Rajendra Kosh", which is only one available encyclopedia of Prakrit, Sanskrit, and Pali words used in Jainism.

Acharya Rajendrasuri was born on 3rd December, 1827 at Bharatpur, Rajasthan in a household of business man named Rishabhdas Parakh. His birth name is Ratna Raj. He had such a brilliant grasping power that at age of 10-12 years he had acquired all the educational studies. He was Having religious bent of mind he renounced the corporeal life and was initiated as Jain yati by Hemavijayaji at Udaipur on Vaishakh shukala 5 Vikram Samvat 1904(in 1848 AD.) and he was now known as Ratnavijay (early name of Rajendrasuri). He had studied diligently the Jain Holy Scriptures, doctrine, literature, grammar, rhetoric, lexicography, etc. under Acharya Pramodsuri and Jain Monk Sagarchandji, the well-known yatis of the age and soon he acquired proficiency. Jain Acharya Dharanendrasuri was so much impressed by the profound scholarship of Rajendrasuri that he appointed him his daftari and entrusted the task of teaching the groups of yati followers. But soon Ratnavijay (Rajendrasuri) was disgusted with the princely and luxurious life of Dharanendrasuri, it was an utter disregard and contradiction to the Jain tenets of non-possession and ahimsa. Consequently Rajendrasuri left Dharanendrasuri in 1864 AD. and this was a turning point in the life of Rajendrasuri.

Now he raised his voice against the corrupt and luxurious life of the Jain yatis and condemned their abundance of possession and insisted on a pious ideal life in accordance with the tenets laid down by Jain Tirthankars and Jain Holy Scriptures. After prolonged deliberations, he issued none-point manifes known as Nav-kalama to for the objective and explained to the Jain world the significance of his nine tenets of reform that the Jain yatis had to follow. It was a vigorous attempts to reform the institution of Jain yati and place it on sound, simple and judicious tenets and get rid of its age old traditions and superstitions.

Although opposed in the initial stages, the attempts of Rajendrasuri were eventually crowned with success. His nine-point manifesto was accepted and recognized by the leading yatis and Jain monk of the age and even Acharya Dharanendrasuri also signed it. Due to this the Jain yatis/Monk had given up their corporeal life and surrendered their princely symbols like silver rods, chanwar, palkhi, arms, etc. to the Jain temples, and tool solemn oath to lead a life of purity, simplicity, celebacy, non-possession, ahimsa, teaching and preaching. Therefore Rajendrasuri reformed and simplifies the Jain yati/monk institution, Tristutik(tin thui) denomination of Jainism, and a new life of revivalism was infused in them. He opposed worship of other Gods and Goddesses in spite of Jain Tirthankars.

Rajendrasuri did not end at the reformation of the Jain yati institution, it was his first task of revival movement. His other achievements were restoration and reconstruction of Jain temples and installation of Jain images and establishment of different socio-religious organizations for the uplift of the Jains and propagation of Jainism. Like a pious, true, diligent monk, devoted to the cause of Jainism. He walked from place to place in Rajasthan, Gujarat, Malwa, etc. teaching, preaching and infusing new spirit of the age amongst the people. He appealed to the masses by delivering his discourses in simple dialects of the people, the common spoken languages of the masses, - Malwi, Gujarati, Marwari, etc.

He inspired the Jain monks to study profoundly the Jain Holy Scriptures. He himself devoted to the profound study of Jain works. He was bitterly opposed to the storage of Jain works in isolated places; he eagerly desired to bring them to light for the propagation of Jainism. He himself wrote collected and edited certain prominent Jain works. He complied the celebrated Jain encyclopedia "Abhidan-Rajendra Kosh". It is a monumental work in seven volumes with more than 90 thousand pages. On the 21st December Friday 1906 AD., Acharya Rajendrasuri laid down for the Moksh Prapti (for paradise) till death in a still Samadhi.

Acharya Tulsi

Acharya Tulsi (1920-1997) was a Jainist Acharya (ascetic). He was the author of more than hundred texts, and the founding father of the Anuvrata. Guru Dev Acharya Tulsi was magnanimous in life and glorious in death. He lives for ever in the hearts and minds of millions of people for whose mental, emotional, and divine upliftment he worked all through his life. Right from his early childhood he exhibited brilliant qualities of head and heart giving indications of his greatness to be and his divine inclinations. He renounced the materialistic world at the tender age of 11 years.

Acharya Tulsi was a great visionary and conceived many innovative programmes and schemes to uplift the mental, ethical and emotional status of his followers and the entire population at large. He had the distinctive quality to translate his vision into actual practice.

Acharya shri Tulsi hailed from a devout household of Jain traders in Ladnun. He was born in 1914 at Ladnun. His Father name was Jhumarmal Khated & mother is Vadana ji. He showed early leadership qualities since his school time. He took his monk's vows at the age of eleven with notable commitment, and by the time he was 16, he had already started attracting acolytes. This young talent through his dynamism and sense of purpose, captured the attention of Kalugani who nominated him to be his successor when he was just 22. That was the rare incident in Jainism history that a 22 year young boy has been given the responsibility of Head of Terapanth group. He surpassed all estimates being made about him by the keen observers of the society. He initiated more than 776 monks and nuns. He has been an accomplished poet, author and also a distinguished religious leader.

Acharya Tulsi showed great dynamism in conceiving and forthrightly implementing the Anuvrat Movement for ethical regeneration of the nation. It was started in on March two, 1949. The five tenets of Anuvrat i.e.Truth, Ahimsa, Non Possession, Non-stealing and Celibacy became the five pillars of this movement for transforming the real life of persons. The Anuvrat Movement launched by Acharya Tulsi on second March 1949 has since inspired millions of people to practice purity and self-discipline in individual life. The ultimate objective of the Movement is to create a nonviolent socio-political world order with the help of a world wide network of self-transformed people.

Thirty-four Years ago, while going through the research journal Dharmdoot during one of his travels on foot he got the notion of editing the Jain Agams (Jain Holy Scriptures) by doing research on them. The Agams in the Jain tradition are as significant as the Vedas are in the Hindu tradition and Pitak is in the Buddhistic tradition. The task was as forbidding as it was complex and difficult. But Sant Tulsi's strong resolve bore fruit and the credit for it should go to him and his able successor's strong will-power and irrepressible zeal. It was a Herculean task to edit, annotate and comment upon Tirthankar Bhagwan Mahavir's precepts dating back to 2500 years ago. It is exclusively the outcome of the untiring efforts of Anuvrat Anushasta Shree Tulsi, Acharya Mahapragya and their selfless army of saints and nuns.

Acharya Mahapragya

Acharya Mahapragya, the tenth Acharya of Terapanth was born in a small and tranquil village of Tamkor in the Jhunjhanun district of Rajasthan on 14 June 1920. Father Tolaram and Mother Baluji named their child

Nathmal. But when he was an infant of one and a half months, his father left this mortal world. Acharya Mahapragya still has vivid memories of his childhood and his father's demise.

In those times there was no school in Tamkor and the only means of education accessible was a tutor's school. Sardarsahar was his uncle's native place. He used to visit Sardarsahar quite often with his mother but the prospect of education was equal to none.

Acharya Shree Kalugani's personality left a profound impact on Nathmal's mind. Both he and his mother pleaded with Acharya Shree for accepting them as his pupils. After that Acharya Mahapragya and his mother left the narrow path of unawareness and joined the highway, which leads towards enlightenment. The path they chose to take reaches out to every door, varying from end to infinity, from immortality to eternity and from spirituality to enlightenment. Acharya Mahapragya entered into monkhood at the age of ten.

The rapport set between Acharya Mahapragya and Acharya Shri Tulsi was extraordinary. From the very beginning, Acharya Mahapragya was quite dedicated towards Acharya Shri Tulsi. Way back in 1955, Acharya Shri Tulsi nominated him as the Chief Secretary of Terapanth. In 1978, once again Acharya Shri Tulsi conferred on him the epithet of "Mahapragya" (a great seer) at Gangasahar, in recognition of his spectacular wisdom and erudition. He was again nominated as the successor-designate on fourth February 1979, at Rajaldesar and his name was changed to "Mahapragya." From then onwards he became known as "Yuvacharya Mahapragya." Gurudev Tulsi also conferred on him the epithet of Jain-Yoga Punaruddharka in recognition of his distinctive researches in the field of Jaiṇ Meditation and Yoga.

Acharya Shri Tulsi announced the relinquishment of his post of Acharya and conferred the same on Yuvacharya Mahapragya on 18th February 1994 at Sujangarh. Later on, in a glorious function at Delhi, held on 5th February 1995, he formally consecrated him as the tenth Acharya of Terapanth.

REFERENCES

Kapashi, V.J.: *In Search of the Ultimate*, V.K. Publications, Harrow, 1984.

Karttikeyanupreksa: Svamikumara, Editor Dr. A.N.Upadhye, Smd. Rajchandra Ashrama, Agosa via Anand (Gujarat), First Edition, 1960.

Radhakrishnan. S.: *Indian Philosophy. 2nd.ed, 2 vols,* Allen and Unwin, London, 1929,1931.

Ramchandran, T.N.: *Jain Monuments of India*, Calcutta, 1944.

Rampuria, S.C.: *The Cult of Ahimsa,* Calcutta, 1947.

Rosenfield, C.: *Gurudev Shree Chitrabhanu, a Man with a Vision,* New Jain Meditation Intemational Center, York, 1981.

Roy Chowdhari, P.C.: *Jainism in Bihar,* Patna, 1956.

Roy, A.K.: *History of the Jains,* Gitanjali Publishing House, New Delhi, 1984.

Sharma, S.R.: *Jainism and Karnataka Culture,* Dharwar, 1940.

Stevenson. S.: *The Heart of Jainism,* Munshiram Manoharlal, New Delhi, 1970.

Tahtinen, U.: *Ahimsa, Non-violence in Indian Society,* Rider, London, 1976.

Talib, G.S.: ed. *Jainism,* Punjabi University, Patiala, 1975.

Tatia, Nathmal: *Studies in Jain Philosophy,* Banaras, 1951.

Tattvartha-sutra: Umasvati, P.V. Research Institute, Varanasi, Reprint Second Edition.

Thomas, F.W.: *Sri Mallisenasuri, Syad-Vada-Manjari,* Motilal Banarsidass Delhi, 1968.

Trsastisalakapurusacaritrani: Canto 10, Hemacandra, Jaina Dharma Prasaraka Sabha, Bhavanagar, First Edition, 1908.

11

Major Sects

Bhagwan Mahavir attracted people from all walks of life, rich and poor, kings and commoners, men and women, princes and priests, touchable and untouchable. Bhagwan Mahavir proclaimed that in the matters of divine advancement, both men and women are on an equal footing. Many women pursued Bhagwan Mahavir's path and renounced the world in search of ultimate truth and bliss. The most significant contribution of Jainism in the social field was the establishment of social equality amongst the four classes: Brahman, Kshatriya, Vaishya, and Shudra including untouchables prevalent in the society.

He organized his devotees, into a four-fold order, namely monks-Sadhu, nuns-Sadhvi, laymen-Shravak, and laywomen-Shravika. This order is known as Jain Sangh. There are about six to eight million Jains live almost exclusively in India. About 100,000 Jains live in North America and other countries.

A few centuries after Bhagwan Mahavir's enlightenment, the Jain religious order (Sangha) grew more and more complex. There established two major sects. In the Digambar denomination monks wear no cloths, while the Shvetambar monks wear white cloths. Basic opinions of both sects on ethics and doctrine are same.

Each major sects has many sub-sects including idol and non-idol worshiping sects. Later generations saw the introduction of ritualistic complexities, which almost placed Bhagwan Mahavir and other Tirthankars on the throne of Hindu deities.

It is usually believed that the Jain sangha divided into two major sects, Digambar and Shvetambar, about 200 years after Bhagwan Mahavir's enlightenment. Some historians believe there was no clear division until the 5th century. The best available information indicates that the chief Jain monk, Acharya Bhadrabahu, foresaw famine and led about 12,000 Digambar devotees to southern India. Twelve years later they returned to find the Shvetambar denomination, and in 453 the Valabhi council edited and compiled traditional Shvetambar Holy Scriptures. The differences between the two sects are minor and relatively obscure.

In Sanskrit, ambar refers to a covering usually, or a garment in particular. Dig, an older form of disha, refers to the cardinal directions. Digambar thus means covered by the four directions, or sky-clad. Svet means white and Shvetambars wear white garments.

Digambar Jain monks don't wear clothes because they believe clothes are like other belongings, increase dependency and craving for materialistic things, and craving for anything eventually leads to grief. Shvetambar Jain monks, contrarily, wear white, seamless clothes for practical reasons, and believe there is nothing in Jain scripture that condemns wearing clothes. Sadhvis of both sects wear white. These differing opinions arise from different interpretations of the same holy texts. There are minor differences in each denomination's literature.

There are both Shvetambar and Digambar stories of the origin of the Digambar denomination. The Shvetambar version says the denomination started 609 years after the death of Bhagwan Mahavir when a Shvetambar named Shivabhuti initiated himself as an ascetic after he was angry at being locked out one night by his mother-in-law and later on decided to follow the way of Bhagwan Mahavir and threw off his ascetic robes. The Digambar version is set in the time of durbhiksha, 'a time when it is difficult to gain alms,' when there was famine and political anarchy in the North. The Digambars migrated to the South under Bhadrabahu, while those that remained became the backsliding Shvetambars who took to wearing clothes. The Shvetambars maintain that Bhadrabahu was at that time in Nepal. Neither version is very old, the Shvetambar story dating from the fifth century and the Digambar story from the tenth century.

The actual historical situation is more complex. It is likely that the fracture into two major sub-groups on the basis of clothing or nudity took place gradually, judging from archaeological and inscriptional evidence. There was no sudden doctrinal split. Bhagwan Mahavir and his devotees were naked monks and the earliest Jin-images are naked. Only in the fifth century is there an image of Bhagwan Rishabh Dev wearing a lower garment. Shvetambar images became usually clothed only several centuries later. The name Digambar took some time to become established in use. Until the fourteenth century a denomination called the Yapaniyas existed, which shows the original flexibility regarding sectarian affiliation. Yapaniyas were a compromise, wearing clothes only when with lay devotees.

The schism appears to have been recognised as early as the first century CE and was certainly founded by the time of the Council of Valabhi in 453 or 466 CE. Dundas explains the Council as The catalyst for the final hardening of boundaries between the Shvetambars and the Digambars. Only Shvetambars came to the Council, held on the Kathiawar Peninsula.

Geography played a prominent part in the schism, with the Digambars prospering in South India and the Shvetambars remaining chiefly in the North. The Digambars claim that when they migrated south with Bhadrabahu to Mysore, Candragupta Maurya, first Emperor of the Maurya dynasty who had become a Jain monk, was with them. They believe that Bhadrabahu and Candragupta Maurya died the holy death of sallekhana, fasting to death, on hills at Sravana Belgola. There is no evidence of this, but many inscriptions in the area from the fifth century CE support a southern migration.

Digambars believe that women can't achieve Moksh in the same birth, while Shvetambars believe that women may achieve nirvana and that Mallinath, a Tirthankar, was a woman. The difference is because Digambar ascetism requires nudity. As nudity is impractical for women, it follows that without it they can't achieve Moksh. This is established on the belief that women can't reach ideal purity yathakhyata, women are if they are not clothed vulnerable to attack and rape by men. Their lack of clothes can, thus, be a hindrance to their leading a holy life. The earliest record of this belief is contained in the Prakrit Suttapahuda of the Digambar mendicant Kundakunda.

Digambars believe that Bhagwan Mahavir was not married, whereas Shvetambars believe the princely Bhagwan Mahavir was married and had a daughter. The two sects also differ on the origin of Mata Trishala, Bhagwan Mahavir's mother.

Sthanakavasis and Digambars believe that only the first five lines are formally part of the Namokara Mantra the main Jain prayer, whereas Shvetambars believe all nine forms the mantra. Other differences are minor and not established on major points of philosophy.

Excavations at Mathura revealed many Jain statues from the Kushana period. Tirthankars, represented without clothes and monks, with cloth wrapped around the left arm, are identified as Ardhaphalaka and cited in some texts. The Yapaniya denomination, believed to have started from the Ardhaphalaka, follows Digambar nudity, along with several Shvetambar philosophy.

Shvetambars are further divided into sub-sects, such as Sthanakavasi, Terapanthi and Deravasi. Some are murtipujak; revering statues while non-murtipujak Jains refuse statues or images. Shvetambars follow the 12 agam literature; voice of all-knowing. Most simply call them Jains and follow general traditions rather than specific sectarian practices. In 1974, a committee with representatives from every denomination compiled a new text called the Samana Suttam.

Digambar, has many different meaning and associations throughout Indian religions. Many representations of deities within these traditions are depicted as sky-clad. Certain traditions and lineages also practice Digambar as a lifelong vow as evidenced by many sadhu throughout India. In the iconography of the Indian religions, Digambar may be understood as enveloped by the quintessential investiture of akasha, space or ether.

DIGAMBAR SECT

Until the leadership of Acharya Bhadrabahu, there was no significant division. After that some divisions gradually arose. Senior Digambar monks wear no clothes, following the practice of Bhagwan Mahavir. They don't consider themselves to be nude — they are wearing the environment or stated otherwise the quintessential, akasha or space. Digambars believe that this practice represents a refusal to give in to the body's demands for comfort and private property — only Digambar monks are required to forsake clothing. Digambar monks have only two belongings: a peacock feather broom and a water gourd. Shvetambar monks usually wear white clothes, maintaining that nudity is no longer practicable. While there are some differences in some practices, the main tenets like Mahavratas, Anuvratas etc. are the same.

The Digambars are also called Digvasanas. The name Digambar means literally 'clothed in the quarters of the sky' and they are called 'atmosphere-clad' or 'sky-clad.' Nudity is the main doctrinal difference between the Shvetambars and the Digambars. Outward appearance is seen by the Digambars as an index of proper understanding of the philosophy. The Digambar view on ascetic nakedness was put by Aparajita in the eighth century. The true monk must be completely naked; even a loincloth is a compromise. He must abandon all belongings and be no longer subject to the social considerations of arrogance and shame. And to obey the vow of non-violence, ahimsa, dirty clothing must be avoided as it attracts tiny creatures which might be crushed. The naked monk must follow the example of the Jins, who were naked. As well, he may not use an alms-bowl, but has to use his hands cupped together as a bowl. He can eat only once a day. Nevertheless, nuns are allowed to be clothed as otherwise they would cause social disruption - even although there is a tradition of naked female yoginis in Hinduism.

There are doctrinal differences with the Shvetambars over the Jins. The Digambars believe that kewalins, ideal saints, such as the Jins live without food. In fact, the Jin can manifest no corporeal activity and no longer has any bodily functions, for if he did his jiva, soul, would then change and he would not be all-knowing. The Jins teach by a magical divine sound. There are also differing accounts of the life of Bhagwan Mahavir. To the Digambars, the embryo of Bhagwan Mahavir was not removed from the womb of Devananda to that of Trisala, as the Shvetambars believe, and they don't follow the Shvetambar account of Bhagwan Mahavir being married and living the life of the householder until he was thirty.

In the Digambar tradition, women can't gain Moksh, nirvana, unless they are first reborn as men. The Digambars disown the Shvetambar canon, claiming that these texts were gradually lost during the first centuries after the Nirvana, death, of Bhagwan Mahavir. They give canonical status to two Prakrit works, Chapters on Karman and Chapters on Kasayas; Passion, both of which they claim were composed on the basis of the lost Drstivada. Of great importance to the Digambars are the works of Kundakunda, such as Essence of the Philosophy.

Basically, the difference in philosophy is minor. Both the Shvetambar and Digambar traditions accept the Tattvarthasutra of Umasvati, who in the second century was the first systematiser of Jain doctrine.

The doctrine and ethics which form the foundation of Jainism are exactly the same for both the Shvetambars and the Digambars, and the five major vows of non-violence, ahimsa, satya, truth, asteya, non-stealing, aparigraha, non-possession, and brahmacharya, celibacy, are fundamental to their philosophy.

Most Digambars are image-worshippers, except for the sects of the Terapanthis (Terahapanthis) and the Taranapanthis.

Gumanapanthis and Totapanthis are minor subsects of the Digambars. They are not very prominent and very little is known about them. Gumanapantha flourished late in the eighteenth century and is named after its founding father Gumana Rama.

The Digambars must have held a prominent position in South India in the early centuries. Jain influence is obvious in Dravidian literature, as in the Tamil epic Silapadikkaram, Lay of the Anklet The Digambars have an extensive literature of their own, mainly in Sanskrit, which has a greater antiquity than that of the Shvetambars, with the exception of the canonical texts of the Shvetambars. There was often a close relationship between Digambar monks and kings. In 981 the giant statue of Bahubali was erected at Sravana Belgola in Karnataka by Camundaraya, a general of an Emperor of the Ganga dynasty. The twelth century Hoysala dynasty supposedly started through the influence of a Digambar monk. There was a powerful ideal of the righteous Jain Emperor.

In the medieval period the Digambar ascetic community split into different sects. The Mula Sangha, the 'Root Assembly,' descended from Bhagwan Mahavir through Kundakunda, split into four sections called Sena, Deva, Simha, and Nandin. Then there were rival Digambar sects such as the Dravida Sangha at Madurai which allowed bathing.

The main figure in medieval Digambar Jainism was the bhattaraka, meaning 'learned man' but who in fact was the head of a group of monks in a matha, monastery, who wore orange robes except when eating or initiating another bhattaraka. Some bhattarakas became Emperor-like figures and there were thirty-six bhattaraka thrones around India. They helped to perpetuate Digambar Jainism. A Rajasthan bhattaraka in the fifteenth century consecrated a thousand Jin-images to send all over India to replace those demolished by the Muslims.

With the Hindu Renaissance, Jainism in South India went into retreat. There may have been a terrible persecution of Jains in the eighth century. Hindu temples in Tamil Nadu show the impaling of eight thousand Jains at Madurai. In Karnataka Jains were slaughtered by the Virashaiva movement which started in the twelth century, but Jains had prominent positions in the Vijayanagar empire established in 1336. However, Jainism continued to decline with many Jains converting to Hinduism. Significant numbers only remained in south west India. Jainism hung on tenaciously, exemplified by the erection of great images of Bahubali at Karkala in 1432 and at Venur in 1604.

In the late sixteenth century a reform movement within Digambar Jainism started in Agra, and was forged in the first half of the seventeenth century by Banarsidass and the Adhyatma movement and his later devotees such as Pandita Todarmal of Jaipur. This profoundly affected Digambar society by largely eliminating the crippling excesses of ritualism and awakening the community to a deeper meaning of its faith.

By the nineteenth century, the bhattaraka thrones had faded into insignificance, except the oldest ones at Mudbridri and Sravana Belgola, which are still prominent and celebrated, and also two in Kolhapur.

Today the Digambars and Shvetambars flourish independently of each other, except for disputes over the administration of pilgrimage sites.

The holiest Digambar site is Sravana Belgola, where there is the fifty-seven foot high image of Bahubali standing in meditation in the kayotsarga posture, arms away from the side, and with creepers growing round his arms and legs and anthills covering his lower legs to symbolise the length of time he has been meditating. The Digambars believe he is the first person in the world to attain nirvana. This was erected in 981 by Camundaraya, a general of an Emperor of the Ganga dynasty, to symbolise the ascetic fighting the divine battle. Bahubali was the son of Bhagwan Rishabh Dev, the first Jin, and when he defeated his half-brother Bharata in a duel, he did not take over as Emperor but renounced the throne and took to meditating in the forest. This is also symbolic of pressures at that time for the Jain warrior between the claims of war and religion.

Since 1398 every ten to fifteen years, depending on astrology, the mastakabhisheka, head-anointment, ceremony takes place, one of the most spectacular in India. Milk, liquid saffron, and other substances in 1,008 pots are poured over the head of Bahubali from a platform by prominent lay persons. Today, flowers are also dropped on the statue from a helicopter.

The statue is on the Big Hill. The Little Hill is also a prominent place of pilgrimage because of generations of Digambar monks who have died there by sallekhana, fasting, testified by nisidhi, memorials of stone reliefs, pillars, images, and temples. A fissure in the rock is called Bhadrabahu's Cave after the supposed leader of the southern migration. Hero stones of those who died in battle are placed near the memorials of the monks.

There are iconographic differences between the Digambar and Shvetambar images. Digambar Jin-images are completely nude and don't show eye-balls. During the dispute over the ownership of Mount Girnar, when the Shvetambars clothed the naked images, this made their worship impossible for the Digambars. Bhagwan Rishabh Dev is symbolised by long hair curling elegantly over his shoulders. The Shvetambars explain his hair by saying that after a long rule as Emperor he renounced the world and started to uproot his hair. After five handfuls the God Indra saw how beautiful the remaining hair was and requested him to stop. The Digambars say that originally Bhagwan Rishabh Dev removed all his hair, but as he sat meditating a jata, mat of hair, grew on his head.

The Digambars don't usually touch the image in a temple and pujas are carried out by a priest called upadhye, who is a rite functionary only. From the sixth century both Digambars and Shvetambars used the eight substances of perfumed material such as camphor, flowers, rice, incense, light, sweets, fruit, and water in the most common puja, the eightfold worship of an image. Nevertheless, Digambar worship is simpler, with flowers and jewellery rarely being used.

The Ganadharavalaya-yantra is a diagrammatic representation of the Purvas and Angas, sacred texts, used in rites of propitiation. An example is to be found in a Digambar temple at Mudbridri, South Kanara. Ambika, the most popular yakshi and who represents maternal fertility, is also known to the Digambars as Kushmandini.

Illustrated manuscripts are chiefly used by Shvetambars, although Digambar devotees did occasionally commission richly illustrated editions of their most sacred texts. Digambar style is less celebratory and festive, being simpler and more austere. In the Lokapurusha, Cosmic Man, the three worlds are portrayed in distinctly different ways depending on whether they are Shvetambar or Digambar as they follow different iconographic traditions. The Digambar is less ornate and the Cosmic Man is naked.

Digambars are found chiefly in south west India, in the states of Maharashtra and Karnataka. In the 1981 Census there were 939,392 Jains in Maharashtra and 284,508 in Karnataka. No sectarian breakdown of these figures is obtainable but the bulk are Digambars.

The native Jain communities of Maharashta, Bundelkhand (MP/UP), Karnataka, Tamil Nadu are all Digambars. In north India, the Saravagis and the Agrawals are also Digambars. In Gujarat and Southern Rajasthan, the majority of Jains follow the Shvetambar tradition, though some Jain communities of these areas like the Humad are also Digambars.

Digambar also has different communities under it such as Saitwal, Lad, Khandelwal, Bagherwal, Aggarwal etc. Chatutath, Pancham,Bogar,Kasar, Saitwal is a well-known and well-organized caste of Marathi-speaking Jain communities. They are high in number. Saitwals are spread all over Maharashtra, South Madhya Pradesh and North Karnatak.Chatutath, pancham,Bogar,Kasar community of digmber jains are stayin in maharastra and karnataka.

The traditional occupation of Saitwals is tailoring. This is a well-educated community and it has given many writers and scholars to the Jain community. They are progressive and social-minded. Most of their surnames are based on their original villages. Parwars chiefly come from M.P and U.P. They are one of the most learned amongst Jains. Most Pandits and Scholars of tirthakshetras are Parwars.

Sub Sects

The Digambar sect, in recent centuries, has been divided into the following major sub-sects: a) Bisapantha, b) Terapantha, and c) Taranapantha or Samaiyapantha.

Those following the Terapanth reforms are called Terapanth and others following more traditional practices are called Bisapanthai. Amongst the Digambars, the Taran Panthi follow Taran Swami.

SHVETAMBAR SECT

The Shvetambar is the other main sect of Jainism, the first one being Digambar. Shvetambar literally means white-clad, describing the practice of wearing white clothes, which sets it apart from Digambar space clad, whose practitioners wear no clothes.

Shvetambars, unlike Digambars, don't believe that monks must practice nudity, or that women are unable to obtain Moksh. Shvetambars maintain that the 19th Tirthankar, Mallinath, was a woman. At present in Shvetambar sects, there are 2,510 Monks and 10,228 nuns, while in Digambars there are 548 monks and 527 nuns (As per 'Smagra Jain chaturmas suchi-2006').

The Shvetambar tradition follows the lineage of Acharya Sthulibhadra suri. Kalpasutra mentions some of the lineages in ancient times. From the Kottiya Gana, this was once important. The Shvetambar ascetic orders are branches of Vrahada-gachchha established in 937 AD. The most important amongst the classical orders today are Kharatara-gachchha (1024 AD.), Tapa Gachchha (1228 AD.) and Tristutik Gachchha.

A major argument was initiated by Lonka Shaha, who started a movement opposed to idol worship in 1476. The Sthanakvasi and Terapanthi (Shvetambar) (1780) orders are offshoots of this movement.

The major reforms by Vijayananda Suri (1827 – 1906) in 1880, as the head of the Tapa Gachchha, led a movement to rejuvenate orders of wandering monks, which brought about the near disappearance of the Yati institutions. Acharya Rajendrasuri restored shraman sanstha in the Tristutik gachchha.

Some Shvetambar monks and nuns cover their mouth with a white cloth muhpatti to practise non-violence even when they talk. By doing so they minimised the possibility of inhaling small organisms.

Sub Sects

Like the Digambar sect, the Shvetambar sect has also been split into three main sub-sects:

- Murtipujaka,
- Sthanakvasi, and
- Terapanthi

Murtipujaka: The original stock of the Shvetambars is known as Murtipujaka Shvetambars since they are the meticulous worshippers of idols. They offer flowers, fruits, saffron, etc. to their idols and consistently adorn them with rich clothes and jeweled ornaments.

Their monks cover their mouth with strips of cloth while speaking, otherwise they keep them in their hands. They stay in temples or in the especially reserved buildings known as upasrayas. They collect food in their bowls from the sravakas or householders' houses and eat at their place of stay.

The Murtipujaka sub-sect is also known by terms like (i) Pujera (worshippers), (ii) Deravasi (temple residents). (iii) Chaityavasi (temple residents) and (iv) Mandir-margi (temple goers) The Murtipujaka Shvetambars are found scattered all over India for business purposes in large urban centres, still they are concentrated mainly in Gujarat.

Sthanakvasi: The Sthanakvasi arose not directly from the Shvetambars but as reformers of an older reforming sect, viz., the Lonka sect of Jainism. This Lonka denomination was established in about 1474 AD. by Lonkashaha, a rich and well-read merchant of Ahmedabad. The main principle of this denomination was not to practice idol-worship. Later on, some of the members of the Lonka denomination disapproved of the ways of life of their monks, declaring that they lived less rigorously than Bhagwan Mahavir would have wished. A Lonka denomination layman, Viraji of Surat, received initiation as a Yati, i.e., an ascetic, and won great admiration on account of the strictness of his life. Many people of the Lonka denomination joined this reformer and they took the name of Sthanakvasi, meaning those who don't have their religious activities in temples but carry on their religious duties in places known as Sthanakas which are like prayer-halls.

The Sthanakvasi are also called by terms as (a) Dhundhiya (searchers) and (b) Sadhumargi (devotees of Sadhus, i.e., ascetics). Except on the crucial point of idol-worship, Sthanakvasi don't differ much from other Shvetambar Jains and hence now-a-days they invariably call themselves as Shvetambar Sthanakvasi. Nevertheless, there are some differences between the Sthanakvasi; and the Murtipujaka Shvetambars in the observance of some religious practices. The Sthanakvasi don't believe in idol-worship at all. As such they don't have temples but only sthanakas, that is, prayer halls, where they carry on their religious fastings, festivals, practices, prayers, discourses, etc. Further, the monks of Sthanakvasi cover their mouths with strips of cloth for all the time and they don't use the cloth of yellow or any other colour (naturally, except white). Moreover, the Sthanakvasi admit the authenticity of only 31 of the Holy Scriptures of Shvetambars. Furthermore, the Sthanakvasi don't have faith in the places of pilgrimage and don't participate in the religious festivals of Murtipujaka Shvetambars. The Shvetambar Sthanakvasi are also spread in different business centres in India but they are found chiefly in Gujarat, Punjab, Harayana and Rajasthan.

It is interesting to note that the two non-idolatrous sub-sects, viz., Taranapanthis amongst the Digambars and Sthanakvasi amongst the Shvetambars, came very late in the history of the Jain Church and to some extent it can safely be said that the Mohammedan influence on the religious mind of India was greatly responsible for their growth. In this connection Mrs. S. Stevenson observes: "If one effect of the Mohammedan conquest, nevertheless, was to drive many of the Jains into closer union with their fellow idol-worshippers in the face of iconoclasts. Another effect was to drive others away from idolatry in total. No oriental could hear a fellow oriental's passionate outcry against idolatry without doubts as to the righteousness of the practice entering his mind, Naturally enough it is in Ahmedabad, the city of Gujarat, that was most under Mohammedan influence, that we can first trace the stirring of these doubts. About 1474 AD. the Lonka denomination, the first of the non-idolatrous Jain sects, arose and was followed by the Dhundhiya or Sthanakvasi denomination in about 1653 AD.

Terapanthi: The terapanthi sub-sect is derived from the Sthanakvasi; section. The Terapanthi sub-sect was established by Swami Bhikkanaji Maharaj. Swami Bhikkanaji was formerly a Sthanakvasi saint and had initiation from his Guru, by name Acharya Raghunatha. Swami Bhikkanaji had differences with his Guru on several aspects of religious practices of Sthanakvasi monks and when these took a serious turn, he established Terapantha in the year 1760 AD.

As Acharya Bh1kkanaji laid stress on the 13 religious tenets, namely, (i) five Mahavratas (great vows), (ii) five samitis (regulations) and (iii) three Guptis (controls or restraints), his sub-sect was known as the Tera (meaning thirteen)-pantha sub-sect. In this connection it is interesting to note that two other interpretations have been given for the use of the term Terapantha for the sub-sect. As per one account, it is cited that as there were only 13 monks and 13 laymen in the pantha when it was established, it was called as Tera(meaning thirteen)-pantha. Sometimes another interpretation of the term Terapantha is given by its devotees. Tera means yours and pantha means path.

The Terapanthis are non-idolatrous and are very finely organized under the total direction of one Acharya, that is, religious head. In its history of little more than 200 years, the Terapantha had a succession of only 9 Acharyas from the founding father Acharya Bhikkanaji as the First Acharya to the current Acharya Tulasi as the 9th Acharya.

This practice of regulating the entire Pantha by one Acharya only has become a characteristic feature of the Terapantha and an example for emulation by other Panthas. It is noteworthy that all monks and nuns of the Terapantha scrupulously follow the orders of their Acharya, preach under his guidance and carry out all religious activities in accordance with his instructions. Further, the Terapantha regularly observes a notable festival known as Maryada Mahotasava. This unique festival is celebrated every year on the 7th day of the bright half of the month of Magha when all monks and lay followers, male and female, meet together at one predetermined place and discuss the different problems of Terapanthis.

The penance of Terapanthis is considered to be very severe. The dress of Terapanthi monks and nuns is akin to that of Sthanakvasi monks and nuns. But there is a difference in the length of muhapatti, i.e., a piece of white cloth kept always on the mouth. The Terapanthis believe that idolatry doesn't provide deliverance and attach importance to the practice of meditation.

Further, it may be stressed that the Terapantha is known for its disciplined organization characterized by one Acharya (i.e., religious head), one code of conduct and one line of thought. The Terapanthis are considered reformists as they emphasize simplicity in religion. For instance, the Terapanthis don't even construct monasteries for their monks, who inhabit a part of the house which the householders build for themselves. Recently their religious head, Acharya Tulsi, had started the Anuvrata Andolana, that is, the small vow movement. which attempts to utilize the spiritual philosophies of the Jains for ethical uplift of the masses in India.

The growth of Terapantha is the last big schism in the Shvetambar denomination and this Pantha is becoming popular. The Terapanthis are still limited in number and even though they are noticed in different cities in India, they are concentrated chiefly in Bikaner, Jodhpur and Mewar regions of Rajasthan.

REFERENCES

Bhattacharya, B.C.: *Jaina Iconography,* 2nd ed, Motilal Banarsidass, Delhi, 1974.

Bhattacharya, N.N.: *Jain Philosophy, Historical Outline.* Munshiram Manoharlal, New Delhi, 1976.

Bothra, P.: *Jain Theory of Perception,* Motilal Banarsidass, Delhi, 1976.

Brown, Percy: *Indian Architecture,* Bombay, 2nd Edn.

Buhler, G.: *Indian Sect of the Jainas,* Edited by Burgess, Jas, Luzac & Co., 46, Great Russell Street, 1903.

Desai, P.B. *Jainism in South India and some Jaina Epigraphs,* Sholapur, 1957.

Devendra Muni Shastri: *Source-Book in Jaina Philosophy,* Sri Tarak Guru Jain Granthalaya, Udaipur, 1983.

Diwakar, R.R.: *Bihar Through Ages,* Calcutta, 1959.

Dwivedi, R.C.: *Contribution of Jainism to Indian Culture,* Motilal Banarsidass, Varanasi, 1975.

Einstein Albert: *Ideas and Opinions,* Bonanza Books, No.9.

Ferfusson, J.: *History of Indian and Eastern Architecture,* London.

Fischer, E., & Jain, J.: *Art and Rituals, 2500 Years of Jainism in India,* Sterling Publishers, New Delhi, 1977.

Garbe, R.: *Encyclopaedia of Religion and Ethics*, T. & T. Clark, 38 George Street, New York, 1920.

Ghosh, A.): *Jaina Arts and Architecture*, New Delhi, 1974.

Glassenapp, H.V: *Doctrine of Karman in Jaina Philosophy*, Bombay, 1942.

Gopal, S.: *Outlines of Jainism*, New Delhi, 1973.

Jain, Champat Rai: *Householder's Dharma*, Bijnore, 1931.

Jain, H., and Upadhye, A.N.: *Mahavira, his Times and his Philosophy of Life*, Bharatiya Gyanpeeth, New Delhi, 1975.

Jain, J. P.: *Religion and Culture of the Jains*, Bharatiya Gyanpeeth, New Delhi, 1975.

Jain, J., and Fischer, E.: *Jaina Iconography, Part One, The Tirthankara in Jaina Scriptures, Art and Rituals, Part Two, Objects of Meditation and the Pantheon. 2 vols.* E.J.Brill, Leiden, 1978.

Jain, Jyoti Prasad: *Jainism: The Oldest Living Religion*, Banaras, 1951.

Jain, Jyoti Prasad: *Religion and Culture of the Jains*, New Delhi, 1977.

Jain, K.C.: *Lord Mahavira and his Times*, Motilal Banarsidass, Delhi, 1974.

Jain, Kailash Chand: *Jainism in Rajasthan*, Sholapur, 1963.

Jain, Kamata Prasad: *The Religion of Tirthankaras*, Aliganj, 1964.

Jain, Muni Uttam Kamal: *Jain Sects and Sub-sects*, New Delhi, 1975.

Jaini, Jugmandar Lal: *Outlines of Jainism*, Cambridge, 1916.

Jaini, P.S.: *The Jaina Path of Purification*, Berkeley: University of California Press, 1979.

Jaini, Padmanabh, S.: *The Jaina Path of Purigication*, California, 1979.

Mookerjee, S.: *The Jain Philosophy of Non-absolutism, a Critical Study of Anekantavada, 2nd. Ed*, Motilal Banarsidass, Delhi, 1978.

Nahar and Ghosh: *An Epitome of Jainism*, Calcutta 1917.

Nevaskar B.: *Capitalists without Capitalism, the Jains of India and the Quakers of the West*, Greenwood Publications, Westport, 1971.

Nyayavatara: Siddhasena, Translated by Vijayamurti Sastracarya, Paramashruta Prabhavaka Mandal, Jauhari Bazar-Bombay, First Edition, 1950.

Padmarajiah, Y.J.: *Jain Theories of Reality and Knowledge*, Bombay, 1963.

Pancastikaya-sara: Kunda-kunda, Edited by A.Chakravarti (Sacred Books of the Jainas, No. 3), Central Jaina Publishing House, Arrah, First Edition, 1920.

Pandey, V.: ed. *The World of Jainism*, pub. by the Author, Bombay, 1976.

Paul Marett: *Jainism Explained*, Lieciciter, 1988.

Pramana-mimamsa: Hemacandra. Edited by Pt.Sukhalal Sanghvi, Saraswati Pustak Bhandar, Ahmedabad, Reprint Second Edition, 1989.

Radhakrishnan, S.: *Indian Philosophy, Vol. I*, George Allen & Unwin, London, First Edition (Revised), 1929.

Radhakrishnan. S.: *Indian Philosophy. 2nd.ed, 2 vols,* Allen and Unwin, London, 1929,1931.

12

Demographic Propagation

One of the oldest religious traditions of India, Jainism has survived side by side with Hinduism during its long history. With fewer than five million adherents and comprising less than one percent of the Indian population, Jainism has demonstrated a notable persistency and patience and continues to exert an influence far beyond its small numbers.

Jainism has been called the only living non-Vedic tradition in India. Jain claims to antiquity seem firmly based and it appears that Parsva and Bhagwan Mahavir were reviving and restoring a religious tradition stretching back into pre-historic times. There are arguments that Jain origins go back to the Indus civilization.

The Jains moved at an early date from the original Ganges region where Bhagwan Mahavir preached. They moved west in one direction and east in another to Orissa and down the eastern coast to South India. Tradition and inscriptions support a migration of Jains to South India from as early as 360 BC. to avoid a famine. The move west focused on the city of Mathura at a similar period and this was a holy city of Jainism until about 1,000 AD. Nevertheless, by the fourth or fifth centuries AD. large numbers had moved further west. Schisms in Jainism are recorded from the earliest times. The separation between the main two branches, Digambars and Shvetambars, was fixed by the first century AD. The Jains of the South are mainly Digambars, while the majority in the North-West are Shvetambars.

Jain history is elusive and needs to be filled out by other sources such as stories, legends, sectarian traditions, and hagiographies. The Jains possess the oldest manuscript libraries in India, and the most prominent collections have only been catalogued this century. Access for scholars is very difficult, and full scholarly study has hardly begun.

Jainism grew in power and significance in the South during the first centuries CE but the Hindu Renaissance of the seventh to tenth centuries caused retraction of Jainism in the South, especially from Tamil Nadu, where only 30,000 Jains remain. In the North-West the Jains were centred in Gujarat and Rajasthan with great temple-cities built on the mountains of Satrunjaya, Girnar, and Abu, and here they suffered from the Muslim incursion. Jainism hung on doggedly in both North and South, and temples, such as at Mount Abu, and the giant statue of Bahubali in Karnataka, were erected.

Nevertheless, there was a long period of downfall. The eighteenth and nineteenth centuries are obscure but there is evidence of downfall in the nineteenth century with many Jains becoming Vaishnavas. Starting at the end of the nineteenth century there was a Jain diaspora with emigration to Africa, and then since the 1970s to England and North America. Economic changes have meant that Jains have moved all over India as well. With Jain monks starting to travel, Jainism must increasingly be considered a world religion.

ORIGIN

Jainism is one of the oldest religion of India. We don't know exactly when it was established. The Jains themselves say that Jainism has existed since eternity and it had like the Jain cosmos no beginning and would have no end. Most of the saints of Jainism belonged to remote ages, millions and billions of years ago. Nevertheless, for practical purposes we may take Bhagwan Mahavir, the last great saint as a historical figure. He was a contemporary of the Buddha.

Jainism first emerged into historical visibility in the sixth century BC. when it was one amongst many religious movements of the period that stressed world renunciation and rejected the religious culture and ritualism of the Brahman priestly class. Western scholars often single out Bhagwan Mahavir (who lived, as per Shvetambar tradition, from 599–527 BC.) as Jainism's founding father. The Jains, nevertheless, maintain that Jainism's teachings are everlasting and uncreated, and consider Bhagwan Mahavir to have been only the most recent of an infinite series of great Jain teachers. In fact, though Jainism's roots predate Bhagwan Mahavir, he played a key role in defining philosophies and practices that became fundamental to Jainism as it evolved. Viable ascetic communities with lay followings formed and grew after Bhagwan Mahavir's death.

Patronized chiefly by newly emerging urban classes (especially merchants) Jainism spread in two directions from its region of origin in the Ganges River basin: down India's eastern coast into the south and westward in the direction of Mathura. The division between the Shvetambars and Digambars crystallized in the fifth century C.E. The south eventually became the heartland of the Digambars; there they flourished and found royal patronage, especially in Karnataka. The Shvetambars became prominent in the west, especially in what is now Gujarat and Rajasthan.

Some account of the life of Bhagwan Mahavir can be obtained from this literature. As per Shvetambars, Bhagwan Mahavir was born on Vaishali a place about 45 km from Patina on Vhaitra, Shukla Trayodasi in 599 BC. He was a Kahatrya price belonging to the Jnatra clan. He died in 517 BC in Pavapuri near Rajagriha. Emperor Shrenika and his son Kunika were the rulers of Magadha during his time. The historicity of Bhagwan Mahavir is sought to be proved by comparing these facts with these obtained from the Buddhist sources. The pali Buddhist texts on the life and saying s of the Buddha are claimed to have been compiled shortly after his death. they mention quite often a Nataputta who belonged to the sect of Niganthas (free from shakels.) As per these sources Nataputta died in Pava thirty years before the death of Buddha. The rulers of Magadha during the Buddha's time were Bimbisara and son Ajatashatru.

It is maintained that the person cited as Nataputta in the Buddhist texts was the same as Bhagwan Mahavir, the Jnatraputra of the Jains. The name of he place where he died in the same in both the sets of sources. Shrenika and Kunika, the two kings cited in the Jain sources were Bimbisara is cited in the (Jain) Dasasuta skandha.

Ajatshatru's son as per Buddhist sources was Udayabhadda. As per Jain sources Kunika's son was Udayin. Since the manes of the sons also are similar Kunika is identified with Ajatashatru.

As stated earlier the Jains Claim that their religion existed from time immemorial and Bhagwan Mahavir was the last great saint and reformer of that religion. The most prominent of these reforms was the introduction of the five vows in place of the four obtaining in the system of Parshva (the twenty-third Tirthankar of the Jains).

The later history old Jainism is markers by a number of schisms. But one might say that different groups existed amongst the Jains even at the time of Bhagwan Mahavir himself. There was an ascetic called keshi who pursued the system of Parshvanatha. He had a long discussion with Gautama a disciple of Bhagwan Mahavir and eventually accepted the latter's view and sincerely adopted the "law of the five vows". Therefore parshva's group and Bhagwan Mahavir's group originally separate were united. Nevertheless news schisms appeared as per Shvetambars even during Bhagwan Mahavir's lifetime. The first schism was by his own son-in law Jamili 14 years after Bhagwan Mahavir's nirvana. The various schisms are known as nihnavas.

The most prominent schism, the eight nihnava as per Shvetambars, occurred amongst the Jains a few centuries after Bhagwan Mahavir. At that time the community broke into the two sects, the Digambars (the skyclad) and Shvetambars (the white-robed). It is interesting to note that the two sects describe the life of Bhagwan Mahavir differently. The Shvetambars say that Bhagwan Mahavir lived as a prince upto the age of thirty. He had married and had a daughter, Anojja or Priyadarshana. His grand-daughter Yashovati was born after Bhagwan Mahavir had left home. Digambars contrarily believe that Bhagwan Mahavir never married.

We therefore see that in the period under discussion Bhagwan Mahavir was preaching perhaps one of the Vratya religions Which was Prevalent in that Part of India. This religion came to be Known as Jainism in later days. Most of the religions in this area advocated an extreme from of asceticism. Gautama, who later became the Buddha, originally joined this main stream. Except for some changes in the Philosophical tenets, Buddha's main modification was that he deprecated the severe asceticism of these religions.

It would therefore appear that Jainism, and many other religions existed from pre-Vedic times in northern India. Only Jainism remained practically unaffected by the impact of Vedism. The other religions which coalesced to form classical Hinduism, were affected by Vedism, albeit, as Dandekar insists superficially.

EARLY RISE

Another prominent development that was taking place in eastern India at the time that the Brahmans were trying established their mastery over the other classes. This the Kshatriyas of the area were not ready to concede. The Ambattha Sutta explains the discussion Buddha had with a Brahmana named Ambattha. At that time the Buddha was staying in the Koshala country. This was perhaps the western limit of his missionary work.

When Ambattha came in the company of the Buddha he behaved in an off-hand manner. The Buddha pulled him up for being ill-mannered to an aged teacher. Ambattha then complained, " That, Gautama is neither fitting nor is it seemly that the Sakyas (who were Kshatriyas) menials as they are, mere menials, should neither venerate, nor value, nor esteem, nor gives gifts to, nor pay honours to Brahmanas."

The Buddha explained to him that these things could not be claimed by an individual merely because he was born a Brahamana. Such veneration was payable only to a recluse or to a Brahmana who had obtained the supreme perfections in wisdom and conduct.

Interestingly enough the Jain Sutras also give instances where Brahmanas claimed superiority by virtue of their birth alone. This was strongly repudiated by the devotees of Bhagwan Mahavir. It appears from the above that the Brahmanas could not claim any superior positions by virtue of their birth alone, in eastern India. A Brahmana had to earn the position by cultivating the same qualities as an ascetic.

We therefore find that in Magadha in the sixth century BC., two prominent things were current in the religious atmosphere. The first is that the most venerated persons in the area were the monks. It did not matter to what order or denomination the monks belonged. All were equally respected. Secondly, the monks were not practicing their austerities to gain paradise or any other pleasureable objects. All that they gained in this word was the respect that the people from the Emperor downwards paid them.

Asceticism, nevertheless, was meant for the wholly committed persons. A common man had to take recourse to the worship of Gods and Goddesses for satisfying his religious instinct. The most popular deities in Magadha at that time were the yakshas. Both Buddhist and Jain canonical works mention the existence of temples of yakshas both of male and female species. In fact as per ancient Jana works there were temples dedicated to various yakshas in every town in northern India. A temple of Bahuputta is cited in Buddhist and also the Jain texts. This temple had been, as per Bhagavati-sutra, the fifth Anga of the Jains, visited by Bhagwan Mahavir himself.

Yakshas were non-Vedic Gods. The term yaksha, occurs six times in the Rigveda, but its meaning there is not clear. The term also occurs several times in the Atharva-veda. In the latter history of Jainism the yakshas became attendants of the Tirthankars.

The traditional Jain belief is that Jainism had existed in the same form from the hoary past, and Bhagwan Mahavir the 24th Tirthankar had carried on the religion exactly as it existed in his time, without any change.

It would appear from the Jain canonical works themselves that the traditional answer is not wholly correct. It is true that at the time of Bhagwan Mahavir there was an older religion whose ideals and methods were almost the as that of Mahivira's and which even his devotees called the older sections of the Church, but at the same time it is also true that Bhagwan Mahavir did introduce two prominent changes in the practices of this older section.

The early teaching of Jainism passed from generation to generation through the oral tradition. A religious council was held in Pataliputra (current-day Patna) in third century BC, where all Jain teachings were recorded and compiled. This collection was later on edited in fifth century AD. The devotees of Jainism slowly began to move to the southern parts of the country.

The differences that rose subsequent to the migration of the monks to the south led to the division of Jainism into two sects-the Digambars or the sky-clad and the Shvetambars or the white-clad. The monks belonging to the sky-clad denomination are naked, while the monks belonging to the white-clad denomination wear white garments. There is hardly any major difference between the two denominations. Jain monks practice ahimsa to the extent that they put a white cloth over their mouths to check them from accidentally inhaling insects. Jainism became popular amongst the royal dynasties like the Ganga, Kadamba, Chalukya and the Rashtrakuta. The rich merchants of Gujarat have patronized this religion.

FACTORS RESPONSIBLE FOR RISE

The 6th Century BC. was a period of religious revolution in various parts of the world. It was an age when great religious teachers, philosophers and thinkers lived. Their ideas made revolutionary changes in all aspects of life. Zoroaster in Persia and Confucius in China preached new philosophies. In India too, the 6th century BC. saw many changes. As many as 62 religious groups developed in the Gangetic plains. They observed countless religious customs and rites. Jainism appeared to put an end to them. Some causes for the growth of Jainism are:

- Religious life in ancient India was in the first place very simple. But in course of time intricate rites and ceremonies began to dominate the practice of worship. Poor people were unable to observe them.
- Religion lost its simplicity. It became expensive and elaborate. Blind faith and superstitious beliefs confused the people.

- Caste system became strict and it created inequality in the society.
- Religious literature was in Sanskrit. The common people spoke in Prakrit and Pall They could not understand Sanskrit.
- The priestly class took advantage of it. They interpreted religion as per their convenience.
- They considered themselves superior and others as inferiors.
- Animal sacrifice became common. People did not like it.
- People wanted a simple religion which would remove the evils in the society.

Bhagwan Mahavir drew his devotees chiefly from the Kshatriya aristocracy and organized them into a regular community with lay and ascetic members of both sexes. There is good reason to believe that before they joined him some of these devotees believed that all belongings, including clothing, should be abandoned, in the pursuit of passionless detachment, while others stopped short of making nudity a requirement. It was this difference, and later disagreement about the contents of the canon of the Holy Scriptures, which were to distinguish the two major denominations of Jainism. No key doctrinal differences emerged, even in later centuries.

In subsequent centuries Jainism spread from east to west across India. From time to time it enjoyed the patronage of kings and princes, under whose auspices it produced some of the most magnificent temple architecture in the world. But with the growth of Hindu devotional theism especially to Shiva and Vishnu, in the Middle Ages, it went into relative downfall. It became concentrated in two areas, where it remains to this day: Gujarat and Rajasthan where the Shvetambars prevail, and the Deccan, or modern Mysore, where the Digambars have their headquarters. But, unlike Buddhism, Jainism continued in the land of its birth. This was probably due largely to its stress on the lay and also on the ascetic calling. In times of persecution it had the resources of an influential and wealthy lay following to fall back on.

Long before sixth century BC. the Vedic religion lost its simplicity owing to costly sacrificial rituals, slaughter of animal, cumbrous ceremonies, indispensability of Brahmin priests and their demand for more and more fees the simple worship of the Vedic tithes degenerated into a lifeless system. The rishis of the Upanishads criticized sacrificial rituals and the worship of Gods and Goddesses. They said that effect of Karma regulated the life of a man. Honest work and purity of life could free him from the cycle of life and death, not costly sacrifices. They also said that a priest was not essential in performing religious rituals. Man can shape his own destiny. These teachings set anew trend in religious thinking. Common man lost faith in Brahmanical religion.

The seeds of the Protest movement lay in the Vedic society. The Vedic society was divided into four clear-cut classes or varnas Brahmanas, Kshatriyas, Vaishyas and Sudras. The Brahmanas claimed the highest position. In the society as also in the state they enjoyed many privileges. They received gifts from the Emperor, they were exempted from the payment of taxes. Not only that, they were also above punishment. In social status the Kshatriyas were next to the Brahmanas. They were warriors and members of the ruling class. They fought for the country and carried on administration. While the social prestigiousness of the Brahmanas and Kshatriyas increased, the prestige of the Vaishyas sank. They were sometime equated with the Sudras. The Sudras occupied the lowest position in the society. They were almost slaves. They were even considered untouchable. This class distinction gave, rise to social tensions. The predomination of the Brahmanas was very much resented by the Kshatriyas. From the Later Vedic age the Brahmana Kshatriya feud started over the question of supremacy in the society. In this connection it may be cited that Bhagwan Mahavir was Kshatriya by caste.

The introduction of new agricultural economy in the north-eastern India was one of the primary causes of the growth of new religions. North-eastern India comprising northern part of Uttar Pradesh and North and South Bihar was covered with dense forest. In the sixth century BC. the forest was cleared with the help of iron implements and the land. was brought under cultivation. For the extension of agriculture it was necessary to preserve Cattle-stock. But the Brahmanical religion stood in the way. Sacrifice of cows was a necessary part of Vedic rites; Hundreds of Oxen were slaughtered in 'Gomedha' sacrifice. The tribal people in some parts of Magadha also killed animals for food. In the interest of agriculture it was necessary to stop animal. slaughter.

Due to the introduction of new agricultural economy there was more [illegible] food. This led to the growth of many cities like Kousambi, Kosal, Kusinagar, Vaisali, Rajagriha, Varanasi, Chirand and so on in north-eastern India. These cities were inhabited many traders and artisans who during this period began to use coins. The use of coins undoubtedly facilitated trade and commerce which made the dealers arid citizens wealthy. These wealthy Vaisyas or the trading class had no social prestige in the Brahmanical society. So,they were in searching of a new religion which would give them social status. No doubt, Jainism satisfied their needs. There was no place of caste-distinction in this religion. So the Vaisyas extended their generous support to Bhagwan Mahavir. Moreover, in ancient India there was continuous warfare amongst different states which were detrimental to the' growth of agriculture and trade and commerce. By preaching ahimsa this new religion helped the progress of agriculture and trade and commerce. The Brahmanical law-Texts or the 'Dharma sutras' had criticized in no uncertain terms the practice of money-lending on interest and sea-voyages which were necessary for business.

Jain texts refer to a community of rich merchants, called Sresthis who had money-lending business. So the Vaisyas became opposed to Brahmanism, and by supporting the new religion they tried to raise their social prestige. From the Later Vedic period the place of women-folk in the Brahmanical society began to deteriorate. On the contrary, women-folk and even the dacoits, were held in high esteem by Jainism. As a result Jainism became acceptable even to the lower- strata or society. The sixth century BC. also witnessed a reaction against private property, abundance of wealth, luxurious life-style and new system of transport and dwelling houses. Some people detested all these things and they longed to return to the primitive life. Old ascetic life began to lure them. Here again, Jainism preached simple, puritan, ascetic life and satisfied the needs of a large section of people. Jain monks were not allowed to touch gold and silver. They were to accept as much as was sufficient to keep body and soul together.

This religion expanded in Magadha and elsewhere because of the strong rulers at Pataliputra. At the time of Alexander the Great's invasion on the borders of the Magadha Empire, it was the Jain rulers who were in firm control at Pataliputra. Alexander's forces were tired and did not advance any further to challenge this empire.

Many centuries later, there was a famine in Magadha and it led to mass migration of the population to South India (current day Karnataka) and after some time, another migration took place to Gujarat (Girnar). The first group was called Shvetambars because they started wearing white clothes, whereas the other ones (Digambars). These were strict and not willing to change. A third influential group developed after migration from Bihar to near Mathura, which tried to patch up between these two groups for a long time. Udaygiri (Orrisa) was also, one of the prominent

Jain centres. In the olden days, this religion was also practised in Sri Lanka. All of this happened about 2000 years back.

JAINISM IN OTHER PARTS OF WORLD

During the 20th century, Jainism evolved into a worldwide faith. Due to age-old trading links, many Jains from western India settled in eastern African countries, most notably Kenya and Uganda. Political unrest in the 1960s obligated many of them to relocate to the United Kingdom, where the first Jain temple outside India was consecrated in Leicester, and then increasingly to the United States and Canada, where they successfully assumed their traditional mercantile and professional occupations. A desire to preserve their religious identity has led expatriate Jains to form trans-sectarian organizations such as the Jain Samaj, established in Europe in 1970, and the Federation of Jain Associations in North America, established in 1981. English-language publications such as Jain Digest and Jain Spirit have presented Jain ideals, such as ahimsa, vegetarianism, and, most recently, environmentalism, to members of the Jain diaspora and the wider world.

Figures for the population of Jains differ from just over three million to twelve million. There are difficulties of Jain identity, with Jains being seen as a Hindu denomination, and some Jains considering themselves Hindus. Certain castes contain both Hindus and Jains.

DEMOGRAPHICS

It is claimed by the Jains that the Census figures are a gross under-estimation because many Jains don't give Jainism as their religion on the census forms for several reasons, and that the population of Jains in India may amount to ten million. During the 1981 Census, the Jains held a major advertising campaign urging Jains to register as such on their census forms.

The 2001 Indian Census records about four million Jains in India. Nevertheless, it should be noted that many Jains were counted as Hindus and one Jain site states there are as many as ten million devotees of Jainism.

The Jains have the maximum literacy rate, 94.1% compared with the national mean of 65.38%. They have the highest female literacy rate, 90.6% compared with the national average of 54.16%. It is believed that the Jains also have the highest per capita income in India. There are about 110 different Jain communities in India and overseas.

Jainism has been spread over mnay countries such as US, UK, Canada, Europe, Kenya, Tanzania and Uganda. The religion has its popularity in some parts of US and many Jain temples have been built there. Smaller Jain communities exist in Nepal, South Africa, Japan, Singapore, Malaysia, Australia, Fiji and Suriname.

There are about 200,000 Jains living outside India. There are an estimated 25,000 in Europe, mainly in England, of Gujarati origin. Many came to escape President Amin in Uganda in the 1970's, and settled chiefly in London, Leicester, and Manchester. There are 21,000 Jains in Africa, mainly in East Africa, 100,000 plus in North America, and 5,000 in the rest of Asia (Cort 1989, 342, cited in Dundas 1992, 232).

The Jain population in India as per 2001 census is 4,225,053 out of the total population of India 1,028,610,328. The states or areas with largest populations are:

Maharashtra	1,301,843
Rajasthan	650,493
Madhya Pradesh	545,446
Gujarat	525,305
Karnataka	412,659
Uttar Pradesh	207,111
Delhi	155,122
Tamil Nadu	83,359

REFERENCES

Acaranga-sutra, Anga-sutrani I: Vacana Pramukha, Acarya Tulasi, Editor Yuvacarya Mahaprajna, Jaina Vishvabharati, Ladnun, First Edition, 1974.

Amar, Muni: *Jainatva ki Jhanki, Sanmati Grantharatnamala No. 12*, Sanmati Gyanpeeth, Seventh Edition, Agra, 1987.

Avasyaka-sutra: Editor Madhukar Muni, Jinagama Granthamala, No.24 Agama Prakashan Samiti, Byavar, First Edition, 1985.

Basham, A.L.: *A Cultural History of India,* Clarendon Press, Oxford.

Basham, A.L.: *Post-script, attached to the article on Hinduism in*

Bhagavati (Vyakhyaprajnapti) in Anga-sutrani II: Editor Yuvacarya Mahaprajna, Jaina Vishvabharati, Ladnum, First Edition, 1974.

Bhargava, D.: *Jain Ethics,* Motilal Banarsidass, Delhi, 1968.

Caillat, C.: *Jainism,* Macmillan Company of Upadhye, A.N., andIndia, Delhi, 1974.

Chakravarti, A.: *Samayasara of Sri Kundakunda,* Translation with Introduction. Bharatiya Gyanpeeth, Delhi, 1971.

Chakravarti, A: *The Religion of Ahimsa,* Bombay, 1957.

Chandogya Upanisad: Edited by Max Muller, F. (S. B. E.) Vol. 1, Motilal Banarasidas, Delhi, Reprint Edition, 1981.

Chatterjee, A.K.: *Comprehensive History of Jainism (up to 1000 A.D.),* Firma KLM, Calcutta, 1978.

Dasavaikalika-sutra: Editor Madhukar Muni, Jinagama Granthamala, No. 23, Agama Prakashan Samiti, Byavara, First Edition, 1985.

Dasgupta, S.N.: *History of Indian Philosophy, Vol. I,* Cambridge University Press, London, Second Edition (Reprint), 1932.

Gopalan, A.S.: *Outlines of Jainism,* Willey Eastern (P) Limited, New Delhi, First Edition, 1973.

Guseva, N.R: *Jainism,* Bombay, 1971.

Hume, Robert Earnest: *Thirteen Principal Upanisads (Trans.),* Oxford, 1921.

Jacobi, H.: *Introduction to Kalpa-sutra.*

Jacobi, H.: *Jaina Sutras, Part 1, The Akaranga Sutra, The Kalpa Sutra, Part2, The Uttaradhyana Sutra,The Sutrakritanga Sutra. 2 vols,* Dover Publications, New York, 1968.

Jacobi, H.: *Mahavira and His Predecessors.*

Jacobi, H.: *Studies in Jainism,* Ahmedabad, 1946.

Jain, C. R.: *Fundamentals of Jainism,* Veer Nirvan Bharti, Meerut, 1974.

Jain, Champat Rai: *Fundamentals of Jainism,* Meerut, 1974.

James, William: *Principles of Psychology, Vol. I,* Macmillan & Co., London, 1918.

Jindal, K.B: *The prefaces,* Calcutta, 1958.

Kalghatagi, T.G.: *Jaina View of Life,* Sholapur, 1969.

Kapadia, H.R.: *Jaina Religion and Literature,* Lahore, 1944.

Kapashi, V.J.: *In Search of the Ultimate,* V.K. Publications, Harrow, 1984.

Law, B.C: *Mahavira: His Life and Teachings,* London, 1937.

Lenin: *Collected Works of Lenin, Vol. 14.*

Madhav Rao, N.: *Jainism A New Look.*

Malavania, Pt. Dalasukhabhai: *Jainism (Some essays),* Translated by Dr. A.S.Gopani, Prakrita Bharati Academy, Jaipur, First Edition, 1986.

Mehata, M.L.: *Jaina Culture,* Varanasi, 1969.

Mehta, M. L.: *Outlines of Jaina Philosophy,* Jaina Mission Society, G. 146, Chickpet, Bangalore - 2, October, 1954.

Ramchandran, T.N.: *Jain Monuments of India,* Calcutta, 1944.

Rampuria, S.C.: *The Cult of Ahimsa,* Calcutta, 1947.

Rosenfield, C.: *Gurudev Shree Chitrabhanu, a Man with a Vision,* New Jain Meditation Intemational Center, York, 1981.

Roy Chowdhari, P.C.: *Jainism in Bihar,* Patna, 1956.

Roy, A.K.: *History of the Jains,* Gitanjali Publishing House, New Delhi, 1984.

Saletore, B.A: *Medieval Jainism,* Bombay, 1938.

Samaya-sara: Kunda-kunda, Bharatiya Gyanpeeth, Durgakund Road, Varanasi, First Edition, 1950.

Sangave, V.S.: *Jaina Community, a Social Survey. 2nd. ed.* Popular Prakashan, Bombay, 1980.

Sangave, Vilas A.: *Life and Legacy of Mahavira:* A Social Study, Meerut, 1974.

Stevenson, Sinclair: *The Heart of Jainism,* Oxford, 1915.

Stevenson. S.: *The Heart of Jainism,* Munshiram Manoharlal, New Delhi, 1970.

Tahtinen, U.: *Ahimsa, Non-violence in Indian Society,* Rider, London, 1976.

Talib, G.S.: ed. *Jainism,* Punjabi University, Patiala, 1975.

Tatia, Nathmal: *Studies in Jain Philosophy,* Banaras, 1951.

Tattvartha-sutra: Umasvati, P.V. Research Institute, Varanasi, Reprint Second Edition.

Thomas, F.W.: *Sri Mallisenasuri, Syad-Vada-Manjari,* Motilal Banarsidass Delhi, 1968.

Trsastisalakapurusacaritrani: Canto 10, Hemacandra, Jaina Dharma Prasaraka Sabha, Bhavanagar, First Edition, 1908.

Tukol, T.K.: *Compendium of Jainism*, Dharwad, 1980.

Upadhye, A.N.: *Lord Mahavira and his Teachings. 2nd. Ed,* Shree Vallabhsuri Smarak Nidhi, Bombay,1983.

Uttaradhyayana-sutra: Editor Madhukara Muni, Jinagama Granthamala No. 19, Agama Prakashan Samiti, Byavara, First Edition, 1984.

Warren, H.: *Jainism in Western Garb, as a Solution to Life's Great Problems,* Edited, with notes, by N.J. Shah. 2nd. ed. Shree Vallabhsuri Smarak Nidhi, Bombay, 1983.

Warren, Herbert: *Jainism,* Arrah, 1916.

Williams, R.: *Jaina Yoga: A survey of Medieval Sharavakachara,* London, 1963.

13

Socio-Political Influence

Religion and politics are inextricably fused. Their separation tantamounts to the parting of blood and body. It was due to this idea that Gandhiji called politics without religion a dirty game. Swami Vivekananda had also considered religion as the core of politics. Papalism pulled the strings in the medieval European politics. Islam has been influencing political forces in many countries.

But religion is a individual affair that should not have anything to do with public matters including politics. Man has made religion in order to develop discipline and also to satiate his divine needs. Any religion that gives birth to riots and violence can't be a religion. Religion can't exist without people. But ironically, man has been exploiting religion to reap political harvest to inject venom and to divide the people.

Most of the politicians routinely visit religious places to seek divine blessings. Although they are staunch believers in religion and meticulously follow religious diktats, they never desist from reminding us that they are pure secularists. Those who claim themselves to be secular socialists socialize with religious leaders for votes.

The religion-politics relationship poses no threat to a country's polity as long as politics doesn't use religion and vice versa. Unfortunately our country witnesses both of them. Today, politics has been religionised and religion has been politicised. Therefore a religion-politics collusion is taking place.

SOCIO-POLITICAL IDENTITY

The most important prospect of the political history of India, right from the times of Bhagwan Mahavir upto the current day, is that India has rarely been politically united. The periods witnessing political unity have been extremely short in the face of prolonged history of thousands of years. The most prominent aspects of our history is that although our political leaders failed us, mainly in attaining political unity, we retained our national unity chiefly because of our cultural unity which our people have developed through ages by their inherent sagacity and wisdom. This cultural unity is expressed through our way of life, our spirit of tolerance and accommodation and our capability of patience and endurance which we have been able to exhibit commonly irrespective of our castes, creed or religion. The main contributing factor to these virtues is the power of assimilation possessed by the Aryan race, settled in the country. Aryans learnt in plenty from the more civilized, original settlers of this land but they also made their own original contribution to heighten the notions which they learnt. When Mohammedans came to India, they, unlike the former invaders, came with their own religion and culture, with the result that they could not be assimilated in the existing Indian culture.

Contrarily, they tried to enforce their own by physical conversions and political, social and economic repression. But by the passage of time even Islam was influenced by Upanisadic thoughts giving birth to Indian Sufism which attracted both Hindu and Muslim masses. Today an average Muslim's social and ethical attitude is not fundamentally different from that of an average Jain or Christian. One can find a difference only in degrees. Therefore our culture, developed by the people of our nation through ages, has saved our national unity, inspite of our political leaders' failure and inspite of the partition of our country on the eve of our political independence.

The roots of above analysis are found in the socio-political environment, prevailing during the time of Bhagwan Mahavir. Those were the times when there was no paramount power to control the whole or even a great bulk of the country. There were small states and republics having monarchical and also non-monarchical forms of government each trying to dominate the other. Political leadership in both the forms of government had failed to unite the country as a one whole. Even in the areas not having monarchy, the political structure was chiefly oligarchical in character, power vested in the hands of the elite.

Socially, on account of the belief that Gods can be pleased to make our life comfortable only by sacrifices, a priestly class with great vested interests grew up and the development of Brahmanical Holy Scriptures, prescribing intricate and highly specialized rules for sacrifices, made the services of the priestly class inevitable even for the ruling princes and political leaders. Nevertheless, the thinkers like Parsva, Kapila, Uddalaka Aruni, Yajnavalkya and many other Rsis of later Upanisadas had started making dents on stronghold of sacrificial priests and princes. These great thinkers had already started a thinking process which was given a revolutionary push by Bhagwan Mahavir and Buddha and which finally proved to be a cementing force of cultural unity inspite of the internecine quarrels between the political leaders of the day.

In light of modern definitions and speculations, the Jain society may be termed as "Jain Community" which states a particular form of social life, its cultural and ethnic notions and values. It is originally established on the Jain principle of equality and equanimity, which stresses on the social and spiritual person, and rejects the concept of God as mediator, and replaces it with the theory of Karma. It stresses on personal purification, which leads the society in peace and order. It regulates not only the current life, but also the future. Unlike the Vedic religion, the Jain Holy Scriptures sets forth the responsibility of ones deeds for deciding his caste.

Jainism doesn't hold caste as a way of people being judged. In other words, caste can't be decided by birth but it is one's own action or conduct, which decides the caste. It is said that by simply shaving the head, one can't be a Muni (monk) and by only adhering to Kasayacivar (saffron clothing) one can't claim to be a Tapasvi, an individual who resides in a jungle can't be called a Sramana. As a matter of fact, they should possess the attributes like Samata (equality and equanimity), Brahmacharya (celibacy), Gyan (knowledge), Tapa (penance) and Caritra (conduct) with the right attitude. This was the Varna system developed on the Rishabh Dev and his son Bharata legend. They have their own system for marriage and other celebrations.

The great devotional movement made an intensive impact on Jain society and made it changed to the great extent. The great Heros Rama, Krishna, Pandavas and others are accepted by Jains as Salaka Mahapurusas and composed a large quantity of literature on their life and works.

Jain Community in its historical and social perspective is a quite distinct, independent and new society with its Congregationalist nature. It has never abandoned the original spirit of Jainism. Thus, the Jain community can't be said to be the part of the Vedic or Hindu community, although it carries profound impact of it in the code of conduct of householders in the later period. Like-wise, in spite of occupying a large portion of business and industry it would not be a true speculation of the Jain community to be recognized only as the business community.

Numerically, Jains form a very small segment of the Indian population. About, 3.19 million devotees, or may be a little more near about 12 millions as per calculation of Jain society, of this religion account for 0.48 percent of the total population as of 1981 census and therefore ranked the sixth largest religious group. Nevertheless, Jains are spread over all parts of India and have contributed a lot in spite of being a small community in the economic, political, cultural, social, and literal, art, architecture and divine fields. They also never indulged in vicious and revengeful activities. Thus the Jain community has its own unique place in the religious and human society.

JAINISM AND POLITICS

Amongst the Muslim, Christian, Buddhist, Sikh and other religious minority communities of India, the Jain community occupies an prominent place from different points of view. The Jains have smallest population amongst the six major religious communities listed by the Government of India in their Census Report. Further, the Jain community is one of the very ancient communities of India. The existence of Jain religion can be traced not only to the Vedic period but even to the Indus Valley period of Indian history. The names of the Jain Tirthankars are cited in the Vedas and there are evidences which show that the Indus Valley people must be worshipping Bhagwan Rishabh Dev, the first Tirthankar of the Jains along with other deities. Therefore hoary antiquity is a special feature of the Jain community and it is pertinent to note that this feature is not present in the other religious minority communities in India.

Except for antiquity, the Jain community has got the characteristic of unbroken continuity. Few communities in the world can claim such a long and continued existence. Even in the past, it appears, I the Jains were never very numerous and did not form an over whelming majority of population in India. It is really a matter of wonder to find haw the Jains could maintain their perpetuity when the devotees of many other religions and denominations, which were prevalent in the past, are not found at present in India. Therefore the survival of the Jains, as a separate being from the hoary antiquity to the current day, can be regarded as their unique feature.

Moreover, unlike other religious minority communities in India, the Jain community is Indian in every sense of the term. The Jains are the native inhabitants of this country and their mythological and historical personages are also from this country: The languages used by the Jains for writing and speaking purposes have inevitably been Indian. The sacred temples and places of pilgrimage of the Jains are located in India only. It seems that the Jains never undertook religious expeditions on a large scale in foreign countries with a view to convert their residents to Jainism. The Jains, thus, have no religious connections or affiliations with people outside India. Hence the total absence of extra-territorial affinities has been a special and important feature of the Jain community. The Jains never look to any foreign country, small or large, for help or guidance in their religious and other matters.

The Jains, although small in number, constitute a separate being and have succeeded in maintaining their unique features. Jainism being an independent religion its devotees have got their own and vast sacred literature, distinct doctrine and outlook on life, and special ethical rules of conduct established on the key principle of Non-violence. The entire activities of the Jains are moulded by the considerations of Non-violence. Therefore, Non-violence forms the very basis of their life and even to the current day strenuous efforts are made by the Jains to avoid Himsa, as far as possible, in every walk of life and in every activity. This utmost importance given to the observance of Non-violence in the life of every person is not found in other communities of India although they may attach some value to the principle of Non-violence. In fact, it can be stated that, the Jain community is the only community in the world which meticulously abides by the principle of Non-violence to the maximum extent possible.

The independence of Jain religion is now acknowledged on all hands. It is established beyond doubt that Jainism is a distinct religion of India and not an offshoot of either Buddhism or Brahmanism. The Jain religion, doctrine, ethics, Gods, temples, sacred places, objects, manners and places of worship, sacred texts, cosmology, mythology, ideology, teachers, monks, vows, holy days, rituals, fastings, festivals, outlook on life and culture with its stress on Non-violence are not only distinct from their Hindu counterparts but also not accepted and pursued by the Hindus. Even in the observance of certain common customs and manners the Jain way of looking at them is quite different from that of the Hindus. For instance, the Hindus regard the marriage as a religious sacrament, while the Jains consider it as a civil contract. Amongst the Hindus adoption is a religious ceremony, this is not so amongst the Jains. As per Jain Law a widow inherits the property of her deceased husband, but this position is not accepted by the Hindus. In the death ceremonies the Jains don't observe the days in memory of the dead. In view of these differences in the principles and practices of Jainism from Hinduism and other religions of India, the devotees of Jainism form a distinct religious community. Therefore this separateness of Jain community from the Hindu community is regarded as the characteristic feature of the Jain community.

Further we find that from ancient times two different types of culture, viz., the Brahmana culture and the Shramana culture, have been existing side by side in India. Of these two cultures, the Hindus represent the Brahmana culture and the Buddhists and the Jains represent the Shramana culture. But Buddhism practically disappeared for a long time from India, the land of its origin, although it triumphantly flourished in other parts of the world, especially in the East. Contrarily, Jainism did not cross the borders of India, yet it persisted, in comparatively small measures, through all these centuries in different parts of India. Therefore the Jain community has served and is still serving as a representative of the Shramana culture in India and it is regarded as a distinctive feature of the Jain community in India.

Although Jain community is a small one it is spread all over India. From ancient times to the current day the Jains are scattered throughout the length and breadth of India. The most outstanding peculiarity of the Jains found in different areas of India is that the Jains got themselves completely assimilated with the people of the region concerned, whether in the North or in the South. The Jains adopted the customs and manners, dress and ornaments, games and amusements, occupations and professions, tools and weapons, housing and furniture etc. of the people of the region concerned. Except for the mere acceptance of these traits of culture, the Jains assiduously tried and greatly succeeded in enriching the various aspects of the culture of the region. In this way the Jains, although small in number, have contributed a great deal to the growth of art and architecture, logic and doctrine, languages and literature, education and learning, charitable and public institutions, and political, materialistic and divine welfare of the people of different areas of India.

These varied and lasting contributions of the Jains to the Indian culture have been very significant especially in relation to their meagre number in India. This shows the total identification of the Jains with the various areas and sections of people in India irrespective of their caste, creed and religion. It can be said to the credit of the Jains that they always maintained very cordial relations with the people of the region. In the long history of the Jains we don't come across any instance when they, although in power, persecuted the devotees of other religions. This outstanding work in the field of culture is regarded as an important feature of the Jain community.

Throughout its long and eventful history the Jain community has produced a large number of reputed personalities in different fields. For instance, in the political field in the past the Jains have contributed the empire-builders like Chandragupta Maurya; extraordinary rulers like Kharvel in Kalinga, Vanaraja and Kumarapala in Gujarat and Amoghavarsha in the Deccan; male military generals like Chamundaraya and Gangaraja; female military generals like Jakkiyavve, Saviyavve and Bhairavadevi; devoted and capable ministers like Bhamashah in Rajasthan and Vastupal and Tejapal in Gujarat; and the renowned Jain Acharyas like Simhanandi and Sudatta who were virtually responsible for the founding of the Ganga Kingdom in the 2nd Century AD. and of the Hoyasala Kingdom in the eleventh Century AD. in Karnatak. In other fields of literature, sculpture, architecture, medicine, social work, etc. the Jains have produced reputed authorities. The gam,. tendency can be noted even at present.

In recent times the Jains have contributed captains of industry, commercial magnates, political leaders, constructive workers, able administrators, social reformers, gifted artists and devoted educationists. In the struggle for liberty the Jains' contribution in the form of men, money and materials was very outstanding. In the post-Independence period the Jains have been rendering valuable services in different fields and on their individual merits and achievements they are securing goodwill of others both for themselves and for their community. As a result we find that the Jain community has secured a place of honour and respect amongst the different communities of India.

FUNDAMENTALISM

In the modern world, comparative religion has become a field of study and also a vehicle for people of other religions to associate themselves with virtues of other religions. Often such comparisons forget or deliberately overlook the differences in the central foundations in the religions. This leads to showing similarities in religions in places where there are no similarities amongst them. This fallacy in comparison is often extended to religious fundamentalism as well. In these comparisons of religious fundamentalism, often the outward manifestations of groups are compared and erroneous conclusions are drawn from them.

The definition of fundamentalism agrees with such past and current behaviour of people of other religions. As per dictionary, the Fundamentalism is a movement or attitude stressing strict literal devotion to a set of fundamental tenets. Often we could see the fundamentalists of monotheistic religions believing in a world created by a God resorting to violence attempting to follow God.

On the contrary, Jains who are resorting to violence due to various reasons could not be labelled as fundamentalists due to the principle differences between Jain teachings and monotheistic teachings. This difference exists because an individual who would rigorously interpret real Jain texts will not find any excuses to resort to violence. Bhagwan Mahavir preached compassion and wisdom and every sutra when interpreted rigorously should lead one to follow the non-violent path.

The issues such as racism, sectarianism, and struggles for power are also equated to Jain fundamentalism if they occur in a wider Jain context. These are also acts by people who are not actually following the Bhagwan Mahavir's words properly. Since regarding the social status or race the Bhagwan Mahavir stated, "an individual doesn't become lower by birth but by actions". Hence, a Jain rigorously following the Bhagwan Mahavir's word will not look down upon other races or thinks one race is superior to another.

Similarly, an individual rigorously following the Bhagwan Mahavir's word would not fall into sectarianism because the Bhagwan Mahavir did not appoint any authority figure to look after the matters of his dispensation after his final nirvana.

CONTEMPORARY POLITICS

The prominent problem, which is undermining the strength of the Jain community for the last so many centuries, is the existence of various religious divisions in the community. Up to the days of Bhagwan Mahavir and even for some centuries later the Jain Church remained one and undivided although some minor schisms had taken place during and after the time of Bhagwan Mahavir. About the end of the first century AD. the Jain Church was eventually split up into two rival denominations which have vigorously maintained the rivalry to the current day. The two main denominations, viz. the Digambar and the Shvetambar, were later kin split up into major and minor sub-sects some of which were revolutionary in the sense that they opposed the established practice of idol worship. Except for the division of the Jain Church into sects, and sub-sects, the Jains were further divided, on a religious basis, into several sections and sub-sections like Sangha, Gana, Gachchha and Shakha.

The Jains did not stop with the creation of a large number of sects, sub-sects, sections and sub-sections in the community, but persistently made and are still making them by various means to perpetuate these divisions. Only a few wend places a common to both be Digambars and the Shvetambars, while each denomination possesses its own numerous sacred places. Even those few common sacred places have, for all these years, become a constant bone of contention between the two denominations as each denomination tries to establish its claim of ownership over them by both fair and foul means. Crores of rupees have been spent and continue to be spent by both the parties on litigation. Usually the members of each sub-sect or sub-section build their own temples or places of worship. Therefore amongst the Digambars the Terapanthis and the Bisapan this have their separate temples and the Taranopan this their own Chaityalayas.

The Murtipujaka Shvetambars have their temples, while the Shvetambar Sthanakavasis visit their Upashrayas only. In big cities practically every prominent Gachchha possesses its temple where all the members of that Gachchha assemble on festival and, other ceremonial days. At Karanja in Vidarbha the members of Sena Gana and Balatkara Gana have their own temples. Further, A many plans the members of some prominent castes have their different temples. Again, the main denominations have their own types of idols, methods of worship, places of pilgrim. age, sacred texts, Samskaras or sacraments, religious teachers and fastings and festivals. These differences have so much been magnified by both the -main denominations that every denomination considers itself as a true devotee of Jainism, while it regards the other denomination as fallen from the real path of Jainism.

The differences have penetrated into the social field also, Formerly, marriages used to take place between the members belonging to different sects and sub-sects; but now there is a marked tendency to restrict the marital relations within the members of a particular denomination or even a sub-sect. Each denomination or sub-sect provides for its students facilities like boarding houses, scholarship funds, research grants etc. There is hardly any association which caters to the needs of students irrespective of sect or sub-sect. Even their religious educational institutions like Gurukulas and Pathashalas are separate for each sect. The members of practically every sect or sub-sect are being organised on an all-India basis. The Digambars have organisations of an all-India character, viz. All India Digambar Jain Mahasabha, Delhi, All India Digambar Jain Sangha, Mathura and All India Digambar Jain Mahasamiti, Delhi; and amongst the Shvetambars each sub-sect has an alt-India organisation, viz. All India Slavetambara (Murtipujaka) Jain Conference, Bombay, All India

Shvetambar Sthanakavasi Jain Conference, Bombay; and Shri Jain Shvetambar Terapanthi Mahasabha, Calcutta.

These organisations have their provincial branches and official newspaper organs through which they try to stabilise their respective positions. It is true that there are some organisations of national and local and regional character like Bharata Jain Maha mandala, Bombay, and Bombay Jain Yuvaka Sangha, Bombay, which are meant for all Jains, but it is a. fact that they are not popular as other sectarian organisations are. Sometimes it is reported that even the religious pontiffs of different sects and sub-sects try to accentuate the religious differences and sever the social relations, if any, existing between them.

Therefore it is quite evident that the Jains have been segregated into different hostile camps on religious grounds. As a result we find that there is -nothing like religious unity amongst the devotees of Jainism and this undoubtedly hinders the progress of the Jain community. Since the Jains have been spread throughout the length and breadth of India, there is a great divergence in their observance of various social customs and manners. In the circumstances the only tie that brings all Jains together is the bond of religion, i.e. they are the devotees of the same religion. It is, thus, the paramount duty of the Jains to see that the feeling of oneness is inculcated in the minds of the Jains by several means. In fact, Jainism is one and undivided so far as its doctrine, key tenets and philosophies are concerned. The Jain Church was united for a long time and its sects-and especially the sub-sects-arose at a comparatively late stage; in its history.

There are not fundamental differences of a serious nature, from the point of view of the current age, between the sects and the sub-sects. As per Jain theory itself nobody, either male or female, can achieve redemption in the present age. It is, thus, quite futile to quarrel on points like 'Savastra-mukti', i.e. whether one can attain Moksh while one wears the clothes; `Strimukti,' i.e. whether a woman can achieve redemption; and `Kewali-Kavalahara`, i.e. whether an omniscient needs food or not. These three are the major points of differences between the Digambars and the Shvetambars and when they are not relevant in the current age there is no reason, why the denominations should give more importance to the minor differences and estrange their relations. The same can be said about the relations between the Terapanthis and the Bisapanthis amongst the Digambars and between the Sthanakavasis and the Terapanthis amongst the Shvetambars as there are not much differences between them. The non-idolatrous sub-sects amongst both the denominations may be allowed to worship in their own way but they should, in no case, be regarded as aliens to Jainism. Therefore more stress, in the first place, should invariably be given on these points of common nature, so that the feeling of hostility may be completely banished from the minds of Jains belonging to different denominations and sub-sects.

With a view to foster this feeling several practical means will have to be adopted by both the denominations. They should celebrate together the birth and death anniversary days of Bhagwan Rishabh Dev and Bhagwan Mahavir together instead of observing them separately. Naturally all other facilities and institutions must be kept free to all Jains. The field of social relations must also be widened. They should not be kept restricted within the members of a particular sect or sub-sect. Efforts should be made to publish the literature stressing the necessary unity in the Jain Church. The religious pontiffs should be made to concentrate their energies on cementing the differences and establishing the cordial relations between the sects and sub-sects. If possible, common Samskaras, fastings and festivals should be evolved, so that many opportunities will be created for bringing all people together and maintaining closer relations between them. When concentrated and sincere efforts are made on above lines, it is hoped, the common religious bond will become firm and will foster the sense of unity amongst the Jains, which is so necessary for organising the Jain community to continue its existence and to increase its prosperity.

REFERENCES

Karttikeyanupreksa: Svamikumara, Editor Dr. A.N.Upadhye, Smd. Rajchandra Ashrama, Agosa via Anand (Gujarat), First Edition, 1960.

Kausambi, *Dharmananda: Bharatiya Sanskrti aur Ahimsa.*

Lalwani, K.C.: *Sramana Bhagavan Mahavira, Life and Doctrine.*

Lalwani. K.C.: *Kalpa Sutra of Badrabahu Svami,* Motilal Banarsidass. Delhi, 1979.

Latthe, A.B: *An Introduction to Jainism,* Bombay, 1905.

Sangave, Vilas A.: *The Sacred Shravan-belagola: A Socio-Religious Study,* New Delhi, 1981.

Sarvartha-siddhi: Pujapada Devanandi, Edited by Pt. Phoolachandra Siddhantashastri, Bharatiya Gyanpeeth, Durgakund Road, Varanasi, 1955.

Schubring, W.: *The Doctrine of the Jains,* Motilal Banarsidass, Delhi, 1962.

Schubring, Walther: *The Religion of the Jainas,* New Delhi 1966.

Shah, Chimanlal J.: *Jainism in North India,* London, 1932.

Shah, U.P.: *'Jainism', New Encyclopaedia Britannica,* Chicago, 1974.

Shah, Umakant P.: *Studies in Jaina Art,* Banaras, 1955.

Sharma, S.R.: *Jainism and Karnataka Culture,* Dharwar, 1940.

Sheth, C.B.: *Jainism in Gujarat,* Bombay, 1953.

Siddhahemasabdanusasanam: Acarya Hemacandra, Bherulal Kamhaiyalal Religious Trust, Chandanbala Apartment, Ridge Road, Valakeshwara, Bombay, Second Edition, 1985.

Smith, Vincent A.: *A History of Fine Àrt in India and Ceylon,* Oxford, 1915.

Sogani, K.C.: *Ethical Doctrines in Jainism,* Jaina Samskriti Samrakshaka Sangha, Sholapur, 1967.

Songani, Kamal Chand: *Ethical Doctrines in Jainism,* Sholapur, 1967.

Srimadbhagavadgita Bhasya: Translated by Dr.A.G. Krishnawarrior, Shri Ramakrishna Math, Madras, First Edition, 1983.

Srimadbhagavat (Two Volumes): Gita Press, Gorakhpur, Third Edition, 1956.

Williams. R.: *Jaina Yoga,* Motilal Banarsidass, Delhi, 1983.

Winternitz, M.: *The Jainas in the History of Indian Literature,* Ahmedabad, 1946.

Zimmer, H.: *Myths and Symbols in Indian Art and Civilization,* Edited by Joseph Campbell, Harper and Brothers, New York, First Edition, 1945.

14

Religious Rituals and Traditions

Jain monks and nuns practice strict asceticism and strive to make their present birth their last, therefore ending their cycle of transmigration. The laity, who pursues less rigorous practices, strives to achieve judicious perception and to do as much good as possible and get closer to the goal of achieving liberty from the cycle of transmigration. Following strict ethics, the laity usually chooses professions that revere and protect life and totally avoid violent livelihoods.

Jains practice Samayika, which is a Sanskrit word meaning equanimity and derived from samaya; the soul. The goal of Samayika is to achieve equanimity. Samayika is begun by attaining a balance in time. If this present moment is defined as a moving line between the past and the future, Samayika happens by being fully aware, alert and conscious in that moving time line when one experiences Atma, one's true nature, common to all life forms. Samayika is especially significant during Paryushana, a special period during the monsoon, and is practiced during the Samvatsari Pratikramana rite.

Jains believe that Devas; demi-gods or celestial beings can't help jiva to obtain nirvana, which must be attained by persons through their own efforts. In fact, Devas themselves can't attain nirvana until they reincarnate as humans and undertake the difficult act of removing karma. Their efforts to achieve the exalted state of Siddha, the permanent deliverance of jiva from all involvement in corporeal existence, must be their own.

Jains are expected to be non-violent in thought, word, and deed, both toward humans and toward all other life forms, including their own selves. Jain monks and nuns walk barefoot and sweep the ground in front of them to avoid killing insects or other tiny beings. Although all life is considered sacred by the Jains, human life is deemed the highest form of life. For this reason, it is considered vital never to harm or upset any person.

While performing holy deeds, Shvetambar Jains wear cloths, muhapatti, over their mouths and noses to avoid saliva falling on texts or revered images. It is incorrect to say that this to avoid accidentally inhaling insects, because apparently it is rare to encounter insects! Many healthy concepts are entwined. For instance, Jains drink only boiled water. In ancient times, an individual might get ill by drinking unboiled water, which could check equanimity, and illness may engender intolerance.

True spirituality, as per enlightened Jains, starts when one achieves Samyak darshana, or true perception. Such souls are on the path to Moksh, striving to remain in the nature of the soul. This is characterized by knowing and observing only all corporeal affairs, without raag; attachment and dwesh; repulsion, a state of pure knowledge and happiness. Attachment to corporeal life collects new karmas, and traps one in birth, death, and suffering. Corporeal life has a dual nature for instance, love and hate, suffering and pleasure, etc for the perception of one state can't exist without the contrasting perception of the other.

Jain Dharma shares some beliefs with Hinduism. Both believe in karma and rebirth. Nevertheless, the Jain version of the Ramayana and Mahabharata is different from Hindu philosophy, for instance. Usually, Hindus believe that Rama was a rebirth of God, whereas Jains believe he achieved Moksh; nirvana because they are free from any belief in a creator – God.

Along with the Five Vows, Jains avoid harboring ill will and practice forgiveness. They believe that atma; soul can lead one to becoming Parmatma; enlightened soul and this must come from one's inner self. Jains refrain from all violence; Ahinsa and recommend that sinful activities be avoided.

Mahatma Gandhi was deeply influenced especially through the guidance of Shrimad Rajchandra by Jain principles such as serene, protective living and honesty, and made them an integral part of his own doctrine. Jainism has a distinct concept underlying Tirthankar worship. The physical form is not worshiped, but their Gunas; virtues, qualities are praised. Tirthankars remain role-models, and sects such as the Sthanakavasi stringently reject statue worship.

Each religion has it's own codes of conducts. These codes are heart of religion and keep it alive. The religious thoughts are shaped by its doctrine. The doctrine can't last unless it has support of conduct. The rites are not monotonous, senseless activities, but each one has profound meaning behind them. Virtues like ahimsa, forbearance, simplicity and straightforwardness are cultivated during religious rites. rites are performed on daily bases and on certain occasions. The rites which are must, are called Essentials (Awashyak), meant for Sadhus and Shravaks. It is believed these essentials were revealed through Tirthanker's vani and then, gandhar bhagvan composed in forty-eight minutes for Sangh.

Another view about origin is that these were prepared after Sudharmaswami's time. Whatever the origin, considering its importance, Acharya Shri Bhadrabahuswami narrated and further, Shri Haribhadrasuri described in detail. Later on, also many Acharys and Sadhus have Written commentaries, every now and then and made it very acceptable and Practicable. We should be able to accept these as 'Essentials'. In modern, progressive Scientific era, when values of everything have been changed; in that time, i.e. about 2000-2500 years old essentials appear very scientific, to live healthier life, physically, and also spiritually. It is our responsibility to understand it and make others, especially to new generation to understand and accept its value. Necessary ceremonies are like sandalwood. We need to scrub it again and again to experience coolness nor you enjoy the fragrance. Similarly these essentials are not occasional ceremonies, but those should be performing everyday, which help us to gain control over our senses.

RELIGIOUS RITUALS

Samayik

It is one of the most prominent and extraordinary strength of Jainism. No other religion has mentioned it. At certain places Jain religion is identified as 'samayik dharma'. This means that even if someone performs just samayik with devotion;. He or she has observed the main tenets of Jainism. Samayik word is originated from word 'sam'- means equal, balanced etc. Samta word is connected to 'Sam'. In a way samayik and samta words are very close and connected as well. At times it looks these words are interchangeable but there is definite difference which is very important. Samta is always present during samayik, but samayik may not be present when someone is in sambhav.

Samta is first step in samayik and total purity of soul is the end result of samayik. Every moment in our life is undulating (visham). Any difficult situation or even a common event makes us very uncomfortable yet we are not aware of it. If we think carefully, soon we will know, our whole life consists of reactions to things, people and circumstances. When one begins a samayik the first condition is to make oneself balanced, i.e. to remain in samata. Ahimsa- In samayik, for 48 minutes, we take vow to keep away from any activity, which creates violence. Here it is not an obvious violence but any activity connected to Kashays. Passions will certainly hurt others will injure our own soul as well. One can attain kashay-free state, only when balanced state is existent.

What is this samayik after all? The word is related to word 'Samay'-time. Bhagwan Mahavir uses word samay for Atma. Samayik means, for that much time to remain in Atmawhich is very rich with joy. This way our Chetana or Conscious stabilizes in time (i.e. kaal)-only current time, here past and future both are absorbed. Past is memory and future is imagination. When conscious gets stabilize in current time, it starts fading kashayas; and this is state of samayik. It is not a ceremony, we do not have to do samayik but we have to be in samayik. In shuddha- samayik one need not to do any thing like dhyan, jap, reading etc. For short time, stop all the activities of mind, speech and body (yoga) and experience the internal peace, light bliss this explains why Emperor Shrenik could not buy samayik from Puniya shravak.

We can see mount Everest from distance, but most people do not have potential to reach up there. Similarly each person can not attain shuddha samayik but if we understand it once, then we may not lose the focus. Initially we may take support of various means- kriyas, jap reading, swadhayaya. This way not in this life; but in near future or in next few lives we may certainly attain this kind of samayik. Talking will not take us, begin walking, it will shorten the path. Putting it simply, samayik is an achievement of being ideal for certain period of time; where one becomes kashaya-free, remains in supreme peace and stabilizes in infinite richness of soul.

Chaturvimsati

When an individual attains sambhav in samayik, spontaneously we think about those great personalities who showed the path of 'samta', next we think about their gunas (charecteries) and one can't avoid praising them. This is the concept behind the chaturvimsati. The Twentyfour Tirthankars, who founded the tirths, we remember their names along with gunas. We recite 'Loggass' for this purpose. It is with profound meaning, its' construction is like Mantra. Constant recital is beneficial to jivas, it helps making Samyaktva very pure. In first verse, there is decision to do stuti of 24 Tirthankars. In second, third and forth verses description of Tirthankars names. Last three verses are like chulika_ means it connects the intention with the effort for it; and in the end, it states gain of desired fruit i.e. Siddhi.

Loggassa is work of shruta-kavali, chaud(14)-Purvadhar gandhar bhagwan's creation, it holds mantra, tantra vidyas and siddhis. In Jainism, Moksh - a karma free state is final goal, and to succeed, samayik is important mean. Moksh-marg means samyak-darshan, ghyan and charitra marg. To remain in this path, sadhak (one who is trying to accomplish) has to do these necessary ceremonies continuously. Darshan takes you to close to the truth, ghyan makes one to understand the truth and charitra let walk on the path of truth. Tirthankars have shown this path after attaining it and we worship them to accomplish the same. Tirthankars' "Nam Smaran" is Nam- Nikshapa. Currently, Tirthankars are not present amongst us, so, we worship the idols to attain their gunas. This is Sthapna-Nikshap.

If we desire to worship through Dravya-Nikshapa; we should be thinking about their life story. For Bhava-Nikshapa we have to contemplate their 'Bhava-Swarup'_ with infinite knowledge, faith, strength and bliss. To take a real support we think of twelve gunas of Arihants (four Aatishayas and eight Pratiharyas). In chaturvimsati-stava, stuti of Tirthankers begin with NamSmaran. Yet to get best, we have to go in bhava – smaran. There is special relationship between the name and his appearance. In a way, name is permanent and appearance is transient. As soon as we say the name, the appearance of name holder will be in front of our eyes; and, immediately one type of relation is established and when bhava is added to it, we will perceive the presence of the same person.

When we recite Arihants' name, his serene appearance will be in front of our eyes, at this time, the particles which are created in our mind affect our karmic body and decrease our instability and distress and slowly we experience peace. In reality nam- smaran (remembering names of Arihants) is related to karma- nirjara and sankrman (transition). If someone, who can not practice any other religious ceremony; and he/she is very unstable, for them, Tirthankars' name jap is only beneficial mean. During kyotsarg, one meditate and recite Loggass; equal to number of shawas (breath), as a result, Loggass becomes Mantra. In short, in Loggass basically there are names of Arihants and prayer to them with great respect. It is a powerful means of karma-niriara.

Vandan

Guru Bhagwants are bridges between us and dharma shown by tirthankers. So third necessary, to bow down to gurus. Guru-vandan is inter-connected with humility.

Humbleness is not an external dealing or behaviour. It is an internal matter. One can reach that far, only after removing self-arrogance. Therefore, becoming arrogance-free means to get empty from inside, and one who is empty from within will automatically bow down to gurus and they certainly make progress in Moksh-marg.

There are four important things needed to obtain humility.

- Listen to gurus respectfully and carefully
- Think over what you have listened
- Confess the same to guru-Bhagwant
- Carry out his order (aaghya)

For guru-vandan, there is external ceremony, which is scientific. When we bow down with five angs (two hands, two knees and head) this activity itself presses on certain glands, as a result secretion of certain substances which in turn controls the arrogance and bring modesty. Therefore arrogance comes down with body as well and Vandan becomes internal and we experience great respect (Aho-bhav)-praise for guru; then only, one becomes eligible to receive knowledge and confess wrong doings (aalochana).

In guru-vandan, shravak or shraman enters in guru's Avagraha i.e. within three and half feet distance from the guru and then touches his feet and take his hands up to his head.

There is great significance of this process or kriya. It is said, from guru's body, constant array of rays coming out, which has a touch of knowledge and sanyam. During vandan, these rays immediately convert and enter in deciple's body.

In short, guru-vandan is religious ceremony in which, one becomes arrogance-free and gets blessings of guru in form of knowledge and sanyam.

Pratikraman

The vitality of sanyam is in kriya and kriya's strength is pratikraman. Samayik is a goal and pratikraman is a tool_ an important means of internal purification of heart.

Commonly used meaning of pratikraman is to turn back from shortcomings or mistakes. Out of all essentials, pratikraman is very significant. In divine world, there are very few religions that have talked about 'turning back'. Everybody desires to go forward. It is special accomplishment of Jainism, to come back from where you do not belong; i.e. where all impurities due to karma-bandh exist. As such during the day, at different times, six essentials should be performed, but if one can not do any/all during the daytime, in Devasi pratikraman, all six essentials are combined.

After savvasavi, from karemibhante to kayotsarg of Nannami

Loggass immediately follows the kayotsarg of Nannami

After Loggass, from muhapatti padilehan to two vandana

From aaloana to Ayariya Uvvajzae

After Ayariya Uvvajzae to until you sit down after one Navakar

After two vandana, one does Pachhakhan.

The Pachhakhan is last, but it is necessary to do Pachhakhan before sunset to be more fruitful, so in Shvetambars it is done in the beginning.

One of the best thing in Jainism, it offers so many alternatives, if you are unable to do what is recommended. Even if, one can do little, with endurance, knowledge and understanding, it can take you towards your goal.

Pratikrman is a process, which keeps us constantly awake, aware about our way of living life. By nature, Jiv every now and then, gets carried away on wrong path. Every morning and evening, find out some time, think and come back. If one can't perform every evening try every fifteenth day-a special thinking, turn back as much as one can. If that is not possible another chance once every forth month. Eventually, at least once year, one should examine, am I on wrong path? Walk back. When soul is making progress in spiritual growth (gun-sthanak); initially thinks about this life and then about past lives and he/she makes efforts to turn back; reaching closure to final goal.

Kayotsarg

This is the last of essentials, usually Kayotsarg is part of samayik-pratikraman and chaitya vandan, and it is done repeatedly. The time period for Kayotsarg is decided along with number of breath. Breathing is survival line for life, (Pran) out of ten prans, swas (breathing) is most prominent, if it breaks life ends as well. On one side, Kayotsarg is connected to swas- Pram and on the other side, it is connected to Navkar Mantra or

Loggas. This way, in Kayotsarg, we recite mantra. Whenever we recite mantras Navkar or Loggas, it brings the picture of the objects in that sutra e.g. When we say Namo Arihantanam try to see tirthankar in Samosaran with eight pratigarya, Chauvisampi Jinvara, remember 24 tirthankars, who are free from life, disease, old age, death and so on. When Kayotsarg is done with bhava, our chetna (conscious) is connected to Tirthankars' and Siddhas' chetna, and in our soul, the Parmatma Shakti is created. In short, Kayotsarg is a profound ocean of spiritualism, if one takes a dive, he may find ratnatrayi.

Pratyakhan

Pratyakhan means vow, wrongful acts of the past; we correct in Pratyakhan; but what about future? If we become lightweight from past, and we are going to increase weight (of karmas) in the future, it will not serve our objective. If we go four steps forward, and five backward, we can never reach our destination. Same wrong acts we do not repeat in the future, and do not do the new deeds, we can take vows. Vows are to control our life. In everyday life we see there are controls every where. Vehicles have breaks, societies have laws and courts etc.

Jain principals of karmas believe, unless you take vows, your ways are open to the areas, where all sinful activities are taking place, you still become part of it, e.g. use of meat, alcohol etc, during Pratyakhan; one shuts the doors to even probable chance to any such activities. The twelve vows of shravak help us to form our boundaries. Pratyakhan always comes after Pratikram, once you are cleaned and then take vows to remain clean.

SOCIAL RITUALS

Fasting

Fasting is common amongst Jains and a part of Jain festivals. Most Jains fast at special times, during festivals, and on holy days. Paryushana is the most important festival, lasting eight days for Shvetambar Jains and ten days for Digambars, during the monsoon. The monsoon is a time of fasting. Nevertheless, a Jain may fast at any time, especially if s/he feels some mistake has been committed. Variations in fastings encourage Jains to do whatever they can to maintain self-discipline.

Some Jains revere a special practice. When an individual is aware of coming death, and feels that s/he has completed all duties, s/he willingly ceases to eat or drink. This form of dying is called santhara. Considered extremely divine and creditable, with all awareness of the transitory nature of human experience, it has recently led to a controversy. In Rajasthan, a lawyer petitioned the High Court of Rajasthan to declare Santhara illegal. Jains see Santhara as divine detachment, a declaration that an individual has finished with this world and now chooses to leave.

Monks, nuns and laity fast as penance and to control cravings. Jains believe fasting purifies the body and the mind, reminding one of Bhagwan Mahavir's stress on renunciation and asceticism. Bhagwan Mahavir spent months fasting and in contemplation. It is not sufficient simply to stop eating when fasting; the person must also stop wanting to eat. Control over one's mind is a major goal. If one continues to desire food, the fast is fruitless.

There are several types of fasts:

- Santhara or total fasting: To give up food and water entirely. This leads to death and is undertaken by someone who has finished all his/her duties and wishes to leave this world serenely. It gives control over when one dies so everything may be completed and an individual may leave of his or her own free will.
- Partial fasting: Eating less than you desire and to simply avoid hunger.
- Vruti Sankshep: Limiting the number of items eaten.
- Rasa Parityag: Giving up favourite foods.
- Great fasts: Some monks fast for months at a time, following Bhagwan Mahavir, who fasted for over 6 months.
- Varsitap: To eat on alternate days and Upavas on the rest, for a whole year. Therefore this fast is very rigorous since it entails a whole year of tap with eating no food on alternate days and eating food on rest of the days, while following the prescribed rules like not eating in the evening after sunset, not eating root vegetables like potatoes, onions, ginger, and various other rules.
- Chauvihar Upvas: To give up food and water for the whole day.
- Upvas: To give up only food for the whole day.

- Digambar Upvas: One may drink water only once a day, before sunset.
- Shvetambar Upvas: One may drink boiled and cooled water after Porsi, provided this is done before sunset.
- Tivihar Upvas: One may drink boiled water between sunrise and sunset.
- Ekasanu: To eat one meal a day at one sitting and drink boiled water as desired between sunrise and sunset.
- Beasanu: To eat two meals a day in two sittings and drink boiled water anytime between sunrise and sunset.
- Ayambil: Eating food once in one sitting. The food contains only cereals and pulses not sprouted and it is spice free and boiled or cooked, without milk, curds, ghee, oil, oil seeds, or green/raw vegetables, fruits and sugar and its products.
- Bela: To give up both food and water or only food continuously for two days.
- Tela: To give up food and water or only food continuously for three days.
- Aththai: To give up food and water or only food continuously for eight days.
- Masaksaman: To give up food and water or only food continuously for a whole month.
- Navkarsi: Food and water is consumed a minimum forty-eight (48) minutes after sunrise. Devout Jains brush their teeth and rinse their mouths only after sunrise.
- Porsi: Taking food and water three hours after sunrise.
- Sadh-porsi: Taking food and water four hours and thirty minutes after sunrise.
- Purimuddh: Taking food and water six hours after sunrise.
- Avadhdh: Taking food and water eight hours after sunrise.
- Tivihar: After sunset no food or juice shall be taken, but one may drink water. Many Jains practise this daily.

CEREMONIAL RITUALS

Birth Ceremony

The actions or deeds, which are done after the birth of the child, are known as birth (Jatkarma) rituals. It is called ceremony because it involves some rituals which are performed after the birth of the child other than the actions. The main aim of these actions is to inculcate some values in the child even while he is ignorant about there importance.

Conception, Simanotanayan and Punsavan rituals are performed when the child is in the mother's womb. These three rituals are called pre-birth rituals and those done after birth of the child are called post-birth rituals. In the pre-birth rituals the values of mother and hereditary values have predominance. The main aim of these rituals is to inculcate good values in the child. So it is tried to improve the life before and after the birth both.

The actions, which are done after the birth of the child, are known as birth (Jatkarma) rituals. It is called ceremony because it involves some rituals are performed after the birth of the child other than the deeds. The main aim of these actions is to inculcate some values in the child even while he is ignorant about their importance. The child lives in a different environment in the mother's womb. It doesn't take food from the mouth and breathe through the nose. Its food is carried through the umbilical cord. The child is inside a pouch during pregnancy, which is filled with water. The child's mouth and eyes are closed with phlegmatic substance to avoid the entry of water in the mouth and eyes. After taking birth, its mouth and nose have to be cleaned.

The child looses the physical attachment with the mother and hence its mouth, ears, nose and lungs have to be cleaned to facilitate the child drink mother's milk and breathe properly. When the child is inside the watery pouch then a type of oily pack covers the body so the watery pouch doesn't harm the skin in any way. After coming out of the pouch, the child is bathed to remove the oily pack from the body. All the necessary actions have to be performed after the birth of the child in order to arouse its five sensory organs. The main aim of birth ceremony is to arouse all the sensory organs. Sushrut has advised to place a little amount of ghee on the child's tongue. Applying ghee or oil on the child's head protects it from cold and catarrh.

In this ceremony the child is made to lick ghee and honey nevertheless the quantity should not be equal. Honey should be three times the ghee; this child should be made to lick with the help of a golden spike. Write Om on the tongue with the help of spike. This has been said in the process of ceremony. The psychologists believe that whatever the child learns till five years of his birth remains with him throughout the life. The main objective of writing Om on his tongue is that whatever he utters will take him on the path of spirituality. The father of the child whispers in his ears -'Vedosi', which means you are a knowledgeable person. The birth ceremony has a divine and scientific importance but nowadays people are under the influence of materialistic comforts and forgetting the importance of rituals. We should get back to the traditions of sages and perform all the rituals so that our future generation gets good qualities and values.

Marriage Ceremony

The Jain marriage custom is governed by the traditional practices which naturally vary from community to community. Some rites are naturally common to all Jain marriage. For the Jains, marriage means a public declaration of a man and a woman's intention to be together for the entire life. The community gives support to the couple by being a part of it. The Jain community assemblies on various occasions have condemned the practice of negotiating a dowry before marriage. Jains believe that there should be no waste of money or time. However, marriage is an once-in-lifetime occasion that has to be celebrated properly and grandly. Jain marriages are mainly conducted by the Jain pundits only

Jains believe in marrying within the community only. They feel that the children therefore born would also become Jains only. They mainly find partners for their eligible boy or girl by word of mouth. They intimate their willingness to get their children married to the other known people in their community. Modern day advertising through newspapers and engaging marriage bureaus are also in vogue these days.

The Jain brides wear sarees only. The preferred colour is red or any other bright colour. The Jain grooms wear the traditional Kurta Pyajama or the Dhoti Kurta.

In Laghana Lekhan, the marriage is fixed. On this occasion, pooja is held at the girl's house and relatives are invited. The lagna, also known as the mahurat is determined by the priest. At the end of the rites, the lagna patrika or a letter telling you about the time of marriage, is sent to the boy's house. It is also customary to send ¾ kg of sweets, especially laddoos at the time of engagement or sagai. The sweets could also be sent in an auspicious time.

The Lagna Patrika Vachan is read out in the boy's house. This is done either on the engagement day or any other auspicious moment. After this the priest reads the letter after the groom has performed the Vinayakyantra Pooja.

Engagement or sagai ceremony is held at the groom's house. The groom would wear the traditional Jain headgear, wash his hands and do the Vinayakyantra. After the Vinayakyantra pooja, the bride's brother applies tilak on the groom's forehead and gifts him a gold chain, a ring, clothes, coconut, sweets and money. The groom is then presented the lagna patrika. The priest reads out the patrika and the groom seeks the blessings of the elders.

After Sagai, the next most prominent ceremony is Mada-mandap, which is held a day or two before marriage. This ceremony is celebrated both at the groom's and also the bride's places. The hour for the occasion is a pre-determined auspicious hour. The priest would perform all the rites.

The barati is a ritual that takes place at the girl's place. It is upon arrival of the barat or the groom's procession that the bride's brother receives the groom and applies tika on his forehead. He is also presented with coconut, money, sweet and clothes. In return, the groom also apply tika on the forehead of the bride's brother and presents him a coconut.

After receiving the groom with all honour, it's time when the married women do an aarti of the groom They also sing the Mangala Geet.

Phere is perhaps the most prominent ceremony in Indian marriages. For the Phere also an auspicious time is being decided. For this the groom and the bride would be taken to the mandap and made them seated. The girl sits to the right of the groom, the groom and the bride changing position after taking the seven vows.

Also known as the kanyapradan ceremony, it has the parents or the uncle of the bride keeping one rupee and twenty-five paise and rice on the right hand of the bride. And then the presentation of the bride to the groom takes place. The father would publicly proclaim this formal presentation of the bride in front all the assembled guests. The groom therefore receives the bride. This occasion is marked with the priest pouring water on the hands of the bride and groom chanting the mantra three times.

The havan starts after the Phere. During the havan, a series of mantras are chanted those of the Peethika, Atha Gathu, Atha Nistarak, Atha Surendra, Atha Parmarajadi and Atha Paramesthi are recited and offerings are made. At the end of these mantras, the Shanti mantra is chanted nine times.

Granthi Bandhan takes place after the havan. In this a married woman takes the corner of the pallu of the bride's sari and then ties it to the shawl of the groom. A mantra is also recited in this occasion. Following which the couple takes four rounds of the fire. In this the bride leads while taking the first round. Then they exchange positions and take another three parikramas around the havankund. There takes place the recitation of Mahaveerakshak stoot in the background. The women also begin singing the mangal geet at this time. A muhurta (auspicious moment) has been already decided previously.

After the phere, the groom and the bride exchange the seven vows separately. When both of them have accepted the seven vows, the priest makes the bride sit on to the left of the groom. After this the bride will be called vamangi, which means she is the left half of the body. This follows with the couple exchanging garlands. Eventually, the havan ends with the Shantipath and Visarjan.

Once the marriage is over, parents and relatives bless the couple. Alongwith the priest also blesses the newly weds and chants a mantra. As in all marriages, a wedding feast for the assembled guests follow this. Now the remaining ritual is left and that of sending the bride to the groom's house. The Jains believe in giving away alms in Jain temples as a thanksgiving to the God.

Jains are rigorously vegetarians. The usual wedding menu consists of the specialities of the localities. The Gujaratis would arrange traditional vegetarian dishes and other may go for the Marwari vegetarian fare. Still others may go for the vegetarian Punjabi dishes.

Death Rites

The Jains cremate the dead as soon as possible. First the body is rubbed with a wet cloth. The corpse is then clothed and placed in a bier and covered with a kafan. The body is tied to the bier and taken to the crematorium. A suitable place without any living organisms like grass or insects is selected so as not to harm them. There a platform of wood is erected.

The body is taken from the bier and placed on the platform with logs of wood over it. Ghee, camphor and sandalwood powder are sprinkled all over the body and the eldest son of the deceased does the last rituals.

The son goes round the pyre three times sprinkling water allover the body. Chanting the Namokar Mantra,he lights up the pyre. Then after sometime they pour milk over the place. The remains are collected in bags and the place is thoroughly cleansed. The remains are not immersed in rivers as they can pollute the water. Instead they dig a hole in the earth and put the remains and sprinkle salt all over, so that it dissolves easily.

The Jains believe that the dead soul would be reborn immediately. So for them death is a festival or Mahotsav. Loud wailing and observing anniversaries are not part of the Jain Tradition.

OTHER RITUALS

Rituals are an integrated part of daily life of a Shravak. In house hold activities, clean the stoves, before lighting, sweep the floor, filter the water boil the water for sadhus, spreading grains for birds first few things to be done. For very pious jains perform pratikraman and samayik etc. The most prominent rites amongst Jains are worship of idols.

1. Daily Puja or Worship
2. Special (parva) Puja or Worship

Daily Puja

In Pujan we worship idol with eight fold offerings. Each puja has specific significance.

There are eight karmas and to destroy eight karma we perform eight kinds of pujas.

Jala (Water) Puja: Water symbolizes the ocean. Every life form continuously travels through Ocean of birth, life, death, and despair. This puja reminds that one should live the life with honesty, truthfulness, love and compassion towards all life forms. This way one will be able to cross the Life Ocean and achieve Moksh or nirvana. The path of nirvana is Samyak Darshan, Samyank Gyan and Samyak Charitra in Jain religion.

Chandan (Sandal-wood) Puja: Chandan symbolizes Knowledge (Gyan). During this puja, one should reflect on Right Knowledge. Right knowledge means proper understanding of reality which includes Soul, Karma, and their relationship. Jainsim believes that the Pat of Knowledge is the main path to achieve nirvana. Bhakti or Devotion helps in the early stages of one's effort for nirvana.

Pushpa (Flower) Puja: Flower symbolizes conduct. Our conduct should be like a flower, which provides fragrance and beauty to all life forms without discrimination. We should live our life like flowers with full of love and compassion towards all life forms.

Dhup (Incense) Puja: Dhup symbolizes ascetic life. While burning itself, Dhup provides fragrance to others. Similarly true monks and nuns spend their entire life selflessly for the benefit of all life forms. This puja reminds that one should thrive for an ascetic life which eventually leads to nirvana.

Deepak (Candle) Puja: The flame of Deepak represents a Pure Consciousness or a Soul without any bondage or an enlightened Soul. In Jainsim, such a soul is called Siddha or God. The ultimate goal of every living being is to become enlightened from karma. By doing this puja, one should thrive to follow Five great Vows: Ahimsa, Truthfulness, Non-stealing, Chastity, and Non- possession. Eventually these proper conducts couple with right faith and knowledge will lead to nirvana.

Akshat (Rice) Puja: The family rice is the kind of grain seeds, which are non- fertile. One can't grow rice plants by seeding the family rice. Symbolically it means that rice is the last birth. By doing this puja one should thrive to put all the efforts in the life in such a way that this life becomes one's last life and after the end of this life one will be liberated and will not be reborn again.

Naivedya (Sweet) Puja: Naivedya symbolizes a tasty food. By doing this puja, one should thrive to reduce or purge the attachment to tasty food. Healthy food is necessary for survival, nevertheless one should no live for to eat a tasty food. Ultimate objective in one's life is to achieve a life where no food is necessary for our existence and that is the life of enlightened soul, who lives in Moksh eternally in ultimate happiness.

Fal (Fruit) Puja: Fruit symbolizes Moksh or Nirvana. If we live our lives without any attachments to corporeal affair, continue to perform our duty without any expectation and reward, be witnessed to all the incidents that occurred surrounding to and within us, truly follow ascetic life, and have a love and compassion to all life forms, we will achieve fruit of Moksh or nirvana. This is the last puja symbolizing the ultimate achievement of our life.

In the end we adorn the idol- Call Aangi- usually very attractive, creates good bhav during Darshan.

Vandan Kirtan

After the idol worship is done, we do bahv puja, recite studies, do chaitya vandan etc.

All the rituals help us in two ways. First, we feel happy, our heart experiences an internal joy. Secondly, it helps in destroying kashayas, plant seeds of good qualities in us and destroy many karmas. Understanding the meaning of all sutras certainly helps us in increasing bhava, joy and instead of a rite, it becomes a daily need. Aarati usually has done in evening. It symbolizes the joy after performing all religious activities in temple. It destroys all karmas and brings bliss to life.

Sthanakvasi and Terapanthi do not believc in idol worship. They just stay in upashraya and do dharma - religious activities.

Special Pujas

Snatra Puja: It symbolizes bathing of the new Tirthankars by devas and devies over mountain meru. It is always performed prior to any puja, Pujan, on birthday celebrations, during opening of new business, and housewarmings etc.

Panch Kalyanak puja: This puja commemorates the five great events of theTtirthankar's life. Basically in this puja, pandit virvijayji has praised Shri Shankheswar Parswanath. This puja is performed during any good event. Five kalyanks are conception, birth, renunciaion nirvana, and Moksh.

Antaray Karma Puja: There are eight poojas, very much like daily Ashta Prakari Pooja. In these poojas,mention about, how different persons created the antraykarmas and they were able to remove those obstacles after performing these poojas. There are other pujas namely, Navpad puja, Barvrata puja, Navvanu (99) Prakari puja including the following:

Pujan: A lengthy rite that almost lasts a whole day and is performed by very learned persons and involves many people in ceremony. Those are done occasionally like during new temple opening ceremony, after someone's special penance like varshitap etc.

REFERENCES

Chakravarti, A: *The Religion of Ahimsa,* Bombay, 1957.

Chandogya Upanisad: Edited by Max Muller, F. (S. B. E.) Vol. 1, Motilal Banarasidas, Delhi, Reprint Edition, 1981.

Chatterjee, A.K.: *Comprehensive History of Jainism (up to 1000 A.D.),* Firma KLM, Calcutta, 1978.

Dasavaikalika-sutra: Editor Madhukar Muni, Jinagama Granthamala, No. 23, Agama Prakashan Samiti, Byavara, First Edition, 1985.

Dasgupta, S.N.: *History of Indian Philosophy, Vol. I,* Cambridge University Press, London, Second Edition (Reprint), 1932.

Desai, P.B. *Jainism in South India and some Jaina Epigraphs,* Sholapur, 1957.

Gopal, S.: *Outlines of Jainism,* New Delhi, 1973.

Gopalan, A.S.: *Outlines of Jainism,* Willey Eastern (P) Limited, New Delhi, First Edition, 1973.

Guseva, N.R: *Jainism,* Bombay, 1971.

Hume, Robert Earnest: *Thirteen Principal Upanisads (Trans.),* Oxford, 1921.

Jacobi, H.: *Introduction to Kalpa-sutra.*

Jacobi, H.: *Jaina Sutras, Part 1, The Akaranga Sutra, The Kalpa Sutra, Part2, The Uttaradhyana Sutra,The Sutrakritanga Sutra. 2 vols,* Dover Publications, New York, 1968.

Jacobi, H.: *Mahavira and His Predecessors.*

Jacobi, H.: *Studies in Jainism,* Ahmedabad, 1946.

Jain, C. R.: *Fundamentals of Jainism,* Veer Nirvan Bharti, Meerut, 1974.

Jain, Champat Rai: *Fundamentals of Jainism,* Meerut, 1974.

Jain, Champat Rai: *Householder's Dharma,* Bijnore, 1931.

Jain, H., and Upadhye, A.N.: *Mahavira, his Times and his Philosophy of Life,* Bharatiya Gyanpeeth, New Delhi, 1975.

Jindal, K.B: *The prefaces,* Calcutta, 1958.

Kalghatagi, T.G.: *Jaina View of Life,* Sholapur, 1969.

Kapadia, H.R.: *Jaina Religion and Literature,* Lahore, 1944.

Kapashi, V.J.: *In Search of the Ultimate,* V.K. Publications, Harrow, 1984.

Karttikeyanupreksa: Svamikumara, Editor Dr. A.N.Upadhye, Smd. Rajchandra Ashrama, Agosa via Anand (Gujarat), First Edition, 1960.

Kausambi, *Dharmananda: Bharatiya Sanskrti aur Ahimsa.*

Lalwani, K.C.: *Sramana Bhagavan Mahavira, Life and Doctrine.*

Lalwani. K.C.: *Kalpa Sutra of Badrabahu Svami,* Motilal Banarsidass. Delhi, 1979.

Latthe, A.B: *An Introduction to Jainism,* Bombay, 1905.

Law, B.C: *Mahavira: His Life and Teachings,* London, 1937.

Lenin: *Collected Works of Lenin, Vol. 14.*

Madhav Rao, N.: *Jainism A New Look.*

Malavania, Pt. Dalasukhabhai: *Jainism (Some essays),* Translated by Dr. A.S.Gopani, Prakrita Bharati Academy, Jaipur, First Edition, 1986.

Mehata, M.L.: *Jaina Culture,* Varanasi, 1969.

Mehta, M. L.: *Outlines of Jaina Philosophy,* Jaina Mission Society, G. 146, Chickpet, Bangalore - 2, October, 1954.

Mookerjee, S.: *The Jain Philosophy of Non-absolutism, a Critical Study of Anekantavada. 2nd. Ed,* Motilal Banarsidass, Delhi, 1978.

Nahar and Ghosh: *An Epitome of Jainism,* Calcutta 1917.

Nevaskär B.: *Capitalists without Capitalism, the Jains of India and the Quakers of the West,* Greenwood Publications, Westport, 1971.

Nyayavatara: Siddhasena, Translated by Vijayamurti Sastracarya, Paramashruta Prabhavaka Mandal, Jauhari Bazar-Bombay, First Edition, 1950.

Padmarajiah, Y.J.: *Jain Theories of Reality and Knowledge,* Bombay, 1963.

Pancastikaya-sara: Kunda-kunda, Edited by A.Chakravarti (Sacred Books of the Jainas, No. 3), Central Jaina Publishing House, Arrah, First Edition, 1920.

Pandey, V.: ed. *The World of Jainism,* pub. by the Author, Bombay, 1976.

Srimadbhagavat (Two Volumes): Gita Press, Gorakhpur, Third Edition, 1956.

Stevenson, Sinclair: *The Heart of Jainism,* Oxford, 1915.

Stevenson. S.: *The Heart of Jainism,* Munshiram Manoharlal, New Delhi, 1970.

Tahtinen, U.: *Ahimsa, Non-violence in Indian Society,* Rider, London, 1976.

Talib, G.S.: ed. *Jainism,* Punjabi University, Patiala, 1975.

15

Society

Jains declined in numbers after the medieval period. In some ways this strengthened Jainism for it produced tight-knit communities of Jains with common interests and a devotion to the faith reinforced by their closeness within the group. In the early nineteenth century we must speak of communities, rather than of a single Jain community, for within the wider structure of the Jain religion Jainism provided, and indeed still provides, for a number of sometimes overlapping allegiances. Besides the broad division between the Shvetambar, strongest in western India, and the Digambar, chiefly in the south, there is the Sthanakvasi denomination (within the Shvetambar division) which rejects the worship of images. The Terapanthi, an offshoot of the Sthanakvasi, dates from 1760 and has become a well- organized and active movement. The Shvetambar, more than the Digambar, have always shown a tendency to form groupings around particular teachers and their successors. Allegiance to a particular temple often can run parallel to household or caste allegiance. We must be honest about the fact that, as in any live and active organization, religious or secular, differences of opinion can arise within the broad unity of the Jain faith.

In the nineteenth and twentieth centuries we can pick out certain mainstreams of growth. With the development of modern communications there has been a notable development of all- India federations of various sorts. Secondly, Jain scholarship, education and writing have broadened out at all levels, whether simple aids for children or learned editions of the sacred texts and university theses on Jain topics. Thirdly, Jains have become much more conscious of the wider public: without seeking to count heads of converts like many religions, Jains have become concerned to spread knowledge of the Jain religion and to encourage devotion to its tenets. Parallel to this there has been a growing (although still small) interest by scholars and others in the West and by non-Jains in India.

Lastly, for the first time in Jain history, Jainism has been carried to Africa, Europe and North America, where Jain communities have settled and flourished.

SOCIAL ORDER

The Jain society is organized into four groups:

- Sadhus
- Sadhvis
- Shravaks
- Shravikas

These are also called the four kinds of organization. The Sadhus and Sadhvis renounce wordily life; assume a life of austerity and discipline and keep moving on the path of self awareness or divine attainment. Besides soaring towards the firmament of divine elevation and growth they also give to all classes of people guidance in respect of ethical religious and divine values that help the proper development of their lives. For this purpose, they adopt such means as discourses, discussions, training programs, meditations, repeating of Mantras; celebrations, devotional festivals, writing articles etc.

The Shravaks and Shravika while remaining as 'grihasthas householder) carry on their wordily duties and conforming to some noble tenets and rules of conduct, also pursue the path of self-realization and divine elevation.

In every town and city in India, there are Jain mandirs (temples), Upashrays (religious centres), Pathshalas (Jain schools), Libraries of Holy Scriptures, Panjarapol (shelter for animals and birds), Ayambilshalas, Choultries (Dharamshalas) and other such institutions. These institutions are under the management of the local or other sanghas (Societies). These societies render service with devotion to Sadhus and Sadhvis who are on padyatri; (who travel on foot).

The members of Jain Societies extend co- operation and sympathy to the fellow members of the society. Most members of the Jain Society offer financial and other aid and help as per their ability and means, for religious and social activities. They render manual service; and they also render service to society with magnanimity.

It is evident that Jainism is an ancient religion of India and that right from hoary antiquity to the current day it has continued to flourish, along with other religions, in different parts of India. Jains, the devotees of Jainism, are, thus, found all over India from ancient times. The Jains are also known everywhere for the strict observance of their religious practices in their daily lives. That is why Jainism could survive in India for the last so many centuries. The Jains, in this way, succeeded in continuing to exist as devout devotees of a distinct religion in India.

But this is not the only distinguishing feature of Jains in India. In fact the most outstanding characteristic of Jains in India is their very impressive record of contributions to Indian culture. In comparison with the limited and small population of Jains. The achievements of Jains in enriching the various aspects of Indian culture are really great.

Perhaps the most creditable contribution of Jains is in the field of languages and literature. It is quite evident that right from the Vedic period two different currents of thought and ways of life known as (a) Brahmana culture and (b) Gramana culture are prevalent in India The gramana culture is chiefly represented by the Jains and the Buddhists and of them the Jains were the first to spread that culture. That is why from ancient times we have the Sramana literature besides the Brahmanic literature. The characteristic features of the Sramana literature are as follows: It disregards the system of castes and fisramas; its heroes are, as a rule, not Gods and Rsis, but kings or merchants or even Sudras. The subjects of poetry taken up by it are not Brahmanic myths and legends, but popular tales, fairy stories, fables and parables. It likes to insist on the despair and sufferings of samsara and it teaches a morality of compassion and ahiritsa, quite distinct from the ethics of Brahmanism with its ideals of the great sacrificers and generous supporter of the priests, and of strict devotion to the caste system.

The authors of this Sramana literature have contributed enormously to the religious, ethical, poetical, and scientific literature of ancient India. A close examination of the vast religious literature of the Jains has been made by M. Winternitz in his 'History of Indian Literature'. In this masterly survey of ancient Indian literature, M. Winternitz has maintained that the Jains were foremost in composing various kinds of narrative literature like Purans, eharitras, kathds, prabandhas, etc. Besides a very extensive body of poetical narratives, the non-canonical literature of the Jains consists of an immense number of commentaries and independent works on dogma, ethics; and ascetic discipline. They also composed legends of saints and works on ecclesiastical history. As fond of story-telling, the Jains were good story-tellers themselves, and have preserved for us many Indian tales that otherwise would have been lost. Kavyas and maha-kavyas too, of renowned merit have been composed by Jain poets. Lyrical and didactic poetry are also well represented in the literature of the Jains.

Except for these, the most valuable contributions have been made by the Jains to the Indian scientific and technical literature on various subjects like logic, doctrine, poetics, grammar, lexico-graphy, astronomy, astrology, geography, mathematics and medicine. The Jains have paid special attention to the arthasastra (or politics) which is considered to be "a corporeal science" par excellence. Therefore there is hardly any branch of science that has not been ably treated by the Jains.

The literature of the Jains is also very important from the point of view of the history of Indian languages for the Jains always took care that their writings were accessible even to the masses of the people. Hence the canonical writings and the earliest commentaries are written in Prakrit dialects and at a later period Sanskrit and various modern Indian languages were used by the Jains. That is why it is not an exaggeration when the celebrated Indologist H.H. Wilson says that every province of Hindustan can produce Jain. compositions, either in Sanskrit or in its vernacular idioms. It is an established fact that the Jains have enriched various regional languages and especially Hindi, Gujarati, Kannada, Tamil and Telugu.

Regarding the Jain contribution to Kannada literature, the great Kannada scholar R. Narasimhacharya has given his considerd opinion in the following terms : "The earliest cultivators of the Kannada language were Jains. The oldest works of any extent and value that have come down to us are all from the pen of the Jains. The period of the Jains' predominance in the literary field may justly be called the 'Augustan Age of Kannada Literature'. Jain authors in Kannada are far more numerous than in Tamil. To name only a few, we have Pampa, Ponna, Ranna, Gunavarman, Nagachandra, Nayasena, Nagavarman, Aggala, Nemichandra, Janna, Andayya, Bandhuvarma and Medhura, whose works are admired as excellent specimens of poetical composition. It is only in Kannacla that we have a Ramayana and a Bharata established on the Jain tradition in addition to those established on Brahmanical tradition. Besides kavyas written by Jain authors, we have many works by them dealing with subjects such as grammar, rhetoric, prosody, mathematics, astrology, medicine, veterinary science, cookery and so forth. In all the number of Jain authors in Kannada is nearly two hundred".

As the Jains have produced their vast literature in these languages from very ancient times. they have certainly played a very important part in the develoment of the different languages of India. The medium of sacred writings and preachings of the Brahmins has all along been Sanskrit and that of the Bauddha's Pali. But the Jains alone utilised the prevailing languages of the different places, besides Sanskrit, Prakrit and Apabhramsha, for their religious propagation and also for the preservation of knowledge. It is therefore quite evident that the Jains occupy an important position in the history of the literature and civilization of India.

Along with literature the Jains have always contributed consi-derably to the growth of the arts in the country. The Jains have taxed their mite to enhance the glory of India in several branches of arts. Compared with their number their contributions appear to be very imposing and unique.

It must be remembered that Jainism did not create a special architecture of its own, for wherever the Jains went they adopted the local building traditions For instance, while in Northern India the Jains pursued the Vaisnava cult in building in southern India they adhered to the Dravidian type. The stupas of the Jains are indistinguishable in form from those of the Buddhists, and a Jain curvilinear stedple is same in outline with that of a Brahmanical temple.

Although the Jains have not evolved a distinct style of architecture, yet it must be said to their credit that they have produced many and finest specimens of architecture in different parts of the country. In this regard it is quite clear that more than any other religion in India the Jains have displayed their intense love of the picturesque while selecting the sites for the construction of their sacred buildings like temples, temple cities, cave temples, stupas, pillars and towers. They have erected their temples either on lonely hill-tops or in deep and secluded valleys.

As the Jain religion considers construction of temples as a meritorious act, the Jains have constructed an unusually larger number of temples throughout India. Nearly 90 percent of Jain temples are the gifts of single wealthy persons and as such the Jain temples are distinguished for elaborate details and exqusite finish.

Of these countless Jain temples, the two marble temples at Mount Abu in Rajasthan are regarded as the most notable contribu-tions of the Jains in the domain of architecture. The two temples are celebrated as unsurpassed models of Western or Gujarati style of architecture which is characterised by a free use of columns carved with all imaginable richness, strut brackets, and exquisite marble ceilings with cusped pendants. The temples are known for the beauty and delicacy of the carving and for the richness of the design. As Cousens remarks:

"The amount of beautiful ornamental detail spread over these temples in the minutely carved decoration of ceilings, pillars, door ways, panels and niches is simply marvellous; the crisp, thin, transluent, shell-like treatment of the marble surpasses anything seen elsewhere and some of the designs are veritable dreams of beauty. The work is so delicate that a common chiselling would have been disastrous. It is said that much of it was produced by scrapping the marble away, and that the masons were paid by the amount of marble dust so removed."

Again, the Jain temple at Ranakpur in Mewar, a part of Rajasthan (which was built in 1440 AD.), is the most complex and extensive Jain temple in India and the most total for the rite of the denomination. The temple covers in total about 48,000 sq. feet of ground and on the merits of its design, the notable art-historian

The immense number of parts in the building, and their general smallness, prevents its laying claim to anything like architectural grandeur; but their variety, their beauty of detail-no two pillars in the whole building being exactly alike-the grace with which they are arranged, the tasteful admixture of domes of different heights with flat ceilings, and mode in which the light is introduced, combine to produce an excellent effect. Indeed I know of no other building in India, of the same class that leaves so pleasing an impression, or affords so many hints for the graceful arrangements of columns in an interior.

The other temples of such superb character are (i) the temple of Parsvanatha at Khajuraho in Bundelkhand in Madhya Pradesh, (ii) the temple at Lakkundi in North Karnataka, (iii) the temple known as Jinanathapura Basadi near gravana-belagola in South Karnataka, (iv) Seth Hathisinghi's temple at Ahmedabad, and (v) the temple known as Hose Vasadi at Mudabidri in South Kanara District of Karnataka.

SOCIAL CONDUCT

Jains have a common complaint that it is not easy to maintain and represent our religious and cultural identity as Jains in the modern world. This is mainly due to the misconception in many people's minds that the Jain religion is very strict and difficult to follow and it impedes our blending in the mainstream society. Evidently, the present religious and cultural traditions practiced, shared, taught and understood here are chiefly extensions of what are being practiced today. However, we are maintaining them so that we can be in a position to create a positive effect on the future generations. By watering the seeds of religious and cultural identity, we are letting our practices and traditions grow and our identity flourish.

Religion and culture have deep-rooted merit and relevance to the physical, mental and materialistic growth of mankind, and to the ethical, divine and philosophical aspects of life. Religion and culture have always responded to human growth. Religion (Dharm) is defined as the ability to sustain the natural order of things. Religion is a reference to universal tenets, laws and duties that bring peace, harmony and progress - the countless possibilities towards a person's divine aspirations - a way to live life harmoniously and to attain ultimate human potential - a mechanism to illuminate the innate nature of things or an inherent duty - a guiding path for those who have gone astray due to an adverse situation or unfortunate circumstances - a life-supporting and life-sustaining process. Religion shows the path of virtue; it reminds us of our fundamental duties and instils values in our lives. Culture means civilization comprised of beliefs, customs, behaviour, conduct and traditions. It encompasses the vital features and elements of governance, administration, traits of people and their behaviour and habits. Culture means belonging to a community and preserving the heritage. Culture embodies the values, philosophy, and norms of a group of people. Religion and culture lay voluntary restraints on our conduct and behaviour. A set of ethics and code of conduct arise out of religious and cultural values.

Social Ethics

Nirvana through the removal of karmic matter from the soul is attainable only through righteous living as per ethical discipline. One should abstain from the five faults (pancapapa) viz, injury (himsa), falsehood (asatya), stealing (steya), unchastity (abrahma) and wordly attachment (parigraha). These vows are of two kinds: Partial vows (Anuvratas) or limited abstention from the five aforesaid faults and Full vows (Mahavratas) or total abstention from five faults. The former is prescribed for householders and the latter for monks. Five kinds or training (bhavana) have been prescribed for each of these vows for the sake of securing stability in them.

The five vratas have been unanimously accepted by the Acharyas, on the basis of Pratimas of Vratas or Paksa, Carya and Sadhana. The difference of opinion is only with regard to the Gunavratas, Siksavratas, Mulagunas and Pratimas. The great Acharya kundakunda described householder's duties on the basis of Pratimas. He simply presented the names of Gunavratas e. g. dik parimana, anarthadanadavarjana and Siksavratas

e. g. samayika prosadha, atithipuja and sallehana. Svami Kartikeya pursued his line but placed desavakasika in place of sallekhana-Vasunandi included sallekhana in Siksavratas. These Acharyas described neither Astamula gunas nor aticaras of vratas.

Jain Acharya argues against the eating of flesh that it can't be procured without causing destruction of life. One who use flesh, thus, commits Himsa, unavoidably. Even if the flesh be that of a buffalo, oxe, tec., which has died of itself, Himsa is caused by the crushing of creatures spontaneously born. He who eats or touches a raw or a cooked piece of flesh, certainly kills spontaneously-born creatures constantly gathering together. In conclusion he says that those who wish to avoid Himsa, should first of all take care to renounce wine, flesh, honey and the two udumbaras (gular and fig) and fruits of Pippala, Pakara and Banyan which are the birth place of small mobile beings.

Jainism is perhaps one of the most scientific religions in world and thus it is still relivant to the society and the world. I don't find any contradiction between Jainism and science. It throws ample light on the real nature of substance or matter as propounded by Jain thinkers. Jain metaphysics approves of the scientific axiom that nothing is destructible. That means nothing can be created out of nothing, or out of something, which doesn't at all exist in one form or the other.

The Jain philosophy is pertinent when it advocates that the cosmos is uncreated, real, everlasting, and infinite with no beginning and end. The modern science has confirmed that this cosmos has automatic working process and the matter is never demolished; it only undergoes changes into different states or modes. This is the law of nature.

The Jain thinkers expressed their opinions that plants and vegetables, earth, water, fire and air have souls and are endowed with only one sense organ of touch. The Jain philosophy of Karma is fully substantiated by the apparent disparities amongst living creatures. This philosophy makes the transmigration of souls a proven fact, and establishes their continuity and immortality.

The Karma philosophy of Jainism also does away with the need of any outside agency, an invisible all pervading, all-powerful and all-knowing supreme being, creator, destroyer, preserver and dispenser of justice, for the purpose of punishing or rewarding humans. Scientists also feel no need of any unknown hand to interfere with the automatic working of the cosmos.

TRADITIONAL VALUES

The problem of falling ethical values is a world phenomenon. Every thoughtful human being is concerned about it. Every man wants to live with dignity—that is his aspiration and need. Why ethical values are falling down is a subject of research. How to re-establish these values, pertains to the sphere of our duty. Extreme preoccupation with economic advancement and a hedonistic approach are responsible for the depreciation of ethical values. The mentality to procure amenities by fair means or foul and the establishment of ethical values don't go together. The more the purity of means is neglected, the greater is the fall in ethical standards. Both ethical and divine values are inevitably linked with the purity of means. In the absence of ethical and divine values, it is not possible even to clearly define humane values.

Non-possessiveness and ahimsa are divine values; integrity or honesty is a ethical one. Only with the growth of a 'purity of means' outlook, can these values be established. In this context it may be said that anekanta, or the relative point of view is the primary value—It is the right vision. The groundwork of training in ahimsa is the right vision. Without a change of outlook, the attempt to establish ahimsa is as if an individual should expect to raise a crop without sowing seeds. Is our approach to money and accumulation of wealth factual? Is our approach to materialistic objects and their use, realistic? If it is realistic, through training in ahimsa, the seed of ahimsa can be sown.

The current day world is afflicted with the problem of a partial viewpoint. A biased one-sided view of economic and materialistic growth has only served to encourage violent behaviour. Without changing this point of view, there is little possibility of promoting non-violent conduct. During the last few decades, interest in ahimsa has grown because of the problems created by violence. Murder, terrorism, growth of destructive weapons, fierce conflict and war—these problems originating from violence breach the peace of society. World-peace is being seriously disturbed. That is why interest in ahimsa has grown. There is a universal feeling that ahimsa is the most appropriate method of resolving the current-day unrest.

CASTE SYSTEM

The Indian caste system explains the social stratification and social restrictions in the Indian subcontinent, in which social classes are defined by thousands of endogamous hereditary groups, often termed as jatis or castes. Within a jati, there exist exogamous groups known as gotras, the lineage or clan of an individual, though in a handful of sub-castes like Shakadvipi, endogamy within a gotra is permitted and alternative mechanisms of restricting endogamy are used (e.g. banning endogamy within a surname).

Though usually identified with Hinduism, the caste system was also observed amongst devotees of other religions in the Indian subcontinent, including some groups of Muslims and Christians. The Indian Constitution has outlawed caste-based discrimination, in keeping with the socialist, secular, democratic tenets that established the nation. Caste barriers have mainly broken down in large cities, although they persist in rural areas of the country. However, the caste system, in various forms, continues to survive in modern India strengthened by a combination of social perceptions and divisive politics.

When Ywan Chwang travelled to South India after the period of the Chalukyan Empire, he noticed that the caste system had existed amongst the Buddhists and Jains. The Jains too have castes in places such as Bihar. For instance, in the village of Bundela, there are severals 'jats' (groups) amongst the Jains. An individual of one jat can't intermingle with a Jain or another jat. They also can't eat with the members of other jats.

STATUS OF WOMEN

The status of women in Jainism differs between the two main sects, Digambar and Shvetambar. Jainism prohibits women from appearing naked; because of this, Digambars, who consider renunciation of clothes necessary to Moksh, say that they can't achieve Moksh. Shvetambars, who allow sadhus to wear clothes, believe that women can achieve Moksh. Some Jains consider women to be inherently inferior, but most do not. However, there are more Shvetambar sadhvis than sadhus and women have always been influential in the Jain religion.

- Mallinath, the 19th Jain Tirthankar; she was female as per Shvetambar Jains, male as per Digambar Jains.
- Marudevi, the mother of Bhagwan Rishabh Dev
- Trishala, the mother of Bhagwan Mahavir

As regards the status of women in the Jain community, we will have to go back to the period of Bhagwan Mahavir who made then a crucial revolt against the existing tradition and extended his solid support to uplift this very important but most neglected organ of the household where they became least powerful and most disregarded and controlled bitterly by men in each and every sphere.

Considering all these nefarious practices and alimentative attitude of men towards women, Bhagwan Mahavir stood against these pernicious social elements and freed them from indignation for their own progress in all walks of life. Some reservations had, naturally to be observed due to the slight physical incapability of women. Hence, some special rules were prescribed for nuns. Although they used to be heads of their units as Pravartini and Ganavacchedini, similar to Acharya and Upadhyaya, they were entirely responsible to the Acharyas. Candana, Puspacula, Subrata, and other well-known nuns of long ago, are referred to in this context. Even the, the patriarchal form of the society was developed and nuns were treated as slightly inferior to monks in certain respects. This nevertheless, doesn't hold women as anything less than human beings who, like all souls, have the right and capability to achieve redemption.

REFERENCES

Acaranga-sutra, Anga-sutrani I: Vacana Pramukha, Acarya Tulasi, Editor Yuvacarya Mahaprajna, Jaina Vishvabharati, Ladnun, First Edition, 1974.

Amar, Muni: *Jainatva ki Jhanki, Sanmati Grantharatnamala No. 12*, Sanmati Gyanpeeth, Seventh Edition, Agra, 1987.

Avasyaka-sutra: Editor Madhukar Muni, Jinagama Granthamala, No.24 Agama Prakashan Samiti, Byavar, First Edition, 1985.

Basham, A.L.: *A Cultural History of India*, Clarendon Press, Oxford.

Basham, A.L.: *Post-script, attached to the article on Hinduism in Cultural History of India*, Oxford University Press.

Bhagavati (Vyakhyaprajnapti) in Anga-sutrani II: Editor Yuvacarya Mahaprajna, Jaina Vishvabharati, Ladnum, First Edition, 1974.

Bhargava, D.: *Jain Ethics*, Motilal Banarsidass, Delhi, 1968.

Bhattacharya, B.C.: *Jaina Iconography*, 2nd ed, Motilal Banarsidass, Delhi, 1974.

Bhattacharya, N.N.: *Jain Philosophy, Historical Outline*. Munshiram Manoharlal, New Delhi, 1976.

Bool Chand: *Lord Mahavira*, Banaras, 1948.

Bothra, P.: *Jain Theory of Perception,* Motilal Banarsidass, Delhi, 1976.

Brown, Percy: *Indian Architecture,* Bombay, 2nd Edn.

Buhler, G.: *Indian Sect of the Jainas,* Edited by Burgess, Jas, Luzac & Co., 46, Great Russell Street, 1903.

Caillat, C.: *Jainism,* Macmillan Company of Upadhye, A.N., andIndia, Delhi, 1974.

Chakravarti, A.: *Samayasara of Sri Kundakunda,* Translation with Introduction. Bharatiya Gyanpeeth, Delhi, 1971.

Devendra Muni Shastri: *Source-Book in Jaina Philosophy,* Sri Tarak Guru Jain Granthalaya, Udaipur, 1983.

Diwakar, R.R.: *Bihar Through Ages,* Calcutta, 1959.

Dwivedi, R.C.: *Contribution of Jainism to Indian Culture,* Motilal Banarsidass, Varanasi, 1975.

Einstein Albert: *Ideas and Opinions,* Bonanza Books, No.9.

Ferfusson, J.: *History of Indian and Eastern Architecture,* London.

Fischer, E., & Jain, J.: *Art and Rituals, 2500 Years of Jainism in India,* Sterling Publishers, New Delhi, 1977.

Garbe, R.: *Encyclopaedia of Religion and Ethics,* T. & T. Clark, 38 George Street, New York, 1920.

Ghosh, A.): *Jaina Arts and Architecture,* New Delhi, 1974.

Glassenapp, H.V: *Doctrine of Karman in Jaina Philosophy,* Bombay, 1942.

Jaini, P.S.: *The Jaina Path of Purification,* Berkeley: University of California Press, 1979.

Jaini, Padmanabh, S.: *The Jaina Path of Purigication,* California, 1979.

James, William: *Principles of Psychology, Vol. I,* Macmillan & Co., London, 1918.

Pramana-mimamsa: Hemacandra. Edited by Pt.Sukhalal Sanghvi, Saraswati Pustak Bhandar, Ahmedabad, Reprint Second Edition, 1989.

Radhakrishnan, S.: *Indian Philosophy, Vol. I,* George Allen & Uniwin, London, First Edition (Revised), 1929.

Radhakrishnan. S.: *Indian Philosophy. 2nd.ed, 2 vols,* Allen and Unwin, London, 1929,1931.

Ramchandran, T.N.: *Jain Monuments of India,* Calcutta, 1944.

Rampuria, S.C.: *The Cult of Ahimsa,* Calcutta, 1947.

Rosenfield, C.: *Gurudev Shree Chitrabhanu, a Man with a Vision,* New Jain Meditation Intemational Center, York, 1981.

Roy Chowdhari, P.C.: *Jainism in Bihar,* Patna, 1956.

Roy, A.K.: *History of the Jains,* Gitanjali Publishing House, New Delhi, 1984.

Saletore, B.A: *Medieval Jainism,* Bombay, 1938.

Samaya-sara: Kunda-kunda, Bharatiya Gyanpeeth, Durgakund Road, Varanasi, First Edition, 1950.

Sangave, V.S.: *Jaina Community, a Social Survey. 2nd. ed.* Popular Prakashan, Bombay, 1980.

Sangave, Vilas A.: *Life and Legacy of Mahavira:* A Social Study, Meerut, 1974.

Sangave, Vilas A.: *The Sacred Shravan-belagola: A Socio-Religious Study,* New Delhi, 1981.

Sarvartha-siddhi: Pujapada Devanandi, Edited by Pt. Phoolachandra Siddhantashastri, Bharatiya Gyanpeeth, Durgakund Road, Varanasi, 1955.

Schubring, W.: *The Doctrine of the Jains,* Motilal Banarsidass, Delhi, 1962.

16

Festivals

Usually, festivals are celebrations and jubilations characterized by excitement, enthusiasm, enjoyments and entertainments; but the Jain festivals are characterized by renunciation, austerities, study of the Holy Scriptures, repetition of holy hymns, meditation, and expressing devotion for the Paramatma. Even those people who are caught in the meshes of ordinary life, as per their ability and conveniences, get free from the corporeal entanglements to the extent possible and become immersed in worship and meditation Renunciation and austerity constitute the very foundation of the Jain Dharma.

Jainism has a very rich life of rites and festivals. It is important to remember that these are not simply empty play- acting but all have a profound significance which is of benefit to the participant or onlooker. The rites should fix the mind on the great religious truths: the person should seek to understand the profound meaning expressed in the quiet or crowded and colourful rites.

The events of Bhagwan Mahavir's life are repeated frequently in symbolic form and the symbols, actions, words and images, unite to bring the Jain devotee's mind and spirit into an understanding of, and union with, the life and message of Bhagwan Mahavir. For many people to whom the more abstruse aspects of religious doctrine are a closed text the rites provide a direction, a focus, for the expression of devotion to the Tirthankar. The devotee worships with his or her mind concentrated and pure, free from violence and harm, and in a condition to disperse the accumulated karma from the soul. The rites are not, naturally, only for simple and unlettered people, but they bring together those whose learning gives them an understanding of the deepest significance of the rites with those content to lose themselves in the quiet ecstasy of devotion.

The daily life of a pious Jain will be interwoven with rite acts. Spreading grain for the birds in the morning, filtering or boiling water for the next few hours' use, these are rite acts of charity and ahimsa. Samayika, the practice of equanimity, loosely translated 'meditation', is a rite act undertaken early in the morning and perhaps also at noon and night. It lasts for forty-eight minutes (one- thirtieth part of the day, an Indian unit of time) and involves usually not just quiet recollection but also usually the repetition of rite prayers. Pratikramana should be performed in the morning in repentance for wrongs committed during the night, again in the evening, and additionally at certain points in the year. During this, the Jain expresses contrition for harm caused, wrong done, duties left undone.

Bowing to the image, and lighting a lamp before it, is a fitting start to the day. More elaborate worship (pug), as described, is a regular daily rite, perhaps in the temple (which the worshipper enters with the words 'Namo Gyanam' 'I bow to the Jin', and, repeated three times, 'Nisihi' to relinquish thoughts about corporeal affairs), but the simpler surroundings of the family shrine can provide a suitable setting.

Worship, or puja, can take many forms. The rite bathing of the image (Snatra Puja) is said to go back to the bathing of the newborn Tirthankar by the Gods (or heavenly beings, not Gods in the all-powerful, everlasting sense). (A simple symbolic act is to touch one's forehead with the liquid used to bathe the image.) Bathing the image also takes place during the Panch Kalyanak Puja, a rite to commemorate the five great events of the Tirthankar's life, conception, birth, renunciation, nirvana and Moksh. Antaraya Karma Puja comprises a series of prayers to help to remove that karma which deludes and hinders the soul. A lengthy temple rite which can take three days to complete is the Arihanta Puja, respect to the arihant (arhat) or omniscient souls, and to a long sequence of other beings. There is a rite of prayer focused on the Siddhachakra, a lotus-shaped disc bearing representations of the arhat, the enlightened soul, religious teacher, religious leader and the monk (the five praiseworthy beings), and also the four qualities of perception, knowledge, conduct and austerity.

It must be said that there is a narrow dividing line between symbolism and superstition. Some people, claiming to be 'judicious', will dismiss all rite acts as superstitious. That is to misunderstand their nature completely: the Jin image has no miraculous powers. Common life is full of rites. from simple greetings to the ritualized conduct of a public confrence. Religious rites must not be seen as an end in themselves: they express, in simple or elaborate symbolic form, the person's craving and intention to follow the example and teaching of Bhagwan Mahavir. The splendor of the temple, the beauty of the words and chants, all help the worshipper towards a reverent state of mind. Some people can do without these external 'props' but they should not scorn those who value them.

In India the European calendar is usually used for business and government matters but religious festivals are usually fixed as per Indian calendar. This calendar is quite straightforward but, as it is established on the phases of the moon, dates are not always the same from year to year as in the European calendar established on the sun.

The serious Jain will fast, more or less completely, and undertake other religious practices, on many days in the year. Ten days in the month of the Indian calendar are kept as fasts by the pious (although others may keep a lesser number). The first day of the three seasons in the Indian year is also of special sanctity. Twice a year, falling in March/April and September/October, the nine-day Oli period of semi-fasting is observed when Jains take only one meal a day, of very plain food. Maunagiyaras falls in November/December when a day of total silence and fasting is kept and meditation is directed towards the five holy beings, monk, teacher, religious leader, arhat and siddha. This day is regarded as the anniversary of the birth of many of the Tirthankar.

Bhagwan Mahavir was born most probably in the year 599 BC. and the exact date is given in the Holy Scriptures as the thirteenth day of the bright half (i.e. when the moon was waxing) of the month of Caitra. In the European calendar this will fall in March or April. The festival to commemorate this, known as Bhagwan Mahavir Jayanti, is an occasion for great celebration. Jains gather together to hear Bhagwan Mahavir's message expounded, so that they can follow his teachings and example. The dreams of his mother before his birth may be dramatically presented and the circumstances of his birth, as narrated in the Holy Scriptures, explained to the assembled people. The image of Bhagwan Mahavir is ceremonially bathed and rocked in a cradle. In many places processions take place through the streets with the image having the place of honour, and in some areas in India this is a general public holiday. One custom associated with the celebrations is to break a coconut at the end and distribute small pieces.

Paryusana is the most prominent period in the Jain year. This is the eight-day period of fasting and religious activities which falls in the months of Sravana and Bhadra (August or September). During the rainy season in India Jain monks cease walking from one town to another and settle in a fixed location with the purpose of reducing the prospect of injury to the living beings now springing to life. Often a town will invite a respected monk to stay in its vicinity during the rainy season (sometimes with a beautifully written manuscript invitation) and the people will receive him with great pomp and rites. A course of lectures or sermons by an ascetic or other respected person is a regular feature of Paryusana.

BHAGWAN MAHAVIR JAYANTI

Bhagwan Mahavir was born most probably in the year 599 BC. and the exact date is given in the Holy Scriptures as the thirteenth day of the bright half i.e. when the moon was waxing of the Hindu calendar month of Chaitra. In the solar calendar this will fall in March or April. The festival to commemorate this, known as Bhagwan Mahavir Jayanti, is an occasion for great celebration. Jains gather together to hear Bhagwan Mahavir's message expounded, so that they can follow his teachings and example. The dreams of his mother before his birth may be dramatically presented and the circumstances of his birth, as narrated in the Holy Scriptures, explained to the assembled people. The idol of Bhagwan Mahavir is ceremonially bathed and rocked in a cradle. In many places the processions take place through the streets with the image having the place of honour, and in some areas in India this is a general public holiday.

PARYUSANA PARVA

The Paryusana Parva is the most prominent festival for the Jains. This is the eight-day period during which many Jains fast and carry out the religious activities. This period falls in the months of Sravana and Bhadra: August or September. During the rainy season in India Jain monks stop walking from one town to another and settle in a fixed location with the purpose of reducing the injury to the living beings now springing to life. Often a township invites respected monks to stay in its vicinity during the rainy season sometimes with a beautifully written manuscript invitation and the people receive them with great pomp and rites. A course of lectures or sermons by an ascetic or other respected person is a regular feature of the Paryusana Parva. The word Paryusana is derived from two words meaning gada a year and a coming back'. It is a period of repentance for the acts of the former year and of austerities to help shed the accumulated karmas. It should be remembered that the austerity is not just to shed karmas, but to control the craving from the sensual delights as a part of the divine training to check the accumulation of the new karmas. During this period some people fast for the all eight days, some for the lesser periods of time a minimum of three days is suggested in the Holy Scriptures, but it is considered obligatory to fast on the last day of the Paryusana Parva. Fasting usually involves total abstinence from any sort of food or drink, but some people do take boiled water during the daytime.

There are regular rituals in the temple and discourses of Kalpa Sutra; one of the sacred texts in the Upashraya during this time. Kalpa Sutra contains the detailed account of Bhagwan Mahavir's life, is read to the congregation. On the third day of the Paryusana Parva the Kalpa Sutra receives a very special reverence and may be carried in the procession. On the fifth day, at a special ceremony, the auspicious dreams of Bhagwan Mahavir's mother, queen Trishala, are demonstrated. Listening to the Kalpa Sutra, taking active steps to check the animal killing, asking and offering forgiveness to all humans, visiting the neighbourhood temples, etc. are some of the prominent activities during this time. The final day of Paryusana is the most prominent of all.

On this day those who have observed the fasts are specially honoured. This is also the day when Jains ask for forgiveness to the household, friends and foes alike for any acts they might have committed towards them in the former year. Thus this annual occasion of the repentance and forgiveness is very prominent. Shortly after Paryusana it is the custom to organize a Swami Vastyalaya-dinner when all the Jains get together and renew their friendship with each other regardless of their socio-economical status.

DIWALI

Diwali or Deepawali is the most prominent festival in India. For the Jains, it is the second most after the Paryusana Parva. For Jains Diwali marks the anniversary of Bhagwan Mahavir's Moksh. Bhagwan Mahavir achieved Moksh on this day in 527 BC. and also of the achievement of total knowledge, nirvana, by his chief devotee, Gautama Indrabhuti. The festival falls on the last day of the Hindu calendar month of Ashvina, the end of the year as per Indian calendar in October or November, The celebration starts in the early morning of the previous day, for it was then that Bhagwan Mahavir commenced his last sermon which lasted till late in the night of Diwali. It is narrated that the eighteen kings of northern India who were in his audience decided that the light of their master's knowledge would be kept alive symbolically by lighting of the lamps. Hence it is called Dipawali, dipa means lamp, or Diwali.

NEW YEAR

The New Year begins the next day of Diwali and is the occasion for joyful gatherings of Jains, with everybody wishing each other a Happy New Year.

GYAN PANCHAMI

The fifth day of the New Year is known as Gyan Panchami, the day of knowledge, when the Holy Scriptures, which impart knowledge to the people, are worshipped with devotion.

PAUSH DASHAMI

This day is celebrated as the birthday of 23rd JainTirthankar Bhagwan Parshvanath. On the 10th day of Posh month of Hindu calendar, hundreds and thousands of Jain men and women perform the tapasya of 3 Upavas-attham continuous fasting for 3 days and by means of recitation and meditation they try to achieve divine welfare. A grand fair takes place in Sankheswar which is a sacred place for Jains. Thousands of people gather here and perform the austerity of 'Attham'.

AKSHAY TRITIYA TAPA

Those noble people who perform the austerity of Varshi tapa complete the austerity on this day by taking sugar-cane juice in the cool shadow of Shatrunjay. First Jain Tirthankar Bhagwan Rishabh Dev performed the Parana (completion of an austerity) on this day after fasting for 13 months and 13 days continuously. This day is considered to be very auspicious for making a pilgrimage to Shatrunjay (Palitana). This falls on the 3rd day of the bright fortnight of Vaishakh month of Hindu calendar.

MAUN-AGIYARAS

It in November/December when a day of total silence and fasting is kept and meditation is directed towards the five holy beings, monk, teacher, religious leader, arhat and siddha. This day is regarded as the anniversary of the birth of many of the Tiirthankaras.

NAVAPAD OLI

The serious Jain layman fast, more or less completely, and undertake other religious practices on many auspicious days throughout the year.

As many as ten days in a given month are observed for the fasts by the pious Jains (although others may observe a lesser number). The first day of the three seasons in the Indian year is also of special sanctity. Twice a year, falling in March/April and September/October, the nine-day Oli period of semi-fasting is observed when Jains take only one meal a day, of very plain food.

YAKSHA PUJA

Jains pay their respect and worship idols of Jins for three reasons:

- He has liberated Himself and achieved Moksh
- He expounded the path of Nirvana
- To get an inspiration to become like Him

The only goal of Jainism is to free ourselves from the corporeal sufferings and achieve nirvana. Jin is an enlightened soul, freed of its materialistic body and resides in the top of the cosmos, called Siddha-loka. The images of Jins are intended to serve as reminders to the faithful of the possibility of nirvana; i.e., they served as role models for both the Jain laity, guiding their ethical code of living, and for the aspirant, Jin providing inspiration and a reminder that divine nirvana is an attainable goal. As a detached soul, removed from this world, the Jin is incapable of responding to a devotee's prayers or requests. This inability to be interventionist, to respond to the prayers and offerings from the faithful, sets Jin images apart from both all Hindu and most Buddhist deities, who can be called upon to ritually correct approaches by a devotee.

In addition to images of Jins, we notice images of Yakshas and Yakshinis; deities in many Jain temples. These deities are seen as neither everlasting nor divine, and they themselves are said to be worshippers of the Jin, true devotees of Jin. In addition, these Yakshas and Yakshinis are full of passions and are wandering through the cycles of births and death just like us. Yakshas are males and Yakshinis are females. They are also called Shasandevtas male ones and Shasandevis female ones. They are guardian deities, angels of order. They are heavenly beings of Vyantar group who have supernatural powers including ability to change their forms and sizes. Either these Yakshas or Yakshinis were appointed by Indra; Emperor of paradise or were positively associated with Tirthankars in their former lives. Although, Tirthankars don't require or ask for any protection, these Yakshas and Yakshinis looked due to their devotion after Tirthankars and came back to protect the Jainism when it became necessary.

The earlier Holy Scriptures like the Sthananga-sutra, Uttardhyayan-sutra, Bhagawati-sutra, Tattvartha-sutra, Antagadadasao-sutra, and Pauma-chariya have frequent references to Yakshas and Yakshinis. Many Jains pay their respect to these Yakshas and Yakshinis for having them provided protection to Tirthankars and to the existence of Jainism. These are the reasons, they are found around the images of Jins and also their personal images in many Jain temples. Yaksha usually found on the right side of the Jin idol while Yakshini on the left side. In Jain temples, they are never situated in superior physical locations in relation to images of the Jins. These are benevolent Yakshas and Yakshinis. There are also malevolent Yakshas and Yakshinis who caused sufferings to Tirthankars and troubles to Jains and existence of Jainism. For instance, Yaksha Sulpani troubled Bhagwan Mahavir in his mediation and inflicted much suffering and there are similar stories in which malevolent Yakshas troubled others as well. We Jains don't pay our respects or worship Yakshas and Yakshinis for the materialistic gains, favour and liberty from fear, illness and disease. We do pay our respect to them for their service to Tirthankars and Jainism. Asking for materialistic gains from them will be quite opposite of the teachings of Jins.

SNATRA MAHOTSAV

The festival of oblation. Snatra Mahotsav is the name given to the ceremony of performing oblations to the image of the Bhagwan; worshipping the Bhagwan with various auspicious things, making offerings to the Bhagwan; and worshipping the Bhagwan with songs. music and dances. It is also called Snatra Puja. The Snatra Mahotsav is performed usually every day, in most Jain temples.

Showing devotion to the Bhagwan and seeking his blessings can be done on any auspicious day or happy occasion. This constitutes an aspect of the very foundation of the Jain dharma.

ATTHAI MAHOTSAV

The festival of eight days. This is a festival of eight days and so it is called Atthai Mahotsav. During these eight days or sometimes five days, many devotional and religious activities are arranged in the Jain temples. The activities include such things as cleaning and decorating the temples, offering prayers to the Paramatma along with songs, music and dances, chanting of hymns of glorification, recitation of songs for worship decorating the images and organizing some other religious and auspicious activities.

REFERENCES

Jain, J. P.: *Religion and Culture of the Jains,* Bharatiya Gyanpeeth, New Delhi, 1975.

Jain, J., and Fischer, E.: *Jaina Iconography, Part One, The Tirthankara in Jaina Scriptures, Art and Rituals, Part Two, Objects of Meditation and the Pantheon. 2 vols.* E.J.Brill, Leiden, 1978.

Jain, Jyoti Prasad: *Jainism: The Oldest Living Religion,* Banaras, 1951.

Jain, Jyoti Prasad: *Religion and Culture of the Jains,* New Delhi, 1977.

Jain, K.C.: *Lord Mahavira and his Times,* Motilal Banarsidass, Delhi, 1974.

Jain, Kailash Chand: *Jainism in Rajasthan,* Sholapur, 1963.

Jain, Kamata Prasad: *The Religion of Tirthankaras,* Aliganj, 1964.

Jain, Muni Uttam Kamal: *Jain Sects and Sub-sects,* New Delhi, 1975.

Jaini, Jugmandar Lal: *Outlines of Jainism,* Cambridge, 1916.

Schubring, Walther: *The Religion of the Jainas,* New Delhi 1966.

Shah, Chimanlal J.: *Jainism in North India,* London, 1932.

Shah, U.P.: *'Jainism', New Encyclopaedia Britannica,* Chicago, 1974.

Shah, Umakant P.: *Studies in Jaina Art,* Banaras, 1955.

Sharma, S.R.: *Jainism and Karnataka Culture,* Dharwar, 1940.

Sheth, C.B.: *Jainism in Gujarat,* Bombay, 1953.

Siddhahemasabdanusasanam: Acarya Hemacandra, Bherulal Kamhaiyalal Religious Trust, Chandanbala Apartment, Ridge Road, Valakeshwara, Bombay, Second Edition, 1985.

Smith, Vincent A.: *A History of Fine Art in India and Ceylon,* Oxford, 1915.

Sogani, K.C.: *Ethical Doctrines in Jainism,* Jaina Samskriti Samrakshaka Sangha, Sholapur, 1967.

Tatia, Nathmal: *Studies in Jain Philosophy,* Banaras, 1951.

Tattvartha-sutra: Umasvati, P.V. Research Institute, Varanasi, Reprint Second Edition.

Thomas, F.W.: *Sri Mallisenasuri, Syad-Vada-Manjari,* Motilal Banarsidass Delhi, 1968.

Trsastisalakapurusacaritrani: Canto 10, Hemacandra, Jaina Dharma Prasaraka Sabha, Bhavanagar, First Edition, 1908.

Tukol, T.K.: *Compendium of Jainism*, Dharwad, 1980.

Upadhye, A.N.: *Lord Mahavira and his Teachings. 2nd. Ed,* Shree Vallabhsuri Smarak Nidhi, Bombay,1983.

Uttaradhyayana-sutra: Editor Madhukara Muni, Jinagama Granthamala No. 19, Agama Prakashan Samiti, Byavara, First Edition, 1984.

Warren, H.: *Jainism in Western Garb, as a Solution to Life's Great Problems,* Edited, with notes, by N.J. Shah. 2nd. ed. Shree Vallabhsuri Smarak Nidhi, Bombay, 1983.

Warren, Herbert: *Jainism,* Arrah, 1916.

Williams, R.: *Jaina Yoga: A survey of Medieval Sharavakachara,* London, 1963.

Williams. R.: *Jaina Yoga,* Motilal Banarsidass, Delhi, 1983.

Winternitz, M.: *The Jainas in the History of Indian Literature,* Ahmedabad, 1946.

Zimmer, H.: *Myths and Symbols in Indian Art and Civilization,* Edited by Joseph Campbell, Harper and Brothers, New York, First Edition, 1945.

17

Religious Places

The holy places of Jainism are the places of Pilgrims, the Jain Temples, Upashray as (The places of abode for monks and nuns) etc. The places of pilgrim are situated either on the peaks of the Mountains or on other best Locations. The Jain temples are the holy places of worship for the Jain Tirthankars / Gods. Where one does the Darshan, Vandan as Pooja and Namaskars. The Upashray are the places of abode for the religious priests, the monks and the nuns. The devotees of Jainism also use them for their own religious rites.

RELIGIOUS PLACES IN INDIA

Shri Bhagwan Mahavirji Tirth

It is situated at village Chandanpur on the banks of the river Gambhir. The nearby railway station of Bhagwan Mahavirji is 7Kms away where buses and taxis are available. On Mumbai –Delhi railway line, Bhagwan Mahavirji station comes between Gangapur and Hindon. From Delhi,Bhagwan Mahavirji is 305 Kms and from Jaipur and Agra is 175 Kms. In Jaipur and Ajmer, there are direct buses to Shri Bhagwan Mahavirji. From Jaipur this shrine can be reached via Mahuva, Hindon and Kheda. It is 60 Kms away from Mahuva village, which is on NH 11.

This idol is believed to have been discovered buried under a mound nearby during the period between 17th and 19th century. The idol looks very ancient, quiet, beautiful and impressive. As soon as the idol was discovered, a magnificent temple was built and the idol installed ceremoniously.

The manifestation of this idol was accompanied by a miraculous incident. It is believed that a cow of a certain household of a low caste was not yielding any milk. On enquiries, it was ascertained that the cow used to stand on a nearby spot on a mound and all her milk used to ooze out there. The owners of the cow tried their best to check her from going to that spot but they did not succeed in their attempts. Then began arising in the minds of the owners several kinds of doubts and fears. Nothing came clear, eventually the mound was dug open and this idol of Shri Bhagwan Mahavir Bhagwan was discovered. With great humility, devotion and caution the idol was taken out and the lucky household felt itself greatly fulfilled. The news spread far and wide and crowds of devotees started to gather at that spot. The mere sight of the Bhagwan satisfied the wishes and ambitions of those who came and day-by-day the number of people went on increasing. At last this magnificent temple was built and with due sanctification rituals, the idol was installed therein. Even this date thousands of devotees visit the temple every day and as per them the mere visit gives them peace never experienced before and fulfils all their dreams.

The annual fair is held here between Chaitra Sukla 13 and Vaishakh Krishna 1. Both Jains and non-Jains such as Min, Gujar, Jat etc., visit this holy place during the fair in thousands and offer their tears of devotion by way of flowers in worship of Bhagwan. Having been impressed by the extra-ordinariness of this shrine, there is a record that kings of Jaipur have donated the village of Alamgirpur-Naurangabad towards the maintenance cost of the shrine such as ceremonial worships, ghee lamps, incense burning etc., The spot where the idol was discovered has been converted into a small structure with a roof and the Bhagwans Foot-Prints enshrined there. The style and architecture of the temple are pleasing to the eyes and the cluster of sikhars gives an idea of a divine city from afar.

Shri Sametshikar Tirth

This supreme holy place was also known in the past as Sametshail. Sametachal, Sametgiri, Sanadhigiri,Samidigiri etc. At present the place is known as Sametshikar and Mount Parshavanth.

Shri Shamalia Parshvanath Bhagwan seated in a lotus posture, in black colour and of height about 90Cms (Lake-temple) in a shrine near Madhuban on Mount Sametshikar 4479 feet above sea-level. This place is also called Mount Parshvanath.

Several Tirthankars of earlier sets of twenty four tirthankars have achieved "Moksh" in this holy place. Even of the present set of twenty four Tirthankars, twenty Tirthankars together with their numerous saint followers have achieved "Moksh" in this most sacred of all places after practicing intense penance. Tradition has it that Shri Saudharmenra himself (Bhagwan of Indras) installed idols at the respective spots where Tirthankars achieved Moksh.

There is no historical record of the period earlier that that of the first century AD. while a reference is found that the Shri Acharaya "Vidyasidh" Padaliptasuriji used to visit this place as on a pilgrimage using his yogic powers of flying in space after the 1st century AD.

In ' Updeshsaptahika' a Jain composition, there is a reference that he used to fly daily to Sametshikar along with other holy places of Abu, Shatrunjay, Girnar and Ashtapad in Mount Kailash, Himalayas for pilgrimage by applying Lepa of ointment on his feet in accordance with Akash Ganmini Vidhya (the science of flying in the sky. His name "Padalipta" itself is indicative(unusual coincidence) of his feet anointed with a paste. In the same way, another of the Shri Acharya Bappathattsuriji also used to visit this place for pilgrimage using similar powers.

During 9th vikram century Acharya Shri Pradyumna Suriji visited this place seven times as on a pilgrimage and got substantial repairs carried out to the temple after a good deal if preaching.

A mention is made in "Vandaruvriti" composed by Acharya Shri Devendrasuriji in 13th Vikram century, of the temples and the idols of this place.

In Kumbharia temples, in one of the stone inscriptions, there is a mention of an installation ceremony performed in this temple at the hands of Acharya Shri paramanandsuriji inVikram Samvat 1345 at the instance of Shri Sharandev's son Virchand who visited the temple in the company of his brothers, sons, grandsons and their respective families.

A mention is also made in the composition of "Yashodharcharit" by Bhattarak Gyanakirtiji in Vikram Samvat 1659 of Nanu, secretary of Maharaj Manasinhji of Akbarpur near Champanagiri having built temples here.

During Vikram samvat, 1670 Shri Kunvarpal and Sonpal Lodha, Oswal businessmen fom Agra visited this place for pilgrimage together with members of their families and friends when repair works to several temples were carried out, there is a reference to this fact in a composition entitled "Sametshikhar Raas" by Shri Jaykirtiji. There after many Acharyas with groups of saints under them and countless Shravak-Sharavika householders have come to this place on pilgrimages.

Several saints have compised "Samet Shikar" Tirthmala, Jain Tirthmala, Purva Desh Tirthmala, etc., and have written tracts which reminds us of its glories of the past centuries.

During Vikram Samvat 1649 Emperor Akbar issued a proclamation presenting this mount of Samet SHikar to Jagat Guru Acharya Shri Hirvijaysuriji. It is told that the original documentation is in the sage custody with Sheth ANandjiKalyanji of Ahemdabad which represents Shvetambar Jain Shree Sangh.

During the years of Vikram samvat 1747 to 1763 Shri Saubhagya Vijayji, Shri Jaivijay Sagarji, Shri HansSomvijayji, Shri Vijaysagarji and other saints have composed Tirmalas which also give detailed description of this holy place.

Up to samvat year 1770, there were three accesses to Mount Sametshikahar, Pilgrims from west used to come via Patna, Navada and Khadagdiha, those from South-east used to come via Manpur, Jaipur, Navagadh and Palganj and the rest used to come via Madhuban.

While describing their pilgrimages, Shri Jayvijayji during 17th century and Shri Vijaysagarji during 18th century have stated that the local men folk here wear only a langoti and don't cover their heads with any cloth. They have curled hair. Womenfolk usually are ugly and frightening. They don't have any tradition to wear head dress, not do their put on brassiers or blouses. These latter words connote only an abuse. These women feel very much surprised when they see women with a head dress or wearing a brassiere and a blouse. Bhils are found here moving about with their bows and arrows. In the forest here are seen fruits, flowers, medicinal plants, wild animals roaming about and countless flowing water-springs.

In some Tirthmalas, it is stated that in the village of Zaria the ruling Emperor is Raghunathsinh whose chief minister is Somdas. A pilgrim tax of eight annas per head from all pilgrims is being collected. In another, narration it is stated that the Emperor of Kartras Shri Krishnasinh also collects a similar tax. The climb to the mountain starts after about four miles' distance from the village of Raghunathpur.

It is also said that once Palganj was the base of this Mount and the pilgrims were required to go to Palganj, meet its Emperor there for permission to climb and the kings' men accompanied pilgrims for a visit to the temple on the top. No proper information is at present available as to the circumstances prevailing on hills then.

In Vikram Samvat 1805 it is recorded that Badshah Ahmadshahof Delhi, who was pleased by the activities of Sheth Mahatab Rai of

Murshidabad, bestowed upon him the title of Jagat Sheth and it is further recorded that in year 1809 the Badshah gave to him as a gift his Madhuban properties. Jaiparnala, jalahari kund, 301 Vighas of land at the base level of Parshavanth Mount and the whole of Parshavanath Mount itself. In year 1812 Badshah Abu Alikhan bahadur declared Palganj-Parshvanath Mount as fully toll free.

It was earnestly desired by Jagat Sheth that temples on the holy place of Sametshikhar needed renovation and heavy repairs and right at that time Shri Devvijayji of Tapa-Gachcha arrived at Samet-Shikhar on a pilgrimage. Jagat Sheth taking advantage of this presence immediately resolved after consulting all of his sevens ons and their families to carry out this massive work of renovation and repairs and entrusted the full responsibility for it to his 4th Son Shri Sugalchand jointly with Shri Mulchandji who was chief executive of his Jaisalmer office. After a short while when jagat Sheth Shri mahatabrai died, the Badshah honoured eldest son Shri Khushalchad with the title of Jagat Sheth in year 1822.

While renovation and repair work was being carried out, Shri Khushalchand was diligently looking for exact spots on which each of the 20 Tirthankars had achieved redemption so as to erect there upon appropriate structures and signs of identity. He had undertaken several trips on elephant from Murshidabad for this purpose but to no avail. It appears thus that the ancient temples and shrines in the course of time may have changed places or even been demolished in total.

Inspired by devvijayji, jagat Sheth by practicing Attham Tama invoked the blessing of Shri Padmavati devi who appearing to him in his dreams directed that wherever on the Mount Swastiks saffron was seen, those were the spots from where the Tirthankars achieved Moksh and at those spots appropriate stupas, foot-prints, shrine etc., were to be designed and constructed.devi also directed that the number of swastiks would correspond to that particular Tirthankar in the chronological order. In this manner by divine guidance and power, 20 spots were decided upon where the stupas, shrines, foot-prints blocks etc were designed and constructed. There is a record that it was ceremonially consecrated at the benign hands of Shri Bhattarak Acharya Shri Dharma Suriji of Tapa Gachchha on the Vasant Panchami day i.e., maha Sukla Panchami on Vikram Samvat 1825. On the block of foot-prints is at present found. The name of Shri Khushalchand of virani gotra. It is possible that on completion of the renovation and repair work by Jagat Sheth, in the satisfaction rituals. Shri Khushalchand may have actually participated or jagat Seth himself would have been of Virani Gotra.

At that time Mount Lake Temple, seven temples in Madhuban, a dharmashala, the temple of the tutelary guardian deity of the mountain Shri Bhomiaji etc., were designed and constructed. It is recorded that the rituals of sanctification for there temples were also performed during the same Muhurut.

The administration of there temples etc., was entrusted to Shri Shvetambar Jain Sangh and in this way all the wishes of Jagat Sheth Shri Mahatabraiji were fulfilled. This monumental work of Jagat Sheth will eternally be remembered by Jain society. It was believed that this was the twenty-first renovation and repairs carried out on these temples. Thereafter many Jain pilgrim groups both large and small started coming to this mount. The stupas, pillars, temples and other commemorative structures remaining in the open sky and often beaten by weather storms, sun heat in the course of time required once again big repairs and renovation and thus during Vikram years 1925 and 1933 after they were carried out, further satisfaction rituals were performed by the benign hands of Shri Jinashantisagarsuriji of Vijay Gachchha and Shri Jinahanssuriji and Shri Jinchandrasuriji of Khartar Gachchha. This was the 22nd renovation and at this time new small temples of Adinath Bhagwan, Vasupujya Bhagwan, Neminath Bhagwan, Bhagwan Mahavir Bhagwan, Everlasting Jineshwar Rishabhanana, Chandranana, Varishena and Vardhaman were constructed. In Madhuban also many small shrines were built.

This mount was given to Jagat Sheth as a gift and yet because of the neglect in some quarters it later became the property of the Emperor of Palganj. During the years 1905 and 1910 this Emperor was in need of money andhe thought of selling or mortgaging it to raise necessary funds. Rai Bahadur Sheth Shri Badridasji, Jewellers of Calcutta and Maharaj Bahadur Sinhji Dugad of Murshidabad having come to know of this intention of the Emperor of Palganj encouraged Sheth Shri Anandji Kalyanji Pedhi of Ahemdabad to buy over the mount and to that end promised to co-operate in a substantial way. The Pedhi thereafter having inspection of the title documents including original proclamation felt it appropriate to buy the mount and arranged for the purchase on the ninth of March 1918 at the price of Rs. Two Lakhs and Forty Two Thousand. The sum was paid to the Emperor and then it once again belonged to the Jain Shvetambar Shree Sangh. In this whole transaction co-operation of these gentlemen was praise worthy and it can be asserted that the transaction became successful only due to the encouragement and co-operation received from them.

In the year of Vikram Samvat 1980, Agamodhdharak Revered Acharya Shri Sagaranandsuriji came here on a pilgrimage and he desired the renovation of these temples once again and due to the efforts of the learned Balbrahmacharini Sadhviji Shri Ranjansriji and Sadhviji Shri Suprabhashriji of his group the renovation having commenced in vikram year 2012 were duly completed in the year 2017. This was the twenty-third renovation.

As stated earlier, this is the place which is hallowed and become most sacred because in the former cycles of time, numberless Tirthankars have achieved Moksh here and even of the current cycle time, twenty of the twenty-four Tirthankars have achieved Moksh here. Rest of the four Tirthankars achieved Moksh elsewhere i.e., Shri Rishabhnath at Astapadh known as Mount Kilash, Shri Vasupujyaji at Champapuri, Shri Neminath at Mount Girnar, and Shri Bhagwan Mahavir at Pavapuri. Besides, countless Acharayas and holy men have treaded upon this soil from times immemorial charging the whole atmosphere, the plants, trees, water, and particles of stone and soil with living vibrations of such utmost purity that mere entry therein immerses every one in the reflections of Supreme Divine, washing away all corporeal thoughts and giving a lifetime experience of ideal esctasy.

Shri Gunyaji Tirth

Gunayaji is a small place on Patna-Ranchi main road from where the temples is only 250 meters away. Cars and buses can go up to the temple. Gunayaji is twenty-three Kms from Pavapuri.

Shri Gautam Swami maharaj seated in a lotus posture, in white colour and of height 30cms in a shrine about three Kms from Navada Railway Station in Gunayaji village, from main road about two hundred meters, in the middle of a lake.

In the history of Rajagirh, a holy shrine named "Gunashil Chaitya" is described and as per one opinion that place may be this "Gunayaji" as colloquialised. Bhagwan Bhagwan Mahavir, several times visited this place and gave sermons seated in Samosarans. As per another opinion, this is the place where the first and the chief disciple of Bhagwan Bhagwan Mahavir, Shri Gautam Swami achieved Kewal Gnan. Anyway, this holy place is very significant because it is contemporaneous to Bhagwan Bhagwan Mahavir. As "Gunayaji" is believed to be a colloquial term of "Gunashil" where Bhagwan Bhagwan Mahavir had paid several visits and further as Shri Gautam Swami, his first and chief disciple achieved here Kewal Gnan, the place has its own special importance.

The architecture of this temple reminds one at once of the Pavapuri Lake-temple. Also opposite the temple there is a Toran which is very attractive. ("Toran" is a decoration by way of an arch generally at the top of gates.)

Shri Kalikund Tirth

Shri Kalikund Parshvanath Bhagwan in white colour seated in a lotus posture, of height approx thirty-five Cms in a shrine in Calicut city. From the temple the Calicut Railway station is approx one Km away so is the bus stand.

It is believed that this temple is more that five hundred years old but the antiquity of this place is difficult to find out as there is no evidence any where. The idol of the Prabhu looks very ancient but there is no inscription found even on the idol. Devotees here call Prabhu, Shri Kalikund Parshvanath from the beginning. Calicut was earlier known as Kojikod, Kozhikode etc., now again it is called Kozhikode.

At various places in India references are found of Kalikund Parshvanath. It is believed that Shri Parshvanath Bhagwan meditated near the mountain named "Kali" and a tank named "Kund" and their Emperor Dadhivahan had built a temple which was named Kalikund. But the exact place and the history is not known till ate. It is but definite that whichever place miracles used to happen, the name of the place was added to Prabhu's name or the place itself sometimes gets the Prabhu's name.

From the antiquity of the idol of Prabhu, the reason for associating the name with Prabhu's name for years and some similarity between the names, most probably this should be the main place of Kalikund Parshvanath. Nevertheless this is a subject of research.

Approx, some 85 years back when foundation was laid for different temple in the courtyard of this temple, 34 ancient idols were found from the earth that are still kept in Shri Adhishvar Bhagwan temple. It is believed that Shri Adhishvar idol is of the time of Emperor Samprati. Other idols too are quite old. No where there is an inscription. It is proven from this there were ancient temples here. Even in the southern regions over here, lot of ancient idols are found. In the state of Kerala, at various places, it is believed that countless idols are excavated from earth. But this is the first time that in the southern side that idols of the time of Emperor Samprati have been excavated from earth.

As per a reference when there was a famine in Bihar state for 12 years, Arya Bhadrabahu Swami with his 1200 followers Muni's had shifted to the southern direction and stayed in Shravenbelgola. His saints then for the propaganda and glorification of Jainism went to Karnataka., Andhra Pradesh, Tamil Nadu and Kerala and executed a lot of good works. Thy helped in the improvement of the language too. They wrote a lot of texts in the respective languages which are available even today. But it is said that even before the Jain culture was found here and people of Jain community lived here. They were called Samanar.

The territory of Emperor of Kaling Desh karkandu was almost full of Southern India and he was the chief disciple and devotee of Shri Parshva Prabhu and for this reason it is possible that Parshvaprabhu would have visited this place also and delivered sermons and religious discourses with which the community people would have been benefited. Like it is referred that Prabhu had visited Gujarat, Madhya Pradesh, Uttar Pradesh etc.,

It is said as stated earlier, that during one of his visits, Shri Parshva Prabhu was meditating at one place near mountain Kali and Pond Kund, where later Emperor Dadhivahan constructed a temple and named Kalikund. That time an elephant from the jungle used to be in the service of Prabhu.

In this place even today lot of mountains, Kunds (Ponds) and elephants are found that can't be seen anywhere else.

On the banks of sea, on mount Malaiyagiri where this town is located lot of ancient idols of Gods are excavated and that reveals that this would have been a big state at one point of time with lot of Jain inhabited and also a big centre for trade.

Here to arrive at anywhere, one has to cross either sea or a mountain. One way from the mountains goes through Karnataka towards Maharashtra till Mumbai. Second through Karnataka towards Tamil Nadu and one more through Karnataka towards Andhra Pradesh. It is possible that many years ago this place would have been desolated due to a cyclone or a devastative earth quake and devotees were unable to visit this place they would have given this name which sanctification of some other idol at other places, one such idol is still there in Dhokla Tirth. But since there is a similarity in the name here its possible that this should be the main place of Kalikund Parshvanath. Nevertheless, this is a area for research.

There is one more Shvetambar temple apart from this. The idol of Shri Kalikund Parshvanath Prabhu is very simple and attractive. In the temple of Adhishvar Bhagwan here, the ancient idols of the period of

Emperor Samprati are very artistic and pleasing to the eyes. The architecture and construction of the temple is totally different and is in a class of its own. All the temples in Kerala, such work can be found.

Bhinmal Jain Tirth

Bhinmal Jain Tirth (Bhinmal) is a Shvetambar Jain temple and pilgrimage centre, in Jalore district, Rajasthan, India. There were several ancient temple constructed in ninth and tenth century by the various dynasties.

Bhagwan Mahavir Swami Jain temple: This Jain temple of Bhagwan Mahavir is the most celebrated. In ancient times this temple was built by Emperor Kumarpal and founded by Acharya Hemachandra, dedicated to 1st Jain Tirthankar Bhagwan Rishabh Dev;after many years 'Bhinmal Jain Sangh' renovated this temple and eventually in 1816 AD. Jain Shvetambar Acharya Jinendrasuri founded new 'Moolnayaka'(main Idol) of twenty-fourth Jain Tirthankar Bhagwan Mahavir. After 145 years in 1959 AD. the temple was in bad condition so again the Jain Sangh renovated it and in 1961 AD.the main idol of Bhagwan Mahavirswami was reestablished by Acharya Vidhachandra suri (5th following Acharya of Acharya Rajendrasuri). Life of Bhagwan Mahavir is carve in colourful way on white marble on the inner boundary wall of the temple. In this temple premises there is one adjoining temple of 'Astapada Tirth' and one nice Guru Mandir dedicated to Acharya Rajendrasuri too.

Parshvanatha Jain temple (Hathi pole): This temple of 23rd Jain Tirthankar Parshvanatha in Hathi pole area of the main town is regarded to be ancient. This temple has great archaeological importance. Golden-coloured idol of Shri Parshvanatha Bhagvan in padmasana posture is the presiding deity. On the image of the main deity, On the idol, there is an inscription of the year 1011 of the Vikram era [954 AD.]. It is believed that the idol was found from a hollow of the ground. Many other idols were also found. The idol of Bhagwan Parshvanatha has supernatural power, according the Jain belief. In the temple premises one adjoining temple of Bhagwan Mahavir is also ancient.

Shantinath Jain temple (Ganesh chowk): This temple was built in 1155 AD.dedicated to 16th Jain Tirthankar Shantinath.

Ganthi Mehata vaas (4 Jain temple complex): In this temple complex there is 4 Jain temple one is dedicated to 16th Jain Tirthankar Bhagwan Shantinath,the idol is established in 1577 AD. by Acharya Hirvijay suri; the second temple is dedicated to 23rd Jain Tirthankar Bhagwan

Parshvanatha,the idol is established in 1626 AD. by Acharya Vijay Devasuri;the 3rd temple is dedicated to 24th Jain Tirthankar Bhagwan Mahavir,the main idol is in Pink colour;4th Jain temple is dedicated to 12th Jain Tirthankar Vasupujyaswami.

Dilwara Temples

The Jain Dilwara temples of India are located about 2½ kilometers from Mount Abu, Rajasthan's only hill station. These temples dating back from the 11th to the 13th century AD are world famous for their stunning use of marble. The five legendary marble temples of Dilwara are the sacred pilgrimage of the Jains. They are an overwhelming blend of simple beauty and exquisite elegance. The marble temples have an opulent entranceway. The simplicity in architecture verily reminds one that Jainism as a religion "encouraged honesty and frugality". The temples reside amidst mesmerizing surroundings of mango trees and wooded hills. A high wall, shimmering luminous in the sunlight, shrouds the temple complex.

Though the Jains built some beautiful temples at other places in Rajasthan but none come close to these in terms of architectural perfection. The ornamental detail spread over the minutely carved ceilings, doorways, pillars and panels is simply marvellous and has to be seen to be believed.

Palitana Temples

Amongst all the Jain temples, Palitana temples are considered to be the most sacred. Located on Shetrunjaya hills there are 863 temples, exquisitely carved in marble. No one is allowed to sleep overnight including the priest, because the temple city has been built as an abode for the Gods. The town is considered by many Jains to be more prominent than the temple covered hills of Bihar, Gwalior, Mt Abu and Girnar. Palitana was the capital of a princely state of the Gohil Rajput clan. It is also one of the greatest tourist attractions in Gujarat for foreign tourists.

Ranakpur

Ranakpur in the state of Rajasthan is one of the five most prominent pilgrimage sites of Jainism. It is home to an exceptionally beautiful temple complex in the Aravali ranges and a must visit for the tourists coming to this region.

Khajuraho

Khajuraho is a village in the Indian state of Madhya Pradesh, located in Chhatarpur District, about 385 miles (620 kilometres) southeast of Delhi, the capital city of India. Khajuraho has the biggest group of medieval

Hindu and Jain temples, famed for their erotic sculpture. The name Khajuraho is deduced from the Hindi word khajur meaning date palm.

The city was once the original capital of the Chandela Rajputs, a Hindu family that ruled this part of India from the tenth to the twelfth centuries. The Khajuraho temples were built over a span of a hundred years, from 950 to 1050. The Chandela capital was moved to Mahoba after this time, but Khajuraho continued to expand for some time. The whole area was enclosed by a wall with eight gates, each flanked by two golden palm trees. There were originally over eighty Hindu temples, of which only twenty-two now stand in a reasonable state of preservation, scattered over an area of about eight square miles.

Unlike other cultural centres of North India, the temples of Khajuraho never underwent massive destruction by early Muslim invaders between. 1100-1400 AD. Due to overgrowth following their abandonment, a number of them survived to be discovered by the British in the nineteenth century.

The colonials undertook the laborious excavation of the temples, which required no small amount of reassembly. Today, the temples serve as fine examples of Northern Indian architectural styles that have gained popularity due to their salacious depiction of the traditional way of life during medieval times. They were rediscovered during the late nineteenth century and the jungles had taken a toll on some of the monuments.

The Khajuraho temples, constructed with spiral superstructures, adhere to a northern Indian shikhara temple style and often to a Panchayatana plan or layout. A few of the temples are committed to the Jain pantheon and the rest to Hindu deities - to God's Trio, Brahma, Vishnu and Shiva, and various Devi forms, such as the Devi Jagadambi temple. A Panchayatana temple had four subordinate shrines on four corners and the main shrine in the centre of the podium, which comprises their base. The temples are grouped into three geographical divisions: western, eastern and southern.

With a graded rise secondary shikharas (spires) cluster to create an appropriate base for the main shikhara over the sanctum. Kandariya Mahadeva, one of the most skilful temples of the Western group, comprises eighty-four shikharas, the main being 116 feet from the ground level. Khajuraho temples achieve the form and glory of bit by bit rising Himalayan peaks. These temples of Khajuraho have sculptures that look very realistic and are studied even today.

RELIGIOUS PLACES OUTSIDE INDIA

Shri Ashtapadh Tirth

As per Holy Scriptures Bhagwan Rishabh Dev who is also called as Shri Adhinath Bhagwan or Adishvar Bhagwan, achieved Moksh from this mountain on Magh Krishna 13 along with his 99 sons and many saints. A reference is found that this shrine was twelve Yojan (ninety-six miles) away from Ayodhya and the height of the mount was eight Yojan (sixty-four miles). It's possible that during the course of time there was a difference in the distance and height of the mountain. It is said that this mount is also called as Mount Kailash. Mansarovar is very close by to this mount. It is learnt that Bharat Charkravarthy, to safe guard this shrine from any Natural Calamaties, had divided this shrine into 8 portions and perhaps that is the reason why it is named as the Ashtapadh. As per "Shiv Puran", Bhagwan Rishabh Dev achieved Moksh from Mount Kailash.

When Bhagwan Rishabh Dev achieved Moksh three stupas were installed and later Shri Bharat Charavarthy constructed massive, mind captivating and attractive 24 small shrines of 24 Tirthankars, the idols studded with precious stones and named it "Sinhnishdha". Later even Shri Bharat Chakravarthy the eldest son of Adinath Bhagwan achieved Nirvana from here along with many Munis. As per another belief, he had achieved Moksh from Hastigiri and hence this is a subject of research. Years later, to further safe guard this mount and Shrines, sons of Sagar Chakravarthy dug large pits near the mount and diverted the river Ganges to flow into it, as per references found. During the course of time since the pit became huge and profound, this shrine was cut of and was not accessible easily. It is understood that due to layers of snow that has covered this mount totally, it is also called "Dhavalgiri".

Emperor Ravana of Lanka while climbing this very mount got so much engrossed in Bhajans of Prabhu that he secured himself a place in future Tirthankars. Bhagwan Mahavir Prabhu's first disciple (Ganadhar) Shri Goutamswamiji had climbed this mount using his powers again broke the fast of 500 Rishi Munis, a reference is fount in this aspect too.

This shrine even today is not seen but Mount Kailash covered with layers of snow is near Tibet and is 6714 Mts (approx 20,200 feet) above sea-level, while Mansarovar which is 22 kms away from the mount is 4560 Mts (approx 13,725 feet above sea level. Hindus and Buddha's consider this as their shrine as well. To reach here one can go via Kathmandu but Indian Government arranges for the pilgrims to reach this place which is also close to China, agreeing mutually with the Chinese and Tibetian Govt.

Siddhachalam

Siddhachalam is the first Jain Tirth outside of India. Established in 1983 by Acharya Sushil Kumarji, it is located on a 108 acre (44ha) site in rural New Jersey. The main temple has idols of Bhagwan Adinath, Bhagwan Parshvanath, Bhagwan Bhagwan Mahavir, Bhagwan Chandraprabhu and Bhagwan Shantinath. There is also a small temple where the main idol is Bhagwan Parshvanath.

Beside these two, there are several Jain derasar (jinalaya) established in various cities outside India:

- The Oshwal Centre located in Potters Bar, UK. The temple is surrounded by landscaped gardens, statues of the 24 Tirthankar, and 54 Otla representing the villages in India that the Visa Oshwal community originated from.
- The Oshwal Mahajanwadi located in Nairobi, Kenya. The temple houses statues of 9 of the 24 Tirthankar.
- The Jain temple in Leicester (UK)
- The Jain temples at Harrow and at Kenton (UK)
- Twenty Jain temples in the USA: at Houston (Texas), Cincinnati (Ohio), Milpitas (California), Philadelphia (Pennsylvania), Pittsburgh (Pennsylvania), Essex falls (New Jersey), Silver Spring (Washington DC), Bartlett (Chicago) etc.
- The Jain temple in Kobe (Japan)
- The Jain temple in Kathmandu (Nepal)

REFERENCES

Bhargava, D.: *Jain Ethics*, Motilal Banarsidass, Delhi, 1968.

Bhattacharya, B.C.: *Jaina Iconography*, 2nd ed, Motilal Banarsidass, Delhi, 1974.

Bhattacharya, N.N.: *Jain Philosophy, Historical Outline*. Munshiram Manoharlal, New Delhi, 1976.

Desai, P.B. *Jainism in South India and some Jaina Epigraphs*, Sholapur, 1957.

Devendra Muni Shastri: *Source-Book in Jaina Philosophy*, Sri Tarak Guru Jain Granthalaya, Udaipur, 1983.

Diwakar, R.R.: *Bihar Through Ages*, Calcutta, 1959.

Dwivedi, R.C.: *Contribution of Jainism to Indian Culture*, Motilal Banarsidass, Varanasi, 1975.

Hume, Robert Earnest: *Thirteen Principal Upanisads (Trans.)*, Oxford, 1921.

Jacobi, H.: *Introduction to Kalpa-sutra.*

Jacobi, H.: *Jaina Sutras, Part 1, The Akaranga Sutra, The Kalpa Sutra, Part2, The Uttaradhyana Sutra,The Sutrakritanga Sutra. 2 vols*, Dover Publications, New York, 1968.

Jacobi, H.: *Mahavira and His Predecessors.*

Jacobi, H.: *Studies in Jainism*, Ahmedabad, 1946.

Jain, C. R.: *Fundamentals of Jainism*, Veer Nirvan Bharti, Meerut, 1974.

Jain, Champat Rai: *Householder's Dharma*, Bijnore, 1931.

Jain, H., and Upadhye, A.N.: *Mahavira, his Times and his Philosophy of Life*, Bharatiya Gyanpeeth, New Delhi, 1975.

Jain, J. P.: *Religion and Culture of the Jains*, Bharatiya Gyanpeeth, New Delhi, 1975.

Jain, J., and Fischer, E.: *Jaina Iconography, Part One, The Tirthankara in Jaina Scriptures, Art and Rituals, Part Two, Objects of Meditation and the Pantheon. 2 vols.* E.J.Brill, Leiden, 1978.

Jain, Jyoti Prasad: *Jainism: The Oldest Living Religion*, Banaras, 1951.

Jain, Jyoti Prasad: *Religion and Culture of the Jains*, New Delhi, 1977.

Jain, K.C.: *Lord Mahavira and his Times*, Motilal Banarsidass, Delhi, 1974.

Jain, Kailash Chand: *Jainism in Rajasthan*, Sholapur, 1963.

Malavania, Pt. Dalasukhabhai: *Jainism (Some essays)*, Translated by Dr. A.S.Gopani, Prakrita Bharati Academy, Jaipur, First Edition, 1986.

Mehata, M.L.: *Jaina Culture*, Varanasi, 1969.

Mehta, M. L.: *Outlines of Jaina Philosophy*, Jaina Mission Society, G. 146, Chickpet, Bangalore - 2, October, 1954.

Mookerjee, S.: *The Jain Philosophy of Non-absolutism, a Critical Study of Anekantavada. 2nd. Ed,* Motilal Banarsidass, Delhi, 1978.

Nahar and Ghosh: *An Epitome of Jainism,* Calcutta 1917.

Nevaskar B.: *Capitalists without Capitalism, the Jains of India and the Quakers of the West,* Greenwood Publications, Westport, 1971.

Nyayavatara: Siddhasena, Translated by Vijayamurti Sastracarya, Paramashruta Prabhavaka Mandal, Jauhari Bazar-Bombay, First Edition, 1950.

Roy Chowdhari, P.C.: *Jainism in Bihar,* Patna, 1956.

Roy, A.K.: *History of the Jains,* Gitanjali Publishing House, New Delhi, 1984.

Saletore, B.A: *Medieval Jainism,* Bombay, 1938.

Tukol, T.K.: *Compendium of Jainism*, Dharwad, 1980.

Upadhye, A.N.: *Lord Mahavira and his Teachings. 2nd. Ed,* Shree Vallabhsuri Smarak Nidhi, Bombay,1983.

Uttaradhyayana-sutra: Editor Madhukara Muni, Jinagama Granthamala No. 19, Agama Prakashan Samiti, Byavara, First Edition, 1984.

Warren, H.: *Jainism in Western Garb, as a Solution to Life's Great Problems,* Edited, with notes, by N.J. Shah. 2nd. ed. Shree Vallabhsuri Smarak Nidhi, Bombay, 1983.

Warren, Herbert: *Jainism,* Arrah, 1916.

Williams, R.: *Jaina Yoga: A survey of Medieval Sharavakachara,* London, 1963.

Williams. R.: *Jaina Yoga,* Motilal Banarsidass, Delhi, 1983.

Winternitz, M.: *The Jainas in the History of Indian Literature,* Ahmedabad, 1946.

Zimmer, H.: *Myths and Symbols in Indian Art and Civilization,* Edited by Joseph Campbell, Harper and Brothers, New York, First Edition, 1945.

18

Art and Iconography

The basic principle of all art or architecture is the transmutation of thoughts into a seeable object or symbolic expression. Architecture further serves as a sort of history. It is a standing and living historical record, rendering a more vivid and lasting picture of a cultural custom than schematic written history does. Jainism is an autonomous and one of the oldest living religions of the world. According to Jainism, in the internal time span there have been cycles of twenty-four Tirthankars in every Avasarpani and Utsarpani division of time. The present cycle of twenty-four Trithankars started with the first Tirthankar Rishabhadev. It ceased with the twenty-fourth Tirthankar Bhagwan Mahavir.

HISTORY

In the field of art and architecture modern and medieval Jains have been the most prolific temple builders in Western India. The notable Jain temples atop Mt. Abu in Rajasthan are triumphs of architecture. The elaborateness and richness of their carvings are truly unexceeded in the world. The great Jain pilgrimage in the Shatrunjay Hills near Palitana in Gujarat, sometimes called the "City of Temples", is an imposing edifice. Its close, systematic grouping of buildings, given striking changes in altitude and very fixed spaces, is another speciality of Jain architecture.

A number of cave-temples have been found in various parts of the Indian subcontinent, West and South. The Jain caves at Ellora in state Maharashtra form a series by themselves and comprise elaborate frescoes and other architectural works. Numerous salient ascetic ideals expressed in Jain and Buddhist sculpture are similar, and modern art historians have a great deal mistaken images of the Buddhas and Jain Tirthankars for one another. The images of Jain Tirthankars are by and large seated in the meditative *padmasana* position "lotus posture", and sometimes in the standing *kayotsarga* posture "body abondoning", or in *ardhapadmasana* "half lotus". The Shvetambar laity has created a unique class of metal-cast images known as *panchatirthis*, or "five holies". The central images on these artefacts comprise of any of the twenty-four Tirthankars in the padmasana pose; two standing, kayotsarga figures seem on each side of the middle image; and two more padmasana images are shaped on either side, above the same kayotsarga figures.

Other outstanding themes within Indian Jain art comprise celestial beings, or angels, as musicians and votaries: some adoring the omniscient Tirthankars, some waving *chamaras*, and some in prayer, kneeling or standing with folded hands, etc. One also finds images of saluting elephants, carrying water-pots in their trunks, pouring at the feet of a kayotsarga Tirthankar figure, on either side. Within the Digambar Jain temples in southern India, the tremendous statues at Shravana Belagola in state of Karnataka, Karkala, Yemur, and Canara are the most prominent monolithic, free-standing statues in the world. The tallest one, of Lord Bahubali at Shravana Belagola, completed in 981 A.D., is over 57 feet high and was cut up from a single block of granite.

The place of Jain paintings in the world's treasury of fine arts is also of significance. An exceptional feature of Jain painting lies in the drift and quality of its lines. Line is so finely drawn in the some Jain schools of painting that few other art traditions bear comparison with it. It has been manifested that the Chinese technique for producing powerful lines was borrowed from India; perhaps time will produce evidence that the Chinese may have learned the skill from Jains artisans. Jain paintings more often than not depict significant historical events, such as the lives and deeds of Tirthankars, ascetics and monarchs, or pilgrimage centers, or exemplifications concerning Jain philosophy and cosmology. Since they confirm a sanctitude of their own in finished form, such works of art were preserved with great veneration in both temples and homes. The Jains have also been keen on illustrating religious texts with miniature paintings whose renditions of man and nature also bear a unique style and taste. The Nahar family collection of manuscripts of the Kalpa Sutra, which considers the lives of the Tirthankars and ascetic conduct, comprises exquisite miniatures which have been gaining the attention of modern art critics. Their interesting changes in drapery, posture and colour, as well as their special stylizations, are quite impressing to the average, unacquainted observer.

The Mughal period of miniature painting importantly shaped Jain miniature art. In fact, it was only in that later date of reference that paintings of buildings, scenery, and portraits become dominant all around the subcontinent.

Archaeological Findings

The ancient Bhagawan Suparshwanatha Jain temple at Midigeshi has the idol of Yaksha Brahmadeva and a stone edict found in the surroundings of the temple tells us some historical aspects of the temple.

A stone adict was found in Elephant Cave in Udayagiri in Orissa. It dates back to 2100 BC. On it is written "King Kharvel took back the statue of Adijin from Kin of Magadh.

Thirthankar Statues has been found in the city of Ramanagar, U.P, India.

In 1949, in Cyprus, A bronze statue of Rishabh Dev dating back to 1250 BC. was found.

ARCHITECTURE

Atadakar Symbols

In further study of Jain architecture the Atadakar Jain symbols comprises Chaitya tree, stupas, Tri-ratna, chaitya-stambha, poorn ghat, flower chaplet etc. Asta-Pratiharya and Ayagpattas were also regarded as significant Jain symbols. The Ayagpattas, rectangular stone-slabs, bore several Jain symbols with or without the image of Tirthankar. Those were the objects of worship. The Ayagpattas determined in the excavations of Kankali-Tila Mathura of the very early centuries are significant.

Tadakar Symbols

With the growth of art forms, iconography obtained significant attention and the images of Tirthankars began to be made. In the later period the worship of Tirthankars in idolatory form became most famous. In the early period of iconography, the Jain idols were laid down at little height from the surface ground in a vedika (alter) like structure. Afterwards, these were roofed and came to be known as Devayatans, Devalayas or Temples. With the progress in building making the simple temple style had drastic change and larger and artistic temples set out to be built. The rock cut caves were also established both to serve as places of worship and as abodes of Jain ascetics for their short period vagabondages.

Temples

The temple constructing deduced its inspiration from the Samavasarana of Tirthankar, in which Tirthankar had his seat in Mulgandha Kuti. Samavasarana was, hence, taken as the model of a Jain temple. Earlier, the Jain temples had a Man-Stambha in each of the four directions, like that of the Samavasaran. Later, one Man-Stambha, in front of the primary entrance of the Jain temple, carried on to be built in numerous Jain temples of India. Temple making is as well said to have its base in the conception of existence of Sumeru and Kailasa, the untouchable mountains, the abodes of Ishta-Dev.

Since it was not possible for the devotees to arrive at these mountains and worship the Ishta, they had in mind raising Sumeru and Kailasa like structures, where the Ishta could come along and be worshipped. These two mountains were thus the examples for temple making as well as for making spires of the temples. The coins of fifth-fourth century B.C. assume spire like structures. Some damaged old seals assume inscription of early forms of temples.

There are literary references of temples which existed even before sixth century B.C. in Mathura, Kampila and other places. Temple constructing seems to have its beginning from North India.

SCULPTURES

Stupas

The stupa was an early form of geomorphological architecture of the Jains as showed by the diggings of Kankali-Tila site at Mathura. As the saying goes, the earliest stupa was made by gods during the time of seventh Tirthankar Suparswanath and was later refurbished in the period of Tirthankar Parswanath. It was known as Vodvo-Stupa. Its mention has been made on the base of image of Tirthankar Munisuvrat of second century A.D. found in Kankali Tila minings. In reality, even by the second century A.D. this stupa had become so ancient that the facts about its source were entirely forgotton and it came to be attributed to gods.

The stupas in general had four Vedicas (Alters) for worship. Though the Jain literature pullulates with references to stupas but the only extant remains are of one or more stupas in Kankali-Tila at Mathura of the centuries right away before and after Christ. Some of the Ayagpattas found in Kankali-Tila diggings bear inscriptions of Jain stupas. Building stupas, nevertheless, seems to have lost privilege with the Jains by the end of the Gupta Period.

Caves

The Jain abstainers formerly did not enter the cities. They opted to have short stay in forests, caves, rock-shelters, etc. outside the populating places. More than two hundred sites in India have the existence of natural or man made Jain caves. Many of the sites in several parts of India have a splendid creation. The man made caves were chiefly produced for the Jain monks and for worship. The earliest among those are four caves of Mauryan period made in the middle of third century B.C. for Ajivak Jain saints in Barabar Hill and Nagarjuni Hill, twelve miles south of Rajgir, two rock cut caves known as twin caves of Son Bhandar at Rajgir also of Mauryan period, and Hathigumpha and Ranigumpha at Udaigiri Hill near Bhuvaneshwar in first century B.C. Afterwards, more prominent caves were made at Vidisha two Jain caves among twenty Gupta period caves, Terpur and Ellora caves in Maharashtra, and at numerous other sites.

The custom of cave making with the Jain images inscribed in them is found in a modernised form in Sittanvasal in the state of Tamil Nadu, Aihole and Badami Jain Caves in the state of Karnataka and Ellora and Terpur Jain Caves. The Ellora group of Jain caves created in tenth-eleventh century A.D. is indeed the most all right instance of cave making in India in character of sculpture and inscriptions. The Jagannath and Indrasabha caves are in full developed forms of Jain temples having vedikas, full size images of Tirthankars, huge columns and roof and wall decorations. It is from Ellora Jain caves that the art of Jain temple constructing continued ameliorating in craftsmanship.

Also in the Tamil region there are numerous rock-carverns at several places which are with or without beds made for the Jain saints right from the second-first century B.C.

Temples

The Jain temples do not seem to have the beginning before the starting time of iconography. Temple architecture is a direct outcome of icon or image worship since at least the historic times. The Buddhist texts talk of the existence of Arhat-chaityas in the Vajji country and Vaisali, which had descended from pre-Buddha and so from pre-Mauryan times. From the fourth century B.C. there is evidence of the existence of Jain images, cave temples and geomorphological shrines or temples. Ramnents of temples discovered from the diggings of Lohanipur, Sravasti and Mathura do not help in evaluating the exact form of the ancient Jain temples. The earliest classes of temples were acknowledged as Yakshayatan and Yaksha-chaitya. The Jain caves which were cognized as cave temples are being regarded dissimilar from Jain temples. The rock cut Jain caves are, nevertheless, of earlier origin. The rock cut caves have their rootage in the pre-Christian era. In the first place, the temples were simple in make. The Vedika and spire are the later additions, as is acknowledged from the temples of Mathura built in second and first century B.C.

The temple making turned popular throughout Mauryan and Shunga periods with ceaseless uptrend in Shak-Satvahan period in first-second century B.C., while the images of Tirthankars started to be inscribed in several components of the temples admitting the columns. Mathura, capital of Saurasena-a significant city from sixth century B.C., Ahichartra, Kausambi, Kampila and Hastinapur were the chief Jain temple centres throughout Kushan period. As in the case of iconography, the temples, highly adorned were constructed in multitude throughout Gupta period fourth-sixth century A.D. After 600 A.D. (post-Gupta period), Nagar Style of temple building became popular in northern India while Dravida style was abundantly assumed in the South. In the post-Gupta period the four styles of temple making became spectacular, viz. Gurjar-Pratihar, Kalturi, Chandel and Kachhapghat. The broad three categorizations of temple building style are Nagar, Vesar and Dravid.

The temple building incurred very good impulse throughout the period sixth-thirteenth century A.D. as it obtained considerable support of the rulers, courtiers and moneyed persons of Gujarat, Rajasthan, Madhya Pradesh, some parts of U.P. and Karnataka. Best of the Jain temples were built throughout this period at many places including Ghanerao, Osia, Mount Abu, Ranakpur, Chittor Fort, Jaisalmer, Jhalrapatan, etc. all in Rajasthan; Gyaraspur, Vidisha and Khajuraho in Madhya Pradesh; Deogarh in Uttar Pradesh; Shatrunjaya-Palitana, Girnar, Taranga, Kumbharia, all in Gujarat; Hampi (Old Vijaynagar), Hellebid, Sravanbelgola, Mudbidri in Karnataka. The Jains in general selected picturesque sights for their temples, assessing rightly the impression of environment on architecture.

CALLIGRAPHY

Calligraphy simply speaking is the art of making beautiful or elegant handwriting. It is a fine art of skilled penmanship. In Jainism calligraphy was not very popular, but they have done very fine calligraphic works in the temples they made in thirteenth and fourteenth centuries. An artistic heritage sweeping over a period of over two thousand years constitutes an amazing variety of sculpture, paintings, ritual objects and textiles. The Jains, in spite of their rigorous ideal of non-attachment to the material world, have developed a cultural heritage rich in its imaginative splendour. A few of Jains calligraphic works are still preserved and displayed in several parts of India.

PRESENT DAY EXAMPLES

Some of the very far-famed Jain temples in India are as under:

- Paraswanath and Adinath temples at Khajuraho (10 century A.D.)
- Vimal Vasahi and Luna Vasahi, Dilwara-Mount Abu (1032 A.D. & 1231 A.D.)
- Adinath temple at Ranakpur (1439 A.D.)
- Neminath and other temples at Girnar (13 century)
- Adinath and other Jain temples at Shatrunjaya (10th century and after)
- Ajitnath temple, Taranga (1165 A.D.)
- Mahavir, Paraswanath and Shantinath temples at Kumbharia (11th century A.D.)
- Adinath Jain temple and Kirti Stambha at Chittor Fort (c-1200-1500 A.D.)
- Maladevi temple at Gyaraspur (late 9th century A.D.)
- Sumantinath Jain temple at Jaisalmer
- Mahavira temple at Ossia (783-92 A.D.)
- Deogarh Jain temples (cir.850 A.D.-13th century A.D.)
- Mahavir temple at Ghanerao.

Indeed the Jain community is proud of the vast and varied sculptures which were built during the last 1700 years-fourth century B.C. to thirteenth century A.D. and it is also a rich heritage of India.

REFERENCES

Avasyaka-sutra: Editor Madhukar Muni, Jinagama Granthamala, No.24 Agama Prakashan Samiti, Byavar, First Edition, 1985.

Basham, A.L.: *A Cultural History of India,* Clarendon Press, Oxford.

Basham, A.L.: *Post-script, attached to the article on Hinduism in Cultural History of India*, Oxford University Press.

Chakravarti, A.: *Samayasara of Sri Kundakunda*, Translation with Introduction. Bharatiya Jnanapitha, Delhi, 1971.

Chakravarti, A: *The Religion of Ahimsa*, Bombay, 1957.

Chandogya Upanisad: Edited by Max Muller, F. (S. B. E.) Vol. 1, Motilal Banarasidas, Delhi, Reprint Edition, 1981.

Diwakar, R.R.: *Bihar Through Ages*, Calcutta, 1959.

Dwivedi, R.C.: *Contribution of Jainism to Indian Culture*, Motilal Banarsidass, Varanasi, 1975.

Einstein Albert: *Ideas and Opinions*, Bonanza Books, No.9.

Ferfusson, J.: *History of Indian and Eastern Architecture*, London

Fischer, E., & Jain, J.: *Art and Rituals, 2500 Years of Jainism in India*, Sterling Publishers, New Delhi, 1977.

Jain, Muni Uttam Kamal: *Jain Sects and Sub-sects*, New Delhi, 1975.

Jaini, Jugmandar Lal: *Outlines of Jainism*, Cambridge, 1916.

Jaini, P.S.: *The Jaina Path of Purification*, Berkeley: University of California Press, 1979.

Nyayavatara: Siddhasena, Translated by Vijayamurti Sastracarya, Paramashruta Prabhavaka Mandal, Jauhari Bazar-Bombay, First Edition, 1950.

Padmarajiah, Y.J.: *Jain Theories of Reality and Knowledge*, Bombay, 1963.

Stevenson, Sinclair: *The Heart of Jainism*, Oxford, 1915.

Stevenson. S.: *The Heart of Jainism*, Munshiram Manoharlal, New Delhi, 1970.

Tahtinen, U.: *Ahimsa, Non-violence in Indian Society*, Rider, London, 1976.

Talib, G.S.: ed. *Jainism*, Punjabi University, Patiala, 1975.

Tatia, Nathmal: *Studies in Jain Philosophy*, Banaras, 1951.

Tukol, T.K.: *Compendium of Jainism*, Dharwad, 1980.

Uttaradhyayana-sutra: Editor Madhukara Muni, Jinagama Granthamala No. 19, Agama Prakashan Samiti, Byavara, First Edition, 1984.

Warren, Herbert: *Jainism*, Arrah, 1916.

19

Mahatma Gandhi, Jainism and India's Freedom Struggle

Mahatma Gandhi, also known as the "Father of India" was a symbol of hope in the British colonial rule, and was a promoter of non-violence, justice and harmony between people of all faiths.

Born in 1869 in Porbandar on the Western coast of India and raised by Hindu parents, Mohandas Karamchand Gandhi found many opportunities in his youth to meet people of all faiths. He was heavily influenced by Jainism in his youth. Gandhi probably took the religious principle of 'Ahimsa' (doing no harm) from his Jain neighbours, and from it developed his own famous principle of Satyagraha (truth force) later on in his life. Gandhi hoped to win people over by changing their hearts and minds, and advocated non-violence in all things. He himself remained a committed Hindu throughout his life, but was critical of all faiths and what he saw as the hypocrisy of organised religion.

Gandhi's Life

Mohandas Karamchand Gandhi was born at Porbandar on the Kathiawar Peninsula of Gujarat into a merchant caste family who were Vaishnavas of the Vallabhacarya tradition who worshipped Krishna. His father was the dewan, chief minister, of Porbandar and later Rajkot. His mother was absorbed in religion and became a follower of the Pranami cult which was influenced by Islam.

The founder Pramanath rejected image-worship and taught direct worship without priests or ritual. This region of India is religiously pluralistic and Muslims and Jains visited Gandhi's home. In fact, his spiritual adviser was Raychandbhai Mehta, a revered Jain layman, who exerted great influence on him, especially with the concept of ahimsa, central to Jain doctrine.

He was married at the age of thirteen. Before Gandhi went to England to study law in 1888 he made three vows to his mother - to abstain from meat, wine, and women. The importance of his mother he acknowledged till the end of his life. He became a member of the executive committee of the London Vegetarian Society and in vegetarian restaurants met Theosophists such as Annie Besant, Fabians like George Bernard Shaw, and Christian visionaries who followed Tolstoy. Their rebellious ideas against capitalism and industrial life and in favour of the simple life and cooperation rather than conflict greatly influenced Gandhi. Returning to India in 1891, Gandhi found his mother had died and he could not easily find work, so he took a one-year contract with a Muslim firm in South Africa. Faced with racial intolerance against Indians, he developed rapidly into a political campaigner. In 1896 he fetched his wife Kasturbai and their children.

Though Gandhi raised an ambulance corps to help the British in the Boer War, victory did not change the attitude to the Indians. Defiance resulted in the birth of Satyagraha and a nonviolent struggle lasting seven years. Kasturbai was the first Indian woman in South Africa imprisoned as a civil resister. Later she was imprisoned several times in India and died in prison.

Near Durban Gandhi had been impressed by a Trappist monastery and he set up a series of ashrams supported by Hermann Kallenbach, a South African Theosophical Jew. One of these was named Tolstoy Farm. He also met C.F.Andrews, an Anglican missionary who spoke for the Indian nationalist leaders. In 1914 Gandhi returned to India. Through Andrews he met Rabindranath Tagore the following year, who called Gandhi a mahatma, "great soul," as the Theosophists had in South Africa. He was to become for millions of Indians simply the Mahatma. In 1919 he announced a Satyagraha struggle, resulting in the Amritsar massacre. By 1920 he was the dominant political figure, and the major campaigns of 1920-22, 1930-34, and 1940-42 led to British abdication. From the 1930's he was based at Sevagram, a village in central India, where he worked on a "constructive programme" to educate rural India, develop cottage industries, and fight untouchability. Though a political leader, the basis of his life was in religion. He achieved a religious goal that combined a life of moral action and spiritual fulfilment.

Gandhi and Jainism

Mohandas K. Gandhi, whom many revere as the Father of India, was not a Jain by birth. His parents were Vaishnavas. Jainism has a strong influence in Gujarat as many Jains live there. Growing up in that state with a pious mother, Gandhi was continuously exposed to the Jain philosophy. Although he was not Jain by birth, he was Jain in spirit because of his ideals and philosophy. Therefore, Gandhi was and was not a Jain. The principle of relativism, *Syadvada*, allows us to make this seemingly contradictory statement. Gandhi was not a Jain from the viewpoint of his birth and what he considered himself to be. On the other hand, he could be called a Jain if one considers his actions and beliefs. An example from Gandhi's life illustrates this wonderful, conflict-resolving principle of relativism.

At the age of 18, Gandhi traveled to England to study law. Gandhi's mother was hesitant to let him leave because she had heard that young, married men became corrupted when they went to England. She consulted Becharji Swami, a Jain monk, who said that Gandhi should take a solemn vow in front of his mother and then he can be allowed to go. "He administered the oath and Gandhi vowed not to touch wine, woman and meat. This done, mother gave her permission. In England, Gandhi's adherence to the vow was tested many times. Once, someone recommended that he eat eggs because eggs were not meat. After taking them for some time, he realized that in his mother's interpretation of the vow, meat included eggs so he quit eating them. This taught the young Gandhi the importance of interpreting a vow in the spirit of the person who administers it; in this case his mother. Gandhi had the choice of following the spirit of the vow or interpreting it explicitly. Both courses of action can be taken but for a pledge, it is necessary to follow the essence of the vow and not the letter to preserve fairness. Fairness and honesty prevent disputes and conflicts. Gandhi strove for this attitude of equality and that is how he was a Jain in spirit.

The central tenet of Jainism is *Ahimsa* (Non-violence) and Gandhi's philosophy rested upon it. He developed a method of political activism called *Satyagraha* which was wholly based upon truth and non-violence. It has been translated as 'non-cooperation' and 'passive resistance.' Gandhi said, "*Satyagraha* is essentially a weapon of the truthful. A *Satyagrahi* is pledged to non-violence.". He used this principle in the Kheda district when there was a crop failure. The officials wanted to collect taxes from the farmers even though they knew the crop was bad and the poor farmers couldn't pay the tax. After trying to petition the officials, the farmers and volunteer political activists signed a pledge saying that they would not pay the taxes because the crops had legitimately failed.

They would also suffer any imprisonment or other legal action the government may impose on them. Instead of rioting and demonstrating, the farmers were for the most part civilized and non-violent so the government had no choice but to give in. The officials could not arrest everyone. This victory demonstrated the power of truth and non-violence which Gandhi had instilled in the people. Like a Jain, Gandhi was also a vegetarian. In fact, he became a complete fruitarian and lived on a purely fruit diet. His diet consisted, among other things, of groundnuts, ripe and unripe bananas, lemon, olive oil, tomatoes and grapes. He completely shunned milk, cereals, pulses and other things. This was how stoutly he believed in the doctrine of *Ahimsa*. His full autobiography is devoted to it.

Gandhi & Jainism Principle of Ahimsa

Ahimsa is a Sanskrit term meaning non-violence (literally: the avoidance of violence - himsa). It is an important tenet of the religions that originated in ancient India (Hinduism, Buddhism and especially Jainism). Ahimsa is a rule of conduct that bars the killing or injuring of living beings. It is closely connected with the notion that all kinds of violence entail negative karmic consequences. The extent to which the principle of non-violence can or should be applied to different life forms is controversial between various authorities, movements and currents within the three religions and has been a matter of debate for thousands of years.

Though the origins of the concept of ahimsa are unknown, the earliest references to ahimsa are found in the texts of historical Vedic religion, dated to 8th century BC. Here, ahimsa initially relates to "non-injury" without a moral connotation, but later to non-violence to animals and then, to all beings. The idea emerges again in the Hindu texts Mahabharata and Manu Smriti, where ahimsa is said to be merited by good Karma. Though meat-eating and slaughter of animals are criticized by some Hindu texts, other texts present counter-arguments in support of hunting and ritual sacrifice. In the 19th and 20th centuries, prominent figures of Indian spirituality such as Swami Vivekananda, Ramana Maharishi, Swami Sivananda and A.C. Bhaktivedanta Swami emphasized the importance of ahimsa. Mohandas Karamchand Gandhi applied ahimsa to politics, by his non-violent satyagrahas.

Ahimsa in Jainism emphasizes vegetarianism and bans hunting and ritual sacrifice. Jains go out of their way so as not to hurt even small insects and other minuscule animals and make considerable efforts not to injure plants in everyday life as far as possible. In accordance to this policy, eating of some foods, whose cultivation harms small insects and worms as well as agriculture itself, is to be abstained from. Violence in self-defense, criminal law, and war are accepted by Hindus and Jains. Though ahimsa is not used as a technical term in Buddhism unlike the other two religions, it condemns ritual sacrifice and war and moral codes emphasize the importance of not taking life.

In Jainism the understanding and implementation of ahimsa is more radical, scrupulous, and comprehensive than in any other religion. Non-violence is seen as the most essential religious duty for everyone (*ahiCsâ paramo dharma%*, a statement often inscribed on Jain temples). Like in Hinduism, the aim is to prevent the accumulation of harmful Karma. When Mahavir revived and reorganized the Jain movement in the 6th or 5th century BC, ahimsa was already an established, strictly observed rule. Parshva, the earliest Jain leader (Tirthankar) whom modern Western historians consider to be a historical figure, lived in about the 8th century BC. He founded the community to which Mahavir's parents belonged. Ahimsa was already part of the "Fourfold Restraint" (*Caujjama*), the vows taken by Parshva's followers. In the times of Mahavir and in the following centuries Jains were at odds with both Buddhists and followers of the Vedic religion or Hindus, whom they accused of negligence and inconsistency in the implementation of ahimsa. There is some evidence, however, that ancient Jain ascetics accepted meat as alms if the animal had not been specifically killed for them. Modern Jains deny this vehemently, especially with regard to Mahavir himself. According to the Jain tradition either lacto-vegetarianism or veganism is mandatory.

The Jain concept of ahimsa is characterized by several aspects. It does not make any exception for ritual sacrificers and professional warrior-hunters. Killing of animals for food is absolutely ruled out. Jains also make considerable efforts not to injure plants in everyday life as far as possible. Though they admit that plants must be destroyed for the sake of food, they accept such violence only inasmuch as it is indispensable for human survival, and there are special instructions for preventing unnecessary violence against plants. Jains go out of their way so as not to hurt even small insects and other minuscule animals. In their view injury caused by carelessness is like injury caused by deliberate action. Eating honey is strictly outlawed, as it would amount to violence against the bees. Some Jains abstain from farming because it inevitably entails unintentional killing or injuring of many small animals, such as worms and insects, but agriculture is not forbidden in general and there are Jain farmers.

In contrast, Jains agree with Hindus that violence in self-defense can be justified, and they agree that a soldier who kills enemies in combat is performing a legitimate duty. Jain communities accepted the use of military power for their defense, and there were Jain monarchs, military commanders, and soldiers.

Though, theoretically, all life forms are said to deserve full protection from all kinds of injury, Jains admit that this ideal cannot be completely implemented in practice. Hence, they recognize a hierarchy of life. Mobile beings are given higher protection than immobile ones. For the mobile beings they distinguish between one-sensed, two-sensed, three-sensed, four-sensed and five-sensed ones; a one-sensed animal has touch as its only sensory modality. The more senses a being has, the more they care about its protection. Among the five-sensed beings, the rational ones (humans) are most strongly protected by Jain ahimsa. In the practice of ahimsa the requirements are less strict for the lay persons who have undertaken *anuvrata* (Lesser Vows) than for the monks and nuns who are bound by *mahavrata* (Great Vows).

The term *ahimsa* appears in the Taittiriya Samhita of the Yajurveda, where it refers to non-injury to the sacrificer himself. It occurs several times in the *Shatapatha Brahmana* in the sense of "non-injury" without a moral connotation. The earliest reference to the idea of non-violence to animals (*pashu-ahimsa*), apparently in a moral sense, is in the Kapisthala Katha Samhita of the Yajurveda, which may have been written in about the 8th century BC. The Chandogya Upanishad, dated to the 8th or 7th century BC, one of the oldest Upanishads, has the earliest evidence for the use of the word *ahimsa* in the sense familiar in Hinduism (a code of conduct). It bars violence against "all creatures" (*sarva-bhuta*) and the practitioner of ahimsa is said to escape from the cycle of reincarnation. It also names ahimsa as one of five essential virtues.

Hindus do not substantially differentiate the soul within a human body from that of an animal. Hence ahimsa as a binding code of conduct implies a ban on hunting, butchery, meat eating, and the use of animal products provided by violent means. The question of moral duties towards animals and of negative Karma incurred from violence against them is discussed in detail in some Hindu scriptures and religious lawbooks.

Some source texts discuss meat eating as a fact without referring to the ethical side of the issue. The Dharmasutra law books written around the 5th or 4th century BC contain regulations for meat eating and lists of edible animals. Medical treatises of the Ayurveda discuss and recommend meat from a purely health-related viewpoint without even mentioning the aspect of ahimsa. Examples are the Sushruta Samhita written in the 3rd or 4th century, which recommends beef for certain patients and for pregnant women, and the Charaka Samhita which describes meat as superior to all other kinds of food for convalescents.

Several highly authoritative scriptures bar violence against domestic animals except in the case of ritual sacrifice. This view is clearly expressed in the Mahabharata, the Bhagavata Purana, and the Chandogya Upanishad. It is also reflected in the Manu Smriti, a particularly renowned traditional Hindu lawbook (Dharmasastra). These texts strongly condemn the slaughter of animals and meat eating. The Mahabharata permits hunting by warriors (Kshatriyas), but opposes it in the case of hermits who must be strictly non-violent. This view has, for the most part, been changed, and now almost all Hindu temples ban meat from temple premises.

Nevertheless the sources show that this compromise between supporters of ahimsa and meat eaters was shaky and hotly disputed. Even the loopholes – ritual slaughter and hunting – were challenged by advocates of ahimsa. The Mahabharata and the Manu Smriti contain lengthy discussions about the legitimacy of ritual slaughter. In the Mahabharata both sides present various arguments to substantiate their viewpoints. Moreover, a hunter defends his profession in a long discourse.

Most of the arguments proposed in favour of non-violence to animals refer to rewards it entails before or after death and to horrible karmic consequences of violence. In particular, it is pointed out that he who deliberately kills an animal will on his part be eaten by an animal in a future existence due to karmic retribution. Ahimsa is described as a prerequisite for acquiring supernatural faculties, highest bliss and ultimate salvation; moreover it is said to protect against all kinds of dangers. The Manu Smriti, Kautilya's Arthashastra and the Vasishtha Dharmasutra point out that ahimsa is a duty for all the four classes (Varnas) of society. The texts declare that ahimsa should be extended to all forms of life. They also give attention to the protection of plants. The Manu Smriti prohibits wanton destruction of both wild and cultivated plants. Hermits (Sannyasins) had to live on a fruitarian diet so as to avoid the destruction of plants.

Mohandas Karamchand Gandhi promoted the principle of ahimsa very successfully by applying it to all spheres of life, particularly to politics. His non-violent resistance movement satyagraha had an immense impact on India, impressed public opinion in Western countries and influenced the leaders of various civil rights movements such as Martin Luther King Jr. In Gandhi's thought ahimsa precludes not only the act of inflicting a physical injury, but also mental states like evil thoughts and hatred, unkind behavior such as harsh words, dishonesty and lying, all of which he saw as manifestations of violence incompatible with ahimsa. Sri Aurobindo criticized the Gandhian concept of ahimsa as unrealistic and not universally applicable; he adopted a pragmatic non-pacifist position, saying that the justification of violence depends on the specific circumstances of the given situation.

Gandhi and Ahimsa: Gandhi's legacy of ahimsa has created a deep impact on the world. He demonstrated to us the immense power of ahimsa by using it as an effective weapon to achieve independence for India without shedding blood. He was deeply influenced by the Jain scholar Raichandbhai. Gandhi has written, "For me there is no religion other than the religion of truth, no duty other than ahimsa. Ahimsa is the greatest religion for me. Gandhi lived ahimsa in his life. According to him violence is bred by inequality, nonviolence by equality.

The Jain Principle of Ahimsa: Jainism is one of the most ancient of the Indian religious traditions. It is also the oldest non-Vedic school of thought. The word 'Jaina' is taken from 'Jina' which means conquerors or victors. Those who destroy all the bad karmas through austerities, penance and practise and observe the vow of ahimsa (nonviolence) in its totality i.e. do not react to any form of provocation or physical injury inflicted upon them in words, thoughts and in their actions become arhats. Jains are the followers of Jinas - the twenty-four Tirthankars. The first Tirthankar was Lord Rishabh and the last Tirthankar was Lord Mahavir (500 years BC). The Jain view of nonviolence enjoins its followers to refrain from indulging in violence in thought, word and action. It believes in the equality of all living beings and in the state of equanimity. Ahimsa results from the equanimous state of mind. Ahimsa in the Jinist tradition means reverence for all forms of life and avoidance of violence in thought, word and deed. A Jain ascetic observes ahimsa in its totality himself. He doesn't encourage others to resort to violence in thought, word and deed nor does he endorse it in thought, word and deed. In Acarang Sutra ahimsa has been proclaimed in the following words:

Injurious activities inspired by self-interest lead to evil and darkness. This is what is called bondage, delusion, death, and hell. To do harm to others is to do harm to oneself. We corrupt ourselves as soon as we intend to corrupt others. We kill ourselves as soon as we intend to kill others. Ahimsa sprouts from a person's inner awakening. It conveys many things simultan-eously whereas the word 'nonviolence' only indicates abstinence from physical violence.

The Jain principle of ahimsa cannot be understood in its right perspective unless we have a clear insight into the Jain concepts of jiva-ajiva (animate and inanimate), asarva- bandha (influx and bondage), samvar-nirjara (inhibition of instincts and impulses and total uprooting of instincts and impulses) and moksha (emancipation resulting from samvar and nirjara. Just as the famous four noble truths of Buddhism namely, suffering, cause of suffering, emancipation and the path leading to emancipation admits that if there is suffering in this world, there is the cause of suffering and there is a cure, a way to end this suffering and attain nirvana, similarly the Jains believe that the world is full of suffering and the cause of suffering is himsa (causing injury to jivas (all forms of life) which includes causing actual physical injury to jivas or causing injury through unpleasant and violent words or thoughts. As a result of himsa (violence) in thought, word and deed, there is influx of karmic matter which adds to the misery and suffering of the jivas who indulge in it in the present life and in the life hereafter and causes karmic bondage leading a jiva to be born in different species in accordance with the nature of his crime and criminality and in order to destroy the karmic bondage ajiva has to repent of his himsa by nirjara i.e. austerities, penance and observance of complete nonviolence (ahimsa) and equanimity of mind and by undergoing rigorous forms of self-suffering and ultimately it will attain to moksha (liberation from the cycle of death and birth).

Lord Mahavir has classified jivas (all forms of life on this planet) into six categories. The very discussion on Jain concept of ahimsa is meaningless unless we perceive the most subtle and complex structure of living organisms on this planet. According to him the entire planet is nothing but a mass of living organisms. His theory of jiva is called shadjivnikaya (six forms of life i.e. prathvikaya (earth), apkaya (water), askaya (fire). vayukaya (air), Vanaspatikaya (vegetation) and traskaya (mobile living organisms). The other philosophers do not recognize earth, water, fire and air as living organisms but according to Mahavir they are. Other religious traditions enjoin their disciples to show compassion towards animals and human beings while some others also agree that vegetation has life and trees and plants feel pain when touched or hit but none of them would believe that the earth or water or air or fire are also living organisms.

Mahavir advises his ascetics to be careful and vigilant and not to cause injury even to earth-bodies, fire-bodies, water-bodies and air-bodies.

A Jain ascetic is supposed to refrain from indulging in violence towards all six kinds of diverse forms of life on this planet. Mahavir's principle of shadjivanikaya is unique. In a way we can even call it something transcendental. Acharya Sidhsen has written referring to Mahavir, "0 venerable one! Your doctrine of shadjivnikaya alone would suffice to establish that you are omniscient. No other proof is required." Truly Mahavir's spiritual perfection and the dawn of ahimsa in him enabled him to attain cosmic vision.

Mahavir's ahimsa is all encompassing and recognizes the right of existence for alljivas (souls) whether they are earth-bodied or jire-bodied or water-bodied or air-bodied or mobile creatures. Alljivas (life forms) are equal. If a householder finds it impossible to refrain from himsa in its totality for his survival, he should be absolutely clear in his mind that he is doing himsa and should ask for the forgiveness of the jivas being killed for his sustenance.

He devised a separate code of conduct for his votaries based on basic vows (anuvrats) which enjoins on them to practise self-restraint and tolerance. For ascetics the five-fold path consisting of the five great vows (Mahavrats), ahimsa (nonviolence) in thought, word and deed, truth, non-stealing, brahmcharya (the practice of chastity in thought, word and deed) and non-acquisitiveness (aparigrah) is a path of complete renunciation of himsa in any form. While the aim of an ascetic is to attain to liberation (moksha), the aim of a Jain householder is to move progressively towards the attainment of liberation. The ecological and environment degradation that has posed a grave threat not only to the existence of humanity which is at the root of the crisis but also to other species of the planet which are facing great difficulties and are almost on the verge of annihilation can be checked even at this stage if the scientific community studies the basic principles of Jainism and advises the people to switch over to the Jain lifestyle rooted in ahimsa. Mahavir says to his disciples, "The Arhats (venerable perfect souls) of the past, those of the present and the future narrate, discourse, proclaim and assert that one should not injure, subjugate, enslave, torture or kill any animal, living being, organism or sentient being. The doctrine of ahimsa is immaculate, immutable and eternal." He further said, "Those who resort to and remain engrossed in violence suffer (the miseries of) transmigration again and again."

Thus the Jain principle of ahimsa is based on the theory of shadjivnikaya (six kinds of life forms classified by Mahavir) while elucidating his most subtle, profound and realistic concept of nonviolence most relevant in the present ecological crisis which in a public hearing in Europe has been described in the following words:

> The important problems are: environmental deterioration in many regions, nearing catastrophic proportions; poverty boarding on indigence for most of the population: intense social differentiation, hastening the disintegration of society; loss of a system of values, with disorientation of much of population; growing criminality, with no guarantees of safely: disappearance of the country's labour potential.

The concept of universal interdependence underpins the Jain theory of knowledge, known as anekantavada or the doctrine of manifold aspects. Anekantavada describes the world as a multifaceted. Everchanging reality with an infinity of viewpoints depending on the time, place, nature and state of the one who is the viewer and that which is viewed.

This leads to the doctrine of syadvada or relativity, which states that truth is relative to different viewpoints (nayas). What is true from one point of view is open to question from another. Absolute truth cannot be grasped from any particular viewpoint alone because absolute truth is the sum total of all the different viewpoints that make up the universe. Because it is rooted in the doctrines of anekantavada and syadvada, Jainism does not look upon the universe from an anthropocentric, ethnocentric or egocentric viewpoint. It takes into account the viewpoints of other species, other communities and nations and other human beings.

Ahimsa is the basic principle of Jainism and is the quintessence of all that it stands for. The age we live in is an age of science and reason. It is also an age of democracy which attaches utmost importance to democracy but most religious traditions consider God as the supreme ruler without whose wish nothing moves in the universe. Contrary to this belief Jainism considers God a perfect liberated soul free from all forms of passions. He doesn't rule the universe but regards all jivas (souls) as equal and bestows on each of them the right to attain to the state of godhood. In other words, all jivas can become gods provided they tread the path of purification and practise equanimity of mind. Their elevation is determined by their deeds and not by God's special compassion. Autocracy is a word not found in the dictionary of the Jains. No Tirthankar (the highest spiritual authority in the Jain tradition) can send any jiva either to heaven or to hell but surely one can attain moksha or liberation by the path shown by them.

Lord Mahavir has also predicted that on account of humanity's abnormal and unethical behaviour, this system will further crumble in the six era and life would be wiped out and the planet's climate would be so hot that a few human beings still left alive would remain hidden in the caves near Himalayas in the day and would live on fish. Let us listen to his warning and do some-thing to arrest this detereorating trend to save the planet by adopting the nonviolent way of living.

Doctrine of Ahimsa and Freedom Movement

During India's freedom struggle, Mahatma Gandhi had forged Non-violence into a political weapon to peacefully push out British imperialism. It can indisputably be said that the technique of non-violent political agitation did obtain a mass base for India's freedom struggle without attracting extreme penalties from the British administration.

Non-violent agitation also enabled nationalist Indian leaders to keep alive the struggle for independence in the absence of an armed insurrection. The roots of our attitude of non-violence go deep into our history. It has been integrated with almost all religions originating in ancient times in the Indian sub-continent viz. Hinduism, Jainism and Buddhism.

The concept of ahimsa was first developed in Jainism, which as we know split from the mainstream of Vedic beliefs very early in Indian history. Jainism disapproves Vedic rituals of animal sacrifice. The concept of Jivadaya i.e. equal respect for all life forms seems to have been first enunciated in Jainism. But ahimsa is more popularly associated with Buddhism perhaps because this religion was more widespread. This concept was also absorbed into Hinduism where it took the form of worship of the cow and bull, ban on animal sacrifices and vegetarianism.

Gandhian approach would need both-courage and freedom-from ill-will. Before launching Satyagraha and during the course of Satyagraha he was ever ready to negotiate and discuss. In the late twenties he was opposed to the exploitation of the textile workers of Ahmedabad by the mill-owners, but he was not found of a strike to end it. In it, and in all other matters in dispute, whether they were small or big in nature or local or national in level, he advocated discussions, negotiations or dialogues, conciliations, arbitrations and adjudication in the last resort. He applied the same method in actions taken time-to-time for the independence of the country. He inspired confidence and faith in his words; he was always dependable.

REFERENCES

Avasyaka-sutra: Editor Madhukar Muni, Jinagama Granthamala, No.24 Agama Prakashan Samiti, Byavar, First Edition, 1985.

Basham, A.L.: *Post-script, attached to the article on Hinduism in Cultural History of India,* Oxford University Press.

Ferfusson, J.: *History of Indian and Eastern Architecture,* London.

Jain, Kamata Prasad: *The Religion of Tirthankaras,* Aliganj, 1964.

Jain, Muni Uttam Kamal: *Jain Sects and Sub-sects,* New Delhi, 1975.

Pandey, V.: ed. *The World of Jainism,* pub. by the Author, Bombay, 1976.

Radhakrishnan, S.: *Indian Philosophy, Vol. I,* George Allen & Uniwin, London, First Edition (Revised), 1929.

Smith, Vincent A.: *A History of Fine Art in India and Ceylon,* Oxford, 1915.

Sogani, K.C.: *Ethical Doctrines in Jainism,* Jaina Samskriti Samrakshaka Sangha, Sholapur, 1967.

Stevenson. S.: *The Heart of Jainism,* Munshiram Manoharlal, New Delhi, 1970.

Trsastisalakapurusacaritrani: Canto 10, Hemacandra, Jaina Dharma Prasaraka Sabha, Bhavanagar, First Edition, 1908.

20

Jainism in Modern World

Teachings of Jainism has an extensive effect on the Indian population in terms of religion, culture, language, cuisine and so on. Jainism has a global impact too, and today we find large population of the Jain community in United States, United Kingdomn, Canada, and East Africa. Jainism today has a very modern outlook; it fits to the modern world aptly. Bhagwan Mahavir propounded a casteless, class less society with no high and low, gender distinctions. His teachings have helped in producing a better surrounding to live in. Jainism teaches us to be truthful and honest, helps in creating a society bereft of theft, lies and general insecurity. Jainism believes in existence of spirit amongst every living matter hence it encouraged vegetarianism and abandonment of animal sacrifice. It is important from the most humane grounds and has brought a change in the society. On the grounds of peace and ahimsa Jainism has immense contributions.

Teachings of Jainism stress on the notions of equality, ahimsa, divine nirvana and self-control. What Bhagwan Mahavir has taught ages back still has its significance in modern day life. Jains are a prominent religious community and Jainism preaches on different tenets of virtue enriching the population.

DIASPORA

Jainism has been a major cultural, philosophical, social and political force since the dawn of civilization in Asia, and its ancient influence has been noted in other religions, including Buddhism and Hinduism.

This pervasive influence of Jain culture and doctrine in ancient Bihar possibly gave rise to Buddhism. The Buddhists have always maintained that during the time of Buddha and Bhagwan Mahavir, Jainism was already an ancient, deeply entrenched faith and culture there. Over several thousand years, Jain influence on Hindu doctrine and religion has been considerable, while Hindu influence on Jain rites may be observed in certain Jain sects. Majority oldest Vedic Hindu Holy books beautifully narrates about various Jain Tirthankars & Jain religion confirming historicity of Jainism from time of Bhagwan Rishabdev & India originally named Bharat after eldest son of First Tirthankar.

With 10 to 12 million devotees, Jainism is amongst the smallest of the major world religions, but in India its influence is much more than these numbers would suggest. Jains live throughout India; Maharashtra, Rajasthan and Gujarat have the largest Jain population amongst Indian states. Karnataka, Bundelkhand and Madhya Pradesh have relatively large Jain populations. There is a large following in Punjab, especially in Ludhiana and Patiala, and there used to be many Jains in Lahore and other cities before the Partition of 1947, after which many fled to India. There are many Jain communities in different parts of India and around the world. They may speak local languages or follow different rites but basically follow the same tenets.

Outside India, the United States, United Kingdom, Canada and East Africa (Kenya, Tanzania and Uganda) have large Jain communities. Jainism is presently a strong faith in the United States and several Jain temples have been built there. American Jainism accommodates all the sects. Smaller Jain communities exist in Nepal, South Africa, Japan, Singapore, Malaysia, Australia, Fiji, and Suriname. In Belgium the very successful Indian diamond community, almost all of whom are Jain, are also establishing a temple to strengthen Jain values in and across Western Europe.

MODERN RELIGIOUS MOVEMENTS

Religious mvement is a kind of social movement that aims to make gradual change, or change in certain aspects of society rather than rapid or key changes. A reform movement is distinguished from more major social movements such as revolutionary movements.

Reformists' ideas are often grounded in liberalism, though they may be rooted in utopian, socialist or religious concepts. Some rely on individual transformation; others rely on small collectives, such as Mahatma Gandhi's spinning wheel and the self sustaining village economy, as a mode of social change. Reactionary movements, which can arise against any of these, attempt to put things back the way they were before whatever successes of the new movement(s), or check any such successes in the first place.

Most Jains still adhere to traditional teachings and practice passed down via the two main communities. What has been termed "modern Jainism" has grown largely out of a number of quite major reform movements of the nineteenth and early twentieth centuries. These movements had a relatively small number of devotees and by no means replaced or superseded the major traditional forms of Jainism. Some specific reform movements still continue to be influential.

SPIRITUAL REVOLUTION

The Jains have divided time i.e. the Kalacakra into two main parts known as 'Utsarpini' and ;Avasarpini'. Each of these is divided into six 'aras', corresponding to the spokes of a wheel. The first Tirthankar, Bhagwan Rishbh Dev taught to the then living humanity the three Rs. i.e. Reading, Writing and Arithmetic besides 'Brahmi' and other 'lipis' to the human world. Therefore the seeds couture and civilization were sown for the future generations of the humanity.

Jainism is a very old religion as per Jains. Bhagwan Mahavir was a historical being, so also Bhagwan Parsva and Bhagwan Neminatha, the 22nd Tirthankar of the Jains. Bhagwan Neminatha is said to be related to and contemporary of Bhagwan Krishna Vasudeva of the Hindus. Taking Bhagwan Rishabh Dev as the first Tirthankar and the time that has lapsed between these Tirthankars as is given in the Sacred literature of the Jains. Jainism enjoys a hoary antiquity. There is reference to Jainism and its Tirthankar in the Bhagavata Puran of the Hindus. Not quarreling over its antiquity, we can safely surmise that the sacred land of Bharata is sanctified and purified by the trinity of three rivers in the form of Hinduism, Jainism and Buddhism. These three great religions of India have gone a long way in bringing about a cultural synthesis and have established and developed and shaped Indian Culture and Civilization. The cultural, social, economic and educational under-currents of these three streams have so undistinguishable merged with one another that it is next to impossible to pin point one or many things that has been solely contributed by one present only. The unision of these under currents is indivisible. Each one eventually aim at 'Moksh', absolution or Nirvana. Call it by any name it aims at the same goal.

The pristine purity and divine attainment of Jainism is indisputable. Right up from the early records of ancient history and antiquity the glorious might and contribution of Jainism is beyond dispute. Jainism and therein can be included Jain monks, religious pontiffs, lay-men and women too who have added to preserve and sustain Indian Culture. The first Tirthankar, Bhagwan Rishabh Dev taught his subjects cooking, building, construction, reading, writing etc. which enabled them to lead a happy social life. Kings like Kumarapala and Kharvel made Jainism a state religion. Personalities like Siddharaja patronized Jainism and gave impetus to literature, art, sculpture, painting, music etc. Even the Muslim monarch Akbar listened to Jain pontiffs and encouraged Jainism in growing Indian culture. Jain Saints like Haribhadra Suri and Kalikala Sarvajna Hemachandra arya are too well-known for their literary accomplishments.

Such Jain monks have tries their deft hand on each and every general of literature. Jains have written Mahakavyas, Kavyas, dutakavyas, samasyapuraka-kavyas, dvisamdhana and saptasamdhanakavyas, Purans, grammear, works on rhetorics, kathas, akhyayikas, dramas, caritas, prabandhagranthas, scientific literature on astronomy, astrology, prosody, didacotic literature on astronomy, astrology, prosody, didacotic literature, commentaries on Sanskrit works etc. etc. To illustrate this by mentioning a few of the outstanding works will serve the objective.

Such works are Trisatisalakapurusacaritam, Upamitibhavaprapancakatha, Siddhahema, Kavyanusasana, Ganitatilaka, Paumacariyam, Desinamamala, Kathakosa, Joisasara, Karalakhana, Ristasamuccaya, Paialacchlnamamala, Tattvarthasutra, etc. The Jains have written in all the principal languages of India. They have written in Sanskrit, Prakrit, Apabhramsa, old Gujarati, Gujarati, Hindi, Marathi, Tamil, Telugu, Malayalam, Kannada etc. South Indian languages woe a good deal for growth as literary languages to Jainism and Jain saints. Apabhramsa language is the sole sphere of Jain authors. Jains have not lagged behind in art, architecture, sculpture, painting etc. The beautiful and world famous temples on Mount Abu, Acalgadha, Sammetsikhara, Satrunjaya, Girnar are enough to show the patronage and enthusiasm given to art and sculpture. Even amongst lay men we have such historical personalities like Jagadushah, Vastupala and Tejpal and in our modern times Jain monks like Vijayavallabhsuri, the Kesari of Punjab, Agamoddharak Sagaranandsuri, Muni Kasturviayaji, Bhuvanavijayaji, Jamburijayaji etc. and philanthropic Sheth Shri Kasturbhai Lalbhai.

Jainism is noted for activism. Its monks and nuns are ever vigilant and active. Buddhism that was born in India was spread and promulgated outside India has been almost driven out from India; whereas Jainism has remained to this day in India on account of its Anekantavada, Non-violence, and strict rules of conduct both for monks, nuns and laity.

Singing the past glory of a thing can't be useful to us. The question that should haunt our mind is the roll of Jainism in our modern times. What can be its contribution in the growth of India, culturally, socially, economically and spiritually.

The Sanskrit word for religion is dharma. It is derived from the root/dhr to sus-tain, to support and hence we have dharanat dharma ucyate. Jainism defines it as : durgation prapatanpranim dharyate its dharmah. All religion eventually objective at absolution and it is to be achieved by one's own endeavour as atmana atmanam uddharet. So religion and spiritualism depends on a person. Norms for this have been laid down but they can't be rigorously pursued and executed.

Jainism which has enjoyed such a glorious past in every sphere and walks of life can continue its past glorious heritage by playing the role of a religion which fosters aims, aspires for the goal that the current Indian Government endeavours to achieve and realize. The 'vratas', the religious ceremonies, religious practices have to be so rationalized and re-oriented that they can well fit in with the change in time. Religions can't remain isolated from society and economic life; it has to be dynamic and not static. Jainism should feel the pulse of changing time and its needs if it wants to translate its past glory into a permanent reality. In the past Jainism was embraced and encouraged by Kings as I think it could translated its well-known doctrine known as Syadvada or Anekantavada. This doctrine of understanding and respecting the view-points of others is the crux of Jainism. If Jainism in modern times is able to bring about a synthesis between its ancient philosophies and social, economic, cultural and political needs of our current century, then it will shine with its glory and grandeur.

FUTURE

As we saw in the Introduction, there have been times when the terms 'Jain' and 'Hindu' have not always been totally distinct and there is evidence that Jain numbers in western India declined in the nineteenth century due to many members of the community becoming Vainavas. In 1930 Charlotte Krause, perhaps the best-informed western observer of Jainism in pre-independence India, published an article in which she discussed the social atmosphere of the religion in the north and the west of the country. She drew attention to what she saw as the predominance of stifling and fiercely observed caste regulations which hemmed in every Jain from birth and the disappearance or conversion to Hinduism of smaller

Jain castes through inability to establish marriage alliances with larger castes which excluded them. Though Krause somewhat weakened her case by contrasting this situation with what she claimed was the unified and 'pure' Digambar Jainism of south India, and despite the large-scale reforms and changes which the Jain caste system has undergone since she wrote, there are still those who conclude that Jainism by its nature as a minority religion must inevitably disappear as a discrete social phenomenon and mutate into little more than another Hindu caste.

Certainly it seems uncontestable that the Jain religion will undergo a degree of readjustment in some regions. Nevertheless, the present sense of identity of its adherents, whatever vicissitudes the community may have experienced in the past, the cumulative weight of a specific historical experience, the richness and coherence of the multidimensional world of learning, ethics, art, rite and social interaction in which Jains have always moved, and the continuity of so many fundamental institutions and practices will ensure that Jainism doesn't succumb, even if its devotees don't dramatically expand in numbers.

Jains have always maintained that their religion is by its very nature and the demands it makes on its adherents more serious and difficult to practise than any other. Not only that, but the odds against being born a Jain and obtaining the opportunity to put the philosophy into practice are extremely long. As one Uvetambara text puts it, there are six things which are difficult for all souls to obtain: existence as a human being, birth in a socially appropriate, ryan country, birth in a good household, hearing the philosophy preached by an omniscient kewalin, trust in the philosophy when heard and putting it into physical action if one has gained faith and taken pleasure in it.

As per Universal History, the numbers of Jains in this world era will decline until the end of the fifth spoke of the wheel when scriptural knowledge will be restricted to the Dauavaikalika Sutra, the ability to engage in ascetic practices will be minimal, and the only survivors will be the shortlived last monk and nun, Duprasabha and Satyauri, along with the last layman and laywoman, the merchant Nagila and his wife Phalguuri, and the last Jain Emperor, Vimalavahana. After their death and reincarnation in various heavens, the sixth spoke of the wheel will end in a conflagration in which human beings who have degenerated to dwarves living in caves, having forgotten the social skills, will disappear and the present world era will come to an end.

But, during this time, Mahavir's contemporary Emperor Ureika will have been in hell expiating the karma brought about by his suicide in depression at having been imprisoned by his son and, in the third spoke of the succeeding world era, he will be reborn as Mahapadma, the next ford maker and the first of a new chain of twenty-four who will preach the philosophy of ahimsa once more.

JAINISM AS A GLOBAL RELIGION

Jains have survived the long gruelling journey but have lost a lot. The main loss has been of self-identity. An individual who has just escaped from a big terrible fire is mainly concerned with his burnt skin and the wounds rather than the torn clothes. The question "Who is a Jain?" is the first step in this search for self-identity. It is an attempt to seek the foundation stone for Jainism Reconstruction and Renaissance.

The move of the world to a more judicious and humane survival is in fact a move towards Jainism. It is time that Jains realized this and took up the leadership in this ongoing historical movement which has changed the world in the past four/five centuries. As men and women across the world (from all races and communities) understand and adopt the "Global Religion of the Modern World" – Jain Dharm– they will not only change their own lives but will also make the world a better place to live in.

GREAT MEN'S VIEWS ON JAINISM

Dr. Herman Jacobi

"In conclusion let me assert my conviction that Jainism is an original system, quite distinct and independent from all others; and that therefore it is of great importance for the study of philosophical thoughts and religious life in ancient India."

Dr. Hertel, Germany

"What would be the condition of the Indian Sanskrit literature if the contribution of the Jains were removed? The more I study Jain literature the more happy and wonder struck I am."

L. P. Tessetori, Italy

"Jainism is of a very high order. Its important teachings are based upon science. The more the scientific knowledge advances the more that Jain teachings will be proven."

George Bernard Shaw

"I adore so greatly the principles of the Jain religion, that I would like to be reborn in a Jain community."

Major-General Forlong

"Lofty ideas and high ascetic practices are found in Jainism. It is impossible to know the beginning of Jainism."

Dr. Hertel, Germany

"The Jains have written great masterpieces only for the benefit of the world."

Mahatma Gandhi

"I say with conviction that the doctrine for which the name of Lord Mahavir is glorified nowadays is the doctrine of Ahimsa. If anyone has practiced to the fullest extent and has propagated most the doctrine of Ahimsa, it was Lord Mahavir."

Dr. Rabindranath Tagore

"Mahavir proclaimed in India that religion is a reality and not a mere social convention. It is really true that salvation can not be had by merely observing external ceremonies. Religion cannot make any difference between man and man."

Lokamanya Bala Gangadhar Tilak

"We learn from scriptures (Sashtras) and commentaries that Jainism is existing from beginningless time. This fact is indisputable and free from difference of opinion. There is much historical evidence on this point."

Justice Ranglekar, Bombay High Court

"Jainism has contributed to the world the sublime doctrine of Ahimsa. No other religion has emphasized the importance of Ahimsa and carried its practice to the extent that Jainism has done. Jainism deserves to become the universal religion because of its Ahimsa doctrine."

Dr. Satischandra Vidhya Bhushan

"The Jain Sadhu leads a life which is praised by all. He practices the vratas and rites strictly and shows to the world the way one has to go in order to realize the atma (soul). Even the life of a Jain householder is so faultless that India should be proud of him."

Dr. Radha Vinodpal

"The right of welcoming the delegates of the universal peace organization belongs to the Jains only. Because Ahimsa alone contributes to the establishment of universal peace. Tirthankars, the propounders of

Jainism, preached to the world the Ahimsa doctrine. Therefore, who else except the followers of Bhagavan Parsvanath and Mahavir can preach universal peace?"

Dr. S. Radhakrishnan, Vice-President, India

"There is nothing wonderful in my saying that Jainism was in existence long before the Vedas were composed."

Shri Jawaharlal Nehru, Prime Minister, India

"Truly speaking, Jainism is an independent and original religion, for it is neither Hinduism nor Vedic religion, but of course it is an aspect of Indian life, culture, and philosophy."

REFERENCES

Avasyaka-sutra: Editor Madhukar Muni, Jinagama Granthamala, No.24 Agama Prakashan Samiti, Byavar, First Edition, 1985.

Basham, A.L.: *Post-script, attached to the article on Hinduism in Cultural History of India*, Oxford University Press.

Bothra, P.: *Jain Theory of Perception*, Motilal Banarsidass, Delhi, 1976.

Brown, Percy: *Indian Architecture*, Bombay, 2nd Edn.

Buhler, G.: *Indian Sect of the Jainas*, Edited by Burgess, Jas, Luzac & Co., 46, Great Russell Street, 1903.

Chakravarti, A.: *Samayasara of Sri Kundakunda*, Translation with Introduction. Bharatiya Gyanpeeth, Delhi, 1971.

Chakravarti, A: *The Religion of Ahimsa*, Bombay, 1957.

Einstein Albert: *Ideas and Opinions*, Bonanza Books, No.9.

Ferfusson, J.: *History of Indian and Eastern Architecture*, London.

Fischer, E., & Jain, J.: *Art and Rituals, 2500 Years of Jainism in India*, Sterling Publishers, New Delhi, 1977.

Garbe, R.: *Encyclopaedia of Religion and Ethics*, T. & T. Clark, 38 George Street, New York, 1920.

Ghosh, A.): *Jaina Arts and Architecture*, New Delhi, 1974.

Glassenapp, H.V: *Doctrine of Karman in Jaina Philosophy*, Bombay, 1942.

Gopal, S.: *Outlines of Jainism*, New Delhi, 1973.

Gopalan, A.S.: *Outlines of Jainism,* Willey Eastern (P) Limited, New Delhi, First Edition, 1973.

Jaini, P.S.: *The Jaina Path of Purification,* Berkeley: University of California Press, 1979.

Jaini, Padmanabh, S.: *The Jaina Path of Purigication,* California, 1979.

James, William: *Principles of Psychology, Vol. I,* Macmillan & Co., London, 1918.

Kausambi, *Dharmananda: Bharatiya Sanskrti aur Ahimsa.*

Madhav Rao, N.: *Jainism A New Look.*

Padmarajiah, Y.J.: *Jain Theories of Reality and Knowledge,* Bombay, 1963.

Pancastikaya-sara: Kunda-kunda, Edited by A.Chakravarti (Sacred Books of the Jainas, No. 3), Central Jaina Publishing House, Arrah, First Edition, 1920.

Pandey, V.: ed. *The World of Jainism,* pub. by the Author, Bombay, 1976.

Radhakrishnan, S.: *Indian Philosophy, Vol. I,* George Allen & Uniwin, London, First Edition (Revised), 1929.

Radhakrishnan. S.: *Indian Philosophy. 2nd.ed, 2 vols,* Allen and Unwin, London, 1929,1931.

Ramchandran, T.N.: *Jain Monuments of India,* Calcutta, 1944.

Srimadbhagavat (Two Volumes): Gita Press, Gorakhpur, Third Edition, 1956.

Stevenson, Sinclair: *The Heart of Jainism,* Oxford, 1915.

Stevenson. S.: *The Heart of Jainism,* Munshiram Manoharlal, New Delhi, 1970.

Tahtinen, U.: *Ahimsa, Non-violence in Indian Society,* Rider, London, 1976.

Trsastisalakapurusacaritrani: Canto 10, Hemacandra, Jaina Dharma Prasaraka Sabha, Bhavanagar, First Edition, 1908.

Bibliography

Acaranga-sutra, Anga-sutrani I: Vacana Pramukha, Acarya Tulasi, Editor Yuvacarya Mahaprajna, Jaina Vishvabharati, Ladnun, First Edition, 1974.

Amar, Muni: *Jainatva ki Jhanki, Sanmati Grantharatnamala No. 12*, Sanmati Jnanapitha, Seventh Edition, Agra, 1987.

Avasyaka-sutra: Editor Madhukar Muni, Jinagama Granthamala, No.24 Agama Prakashan Samiti, Byavar, First Edition, 1985.

Basham, A.L.: *A Cultural History of India,* Clarendon Press, Oxford.

Basham, A.L.: *Post-script, attached to the article on Hinduism in Cultural History of India*, Oxford University Press.

Bhagavati (Vyakhyaprajnapti) in Anga-sutrani II: Editor Yuvacarya Mahaprajna, Jaina Vishvabharati, Ladnum, First Edition, 1974.

Bhargava, D.: *Jain Ethics,* Motilal Banarsidass, Delhi, 1968.

Bhattacharya, B.C.: *Jaina Iconography,* 2nd ed, Motilal Banarsidass, Delhi, 1974.

Bhattacharya, N.N.: *Jain Philosophy, Historical Outline.* Munshiram Manoharlal, New Delhi, 1976.

Bool Chand: *Lord Mahavira,* Banaras, 1948

Bothra, P.: *Jain Theory of Perception,* Motilal Banarsidass, Delhi, 1976.

Brown, Percy: *Indian Architecture,* Bombay, 2nd Edn.

Buhler, G.: *Indian Sect of the Jainas,* Edited by Burgess, Jas, Luzac & Co., 46, Great Russell Street, 1903.

Caillat, C.: *Jainism,* Macmillan Company of Upadhye, A.N., andIndia, Delhi, 1974.

Chakravarti, A.: *Samayasara of Sri Kundakunda*, Translation with Introduction. Bharatiya Jnanapitha, Delhi, 1971.

Chakravarti, A: *The Religion of Ahimsa,* Bombay, 1957

Chandogya Upanisad: Edited by Max Muller, F. (S. B. E.) Vol. 1, Motilal Banarasidas, Delhi, Reprint Edition, 1981.

Chatterjee, A.K.: *Comprehensive History of Jainism (up to 1000 A.D.)*, Firma KLM, Calcutta, 1978.

Dasavaikalika-sutra: Editor Madhukar Muni, Jinagama Granthamala, No. 23, Agama Prakashan Samiti, Byavara, First Edition, 1985.

Dasgupta, S.N.: *History of Indian Philosophy, Vol. I*, Cambridge University Press, London, Second Edition (Reprint), 1932.

Desai, P.B. *Jainism in South India and some Jaina Epigraphs*, Sholapur, 1957)

Devendra Muni Shastri: *Source-Book in Jaina Philosophy*, Sri Tarak Guru Jain Granthalaya, Udaipur, 1983.

Diwakar, R.R.: *Bihar Through Ages*, Calcutta, 1959

Dwivedi, R.C.: *Contribution of Jainism to Indian Culture*, Motilal Banarsidass, Varanasi, 1975.

Einstein Albert: *Ideas and Opinions*, Bonanza Books, No.9.

Ferfusson, J.: *History of Indian and Eastern Architecture*, London

Fischer, E., & Jain, J.: *Art and Rituals, 2500 Years of Jainism in India*, Sterling Publishers, New Delhi, 1977.

Garbe, R.: *Encyclopaedia of Religion and Ethics*, T. & T. Clark, 38 George Street, New York, 1920.

Ghosh, A.): *Jaina Arts and Architecture*, New Delhi, 1974

Glassenapp, H.V: *Doctrine of Karman in Jaina Philosophy*, Bombay, 1942

Gopal, S.: *Outlines of Jainism*, New Delhi, 1973

Gopalan, A.S.: *Outlines of Jainism*, Willey Eastern (P) Limited, New Delhi, First Edition, 1973.

Guseva, N.R: *Jainism*, Bombay, 1971

Hume, Robert Earnest: *Thirteen Principal Upanisads (Trans.)*, Oxford, 1921.

Jacobi, H.: *Introduction to Kalpa-sutra.*

Jacobi, H.: *Jaina Sutras, Part 1, The Akaranga Sutra, The Kalpa Sutra, Part2, The Uttaradhyana Sutra, The Sutrakritanga Sutra. 2 vols*, Dover Publications, New York, 1968.

Jacobi, H.: *Mahavira and His Predecessors.*

Jacobi, H.: *Studies in Jainism*, Ahmedabad, 1946

Jain, C. R.: *Fundamentals of Jainism*, Veer Nirvan Bharti, Meerut, 1974.

Jain, Champat Rai: *Fundamentals of Jainism*, Meerut, 1974

Jain, Champat Rai: *Householder's Dharma*, Bijnore, 1931

Jain, H., and Upadhye, A.N.: *Mahavira, his Times and his Philosophy of Life*, Bharatiya Jnanpith, New Delhi, 1975.

Jain, J. P.: *Religion and Culture of the Jains*, Bharatiya Jnanpith, New Delhi, 1975.

Jain, J., and Fischer, E.: *Jaina Iconography, Part One, The Tirthankara in Jaina Scriptures, Art and Rituals, Part Two, Objects of Meditation and the Pantheon. 2 vols.* E.J.Brill, Leiden, 1978.

Jain, Jyoti Prasad: *Jainism: The Oldest Living Religion*, Banaras, 1951

Jain, Jyoti Prasad: *Religion and Culture of the Jains*, New Delhi, 1977

Jain, K.C.: *Lord Mahavira and his Times*, Motilal Banarsidass, Delhi, 1974.

Jain, Kailash Chand: *Jainism in Rajasthan*, Sholapur, 1963

Jain, Kamata Prasad: *The Religion of Tirthankaras*, Aliganj, 1964

Jain, Muni Uttam Kamal: *Jain Sects and Sub-sects*, New Delhi, 1975

Jaini, Jugmandar Lal: *Outlines of Jainism*, Cambridge, 1916

Jaini, P.S.: *The Jaina Path of Purification*, Berkeley: University of California Press, 1979.

Jaini, Padmanabh, S.: *The Jaina Path of Purigication*, California, 1979

James, William: *Principles of Psychology, Vol. I*, Macmillan & Co., London, 1918.

Jindal, K.B: *The prefaces*, Calcutta, 1958

Kalghatagi, T.G.: *Jaina View of Life*, Sholapur, 1969

Kapadia, H.R.: *Jaina Religion and Literature*, Lahore, 1944

Kapashi, V.J.: *In Search of the Ultimate*, V.K. Publications, Harrow, 1984.

Karttikeyanupreksa: Svamikumara, Editor Dr. A.N.Upadhye, Smd. Rajchandra Ashrama, Agosa via Anand (Gujarat), First Edition, 1960.

Kausambi, *Dharmananda: Bharatiya Sanskrti aur Ahimsa.*

Lalwani, K.C.: *Sramana Bhagavan Mahavira, Life and Doctrine.*

Lalwani. K.C.: *Kalpa Sutra of Badrabahu Svami*, Motilal Banarsidass. Delhi, 1979.

Latthe, A.B: *An Introduction to Jainism*, Bombay, 1905

Law, B.C: *Mahavira: His Life and Teachings*, London, 1937

Lenin: *Collected Works of Lenin, Vol. 14.*

Madhav Rao, N.: *Jainism A New Look.*

Malavania, Pt. Dalasukhabhai: *Jainism (Some essays),* Translated by Dr. A.S.Gopani, Prakrita Bharati Academy, Jaipur, First Edition, 1986.

Mehata, M.L.: *Jaina Culture,* Varanasi, 1969

Mehta, M. L.: *Outlines of Jaina Philosophy*, Jaina Mission Society, G. 146, Chickpet, Bangalore - 2, October, 1954.

Mookerjee, S.: *The Jain Philosophy of Non-absolutism, a Critical Study of Anekantavada. 2nd. Ed,* Motilal Banarsidass, Delhi, 1978.

Nahar and Ghosh: *An Epitome of Jainism,* Calcutta 1917

Nevaskar B.: *Capitalists without Capitalism, the Jains of India and the Quakers of the West,* Greenwood Publications, Westport, 1971.

Nyayavatara: Siddhasena, Translated by Vijayamurti Sastracarya, Paramashruta Prabhavaka Mandal, Jauhari Bazar-Bombay, First Edition, 1950.

Padmarajiah, Y.J.: *Jain Theories of Reality and Knowledge,* Bombay, 1963

Pancastikaya-sara: Kunda-kunda, Edited by A.Chakravarti (Sacred Books of the Jainas, No. 3), Central Jaina Publishing House, Arrah, First Edition, 1920.

Pandey, V.: ed. *The World of Jainism,* pub. by the Author, Bombay, 1976.

Paul Marett: *Jainism Explained*, Liececiter 1988

Pramana-mimamsa: Hemacandra. Edited by Pt.Sukhalal Sanghvi, Saraswati Pustak Bhandar, Ahmedabad, Reprint Second Edition, 1989.

Radhakrishnan, S.: *Indian Philosophy, Vol. I*, George Allen & Uniwin, London, First Edition (Revised), 1929.

Radhakrishnan. S.: *Indian Philosophy. 2nd.ed, 2 vols,* Allen and Unwin, London, 1929,1931.

Ramchandran, T.N.: *Jain Monuments of India*, Calcutta, 1944

Rampuria, S.C.: *The Cult of Ahimsa,* Calcutta, 1947

Rosenfield, C.: *Gurudev Shree Chitrabhanu, a Man with a Vision,* New Jain Meditation Intemational Center, York, 1981.

Roy Chowdhari, P.C.: *Jainism in Bihar,* Patna, 1956

Roy, A.K.: *History of the Jains,* Gitanjali Publishing House, New Delhi, 1984.

Saletore, B.A: *Medieval Jainism,* Bombay, 1938

Samaya-sara: Kunda-kunda, Bharatiya Jnanapitha, Durgakund Road, Varanasi, First Edition, 1950.

Sangave, V.S.: *Jaina Community, a Social Survey. 2nd. ed.* Popular Prakashan, Bombay, 1980.

Sangave, Vilas A.: *Life and Legacy of Mahavira:* A Social Study, Meerut, 1974

Sangave, Vilas A.: *The Sacred Shravan-belagola: A Socio-Religious Study,* New Delhi, 1981

Sarvartha-siddhi: Pujapada Devanandi, Edited by Pt. Phoolachandra Siddhantashastri, Bharatiya Jnanapitha, Durgakund Road, Varanasi, 1955.

Schubring, W.: *The Doctrine of the Jains,* Motilal Banarsidass, Delhi, 1962.

Schubring, Walther: *The Religion of the Jainas,* New Delhi 1966

Shah, Chimanlal J.: *Jainism in North India,* London, 1932

Shah, U.P.: *'Jainism', New Encyclopaedia Britannica,* Chicago, 1974.

Shah, Umakant P.: *Studies in Jaina Art,* Banaras, 1955

Sharma, S.R.: *Jainism and Karnataka Culture,* Dharwar, 1940

Sheth, C.B.: *Jainism in Gujarat,* Bombay, 1953

Siddhahemasabdanusasanam: Acarya Hemacandra, Bherulal Kamhaiyalal Religious Trust, Chandanbala Apartment, Ridge Road, Valakeshwara, Bombay, Second Edition, 1985.

Smith, Vincent A.: *A History of Fine Art in India and Ceylon,* Oxford, 1915

Sogani, K.C.: *Ethical Doctrines in Jainism,* Jaina Samskriti Samrakshaka Sangha, Sholapur, 1967.

Songani, Kamal Chand: *Ethical Doctrines in Jainism,* Sholapur, 1967

Srimadbhagavadgita Bhasya: Translated by Dr.A.G. Krishnawarrior, Shri Ramakrishna Math, Madras, First Edition, 1983.

Srimadbhagavat (Two Volumes): Gita Press, Gorakhpur, Third Edition, 1956.

Stevenson, Sinclair: *The Heart of Jainism,* Oxford, 1915.

Stevenson. S.: *The Heart of Jainism,* Munshiram Manoharlal, New Delhi, 1970.

Tahtinen, U.: *Ahimsa, Non-violence in Indian Society,* Rider, London, 1976.

Talib, G.S.: ed. *Jainism,* Punjabi University, Patiala, 1975.

Tatia, Nathmal: *Studies in Jain Philosophy,* Banaras, 1951.

Tattvartha-sutra: Umasvati, P.V. Research Institute, Varanasi, Reprint Second Edition.

Thomas, F.W.: *Sri Mallisenasuri, Syad-Vada-Manjari,* Motilal Banarsidass Delhi, 1968.

Trsastisalakapurusacaritrani: Canto 10, Hemacandra, Jaina Dharma Prasaraka Sabha, Bhavanagar, First Edition, 1908.

Tukol, T.K.: *Compendium of Jainism*, Dharwad, 1980

Upadhye, A.N.: *Lord Mahavira and his Teachings. 2nd. Ed*, Shree Vallabhsuri Smarak Nidhi, Bombay,1983.

Uttaradhyayana-sutra: Editor Madhukara Muni, Jinagama Granthamala No. 19, Agama Prakashan Samiti, Byavara, First Edition, 1984.

Warren, H.: *Jainism in Western Garb, as a Solution to Life's Great Problems*, Edited, with notes, by N.J. Shah. 2nd. ed. Shree Vallabhsuri Smarak Nidhi, Bombay, 1983.

Warren, Herbert: *Jainism*, Arrah, 1916

Williams, R.: *Jaina Yoga: A survey of Medieval Sharavakachara*, London, 1963

Williams. R.: *Jaina Yoga*, Motilal Banarsidass, Delhi, 1983.

Winternitz, M.: *The Jainas in the History of Indian Literature*, Ahmedabad, 1946

Zimmer, H.: *Myths and Symbols in Indian Art and Civilization*, Edited by Joseph Campbell, Harper and Brothers, New York, First Edition, 1945.

Index